A Promise To Keep

Also by Lilian Harry

Goodbye Sweetheart
Keep Smiling Through
The Girls They Left Behind
Moonlight & Lovesongs
Love & Laughter
Wives & Sweethearts
Corner House Girls
Kiss the Girls Goodbye
PS I Love You
A Girl Called Thursday
Tuppence to Spend

A Promise to Keep

LILIAN HARRY

ORION

For Aidan

First published in Great Britain in 2003 by Orion,
an imprint of the Orion Publishing Group Ltd.

A CIP catalogue record for this book is available
from the British Library.

Typeset by Deltatype Ltd, Birkenhead, Merseyside

Printed in Great Britain by Clays Ltd, St Ives plc

The Orion Publishing Group Ltd
Orion House
5 Upper Saint Martin's Lane
London, WC2H 9EA

FOREWORD

Once again, I owe a debt of gratitude to Helen Long, whose book *Change Into Uniform* inspired both this novel and the previous 'Thursday' story, *A Girl Called Thursday*.

Helen Long was a remarkable woman. A debutante in the 1930s, she volunteered as a Red Cross VAD and served in Haslar Royal Naval Hospital in Gosport, Hampshire, and then in Egypt. She was one of the first members of the RN Blood Transfusion Service, and after the war became one of the first BEA air hostesses, before marrying Dr Aidan Long, whom she had met at Haslar.

Helen wrote several other books, the most significant being *Safe Houses Are Dangerous* – the story of her uncle, Dr Georges Rodocanachi, and his wife, Fanny, whose flat in Marseilles was the headquarters of the O'Leary escape line, bringing many Allied servicemen to safety from occupied France. She contributed frequently to such magazines as *The Lady* and in the last year or so of her life was awarded the Silver Rose Bowl of the Society of Women Writers and Journalists for her writing. Sadly, she died in 2001 while I was writing *A Girl Called Thursday*, and I was never able to meet her. I have, however, had the pleasure of meeting both her husband, Aidan, and her son, David, who have been most helpful and encouraging.

As the Royal [Naval] Haslar Hospital features strongly in both books, some readers might like to know its situation today. Unfortunately, although the hospital is still functioning, it is on a much reduced scale. Currently run by all three Services and the NHS it serves local as well as Service patients, but its excellent Accident Treatment Centre is confined to dealing with injuries only. Patients with life-threatening conditions have to make the twelve-mile journey through the bottleneck of the Gosport – Fareham road to the Queen Alexandra Hospital at Portsmouth – a journey that can take well over an hour. The town of Gosport is in constant fear of its complete closure, which would be a sad end to an historic and still desperately needed hospital. The Save Haslar Task Force has been working to prevent this, and I wish it all success.

I would also like to thank Surgeon Captain Jarvis and his staff at the hospital who gave me so much assistance with my research and kindly allowed me to use their marquee as a launch venue for *A Girl Called Thursday*.

A WORD OF EXPLANATION

Some terms may be unfamiliar to new readers:

VAD: Voluntary Aid Detachment – volunteer nurses (mostly unregistered) who served as assistants with the armed forces
QAIMNS: Queen Alexandra's Imperial Military Nursing Service
QARNNS: Queen Alexandra's Royal Naval Nursing Service
SBA: Sick Berth Attendant
BGH: British General Hospital (Egypt)
DUKW (pronounced 'duck'): wheeled amphibious personnel carrier
Pompey: local name for Portsmouth

Chapter One

'*Thursday*!'

Thursday Tilford, enveloped in a mass family embrace, laughed and cried and kissed all at once, and finally begged for mercy.

'You're suffocating me! I can't breathe!' They stepped back and she found herself with just her mother's arms still around her. Tears brimming from her eyes, Thursday held her close for a moment.

'Oh, love,' Mary said at last, pulling a hanky from her sleeve and wiping her wet cheeks, 'it's *so* good to have you home again.'

'It's good to be here. But it's not for long, mind,' Thursday warned her. 'I've only got a few days' leave and then it's back to Haslar. The war's not over yet by a long chalk.'

'No, but it could be soon,' Jenny piped up. She had gone back to her favourite position on the hearthrug where she had been playing with little Leslie. 'They say there's something really big going on all along the south coast – tanks and all sorts heading for the beaches, and—'

'And you didn't ought to be talking about it!' her father said sharply. 'For goodness sake, our Jenny, the war's been going on for nearly five years; you ought to know by now about walls having ears and all that. I hope you're not opening your mouth like this when you're working down at the hospital.'

'Course I'm not,' Jenny said in an injured tone. 'It's just in the family. Anyway, Thursday'll be there to see for herself soon. I bet Portsmouth's one of the main places the invasion's going from—'

'Jenny! That's *enough*.' Walter gave her an angry glance. 'Family or not, we didn't ought to discuss it. It's too easy to let something slip when we shouldn't – not that *we* know any secrets,' he admitted, 'but you just don't know who might be listening or what they might pick up on. Least said, soonest mended.' He opened his tobacco pouch and stuffed his pipe, pressing the baccy down hard with his thumb. Jenny folded her lips wryly and shot Thursday a comical look. Thursday felt her lips twitch. Not much had changed at home, she thought. They might all be two years older than when she had last seen them, and Jenny training as a nurse at the Royal Infirmary, but Dad was still doing his best to rule the roost and Jenny still cheeking him and getting away with it.

'Never mind all that,' Mary said, giving Thursday's arm a little shake. 'Come and sit down, love, and I'll make a cup of tea. We're all pleased to see you back safe and sound, and that's the main thing. I can't tell you how worried I was, all the time you were at sea.'

'We're all waiting to hear about Egypt,' Jenny added. 'Aren't we, Dizzy?'

Denise nodded. She had pulled Leslie back on to her own lap and he leaned into her and slid his thumb into his mouth. Thursday knelt beside her cousin and gazed at her little godson, marvelling at his soft cheeks and long lashes. 'I've missed two whole years of him,' she mourned. 'He was still a baby when I went away – he's a real little boy now.'

'Three years old,' Denise said proudly. Her face clouded a little. 'His daddy hasn't seen him since he really was a baby.' She looked at Thursday. 'How was Vic when you saw him? He's hardly told me anything.'

Thursday hesitated. She'd still not decided how much to tell Denise about the injuries her young husband had received in Africa. 'I'll come round and have a chat tomorrow,' she said quietly. 'We can't talk properly in this scrum. But he's all right, Dizzy, and he talked about you and Leslie the whole time. You don't have to worry about that.'

Her Uncle Percy cleared his throat. 'The main thing is, he's safe, or as safe as anyone can be these days. And Denise knows she's always got me and her mother to turn to.'

'That's right,' Flo agreed. 'It's just as well she stopped at home with us when Vic was called up. She can carry on with her job and I can look after the baby. Not that he's any trouble at all, the dear little soul,' she added, chucking her grandson under the chin so that he giggled and curled himself more deeply in his mother's lap.

Thursday smiled and turned to take a cup of tea from her mother. 'How about our Steve, have you heard from him lately?'

'Oh yes, he writes regular. He doesn't say a lot, mind you, they're not allowed much paper for a start, but he seems to be going on all right and I don't think they treat them too badly either in prison camp. They have football matches and get up concerts and that sort of thing, and we're allowed to send parcels, when there's anything to send, which isn't all that often. I don't think the food's very good but at least he's alive and more or less safe.' She shook her head. 'I don't like thinking of him treated like a criminal, but I don't mind admitting I'd rather that than have him fighting.'

Thursday nodded. The Tilfords were lucky that Steve was a POW. She thought sadly of her cousins Mike and Leslie – Mike posted missing, believed killed, at Dunkirk and Leslie shot down in his Spitfire. No wonder poor Auntie Flo thought the world of her grandson, named after them. He and Denise were all she had left now.

It was obvious that Leslie was the apple of everyone's eye. It seemed almost impossible to believe that Uncle Percy had refused to look at him when he was born. He and Flo had been horrified when Denise, at only fifteen, had admitted that she was pregnant, and furious with Vic even though he'd believed her to be eighteen. The fact that Denise had lied to him didn't excuse him taking advantage, Percy had raged. They weren't married, not even engaged, nor likely to be if Percy had anything to do with it. He'd wanted the girl sent away somewhere quiet to have her baby and get it adopted, but at this Flo had put her foot down. Out of wedlock or not, she told Percy, this was their grandchild, and it could be the only grandchild they'd ever have. They couldn't, they just *couldn't*, let the baby go to strangers.

Walter and Mary had been just as dismayed. Girls who had babies without being decently married were ostracised, and the whole family tainted. Flo's stance had surprised them – she'd always been one to worry about what the neighbours would say – but she'd been so determined that everyone had had to accept it, and with Denise flatly refusing to give up the baby, Percy had been forced to agree to their marrying as soon as Denise turned sixteen. And, as Mary had observed, babies brought their love with them. Even if they hadn't been wanted, they all seemed to make themselves a place in the family, and little Leslie Michael Stephen – named after his two uncles and Thursday's brother Steve – had been barely a fortnight old when he'd won his grandfather round. Even Vic, who had got his call-up soon after his son's birth, had been accepted, especially by Flo who had never forgotten the way he had comforted her when she'd got the news about Leslie. 'As good as a son to me,' she'd said, and refused to let Percy say another word against him.

As Mary handed round the tea and a plate of biscuits, Thursday sat in her mother's armchair, trying to get used to the feeling of being at home again after two years in Egypt. She looked round at the familiar room and the faces she'd missed so much. There'd been changes while she'd been away. The saddest was that her little dog, Patch, had died. Mary had written to tell her he was ill with distemper, and Thursday had known at once what the next letter would say. When it arrived, she'd left it unopened for a whole day, waiting till nightfall to read the bad news. Oh Patchie, she'd thought, the tears dripping on to the sheet of paper, oh Patchie. And she'd remembered how he'd come to her as a puppy on her twelfth birthday, struggling out of the cardboard box in which her father had brought him home and licking her face as she lifted him into her arms. He'd been with her during all her growing-up years, her special friend, rushing to meet her when she came home from school or work, sleeping on her bed whenever he could sneak up the stairs, keeping so close to her that Steve had once said he was glued to her leg. And now he was dead. Patchie. Her Patchie.

Thinking about him brought the tears to her eyes again. Now she was home, it was as if he'd only just died, and the sorrow of knowing he would never rush to her again came as fresh as on the day she'd received her mother's letter. Then, catching Mary's eye, she blinked back the tears and smiled. I've cried for him once, she thought. I'm not going to spoil this homecoming by doing it all over again.

'Is Auntie Maudie coming over? I want to see her before I go back.'

'She's on duty a lot this week. I thought we'd pop over to Ledbury on the train one afternoon. Day after tomorrow, if that's all right with you.'

'I'll come too,' Jenny suggested. 'We can talk about operations and things.'

Mary frowned. 'You know I don't like—'

'It's all right, Mum, I'm only teasing. But you can't expect three nurses to get together and not talk about their job! I always have a natter with Auntie Maudie when I go over, and she's sure to be interested in what Thursday's been doing.'

'Of course she will,' Thursday said. 'And I want to thank her again for the little nurse's watch she lent me. Uncle Bill gave it to her in the First World War, and I've worn it all the time. It's been a godsend on the wards.'

'Well, so long as you don't start talking about blood,' Mary said, and everyone laughed. 'Now look, we didn't know just what time you'd be getting home today so I haven't done anything special, just a few Spam sandwiches, but we're all here again for Sunday dinner. Your father's going to kill one of the hens—'

'Not Aggie!' Thursday broke in, and her mother gave her an exasperated look.

'No, not Aggie, I daresay she'll outlive us all if you've got anything to do with it. It's one of the others, that you don't know so well. And don't go down the garden giving them all names – you know once they've got names nobody likes to eat them. There's plenty of veg from the allotment, and some soft fruit for pudding, so it'll be a real old-fashioned Sunday dinner. When d'you have to go away again?'

'I knew you'd ask that,' Thursday said. 'I'm just surprised you've waited so long – usually you ask the minute I walk through the door. "Hello, Thursday, nice to see you, when are you going again?" Can't wait to get rid of me, as usual.'

'You know I didn't mean that!' Mary's face was pink as everyone laughed again. 'Oh, you're awful, the lot of you. I can't say a word without getting picked up on it . . . I only want to know so that I can make arrangements. And so I don't wake up one morning to find you've gone.'

Thursday gave her mother's arm a squeeze. 'You know I wouldn't do that. And I'm only teasing, you know that too. I've got a week – so that's next Wednesday, thirty-first of May.' She stretched her arms, nearly knocking her cup off the arm of her chair. 'A whole week at home! Luxury.'

'Time to tell us all about Egypt,' Jenny said wistfully. 'I wish now that I'd volunteered as a VAD, instead of going for State

Registration and getting stuck here in Worcester. Would have done, if I'd known you could go to places like that.'

'You're better off as you are if you want to be a real nurse. We're just dogsbodies most of the time, doing all the dirty work, though we do get to talk to the patients a bit more – the QARNNs just don't have the time. But we'll never be trained like you are.' Thursday took another ginger biscuit to show her appreciation, aware that her mother would have saved these specially for her return. 'Anyway, what I want to know now is what's been going on while I've been away. How about Mrs Hoskins – is she home or is she off with that fancy man of hers again? And that boy who got sent to approved school – is he back terrorising the neighbourhood? I've got a lot of catching up to do.'

Jenny giggled. 'You certainly have! Freddy Barnes went into the Army and he's won two medals already – his mum's like a dog with two tails. As for Mrs Hoskins, she's had so many fancy men even she's lost count, and—'

'Pipe down, Jenny!' Mary said sharply. 'You know what we think about that sort of gossip. I'm surprised at you for encouraging her,' she told Thursday. 'I'd have thought you'd have learned better, being with those other girls. They tell me a lot of the VADs are real upper-class.'

Thursday grinned. 'They are. But they like a good gossip as much as anyone else. It's just upper-class gossip, that's all. You should hear what they say about the lords and ladies they know and what goes on in big houses with all those bedrooms. Why, Louisa Wetherby once told me—'

'*Thursday*!' her mother expostulated, and the girls dissolved in giggles.

Thursday winked at her sister and cousin, and whispered, 'Tell you later,' and then said aloud, in a demure voice, 'Sorry, Mum. Let me get you another cup of tea, and then you can tell me all the things you want to tell me about, all right?' She got up and took her mother's cup, then bent suddenly and kissed her. 'D'you know what? It feels *much* more like being at home when you tell me off than when you treat me like an honoured guest. So just carry on that way, will you? Because that's what I've missed most.'

Mary shook her head at her. 'Stop it do, or you'll have me in tears again. As if I've ever told you off! Didn't tell you off enough, that's what your father always used to say.'

Thursday smiled and went out to the kitchen. She filled the kettle and put it on the stove, then stood leafing through the pile of cookery books and pamphlets her mother had collected. *Potato Pete's Recipe Book: Two Ways of Reconstituting Dried Eggs*, and *Try Cooking Cabbage This Way* . . . She turned to find her Cousin Denise standing beside her. The younger girl looked at her.

'You will tell me the truth about Vic, won't you – what happened to him and – and how he is now. I'm sure there's more than he's told me, and I've got to know.'

Thursday laid her hand on her cousin's arm and nodded. 'I will, I promise. But you mustn't worry, Dizzy. He's just the same as he ever was, really. And he misses you and Leslie all the time.'

Denise nodded and sniffed, brushing her hand across her eyes. 'I miss him too. I really do love him, Thurs, I always did. It wasn't just a – what did they call it? – infatuation. We really did love each other. That's why I lied to him about my age. I was so scared I'd lose him if he knew the truth.'

'Well, that's all over now.' Thursday warmed the teapot with a drop of hot water from the kettle. 'You're married and you've got your little boy, and one day soon Vic'll come home and you'll be able to get a place of your own and settle down properly.' The kettle boiled and she made the tea. 'Go and get the cups, Dizzy. I'll come and see you tomorrow and tell you all about when I saw him in Egypt.'

She stood for a moment alone in the kitchen, listening to the chatter from next door. There would be a lot of talking to do in the next few days, a lot of stories to swap and a lot of reassurance to give. And then she would be going back to Haslar, the Naval hospital on the shore of Portsmouth Harbour where she had first become a VAD. Another kind of homecoming, in a way. I wonder how much will have changed there, she thought. And I wonder what's going to happen next. Something big, Jenny said – perhaps even an invasion. Can this really be the beginning of the end of the war, after all this time?

Denise came back with the cups and Thursday began to fill them with tea. Just for now, she'd forget all about it. Just for now, it was enough to be at home in Worcester with her family.

During those few days' leave, Thursday saw Denise only a couple of times. She was working long hours at the glove factory, making khaki gloves for soldiers, navy-blue ones for sailors, grey ones for airmen and leather ones for officers. 'Once this is all over I'm never going to look at a glove again,' she declared, coming in for a late supper after three hours' overtime when Thursday was round at her aunt's the next evening. 'I'd rather have chilblains!'

She lay back in her mother's armchair, her eyes closed. Thursday looked at her pale face and thought of Vic, lying in his hospital bed. They're just kids, the pair of them, she thought, and they're not the only ones either. This whole war's being fought by kids.

'I had a letter from Vic today,' Denise said, opening her eyes suddenly. 'I told him you were coming home. He says you just about saved his life, Thurs.'

Thursday coloured. 'I didn't do much. I just sat beside him at night. I think it helped that I could talk about you and Leslie, that's all.'

'Well, whatever you did he thought a lot of it. And so do I.' Denise closed her eyes again. 'I'm glad you were there.'

Thursday bit her lip and nodded. 'I'm glad I was there too. It was strange having someone from the family out there in Alex. We hardly knew each other before – when you got married – but we got to know each other quite well in the hospital. He's a nice chap, Dizzy. You're lucky – you've got a good husband.'

'Well, I always knew that!' Denise said, with a flash of her old spirit. 'Knew that right from the start. But then you do, don't you – when it's the right one.' She closed her eyes again. 'That's if he still thinks I *am* the right one.'

'Oh, he does!' Thursday hesitated, then took a breath. 'Look, it's a long time since I saw him and I expect it's different now, but – well, he was wondering if you'd still fancy him. You see—'

'But of course I'll fancy him!' Denise exclaimed. 'I fancied him the minute I first saw him. Why on earth shouldn't I?'

'Because he doesn't look quite the same.' Thursday searched for the right words. She'd known for a long time that this moment must come, that she would have to prepare Denise for her first meeting with Vic. 'Dizzy, he was badly burned. His face was blistered all over – and parts of his body too. It's probably not so bad now as when I last saw him, but he's bound to be scarred.' She looked helplessly at her cousin. 'I'm sorry, but you ought to know – so that it isn't too much of a shock.'

There was a short silence. Then Denise said in a small voice, 'Is it very bad?'

'Quite bad,' Thursday said honestly. 'I'm really sorry, Diz.'

Denise bit her lip. She looked at Leslie, who was on the floor engrossed in a game with some old lead soldiers. Then she took in a deep breath and shrugged.

'I don't see that that's so awful – so long as he's not still hurting from it. He'll still be the same old Vic underneath, won't he?'

'Yes,' Thursday said with relief. 'He'll be the same old Vic. He was in Egypt, anyway. We got on really well.'

'That's all right then,' Denise said. She lifted her chin a little and looked Thursday in the eye. 'You know what Gran says – handsome is as handsome does, and I reckon my Vic will always be handsome to me, no matter what other people think. But thanks for telling me. I wouldn't want to look as if I was upset by it, the first time we see each other again.'

Thursday nodded, relief washing through her. It had been one of the things that had haunted her about coming home – the necessity of telling Denise about Vic. Even now, she wasn't sure that she'd really prepared her for the puckered, dead-looking skin that covered all one side of Vic's face now and stretched down his body. Perhaps later on she'd tell her more, but she'd learned that such shocks took time to absorb. Denise would ask for more information when she was ready.

'He really does love you, Dizzy,' she said quietly. 'He told me that. He just wants to get back to you and Leslie. Nothing else really seems to matter to him.'

'It doesn't matter to me either,' Denise said. 'Just to have us together again, a proper family – that's all we want.' She paused. 'All anyone wants, I suppose. Funny that it takes a war to bring it home to people what's really important about life.'

The brief leave over, Thursday set out on the familiar train journey to Portsmouth. And as she walked down the pontoon from the railway station and stepped aboard the waiting pinnace, she felt herself jerked back four years, to the moment in 1940 when she had first stared out over Portsmouth Harbour.

Four years! Four – no, *five* – years of war, years that had torn her and millions of other young men and women from their homes and families and thrown them into lives they could never have dreamed of. Thrown many of them to their deaths, she thought sadly, remembering the long lists of names in newspapers, the reports on the wireless, the soldiers and sailors she had herself nursed, both here in England and during her years abroad. And here she was, home again, and still it wasn't over.

'Come on, love,' urged the matelot waiting to cast off. 'You're not here on your holidays, you know. Mind you,' he added, glancing at her, 'you look as if you 'ave been. Look as if you've been in the South of France sunning yourself, you do. And what's that ribbon you're wearing? Been serving overseas?'

Thursday nodded a little self-consciously. She'd been proud to be presented with the medal that indicated her service abroad, but reluctant to display it until her father had told her, bluntly, that it was her patriotic duty to do so. 'That's an encouragement to others, that is,' he'd said, knocking his pipe out on the fender. 'It's good for people to know what girls like you have been doing to serve your country. It gives 'em summat to hold up their heads about, summat to hope for. You wear it, and be proud to.'

'So where you been, then?' the matelot asked now, still eyeing the ribbon. 'Africa?'

Thursday nodded. 'Egypt. I've been there two years. But I was at Haslar before that, and now they've sent me back. It feels queer, coming home again after all this time and the war still on. Somehow I always thought we wouldn't come back till it was over.'

'Maybe it won't be too long now,' the sailor said cryptically, looking out over the busy scene. Thursday followed his glance. The harbour was thronged with ships – some tied up at the main jetties in the dockyard, others moored out in the harbour, with smaller boats, ferries and tugs bustling between them. And as the Naval pinnace made the short crossing to the Gosport side she could see through the entrance that the Solent itself was just as crowded. Something was obviously going on – something big.

'What is it?' she asked curiously, but the sailor glanced at her sideways and tapped his nose.

'What we don't know can't hurt us. But you must've seen the roads, all jammed up with Army stuff. Been coming in for the past few weeks, so I've been told – lorries, tanks, DUKWs, you name it, it's there. American, too, a lot of it. Second Front, innit? And they say it's all being master-minded from just over Portsdown Hill.' He seemed to remember his first words and shut his mouth firmly. 'Shouldn't have said that.'

Thursday looked at him. There was nobody else in the boat, but everyone knew that you had to be careful what you said, especially about anything military. *Careless Talk Costs Lives* – the notices had been everywhere at the beginning of the war, and there had been cases of people put into prison for making casual remarks that could have been helpful to the enemy. A girl only had to be overhead in a teashop, telling a friend that her sweetheart's ship was sailing that night, and it could end in the ship's being torpedoed and sunk. Spies and Fifth Columnists, it seemed, were everywhere.

She turned her eyes again towards the crowded harbour. There was clearly a big 'flap' on, and from the look of the ships and the determined air of the smaller boats hurrying between them, it was obvious that the matelot was right – it was the long-awaited Second Front. Everyone was expecting it, had been for months – it was why she and the other VADs had been brought home. The theatre of war was moving back to Europe.

Jenny had been right too. It was the invasion. The invasion of Europe by Britain, and by her allies – America, Canada, Australia and the rest. This was what the country had been waiting for.

'I came by train,' she said, 'and it was packed with Navy types. But you're right, we did see a lot of Army vehicles on the roads, and all along the country lanes. You mean they're planning to take them all on ships? But how?'

He shook his head. 'We don't talk about it, not more'n we can help. There ain't no need. Everyone can see what's going on, and we all know the beaches have been closed for months. Gawd knows what they've been doing there, building bloody great concrete towers it looks like – not that you can see much past all the barbed wire. We might have our own ideas what they're for but we don't ask. And if you take my advice, you won't neither.'

Nothing's changed, Thursday thought, remembering how she and Patsy Martin – Patsy Greenaway now – had come to Portsmouth by train on that bitterly cold, snowy day in 1940, not daring to talk about where they were going or why, in case there was a spy in the carriage with them. It all seemed a very long time ago: the train getting stuck in huge snowdrifts so that the passengers – mostly soldiers – had climbed out to help dig a way through; their surprise at the harbour station with its wooden platform and glimpse of the sea surging beneath them; the massive icicles that had formed beneath the structure; the sloping pontoon to the Gosport ferry crowded by the workmen swarming out through the dockyard gates.

And the ships! It was like a different world, different from anything either she or Patsy had ever seen, except in pictures or at the cinema. The frigates, the destroyers, the enormous, towering bulk of the aircraft-carrier *Ark Royal* looming over them in their tiny pinnace. One of the greatest ships of the Royal Navy, she thought sadly, remembering the flight of aircraft it had taken to the beseiged island of Malta, the battles it had fought, the pride everyone had felt in its name. And now it was gone, sunk by a U-boat off Gibraltar.

The sailor brought the pinnace alongside the Haslar jetty, and Thursday turned her head and looked up at the hospital where she had begun her days as a VAD. How ignorant we were, she thought. We knew nothing about the Navy, nothing about nursing. We had no idea of Haslar's history: nearly two hundred years old and one of the first real Naval hospitals. And we certainly had no idea of what we were going to face. The ships coming back from Dunkirk. The wounded sailors, some of them no more than boys. The men who would die before our eyes.

She thought of Tony West, who had kissed her before he went to sea and then come back with his face so badly damaged he would never kiss again. And Susie, the little girl whose leg had been amputated on the night of the big Blitz. And all the others who had passed through Haslar's wards – Stoker Davis, with his amazing tattoos, who had been a hero at sea yet made a fuss like a baby when he was given an enema; the young German, Heinz Schmidt; the sailor who had told her about the great queues of men standing in the water at Dunkirk, being shelled and machine-gunned as they waited for rescue, watching their comrades die around them. And that brought her back again to Tony, one of the first to arrive with his terrible injuries, his torn and broken face . . .

We didn't have a clue what war could be like when we first arrived, she thought, gazing along the paved way that led from the jetty straight through the entrance and under the arcade. We had no idea that these tramlines would be used for trolleys to bring men from the boats to the wards, just like they'd been used for the past two hundred years. We didn't know anything about the Navy or the way it worked, or the words it used; we didn't know what the matelot meant when he told us to "turn starboard" – we didn't even know what a *matelot* was. Her lips twitched again, and she gave the sailor who had brought her over – a matelot himself, in his square rig uniform – a sudden grin.

'Well, thank Gawd for that,' he said, raising his eyebrows. 'Thought you'd been turned into stone. I was just about to pinch you to see.'

'You'd have found out pretty soon I wasn't,' she said, laughing. 'I can pack quite a punch when I'm pinched! Sorry, I was just taking it all in – thinking about the first time I came here. It seems so long ago.' She bent to hoist her kitbag on to her shoulder. 'Thanks for bringing me over. I'd better go and find out where I'm supposed to be. I wonder what changes there'll have been.'

'Not many. A place like this don't change much. Pity we can't say the same about the town.' He glanced past her at the buildings of Gosport across the creek, and Portsmouth on the far side of the harbour. 'Taken a fair battering round here – but you'd know about that, if you were here in forty-one.'

'Yes,' Thursday agreed, thinking again of the Blitz. 'Yes, I do.'

She climbed on to the jetty and walked slowly along the marble-smooth paved way that had been trodden by so many thousands of feet over the past two centuries. Haslar Hospital, so difficult to reach by land from Portsmouth, had been ideally situated for bringing wounded sailors from ships in the harbour and the Solent. Standing on the very edge of a low cliff, now retained by a steeply sloping sea wall, it looked straight out across the Solent to the Isle of Wight, yet here on the other side it was sheltered by the neck of the harbour and its own twisting, narrow creek. The phrase 'Up the creek without a paddle', she'd been told when she first came here, had actually originated in Haslar Lake, as it was called, and probably came from the days when sailors brought here had had only a small chance of surviving.

Treatment was better now, especially with the wonderful new drug, penicillin, which had just been brought in – but there had still been plenty of deaths. All the same, Thursday felt proud as she passed under the low, vaulted roof of the arcade and remembered how she and the other new VADs had stood here and cheered so loudly that Madam had come to see what all the noise was about, and reminded them that they were in a hospital. And even prouder when she recalled those dark days after Dunkirk when the wounded men had poured in, coming by boat and being trollied up the tramlines just as in the old days, and coming into this arcade to be sent to the wards . . .

So many memories, she thought, pausing at the other side of the arcade to gaze across the wide quadrangle at the avenue of trees leading to the little church, and at the gracious Georgian façades of the buildings that stood at each side. So many friends, so many patients. I wonder where they all are now. I wonder if there are any still here . . .

'Tilford!'

Thursday jumped. The voice was unmistakable and, when she turned, the woman striding towards her seemed to have stepped straight out of her thoughts. The tall, elegant figure emphasised by the belt clipped round its narrow waist, the thin, aristocratic face, the bright brown eyes and, most of all, that crisp, clear voice.

'Madam!'

'So you haven't quite forgotten us, then.' Miss Makepeace, the Red Cross Commandant at Haslar, who had been in charge of all VADs there since the war began, surveyed her just as she had done on that cold, snowy afternoon when Thursday and Patsy Martin had first arrived. It was a cool, assessing look, as if she were sizing you up and considering your fitness for the job, and once again Thursday found herself holding her breath and hoping she would not be found wanting. Then that familiar warm twinkle came into the bright eyes, the firm lips twitched into a smile, and the smooth brown head nodded as if some test had been passed. 'It's good to see you again, Tilford.'

'It's good to see you too, Madam.' Thursday glanced around the big open space. 'It's good to be back.'

Miss Makepeace gave another sharp nod, as if that were only to be expected. Where else would one want to be, but at Haslar? But Thursday felt a small twinge of guilt as she spoke, for her words weren't entirely true. It *was* good to be back, in a way, but the past two years had been filled with so many new sights and sounds and experiences, that coming back to where it had all begun seemed to be something of an anti-climax. There was nothing new to discover here in Haslar. She knew it all so well. And she was so much older now than when she had first arrived – so much more experienced, so much wiser, so much sadder . . .

Worst of all, Dr Connor Kirkpatrick wasn't here – and Haslar without Connor was an empty place.

Madam was watching her, those bright brown eyes as keen as ever, missing nothing. 'You won't have much time for nostalgia, Tilford. There's plenty of work on its way, as you may have guessed. You'll find some of your old friends here, I dare say, so there'll be lots of news to catch up on, but the first priority is to find out where you'll be working. Sister Tutor will decide that, but you can have a meal first and get settled in. You're in your old dormitory – I expect you can remember the way.' She turned, as if Thursday were already dismissed from her mind, then turned back and gave her that warm, well-remembered smile. 'I've had excellent reports of your work in Egypt. Of all my girls, in fact. Well done – I'm proud of you.'

Thursday blinked back the sudden tears. 'Thank you, Madam.' She hefted her kitbag on to her shoulder and began to climb the familiar stairs to the dormitory. Nothing had changed here either, she thought, treading the old brown linoleum between the brass strips on the edge of each step. She wondered who would be in the dorm with her. Old friends, Madam said, but the last she'd heard of Patsy, she was in Scotland. And Jeanie Brown had been posted abroad at the same time as Thursday, only two or three months after Patsy's wedding to Roy Greenaway in June 1941, and someone had told Thursday that they thought she'd been killed. And what about Helen Stanway, who had shown them all around the hospital on their first day, tall, bony Ellen Bridges from Dorset, Anne Davis from Kent, and Susan Morrison from near Guildford? Where were they all now? Would she find any of them waiting for her in the dormitory?

And of course, there was Vera Hapgood, she thought with a wry smile. The least popular girl at Haslar, sallow-faced and brooding, with a sarcastic and bitter tongue. What had happened to *her* in the past two years? Would she be back at Haslar?

The only ones Thursday knew about were her great friend Elsie Jackson, from Portsmouth, and Louisa Wetherby – Louisa who was 'posh' and had been to boarding school in Great Malvern, not far from Thursday's own home in Worcester. She, Elsie and Thursday had been together in Alexandria, working side by side in the same wards, and had become good friends despite the difference in their backgrounds. We've been through too much together not to be, Thursday thought. It doesn't make any difference when you're emptying bedpans together. And we've all learned a lot since we started here as VADs together, way back in 1940.

The sense of having stepped back into the past was even stronger as she came to the door of the dormitory. How many times had she climbed those stairs, worn out after a day on the wards or a night on the town? How many times had she run out, still fastening her cap, terrified of being late for duty? *'Navy time is five minutes early, nurse . . .'* She could hear Sister Burton's voice now, reproving any girl who was even a few seconds late, and she remembered the jokes about the ship sailing without you if you weren't on time. And Haslar *was* a ship, in Navy terms – a ship where every man, however badly wounded, was on active service, and every nurse's task was to get the patients fit to return to sea. In order to maintain the atmosphere and discipline of a real ship, the terminology was the same: 'deck' for floor, 'heads' for lavatories, 'quarterdeck' for the long, tree-lined avenue leading to the little church of St Luke.

The familiarity of it all flooded back and, as she pushed open the door, Thursday almost expected to see exactly what she had seen on that first January day and so often afterwards – the rows of beds with their neat counterpanes, each with a blue anchor embroidered on its centre, and the girls either sitting or lying on them or clustered around the stove in the middle of the long room, drinking cocoa. Elsie Jackson, half asleep as usual. Patsy, darning her stockings. Jeanie knitting a navy-blue balaclava or socks. Ellen Bridges reading *Woman's Own*, Louisa Wetherby writing a letter home, Vera Hapgood sitting apart from them all, as if she were better in some way. And Anne and Susan playing draughts or snakes and ladders, looking up to suggest a game of Ludo with some of the others . . . The picture was so clear in her mind that it came as a shock to see the beds replaced by two-tier iron bunks, and an even bigger shock to see the different faces turned towards her. The strange, unknown faces.

Thursday stopped abruptly, feeling almost as if she'd been thrown into a different world. The faces blurred before her, swam a little and then settled again into sharp focus. She was able to see their expressions – enquiring, friendly, smiling. And then, with a sense of joyful relief, to recognise one or two.

'Elsie, you bad penny! And *Patsy* – I didn't think you'd be here! Oh, and Ellen and Susan too – oh, it's lovely to see you all again.' She found herself enveloped in hugs, returning them with tears running down her cheeks. 'Look what you're doing, you're making me cry! Oh, it's so *good* to be with you, you horrors.'

'You're making us cry too,' Patsy said, grinning through her own tears. She'd hardly changed at all, Thursday thought, still as small and bright-faced, her dark curls as exuberant as ever. 'Just shows how awful it is to think we're all back here where we started.' She turned and held Thursday's hand high in the air, as if showing her off to the rest of the girls in the long room. 'This is Thursday Tilford. She was here with us in 1940 and 1941, all through the Blitz. Not a bad nurse, all things considered, and she makes a smashing cup of cocoa.'

The girls looked at her with varying expressions. Some of them must be quite new, Thursday decided, for they looked no older than twenty or twenty-one, the age at which VADs were taken on. Others were her own age or older, and clearly at least as experienced as she. Thursday wondered where they had been serving and what stories they could tell. She smiled around at them, and they grinned back and waved or lifted their cocoa mugs in salute. It's all right, she thought with relief. We'll be friends. And then, catching the dark, sardonic eye of Vera Hapgood – well, most of us will.

For the time being, however, it was her own old friends she was interested in. Patsy had saved her the bunk above her own – 'you being so much taller than me' – and Elsie's was next to it. The three of them sat down together and gazed at each other. Two years – it wasn't so very long, really. You wouldn't expect many changes in that time. And yet, even though Patsy seemed much the same, there *were* changes – a splay of tiny lines at the corners of her eyes, and around her lips, lines that made her look as if more than two years had passed. And when you studied her more closely you could see a haunted expression in her eyes. Thursday, staring at her, felt a sudden stab of fear.

'What's happened?' she asked. 'Where've you been these past two years? I seem to have lost touch. Is everything all right, Pats? Is – is Roy all right?'

Patsy nodded. 'He was, last time I heard. But there don't seem to be any letters getting through now, and you've seen what's happening – all the troops coming south, the ships crowding into the Channel. People say it's the Second Front – the invasion. And Roy's ship . . .' To Thursday's dismay, she saw tears gather in her friend's eyes. 'I don't know if I can take much more of all this worry,' she said defeatedly. 'He's been sunk twice – caught in an engine-room fire, nearly drowned. I mean, for God's sake, he's not a *cat*, with nine lives. He's just an ordinary sailor. How lucky can anyone be?'

'I don't know,' Thursday said. She thought of the day they'd met Roy Greenaway and the other two sick-berth attendants they'd gone around with – Doug Brighton and Tony West. Three breezy young sailors, looking forward to getting back to sea as soon as the VADs were sufficiently trained to replace them on the wards. Three cheeky, bantering young men who had cycled over Pneumonia Bridge into Gosport and taken them to tea at the Swiss Café or gone dancing at Lee and Grange. Three young men with their whole lives to look forward to – and now Tony was dead and the other two still facing peril. 'I just don't know, Pats. I can't say he'll be all right, because none of us knows what's going to happen. But we can think about him – pray, if you like. They say it helps.'

'Do they?' Patsy said tonelessly. 'It didn't help Tony, or all those other young chaps who got killed, did it? They're just as dead as if nobody'd given them a thought.'

They were silent for a moment, then Elsie spoke in her old, brisk, matter-of-fact tone. 'Come on, Pats. No use looking on the black side. We're here to do a job of work and we're not going to be much use if we sit about grizzling.'

Patsy looked at her and then grinned. She reached out and took Thursday's hand. 'It's all right, Thurs. I'm not the only one with a bloke out there. And at least we've had our share of happiness. And now we three are back here together, and there's a lot of hard work coming. It's the best thing, hard work – especially our sort.' She straightened her shoulders and went on determinedly, 'It's going to be good, us being here together again. It's going to be really good, Thursday.'

'Yes.' Thursday squeezed her hand and then got up and went to the window. She looked out over the hospital grounds, at the wall that ran alongside the top of the sloping sea wall. She could just see the green bulk of the Isle of Wight across the Solent. The sea was crowded with ships, some at anchor, some steaming for the harbour entrance. She gazed at them and thought of Patsy's words and of the sailor who had brought her across in the pinnace.

Something big was about to happen. And when something big happened in wartime, it always meant casualties.

There would be plenty of hard work to do in the coming weeks and, as she thought of what lay ahead, Thursday braced her shoulders and lifted her chin. Whatever had happened to them since they had last been here, she and the other VADs would be ready for it.

And I'm looking forward to it too, she thought. Not to the wounded men, but to helping them get better. And to working here with Elsie and Patsy, and whoever else is here too.

Patsy was right. It was going to be good.

Chapter Two

Sister Tutor was as brisk as Madam had been. 'Let me see, you did some theatre work when you were here before, didn't you? And you've done mixed ward nursing and theatre while you've been away. Well, we're going to need plenty of good theatre nurses in the next few weeks, so unless you've any objection to working underground I'd like you to go there. There's a Naval training course you could do as well, with qualifications if you pass the examination. I understand you were considering going in for full State Registration after the war. Are you still interested in that, or have your experiences in Egypt put you off the idea?'

Thursday hesitated. Her experiences in Egypt, she thought, ought to be a qualification in themselves but she knew there was far more to nursing, especially in peacetime. Tending wounded men was no preparation for illnesses such as cancer or heart disease, or any of the multitude of other complaints that could bring patients into hospital. She thought of the years of training that she would still have to do, and felt suddenly weary.

'I don't know, Sister,' she said honestly at last. 'I've spent such a long time as a VAD, I'm not sure how I'll feel about it after the war.' *After the war.* The words sounded strange, almost meaningless. They'd been spoken for so long, and yet the end of the war seemed as far away as ever. Further, in fact, for when they had first been spoken, everyone had been expecting the war to be 'over by Christmas'. And then the following Christmas . . . and then, slowly, hope and expectation had been put to the back of the mind as the nation gritted its teeth and resigned itself to years of endurance.

Sister Tutor regarded her for a moment, then nodded slightly, as if recognising the weariness of Thursday's heart. Perhaps she had seen it before, in all the girls who had come back to Haslar after their service abroad; in all the men and women who had suspended their lives five years ago to fight this war, who had lost friends, relatives and lovers. Perhaps she too felt the deep fatigue and longed for it to be all over.

'Well, there's no need to decide that now,' she said at last. 'I'll put you down for the Naval course anyway. There'll probably be plenty of others wanting to do it, too, so there's no guarantee you'll get a place.' She glanced down at her list again. 'Meanwhile, I'd like you to report to Ratings' Medical. Sister Burton is in charge there – you'll remember her, I'm sure, and I've no doubt she'll remember you.'

I bet she will, Thursday thought as she thanked the Sister and made her way to the ward where she had begun her days as a VAD. Once again she felt she had come full circle, but she was no longer the innocent she had been then, and she felt slightly resentful at the thought of meeting Sister Burton again. Just what *would* she remember about Thursday? The day she'd taken nearly an hour over her first blanket bath? The day she and some of the other girls had got into a heated and noisy argument while rolling bandages? The day she and Tony West had colluded to give Stoker Davis an enema he'd never forget?

Tony. He'd died on this ward. Thursday hadn't been looking after him herself – Jeanie Brown had been specialling him – but she'd been to see him as often as she could get away, holding his hand and gazing down with tears of pity in her eyes at his ruined face. And it was here, she thought, that she'd first met Connor. Connor Kirkpatrick, who had given her his smile and walked away with her heart.

Connor, somewhere between Africa and the Far East.

Connor, who had given her the little Naval brooch of a silver crown. Connor, who wore her cloth VAD badge next to his heart.

Connor, who was, as her sister Jenny had remarked, a 'bit out of her class' but who didn't seem to care. Connor, who wrote her such loving letters, who had – almost – made her a promise.

Did I do that too? she wondered as she tapped her way swiftly through the polished corridors. Did I really make him a promise? *Did* we promise each other anything with that little brooch, and that cloth badge? Or was it just wishful thinking, something that couldn't possibly last for years of separation? And how will we know whether it's lasted or not? Won't we be different people, when we meet again at last?

And had there been anyone else for him during all that time – as there had, perhaps, been someone for her?

Sister Burton was in the ward, looking exactly as she had two years before. She was on Captain's rounds when Thursday came through the double doors, walking smartly a step or two behind the Naval doctor, with a QARNN and a VAD close behind them. The Queen Alexandra nurse glanced briefly at Thursday and walked on, but the VAD gave her a warm grin and a wink behind Sister Burton's back. Thursday felt cheered. At least somebody wasn't trying to give her the impression she wasn't welcome any more.

To be fair, neither did Sister Burton when the doctor had departed and she was able to give Thursday her attention. She took her into the little office and sat down behind the desk, indicating that Thursday should take the other chair. 'Well, Tilford. So you've come back to us. I dare say it feels rather strange, doesn't it?'

'Yes, Sister.'

The smooth head nodded. 'Coming back always does. But you'll soon settle in again, I'm sure. Your overseas experience will have taught you how to do that.' She smiled suddenly. 'In fact, it might be a good idea to treat Haslar as a foreign country, accepting the differences instead of letting them upset you. Just until you get used to it.'

'It isn't Haslar that seems different,' Thursday said. 'Not the hospital itself, I mean – that all looks just the same. It's – it's – I don't quite know what it is,' she finished helplessly, and Sister Burton smiled again.

'It's you who are different, Tilford. And the people here too – some of them, anyway. So many of the nurses and VADs are new to you – it's odd to see all those strange faces in the places you know so well, doing the jobs you remember others doing. But I'm the same and so is Miss Makepeace, and I believe there are a few of your old friends here too – Greenaway, or Martin as she then was – and Jackson, and Hapgood. And you'll soon make friends amongst the others, I know.' There was a moment's silence and then she spoke more briskly, in her old, rather terse voice. 'Not that you're here for socialising. There's work to be done, Tilford, and there'll be more very soon. I want you to give your all to my ward, just as you did before. There are sick men to be nursed and, as usual, neither enough time nor enough nurses to do it. Come with me and I'll introduce you to the QARNN who's my staff nurse, and she'll tell you what to do.'

She rose to her feet, and Thursday stood back automatically to allow her to pass. The Sister paused once more and looked her in the eyes, and once again Thursday saw the warmth behind her cool gaze.

'You're very welcome here, Tilford,' she said quietly, and nodded. 'Very welcome indeed.'

'So how did you get on?'

The girls were back in the dormitory, lying on their beds after their first day's duty. Elsie had worked in the Zymotics block, where infectious diseases were treated, and Patsy had been sent to Officers' Medical. Like Thursday, she had applied for the course in theatre work and Thursday hoped they would both get it. It would be good to work with Patsy.

At Elsie's question, she rolled over to face the yellow-haired girl. Elsie was looking tired, she thought, but then so did they all. Scarcely back in England a week, after the long journeys from their foreign postings, they'd hardly had time to find their feet before being rushed off them. And the Second Front hadn't even begun yet. When the invasion took place – and everyone said it must be soon, now – they would be lucky to lie on their beds at all.

'I don't really know,' she said thoughtfully. 'I keep feeling as if I'd stepped back into the past and yet it's different – as if it's out of focus. It's like a dream, when you sort of know the place you're in but it's all different and you can't find your friends in the crowd. And I can't make out who all the strangers are.' She paused. 'I keep thinking of the ones who used to be here.'

'Like Jeanie,' Patsy agreed soberly. 'It was dreadful, what happened to her. She'd not long arrived in Singapore when the Japanese bombed Pearl Harbor. They just overran the whole place – nobody had a chance.' Her eyes were full of tears. 'The ones that got away in ships were bombed and sunk, and you can imagine what happened to those who were left behind – the same as in Hong

Kong, raped and murdered.' Tears spilled over and ran down her cheeks. 'It's awful to think of Jeanie being treated like that. She was always so sweet and gentle.'

'Patsy!' Thursday stared at her, appalled. 'Nobody told me that. I knew she was supposed to have been killed, but I thought it was in a raid or something. Not like *that*.'

'Are you sure, Pats?' Elsie asked, as shocked as Thursday. 'Some of them were taken prisoner, weren't they? I mean, does anyone know for certain?'

'Well, I don't know – I've always thought she was killed. But even if she was taken prisoner,' Patsy shuddered, 'they treat them just as badly, don't they? I mean, we've heard some dreadful rumours about the Japanese POW camps.'

'Let's hope that's all they are, then – rumours.' Thursday felt shaken. She knew a little of what had happened in Singapore, through Connor's letters as well as through the news that had leaked out. Suddenly she felt that she couldn't lie here any longer. She swung her legs off her bed and stood up. 'Let's go into Gosport. I want to see if the Swiss Café's still there. And good old Pneumonia Bridge, and Bemister's Lane. Come on – it'll be like old times, and we might not get many more chances for a while.'

'We'll have to walk.' Patsy got up too. 'I left my bike in Scotland. It was such a wreck it wasn't worth dragging back.'

'I sold mine when I went to Egypt,' Thursday said. 'How about you, Elsie?'

'Mine's at my auntie's in Portsmouth. I thought I might bring it over sometime. But I don't mind the walk now. It's not that far.'

They brushed their hair and set off, feeling better for having something to do. As they crowded through the door, Thursday glanced over her shoulder and saw Vera Hapgood sitting alone, her face sallow under the fading tan, her mouse-coloured hair hanging straight on either side of her thin cheeks, her eyes brooding and unhappy.

Thursday felt a twinge of guilt. 'Come on, Vera. Come into Gosport with us.'

The other two turned and stared at her in surprise. Vera caught their glances and shook her head, a small, bitter smile twisting her lips. 'No, thanks. I don't want to push in where I'm not wanted.'

Thursday opened her mouth, but before she could speak Elsie

had hustled her through the door and down the wide stairs. At the bottom, Thursday pulled her arm away and flung them both an accusing look.

'What did you want to do that for?'

'Why do you think? Why on earth did you ask *her* along? Talk about a wet blanket! You know what she's like, Thursday, we were never pals with her.'

'That was two years ago.' Thursday followed them out of the door. 'We've grown up a bit since then. She's still nursing, isn't she? Doing the same sort of work as you and me and the rest of us. She's not as bad as you think, Elsie.'

'I'll believe you, thousands wouldn't.' Elsie gripped her arm again as if afraid Thursday was going to run back to the dormitory and fetch Vera down by force. 'Some day we'll ask her along again and see if it's true, if you want to. But not today, eh? Today, it's just the three of us, the way it always used to be. A walk down Memory Lane, see? A look round Gosport to see if it's changed much since we were here last. A cup of tea and a bun in the Swiss Café and a stroll down the High Street. Wander round Woolworth's and Littlewood's. See if they've still got that parrot in the window of the Isle of Wight Hoy. Lean on the ferry railings and look at the ships. Why, we could even go over on the ferry and have a look at Pompey.'

Thursday laughed. 'We'll never have time to do all that! All right, Else, it's just the three of us this time. I won't push Vera on you if you really don't want her, but you ought to give her a chance, all the same.'

'We will,' Patsy said as they swung out through the gates, giving the sailors on guard a cheery wave. 'We will. Only not just yet, all right? Let's get to know each other again first.'

Gosport had changed more than they expected. Somehow, they had forgotten the bomb damage of the Blitz and remembered the town as it had been when they'd first arrived. The overgrown jungle of the bombsites took them by surprise, and the sight of the burned-out shell of the Ritz cinema, still standing beside the moat that surrounded Walpole Park, shook them. They gazed at it, remembering the films they'd been to see, remembering the young men who had taken them there.

'Roy and me used to sit in the back row,' Patsy said at last, turning away. 'I don't know that we ever saw much of the film, but we enjoyed ourselves!'

They walked down the High Street, popping into the sweetshop to furnish themselves with bags of sherbet bonbons and toffee crunch. Although the hospital kept their ration books, they were able to use their own sweet coupons and had enough for a few ounces of sweets each. Chewing happily, they sauntered past the Swiss Café where they had enjoyed so many teas and buns, and went into Woolworth's.

'Everyone always comes into Woolworth's,' Elsie remarked as they browsed around the counters. 'It's nice to be able to just look, without feeling you've got to buy something. Not that I've ever managed to come out without buying something,' she added, stopping to examine the array of Pond's lipsticks and face creams. 'This is quite a pretty colour.'

'It would suit you too,' Patsy said, narrowing her eyes at the pale pink. 'Better than that red you're wearing now. It's too bright for you, that is.'

'I like a bright lipstick. That one wouldn't look as if I'd got any on at all.'

'Yes, it would, it just wouldn't be so bright. That red sort of drains your colour. Why don't you get it, Else?'

'I might. I was thinking of some new scent. *Evening in Paris* – I like that one. I wore it a lot in Egypt. Mind you, you needed scent there, didn't you, Thurs? It was more like *Evening in Sewers* sometimes. Specially when it was hot.'

They laughed and strolled on. It was strange to be back, Thursday thought, struck once again by a wave of the feeling that all this had happened before. They'd wandered round Woolworth's like this so many times, discussing the few lipsticks and scents available – not that there'd been much to discuss. The shortages of rationing had just begun to bite then, and there was little in the way of luxury goods. Factories had better things to do than produce cosmetics – or maybe they weren't better things, she thought wryly, remembering the injuries she and the other nurses had to deal with day after day. Maybe it *was* better to produce frivolous things like lipstick and cold cream than bombs and bullets.

There was even less to choose now. It had been one of the shocks of their returns to find that five years of war meant that luxuries were in shorter supply than ever before; everyone had become expert at making things last. Lipsticks were used down to the very last smear in the tube, and scraps of soap gathered together in jars to be melted and hardened into a lump. Washing-up soda was swished in the hard water and then taken out so that it wouldn't dissolve too quickly. Stockings were darned to within an inch of their lives, jumpers unpicked and reknitted into mittens or socks, and shirt collars turned and turned again. New clothes were something you saved your clothing coupons for, and then struggled to find something to buy with them. Make do and mend had become a way of life.

They walked down to the ferry and leaned on the rails, gazing out over the harbour. As always, it was full of ships, some of them moored to the jetties of the dockyard opposite, others riding at buoys in the middle. The harbour stretched away towards the green bulwark of Portsdown Hill, pocked with the white craters of the chalkpits, and other ships could be seen in the upper reaches. The girls stared at them.

'It's going to happen soon, isn't it?' Patsy said at last. 'I mean, look at them. They're not here on their holidays.'

'I still don't understand it,' Elsie said. 'I was round my gran's over near Ann's Hill last weekend – my mum's been stopping with her since she got poorly – and there's long queues of Army stuff pouring in, just clogging up all the roads and lanes. I walked up Leesland Road and there were tanks coming through; the kerbstones were all squashed and marked with their tracks. It's not just our boys either, it's Canadians, and American GIs, thousands and thousands of them. Gran told me they came through in jeeps one morning, chucking bars of chocolate and chewing gum, and even money, out at the kids on their way to school.'

'Where were they going?' Thursday asked.

'Stokes Bay, apparently.' She shook her head. 'All those thousands of men and tanks and lorries and God knows what, all heading for the beaches. What are they going to do when they get there, that's what I want to know. How can they get all that stuff on board ships? I mean, they're huge, those tanks, and there's DUKWs and—'

'Ducks?' Thursday interrupted. 'What are they, for goodness sake? The coxswain on the pinnace mentioned them.'

'Oh, you know, those amphibious things – look like a cross between a tank and a flaming great lorry, and they can go on land and water. It's *DUKW*. I can never remember what it stands for. I suppose they can drive them across the Channel, but I can't see how they'll get the rest over.'

'Well, ours is not to reason why,' Thursday said, stepping away from the railings. 'We probably shouldn't even be wondering about it. They must know what they're doing.'

Elsie nodded. 'Gran says the beaches have been wired off for months now; nobody can get near without a permit, and there's been no end of building work going on there. The man next door to her says they've been constructing a bridge but that's daft. At least,' she added doubtfully, 'I suppose it is.'

'I heard it was a tunnel,' Patsy said. 'That would make more sense, wouldn't it? A tunnel right through to France and then our boys could pop up right under the Germans' noses.' She bit her lip and turned away abruptly. 'Whatever it is, I just hope it gets this horrible war over as quickly as possible, and without thousands more people getting killed, too.'

Sober again, they walked back to the Swiss Café and pushed open the door. Once again, Thursday felt that sense of *déjà vu*. The first time I ever came in here, she thought, was with Tony West and we sat at this very table and had toasted tea-cakes. Oh, Tony . . .

For a little while, she'd thought herself in love with the merry-faced SBA. Then he'd gone away, and although she had written to him the feeling had faded – until he came back, so grievously wounded, and died of his terrible injuries. It had taken her a long time to get over the mixture of grief and guilt she had felt then, and it wasn't until she had met Connor that she'd been able to let herself think of love again. And then Connor too had gone away . . .

'Penny for them?' Elsie said, watching her, and Thursday blushed.

'Oh, you know – I was just thinking about all the times we used to come in here. It hasn't changed at all, has it?' She looked around the walls. 'Got a bit shabbier, that's all.'

'It needs a lick of paint,' Elsie agreed, 'but so does everywhere. I think they're only making grey now, for battleships.'

They were silent for a few minutes, until the tea and plate of buns arrived. Then Patsy glanced at the other two. 'Well? What have you been doing all this time? How was Egypt?'

'Sandy,' Thursday retorted with a grin. She smiled reminiscently. 'You know, I never thought I'd get sent anywhere like that. I mean, me going to Egypt with all those camels and pyramids and things. My mum's never been further than Weston-super-Mare! Dad was in France, of course, in the First War,' she added, 'but that was no picnic.'

'And Egypt was?' Patsy asked. 'You mean you had a good time?'

Elsie glanced sideways at Thursday, then grinned. 'Well, of course we did, whenever we got the chance. What do you take us for? Weren't going to sit in the mess with our knitting and pass up all the dances, were we? *You* wouldn't have!'

'No, I wouldn't.' Patsy smiled. 'I didn't even in Scotland. You've got to have a bit of fun, and Roy never minded.' She winked. 'So tell us what it was like, out there under the desert stars. Did any tall, dark and handsome sheiks carry you off to their tents and have their wicked way with you?'

Elsie laughed outright. 'Think I'd be here now if they did? I always fancied myself sitting on a gold cushion being fed with dates . . . But there were plenty of soldiers about, just waiting for a bit of home comfort.'

'Soldiers?' Patsy said. 'But we're Naval VADs.'

Thursday nodded. 'Yes, there were a few Navy people there because it was a Naval base, but the hospital itself was a military one. And I can tell you, they don't half do things different. No nice china plates like we've got here, with a pretty blue anchor on them – they use *tin* ones! And tin mugs, that nearly burn your lips off if you're not careful.'

'Not that we had all that many of them,' Elsie added. 'Not enough room on the merchant ships for stuff like that, see. Some of our blokes had to make mugs out of old beer cans. But it wasn't just that kind of thing, it was the way they wanted things done – like hospital corners. I mean, you'd think the way we tuck the sheets in at Haslar would be good enough for anyone, wouldn't you, but no, it had to be done different, the *Army* way, and woe betide you if they weren't right on Colonel's Rounds.'

'*Colonel's* Rounds? But they have Captains in the Army, don't they?'

'Yeah, but an Army Captain's not like a Naval one. And that's another thing we had to learn – all the ranks. I tell you, it was like going back to flaming school. And now I'm back with the Navy I've got to start all over again and I just *know* I'm going to get in a muddle at the wrong moment.'

The other two laughed at Elsie's woebegone face, and then Thursday said, 'Still, we enjoyed it. We had a good time.' Her face clouded. 'But there were plenty who didn't. We got the casualties from El Alamein, and all those desert battles – pretty knocked about too, they were. You know the sort of thing.'

Patsy nodded. They had all seen plenty of battle injuries, here at Haslar and on their postings. Nobody needed to be told about the limbs blown away, the terrible abdominal injuries, the faces ruined beyond repair, the agonised and lingering deaths.

There was another silence. Thursday glanced at Elsie's face and poured another cup of tea. She pushed it gently closer to Elsie's hand. They had all seen too much suffering and death, and although you were supposed to develop a suit of armour and not allow it to upset you, nobody could ever be truly protected.

'Let's forget it for a while now,' she suggested. 'We're going to see it all again pretty soon, unless I'm much mistaken. Tell Patsy how many boyfriends you had out there, Elsie.' She winked.

'Quite a few, I'd guess,' Patsy said with a grin.

Elsie brushed a hand across her eyes and tried to look coy. 'I don't know why you should think that, I'm sure. Well – maybe one or two. *You* know.'

'Yes, *we* know,' Patsy said. 'One or two hundred, that's what you mean.'

'No, I don't! Anyway, I never counted,' Elsie said, reducing both the others to giggles. 'Well, all right, there *were* quite a few. But there's bound to be, isn't there? They keep going away. And you've got to give a bit of comfort to the boys while they've got the chance.'

'So long as it's not too much comfort,' Patsy said with a grin at Thursday. 'Or was it a case of, if you can't be good, be careful?'

'Not at all,' Elsie said with unaccustomed dignity. 'More a case of, if you can't be careful, be good! Look, it's different out there under the desert stars, ain't it, Thurs?'

'I think you'd better tell Patsy about your romantic adventures when we're somewhere a bit more private,' Thursday told her, glancing around the crowded café, and then, noticing the wall clock, 'Hey, look at the time! We'd better get our skates on or we'll miss supper.'

'Thursday! And you've only just eaten a whole tea-cake. I don't know where you put it, I honestly don't.' Elsie looked at her friend's slim figure and patted her own stomach ruefully. 'It's not fair. I don't eat half as much as I used to, and I still can't shift it.'

'It's puppy fat,' Patsy told her solemnly. 'It'll go when you grow up.'

'Well, if I'm not grown up at twenty-six, I don't reckon I ever will be. Puppy fat indeed! Must be a blooming big puppy, that's all I can say.'

The girls laughed as they paid the bill and scurried along the High Street to dive into the narrow opening of Bemister's Lane. Pretty soon, they were panting up the steep incline of Pneumonia Bridge, the narrow walkway that had been built to replace the original bridge destroyed early in the war. They ran down the other side and between the high brick walls to the hospital entrance, passing the sailors on guard to arrive at their quarters in D Block just in time to sign in for supper.

We did this so many times, Thursday thought as she sat at the table, eating shepherd's pie. And yet we've changed a lot, since the last time we sat here together. We've been through all kinds of experiences, some we'll never even be able to tell each other about.

We're different – every one of us.

Chapter Three

Elsie's reminiscences about Egypt brought Thursday's own memories to mind as she lay in bed that night, aware of the other girls around her on the iron bunks. Some were already asleep, breathing steadily or snoring gently. Patsy was making that funny little snuffling noise she sometimes made when she was dreaming, and Elsie was clicking her tongue at the back of her throat in the way that had sometimes nearly driven Thursday mad, and which she had missed so much when the other girl was sent to a different hospital in Cairo.

It wasn't only the other VADs that she'd missed, of course. Her family had been very much in her thoughts while she was in Egypt. She'd lain awake like this on so many nights, thinking of them and wondering what they were doing at that precise minute. Her father Walter, working at the porcelain factory where they were now making parts for aeroplanes and military vehicles; her sister Jenny, who had volunteered as an orderly at Worcester Royal Infirmary and was now halfway through her SRN training. Her mother Mary, who struggled to hold the family together, who had wanted Thursday to marry Sidney Fletcher. And her brother Steve, whom they'd thought killed at Dunkirk with his cousin Mike and heard – on the very day of Patsy's wedding, almost three years ago to the day – was still alive and a prisoner of war in Germany.

Patsy's wedding! With a shock, Thursday realised that the anniversary was only a few days away. Friday 6 June, it had been and now it was Saturday 3 June. She thought of that day, of the service in the village church only a mile away from the hospital, of the sunshine and the pretty dresses that had been somehow cobbled together, of the joy in Patsy's and Roy's faces. They never seemed to have stopped bickering during their courtship, but there was no doubt, when you looked at their radiant happiness, that they were meant for each other.

Thursday's heart ached. The tears rose to her eyes and she turned her face into the pillow so as not to disturb anyone with her weeping. Connor, she thought, Connor. We never even got as far as being married before you went away, and that was even longer ago than Patsy's wedding. And then she scolded herself for her selfishness and self-pity.

So much had happened since she had first come to Haslar and learned what nursing was all about, what war really could mean. It meant courage, too. Thursday and the other VADs had had to call upon more reserves of courage than they'd ever thought possible. She thought back to the air raids, when they had had to help patients down from the wards to the basements and wait for the bombing to stop – except that Thursday hadn't always waited. A small smile touched her lips as she recalled the day she'd crept back up to the wards to be with the men with broken limbs who'd had to be left there, strapped to Balkan beams and unable to move, and found Madam there as well. And the time the big, creaky lift had stuck and Elsie had got a sing-song going inside. Then there was the Blitz itself, on 10 January 1941 . . .

I wasn't even in Haslar that night, she thought. I was up on Portsdown Hill with Connor in a borrowed car, and when we heard the sirens go and the planes come over, it was like fireworks night. Getting back to the hospital was a nightmare of bombs and explosions and incendiaries. She remembered the frantic dash through streets that were already aflame, the desperate pleas of injured people, the flying debris and the thick, acrid smoke. And then she remembered Susie.

The little girl's uncle had been almost mad with distress. He'd been looking after his sister and two young children and he'd gone out as soon as the raid began, on fire-watching duty. His sister had stayed in the house with the baby, who was poorly, and when the house had been hit it had caught fire immediately. He'd managed to get little Susie out, but there was no chance for the others, and Susie herself was so badly hurt that Connor had had to amputate her leg there and then. Thursday had helped him and then they'd taken the little girl back to the hospital in the borrowed car. Connor had said afterwards that his friend, whose car it was, would never be able to get the bloodstains out.

Oh, Connor, she thought. *Where are you now?*

It all seemed so very long ago. It was only two days later that Connor had gone away, leaving Thursday with the little brooch in the shape of a Naval crown. She'd stayed another six months at Haslar before being posted to Egypt, and her life had taken a new turn. Images swirled in her brain, half memory, half dream. She could see a succession of faces passing in front of her. Connor . . . Susie . . . Denise and Vic . . . her brother Steve and her cousins Mike and Leslie . . . her mother and father. Then Connor again. She jerked awake suddenly, her heart thudding. She had woken so abruptly that she felt sick and dizzy, and she lay still, trying to steady her breathing, to calm down.

I've got to stop this, she thought, listening to the quiet breathing all about her. I've got to get to sleep. There's a big flap due any day now, and I'm going to need all my strength. I haven't got *time* to lie here going over the past.

Feeling calmer, she turned over again and then felt under her pillow for the little brooch. She felt its shape, the points of the crown, the smooth surface. It had been given her with love, she knew that. Connor had said he wished it could have been a ring. And then they'd been plunged into the Blitz, and there had been no more time. He was gone, leaving Thursday in a mist of tears before she wiped them away, pulled back her shoulders and found a smile to take on duty with her. Neither of them had had any idea that their separation would last so long.

Three years. Three years of hard work, of the fascination of a new land, of unexpected joys and sorrows. We're different people now, she thought, fingering the tiny brooch. What will it be like when we meet again?

And what of the other brooch, packed in its little white box at the bottom of her case? The brooch that was shaped like a star.

With questions still echoing in her mind she drifted away, at last, into sleep.

Connor had sailed for Singapore in January 1941. A British Crown Colony since 1867, it was a major port in the Far East and a popular 'draft' for sailors. Ratings and officers were able to take their wives for the two- or three-year tour of duty, and they lived a pleasant way of life, with servants and nannies, and plenty of time to meet for lunch or cocktails.

Not all the wives took an easy life, however; some were working as VADs in the Naval hospital, and Thursday had hoped that she might get her own posting there, and so be able to meet Connor again when he was in port. But what had happened to Singapore in February 1942 put a cruel end to all such hopes.

The threat from the Japanese had been growing all through the previous year. Now, first Hong Kong and then Singapore were overrun, the men, women and children who had thought themselves safe, raped and murdered. In the hospitals, nurses and patients were bayoneted to death; in the streets, women and children were cut down or shot. The island was in chaos, with casualties flooding into the hospitals while those same hospitals were desperately trying to evacuate. As the Japanese soldiers arrived in their tens of thousands, the British, Australians and Indians who had been prepared to defend Singapore to the death, were ordered to leave.

Connor wrote to tell Thursday about it much later, from Java. His own ship, the *Livid*, had been one of those which left Singapore in the second week of February, loaded with civilians. It was one of the last of the Naval ships to do so. As it steamed away from the island, those on board looked back to see a thick black plume of smoke rise from the oil terminals in the dockyard, and knew that the Naval base had been deliberately fired, and abandoned.

It was one of the worst moments of my life, he wrote, *to see that great Naval base, the whole reason for Singapore's existence, scuttled like a ship and left deserted. If Dunkirk was a defeat, what could you call this? I felt so terrible about those poor souls left behind. We'd heard a bit about the awful things the Japanese had done in Hong Kong and we knew they'd show no mercy. And we couldn't do a thing about it – all we could do was get our own people to safety, and hope for the best for the others.*

Even this simple hope was doomed. Every ship leaving Singapore, whether it be Naval or Merchant, had to run the gauntlet of the Japanese bombers. The *Empire Star*, carrying over two thousand people, was hit three times but managed to limp to safety in Batavia. Others were sunk and their cargo of refugees either drowned or were washed up on the shore, to be captured or to die.

They kept evacuating to the last moment, Connor wrote. *By 14*

February they were down to little coastal steamers. They were loaded with civilians, as well as nurses still trying to look after the sick and wounded. They set up sick bays wherever they could – on the decks, in the holds – but all to no avail. Thursday, reading his letter, could sense the long pause while he tried to find words to tell her what had happened; she could almost hear his heavy sigh as he finally wrote, quite baldly: *They were bombed out of the water – almost all the eighty or so vessels that left Singapore that day. We don't know what happened to the people – how many were killed or drowned, how many struggled to land on one of the hundreds of little islands, nor what befell them if they did. We don't know what the Japanese did to those who were left in Singapore, but we fear the worst . . .*

Chapter Four

Thursday woke next morning with a headache and heavy eyes. She felt as if she'd been crying all night, and perhaps she had – crying in her dreams for the hundreds of women and children who had been killed trying to escape from Singapore, for all the soldiers and sailors who had gone with them, for all those who had died since the war began.

She leaned over her bunk and looked down. Patsy was just waking in the bed below her. She opened her eyes, frowned a little as if wondering where she was, then closed them again, squeezing them tightly. She's thinking about Roy, Thursday realised, drawing back quickly. She must go through it every time she wakes up – thinking about him and then remembering he's somewhere at sea on one of those ships, waiting to go to France. She's wondering where he is and if she'll ever see him again.

After a moment or two, she heard the other girl move and peeped down again. Patsy glanced up at her and grinned. 'Hello, you.' Her eyes were damp but the anxiety had gone, pushed resolutely aside. 'Talk about flaming June, eh!'

Thursday looked towards the tall windows. Someone had removed the blackout and she could see the sky, grey and overcast. It was very different from the blue, sunny skies of Egypt, but the work, she knew, would be the same. She dropped down from her bunk to the floor. Elsie was already up and heading for the washroom, her dollybag, made from an old towel, swinging from her wrist. Thursday followed her and found herself at the row of washbasins with Vera Hapgood between herself and Elsie.

The sallow girl gave her a brief glance. 'So you've come back at last.'

Thursday was determined to be friendly. 'Yes, here we all are, just like a purse full of bad pennies. Did you get posted anywhere interesting, Vera?'

The glance turned to a sneer. 'You know flipping well I didn't. It was all right for you lot, swanning about in Africa. *Some* of us had to stay here and hold the fort.'

'You mean you've been at Haslar all this time? But I thought all the mobile VADs—'

'Well, you thought wrong,' Vera told her bluntly, and pushed past. 'Excuse me. *Some* of us have got work to do, if you don't mind.'

As she stalked out of the washroom, Thursday met Elsie's eye and grimaced. Elsie made a face back. 'You surely didn't expect her to have changed. She's got an even bigger grudge now – thinks we've had it easy, sunning ourselves while she and the others have had to stay in England.'

'Or Scotland,' Patsy remarked, taking Vera's place between them and turning on the tap. 'I can tell you this, some of us think it's the people who stayed at Haslar who had it easy. It's darned cold up there!'

'I don't think anyone's had it easy, wherever they've been,' Elsie said soberly. 'Not nurses, anyway. It stands to reason, doesn't it? We've been sent to the front line, wherever it is, because that's where the casualties are. And even if we weren't near the front line we were still busy getting sick and wounded men fit to go back into action. It hasn't been a rest cure for nurses, whoever they are.'

'No,' Thursday agreed. 'I was thinking last night about the ones who were in Singapore. Hundreds of them died then. As for the ones who got away – most of them ended up in Japanese hands.' She shuddered. 'Connor's told me a bit about it, but no one knows exactly what's happening to them. It doesn't bear thinking of.'

The others looked at her. Patsy said, 'So he's still all right, then, Surgeon Commander Kirkpatrick? I didn't like to ask before.'

'Oh yes,' Thursday said. 'He's all right. Had a few close shaves, and I suppose there'll be more, but so far, *Livid*'s managed to stay in one piece. Goodness knows how.' She opened a round tin of toothpaste and rubbed her toothbrush across the pink block inside. 'He tries to write as often as possible, but of course when they're in action . . .'

The others nodded. Thursday saw Patsy bite her lip and knew she was thinking again of Roy, somewhere at sea. The familiar terror clutched again at her own heart. Even now, something similar might have happened to Connor. Any day, she might switch on the wireless to listen to the news and hear that his ship had been sunk, but she wouldn't know if he had survived until someone wrote to tell her. He might be killed by bullets or bombs, or drowned in the sea he loved so much, and she wouldn't know; she would have no idea.

I *would*, she thought, scrubbing her teeth fiercely. I *would* know. I'd know the minute it happened, I'd feel it inside, I'd feel his pain . . . But she couldn't be sure, and the dread had been with her so long, it was now a part of her.

She picked up her washing things and went back to the dormitory. In silence, she began to make her bed, stretching up over Patsy's to smooth out the white counterpane and make sure the blue embroidered anchor was exactly in the middle. That was something that wouldn't have changed, here at Haslar! And neither had the strict Naval discipline, the demand for punctuality – 'Naval time is five minutes early' – nor the consistently high standards expected of the Queen Alexandra nurses – the QARNNs – and the VADs.

The dormitory was bustling now with girls getting ready for breakfast before going on duty and relieving the night staff. Thursday jerked herself out of her musing, and gave her counterpane a final tug. It was time to stop being self-pitying and get back to work. She put on her cap, made sure the white kirby grips were holding it firmly in place, gave a last twitch to her apron and checked that the little silver watch her Aunt Maudie had given her was pinned to her bib. Thursday had promised to take care of it and return it to her aunt when the war was over. She looked on it as a talisman, to keep her safe and to remind her of home.

Ready at last, she hurried across to the ward. She was almost at the door when she heard brisk footsteps behind her and turned quickly, her face lighting up with pleasure.

'Louisa! I wondered where you'd got to.'

'I had a few days' extra leave because my father's ill.' The tall blonde girl caught her up and they smiled at each other. 'It's good to see you again, Thursday. I was wondering if there'd be anyone here that I knew.'

'There are plenty. Patsy's here, and Elsie, and Ellen Bridges, and Susan – and Vera Hapgood,' she finished with a grin.

Louisa made a face. 'Well, it can't be all good news, I suppose! Or maybe she's improved with time.'

'I don't think so. She and Elsie have already had one dust-up. But what about you, Louie? Is your dad better now?'

Louisa shook her head. Her thin, aristocratic face was sombre and her blue eyes shadowed. Her father had a title of some sort – an Honourable, Thursday thought – but she never talked about it and had always mucked in with the rest, and while they were in Alexandria the two had become good friends.

'He's not going to get better. It's his heart, you see. He just has to rest as much as possible, but you can see he's getting weaker all the time.'

'Oh, Louie – I'm sorry.' Thursday touched her friend's arm. 'It must have been awful, having to come away and leave him and your mum.'

'Yes, it was, but I'm not the only one with problems at home. And we're going to be needed here.' Louisa glanced at her. 'Have you seen all the troops?'

Thursday nodded. 'The place is full of them. Lorries and all sorts, clogging up all the roads, and thousands and thousands of soldiers. It's like a massive queue, stretching right out into the country.'

'It's the invasion,' Louisa said soberly. 'It must be any day now. And d'you know, down in Falmouth they've got another fleet – of *cardboard* ships! Well, wooden ones anyway, knocked up out of plywood or something, and painted to look like real ships. My brother told me about them. And all round the east coast they've got planes and ships racing about like mad, pretending they're a crowd, to make the Germans think we're invading from there!'

Thursday stared at her. 'It sounds daft. It'll never work, surely. Mind you, there are some funny stories going round about what's happening at Stokes Bay. Someone told me they've been building some huge concrete things out there for months. And then they just disappeared. I heard they'd been towed out to sea and sunk but I can't believe that, can you? It doesn't make sense.'

Louisa shrugged. 'Nothing about this war makes sense. And I suppose we shouldn't be talking about it, even here. Anyway,' she moved forward briskly, 'we'd better get our skates on and get into the ward or Sister Burton will have our guts for garters.'

'Mind you,' Elsie said as they scrambled through their lunch a few hours later, 'it wasn't all bad in Alex, was it, Thurs? To tell the truth, it was pretty good a lot of the time.' She grinned wickedly. 'Specially when the Yanks arrived! They were so different from our lot – fresh from home, raring to go, plenty of money to spend, and—'

'And you all ready to help them spend it,' Vera Hapgood butted in. 'You always were a tart, Elsie Jackson!'

There was a sudden silence. Elsie's skin flushed a bright red and her eyes darkened with anger. She shot her hand across the table, grabbed the edge of Vera's plate and tipped it over, depositing gravy, meat and vegetables in the girl's lap. Breathing hard, she followed it with Vera's glass of water, and then she jumped up to face her old enemy, who by now was also on her feet and screaming abuse. The other girls sat by, horrified.

'Stop it, Elsie, for goodness *sake*!' Thursday grabbed Elsie's arm. 'And you stop that noise, Vera or you'll have Madam in here and you know what'll happen then. We'll be up before the Captain. Look, it was an accident, all right? If anyone asks, it was an *accident*. We'll settle this afterwards but for now just get the mess cleaned up, both of you, and stop behaving like children!'

The two enemies glared at her. 'What do you mean, an accident?' Vera demanded. 'She did it deliberately, you all saw it, and I don't care if we do come up before the Captain. I'll tell him what happened, and I'll tell Madam too. I'll get her thrown out—'

'Get *me* thrown out?' Elsie squawked. 'What about you, and what you called me? You'll be the one to get chucked out and I'll tell Madam myself!'

'You won't,' Thursday stated. 'You won't tell anyone, either of you. You're not babies in high chairs – you're twenty-six-year-old *women*, for goodness sake, far too old to throw food at one another. And neither of you is getting thrown out. You're VADs, remember? Nurses! You're needed here, and you're going to be needed even more when D-Day comes.' She stared at them. 'How can you even *think* of getting each other thrown out when there are men to be nursed, men who've risked their lives? What does it matter *what* she calls you?' she asked Elsie, and then turned to Vera. 'Not that you didn't deserve it. You'd better go and get yourself cleaned up and into a decent uniform before Madam does see you. *She* won't have the patience to listen to tale-telling and you'll *both* be for the high jump!'

Vera gave her a furious glance and then ran from the room. Elsie, looking mutinous, took the dustpan and brush from the girl who had run to fetch it, and set about cleaning the floor. She dumped the mess into the swill-bucket where leftover food was collected for the pigs at the farm along Clayhall Road, and came back to the table.

'Lucky we're near the door,' she said. 'Not too many people noticed, what with all the racket going on in here anyway. Sorry, Thurs, maybe I did fly off the handle a bit, but she just caught me on the raw. I mean, I was just trying to jolly things along a bit, that was all. We *did* have fun out there, but there was no harm in it. And I was never – well, what *she* called me.'

'No, of course you weren't,' Thursday said. Elsie had certainly kicked over the traces a bit during her time in Egypt, but that wasn't being a tart. 'But we've got to rub along together here, Else, just like we used to. And like we had to abroad, too,' she added, thinking of other 'Veras' she had met. 'There's always someone we won't get along with.'

'Nobody gets along with *her*,' Elsie muttered, but she sat down again and took a sip of water. Then she grinned. 'Well, there's one good thing come out of it – there'll be a spare helping of pudding at this table! What do you reckon, girls? Shall we save it for Her Ladyship, or shall we share it out amongst ourselves?'

'It's got to be soon.'

The thought was in everyone's mind, the words on everyone's lips. Thursday, taking a patient's temperature later that day, glanced out of the window at the Solent and blinked. The strip of water between Portsmouth and the Isle of Wight had been busy before – now it was packed with ships, crowded so thickly that she felt she could have walked to the Island across them. American as well as British, they floated at anchor, a solid grey mass of steel bulwarks on the grey swell of the sea, shifting beneath an iron-grey sky. And above them, hovering just below the swollen clouds, a vast flock of silver barrage balloons, each tethered to a ship by an almost invisible steel cable.

They look like kiddies going to a party, Thursday thought, then bit her lip, realising the kind of party it would be. There were thousands of them there. Thousands. She remembered what Elsie had said about the tanks and lorries and – what was it? – DUKWs. And all sorts of other queer vehicles that had been seen driving through Gosport. They must be intending to take them across on all these ships. But how did you get things like that on a ship, straight off the beach? And what would happen when they reached the other side? Surely it would take ages to disembark, and the Germans would be certain to find out. It could be Dunkirk and Dieppe all over again.

She shivered and turned away, hoping the authorities knew what they were doing. Mr Churchill, Field Marshal Montgomery – 'Monty' – General Eisenhower and the French leader, General de Gaulle – they must have thought it all out and decided it would work. The men she'd seen sitting by their vehicles at the roadside seemed cheerful enough, too cooking sausages on Primus stoves and chatting to the people from the nearby houses. They seemed ready to go, and keen to get into action.

And in a few days' time they'd be back again, some of them, she thought. Wounded and injured and dying too, the boys who were laughing and joking on their way to Stokes Bay today. On their way to D-Day and the invasion . . .

A muffled gurgling sound from the patient she was checking made her jump, and she turned back to see him pointing to the thermometer in his mouth. Catching her breath, she whipped it out quickly and held it up to the light.

'Blimey, nurse, I thought you'd turned to stone and I'd got that thing stuck in me gob for the duration,' he said. 'What's so interesting out there? Jerry climbing up the sea wall, or your boyfriend waiting to take you to the pictures?'

Thursday looked at him guiltily. For a few moments, she had forgotten where she was, forgotten everything in her amazement at the sight of all the ships. Then she smiled and shook her head.

'Sorry. I lost track for a minute. Your temperature's up again, Stoker Morrison. You'd better lie down and rest for a while, and no getting out of bed, all right? No excitement until it's gone down again.'

He wrinkled his face in disgust. 'And there was me thinking I'd be able to get out and 'ave a look at the sea. Oh well.' He slid down between the sheets again and gave her a rueful grin. 'I got to admit, I 'ave got a bit of an 'eadache. Spot of shut-eye won't do no 'arm. And I don't suppose there's all that much goin' on, is there?'

Thursday glanced again out of the window, at the massing fleet of ships. 'No,' she said, 'not all that much, really . . .'

The gliders began to come over early in the morning, two days later. It was 6 June.

There had been a growing tension in the air for days now. All the nurses and some of the patients were aware of the flotilla packing the Solent, but nobody dared speak of it. It was as if they felt that to talk about it might make it vanish, as if it weren't really there at all but was just a dream. They went about their work, glancing out every now and then to reassure themselves, and dreading the sound of the air raid siren and German bombers. Surely they must know . . . Or perhaps the diversionary tactics of the wooden ships at Falmouth and the frantic activity off Dover had tricked them into thinking the danger was coming from those areas instead. You wouldn't think they'd be so easily fooled, Thursday thought. You wouldn't think they'd even try such schoolboy antics! But maybe it was their sheer, childish simplicity that had made them so successful. Or perhaps it was the unseasonal weather – wet, cold and windy, not at all the sort of conditions when an invasion might be expected.

She was standing at the dormitory window after a restless night when she saw the first flight of bombers approach, each towing a great, silent aircraft across the skies. For a moment, she stood transfixed, staring in disbelief. Then a swarm of them appeared, the bombers growling their deep, threatening note and the gliders like huge birds of prey. She turned to the other girls, some of them still asleep, some yawning and stretching and beginning to climb reluctantly from their bunks.

'Look! *Look!* It's the invasion – it must be – it's started. It's *started*!'

Louisa was at her side at once. Elsie, rubbing her eyes, stumbled over in her nightie and gazed blearily out. The other girls crowded round, pointing and exclaiming.

'They're so quiet! Haven't they got engines?'

'Course not – they're gliders, silly. The bombers'll take them nearly over to France and then let go.'

'I know what gliders are, thanks very much, Ellen Bridges. But these are enormous – how can they stay up there without engines?'

Nobody seemed to want to explain the theory of aerodynamics at that moment. They stood in silence, watching as the aircraft swooped across the Solent and disappeared over the Isle of Wight, and then Elsie gave a yelp.

'The ships! They've gone!'

'Good heavens,' Thursday said wonderingly. 'So they have.'

'I don't believe it,' Louisa Wetherby said. 'It's not possible – so quickly. They were there yesterday, masses of them. The order must have been given in the night and they all just – went.'

'Or very early this morning,' Thursday agreed. She stood on tiptoe, straining her eyes to see through the slanting rain. The sea was grey and bleak, the waves tossing and breaking, spraying white foam into the air. 'Look, you can just see their shapes, out past the end of the Island. They're on their way now.' Excitement welled up in her and she turned and flung her arms around Louisa, hugging her and jumping up and down. 'They're on their way to France! The invasion's started! We're going to win the war at last – we are, I know we are! Oh, Louie, Elsie, Patsy—' She stopped abruptly. 'Where's Patsy?'

'Here I am,' said a quiet voice, and Patsy appeared from the washroom. She looked pale and her eyes were rimmed with pink. 'Sorry, Thursday – I just had to nip into the lav. What's going on?'

Thursday stared at her. 'It's the invasion, Pats – it's started. The ships have all gone.' Realisation dawned, and her hand flew to her mouth as she pushed past the other girls to her friend's side. 'Oh, Patsy – I almost forgot. It's the sixth of June, isn't it. Your wedding anniversary.'

Patsy nodded as the other girls stared uncomprehendingly, and then those who had been at Haslar three years earlier crowded about the two. Patsy was enveloped in a sea of comforting arms and for a few moments she stayed there, then she pushed them gently aside.

'I'm all right. It was just – you know, waking up and realising. I needed to be on my own for a minute or two. I'll be all right now.' She moved to the window. 'What did you say? The invasion? How d'you know?'

'The ships have gone, see?' Thursday stood beside her, her arm laid lightly across Patsy's shoulders as she pointed. 'And there were huge gliders going over – look, there's another lot. What d'you think they're carrying? They look almost big enough to carry tanks and lorries, but it doesn't seem possible, does it?'

Patsy nodded. Then, after staring for a minute or two more, she turned and gave them a triumphant smile.

'You know what this means, don't you? It means we're going to win the war! That's a real invasion, that is. And,' her voice sobered, 'if there are troops on those ships about to land in France, a lot of them will be coming back wounded. It'll be Action Stations here at Haslar, just like after Dunkirk. And we'll do our best for them, just like we did then. Now I don't know about you, but I'm going to get a good breakfast inside me, because if last time is anything to go by, we might not get time for a good square meal again till heaven knows when!'

Chapter Five

The official announcement came soon after breakfast. Today was D-Day and the hospital was at Action Stations. No patients were expected for twenty-four hours but it might be less, and everything must be ready. The operating theatres in particular must be on standby.

With the VADs gathered together, Sister Tutor read out the names of those selected for the theatre course. 'Bowden, Cockroft, Tilford, Wetherby and Mears will report immediately to Surgeon Commander Sharp. The rest of you, return to your wards at once. There'll be plenty to do to prepare for our new patients.' She looked down from her dais and her calm gaze rested upon their upturned faces. 'I know that we can all rely upon your hard work and dedication in the days ahead. Some of you are new and may feel a little nervous about what you may be called upon to do. Others were here after Dunkirk, and many of you have served overseas and in other hospitals where emergencies have stretched you to the limit. I know you will all work together as a team, remembering that the patient must always come first and orders must be obeyed without question. That's the way the Royal Navy has always functioned, and that's the way we shall succeed now. Good luck to you all.'

The girls filed soberly out of the room. Thursday found herself beside Patsy and gave her arm a squeeze. 'All right, Pats?'

The other girl gave her a faint smile. 'To tell you the truth, I'll be glad to have something to do. It'll take my mind off – you know.' Her voice wobbled a little but she drew in a breath and continued, 'It seems awful to say it, somehow. It's our wedding anniversary – I *ought* to be thinking of him. And I am – deep down, I always am.'

Thursday nodded. She thought she understood. Connor too was

far away, and before he left he'd told her that he didn't want her to consider herself tied to him. 'I don't want you moping while the other girls have fun, Thursday. I don't want you living like a nun – I want you to be the Thursday I know and love, the one who's always got a smile and a laugh, who goes out on her bike and has tea at the Swiss Café and goes dancing. I want you to make the most of every day, because all we've got, these days, is today. And then write and tell me all about it!' he'd finished with a grin.

At least Roy and Patsy were married; at least they'd had a little time of happiness together. Thursday looked at her bare left hand, and wished there had been time for that. She and Connor had never had the chance, and perhaps never would. As he had told her, three long years ago, life was too uncertain these days to be sure of anything.

Thursday had done as he had told her. After a time during which she hadn't wanted to do anything or go anywhere, she had begun to go out with the other girls again, to go dancing. It had been good to be held again in a man's arms, if only for a few minutes, and she'd felt comforted and hoped that Connor was finding the same comfort. And when she'd been posted to Egypt it had been impossible to hold herself apart. It was a different world and friendships, flirtations and even romance blossomed under the African skies. But always – always, at the back of her mind – there had been Connor. As Patsy said, deep down you were always thinking of the man you loved.

'I'm glad I'm going to be in theatre,' she said. 'And Louisa, too. But I'll miss being with the patients on the wards.'

'That's why I didn't volunteer,' Patsy said, and Elsie, coming up behind them, agreed.

'I did a bit of theatre in Egypt, remember, and decided it's not for me. I'm better with the patients when they're awake. They seem to appreciate a joke better then!'

The other two laughed. 'Even yours?' Thursday asked wickedly, and Elsie thumped her arm. 'Well, you'll be able to keep us up to date with what's happening up above, then. We're going to be like moles, down there in the dungeons.'

Although Haslar had normal operating theatres in the main hospital, there was also a vast network of cellars beneath the buildings, and several of these had been fitted out as emergency theatres. Others were used as air raid shelters, and there had been so many evacuations during the raids and Blitz of 1940 and 1941 that the men had begun to joke ruefully that they might as well stop down there for the duration.

Thursday and Louisa made their way down the wide stairs beneath the arcade. There was a large lift which could be used for bringing down patients, but to save electricity it was used only when absolutely necessary. There were two large theatres here and the girls who were to take the course and work here made their way to the first one, where Surgeon Commander Sharp held court. They did not expect to meet the man himself, knowing that he would almost certainly be operating at this moment, but when they saw the QARNN who was waiting for them their faces lit up.

'Stanway!' Thursday wanted to hug her old friend, but didn't quite dare. 'We weren't sure you were back.'

Helen Stanway smiled at them. She'd been at Haslar when they'd first arrived as raw recruits, and had shown them round the hospital. Thursday remembered how they'd all cheered as they stood under the arcade, so loudly that Madam had come to see what all the noise was about. Helen had been a rock for the younger girls, firm and cool but always sympathetic – as long as you did your job well. She had neither time nor sympathy for sluggards.

'I'm glad to see you all again,' she said, her grey eyes moving over their faces. 'We must get together one day and talk about all our experiences. But that won't be for a while, I'm afraid – for the next few weeks we'll be at crisis level. There'll be a lot of patients arriving here very soon, and we're all going to be stretched to our limits.' She smiled again. 'I know not one of you will mind that at all!'

Briskly, she went through the list of names. Some of the girls, including Thursday, had already done theatre work and their experience would be valuable. Others barely knew a scalpel from a suture and would have to be taught – and taught quickly. They were here not merely to learn, but to assist, and there would be no time for mistakes.

'We'll be working a three watch system, eight hours at a time, over twenty-four hours, and we expect operating to be continuous. Each theatre has three tables, which will be running simultaneously, so at any one time you'll find six operations in progress. Each table has the complete team available, of course – a surgeon, anaesthetist, Sister and two VADs, or sometimes SBAs if they're available; most of them are at sea, of course, aboard ships.' She looked at them gravely. 'If you haven't encountered battle casualties before, you may find the sights and smells a little upsetting to begin with, but remember that these men are war heroes, *every one of them*, and they deserve our best attention. *We* haven't been to war, we haven't had to land on foreign beaches and face enemy attack, we haven't fought and been shot or bombed or bayoneted. All we've had to do is wait in comparative luxury for them to be brought to us. A few unpleasant moments are nothing – *nothing* – compared with what they've endured, and it behoves us to do our absolute best to bring them back to health. So we do *not* think about ourselves, but about them. At every moment.' She paused and there was a silence as she let her eyes move over their faces again, and then her smile broke out once more. 'I know I can rely on every one of you,' she said simply, and gave a quick, firm nod.

The girls were then assigned to their duties. Each would work at a certain table in one of the two theatres. Thursday found herself in 'A' with Louisa, while Ellen Bridges and Joy Cockroft were at the next table. Ellen had done a little theatre work, but Joy was completely new to it and by the end of the morning she was looking flustered and bewildered.

'I don't think I should have volunteered for this,' she said in distress. 'I'm going to be absolutely useless. I'm terrified I'm not going to be able to give the surgeon the right instruments.'

'You won't have to give him anything, not at the beginning,' Ellen told her comfortingly, 'and we all find it a bit strange to start with. You'll soon get used to it.'

'I hope so,' Joy said. 'I don't know what I'd do if someone died because I was so useless.'

'Go on, nobody'll die – not because of you, anyway.' Ellen looked at her. Joy, a diminutive redhead, was two or three years younger than most of them and new to Haslar. 'Where were you before you came here?'

'Well, I started as a Nightingale at St Thomas's Hospital in London. It's Florence Nightingale's hospital, so the nurses there are called after her. But then I got ill and had to leave, and when I was better I thought I'd volunteer. I want to go back to training as an SRN after the war,' she added. 'If they'll have me, that is.'

''Course they'll have you! They'll jump at anyone who's done

Naval nursing, especially if you'd already been there before the war. Look, you needn't worry about the theatre work. Madam and Tutor wouldn't have put you down for the course if they hadn't thought you could do it.'

'But how would they *know*?' Joy asked worriedly. 'Suppose they've made a terrible mistake?'

Ellen smiled at her. 'Madam and Sister Tutor *never* make mistakes. Now, come on – we'll go through the instruments again. Scalpel?'

'That's the knife the surgeon uses to cut into the patient's flesh.'

'Right. Forceps?'

'They're little pincers used to pick up swabs or take out organs – like sugar tongs.'

'Right.' The lesson continued as they made their way to the mess for lunch. Ellen beamed at her pupil. 'You see? You know all that. You don't need to worry at all. You'll be an excellent theatre nurse.'

Joy grinned. 'Well, if you really think so . . .'

'I know so. And I'll tell you something else.' Ellen leaned close to her as they queued for their helping of toad-in-the-hole and cabbage. 'I'm like Madam and Sister Tutor – I'm *never* wrong!'

The first casualties began to arrive next morning. Thursday, taking the chance of a breath of air along the sea wall before going on duty, saw the ships heading back across the Solent in grim convoy and turned at once to run back through the gate.

'They're coming! I've seen the ships – they'll be here any minute.' She burst into the dormitory and snatched up her cap and apron, pinning on her watch with shaking fingers. 'Come on, Ellen – Lou – we'll be wanted in theatre.' She ran out again, followed by the others, and together they scurried across to the arcade to the basement while the other girls ran on to the jetty where the pinnaces would arrive.

The theatre staff were already gathering at the theatre doors when the alarms began to sound. Helen Stanway gave the girls a nod of approval. 'Good. Get yourselves scrubbed and ready. Tilford, Wetherby, Bridges and Cockroft, you'll be on Surgeon Commander Sharp's team. Bowden and Wetherby, you can man the autoclave; there'll be plenty of sterilising to do. Tilford, you'll be dirty nurse. Bridges, Cockroft and Mears, go through to B Theatre where Sister

Weston will give you your orders.' Her voice was calm and clear, steadying the jittering nerves of the girls.

I oughtn't to feel like this, Thursday thought. I should be used to it by now. Once the flow had begun, there would be no time to worry, no time to think of anything other than the work to be done. But those last few moments, waiting for the first casualties to arrive, not knowing just what their injuries might be, were always nerve-racking.

Down by the jetty, the other girls were equally tense. Elsie had gone over to Zymotics, but Patsy, Susan and Vera Hapgood were amongst those who were to receive the patients as they arrived and get them to the wards they were assigned to by the Naval doctors. The trolleys were already in place on the tramlines that had been laid when Haslar Hospital was first built, and matelots stood ready to push them through the arcade, while the walking wounded would be helped by VADs.

'Blimey, this takes me back,' Patsy muttered as they stood there, watching the grey battleships steam slowly through the narrow harbour entrance. 'It's just like it was after Dunkirk, except that they're being landed by Naval pinnaces instead of ferry boats.' Her voice was taut with strain and Susan Morrison squeezed her arm.

'Your Roy'll be all right. He's lucky, you know he is.'

'*So* far,' Patsy said under her breath.

'It's not going to be like Dunkirk,' Susan told her. 'That was all such a rush, and nobody expected it. A lot of planning has gone into D-Day. I mean, all those things they were building out at Stokes Bay – we used to wonder whatever was going on out there. And look what they turned out to be – concrete *harbours*! I mean, who'd have dreamed that was what they were? Who could have thought of it? I bet the Germans never had the slightest idea. And even if they did realise we were going to invade, they didn't know where we were going to go. I reckon we'll have really caught them on the hop.'

'I hope so.' Patsy thought of all the defeats that had been suffered so far – Dunkirk, Dieppe, Hong Kong, Singapore. Yet there'd been victories too – El Alamein, Monte Cassino, Tobruk. And this new invasion could be the greatest victory of all. 'Oh, Susie, I really do hope so.'

The first pinnace was forging towards them across the choppy water. Patsy's eyes scanned it anxiously. 'Oh, those poor blokes, they'll be getting bounced about all over the place. Couldn't they have picked better weather for an invasion?' She moved forwards, her heart skipping. If Roy was in one of these boats . . .

He wasn't. And once the casualties began to come off, there was no more time to think about him. Just as they had done after Dunkirk, Patsy and the other girls were soon embroiled in a state of ordered chaos as the pinnaces came and went, each unloading its cargo of wounded men. Men, some of them no more than boys, boys who had been too young to fight when the war began, with broken arms or legs, bandaged heads, torn and shattered bodies; men and boys whose flesh had been shot or burned away, men with injuries that would maim and cripple them for the rest of their lives; men and boys who had been sitting by their lorries and tanks in the roads and lanes leading to Stokes Bay and other beaches only a day or two before, cooking sausages over Primus stoves and telling tales to the children who gathered around them.

Patsy felt a moment of grief for the young soldiers who had gone off so bravely and been wounded so soon. But there was no time for sorrow. There was too much work to be done. She moved into place and reached out her arms to a young, bewildered Tommy with a uniform caked in blood and salt. 'It's all right, love. It's all right. You're safe now. We'll look after you. It's all right . . .'

'There've only been a few so far,' Helen Stanway told Thursday and the others as they scrubbed their hands at the washbasins, 'but we're expecting a steady flow from now on. The ships are bringing them back as fast as they can.'

It sounded ominous. Thursday recalled Dunkirk – the thousands of men brought home weary, injured, defeated . . . But there were bound to be wounded, she reminded herself. They were going into battle. There would be men injured and killed right from the start. At least they *could* be brought back. They didn't have to be taken prisoner, or left to die in a foreign field.

She took her place at the operating table. The team was in position and the first patient under anaesthetic. She looked down at the prone body. It was a sailor who had been badly gashed by some jagged lump of metal; his torso was torn and shredded, his liver protruding and a white fragment of bone piercing the wall of his chest. Thursday felt a quick pang of pity and then, with resolution, she thrust aside all emotion and concentrated on simply doing her job, just as Sister Tutor had taught her when she had first come to Haslar.

'Right,' the surgeon said quietly, and turned to the nurse who stood at his side. 'Scalpel . . .'

They lost all sense of time. With their work taking such deep concentration, the girls found that the hours could tick by like minutes, and it wasn't until the watch was over that they realised just how exhausted they were. Thursday came off duty after each watch feeling dazed, her legs aching from the hours of standing, her mind numb from concentration. Spare time became a thing of the past; they ate their meals like automatons, washed and fell into bed to sleep like logs. The time went past in a blur and as Thursday came off duty one sunny afternoon, she was startled to realise that five days had gone by.

She climbed the stairs and stood outside for a moment, drawing in great lungfuls of fresh air. The light was dazzling, and she had the same feeling of surprise as when she came out of an afternoon in the cinema to find it was still daylight. Blinking, she put out a hand to steady herself against the wall and found Louisa at her side.

'What we need,' the tall girl said, 'is a cup of tea.'

'What I need is eight hours' sleep,' Thursday said. 'Or maybe a swim. Or a long country walk. But a cup of tea's a good start, and I don't suppose the others are very likely anyway.'

They walked back to the mess together, not speaking. Both had worked in operating theatres during their time abroad, and Thursday had worked here at Haslar, with Connor. They were accustomed to the concentration, to the continuous flow of patients, to the numerous different injuries. But it always took a while to adjust, to return to real life. Thursday remembered going back to the mess one day after assisting at a double amputation and finding leg of lamb being served for dinner. The very word 'leg' seemed offensive, but she'd been sharply taken to task by one of her colleagues, who had told her that if she wanted to be a 'real' nurse she'd got to learn to leave such fastidiousness behind. 'You won't be any use to the patients if you're going to turn into jelly because animals have got legs as well as us, and we eat them. It's the patients who matter – not your silly feelings.'

Thursday, abashed, had taken the warning to heart. She didn't want to find herself back on the wards, taking temperatures and pulses, even though she knew that was just as useful in the general nursing of the patients. And it wasn't as if she didn't *like* leg of lamb . . .

All the same, she always needed those few moments of adjustment from the theatre to the outside world, and she'd learned to accept this and allow for it.

'What d'you think you'll do once the war's over?' she asked Louisa. 'Will you stay in nursing – go for State Registration? I don't suppose they'll want VADs any more.'

Louisa shook her head. 'I don't think so. I think I'll have had enough of it by then. Besides,' she blushed a little, 'there's Andrew.'

'Oh.' Thursday looked at her friend. 'It really is serious, then?'

'I think so. We've been writing to each other ever since he left Alex. Well, it was serious even before then, only we didn't somehow want to commit ourselves – everything's so uncertain, it seemed almost like asking for bad luck. But since we've been apart – well, you know how it is.'

Thursday nodded. She knew exactly how it was. It had been the same for herself and Connor – the brief courtship, the exchanged messages, the promise. Only he hadn't wanted her to make any promises. He hadn't wanted her to tie herself down; he'd wanted her to live her life, go out and have fun while she had the chance.

All the same, he hadn't – she was sure – wanted her to fall in love with someone else. And she *had* promised – she'd made the promise to herself, that she would keep faith with him, that she'd wait until they were together again. She'd promised him in her heart, and it was a promise she wanted desperately to keep.

'I want to marry Andrew,' Louisa said, 'as soon as he comes home. We've been talking about it, in our letters. He'll leave the Army then – he isn't a regular – and go back into his father's business. They run a car manufacturing company in the Midlands. There'll be plenty of new vehicles wanted once things settle down again – cars and buses, lorries, all sorts. He'll need a wife who's at home, not working nights in a hospital.'

'Oh, that's lovely,' Thursday said. 'I'm so pleased. So really you're engaged, aren't you?'

'Not officially.' Louisa blushed again. 'I mean, there isn't a ring yet, and I think Andrew will want to propose properly when he gets back. We don't want to rush things. We'll have to get to know each other again. Everything's going to be different after the war, isn't it? Life will change completely. We'll have to get used to peace all over again.'

'Yes, I suppose we will.' Thursday rubbed her chin wryly. I can't even cope with coming out of the theatre without a bit of time to adjust, she thought. How am I going to manage to come out of the war?

Peace seemed, suddenly, to be rather a frightening idea.

'Well, it won't be for a long time yet,' she said. 'There's going to be a lot more spilt milk going under the bridge, as Elsie would say, before we have to cross that particular one.'

'Or a lot of spilt blood,' Louisa said soberly, and they pushed open the door of the mess and went to get their tea.

The medical wards were just as busy. Patsy, Susan, Vera Hapgood and the others were almost run off their feet, yet they still managed somehow to spend a little time with each patient, chatting to them as they carried out their mundane tasks and trying to give them what comfort they could. Unburdening themselves of their experiences seemed almost as important to the men as having their wounds attended to, especially as few of them could receive family visitors. The ban on visiting the coast, together with the difficulties of transport, made travelling from other parts of the countries almost impossible.

'It was bloody mayhem,' one of the Commandos said. With other Royal Marines and American Army units, he'd been in the first landings and now, less than a day later, he was back in England, with Patsy beside his bed helping the QARNN to change his dressings. 'Dozens of poor blighters were shot down in the first wave, but there were so many of us coming off the landing craft, and with the blokes at the guns firing away like madmen, see, they just couldn't get us all. I reckon our boys saw a few of them off an' all,' he added with satisfaction. 'And once we got to the beachhead, we could take cover under the Atlantic Wall. That's the dirty great concrete walls they put up as sort of fortifications,' he explained, seeing Patsy's mystified face. 'Any road, once you could get under the lee of that, you were out of the way of enemy fire, see, and there were so many of us, we took the Jerries by surprise. They never expected such a mass.' He lay back, wincing as Sister Burton began to clean the gaping wound in his thigh. 'Here, you're not putting that iodine muck on that, are you? It bloody stings, that does.'

Patsy grinned at him. 'Don't tell me you're frightened of a little bit of iodine! Not after you've just been in an invasion!'

'Yeah, well, that's men's work, innit. Iodine's what women put on their kiddies' knees when they falls over in the playground.' He gave a little yelp as Burton swabbed the wound. 'Here, you done that on purpose!'

'I'll do worse than that if you don't behave yourself,' the QARNN told him calmly. 'You're in a Naval hospital now, remember. We expect our patients to be tough. You won't get your Sergeant Major coming round to bring you tea and sympathy.'

The Commando looked entreatingly at Patsy, and she grinned again and winked. 'Never mind, if you're good *I'll* bring you some tea. That's what we VADs are for.'

'Not until you've finished with dressings and bedpans,' Sister said smartly, winding a bandage around the muscular thigh. 'And then only if I haven't found some other jobs for you to do.' She stood back and regarded her work. 'You'll do. A week or so in here and you'll be fit to go back again.'

'Well, if that ain't the best news I've heard since my brother told me Father Christmas wasn't real,' he said morosely, watching her walk briskly away down the ward. 'Still, it'll be better than being in here with that martinet ruling the roost. How d'you put up with it?'

'It isn't Sister Burton we have to put up with,' Patsy told him. 'It's you patients! Just think how nice it would be in here without you lot – nice tidy beds, no newspapers all over the place, nobody cluttering the place up with mugs of cocoa.' She gave an exaggerated sigh of wistfulness. 'That's why we do our best to get you fit again – just so we can have a bit of peace.'

'Peace!' he said, and lay back on his pillows, looking suddenly white. 'Peace, that's what we all want.'

Patsy touched his hand for a moment, then slipped away. The wards were filling rapidly now; as well as by sea, men were being ferried back to England by air. The man in the next bed to the Commando was one of the parachutists who had been dropped from a glider, and parachuted straight into a clump of trees.

'Just hanging there, I was,' he told Patsy in a whisper as he looked up at her from his prone position, 'with all the cords and silk and stuff tangled up round me like a bloody cat's cradle, and then these German soldiers appeared out of nowhere and started machine-gunning me. Thought I was a goner, I did straight, and then some Tommies come out of the trees and shot *them*! Well, you should have seen 'em skedaddle – wasn't expecting it, see. So the Tommies cut me down and took me off to the field hospital, and then this Dakota landed in a field nearby and they loaded me on board with some other blokes and here we are in Haslar.'

'My, you were lucky,' Patsy observed. 'If those Jerries had been better at shooting . . .'

'Well, you can't aim a machine-gun all that accurately, see. I mean, it sprays out bullets all over the place, doesn't it? You just trust to luck one of them will hit something vital – and generally one does. So I guess I *was* pretty lucky, when you think about it. Just got a few cuts and bruises and that, and my arms almost torn out of their sockets, and this bit of back trouble, that's all. And I tell you what,' he winked painfully, the deep scratches on his face pulling at the scraped skin, 'there was this real little doll of a nurse on board that Dakota. Got a date with her, I have, the minute I'm out of here.'

Patsy gazed at him. The 'bit of back trouble' he referred to was a fracture that might leave him paralysed from the waist down for the rest of his life. Nobody had told him yet. She wondered if the nurse in the Dakota had realised it.

'I didn't know they had women nurses flying into France,' she said.

'Only just started, see. Nightingales, they call 'em.' He closed his eyes, exhausted, and Patsy went on to the next man, her heart full of sorrow for the waste of so many young lives, and with a deep gnawing anxiety for Roy.

'It must be nice to be able to talk to the patients,' Joy said a little wistfully when they all met at suppertime. 'Chat to them, help to cheer them up and all that. Ours are either fast asleep or just nodding off.'

'Take it from me, they're better off that way,' Patsy advised her. 'You've seen patients who are in pain all the time. It's a lot worse, I can tell you, when they're straight from the battlefield. You have to get used to seeing men with their arms and legs torn off, or hanging by a thread – men with their insides almost ripped out – men going mad with it, screaming in agony, crying for their mothers and dying in front of your very eyes. *You* see them when they're out of all that. You can tidy them up and do whatever's necessary without hurting them, without hearing them scream. If you'd ever tried changing the dressings of a man who's been badly burnt or had half his face torn away, you'd know what I mean,' she added.

Joy turned pale. 'I don't know whether I'm going to be any use as a nurse either way,' she said. 'I'm so scared of doing the wrong thing. And the amputations – all those poor boys having their arms or legs cut off.' She laid down her knife and fork. 'I've been thinking of going to Madam and telling her I'm no good.'

The others stared at her. 'You don't mean it,' Thursday said at last.

'I do.' The little redhead was close to tears. 'I nearly dropped the scalpel this morning when Sharpie gave it back to me. *Dropped* it! It would have got dirty on the floor and – and –'

'And had to be sterilised. Which is what was going to happen to it anyway,' Ellen pointed out. 'Look, all you need to do is try to relax a bit. Forget about yourself and how frightened or useless you are – just think about what you're doing. We all go through this, you know, when we're new. And you've been thrown in right at the deep end. We haven't stopped for the entire watch, ever since it started. It's as if they were coming in on a conveyor belt.' She slipped her arm round Joy's shoulders and gave her a squeeze. 'You'll be all right. You're just tired, that's all.'

'We're all tired,' Thursday said. 'I'm exhausted! I feel as if I haven't seen the outside world for months.'

'It's the smell, too,' Joy went on. 'Gas gangrene – I've never smelt anything so horrible. I don't know how I stop myself being sick when I go down those stairs.' She leaned her elbows on the table and put her face in her hands. 'Honestly, I'm no good at it. I'm a rotten, rotten nurse.'

The others glanced at each other. Then Ellen got up. 'I'm going to go and see Madam, ask if you can have a bit of time off. You're all right, really, Joy, you just need a break.' She glanced at the others. 'Maybe we all do. Even a walk along the sea wall would do us good.'

Madam agreed. 'You've been working at full stretch for nearly a week. You need a good blow of sea air. The barricades have been removed from Stokes Bay and Gilkicker now – run down there and have a few hours on the beach. I dare say there'll be plenty of other people doing the same, now that the weather's cleared up.'

The girls went out in a gang. Most of them had bikes now, and they pedalled along Clayhall and into Anglesey Road to reach Stokes Bay. The wind and rain of the previous week had cleared away, leaving blue skies and warm June sunshine, and as Madam had said, there were plenty of local people making their way there too. It was so long since anyone had been allowed out to the beach, and now that the great rolls of barbed wire had been removed everyone wanted to see the sea again. For Gosport people, the sea was a part of their lives; you couldn't help but be aware of it, either out at the Bay or Lee, or down at the ferry when you wanted to cross the harbour to go to 'Pompey'. They knew it in all its moods – grey-green under cloudy skies, swelling ominously as the wind got up, slashing against the jetties and sea walls when it was stormy. And blue and calm, as it was today, with just a few 'white horses' far out where a summer breeze blew the tops off the waves in a spray of foam.

The girls propped their bikes together on the shingle and gazed at it.

'It looks so peaceful,' Thursday said at last. 'You wouldn't believe that only a week or so ago, there were hundreds of men here with tanks and lorries and heaven knows what else, going aboard all those ships. And look – those must be the Mulberry Harbours! They've brought them back.'

They stared at the huge concrete blocks anchored just off the shore. Now that they knew what they'd been used for, it was easy to see that they could have been slung together to make artificial harbours where the troops could land. 'Mind, I still don't see how it is they float,' Elsie said, shaking her head. 'I mean, they're *concrete*. I just don't understand it.'

'Just as well you weren't in charge, then,' Ellen said cheerfully. She linked arms with Joy. 'Come on. Let's have a walk along the beach. I want to paddle!'

They set off, but within moments the walk had turned into a run and then a wild chase along the shingly beach. Shedding all their responsibilities, the nurses became children again, racing each other along the edge of the waves. Then Thursday sat down and pulled off her shoes, tying the laces together to sling them around her neck.

Holding her skirt above her knees, she waded into the water, gasping a little at the first icy shock, then laughing with delight as she went deeper. The others followed, lifting their faces blissfully to the sun, and emerged at last to sit on the shingle while their feet dried. Patsy lay back and stretched her arms above her head.

'We'll have to get out our bathers,' Thursday said. 'We'll be able to swim off the sea wall again. It must have been miserable for people not to be able to go for a dip.'

'Mm.' Patsy sounded uninterested and Thursday glanced at her. Patsy had been the keenest swimmer of them all.

'Didn't you do any swimming while you were in Scotland?' she asked idly, letting some sand trickle through her fingers. Stokes Bay was mostly shingle but there were occasional patches of sand, jealously commandeered on Sundays by families with small children.

Patsy sat up and picked up a handful of seaweed. She started to pop the little bladders. 'Not really. We couldn't swim in the harbour and the coast was too far away to go there often – and the water was freezing. And sometimes there were really big jellyfish.' She dropped the seaweed as if it was of no further interest, and stared towards the Island.

Thursday glanced her. She knew that Patsy was worrying about Roy. There had still been no word from him. 'But it must be lovely up there, surely,' she persisted. 'I've seen pictures of the coast – all the little islands. They looked beautiful.'

'Oh yes,' Patsy said, shrugging. 'The scenery's lovely. And the water's so clear, you could see the bottom even when it was quite deep. And the coast is beautiful. We had a couple of trips out there, but that was all.' She looked at the other two. 'I dare say you got plenty of swimming in Egypt. It must have been like being on holiday, when you got time off.'

'*When*,' Elsie said sardonically. 'It wasn't no beach holiday, I can tell you, even if we did have plenty of sand.'

'Bet it was nice and hot, though,' Patsy said wistfully. 'I could've done with some of that sunshine. I don't reckon there's *anywhere* colder than Scotland.'

Thursday thought of the skies above Alexandria. They had been a hard, metallic blue, quite different from the gentle azure of this English afternoon, and the sun had burned with a relentless white heat. But the Mediterranean had been delicious to bathe in, just cool enough to refresh sweating skin yet warm enough to stay in for hours. She thought of the girls and men who had gathered there during their off-duty hours, sometimes during the day, sometimes in the evening. The stars had hung above them, huge and brilliant, almost close enough, it seemed, to touch. Like diamonds . . .

She moved sharply, dropping her handful of sand back on to the shingle of Stokes Bay beach. 'Isn't it time we were getting back?'

Patsy glanced up, surprised by her tone, but Elsie looked at her watch and nodded. 'I suppose it is. We don't want Madam thinking we've forgotten about our next duty.' She heaved herself to her feet. 'It's been good, though, hasn't it? Being able to come out here again and behave like kids let out of school.'

Joy got to her feet too, nodding. 'It has. I feel a lot better.'

'There,' Ellen said, 'you see? That was all you needed, a break and some fresh air. So no more talk about not being any good as a nurse, all right?'

'Well – maybe.' Joy brushed back her auburn curls. 'I'll see for sure when we get back to the theatre. And I hope someone's cleared away all those amputations. It was seeing that big heap of arms and legs piled up outside the theatre door, that started me off in the first place. I mean, they're bits of *people*, and they're treated just like so much rubbish.'

'And that's all they are,' Elsie said firmly. 'No use to nobody. You've got to forget that side of it, Joy. Get your suit of armour on, like the rest of us do.'

Joy nodded a little doubtfully. Thursday watched her, remembering how hard it had been for her too, in the early days. And even now, she was sometimes caught unexpectedly by some sight or sound that reminded her that these patients were men who had home lives – wives, children, parents, brothers and sisters. And a lifetime to go through, without the arm or leg – or both – that had been lost in Normandy or here in Haslar Hospital. It was hard to remain objective when you thought of that.

It was like remembering the sun-soaked days and starlit nights of Alexandria. You just had to push the thoughts and memories away. You *had* to – or you wouldn't be able to carry on.

Chapter Six

The suit of armour was certainly needed after D-Day. Haslar was the first port of call for many of the most severely wounded – military and Air Force personnel as well as Naval. Once any emergency treatment had been carried out and the patients were fit to be moved, they were sent on to other hospitals and their beds freed for the next wave of casualties.

The VADs on the medical wards found themselves listening to more horrific tales as the men recovered. 'You wouldn't credit some of the stuff we took over,' the Commando told Patsy. Mostly silent and withdrawn, he seemed to find relief in talking to her and Sister Burton didn't chivvy Patsy away when she saw her standing by his bed. 'Not just tanks and jeeps, I don't mean, but all those contraptions they call Funnies – crab tanks, and crocodiles, and flame throwers. There was swimming tanks too, supposed to float – and some of them might have but all the ones I saw sank like bloody stones.' He shook his head. 'Tested 'em in calm water, see, but when we actually made the landings we had all those storms, didn't we, the wind whipping up the bloody waves like the sides of houses. Total bloody nightmare. Poor bleeding sods inside didn't stand a chance, not a chance.'

Thursday nodded soberly when Patsy reported this. 'We had a patient in the theatre today. He was rambling as he went under, but we all thought that what he said must be true. It was horrible. Men shot the minute they landed on the beach, and nobody to help them. You couldn't stop, he said, you just had to go on, even if it was your friend, even if it was your *brother*. He saw his best friend with almost all his face blown away . . .' She shook her head. 'He said the medical orderlies tried their best to get all the injured back on the ships, but there were crowds of men still coming off, trying to land. And there were *hundreds* drowned, weighed down by all their equipment. Bodies everywhere, he kept saying, bodies everywhere . . . It was so horrible to hear him, poor man; we were all thankful when he went under the anaesthetic. At least he could forget for a few hours.'

Most of the VADs and the QARNNs had seen war wounds before. They knew that bullets, bombs and grenades could tear through the body, ripping it apart, shredding muscle and shattering bone. Often, it seemed impossible to repair the horrific damage; often, a patient who had miraculously survived the journey back across the Channel died even as he came into the theatre, or while the surgeon was operating. Some died later, as if unable to fight any longer.

'But we save a lot,' Louisa said as they sank on to their beds one day after a particularly grim watch. 'Even if they've lost a leg or an arm, they'll get better. They'll still be able to have their life.'

'And they're not all amputations,' Ellen agreed. 'Even though it does seem like it, when you see those arms and legs piled up outside the theatre door.'

'I just wish the porters would take them away,' Joy said again, but everyone knew that they were so busy transporting the incessant stream of patients in and out of the theatre that there was barely time to clear up the detritus of the operations. Now and again, it got too much for anyone to tolerate for another moment, and then there would be a frenzy of cleaning up; the rotting body parts would be removed to the hospital incinerator and the floors scrubbed and disinfected. But nothing could disguise the overpowering smell of gas gangrene that permeated the basements.

The first German casualties took them all by surprise. Thursday was sitting by with the autoclave, sterilising the vast array of instruments that had been used in the latest wave of operations, when she heard the first scream. A thrill of fear ran through her and she looked up, wondering what could be happening to make a man scream like that. Surely, after all that had happened, the enemy couldn't be invading now . . . And then the screams came closer and the doors swung open to admit a patient on a trolley.

The theatre staff froze. They were used to patients in pain, and did their best to ease it as quickly as possible. Even before they arrived in theatre, they would have been given injections to calm them, yet this patient wasn't calm at all. And his screams didn't seem to be of pain.

He's terrified, Thursday thought. He's frightened to death – but why?

The man was yelling words she didn't understand, and then she had a sudden memory of young Heinz Schmidt, the German she had nursed here at Haslar in the early days of the war, and realised that this man too was a German.

'Whatever's the matter with him?' she asked Louisa in a low voice.

'He thinks we'll operate without an anaesthetic,' Louisa whispered back. 'Apparently that's what they've been told. He's got an abdominal injury and a broken leg, and lacerations, and he thinks all that will be done without any anaesthetic at all. No wonder he's frightened, poor man.'

The anaesthetist approached the trolley and the screams intensified. Even though they all knew that in a few moments he would be unconscious and the screams would cease, everyone in the theatre was affected by the fear that radiated from the injured man. Accustomed as they were to terrible injuries, they were also accustomed to men who either tried to hold back their groans or, if they couldn't do that, at least had a basic trust in the doctors and nurses around them. By the time the noise died down, half the nurses were trembling and the surgeons were even more brusque than usual. Outside the theatre, other patients waiting their turn were shocked and anxious.

'What's going on in there, nurse?' Thursday heard one ask as she slipped outside to fetch something. 'It sounds like a pig's being killed.'

'It's a German patient. He thought we wouldn't use anaesthetic on him.'

The man snorted. 'Blimey, it's a pity we do. They probably treat our boys that way, that's why they think we do it too. Too soft, that's what we are.'

Thursday went back to the theatre, the words echoing in her mind. Was the man right? Were the Germans really so inhumane to their prisoners? She thought about her brother Steve, whom the family had thought dead for almost a year before they discovered that he was actually in German hands. Had they operated on him without anaesthetic?

'Of course they don't,' Louisa said when Thursday admitted her fears later that day. 'They've signed the Geneva Convention, haven't they? There are rules about that sort of thing. They might not treat prisoners like royalty, but they're not that brutal. Anyway, you've had letters from him, haven't you? He hasn't said anything?'

'No, he hasn't,' Thursday said, relieved. 'You're right, Lou. He hasn't even had any operations, as far as we know – never got injured.' She grinned a little shamefacedly. 'It was that man screaming like that – it got me in a panic.'

'Yes, and that's how they brainwash us,' Louisa said soberly. 'All that propaganda we used to hear, about Germans eating babies and that sort of thing – it frightens everyone and when people are frightened they lose their heads and can't fight. It's like another sort of weapon.'

Thursday thought for a few minutes. 'Yes, but what about all those things we've been hearing about Hong Kong and Singapore? For all we know, the Japanese *are* treating people like that. We don't know what's happening to their prisoners. They never signed this Convention, did they?'

'No, they didn't. But they're human beings, just the same. Surely, once people are prisoners and can't do them any more harm, they won't behave like animals. Surely . . .'

But her voice was less certain and they looked at each other with fear, thinking of Jeanie Brown and the other nurses and civilians now in Japanese hands. Nobody knew what was happening to them – but everyone feared the worst.

'It's horrible, this war,' Thursday said at last. 'Horrible. And I can't even remember now why it all started. Hitler, taking over a few countries in Europe – and now it's spread all over the world. When's it going to stop, Louie?'

The other girl put her arm round Thursday's shoulders. 'We're on the last lap now. We must be. We may be getting a lot of casualties here at Haslar, but most of the men who went over on D-Day are still there, fighting and driving the Germans back. We've got them on the run. And when we've finished with them we'll sort out the Japanese too. You'll see. We're winning now, Thursday – we really are.'

It was almost a fortnight before the flood of casualties began to ease off. 'They say there's thousands dead,' Elsie said, coming over from Zymotics, 'and I don't know how many have come through Haslar. However many did they send over there in the first place?'

'Thousands more, I suppose.' Thursday was in a strange state of fatigue and exhilaration. The constant demands of the work in the hot, steamy underground theatres with their lack of fresh air and sense of being cut off from the outside world kept her and the others on a rush of adrenalin, so that they felt almost as if they were floating an inch or two above the ground. They did their work in a dream of efficiency, working on a different level of consciousness, and it was only when they came off duty that they began to realise how utterly exhausted they were. Yet even then, there wasn't time to relax – apart from the odd walk along the sea wall or swift dash into Gosport; their whole beings were wrapped up in the theatre and what must be done there. And those brief moments off duty seemed unreal. Walking round Woolworth's one day, looking for oddments of toiletry or cosmetics, Thursday was overtaken by a sudden exasperated impatience. She flung down the lipstick she had been examining and stalked out, wanting only to get back on duty.

But most of their off-duty time was taken up either with sleep, or with writing letters. Everyone had husbands, sweethearts or family at home to write to. Thursday divided her time between her mother and father, back home in Worcester, and Connor, somewhere in the Far East. Yet even as she covered the sheets of paper with her sloping handwriting, she knew that she couldn't tell her family what she could tell Connor, for the descriptions of her work and her stories of what the men had endured were beyond their imaginings. Even her letters to Connor, who was himself a surgeon, must run the gauntlet of the censor.

Writing to Connor, whether the letters reached him or not, was a safety valve. Thursday and the other girls could talk together about what they were seeing and hearing, but what they really wanted to do with their off-duty time was forget it. At the same time, it would have preyed too much upon their minds – in spite of the suits of armour – if they hadn't been able to express their thoughts and feelings to someone else.

'It's Saturday tomorrow,' Elsie said. She was stretched on her bunk in her underclothes, her skin still faintly golden from the tan she had acquired in Egypt. 'We've got the night off. Let's go out – have a bit of fun.'

Thursday rolled over and peered down. 'Where shall we go?'

'Kimball's? The Savoy?' They were the two best-known dance halls in Portsmouth. 'Or we could go to South Parade Pier, they get some good bands there. They had Joe Loss the other week. Come on. We've been working flat out ever since we got here. It's time we let our hair down a bit.'

Still hanging over the edge of her bunk, Thursday looked down at Patsy. 'What d'you think, Pats?'

'I don't know. I don't know if I feel like it.' Patsy sounded weary, her voice flat and depressed. Thursday and Elsie glanced at each other.

'Come on, Pats,' Thursday said gently. 'Elsie's right, it'll do us good. We haven't had a proper night out since we got here.'

'I don't know if I want a night out.'

Thursday hesitated. She knew how Patsy was feeling – as they all were, suddenly flat after the sustained effort of the last two weeks. She knew, too, that this was the very moment when they most needed to relax – to go somewhere with bright lights and music and dancing, to laugh and make jokes and kick over the traces. Just for one evening.

'Come on, Pats,' she said again. 'It'll do you good.'

'There's only one thing that'll do me good,' Patsy said, staring out of the window. 'And that's a letter from my Roy.' She sat up. 'It's a fortnight now since D-Day and I haven't heard a word. What's happened to him? Why can't he write?'

Thursday gazed at her helplessly. 'You don't even know for sure he was there. His ship could be anywhere—'

'It's bound to have gone there,' Patsy said. 'You know it is. And what about that man you told me about, Thursday, the one who said the medical orderlies were going ashore, trying to get the men back? Roy could have done that, he could have got shot, or drowned, or *anything*. If I could just get a *letter* . . .'

There was a short silence. The girls looked at each other.

'Look,' Elsie said at last, in her commonsense voice, 'you know as well as I do there's going to be no letter coming tonight. Tomorrow morning's the soonest the next post can come, and it's not going to come any quicker for you sitting here moping about it. Come on, come out with us – the time'll pass all the quicker. I don't see how they've got time to write letters anyway,' she added. 'You know what it's been like over there. I don't suppose there's anywhere they can buy stamps!'

Patsy stared at her and then burst out laughing. Her laughter had an hysterical edge to it, but Elsie took no notice. She put her arm round Patsy's shoulders and held her tightly. 'That's it, Pats. You have a good laugh. Have a cry, if you want. But come out with us tonight. A bit of jitterbugging, that's what you need. A bit of a cuddle with some nice bloke. It won't do any harm, and it'll do a hell of a lot of good! Is that agreed, then?'

Patsy nodded, sniffing and reaching into her sleeve for her hanky. She smiled a rather watery smile.

'All right, Elsie, you win. I'll come and jitterbug with you. I ought to get back into practice anyway, for when the war's over and Roy comes home. He was always a good dancer. We used to talk about going in for championships, you know.'

'That's right,' Elsie said, giving Thursday a nod over Patsy's head. 'You get some practice in. It won't be long now, and you'll be jitterbugging champions of Pompey – you and Roy together!'

The Savoy dance hall was almost opposite South Parade Pier, in Southsea. To get there, the girls crossed the harbour via the 'floating bridge' – the chain ferry which carried cars from Gosport to Old Portsmouth. From there, it was only a mile or so to cycle to Southsea, mostly along the seafront.

'It's strange to think that this was all wired off just a week ago,' Thursday commented as they pedalled along. She gazed out across the strip of water between the mainland and the Isle of Wight. There were people on the beach even now, enjoying the long June evening. It would be late tonight before the light faded from the sky – double summer time kept darkness at bay until gone eleven. Yet nobody could doubt that the country was still very much at war. The Solent was still busy with ships, crossing to and fro to take fresh troops to France and bring back the wounded. More injured men for us to nurse, she thought, more young soldiers and sailors with their lives changed for ever . . .

'People still can't come here from other places, though,' Patsy said. 'You still need a permit to come to the south coast. There was a woman the other day in one of the pubs in Gosport, she was caught in a spot check and didn't have her identity card on her – they arrested her and took her off to the police station. She was all night in a cell before her hubby came in next day and got her out, but she's still got to go to the court and pay a fine.'

'Well, as long as they're still sending men over I suppose they've got to be careful,' Elsie said. 'There's plenty of information for spies to pick up. Which ships are going out, and that sort of thing. Wonder if there'll be any decent blokes at the dance tonight?'

'I don't care what they're like, so long as they can dance,' Patsy observed. 'That's all I'm interested in.'

Thursday said nothing. She felt suddenly lonely, and wondered why she'd come. Like Patsy, she really only wanted to dance with one man but Connor was thousands of miles away and it would still be a long time before he could hold her in his arms. She remembered the dance they'd been to at Grange, in Gosport, and how they'd swirled round the floor together. And next day, Grange had been bombed and some of the people who had been there with them had been killed.

And yet, although she was missing Connor desperately, she still wanted to feel the closeness of a man's body against hers, the warmth and strength of male arms around her. It would satisfy at least a pang or two of the hunger that seemed a part of her these days. I'll be twenty-six in November, she thought, and I've never made love with a man, not properly. By the time my mother was this age, she had three children. I'll be an old hag of thirty before I start a family – if then!

They arrived at the Savoy and propped their bikes together. It wasn't very romantic, arriving by bike, but the only other way was to walk, or go by pinnace to the main jetty and catch a bus. And there was getting back to consider too. It would still be light enough to cycle, if they left by eleven, and they could catch the floating bridge on its last crossing.

If they missed that, it meant a wild dash round to the main ferry – a ride of over a mile – for the last of the boats, or the pinnace. And if they missed *that*, it meant a long wait until 5 a.m. when the boats began to run again, and a severe reprimand from Madam. Being 'adrift' was a serious offence, in the Navy.

The dance had already begun as they walked into the hall and people were swirling around the floor. Like the Pier, the Savoy boasted some of the best-known bands for its dances, with leaders like Ambrose, Joe Loss and Nat Gonella. The Squadronnaires, recruited from the RAF, came sometimes, as well as The Skyrockets and their Naval equivalent The Blue Mariners. Both Thursday and Elsie had seen some of these bands during their foreign service, as well as singers and entertainers like Vera Lynn, Gracie Fields, and Tommy Trinder with his broad grin and catch-phrase, 'You Lucky People!'

The band tonight wasn't a famous one, but it played all the favourite tunes of the day – 'I Know Why and So Do You', 'Tangerine', 'In the Mood' and 'Moonlight Serenade'. There were plenty of partners available and the girls were snapped up as soon as they came in. Thursday found herself in the arms of a tall, fair-haired American, dancing a tango that left her breathless. Their bodies were close and she could smell a mixture of coal-tar soap and sweat that was oddly attractive. A very male scent, she thought, inhaling it; a very *exciting* scent. She closed her eyes, letting herself float in his arms, then flicked them open again as he bent her backwards to the swoop of the music, and found herself staring up into his face.

'Say, you're quite a mover,' he drawled, letting her come upright again and finishing the dance with a flourish. 'Will you do the next one with me as well?'

Thursday nodded. Dancing had been a major pastime in Egypt, and she loved the feeling that she could let her body mould closely to her partner's without any sense of betrayal towards the man who held her heart. Even the kisses exchanged during the last waltz, passionate though they might be, were only for that evening – a mutual recognition that love could last for as much as a lifetime, but as little as an evening. It was just as real sometimes, she thought, as they swung into a fast foxtrot, but it would be over by the time she reached the ferry, and no hard feelings on either side. That was the trick of it, like putting on your suit of armour at the hospital. You could let yourself feel, let yourself love a little, but it had to come to an end, just as the dance itself came to an end. With the playing of the National Anthem and that last goodnight kiss, your little holiday from real life must be finished, and real life resumed. But you felt refreshed by your evening. It helped everyone to carry on.

Of course, if you were like Elsie, still single and heartwhole, you could let the romance continue. Elsie looked as if she was going to do so tonight, Thursday thought, catching a glimpse of her friend drifting by, her arms wound round the neck of a sturdy matelot, eyes blissfully closed.

'So you're a nurse, are you?' her partner said, walking her back to her seat at the end of the foxtrot. 'Here in Portsmouth?'

Thursday shook her head, then nodded. 'Well, almost. I'm at Haslar. It's in Gosport, on the other side of the harbour. A Naval hospital.'

He nodded. 'I know it. Buddy of mine finished up there a week or so ago. Went over in the first wave of landings and copped a packet, but he's going to be OK. Lost a foot, unfortunately, so his war's over. He's in one of our hospitals now.'

'Oh.' Thursday looked at him, wondering if she might have assisted in the operation the man must have had. 'I'm sorry.'

The GI shrugged. 'Could have been worse. At least he's still alive, and a guy can do a lot with an artificial foot. Even dance!' The music was striking up again and he grinned at her. 'Feel like doing something more lively?'

Dancers were already crowding the floor and Thursday found herself twisting and gyrating in time to the jazz, her feet tapping wildly as her partner twirled her around. He pulled her close, caught her by the waist and swung her high in the air, then down again and between his legs. Thursday gasped with shock and exhilaration, tried to anticipate his next move and then gave up as she found herself almost on his shoulders. Just don't let him drop me, she prayed, and then forgot even that in her elation. Oh, this was wonderful, this was marvellous; it was exciting and arousing, it was like flying, it was like being a part of the music, a part of the dance, a part of the tall, fair GI who was her partner . . .

The music ended so abruptly that she felt dizzy. She swayed and felt his arms around her, firm and strong as they had been during the dance but with an added tension that transmitted itself to her body. She stood still, close in his embrace, and then looked up into his face.

He had very blue eyes. Clear blue eyes. Honest, direct eyes, with very wide pupils. She looked into them and caught her breath.

There was a moment of silence.

'I don't even know your name,' he murmured.

'It's Thursday.'

'Thursday?'

She nodded. Her voice was low, shaking. 'What's yours?'

'Earl.'

'Earl?' She laughed. 'That's like being called Duke. Or Prince.'

'Well, it's no stranger than being called a day of the week.' He gave her a quizzical glance. 'Let's go outside for a minute. Get some fresh air.'

'I . . .' Thursday hesitated. She flicked a look around the big room, wondering where the others were. She spotted Elsie, now sitting on the sailor's lap, but Patsy was nowhere to be seen. 'I ought to stay with my friends,' she said lamely.

'Aw, come on. They're OK. You all came for a bit of fun, didn't you? A night off from the war?' He took her gently by the arm and drew her towards the door. 'I'm not going to make a pass at you – not unless you want me to, anyway!'

That's just the trouble, Thursday thought as she allowed him to guide her outside. With the exhilaration of the dance still fizzing through her body and the warmth of his embrace still lingering about her, she might well want him to make a pass at her. I'm only human, she thought, and I'm nearly twenty-six, and it's such a long time since Connor went away. And there've been other men to dance with since then, other men to hold and kiss me, other men to love a little – and every time it gets more difficult not to fall all the way in love. Sometimes, it had been almost impossible.

Once, it had been quite impossible. It was only the thought of the promise she had made, the promise she knew she must keep even though it had been made only in her heart, that had kept her from taking that final step.

Earl led her out into the soft light of the evening and they walked across the road to the promenade. The shingle beach was washed now by soft wavelets, a clear turquoise laced with creamy foam – a far cry from the grey, sullen swell and crashing waves of D-Day. Thursday stared at it, remembering the great armada that had massed here, each ship like a child at a pre-war birthday party with its big grey balloon floating above. She remembered the thunder of the aircraft as they passed overhead, wave upon wave of Spitfires, Hurricanes, Dakotas and the huge American Flying Fortresses. And the silence of the gliders, carrying troops and vehicles to land beyond the shores, to take the enemy by surprise.

'I guess that's where I'll be heading soon,' Earl murmured, breaking into her thoughts.

She turned and looked at him. 'To France?'

'Sure. They won't leave any of us behind, not as long as we're fit and ready for action.' He grinned at her and flexed his muscles. 'Gee, I hope not, anyway! I'm sure ready for it. Teach those bastards – sorry – a lesson. It was plenty time for us to come into the war.'

'I suppose that's something we can thank the Japanese for,' Thursday said, and then thought of Jeanie Brown. 'I wish they hadn't done what they did, though. It wasn't anything to do with them – why did they have to join in?'

'The way it was explained to us, they'd been after China for years. I guess they saw a chance and took it, and then found Russia getting in their way. That meant they'd got to take Hitler's side, and get rid of our bases in the South Pacific.' He snapped his fingers. 'Pearl Harbor!'

Thursday nodded. It sounded simple enough, put like that, yet it was terrible that the world was at war simply because of greed. Why did leaders want more and more power? Why couldn't everyone be satisfied to live simply in their own homes, peaceful and content?

The sun was going down slowly, turning the sky to the colour of apricots with a soft green shadow merging into the far horizon. A shimmering path lay like a carpet of gold leaf across the sea, shifting gently with the swell, broken in places as a ship crossed. A few people were bathing, reluctant to let the day end, and couples were walking arm-in-arm along the prom.

'It's hard to believe they're fighting over there,' Thursday said softly. 'Men killing each other. The wounded just lying there helpless while others run past and leave them.'

'There's nothing else you can do,' Earl told her. 'You're there to fight, and if you stop you're likely to get killed as well. You can prop a bloke up, put a cigarette between his lips, but any more than that and you're risking others' lives as well as your own.' He stared out over the crowded waters. 'It might be your best buddy shot down, and you still can't do more than that.'

Thursday glanced at him. 'Is that what happened to you?'

'It has done,' he said briefly, and then took his eyes away from the ships. He turned to look down into her face. 'Don't let's talk about it now, Thursday.' He grinned. 'I still can't get over that name of yours! Come on – let's forget it for a while. Real life'll come back soon enough. Let's do what the song says – let's face the music and dance!'

She laughed, and then reached up and touched his face. 'That's what it's for, isn't it – dancing? To help us forget, for just a little while. It does us good.'

'It'll do me good,' he said seriously, 'to have this evening to remember when I'm over there.' He nodded out towards the sea. 'It'll do me good to remember you, Thursday, and think of the dancing we had together. And maybe a kiss or two as well.' He bent his head and touched her lips with his.

Thursday stood quite still. She closed her eyes. Earl's arms were warm and hard about her body, his lips tender yet searching. She let her own arms creep up round his neck, and pulled him suddenly tight against her, caught by a rush of desire. I want to be loved, she thought, letting herself relax against him. I want to know what it's like to be loved, to love someone. I want to *feel* it . . .

Earl lifted his lips away at last. They pulled slowly apart. She slid her arms down from his neck and rested her palms against his chest. He reached up and took her left hand and looked at it.

'You're not married? Not engaged?'

She hesitated. 'Not exactly.'

'There's a feller, though? Someone you think a lot of?'

She nodded. 'He's in the Far East, on a ship. He's been away for three years now.'

'Three years,' he said. 'That's a hell of a long time to wait.'

Thursday looked down for a moment, then raised her eyes to his. 'He didn't ask me to wait,' she said. 'I wanted to. I made a promise – to myself, really. But it is a long time. I didn't know it would be so long – I didn't know what it would be like.'

There was a little silence. She could feel her heart thudding. She didn't really know what she was saying to him – that she wanted to keep her promise, or that it had been too big a promise to make? Suppose he asked her to break it, on this lovely June evening, with the peace of the seafront disturbed only by dance music sounding from the pier? Had she kept her promise long enough?

*

'I want you to have fun,' Connor's voice said inside her head. 'I want you to be the Thursday who goes dancing – who always has a smile and a laugh. I don't want you to stay at home moping.'

He must have known the risks. He must have known the temptations. That was why he hadn't wanted to tie her down, hadn't wanted her to make any promises. He hadn't wanted her to face the dilemma that such a promise could cause.

But I made it, all the same, she reminded herself. I made it to him even though he didn't know it. And a promise is a promise.

Earl was watching her face. He cupped his hand against her cheek and lifted her lips to his again. His kiss this time was tender, but he withdrew before it became deep again. He smiled into her eyes.

'Let's go back inside,' he said quietly. 'I've got a girl at home myself. I don't want to have any shadows between us when I get back home. I don't think you want shadows either. Not really.'

Their arms around each other's waists, they went back across the road and into the dance hall again. The band was playing 'That Lovely Weekend' and couples were moving slowly around the floor, arms wrapped tightly around each other, the girls with their cheeks resting against their partners'. Earl held out his arms and Thursday went into them and, like the others, laid her head on his shoulder.

They would never spend a weekend together, nor even a night. They would probably not even meet again. But for this one evening they could give each other comfort – and leave no shadows.

The dance finished at ten, an hour before blackout, and the girls kissed their partners good night and collected their bikes.

Patsy sighed happily. 'You know, I really enjoyed that. It was lovely to dance again. That GI I was dancing with was so good – almost as good as Roy. He was nice, too.' She grinned. 'Gave me a lovely good-night kiss!'

'Mine was nice too,' Elsie said dreamily. She was clutching a small bar of chocolate that she and the Naval rating she'd met in the Paul Jones had won in the Spot dance later on. 'And yours looked a real dish, Thursday!'

Thursday smiled, but she felt a little sad. Earl was a nice man, an attractive man, and one she felt she could have fallen in love with, had things been different. But he was right – he was going away in a few days. Neither wanted a shadow in their life. I wonder how many men a girl could fall in love with, she thought as she started to pedal down the road. In the ordinary way, you probably wouldn't meet more than one or two, but these days, with so many people moving about all the time, you could meet a dozen or more. Could any one of them be 'Mr Right'? If she hadn't known Connor, would Mark Sangster whom she'd known in Egypt, have been the one for her? And if she hadn't met either of them, could it have been Earl – or half a dozen other men she'd met in the past few years?

If it hadn't been for the war, she mused, following the other two girls, would I really have settled down with Sidney, like Mum wanted me to, and lived happily ever after?

The thought made her giggle, and Patsy looked over her shoulder. 'Come on, slowcoach, we'll miss the last ferry if you don't get a move on.'

'Coming,' Thursday said, and put her musings out of her mind. It didn't do any good to wonder. Life was what it was, and you just had to go along with whatever did happen.

By the time the girls reached Gosport again and were pedalling as fast as they could past Trinity Church on their way to Pneumonia Bridge, it was almost dark.

'Oh, that did me good,' Patsy said again. 'Thanks for making me come. It was a smashing evening.'

'We're only just going to make it back in time, you know,' Elsie said, puffing as she got off her bike to push it up the steep slope. 'I bet Madam's there now, looking at the signing-in book and checking her watch.'

'We've still got seven minutes.' They reached the top of the bridge and freewheeled down the other side to swoop round the corner and into Clayhall Road. The high brick wall of the hospital rose beside them and they skidded to a halt at the gate, fishing for their passes to show the sailors on guard. Waved through, they puffed into the sheds, threw their bikes into the racks and rushed into D Block.

Miss Makepeace was waiting on the landing. Her face was grave, and Thursday felt a lurch of her heart. She paused, one hand on the banister, one at her throat.

'We're surely not late, are we, Madam?' Patsy gasped. 'We came as fast as we could.'

'My watch says there's still three minutes to go,' Elsie panted. 'We're really sorry—'

'You're not late. At least, I don't think so.' Miss Makepeace's voice was serious. She turned to Patsy. 'Greenaway, I'm very sorry. I'm afraid there's a telegram for you.'

'A telegram?' Patsy's voice was a whisper. She looked at her friends, then back at the Red Cross Commandant. 'A *telegram*?'

Madam handed it over. Patsy's fingers closed about the little brown envelope and she stared at it. Thursday moved closer and put her arm about Patsy's shoulders.

'Would you like me to open it for you?'

Patsy shook her head uncertainly. 'No. No, I'll do it.' With shaking fingers, she began to tear at the flimsy paper. It seemed to take an age before she had it open and drew out the greyish scrap inside with its letters stuck unevenly across it. She frowned at it, her lips moving slowly, not seeming to understand what it said, and then, shaking her head in denial, read it again.

'It's not true,' she said blankly. 'It's not true. He was going to send me a card. We're going to be dancing champions. It can't be true. It *can't*!'

Thursday reached out and took the telegram from her fingers. She read it quickly and felt the tears fill her eyes.

'Oh, Patsy,' she said. 'Oh, Patsy . . .'

Chapter Seven

Miss Makepeace wanted her to take a few days' leave, but Patsy shook her head. 'What's the point? What would I do? There's no – no *funeral* to go to. And there are patients coming in all the time. I can't leave now.' She spoke in a dull, flat voice, and Thursday caught Madam's brown eyes resting on her anxiously, but the Commandant said no more. She sighed a little and nodded.

'Very well. But if you do decide you want a few days, you must come to me immediately, do you understand? There's to be no bravely carrying on if you don't feel up to the job. I won't have the patients' lives put at risk.'

It sounded rather harsh, thought Thursday who had gone to Madam's office with Patsy early next morning, but perhaps it was the best way. Madam was right – everyone who worked in the hospital must be 'on top line'. A moment's carelessness could cost a man his life.

'I'm looking to you to keep an eye on her, Tilford,' Madam said as Patsy turned to leave the office. 'Come to me the moment you think she needs help. The shock's numbing her at the moment and it may carry her through several days, but the grief's bound to hit her eventually. We can't afford any breakdowns.' The bright brown eyes regarded Thursday. 'I'm as much concerned for Greenaway as for the patients, you understand. She's been an exemplary VAD and this is a terrible blow. We must all take care of her.'

'Yes, Madam.' Thursday hesitated. 'She seems to be in another world, somehow. Almost as if she's decided not to believe it. I listened in the night but I don't think she cried, not at all.'

Miss Makepeace nodded. 'Some people do react in that way. It can mislead us into thinking they don't care, or that they're dealing with the whole thing very bravely. It usually means that, as you say, they just won't accept the truth, and that can be very dangerous. Because one day they *have* to accept it, and it can trigger a much worse reaction than if they began to grieve straightaway. You must keep an eye on her, you and Jackson especially. I know you've always been good friends. Don't forget – come to me the moment you feel any anxiety.'

'Yes, Madam.' Thursday felt the familiar warmth of knowing that she could rely on and trust the Commandant implicitly. It had been like that from the beginning, she thought, from that very first snowy evening when she and Patsy had arrived at Haslar as new and rather scared VADs. One glance from those brown eyes, one word spoken in that clear, steady voice, and they had known that they had come, like the ship Haslar Hospital operated as, into safe harbour.

All the girls were equally concerned for Patsy. Several of them had also lost husbands or sweethearts, and all of them knew some young man who had gone off to war and never returned. Thursday's cousins Mike and Leslie had both been killed in action, Elsie's brother Dave by a bomb, Louisa's cousin in Bomb Disposal had been blown up by a mine, Helen Stanway's father lost at sea . . . the list was endless. But Patsy had been married from Haslar, and Madam and a number of the VADs had been present at her wedding. They'd all known Roy, right from the moment he and Patsy had met, and so the blow seemed all the harsher.

For Patsy, it was as if she had been turned to stone. The shock, hitting her like a blow, ran like ice through her body, and froze her heart. After that first moment of denial, she was swept by a feeling of inevitability. It had always been going to happen. Roy had escaped death twice, three times, already. Perhaps even more. But now his luck had run out and he was gone.

She refused to talk about it, even to her friends. When the letter came a few days later from the First Lieutenant, she read it almost as if it were about someone else. Roy had gone with two other SBAs on to the beaches, working with the wounded, trying to treat them where they lay and get them back on to the ships that had only just landed them. Under heavy fire, he had refused to take shelter and continued to work, saving a number of lives before disappearing in a blast from a storm of grenades. In the confusion, two other SBAs had been killed as well as the ship's doctor, and men were ordered to return to any ship they could reach. It was days before it was known just who had been saved and who killed or injured, and Roy's death had only been confirmed when his identity tag had been discovered. The letter gave no other details, but Patsy had heard enough from other sailors to know that this meant there had been no body; only pieces.

Her Roy, blown to pieces. She tried the words out in her mind and they meant nothing. She couldn't imagine it. It was as if a steel curtain descended between the words and their meaning. It was a curtain she almost welcomed, knowing that beyond it lay a pain too sharp to face.

'I don't want time off,' she repeated tonelessly when Thursday tried to urge her to go home for a few days. 'It won't do anyone any good. I've got a job to do here. Leave me alone.'

She went back to the ward and concentrated fiercely on the men she was nursing. They needed her. They were still alive. Like Roy, they had escaped death. Like Roy, they might not escape next time, but for now they were in her charge and she could do something for them. She could make them comfortable, give them medicine to make them better, tend their wounds, listen to their stories and make them laugh again. With them, she could be in control, and as long as she was in control she could manage.

If she went home, she wouldn't be in control. She would be the one who was being looked after, and then that steel curtain might lift and she would have to face what lay on the other side.

The worst time was when she came off duty.

'I just don't know what to do for her,' Elsie said to Thursday as they walked along the sea wall together during another brief spell off duty. 'Work's all right, but she's got to have some time off as well. But what can she do? She won't want to go dancing or to the pictures, I can understand that, but it's not good for her to sit on her bed and just do nothing.'

'She doesn't even cry,' Thursday agreed. 'She just sits there, looking at his photo, or going through his letters. I wouldn't want to stop her doing that, mind, it seems right to want to go over it all – but she ought to cry as well. It's not natural.'

'It's like Madam said. Some people can't cry, not at first.'

Thursday thought of her mother, waiting month after month for news of Steve after Dunkirk. She'd refused to believe he was dead, even though everyone knew he must be, and she hadn't cried either. She'd held in all her grief, keeping her lips tight, until they'd really begun to fear for her. If she didn't crack soon, Thursday had thought, she'd break into a million pieces, like a glass shattering. But in the end she'd been proved right – Steve *wasn't* dead, he was a prisoner of war in somewhere called Colditz Castle, and one day he'd be home again. Mary's grief had turned to joy and then to practicality as she'd set about sending him cakes and other comforts. It wasn't going to be like that for Patsy.

'I don't think there's anything we *can* do,' she said to Elsie now, 'except just let her go the way she wants and be around when she needs us.'

The road ran under the high brick wall of the hospital and along the top of the sloping sea wall. At high tide the sea lapped halfway up the steep incline, and you could swim straight into deep water. Even at low tide, it revealed only a strip of shingle at the foot. The girls walked as far as they could, along to where the road turned inland towards Anglesey and tarmac gave way to the scrub of the golf course. Like the rest of the beach, this strip had been wired off during the past few months and the smooth greens of the golf course allowed to revert to scrub. The old moat still ran around Fort Gilkicker and there were defences and gun emplacements all the way along.

'This would have done Patsy good,' Thursday remarked as they turned to walk back. 'A bit of sea air and exercise. We'll have to make her come out with us next time.'

They sat down on the top of the slope and turned their faces to the sun. The brief spell of fine weather had cheered them a little, although there was a steely look to the sky now that threatened rain. The Solent was still crowded with ships plying back and forth, still protected by their silvery barrage balloons, and they watched them silently. Above the balloons there was a steady stream of aircraft, each squadron on its way to France both to give air cover to the invading troops and to ward off any air raids the Germans might make on England. D-Day had been only the beginning of an invasion which was still under way.

Thursday gazed out over the scene, then frowned. Her heart gave a sudden lurch and she gripped Elsie's arm. 'Look! Look, Else –

look over there, just past the Island. It's a plane – at least, I think it is – all by itself. I've never seen anything like it. Look at its tiny wings. What d'you think it is?'

They stared, shading their eyes against the brightness. The aircraft was small and black, flying like a dart towards the coast. Thursday felt a knot of fear low down in her stomach. She gripped Elsie's arm more tightly.

'I don't like it,' Elsie said in a low voice. 'I don't think it's one of ours. What can it be? It's too small to be a bomber.'

'It's very high,' Thursday said uneasily. 'Maybe we can't judge its size properly.'

The plane seemed to be flying in a dead straight line, purposefully heading north. It crossed the coastline and disappeared, apparently without having been noticed. Thursday and Elsie looked at each other.

'Let's get back.' Elsie got to her feet. 'There was something about that thing that scared me, Thurs. The way it flew – as if it knew just where it was going, and nothing and nobody was going to stop it. And I reckon it was one of *theirs*. I'm sure it was.'

'The secret weapon people have been talking about?' Thursday suggested doubtfully. 'Hitler's secret weapon?'

'I dunno. All I know is, I want to get back to the hospital. We've been out long enough, Thurs. I want to get back where we know what's what and who people are. I want to get back where I feel *safe*.'

Nowhere was really safe, But Thursday, following her friend as she half-ran along the sea road, knew just what Elsie meant. Out here, in full view of every ship in the Solent, of any plane that came over, they felt exposed and vulnerable. Attack could come from any quarter. People had been strafed and machine-gunned in their own streets, at their own front doors.

Terror gripped her heart as she scurried back to the hospital gates, and although the day was still as bright, she felt as if the hounds of darkness were snapping at her heels.

Over the next few days, the truth emerged.

The strange aircraft was indeed a new weapon – and the most terrifying one yet. Officially, it was called the V1 but it soon acquired more common names – the buzz-bomb or doodlebug because of the noise it made and, most accurately, the flying bomb.

For that was exactly what it was – a pilotless aircraft which was wholly bomb, packed with explosive and with just enough engine power to reach its target.

Its target, on the whole, was London. Anywhere in London. There was no pretence now that the targets were military. The flying bombs were aimed at a city full of people confident that the war was almost over, that air raids were a thing of the past and it was safe to come home. Suddenly, it wasn't safe at all. Death could flash out of a blue or stormy sky, day or night, too quickly for a siren to be sounded and giving no time to take cover. The country was once again on permanent alert, and all you could do if you heard it was pray. If the engine stopped above you, it simply fell and you had just fifteen seconds before the explosion to throw yourself on the ground. If you stayed on your feet, you could be flung across the street by the blast, peppered with debris or simply scattered in small pieces. If the bomb fell directly on you, there was no chance at all of surviving.

'I dunno,' Elsie said as they sat outside the next evening. Even at nine o'clock the sun was still high and warm and they had dragged chairs out in front of the block. 'It's like two steps forward and one back. They're sending these flaming things over all the time. They said on the news that there was over seventy hit London yesterday, and what about that one that killed all those people in that Army chapel just by Buckingham Palace? Over a *hundred*, it said on the news.' She shook her head. 'They're worse than ordinary planes – at least you get some warning when there's a proper raid on, and you know it's people up there. It seems worse, somehow, knowing that there's no one flying these ruddy things. It's as if there's nothing anyone can do. I mean, there could be one coming over at this very moment and we wouldn't know till it was almost here.'

They all glanced uneasily up at the sky. Elsie was right, Thursday thought, there was something horribly menacing about these new weapons. It was because the Germans weren't taking any risks, she thought. There was no pilot, so nobody could get killed. And there seemed to be hundreds of them, perhaps thousands. Would they be the weapons that finally won the war? Had the invasion and all the injuries and loss of life on the Normandy beaches been in vain?

The flood of casualties had eased a little, although there were still plenty of new cases arriving. Many of them were smothered in the sand of the beaches where they had lain for hours, waiting to be rescued. The wards and operating theatres were busy, and off-duty time precious. Thursday spent much of hers writing letters, either to Connor or to her family in Worcester.

It seems an age already since I saw you all, she wrote to her mother. *Madam says we shall all have a week sometime during the summer, if things go on as they are doing, but I don't know when it will be. We're still flat out here, although the first wave has slowed down a bit. I'll probably just turn up on the doorstep one day with my suitcase! Take care of yourselves and give my love to Denise and my godson.*

She folded her letter and slipped it into an envelope. It was funny, she thought, she missed her family more now that she was back in England than she had while she was in Egypt. The few days she'd had at home had been all too short, giving her no more than a tantalising glimpse of the family life she'd left behind when she first volunteered as a VAD. Too short to get used to the changes – the fact that she'd never see her cousins Mike and Leslie again, nor her dog Patch.

She remembered the day the letter had come, telling her about Patch's death. Louisa had come into the room and found her crying. She'd sat down beside her, her arm around Thursday's shoulders, asking what had happened. 'Is it your brother? Or one of your parents?'

Thursday shook her head and held out the single sheet. 'I shouldn't be crying. Not when so many awful things are happening. But he was *my* dog. He understood—' Her voice choked and Louisa's arm tightened about her.

'It's all right, Thursday. You can cry. I know what it's like – I lost my own dog a little while ago. He was a Labrador and he loved everyone, but he was my dog just the same. He was special.'

'That's just what Patchie was – special.' Thursday drew a sobbing breath. 'But it seems wrong all the same. I mean, my auntie's lost both her sons, and we thought our Steve was dead too, and I was really upset, I really was, but I never cried like this for any of them. And when Tony died – I *wanted* to cry for him, but I couldn't, not like this. It seems wrong – as if I thought more of him than I did of them.' She choked again, the tears streaming down her face. 'I don't know what's the matter with me, Lou. I just can't seem to stop.'

'It's all right. It doesn't matter. Just let it go – let it go.' Louisa kept her arm around Thursday's shoulders, murmuring soothingly to her all the while. 'Just cry. Cry as much as you want. It doesn't matter.'

Later, Thursday realised that she had been crying for her lost cousins, for her first sweetheart, Tony West, for her brother, and – perhaps – for all the young men and women she had nursed through the past few years, just as much as for her dog. Patch's death had given her the right to let go of all the grief she had kept pent up inside her, and the pain of all the years of war had been lanced like a boil by the loss of one small mongrel dog. And it had done her good; when the first searing anguish was over, she'd been able to face the war again and return to her duties with a calmer heart.

She and Louisa, already friends, had forged a special bond that evening. From totally different backgrounds, they had discovered common ground in the fact that Louisa had gone to a boarding school in Great Malvern, only a few miles from Thursday's home in Worcester. On the way out to Egypt, with plenty of time at sea for talking, they'd discovered more about each other. Thursday had told Louisa about her home and family and Louisa had in return given Thursday a glimpse into her own, very different, life.

'People think that someone like Daddy's got pots of money, of course,' she'd observed, 'but he has to work for it, just like anyone else. I mean, he did inherit all the land and everything, but it has to pay its way. The farms are what we live on – the rent from the tenants and the income from Home Farm – that's the one Daddy runs himself. And all the tenant farms have to be maintained and looked after – they're not exactly a gold mine.'

They sounded like one to Thursday, whose father had worked all his life in the porcelain factory and wanted nothing more for his children than an apprenticeship to a decent trade. She tried to imagine living in a huge house, with separate bedrooms for everyone and still some to spare, and enormous gardens and not one farm but half a dozen. 'Will your brother take it over one day?' she asked.

Louisa nodded. 'It'll go to Robert – he's the eldest son. It has to – there's an entail on it. There's a trust for me as well, and one for Dominic, and he'll probably take over one of the farms. He loves being on the land.'

'Why didn't you stay at home, then?' Thursday asked. 'You could have been a Land Girl and lived in comfort, instead of roughing it as a VAD and spending all day emptying bedpans.'

Louisa laughed. 'And it wouldn't have seemed like war work at all! Not that we live in luxury, Thursday. I'm sure it seems like it to you, but at home we live quite simply. Well, all right, we do have maids and gardeners, we could never manage the house and garden without. But we don't dine on caviar every night and drink champagne for breakfast. Mummy does most of the cooking and gardening, and we all had to help. And Mummy and Daddy have always insisted that we must be able to look after ourselves. I've always washed my own undies, for instance, and we had to do that at school too. And *that* wasn't the lap of luxury either; in fact, it was just like being at Haslar!'

It still seemed a luxurious way of life to Thursday. 'But you used to go to balls and society parties in London, didn't you? And do the "Season"?'

'Oh yes,' Louisa said carelessly, as if it didn't much matter. 'I was presented at Court and all that kind of thing. That was quite fun, especially meeting the King and Queen – he's sweet, very shy but really nice, and she's lovely – but it all seems a bit unreal now. Like playing at life instead of living it. In fact, now I come to think about it, that's really what we were doing.' She turned her head and looked at Thursday gravely. 'This'll probably sound funny to you, Thursday, but I'd rather be doing what we're doing now – helping to nurse men who've been wounded in war, even if it does just mean emptying bedpans – than going to all those dinners and balls. It's as if all that was a dream and now I'm awake and can get on with real life.'

Thursday nodded. 'I know what you mean. Being a VAD has given me the chance to do things I'd never have been able to do before. I suppose the war's done that for a lot of people,' she went on thoughtfully. 'Especially girls. Without it, we would have been expected to just settle down and get married and have a family, without ever moving further away from home than the next street. But now – well, women are doing all sorts of jobs. Driving buses, flying aeroplanes, being wireless operators, doing important jobs in offices – there's no end to what women can do now.'

'There's no end to what women can do, full stop,' Louisa said with a smile, and then added, 'but I wonder what will happen after the war. When the men come home they'll want their old jobs back again, won't they? And what will we women do, now we've tasted freedom? Are we just going to give it up? Or are we going to fight to keep hold of it? It'll be interesting to see.'

Louisa's words stayed in Thursday's mind. Sitting by the autoclave in the hot, steamy underground theatre, sterilising the instruments, she thought about the end of the war and what it would bring. For so long, it had stretched ahead without any promise of a conclusion, but now, with the Italian capitulation assured and the invasion forging ahead, everyone was beginning to think about the possibility and to make plans. Many of the beaches were open again – although the ban on visitors to the forbidden ten-mile zone was still in force – parents were calling for the evacuated schools to be returned to the city and there was even talk of rebuilding the blitzed city centre. What a job that would be, Thursday thought. She'd been over to Portsmouth with Elsie, to visit the Jacksons, and had noticed that although a lot of the rubble had been tidied up, the gutted Guildhall still stood in ruins, along with most of the big shops along Commercial Street. It would take years to put them all back the way they had been.

However, the important thing was that they were thinking about it. Making plans. And perhaps that was what she ought to be doing too.

Thursday fished out the sterilised instruments and put in a fresh load. Did she want to continue nursing? There'd been a time when she'd been determined to go for state registration as soon as the war was over, like her sister Jenny and their Aunt Maudie, but now she wasn't so sure. I wouldn't have missed it for the world, she thought, but what will it be like afterwards? It'll still be worth doing, I know – nursing will always be worth doing – but will it be quite the same without the urgency of war?

It was only the war that had brought her into nursing; on leaving school, she had been apprenticed to a tailor in Worcester. But did she want to go back to tailoring or dressmaking? Would she even want to go back to Worcester?

Louisa's right, she thought, we've seen and done a lot more than our mothers ever did, or ever even dreamed of. And it's changed us.

We're different people – and we don't know quite what people we're going to be when all this is over.

We're *used* to war, she thought with a kind of horror.

In the dormitory, when they had finished their morning shift, she tried to explain her feelings to the others. 'I don't know *what* I'm going to want to do. It's all going to be so different. People trying to settle down – to get the country back together. Men coming home and wanting their old jobs back – or maybe not being fit enough to work at all. It's not going to be like it was in 1939. We're all older, for a start, and we've done so much. Look at Elsie and Louisa and me – we've been abroad, and not just on holiday – we've *lived* there. We'd never have done any of that – well, you might, Lou, but *we* never would. We'd have been stuck in backstreets all our lives. Marrying the first boy we went out with, renting a few rooms or a little house somewhere near our mums and having three or four kids. And nothing else to look forward to at all. We're not going to settle for that now, are we? *Are* we?' She looked around at them.

'Well, I would,' Patsy said tautly. 'I'd settle for it any day of the week.'

Thursday thumped her forehead with her palm and stared at her friend, horrified. 'Oh, *Pats*! I'm sorry – I never thought. Trust me and my big mouth, every time I open it I put my foot in it! I'm really sorry, Pats. I'm so *stupid*.'

Patsy shook her head. Her eyes were bright and her lower lip was folded in tightly between her teeth. She reached beneath her bunk suddenly and groped for her shoes. 'I'm just going out for a walk.'

'I'll come too.' Thursday slid down from her own bunk but Patsy turned on her sharply.

'*No*! No, I don't want you to come. I don't want *anyone*.' She was making for the door, and although her head was high they could all hear the break in her voice. They looked at each other in alarm and Thursday, her own shoes in her hand, stood helpless and dismayed.

'She looked awful,' Elsie said. 'White as a sheet. Oh, *Thurs*!'

'It's all my fault,' Thursday said. 'I don't know what I was thinking of. Saying all that about getting married and settling down as if it was something no one in their right mind would want. Oh, I'm such an *idiot*. Poor Patsy. What are we going to do? We can't just let her go off on her own like that.'

'Maybe it's what she needs,' Elsie said. 'Maybe she'll have a good cry and let it all out. You know she's been bottling it up. It's not good for her.'

'But she's on her *own*,' Thursday said. 'She needs someone with her. I'm going after her.' She thrust her feet into her shoes and bent to lace them up. 'I won't say anything, I won't even stay with her if she doesn't want me, but I can't just let her go off like that, all upset. I'm her *friend*. At least,' she added dolefully, 'I was. She may never want to speak to me again, after this.'

'Of course she will. It's not that bad, Thurs.' Elsie touched her arm. 'She knows you didn't mean it. Something was bound to set her off sometime.'

'Well, maybe. But I've got to go after her, anyway. Just to make sure . . .' Thursday ran to the door and hurried down the stairs. At the entrance to the block, she stood for a moment looking to see where Patsy had gone. There was no sign of her heading out towards the sea wall, nor along the quarter deck leading to the little church. Then her eye caught a flicker of movement and she saw the familiar figure walking rapidly towards the Clayhall Road gate. Of course! She was going to Alverstoke, where she and Roy had been married. Swiftly, Thursday ran after her, then slowed as she realised that, as Elsie had said, Patsy might want to be alone. I won't let her know I'm here, she thought. I'll just go along to keep an eye on her, just in case she needs me . . .

Patsy was walking quickly. She could feel the tears building inside her, pressing against her heart and her throat like a dam about to burst. They had been building ever since the telegram had arrived, but the steel curtain had kept it back. Now the curtain was dissolving, turning to glass, and she could sense, almost see, the grief that lay on the other side. Soon the glass itself would shatter . . .

She knew only that she had to get away from the hospital before she could let the dam shatter the fragile glass. She had to be somewhere that meant something special to herself and Roy. There were a hundred places – the sea wall where they had walked, holding hands, the road past Gilkicker Fort where they had cycled to Stokes Bay, Lee Tower where they'd danced, Pneumonia Bridge where they'd crossed Haslar Lake into Gosport to have tea at the Swiss Café or a bun and mug of cocoa in the Dive. The ferry to Portsmouth, where they'd huddled against the funnel on cold nights, coming back from the pictures. The entire place was filled with memories, memories she hadn't dared face until now.

She walked down Clayhall Road and along the old railway line, stopping on Jackie Spencer's bridge to lean on the iron parapet and gaze across the head of Haslar creek towards Alverstoke and the church tower. The day was fine and clear, and the tide was in; the water lay like a blue lake and the tower was pale grey against the cloudless sky. You could almost imagine, she thought, that there was no war on at all.

It was just like this the day we were married, Patsy reflected. A warm, sunny June day, three years ago. She remembered what fun it had been getting ready for the wedding – the other girls' panic as they discussed what to wear, the excitement of planning. Most of them had been in uniform, of course, but for Thursday and Elsie as bridesmaids and herself as a bride there had got to be something pretty. Thursday had made herself a lovely frock and then, because Patsy had no wedding dress, insisted that she wear it instead. And Elsie had worn a nightie, with Vera Hapgood's waistcoat over it!

I felt like a film star, walking up the aisle to marry Roy, she thought. Nobody could have been happier than me that day. And we had such a lovely honeymoon, those few days in Cornwall. And since then too, whenever he managed to get some leave. It was all like a dream. And now . . .

Now the dream had come to an end, and with it had ended their dream of a future together. Nothing special. Nothing glamorous. Just an ordinary, quiet life, in a little house somewhere with a family of their own – children, grandchildren, the two of them growing old together. Darby and Joan.

And now it would never happen. It was over. The dream had been destroyed and with it all their hopes and plans, and the children and the grandchildren would never be born.

For a moment, Patsy seemed to see the wedding procession – herself, her friends, the nurses and VADs, Madam and even two of the doctors – walking along the road that led beside the creek to the church. The picture faded and she saw just herself and Roy, a few years older, walking arm in arm, while in front of them ran three or four children. It was a hazy picture and the figures seemed to blur into each other as she peered through the mist that had gathered before her eyes. And then those figures too shimmered away, and there were others – grown men and women she only half recognised, and yet more children, running and calling and laughing. Children who should have belonged to the future; children whose very existence had been snatched away from them.

'Oh, *Roy*!' she cried, reaching out as if she could gather them all to her breast. 'Oh, Roy! Roy! *Roy*.' And as the last fragile barrier of glass shattered in her mind, the pictures dissolved and the tears burst at last through the dam, and she laid her head on her arms and began to weep.

Thursday, following at a distance, had stopped when she saw Patsy on the bridge. She raised one hand to her mouth, biting her knuckles anxiously, praying that Patsy wasn't going to do anything silly. People had jumped from that bridge in the past, she'd heard, knowing that although the water wasn't deep, an outgoing tide would sweep them rapidly out into the deeper waters of the creek and the harbour, beyond rescue. As she heard Patsy's cry, she started forwards, afraid that if Patsy were indeed that desperate, she wouldn't be able to reach her in time. And then she saw her friend's head droop on to her arms and saw the shaking of her shoulders as she began to cry.

Elsie had said that was what she needed – to let out all those tears that had been building up, to face up to her sorrow. And Madam had said the grief would hit her eventually and that Thursday and the others must be ready to help her when it did. Thursday felt a great wave of thankfulness wash over her that she had followed her here. Patsy was crying now as if her heart had broken – as indeed it had – and she needed to be allowed to do it. But she also needed a friend, a pair of loving arms about her, someone who would share her grief.

Quietly, Thursday came nearer and waited. She laid one arm across Patsy's shoulders and whispered in her ear. 'It's Thursday, Pats. I'm here with you. Cry all you want. Just cry. It'll do you good.' Her voice broke and she felt the tears come to her own eyes. 'I'll cry with you.' A sob rose in her throat. 'Oh, Patsy – poor Roy. Poor, *poor* Roy.'

Patsy turned towards her. She put her arms around Thursday and laid her face against her shoulder. They held each other tightly and their tears mingled, while below them the water lay cool and still, and at the head of the creek the church tower stood calm and grey against the blue sky.

When at last their tears eased, they walked on across the bridge, their arms around each other's waists. They walked beside the creek where Patsy had seen the dream figures, the sons and daughters and grandchildren who would never be, and they walked to the church where Patsy and Roy had been married. There, looking up at the altar, they wept again but, when they left the church to make their way slowly back to the hospital, the anguish that had frozen Patsy's heart had been released. She would never forget Roy – they both knew that. But while the memories would always be precious, the grief would slowly grow more bearable, and she would be able to live and laugh again. The steel curtain had gone for ever.

When the two girls came back to the hospital and met the others, Elsie gave Thursday a questioning look but made no comment on their reddened eyes and treated Patsy with the quiet gentleness that Thursday had sometimes seen her using on the wards, when nursing a patient who was particularly ill. It was what made her such a good nurse, she thought – that ability to know when to soften her laughter, when to soothe a man instead of jolly him along. It was what made her the friend that both Patsy and Thursday needed today.

'She's had a good cry,' she told Elsie privately later. 'I dare say she'll cry again, now she's started, but it'll be good, healthy crying. And she's going to ask for a few days' leave when she feels ready for it. Just now, nursing the men's better for her than time off.'

'It's good for her to do something for other people,' Elsie agreed. 'Perhaps she'll take up nursing permanently – once the war's over, I mean. She'll need to have something worthwhile to do, to fill up the gap Roy's left. I reckon we're all going to need something. It won't be easy to go back to what we used to be.'

Thursday nodded. But when she went to bed that night she lay for a long time staring into the darkness, thinking about Patsy and thinking again about the end of the war. I don't think I'll be able to go back to being the old Thursday, she thought, I really don't. I *am* different now. I'm going to want to do something else with my life – and I'm not sure it'll be getting married and settling down. Not straight off, anyway. I'll need some time to find out about myself, and to see what the world's going to be like when there isn't any more war.

And what about Connor? Would he be different too? Would he be as attracted to the new Thursday as he was to the old? Would she still feel the same about him, when they met again, or would the years have made too much difference?

I still feel I love him, she thought, but will it last? We only knew each other for a little while. And he's a doctor – properly educated, from a nice house with parents that people look up to. Is he really still going to be interested in a little VAD from a backstreet in Worcester with a dad who works in a porcelain factory and a mum who helps make soldiers' uniforms?

Her inner panic grew and tightened. I almost wish the war wouldn't come to an end, she thought, and then felt horrified with herself. That's a wicked thing to think, Thursday Tilford, she told herself angrily, and you're a wicked girl to think it. If that's the best you can do, you'd better stop thinking altogether and do what Louisa says – just wait and see.

She turned over, punched her pillow as if it were responsible for her thoughts, and fell asleep.

The initial crisis was almost over. By the time the casualties reached Haslar, the journey had proved almost too much for some of them, even though they'd been nursed all the way. The QARNNs and VADs took them in briskly but tenderly, made them comfortable and did whatever they could.

Thursday enjoyed her theatre work but occasionally found herself longing for a conscious patient, one she could talk to and offer comfort to. She understood Elsie's preference for the wards and wondered if she should ask to go back to them herself.

'Not at the moment,' Miss Makepeace said briskly when Thursday discussed it with her. 'You're a good theatre nurse and you're needed there. I know you're a good ward nurse too, but if we take you out of the theatre we'll have to put someone else in, and that could mean a loss of efficiency while she learns the procedure.'

'It's not as if I'm doing anything really important,' Thursday ventured. 'I mean, you know we VADs just do the ordinary things – sterilising and that sort of thing. We're not helping with the operations themselves.'

Madam stiffened and fixed her with her bright brown gaze. '*Everyone's* task is important in a theatre. You're part of a team, Tilford, and a team can't function properly if one of its members isn't fully effective. I hope you're not going to tell me that your work isn't up to scratch.'

'No, I'm not, Madam,' Thursday said hastily. 'Of course I'm not. I always work as well as I can. I just felt—'

'You feel restless,' the Red Cross Commandant said, her tone softer. 'You're back here at Haslar after having been abroad for two years, people are beginning to talk about the end of the war and you're feeling uncertain. It's understandable, but you mustn't let it affect your work. We still have many casualties and we don't know what may happen next. The war is by no means over, and your work is as vital now as it was at the beginning. Remember that, Tilford.'

'Yes, Madam.' Thursday left the office, feeling a little better but still aware of the questions in her mind.

The flying bombs were coming over every day now. Mostly, they were aimed at London but you never knew, as they flew over, whether their fuel might run out at any moment. Some dropped on Portsmouth and other towns, and everyone felt the same dread when they heard the unmistakable sound of the engine. And even if it didn't stop right overhead, the blast could cause damage for a quarter of a mile all round. In less than two weeks, over fifteen hundred people had been killed and nearly five thousand badly hurt. They really were weapons of terror.

Gosport and Portsmouth were still busy, their beaches a constant scene of activity as ships reloaded with men and provisions. The strange tension of the week before D-Day had mostly evaporated, but the flow of soldiers ready to go over and fight seemed endless. They knew now what they were going to, knew that the Atlantic Wall had been breached and the beaches captured, but they were still very aware that the battle had only just begun. The whole of occupied France waited for liberation and peace and, after that, the rest of Europe. There was a lot more fighting to do before peace could be declared.

Peace. It was a strange word, stranger still after five years of war. For a little while, you heard it everywhere – '*when peace comes*' – and then it stopped as people began to realise that it was still somewhere in the future. Another Christmas, at least, would come and go before peace became a reality.

Thursday pushed her restlessness away. There was work to do, casualties to be nursed and operated on, and dreams and memories must take second place. She went through the days, working her duties, walking along the sea front, writing to Connor and to her family. It was a good day when a letter came, a disappointing one when none arrived. Sometimes she would go a week or more without hearing from Connor, and then a bundle of letters would arrive together. This had happened so many times that they had agreed on a numbering system, so that the letters could be read in order. After two years apart, Connor's letters had reached number 275.

My darling, he wrote, *it seems such a long time since I saw you – and England. I miss the seasons almost as much as I miss you. When I think of the short time that we knew each other – from autumn into winter – I realise that I can only associate you with the bitter cold of January, and the terror of the Blitz. We didn't even have a Christmas together. I don't know you with the spring breezes ruffling your hair, nor with the summer sunshine on your face. We've never swum together in the sea, nor walked in meadows or on the moors, nor sailed in the little tub of a dinghy I kept in Haslar Lake. But we* WILL *do those things, my dearest. When all this is over and we're free to live our lives again, we'll do all those things. I'll take you to Devon, to see my family, and we'll walk on the moors and beside the sea, we'll swim and cycle and ride the two old horses that live in the paddock, we'll do all those things together that we ought to have been able to do when we were young and carefree. And we'll love each other again, as I loved you before I left you – as I love you now.*

Thursday folded the letter and put it in her pocket. The words and the passion made her heart beat faster, yet she was aware of a touch of uneasiness. Suppose they *didn't* love each other when they met again? Suppose the changes were too much?

'Don't be daft,' Elsie said robustly, 'of course you will. Anyone could see you two were made for each other. Once he's home again and you've had a proper kiss, it'll all be just like it was before, you'll see.'

'But suppose it isn't?' Thursday repeated, and Elsie shrugged.

'Well, it won't be the end of the world, will it? You're not married – not even engaged. If it doesn't work any more, you can just say goodbye. There'll be other fellers, Thurs. There's plenty more fish in the sea.'

There were indeed, Thursday thought. Plenty. She'd already met some of them, both in Egypt and on the way out there . . .

Chapter Eight

It had been strange, on that day in 1942, to find herself on board a luxury liner, setting sail for some unknown destination. Along with Elsie, Louisa and a dozen other girls from Haslar, Thursday had been instructed to report to the dock at Avonmouth, with her luggage carefully marked with the code number which would, she hoped, ensure that it arrived at her destination with her. None of them had any idea where they were going, and were told that if they did begin to guess they mustn't put any hint in their letters home. They weren't the only ones to be going in the convoy, and if any ship were lost, information could be picked up by the enemy and used to destroy the rest. 'You don't want thousands of deaths laid at your door.'

'Makes us sound as bad as Hitler!' Elsie had said as their train from Paddington tore through the countryside. 'As if we'd be so daft.'

'Well, some might. And it's easy enough to let something slip. That's why they don't tell us anything – we might give it away without even realising it.'

'Fat chance,' Elsie remarked, 'when our letters'll be censored anyway. Where on earth d'you think we are? We could be halfway to Scotland for all we know, now they've taken away all the nameplates on the platforms.'

The train snorted its way into the terminus at last and they crowded on to a coach, its blinds drawn. 'Just in case we recognise anywhere and tell the Jerries!' Elsie said with a grin as they rattled through the streets. At last they stopped, but instead of being at the docks as they had expected, they were told to get off. 'Embarkation won't take place until tomorrow,' the Red Cross official informed them. 'You'll all be staying the night at various small hotels and guest houses. I'll need to check off your names as you get off, so that we'll know where you are, and you must be ready and waiting just here at seven a.m. tomorrow. Don't be late.'

'Or the ship will sail without us!' Elsie murmured, in the phrase that had become a byword at Haslar, where they'd been taught that 'Naval time is five minutes early'. 'Only this time, it really will!'

'This is Bristol,' Louisa said, staring round at the buildings. 'I thought it would be. I came here once on a school trip. The dock's called Avonmouth. You can see the ships over there, see?'

They glanced across and saw the usual tangle of dockyard paraphernalia – cranes, masts, derricks – and the funnels of the ships lying alongside. Thursday felt a little leap of excitement within her as she gazed at them. 'They look different from the ships in Portsmouth. Bigger. And their funnels are different.'

'That's because they're passenger liners. I've heard nearly all the Cunard liners have been requisitioned for service – even the *Queen Mary*. Wouldn't it be a hoot if we were to sail on her?'

Their hotel was a tall narrow building in the middle of a terrace a street or two away. They approached it rather warily, watched by a few girls in civilian clothes who leaned against a wall, smoking cigarettes. Business girls, I suppose, Thursday thought, for they'd been told that most of the buildings in this area were actually hostels where working girls or businesswomen lived. These looked as if they were dressed for an evening out, with low-cut blouses and plenty of make-up. They eyed the three VADs with some suspicion.

Louisa stopped and looked up at the doorway. 'Can you tell us if this is the Pleasant View Hotel?'

At the sound of her voice, with its cut-glass accent, the girls glanced at each other and raised their eyebrows. A couple of them began to snigger and one, with a cloud of red hair and a scarlet blouse, took her cigarette from her mouth.

'You stopping here, then?' she asked brusquely.

'Only the one night,' Thursday said, disliking the way they had sneered at Louisa's voice. 'We're—' She stopped abruptly, remembering that they were under strict instructions not to divulge information. 'We're going on tomorrow.'

'Nurses?' the girl asked, staring at their uniform.

'Look, is this the Pleasant View, or ain't it?' Elsie butted in. 'Not that it's a very pleasant view from where I'm standing!' She stared at the civilians. 'Still, I suppose you do some sort of war work as well, doncher?'

At this, the sniggers erupted into loud guffaws as the Bristol girls turned to each other, their faces red with mirth, punching each other on the arm and repeating, 'War work! Blimey, that's rich! War work!' until the VADs, staring at them with increasing exasperation, shrugged and turned away.

'It's no good talking to them,' Elsie said. 'Anyway, I've just seen a notice in the window – see? *Pleasant View – Vacancies Day and Night* – that's a funny way of putting it, isn't it? – *and Services Offered*. Wonder what they mean by that?'

'Well, never mind, it doesn't affect us.' Louisa lifted her kitbag and mounted the three steps to the front door. 'Come on – I want to get rid of this luggage and find something to eat. That Red Cross woman said there's a restaurant round the corner that we can use.'

Their room was cramped, with one double bed and a single camp bed that had obviously been hastily pushed in along the wall. There was a tiny washbasin, one chair and a small cupboard where the girls could hang their clothes. They looked at it in some dismay, then Louisa shrugged. 'I dare say we'll see worse than this before we're through. Anyway, since all I intend to do is sleep, what it looks like isn't going to bother me too much.' She felt the bed. 'Gosh, this is as bad as boarding school. One lump or two?'

By nine o'clock they had eaten fish and chips at the café round the corner and were back in the room, getting ready for bed. Thursday and Elsie decided to share the double bed and Louisa took the rickety single. They had just begun to undress when they were startled by a knock on the door.

Thursday, who hadn't yet removed anything, opened the door and peered out. 'D'you want something?' She could see a large man, lit dimly by the faint bulb hanging unshaded over the landing.

The man stared at her and she felt a small twinge of unease. 'Who're you? Ain't Rosie in there?'

Thursday shook her head. 'No. You must have the wrong room.'

There was a brief pause, then the voice said, sounding dissatisfied, 'She must be. Thass her room. Where is she?' He began to push the door further open.

Alarmed, Thursday pushed back. 'It isn't her room! It's ours. Stop it – you can't come in. Go *away*.'

'Go away?' He stopped pushing to stare at her again, and Thursday took the opportunity to close the door. Before she could close it fully, he had his foot inside. 'Whatcher mean, go away? I'm a customer. If Rosie ain't here, I'll have someone else.' He peered at her. 'You look all right. You'll do.' And he started to push again.

'No!' Thursday shouted, and looked over her shoulder desperately at Louisa and Elsie, who were staring open-mouthed. 'Go away! Go *away*! You can't come in – you *can't*! Oh, help me, for goodness sake, help me!'

The other two leaped to her side. Elsie lent her weight to the door and Louisa took one look at the foot stuck in the way and stamped on it hard. The man yelped and jerked back, and they shoved the door shut and looked for the key.

'There isn't one! There isn't even a bolt.' He was still pushing from the other side, shouting words even Elsie had never heard before. 'Oh, what shall we do, what shall we do?'

'Use a chair.' Louisa grabbed the kitchen chair that stood beside the bed and pushed its back under the door knob. Cautiously, they stood back and saw with relief that it was holding, although Thursday thought it looked pretty flimsy and wouldn't hold if the man became really determined. However, after one or two more desultory pushes he gave up and they could hear him talking to someone else on the stairs. There was a brief conversation and then his footsteps sounded, going on up the next flight. They heard another door close and the mumble of voices overhead.

Thursday sat down suddenly on the bed. Elsie fixed the chair more securely under the door knob and Louisa sat down beside Thursday and put her arm round her shoulders. 'Are you all right?'

'Yes, I think so. What a horrible man. I wonder why he thought this was Rosie's room? I can't believe she'll be very pleased to see him when he does find her.'

'Oh, I dunno,' Elsie said, surveying the chair grimly. 'I think she'll be pleased enough to see him. Depends what he pays, of course.'

'Pays?' Thursday echoed. 'What d'you mean, *pays*?'

'Well, didn't you hear what he said? Customer, in't he? And that's what that notice means – *Services Offered*. This place ain't a working girls' hostel at all – well, it *is*, but only in a manner of speaking.' She caught Thursday's still bemused glance. 'It's a bloody knocking shop, ain't it!'

'A knocking—?' Thursday began, and Louisa interrupted.

'A brothel, Thursday. That's what Elsie means. A place where men can come and pay girls to have sexual intercourse with them. Prostitutes. That's what those girls outside were.'

'And that's why they screamed their heads off laughing when I said that about war work,' Elsie said. 'I had me doubts about them then. But I never thought the Red Cross would stick us in a place like this!'

'I suppose they didn't know,' Louisa said. She glanced at the chair. 'We'd better keep that there all night – we may get some more callers asking for Rosie. And I'll tell you one thing – I'm not going to undress! I'm not taking any chances.'

'Undress?' Thursday said, still feeling shaken. 'I don't think I'm even going to lie down. And I'm dead certain I'm not going to sleep.' She groaned as more footsteps came up the stairs and someone else knocked loudly on the door. 'Go away!' she shouted. 'Rosie's not here – and neither is anyone else!'

'We're not open for business tonight!' Elsie yelled, banging back. 'Try next door!'

The caller left, grumbling. But the next one was not so easily persuaded, and it took several minutes of bitter argument before he too departed. The girls wedged the chair more firmly and looked at each other with resignation.

'It's going to be a long, long night,' Elsie said, flopping on to the bed. 'I don't think there's much chance of us missing the boat tomorrow. I reckon I'm going to be first aboard!'

'Blimey,' Elsie said in awe, 'it might not be the *Queen Mary*, but it's not far off!'

They stared up at the great ship, its prow rising sleek and elegant above the dock. The familiar Cunard colours had been covered with battleship grey, but there was no mistaking this for a Naval ship. The girls gazed at her in awe.

'We're not really going on that,' Thursday said. 'It's a joke. They're going to let us look at it for a bit and then take us away and shove us on a ferry boat. That's for special people.'

'What d'you mean, *special* people?' Elsie demanded. '*We're* special people – we're VADs! Anyway, I'm not taking any chances – I'm getting aboard before they realise they've brought us to the wrong place. Come on!'

Giggling with excitement, they dragged their luggage closer to the dockside. With the dozen other girls, who had emerged from various establishments nearby (most of them apparently more respectable than the one Thursday and her friends had been allocated) they piled it all together and then sat and watched as a long line of soldiers and sailors made their way up the gangplank. Embarkation had obviously begun some time ago, the men were filing on to the ship like ants and there were still yet more to come. 'Hundreds of them,' Thursday said in amazement. 'Thousands! How many people can a ship like this hold, Lou? It'll burst if many more go aboard.'

'Well, in peacetime they'd have a bit more room, I suppose. I don't really know. Daddy was going to take us to America but then the war came along, so we didn't go. I've never been to sea on a ship like this.' She gazed up at the towering prow. 'And look at all the military stuff they're lifting on board, too! Tanks and lorries, and all the luggage . . . I hope ours doesn't get mixed up with that lot, we'll never get it back again.'

Thursday giggled. 'We'll find ourselves with rifles and grenades, and some poor soldier will have a bag full of navy-blue bloomers! Oh look, someone's calling us over. It must be our turn to go aboard.'

Suddenly subdued, they picked up their cases and kitbags and made their way over to the gangplank where a Red Cross officer was standing with a list. As each girl drew near, she asked her name and ticked it off. Thursday waited for the inevitable comment but it didn't come; instead, the woman made a swift pencil stroke and nodded her past.

'Well, this is it,' Thursday said quietly to Louisa, who was just behind her. 'Goodbye to England. I wonder when we'll be back.'

'And what will have happened by then,' the other girl nodded. She hefted her suitcase a little higher. 'Go on, Thursday. No backing out now!'

Thursday shook her head. She had no intention of backing out. She was too excited at the thought of going abroad for the first time, too intrigued by the mystery of their destination. All the same, she couldn't quite bring herself to take that final move away from

English soil, and she hesitated, touching the dockside with her foot until the very last moment.

'Go *on*, Thursday, for heaven's sake,' Louisa said again from behind her, and gave her a gentle push. With a little sound that was half gasp, half sob, Thursday stepped hurriedly up the narrow ramp. In a moment, she was on the deck and then inside the ship. I'm on my way, she thought, dazed. I'm on a ship, a *liner*, and I'm going abroad . . .

Elsie was just in front. She turned and gave Thursday a broad, though slightly wavering, grin. 'Well, here we are, Thurs. Proper sailors at last. We joined the Navy to see the world –'

'And what did we see?' Thursday finished. 'We saw the sea! Well, I hope we're going to see some land again, because—'

'Never mind what you want to see,' a voice broke in. 'What you're going to see now is your cabins. We got a lot of personnel to get aboard today, so if you don't mind, ladies . . .' The sailor, looking remarkably like the matelots they were accustomed to seeing around Haslar, swung their kitbags on to his shoulder and set off at speed along the steel-lined passageway. The girls followed him, squeezing past the people who wanted to come the other way, people who all seemed to know where they were going. It seemed that the whole of the Army and Navy were trying to cram aboard this ship which, big though it was, was surely never built for a crowd this size. We're going to be crammed in like sardines in a tin, Thursday thought as they followed their guide along gangways, up and down steep ladders and then through more narrow passages and past door after door until at last he stopped and threw their bags into an empty cabin.

'There you are. This one'll do. Four bunks, see, so the next one that comes along'll be in here with you. This is deck E and you'll find the mess deck is on C. Better get yourselves up there pronto and see what time your meals are – they're being served in rotation, see. This here's sea-water soap. There'll be a roster for baths as well. It don't lather up like the Palmolive you're used to, but it's the best you'll get. Fresh water's like gold on board ship, so don't go splashing it about, all right?' He glanced behind him into the passageway to where a tall, slender girl with a cloud of pale blonde hair was standing. 'All right, love, you're in here with these three. They'll give you the gen.' He gave them all a brisk nod and a sudden grin: 'Have a good cruise, girls, and if you want to hand out any tips, I'm your steward for the trip, OK?'

'What did he mean by that?' Elsie said, staring after him.

Louisa laughed. 'A joke, I should think! We won't get stewards and we'll probably never set eyes on him again.' She looked at the newcomer. 'We're from Haslar Royal Naval Hospital. Where are you from?'

'Plymouth. Devonport Naval Hospital.' The girl had a firm, confident voice, with no hint of a west Country accent. She talked like Louisa, and Thursday knew at once that she came from the same kind of background. 'My name's Priscilla Lacock.' She came into the cabin and looked round, raising her fine eyebrows humorously. 'Good Lord, is this the best they can do? Bunks? I thought we'd get cabins to ourselves at the very least!'

The girls stared at her. She was wearing the same uniform as they wore – dark-blue costume with VAD badge sewn on the sleeve, black tie and white blouse, but somehow, on her slender figure, it looked more elegant.

'I think they want to get as many people as possible aboard,' Thursday said at last. 'It isn't a luxury cruise.'

Priscilla grinned. 'We're lucky not to be travelling in the hold, like slaves always used to.' She dumped her suitcase on the deck. 'I suppose you've already picked your bunks?'

'Not really,' Elsie said. 'We've only just got here, see. But I always have a lower one if I can – no one'd want to risk sleeping under me anyway, in case I bring the whole lot down,' she patted her full hips ruefully, 'and Thursday here has the one over me because she's tall and can get up easier. So it looks as if it's between you and Lou for the other two.'

'First come, first served,' Priscilla said cheerfully. 'You were here before me. Only thing is, I get claustrophobia in small spaces so I wouldn't mind having the lower bunk so that I can see out of the porthole.'

'OK by me.' Louisa glanced around the tiny cabin. 'Look, let's leave our unpacking until later – not that we've got much room to unpack anyway. I want to see what's happening on deck – we'll be sailing pretty soon, I wouldn't wonder. Come on, let's see if we can find our way back.'

'It's finding our way back *here* that'll be the clever part,' Thursday remarked. 'Perhaps we ought to take a ball of string and unwind it as we go, so that we've got something to follow.'

'And if everyone else does that too, we'll be knitting a Fair Isle jumper between us!' Elsie grinned and they crowded out of the door and made their way through the busy passageways. They emerged on to the top deck and stared around eagerly. 'Oh, look – they're putting up a barrage balloon!'

'Let's find ourselves a place out of the way,' Louisa suggested. 'How about over here, under this lifeboat? We won't be in the way and we can see everything that goes on.'

They squeezed into the niche together and watched eagerly as the huge balloon was fastened to the deck by a wire hawser. Like a silver airborne whale, it floated high above, a protection against enemy aircraft when the ship put to sea. There was a bustle of activity as it was secured and the sailors and dockyard workers removed all the gangplanks and the moorings, until at last only the bow and stern lines remained. Then they too were removed and the ship began slowly to move, nudged on its way by the tugs that fussed around it. Thursday's heart gave a leap as she realised that they were really on their way.

'I came down here once to see my aunt off to America,' Priscilla murmured. 'You should have seen it then. The ship all festooned with little flags, and people throwing coloured paper streamers to each other, a band playing and everyone singing, everyone excited – some people laughing and cheering, others crying because they were going away, or being left behind.'

'What were they singing?' Elsie asked, but her voice was drowned by a sudden great wave of sound as the thousands of men aboard the ship, joined by those still on shore, broke into song, and the girls fell silent to listen.

' "Now is the Hour",' Thursday said softly when the song ended. 'It's what people always do sing, isn't it? And "Wish Me Luck, as You Wave Me Goodbye" . . . I couldn't join in, could you? It would have made me cry.'

'I'm crying anyway,' Elsie said, feeling for a hanky. 'Oh God, Thurs, do you realise we're going abroad? I've never been further than the Isle of Wight before! And we don't even know where we're going. It could be Africa, India, *anywhere*! I can't believe it.'

'Well, you did volunteer to be mobile,' Thursday retorted with a grin. 'You didn't expect to stay at Haslar for the rest of the war, did you?'

'I dunno. I dunno what I expected.' Elsie looked down at the dockside, now drawing further away as the ship moved out to the open sea. 'I just know it feels funny now, to think of going away from England and not know where we're going or how long we'll be gone.'

'Yes,' Thursday said, thinking of her family at home, of her mother and father, of Jenny starting work in the local hospital, of Steve in his prison camp, of her aunt and uncle and Cousin Denise with her new baby . . . Keep them safe for me, she prayed suddenly, clasping her hands together. And keep all the brave soldiers and sailors and airmen safe as well – though obviously they can't *all* be kept safe, not in wartime – but please, Lord, please keep as many safe as possible, and let me and Elsie and Louisa and the others come home when it's all over and find our families still all right . . . and let us win this war, please, so that the world can go back to being peaceful and happy once again . . .

Chapter Nine

The voyage had taken several weeks. Along with the other girls, Thursday had soon slipped into a pleasant routine – meals taken in the big dining-hall, PT every morning, boat drill, card games, draughts or chess to while away the time or, as the ship sailed into warmer waters, sunbathing in the little portion of deck allocated to the VADs.

'Tell you what,' Elsie said, stretching herself out with her kapok lifejacket as a cushion under her head, 'this might not be a luxury cruise, but it's flipping well nearly as good. Getting waited on at mealtimes, nothing to do but enjoy ourselves – and five thousand men to help us do it! I think I've died and gone to heaven, that's what.'

Thursday chuckled. 'I must say, it's rather nice to have all this attention. And they're all so polite! Why, at the Housey-Housey last night one of the Corporals insisted I share his card, wouldn't take no for an answer, and then made me take the prize we won. He was really nice,' she added reminiscently.

Elsie gave a hoot of laughter. 'We could see that! And what happened when you went out on deck with him, Thursday, eh? Tell us that. Though I bet you won't be telling the dashing Commander Kirkpatrick next time you write!'

Thursday blushed. 'There's nothing between me and Johnny.'

'Johnny, is it? A minute ago he was just "one of the Corporals". And you were looking very pleased with yourself when you came to bed – *eventually*.'

Thursday gave her a sideways glance and folded her lips demurely. She had no intention of telling Elsie how the young soldier had stood beside her on the upper deck, his head close to hers as they gazed down at the phosphorescent shimmer of the waves. Behind the ship its wake foamed and glittered so that despite the stringent blackout imposed, it seemed impossible that they weren't visible for miles. Around them, they knew, were all the other ships of the convoy – a dozen or so more troopships carrying thousands of soldiers, airmen and Marines to their next theatre of war, accompanied by a protective ring of Naval battleships; yet each was completely darkened, no glimmer of light betraying the crowds within.

Above, clustered as thickly as blackberries on a bush, hung the stars, their formations strangely different from the ones Thursday had been used to. She'd never been particularly interested in the constellations, knowing only the familiar shape of the Plough, but she was aware, nevertheless, that these were different. She felt that she could stand here and gaze at them for hours, or at the moon which, as it seemed to rise from the depths of the ocean, was like an enormous globe hung there to light them on their way.

If only you were here, Connor, she thought sadly, her heart aching. It would be so lovely to stand at the rail with you, watching the phosphorescence and the stars, holding your hand and waiting for you to kiss me. Or perhaps I wouldn't wait . . . A tingle of desire ran through her as she thought of being in Connor's arms, held close to that body which had become so familiar, so precious. I've never had any real loving, she thought regretfully. There was only Sidney, who never did more than give me a peck, and Tony who was killed before we'd even begun to fall in love – and Connor, who went away so soon. I'm twenty-four and I've never done more than kiss a man – and even those kisses have been pretty demure.

And now here she was on board ship, a little world of its own – one of just a dozen girls amongst five thousand men. It was unreasonable not to expect the girls to pair off with some of the men – indeed, Elsie had remarked with a grin that she hoped the voyage would last long enough to get round them all – and it was also unreasonable not to realise that among these five thousand there would be more than one who might prove a sore temptation. But all I want is a kiss or two, Thursday thought longingly, acutely aware of the soldier at her side. There can't be any harm in that.

She hung over the rail, gazing at the sea. It was a continual fascination, this shifting, shimmering swell of brilliance, and there was always the chance of a school of flying fish, attracted by the paravane which was hung beside the deck to deflect mines and hurling themselves through the air to land gasping on the deck. One of the sailors had gathered the girls around him a few days ago, showing them a dozen or so of the strange creatures and fanning their 'wings' out to show how they really could glide through the air after leaping out of the water.

'I wonder where Horace went,' she said dreamily. Horace had been their name for the barrage balloon which had accompanied them out of Bristol and then gradually detached itself and floated away through the sky alone as if on its own mysterious errand. A few still flew above the convoy, but several more had managed to escape their ships and gone off after Horace, like a school of airborne whales determined not to be shackled.

'Dunno.' Johnny stood very close, his shoulder touching hers. 'Hope he's enjoying himself, wherever he is. As much as I am,' he added softly.

'Mm. It's like a dream, isn't it, this voyage? It's like time out of the war, out of the world itself. I know we get the daily bulletins so we know more or less what's going on, but it doesn't seem to affect us much. Even though we know it could all change, and we could be attacked at any moment.'

'That's why we have these boat drills every day,' he said. 'Just to make sure we don't forget what we're going for. And we blokes have a lot of training to do, to keep our fitness up,' he added. 'Wouldn't do for the Tommies and Marines to come off the ship too weak and flabby to carry their own kitbags!'

'The boat drills are so boring, though. You should hear what Elsie says about them! I hope we don't ever have to use them. Did you know, if we do have to take to the boats, we VADs all have to go to a separate one? We'd be all on our own in a boat with nearly forty men. We're supposed to *inspire* them, if you please – in the middle of the night, our hair all in curlers and wearing navy-blue bloomers! I don't know what sort of inspiration that would be.'

'It would inspire me,' he said, 'if you were the one in our boat.'

There was a tiny silence. Johnny slid his arm around her shoulders. Thursday turned her face towards him and found him very close, his breath warm on her cheek. She opened her mouth a little, but the words were lost in his kiss and, after a moment of surprise, she found herself kissing him back.

'Oh, Thursday,' he said at last, 'you are a lovely girl.'

Thursday said nothing. Her thoughts were whirling, but the response of her body had shaken her even more. She stared at him, wanting him to kiss her again. Oh, I've missed this, she thought. I've missed it so much . . . Then she put her hands lightly against his chest and held him away.

'I'm sort of engaged,' she said. 'Not formally with a ring, or anything – he said he didn't want to tie me down – but I'm trying to keep my promise.'

'That's all right,' he said. 'I'm not going to do anything you wouldn't want. And I don't want to mess anything up for you – I've got someone myself, back home. But it seems an awful waste to be out here, with all this,' he gestured at the deep black sky, peppered with stars, at the glittering spray beneath them, 'and not have a little bit of romance to remember. It's like you said – it's a different world out here, on board this ship.' He kissed her again, and Thursday wound her arms around his neck and relaxed against him. Oh, this is good, she thought, so good, to feel a man's body close to mine. And Connor wouldn't mind, I'm sure he wouldn't. We had so little time, and this will only be an interlude. A lovely, happy, innocent interlude . . .

She knew that she did look different when she returned to the cabin at last. The other girls were all in their bunks, and only Elsie was awake. She had looked at Thursday in the tiny light cast by Thursday's small torch as she undressed, and raised her eyebrows in question.

But Thursday wasn't going to tell her about those moonlight kisses. Not now. Not ever. They were just a shipboard romance. All the same, when the ship arrived at Cape Town and Johnny disembarked, the two of them had cast away all pretence and, like a dozen others, clung together sadly in the knowledge that their romantic interlude was over and they might never meet again.

Life on board ship wasn't, they all agreed, a luxury trip. The food was good, and well served, but apart from that facilities were basic. With so many more people on board than the liner was built to accommodate, conditions were cramped, particularly for the men, but the greatest adversity was the shortage of fresh water which was strictly rationed and turned on only twice a day. During these two periods, the girls were allowed to take as much as they could carry, and they arrived at the taps with every container they could think of – billycans, tooth mugs, empty shampoo bottles – and, if they were lucky enough to be there without an impatient queue behind them, took the opportunity to wash their hair. Apart from that, their washing was limited to the saltwater baths and the soap that lathered reluctantly and left them feeling as sticky and hot as they'd felt before.

'I'd give twenty pounds for a decent shampoo,' Elsie remarked, brushing hopelessly at her long yellow hair, 'and some setting lotion. All me curls are dropping out in this heat.'

'Well, you certainly work hard enough at keeping them in,' Priscilla said. 'Sitting in your bunk every night wrapping those rags round it. I thought it was only little girls who wore ringlets.'

'Well, now you know it's big girls as well,' Elsie retorted. 'We can't all have natural waves.'

Priscilla tossed her head and her cloud of fine, pale hair wafted like a mist around her head. It wasn't exactly wavy, Thursday thought, but it seemed to settle naturally into a nice shape. Her eyes were nice too, a light grey that could look blue or even green to reflect the sea and, although her face had the aristocratic features that could sometimes look a bit snooty, the minute she gave you that wicked grin of hers you knew she would be all right.

'Got to admit I thought you might be a bit of a snob, when I first saw you,' Elsie remarked one day as they tried to get dressed all at once in the tiny cabin. 'You looked so posh, what with your smart leather suitcase and all.'

'You should have known me when I first went to Devonport,' Priscilla told her. 'I was OK with the girls who'd been to boarding school like me – we were used to iron beds and lousy food – but I couldn't get used to the working-class girls at all. They'd only ever shared with their sisters; they didn't like undressing in front of the rest of us, they hated the food and they cried all night for their mothers! We were accustomed to being away from home, you see, so it came more easily. And I'm afraid some of us *were* terrible snobs. We thought that just because we'd had an expensive education we were God's gift to wounded sailors. We soon learned differently about *that*!'

'I was surprised to find girls like Elsie and Thursday in the VADs,' Louisa admitted. 'The pay's so awful I thought it would be only girls like us, who had families who could send us a bit extra, who'd be able to do it.'

'Doesn't make any difference to us,' Elsie said. 'Shop wages aren't up to much. We're not used to getting a lot of pay anyway, and we do get all found now – all our clothes, food and a bed to sleep in. And if we can find a bloke to take us out we don't even have to pay to go to the pictures. I mean, that's the way it is, isn't it? Girls never do get much pay.'

'Not even if they do the same job as a man,' Thursday agreed. 'Shift over a bit, Elsie, I haven't got room to put my stockings on with you taking up all the space.'

The rest of the VADs – most from Haslar, two or three from Plymouth – had settled down well too and become good friends. They sunbathed together in their private portion of deck, did their PT and boat drill and mourned the possibility that if the ship did have to be abandoned, they would be split up.

'It don't bear thinking of,' Elsie said. 'I mean, on our own in a boatload of men, how are we going to manage about spending a penny and all that? Nobody bothers to tell you that when we do boat drill.'

'Let's hope we never have to find out,' Thursday said. They were on deck, carrying their bulky kapok lifejackets as usual, making for their sunbathing spot. 'We're pretty well looked after by all these ships. Mind you, it cuts both ways – with so many steaming along in a gang, it's a wonder the Germans don't find us easy.'

Each morning the girls went out on deck to make sure their companion ships were still there. They counted them carefully, able by now to recognise each one by name, and there was inevitably consternation when one was missing. Mostly, the errant one returned during the day having been off on some mission, and they breathed a sigh of relief.

Every evening there was some kind of entertainment. The men got up concerts and Thursday was surprised to find how talented many of them were. Some of them formed a choir and sang songs that varied from Victorian ballads to all the latest hits; others did their turns alone, or performed sketches together. There was Housey-Housey too, and the girls joined in with enthusiasm, marking their cards to the calls: 'Clickety-click – number six. Nelson's eye – number one. Two fat ladies – eighty-eight. Was she worth it – seven and six.'

'I don't know how you can do it so quickly,' Priscilla complained. 'I'm always half a card behind the rest of you. It's so hot and stuffy down there too, I can't breathe – all that cigarette smoke, and no portholes open.'

'Well, we can't, can we,' Thursday said reasonably. 'We've got to keep the blackout. And you smoke, in here.'

'That's different. There are only four of us in here. There are hundreds in that lounge.' She put on what Elsie called her snooty look and drawled exaggeratedly. 'The First Class Lounge is bad enough, darlings – but *Second* Class – ugh!'

'Never mind,' Louisa remarked from the bunk where she was lying in her panties and camisole. 'Nobody would expect you to lower yourself to go in there, so they don't have to lay on anything special for you.'

Priscilla made a rude face at her. 'I don't know why I had to find myself sharing a cabin with you,' she declared. 'Elsie and Thursday are all right, but you upper-class girls – well!' She got off her bunk and pulled on her white dress. 'It's so *hot* in here. I'm going up on deck – see if I can find some fresh air.'

'She's a card, she is,' Elsie said as Priscilla wafted out of the cabin. 'I tell you what, Lou, if it hadn't been for the war and being a VAD I'd never have met people like you and Priss. It's opened my eyes a bit. I never thought I'd be able to even talk to anyone who'd been to a posh school and had pots of money, and I never thought they'd bother to talk to me either.'

'It's the same for us, I suppose,' Louisa said. 'We wouldn't meet people like you – not to live and work with. We wouldn't even have got jobs at all, we'd just do the Season and find a husband to keep us. It's been an eye-opener for people like me and Priscilla too. It's done us good.'

'Yes, but you weren't ever snooty,' Elsie said. 'Priss was to begin with, she's told me that herself. And that girl who knew her at Devonport, Daisy Roberts, she says she was a real pain in the you-know-where. Thought anyone who came from a house with less than six bedrooms was straight out of a slum. Daisy says she treated them like dirt at first. *You* never did that.'

'My father would shoot me if I did. He's always told us that anyone who does a decent day's work for a living is worthy of respect, whatever the job is. And those who do the most disgusting jobs – taking away rubbish or working in the sewers – are entitled to the most respect of all.'

'Blimey,' Elsie said, 'he sounds more Labour than my dad.'

'I don't think it's a matter of politics,' Louisa said thoughtfully. 'Just realising that everyone's human and we can't all live in big houses – but that doesn't make some of us better than others.'

'But why *do* some live in big houses and have more money?' Thursday asked. 'Your father – or someone a long way back – must have been better in some way, to get it in the first place.'

'I don't think so. We just got handed a parcel of land by William the Conqueror. We're probably the last people to deserve it, if the truth were known! And look at all the people who made their money from slavery. Not much to be proud of there. Anyway, having land and money means responsibility too. What we've got is a sort of – of *trust*. We've got to look after it. It's not really ours, all that land and money; it's just been passed to us to take care of while we're here, and pass on to the next generation of the family. We're lucky, that's all.' She sat on Prisiclla's bunk to peer through the porthole. 'D'you think anyone knows where we are yet? Someone said they thought we were heading for Cape Town, but we could be anywhere. This endless sea – we could be like the Flying Dutchman, steaming around the ocean for ever, totally lost!'

Thursday laughed. 'Perhaps we are. Perhaps the war's over and nobody's told us because they've forgotten we ever existed.'

'They'd better not forget,' Elsie said darkly. 'I don't mind playing Housey-Housey or draughts and getting up concerts for a few weeks, but I'm blowed if I'm going to do it for ever! Even Mr Churchill can't expect *that*.'

The convoy steamed on. The dozen troopships were still accompanied by their protective ring of destroyers and battleships, all now easily recognisable to the VADs. The girls hung over the rail, gazing at them.

'They're glorious, aren't they,' Thursday said softly. 'Beautiful ships, and yet so sort of *formidable*, with all those guns and things. I feel absolutely safe with them there. Nothing can hurt us while they're looking after us.'

She knew in her heart that this wasn't really true. It would only take a few German bombers to come over, or some submarines to skulk under the surface of the smooth blue sea, for all hell to break loose. She closed her eyes, imagining for a moment the battle that would ensue, the shells exploding, the aircraft shot down, the ships sinking in a mass of flames . . . Dear God, don't let it happen, she prayed. Please, please don't let it happen.

'I don't want to scare anyone.' Elsie said suddenly, frightening Thursday so much that her heart seemed to fall like a stone right through her body, 'but could that be land over there?'

Thursday craned her neck. 'It's a smudge. It's probably smoke.' Her heart thumped again. 'You don't think it's ships?'

'No,' Louisa said, 'it's not. It *is* land. We're arriving somewhere.'

They stared anxiously, still uncertain, and then Thursday noticed something else. 'What's that? Look – over there. There's something in the water.' Her fears seemed to surface with the sudden turbulence only fifty yards or so away. 'Oh, my God, it's a sub!'

'It's not! It's a whale! It's a *whale*!' Louisa was almost jumping out of her skin with excitement. 'I saw one once when we went to Norway. Look, it's coming right up – it's going to spout! Oh, did you ever see anything more glorious!'

They watched, enthralled, as the huge creature rose to the surface like a black, glistening mound and sent a fountain of water high into the air. By now, word was being passed round the ship and men were running from everywhere to hang over the rails on that side of the decks. Aboard other ships, people could be seen doing the same, so that the whale had an audience of thousands on every side. As if enjoying the attention, it dived and rolled to the surface in a series of glittering displays, then with an almost wicked look in its eye, stood on its head and flourished its tail like a magnificent flag of victory.

'Oh,' Thursday said, tears in her eyes at the beauty of it. 'Oh . . .' The next second, her ears were blasted by the sound of the ship's sirens. 'Action Stations!' she gasped, and stared in terror at her companions. But there was no time to do more than give each of them a swift hug, and then race to her position by the lifeboat. Thank heavens for all that drill, she thought as she panted along the decks. At least everyone knows where to go. But what could it be?

There were no planes, so it must be subs, or maybe that smudge they had seen was smoke from German ships after all. She reached her lifeboat and scrambled into place beside it, waiting to hear the sudden rattle of gunfire or the shattering roar of an explosion, and then saw that the sailor in charge of it was grinning.

'What is it? What's so funny? Are we being attacked?'

'Not on your life,' he said cheerily. 'It was the only way to trim the ship, see? What with the whole five thousand of you all rushing over to one side to see that blooming whale, we were in a fair way to keeling over. This was the quickest way of getting you all away, I reckon.' His voice was drowned by the siren, sounding the return to normal. 'See? And didn't you notice you had to run uphill to get here?'

Thursday felt the deck shift beneath her feet. He was right – the ship *had* been listing as everyone raced to see the whale. She grinned, a little ashamed of her fear, and he patted her arm. 'It's all right, nursey. The good old J25 ain't going down yet. And if I'm not much mistaken, we're about to make landfall too. Be smashing to get some terra firma under our feet again, won't it!'

Thursday turned again. The smudge that Elsie had pointed out had become clearer. It was definitely land. But she knew better now than to race to the rail to stare at it. The call to Action Stations had been a false one, but nobody wanted another.

'Well, that was exciting, wasn't it!' Elsie said when they met again. 'And it *was* land I saw – it's getting clearer every minute. The question now is—'

'What land is it?' Thursday finished. 'And is this where we'll leave the ship, or will we go even further?'

The land had been, as they'd suspected for some time, the coast of South Africa. The prospect of firm ground beneath their feet was, as the matelot had said, an exciting one and the atmosphere on the ship was almost like the end of term at school as last-minute concerts were arranged, parties held in various corners and addresses exchanged with newfound friends. With so many men available for so many weeks, the girls had had as much choice of partners as any girl could possibly ask – yet it was surprising, Thursday thought, that there hadn't been more real, full-blown love affairs. Romance there had been in plenty – she recalled her own lingering hours spent at the rail with Johnny – but for the most part they'd known it couldn't be serious. As soon as land was reached, they would be separated, the girls going on to destinations yet unknown, the men to be plunged back into battle. Their brief idyll would be over and they would never see each other again.

For two of the VADs, however, it had turned out to be more serious. Daisy Roberts, a small, quiet girl from Devonport, had struck up a friendship on the very first day with a young airman and by the time the ship docked at Cape Town, they'd announced their engagement. And Priscilla had stunned them all by arriving in the cabin one evening flourishing a sparkling diamond ring on her left hand.

'A *ring*?' Thursday exclaimed, staring in astonishment. 'But who is it? And how on earth did he come to have a ring with him?'

Priscilla grinned. 'He's one of the ship's officers – Lieutenant-Commander Hillier. I met him the night we were asked to "take wine" with them. And it's none of your business why he had a ring with him.'

'Pardon me for breathing,' Thursday said. 'It's just a natural question. You've kept it jolly quiet, all the same. I suppose all those little jaunts up on deck to get some fresh air had something to do with it!'

'Well – maybe.' Priscilla stretched her hand out and admired the flashing stone. 'Aren't you going to wish me happiness?'

'Of course we are, you goof!' Thursday flung her arms around Priscilla. 'Even though you don't deserve it, after keeping it all so secret. We hope you'll be very happy. And Lieutenant-Commander Hillier too,' she added. 'What's his Christian name, by the way? Or haven't you got that far yet?'

Elsie gave a hoot of laughter and Priscilla shot her a withering look. 'His name's Quentin.'

'Quentin,' Elsie repeated expressionlessly, her lips twitching.

'Yes, *Quentin*, and you needn't say it like that – just because it's the sort of name your family would never dream of using! Oh,' as they all began to giggle, 'it's simply no use at all talking to you three! For heaven's sake, stop *laughing*, will you!'

'Sorry,' Thursday said, trying to straighten her face. 'Honestly, Priss, we're all pleased for you. We're not really laughing at you. It's just such a surprise, that's all.'

'Mind you,' Elsie said, her face twitching again, 'I'm not sure you've really given it enough thought, Priss. You know what your name is going to be, don't you? Priscilla Hillier. It's a bit of a tongue-twister.'

'It's not such a bad name as all that,' Louisa defended her. 'Neither's Quentin. I've got a second cousin once removed called Quentin. It's a very old name. There's a saint in Scotland, I think, and Walter Scott used it in one of his novels.'

'All right, you've convinced us.' Thursday said, and rolled off her bunk. 'Come on, let's see if the water's on. All my bottles are empty, and I want to wash my hair before tonight's concert.'

'Don't say *you're* going to try to trap a nice Lieutenant-Commander,' Elsie said slyly, and ducked away from Priscilla's punch. 'Well, *I* am! I'm not letting our Priss outdo me.'

Laughing, they squeezed out through the narrow door and into the passageway. As they went, Thursday gave a quick glance out of the porthole. The land was definitely getting closer. Africa! she thought. Whoever would have thought that Thursday Tilford, from backstreet Worcester, would ever go to Africa?

Chapter Ten

Back at Haslar in August 1944, Thursday found it hard to believe that she'd actually lived in the elegant house where she, Louisa and Elsie had been put up while waiting to start the next stage of their journey. Dreamily, she recalled their first sight of Table Mountain, draped in its white tablecloth of cloud, their first tentative venture into the town, the dances and parties they'd been invited to, the strange and delicious foods – fruits she had never heard of, like mangoes, lychees, guavas and passion-fruit – and the beautiful flowers and trees that grew in the gardens. They'd been treated like queens, she thought, and hadn't they just lapped it up! After the cramped conditions on board ship and with the prospect of yet another voyage, a touch of luxury was what they'd craved.

And the food parcels they'd been able to send home! Thursday had hugged herself with glee, imagining her mother's face when she found dried fruits, jams and sugar such as she hadn't seen for months. There was chocolate too, to be tucked into the corners, and a bar or two to be kept for themselves in this land of plenty, and no rationing. She ordered another box for her aunt, and marked one of the bars of chocolate specially for Denise and little Leslie.

'I could do with one of those food parcels now,' she remarked to Elsie when they met after their duty for a stroll round the grounds. 'You know, the ones we sent from Cape Town. The shortages seem worse than ever here now. Everything on coupons or points – what use is two ounces of sweets to anyone? And one egg? They might as well not bother at all.'

'Did you reckon we'd be this long in the VADs when you first volunteered?' Elsie asked. 'I know we all knew by then that it wouldn't be over by Christmas, but I don't think we believed it'd go on like it did. And look at us now – four flipping years since we first came to Haslar, and here we are again, wiping men's bottoms and changing their dressings, just as if we'd never been away.'

'You're not sorry you joined though, are you?'

'Flipping heck, no! Best thing I ever did. I mean, how else would I have ever got to go to Egypt? I know it wasn't no picnic, but we had some good times too, didn't we, Thurs? Remember the Pyramids that night? And the poor old Sphinx with sandbags up to his chin? At least they didn't have no trouble getting the sand! Oh, yes – and remember that camel, the one what stood on Prissy-Cilla's foot?'

Thursday laughed. 'You'd have thought it had broken her leg, the way she screamed. It hadn't even broken her toe. I never knew their hooves were all soft and warm till that Arab boy showed us.' Her face saddened. 'Poor Priscilla . . .'

Elsie nodded soberly. After a few moments she said casually, 'Ever hear from that Army chap again? What was his name – Martin, Malcolm?'

'It was Mark,' Thursday said, colouring. 'As you very well know! No, I haven't heard from him. I don't expect to, either. We said goodbye when he went away, and that was that. I don't even know where he is now.'

'Daresay you could find out,' Elsie suggested offhandedly. 'You know his unit.'

'I don't want to find out!' Thursday caught herself up, surprised herself by the sharpness in her voice. 'Sorry, Elsie – I didn't mean to snap. But when we said goodbye, we knew that was what we meant. It was never more than a friendship, anyway.'

Once again, Elsie didn't reply. They walked along the avenue of cherry trees, each lost in her own thoughts. Then Thursday sighed and said, 'I haven't forgotten him – how could I? I haven't forgotten any of them – Johnny on the way out to Cape Town, Tom and Peter when we were going to Egypt, and all the men we got to know while we were in Alex. They were all special, but they could never take Connor's place, any of them.'

'Not even Mark Sangster?'

There was a brief silence. Then Thursday shook her head. 'Not even Mark.'

They arrived at the door of D Block and stood for a moment in the late-afternoon sunshine. Thursday closed her eyes and lifted her face, letting her thoughts waft back to those hot afternoons and cool evenings in Alexandria, where she had met and nursed so many young men. And back, inevitably, to Mark.

No, she told herself as Elsie touched her arm and she stepped aside to let a group of other VADs come through the door. Nobody has ever taken Connor's place in my heart. Not even Mark Sangster.

Troops were still arriving daily to embark for France, and in August the *Portsmouth Evening News* showed a photograph of hundreds of ATS girls boarding a troopship bound across the Channel. Since they would certainly not be sent to any fighting zone, this was considered the most hopeful sign yet, although it still seemed at times as if the war were a matter of two steps forward and one back. You could feel confident at one minute that the Allies were winning, and then in despair the next over some other defeat. And still being waged, as viciously as ever, was the war in the Far East.

Thursday lived for Connor's letters. She never really knew where he was, just that his ship was out there somewhere, in the Indian Ocean or the South China Sea. She wrote every day, adding a little to her letters each evening and posting them two or three times a week. Some news, she knew, would be censored, so there was no point in telling him that the ban on travelling to the Isle of Wight had been lifted at last so that relatives could see each other for the first time in eighteen months, nor that the ten-mile forbidden zone all around the south coast had been removed, but she could tell him that Paris had been liberated and that the defence against the V1s was succeeding and that out of almost a hundred launched that month, only four had got through.

Our boys go up in their Spitfires and tip their wings to turn them off course, she wrote, wondering if this would be crossed out but determined to pass the news on if she could. *As often as not, they go straight down into the sea. Hitler must be hopping mad!* And one evening, after a walk on the sea wall with Patsy: *We've just seen the most amazing thing. The sun was going down into a fairly clear sky when we saw some enormous crimson V signs high up above it. Everyone saw them and nobody can talk about anything else. Louisa thinks the Air Force has sent some planes up to lay a coloured trail, like the sky-writing they used to do before the war, and Elsie reckons it's an omen – a miracle, sent by God, to tell us we're winning. I never realised Elsie was so religious! What do you think it could have been?* A day or so later, giggling to herself, she added a postscript: *Hundreds of people saw the V signs in the sky and wrote to the local paper about them. The Air Force won't have it that it was anything to do with them, and pass it off as just cloud formations. But a lot of people agree with Elsie that it was an omen – and even if it wasn't, it's done a lot of good. Patsy's been a different girl since then, and if it's helped her it's probably helped a lot of others too, so who cares what it was really! And it really does look as if the war MIGHT be coming to an end – some of the Home Guard have been stood down and we're having 'dim-out' instead of 'blackout'. That means we can have ordinary curtains up on the windows instead of those horrible black ones (that's if anyone has still got their old ones, and hasn't cut them up to make clothes or had them eaten away by moths!) and there'll even be a few streetlights to show us the way home!*

After her breakdown on Jackie Spencer's bridge, Patsy had begun to emerge from her shell. Still a pale, subdued ghost of her former self, she could at least be persuaded to come for a walk or a cycle ride, and once she'd been with Elsie and Thursday to the Theatre Royal in Portsmouth, to see to see the new Walt Disney cartoon film *Snow White and the Seven Dwarfs*. Glancing sideways as the dwarfs heaved their shovels on to their shoulders and marched off to work, singing, 'Hi-ho, hi-ho, it's off to work we go,' Thursday had seen Patsy giggling helplessly, and blessed Walt Disney for his ability to make people laugh.

The sight of the V signs in the sky had stopped Patsy short as she walked along the sea wall, and the flush in her cheeks, as if the sunset had touched her as well, as she stood with upturned face and brightened eyes, made her look more like the old Patsy than Thursday had seen for weeks.

'I'm going home for the weekend,' she said a few days later. 'Madam's given me some leave, and Mum's been on at me to go home ever since . . .' her voice shook but she went on determinedly, 'since Roy died.'

'Oh, Patsy, I'm glad. You need to get away, and be looked after for a while. Pity it can't be longer than a weekend, though. You need a couple of weeks at least.'

Patsy shrugged. 'Who gets a couple of weeks' holiday? Two or three days'll be enough for me. Anyway,' she lowered her voice, 'I've got an idea something big's going to happen. Madam didn't exactly say so, but I got the impression we're going to be on standby again.'

Thursday stared at her. 'Why? What d'you think's going to happen? The Germans can't be going to push us back again, surely. We're well into France now.'

'I don't know,' Patsy said. 'I just got the feeling, that's all.'

'Well, we'd better not talk about it then,' Thursday said, glancing round the busy mess-hall. 'Anyway, you don't need to worry about it, Pats. You go home and have a good time. Me and Elsie and the others will hold the fort.'

Patsy went off a day or two later, crossing the harbour in the Naval pinnace to catch the London train at the station built out on its stilts above the edge of the harbour.

'I hope she'll be all right,' Joy Cockroft said anxiously. Since Patsy had taken her under her wing when she'd first arrived, she'd followed the older girl around like a puppy. 'There've been a lot of reports about gas explosions. All over London, they reckon. I can't help wondering if it's not some new secret weapon Hitler's got.'

'Don't be daft,' Thursday said briskly. 'If it was anything like the doodlebugs you'd hear them coming – and you know they've told us there won't be any more of those. These are just explosions, and Patsy's not going anywhere near a gas main, anyway. She's only going to change trains for Evesham. Tell you what, we'll go over to Southsea tomorrow afternoon – they say there's lots of shops open and people are coming from all around, even from London. Poor souls, they haven't been able to come down to the seaside all summer.'

The shopping centre at Southsea had been virtually reduced to rubble, with the big shops Handley's and Knight & Lee's taking the brunt of the Blitz, yet, as Thursday said, there were still plenty of shops which had managed to stay open. Mostly, women were looking for household utensils which were beginning to appear again – pot scourers, wooden spoons, mops and china. It was all utility, of course – not bone china, Thursday thought a little critically, remembering the porcelain her father had made in Worcester – but it was selling in huge quantities. People had been making do with old china for years now, having to salvage whatever they could from their bombed houses, and it wasn't at all uncommon to be offered tea in a cup with no handle.

The girls were more interested in stockings and make-up. A fortnight earlier there had been a consignment of nylon stockings from America and the queue had stretched for half a mile. They made for the lingerie counters and were lucky enough to come away with two pairs each.

'Well, that's my week's pay gone,' Thursday said ruefully. 'D'you know, one of the best things about peace coming will be getting paid a decent wage again. It's no wonder it's mostly upper-class girls who volunteered to be VADs – nobody else could afford it. If my dad hadn't sent me the odd Postal Order, I don't know what I'd have done.'

'Well, we do get fed, and have our uniforms provided,' Elsie said fairly. 'But you're right, Thurs, it's never left much for our bits and pieces, or going out. But at least there's always been plenty of blokes around, ready to buy a drink or take us to the flicks!'

It seemed a waste to be going to Southsea on a Saturday afternoon and not go on to a dance at one of the three popular venues, the Savoy, Kimball's or South Parade Pier. They'd looked in the paper to see which had the best band, and decided on the Pier, so they collected their bikes from the rack and cycled out to the front to find a café for some tea.

'Beans on toast and a pot of tea,' Thursday said, 'and then I'm cleaned out till next week.'

'You've got enough for the ferry, in case we miss the pinnace?' Joy asked anxiously.

'Oh yes – and a penny for emergencies!' Thursday grinned. 'Listen, it says in the paper there's going to be a big RAF parade to the cathedral tomorrow – it's September the seventeenth, Battle of Britain Day. There'll be Navy and Army people there too. Wish we could go and see it.'

'They'll be having a special service in St Luke's, though,' Elsie said. 'It don't seem possible it was four years ago, does it? Remember how we used to watch the dogfights from the hospital? And that day we had the first big air raid and you went for the men because they were cheering when a Jerry plane got shot down? Cor, I reckon you'd have stood up to Madam herself that day, you were in such a blazing temper.'

'Well, it seemed so awful to laugh because some poor man was being burned to death, even if he was a German. But they never thought of it that way, did they? It was just a fight to them. They didn't seem to realise there were human beings in those planes.' She sighed. 'I suppose they were right, in a way. We wouldn't have a chance of winning if the men all started to feel sorry for the enemy. But I couldn't help thinking of my Cousin Leslie, who was probably up there in the thick of it – and that young German we had in the ward. He was just an ordinary boy, like ours, and he didn't have any real quarrel with us. It was just Hitler, telling them lies and working them all up.'

'Your cousin did get shot down later on, didn't he?' Elsie said, and Thursday nodded.

'Yes, he was killed. Poor Auntie Flo – she lost both her boys. Leslie shot down and Mike at Dunkirk. At least our Steve's still alive, in the POW camp.'

'I remember coming over to Pompey to see if Mum and the family were all right,' Elsie said quietly. 'It was the first time I'd seen what an air raid could do. I couldn't believe it – houses smashed to bits, furniture all broken and lying out in the gutter, everyone scrabbling in all the rubble looking for people that had been buried . . . Fire and smoke all over the place – ambulances and fire engines rushing about . . . And that little dead baby, just lying in the gutter, covered in blood. That was the worst of all. A *baby*.'

The other two nodded. They'd seen many more sights as bad since then, but the first time was always the worst. It was always a shock, to see what war could do.

'It's got to be over soon,' she said. 'It's just got to be.'

And it seemed, the next morning, as if she was right. The word ran round the hospital again – 'by Christmas'. Field Marshal Montgomery himself had said so. The girls had seen the evidence themselves, as they crossed the grounds from D Block to the hospital to go on early duty, and heard the sound of a steady roar from above. They stopped, staring upwards, and then caught at each other's arms. 'Look! Look at that!'

Yet again, the sky was almost black with aircraft, moving steadily towards the sea. Elsie shaded her eyes with her hand. 'It's planes. And *gliders* again! Enormous ones. But why would we be sending gliders over now? We're not invading France again, surely.'

'Well, we're invading somewhere, that's for sure,' Thursday said slowly. 'That's the same sort as went over before, remember? What was it they were called? Horsas – the ones carrying troops and tanks and things. And look at those huge planes towing them – they must be carrying men as well.' She dropped her hands and turned to them, her face alight. 'This is what Madam was hinting at! This is the new flap – what we're on standby for. It *is* an invasion – I don't know where, but it is, all the same – and they're expecting casualties. They always do.'

'Well, it won't be for a day or two,' Elsie said, staring up again. 'They're only just setting out. There won't be any casualties yet.'

'They won't be long coming, all the same,' Thursday said grimly. 'They're bringing them back by air now, remember, in those Dakota air ambulances. And going by the last lot, Haslar's going to need all the nurses it's got. We'd better get on duty now, anyway. There won't be any news for a few hours and we've got men here now, waiting for us. There's a long list of ops in the theatre this morning and your bed patients will be wanting their bedpans!'

For a few days there was little news. The whole country was aware that something big was happening – the biggest operation since D-Day itself – and there were numerous rumours. But most people were still too aware of the dangers of gossip to take too much notice. They watched the steady flights of planes and gliders heading out over the south and east coasts, and kept their lips tight.

Thursday concentrated on her work. In a day or two, the first casualties would begin to arrive, she thought. But she wasn't prepared – nobody was prepared – for the number that began to arrive, nor for the number of those who would never come back.

To begin with, the news had been good. When Thursday came off duty on the third or fourth day, it was to find people hurrying towards the blocks, calling out that there was a special broadcast, that Field Marshal Montgomery himself was making an announcement. She raced up the stairs from the basement and joined the throng hurrying back to the mess, where other VADs and QARNNs were already gathering. Glancing around, she caught sight of Louisa and Elsie, clustering with the others round the wireless. Thursday joined them and craned her neck to listen.

'It's Monty himself!' Louisa whispered, making room for her. 'He's making the announcement now – Operation Market Garden, it's called. They're going to capture all the bridges over the rivers between Holland and Germany. They've dropped thousands of American and British paratroopers at Maas and Arnhem, and tanks as well – that must be what we saw going over in those planes and gliders – and they're going to take the bridges over the Rhine itself, and then the land troops will be able to advance. He says if it all goes well, the war will be over by Christmas!'

Thursday stared at her. 'By Christmas?'

'Yes!' Louisa cried jubilantly. 'Just think, of it, Thursday – all this, over by *Christmas*!'

'But they said that before,' Thursday said blankly, thinking of all the times when that very phrase had been used in the past. Could it possibly be true this time?

Within another day or so, they knew that Operation Market Garden had gone disastrously wrong. On the first night, the Germans had captured the battle plans from a crashed glider and, wherever the troops went after that, they were expected. The bridges and their surrounding towns were defended and the paratroopers, who had expected to land in secrecy, found themselves machine-gunned as they floated down from the sky. The forces trying so desperately to hold the bridge at Arnhem surrendered at last, and the whole operation was abandoned.

Of the ten thousand men who had crossed with such brave hearts and high expectations, less than a quarter returned. Over a thousand were killed in those few terrible days, the rest taken prisoner.

The war would not be over by Christmas. Monty's daring plan had come to nothing – worse than nothing, for so many men had been either killed or taken prisoner, each one a highly trained soldier or paratrooper, each one a desperate loss to the Allies. And of those who had escaped, so many were wounded, either shot or burned, and once again Haslar, barely recovered from the D-Day crisis, was one of the receiving hospitals for wounded men straight from the war. Arriving by sea through Portsmouth or by air through various RAF stations, the familiar stream of bandaged, bloody and dirty soldiers and airmen were carried in and the nurses and doctors worked with scarcely a pause to tend them. Thursday and Louisa scoured tables, scrubbed floors, sterilised instruments and laid them out ready for the surgeons, and wheeled in the patients on their trolleys, tending them in their last few moments of consciousness before the surgeon began his work.

'You know,' Thursday said as she sat for a few moments beside Louisa at the autoclave, 'I sometimes think that's the most important thing we ever do. Just holding their hands when they come into the theatre, and giving them a smile. It's the last thing they see before they go under – and I'm sure it must do them good to see a smile, to think for that last few seconds that there's someone there who cares.'

'But we all care,' Louisa said. 'The QARNNs and the surgeons care. They wouldn't be doing it if they didn't.'

'I don't know. Sometimes, I think some of them just see the patients as interesting jobs to do. Like mending a clock and being pleased that you've got it going again. They don't really see them as people who are going to sit up in bed again and walk about and do all the things real living people do. They're just – jobs.'

Louisa thought for a moment. 'Well, maybe some of them are like that,' she admitted. 'Surgeon-Lieutenant Brown, he's a bit cold, I admit. But Connor wasn't like that.'

'No,' Thursday said. 'He wasn't. But how do I know what he's like now, Lou? This armour we're supposed to put on – some people forget to take it off again, and that's what makes them seem so hard. How do I know Connor hasn't become one of those people?'

'Can't you tell from his letters?'

'I don't know,' Thursday said sadly. 'It's been so long, and there've been so many letters. Sometimes I think we've just learned how to write them – we've got so used to it that the things we say have turned into a habit. I just don't know any more.'

Louisa stared at her in dismay. 'You're not having doubts again, are you, Thursday?'

But Thursday could not answer. She turned away. No, she told herself fiercely, I've never doubted what I feel for Connor, *never*. I love him. And he loves me. I know it's true. I *know* it . . .

The men continued to come, and once again they had terrible stories to tell. Stories of paratroopers being riddled with bullets as they hung, helpless, on their floating parachutes. Others coming down in trees, too tangled in their 'chutes to be able to escape the jeering Germans. Dying men hanging in hedges or on fences, bleeding to death. Ground troops walking into ambush, fighting desperately amongst the houses of terrified civilians. Soldiers attacked with flame-throwers as they struggled to hold the bridges that were so vital for success.

'It gets worse and worse,' Thursday said despairingly. And by now it had been admitted too that the 'gas explosions' in London really were yet another terrible weapon, sent by Hitler to kill and terrorise the capital. 'V2s, they're called. They come so fast all you hear is a double thunderclap, and then a noise like an express train rushing past – and then the explosion. There's nothing you can do about them. Our boys can't even go and tip them off course, like they could the doodlebugs. They go too fast, faster than anything's ever gone before.'

'They're talking about evacuating everyone out of London,' Elsie said. '*Everyone*. My auntie lives at Putney. She's always said she'd never leave, but she's so frightened now she'd go anywhere just to get away from them. It's awful.'

'I don't know if this war's ever going to be over,' Thursday said gloomily. 'Sometimes I think we're going to be here for ever, Elsie, until there are no men left to send away.'

'They ought to put Mr Churchill and Hitler into a boxing ring and let them slug it out,' Elsie said with an attempt at a joke. 'I bet I know who'd win – Churchill! He'd only need to fall on Hitler to squash him!'

Thursday went back to her duty. She was feeling low today, as if she truly believed that the war would never end. And yet she knew that she would never give in. However much of a struggle it was, however low she felt, she only had to look at the next patient to know that she would carry on to the bitter end.

The theatre was ready again. She stood by the door, waiting for the trolley. It came through, and she looked down at the face of the man who lay there, ready as always with her smile of comfort.

As the dark eyes met hers, she saw the recognition, felt her own like a flash of blinding light in her brain, and in that moment the years swung away from her and she was back in Alexandria. Her heart kicked, and she gave a small gasp and laid her hand on the edge of the trolley to steady herself.

'Nurse?' said a sharp voice behind her. 'Nurse? Are you all right?'

'Yes,' Thursday said dazedly, as she looked down again and saw the same shock reflected in the wide dark eyes. 'Yes – yes, Sister, I'm all right.'

She touched the hand that lay on the trolley and summoned up her smile. 'It'll soon be over now,' she said, as she always did. 'You're going to be all right. You're here in Haslar Hospital, and you're going to be all right . . .'

The trolley moved on, away from her, and she watched as the patient was moved carefully from the trolley to the table. She saw the nurse begin to unwrap the dressings and remove the splints, the anaesthetist prepare his instruments. She saw the man on the table close his eyes as the medication took its effect.

Mark, she thought. *Mark* . . .

Mark Sangster. The only man who had ever come anywhere near making her doubt the promise she had made to Connor.

Chapter Eleven

From Cape Town, the convoy had sailed up the east coast of Africa and through the Red Sea to Suez, stopping briefly only twice, at Aden and Durban. There, they had stood at the rail staring at the blaze of lights.

'D'you mean to say there's no blackout here?' Elsie asked in disbelief. 'After all the rules and regulations we've had on board – sentries posted at every doorway and all hell let loose if you dare light a fag? Don't they know there's a war on?'

'Perhaps it's all over,' Thursday said. 'Perhaps the war's finished and they've forgotten to tell us.'

'It's a mirage,' Louisa grinned. 'It's the heat – we're seeing things.'

Everyone on board was suffering from the heat. For the men, living in such cramped conditions with areas like the ship's swimming pool and billiard rooms packed with bunks six or seven tiers high, it was particularly bad and the ship's hospital was full of cases of heat exhaustion and sunstroke. Thursday had suggested that the VADs volunteer to help with the nursing, and the girls found themselves reporting for duty, wearing their new white tropical dresses, and discovering for themselves just how difficult it was to nurse patients in the confined quarters below deck.

'It's making the beds that's the most awkward,' Louisa commented, rubbing her back. 'I know they've got to be like boxes, to stop patients rolling out in high seas, but it makes it jolly tricky to do hospital corners!'

'Still, it's nice to be working,' Thursday said. 'I was getting fed up with Housey-Housey and ship's concerts. It's good to feel useful again.'

'Keeps our hand in too,' Elsie agreed. 'I was beginning to think we'd have been at sea so long we'd have forgotten what to do when we arrived wherever it is we're going!'

Everyone had been pretty sure by then that they were heading for Egypt. As Louisa, who had been good at geography at school, had said, where else could they be bound? And with the war in the African desert getting worse, there were sure to be lots of casualties. The nursing Sisters in the hospitals there were going to need VADs to do the menial tasks.

At Suez, there was just time to rush into town and send telegrams home. Mum and Dad will be wondering where on earth I've got to, Thursday thought, for no news of the convoy's position would have been broadcast and there had been no way to receive letters from home, although they'd been able to write from Cape Town. She stared at the list of standard texts which could be sent. There was so much she wanted to say, and almost all of it forbidden. It seemed such an anti-climax to their long voyage to be able to say no more than: *Safe and well. Fondest love, Thursday* – but she knew that it would be thankfully received at home.

'The last leg, thank God,' Elsie said as they set off for Cairo. 'At least, we hope so. I tell you what, Thurs, I'll be jolly glad now to get back on dry land and be in a proper hospital again. The only ship I'm ever going to go on again when we get home is the Gosport ferry!'

The 64th British General Hospital in Alexandria was a military one situated in a Naval base, although in peacetime it had been a public school. Like Haslar, it was set in broad grounds with an avenue of trees leading from the central doors, but there the resemblance ended.

It had been hard enough, when they'd first arrived at Haslar, to get used to Naval discipline and jargon – calling the floor the 'deck', the lavatories the 'heads' and so on – but now they had to adjust all over again, this time to Army procedures and different ways. The Wardmaster on Thursday's ward was a Regimental Sergeant Major and the ward Sisters, all members of the Queen Alexandra Royal Military Nursing Service – QARMNS, as opposed to the QARNNS the Haslar girls were used to – were inclined to be disparaging towards the new arrivals and found fault with every small misdemeanour. Even bedmaking became an issue – the 'hospital corners' which had become second nature were suddenly all wrong and had to be done in a different way. Thursday raged inwardly at what seemed to her to be an unnecessary fussiness – how could it *really* matter how the sheets were tucked in? – but, like the others, she knew that even the smallest point of discipline mattered in the Services, and it was easier in the end to do as you were told. And as Louisa reminded her one day, Miss Makepeace, back at Haslar, would be relying on them to make a good impression. 'We can't let Madam down,' she said, and it became a byword whenever the going seemed especially difficult. However, they were all too pleased to be working again at last to allow small irritations to disturb them for long, and soon got back into the hospital routine.

'Blimey, it's a bit different here to Haslar,' Elsie said, encountering Thursday in the sluice where she was washing out bedpans. 'I've never even heard of half the things these poor sods have got. Dysentery, malaria, diptheria, typhoid—'

'Typhus,' Thursday continued, 'and jaundice, and enteritis, and desert sores—'

'And God knows what else. You name it, these poor blighters've got it. And there never seem to be enough bandages or dressings or medicines to treat 'em all. They say the boss carries his sulphaguanidine about in his pocket all the time, won't let it out of his sight and only gives it to the blokes who've got really bad dysentery.' She shook her head. 'It's the gas gangrene that gets in my craw. I think that's the worst stink I've ever smelled. I don't reckon those cones we burn to get rid of the pong do all that much good either – I'm not sure but what they aren't worse! And you know, soon as you feel those little bubbles under the poor bloke's skin, that he's a goner. They can't do nothing for that.' She was silent for a moment, then straightened her shoulders. 'And the *sand* – don't nobody *never* suggest going to the beach again. Sandcastles! I've seen enough sand to build *Windsor* Castle.'

Thursday nodded. The desert sand seemed to get everywhere. It came in on the bodies of the patients and it didn't matter how often you bathed them, they still seemed to have it in their beds. 'It's like laying between sheets of bloody sandpaper,' one of them complained. 'Can't you do nothing about it, nurse?'

'Well, I've tried,' Thursday said helplessly. 'I've bathed you three times already, and there's all the others to do as well. I just don't know where it all comes from.'

'We're made of it,' the Sergeant in the next bed said lugubriously. 'Spend enough time out in the Blue and that's what happens to you. Your skin turns to sand. You never get rid of it. I had an uncle in the First War, he come home covered in sand, and my auntie said she wouldn't sleep with him no more because it was like he needed a shave all over. Never got rid of it, he didn't.'

'Well, if I don't get rid of this,' the first man said, 'I'm going to go right round the bloody bend. I tell you, it's bad enough being riddled with bloody bullets, but this is adding insult to injury. If I'd wanted a beach holiday I'd have gone to bloody Brighton.'

'I'll give you one more bath,' Thursday said, 'and that'll have to do till tomorrow.' Tenderly, she washed the soldier's bony buttocks. The men were all so thin, she thought, and burned almost black by the sun. How could they have survived out there, not only under fire but prey to all these horrible diseases as well?

She patted the soldier's skin dry. 'There. I hope you'll feel more comfortable now.'

'Oh, I will,' he said, and winked. 'It's worth a bit of desert sand to get a cuddle from a pretty young nurse.'

Thursday gave him a reproving look and moved on to the next patient. He had a leg in plaster from toe to thigh, and a look of extreme suffering on his face. She stared at him in alarm.

'What is it? Are you feeling ill?'

'Blimey, I almost wish I was,' he groaned. 'It's the flaming bed-bugs, they're driving me mad. They're bloody hell, they are. Worse than flaming vampires. Talk about Dracula.' He shifted awkwardly in his bed. 'Can't you have a feel down me plaster? I'm sure there's one down there. Just up above me knee, it is. Look, try this knitting needle, see if you can't catch the little blighter.'

Thursday took the needle and poked it under the plaster. Whether she was reaching the bed-bug or not, she had no idea, but after a few moments the Corporal grunted with satisfaction and she withdrew the needle. 'That better?'

'Well, you've either killed him or frightened him to death, love. He's stopped biting anyway. Cor, they're bleeding hell, they are. I dunno what God made them for, no good to man nor beast. Thanks, love, I'll give you a shout next time I wants a bit of a scratch, shall I?'

'Not if Sister's about, please. I don't know what she'd do if she saw me poking a knitting needle down your plaster!' Thursday looked at the implement. 'What are you doing with a knitting needle, anyway? Making balaclavas for your mates?'

'Blimey, they don't want no balaclavas out here!' He grinned. 'Sister give me it. Got fed up with me asking for a scratch, she did, and give it me so I could do it meself. But it's much nicer when a pretty young nurse does it!'

Thursday stared at him, then laughed. 'You mean you could have done it yourself? Well, of course you could – you old rascal, you! You got me here under false pretences.'

He winked. 'Is there any other sort? Come on, Nursey, you got to allow us a bit of comfort – specially after what we bin through for our country, eh?'

Thursday shook her head at him and hurried away. She was behind with her routine now and the next two patients got their baths in double-quick time. By the grins on their faces, though, she could see that they didn't mind. The whole ward had enjoyed seeing her poking about with the knitting needle in the Corporal's leg plaster, and for the next three days she had to endure a barrage of teasing about knitting, and requests to kill bed-bugs in various delicate parts of the men's anatomy.

There seemed to be no way of getting rid of the bugs. The school buildings had been taken over so quickly for use as a hospital that there had been no time for proper fumigation and the hydrocyanic acid which would have been used was too dangerous when the wards were occupied. All that could be done was to stand the legs of each bed in tins of paraffin to stop them climbing up, and apply a blowtorch to the beds of the up-patients. Even that only got rid of them for a short while.

Bed-bugs were mostly a problem at night, hiding in even the tiniest cracks and crevices during the day. But that didn't mean the men – or the nurses – were free from irritation, for as soon as dawn broke the sandflies arrived, clouds of them searching voraciously for flesh to bite. They were especially fond of open wounds, however small, and nearly all the men suffered from the 'desert sores' they caused, but the greatest danger they brought was diphtheria and there had been an epidemic not long before Thursday and the others arrived.

'I'd never even heard of half the diseases we get here, when we were at Haslar,' Elsie said. 'I must say I'm jolly glad of my mosquito net to sleep under, though. Once you get malaria, you've got it for life, Sister told me – and that's if you survive the first lot!'

'Just think yourself lucky not to have been sent out to the desert,' one of the QARMN Sisters told her. 'I was there for three months. We slept in tents and had to iron our uniforms with a flat-iron that we heated up on an oil stove. And you didn't skimp the ironing – it was the only way to kill off the bugs that had got through the wash! It wasn't just bugs and flies and mosquitos, either – we were absolutely overrun with rats.'

'Rats!' Priscilla said with a shudder. 'Oh, how revolting.'

'You don't have time to be revolted,' the Sister said. 'There are too many. They're everywhere. We had to take sticks with us when we went to the latrines, to beat them off, and they used to nest right down beside the tent walls and come in and run over the beds. It was worst of all for the patients who were in plaster – the rats would come in and chew it. They'd gnaw holes in the mosquito nets to get at it. We had to give the men sticks to beat them off with.'

The girls listened in horror. They'd all seen desert rats by then, but the hospital itself was largely clear of them. A few bed-bugs seemed a mild kind of torture in comparison.

'It's luxury here,' the Sister went on. 'You grumble about the sand, but out there in the desert the wind never stopped blowing, so it was like having sand kicked into your face the whole time, and we only got one bucket of water each a day – for *everything*! And when all you wanted at night was a long, cool shower to get the sand and the sweat and the bugs off you, that really *was* torture.'

'I'll never moan again,' Elsie promised, but the Sister smiled.

'Yes, you will. There'll be plenty of other things to grumble about – you'll find out! But there's plenty to enjoy as well, and we're doing valuable work, so I don't think it'll seem too bad.'

The biggest surprise to the girls was to find themselves nursing men with such everyday diseases as chicken-pox, mumps and measles. The Australian soldiers, who weren't accustomed to these childish illnesses, caught them almost as soon as they boarded the troopships that had been British liners in a previous life, and a lot of them arrived at Suez covered in spots or with painfully swollen necks. After several weeks at sea, many of them were over the worst and more than a little disgruntled to find themselves told they must stay in quarantine. Priscilla, going round her ward at midnight, would find their beds stuffed with pillows while the men were out sampling the nightspots. 'And spreading a few spots of their own around the locals,' she reported with irritation. 'Honestly, how selfish can you get!'

'Well, they've been cooped up at sea for weeks, they must be really fed up,' Elsie said. 'Poor sods, they're desperate for a bit of fun.'

'It won't be much fun for us when the other regiments go down with measles,' Priscilla said, but Thursday shook her head.

'They'll have had all those things when they were children. Why, my mum invited all the neighbours' children in when me and our Steve had chicken-pox, just so we could all get it over with. And she was dead keen for him to catch mumps. They say it's really bad for boys if they don't get it till they're grown up.'

Apart from Diggers' Plague, as some of the girls called it, most of the men they were nursing now were either serious medical or orthopaedic cases, kept at the hospital until they were fit to be moved to the canal zone. It was more like civilian nursing in a way, Thursday thought – an even routine of bathing, dressing, bedmaking and bedpan duties. She knew that there had been a good deal of fighting out in the desert but just now there seemed to be a moment of abeyance. It would start again, of course – they hadn't accompanied all those thousands of troops out here for nothing – but just for a while there was time to breathe. Time to wander out at night and look at the myriad stars; time to wonder at the tales the men told of creatures they encountered out in the desert – chameleons, scorpions, tarantulas; time to make new friends, to explore their surroundings and get to know the night-life of a town that was full of bars and restaurants, with plenty of British and American uniforms to be seen, and plenty of offers to take a pretty young nurse to dinner or for a drink.

'Come on, Thurs,' Elsie urged. 'That smashing young Sergeant says he can find a partner for you and we'll go dancing. Let's make the most of what fun there is around here. We might never get the chance again.'

Thursday pushed her writing-pad aside and went to get ready. Elsie was right – you didn't know what life held. Only a few weeks ago there had been a serious panic in Alexandria, when it was thought that the Germans were about to invade, and the Navy had been evacuated. In the British Embassy, the staff had burned all their papers to prevent their falling into enemy hands, and the Eighth Army had been pushed back as far as El Alamein, only sixty miles away. Although so far the Allied troops had managed to hold the defence, you never knew what was going to happen next. It was foolish not to snatch at what fun and happiness there was.

I'm not breaking my promise to you, Connor, she thought as she changed into a clean white dress, examining herself closely for any fleas or bed-bugs that she might have collected during the day, but it's going to be so long until we meet again, and life is here and now. It seems almost like tempting Fate to think about the future, when we don't even know if there's going to be one.

So she went out with Elsie and her Sergeant and the young soldier who had been brought along as her partner, and danced in his arms, closing her eyes and her mind against tomorrow. And later, they walked under the stars, their arms about each other's waists, and when he paused beneath a palm tree and took her in his arms she lifted her face for his kiss and allowed him to hold her close.

'It's been a marvellous evening, Thursday,' he whispered. 'I wish I could ask you for another date, but we might not be here much longer. I'll look you up when I get back, OK? See if you still remember who I am?'

'OK,' she whispered back, and wondered if he ever would – indeed, if he would ever even come back. So many young men were going away, out into the desert, literally into the 'Blue', and how many would come back? And of those who did, how many would be whole and undamaged, with two arms and legs, two eyes, and a face that wasn't seared by flames or smashed by bullets? She gripped him tightly in her arms and kissed him again. 'It's been a lovely evening. I won't forget you. Good luck – wherever you go.'

'Thanks.' They stood in silence for a moment, warm and close under the gently sighing fronds of the palm. 'Thanks, Thursday. And good luck to you, too.'

Later, as she ducked under the mosquito net and climbed into bed, Thursday noticed the half-finished letter to Connor. And good luck to you too, my darling, she thought. Good luck to all the men out here in the desert, or wherever you are, good luck to those still in Europe and those in the Far East – especially those in Japanese POW camps. Good luck to the nurses too, and all the civilians everywhere who have been caught up in this horrible war that's spread like a sore over the world.

Good luck. It's what we all need.

In the third week of October, almost before the VADs had become acclimatised to their new surroundings, they were thrown once more into battle stations as General Montgomery ordered the attack on El Alamein and gunfire roared once more in everyone's ears.

'Oh, my goodness!' Thursday clutched her friend as the ground shook beneath their feet. 'What's that?'

'It's the guns.' Louisa was pale. 'It's all right – they're miles away. It's just that the sound travels, and the vibration carries a long way too.'

'Well, I hope you're right. I feel as if we're in the front line.' Elsie took out a packet of cigarettes and lit one, her fingers shaking. 'Want one, Lou?'

Louisa took one but Thursday shook her head. She'd never taken to smoking – her father had always said he didn't like to see a woman with a fag hanging out of her mouth, and anyway it turned your fingers yellow and your teeth as well. Why I should think about all that now, in the middle of a big battle, heaven only knows, she thought, but the smallest things could remind you of home. Like that little dog she'd seen in Cairo that had looked just like Patch. And the white cat that had reminded her of her Auntie Maudie's Snowy. A fresh burst of gunfire broke into her thoughts and she reached out involuntarily for Elsie's hand.

'It's as bad as the Blitz,' Elsie said as the girls crowded together, listening to the distant thunder and staring, fascinated, at the brilliant flashes of light along the horizon. 'There must be hundreds of guns.'

'A thousand, I heard someone say,' Thursday said. 'It's a terrific attack. And they've got armoured cars and tanks and God knows what to back them up. They were brought over in the holds of the convoy.'

‘I felt sorry for the men, having to set off on a route march the minute they landed,’ Elsie observed. ‘I mean, all that PT and training on board just isn’t the same as marching off into the desert with a heavy pack on your back.’

‘Well, we’ll be seeing some of them soon,’ Louisa said, drawing on her cigarette. ‘It won’t be long before the casualties start to arrive.’

They had been busy ever since early that morning, when the order had come through to prepare the hospital as a casualty clearing station. As swiftly as possible, all the patients who were fit to be moved were packed on to the trains that waited at the hospital gates, and those who were left shifted so that there could be empty wards for the new arrivals. Here, beds were rapidly remade and everything made ready for wounded men – dressings and bandages newly sterilised, medicines and lotions lined up in cupboards and on shelves, stretchers stacked along the walls in case there were too few beds. One ward was set aside for blood donating, and in between their duties, Thursday and the others queued up to give their pint, barely resting for five minutes afterwards before they were up again and scurrying about to carry out the Ward Sister’s demands. One, coming upon Thursday as she made gallon after gallon of fresh lime juice, paused to speak to her.

‘You’re doing very well, you girls,’ she said. ‘I must say we thought you were going to be something of a burden rather than a help, but you’re all working very hard. What’s more, you can think for yourselves – you don’t have to be *told* all the time. Well done.’ And she marched away, leaving Thursday staring after her open-mouthed.

‘What did she think we were, morons?’ she asked indignantly, telling the others about it now. ‘As if we hadn’t already been through the Blitz! The trouble is, they think if you’re not State Registered or in the QA, you can’t be a proper nurse at all!’

‘Well, we’ll soon show ’em their mistake,’ Elsie said stoutly. ‘Won’t we, Lou?’

Louisa nodded. ‘Some of them think we’re either mindless shopgirls or mindless debutantes! Sister Freeman told me the other day that she hoped I hadn’t wasted space bringing out my ball gowns, because I wasn’t going to get much chance to use them. I didn’t like to tell her I’d already been dancing at Shepheards, when we were in Cairo!' She chuckled. 'Or that the very attractive Lieutenant Colonel who took me was my cousin!'

Within a few hours, the casualties had begun to arrive. The first of the exhausted men, their wounds roughly bandaged or splinted at a First Aid post just behind the front lines, were Australians, quickly followed by New Zealanders, South Africans and the Scottish Highlanders who had sounded the call to arms on their bagpipes. And once they had begun, there was no chance for conversation for many hours, many days. Once again, the girls were plunged into the heartbreaking exhilaration of receiving a long line of injured soldiers, knowing with one glance that many of them were not going to survive and doing their utmost to give them comfort as they tended their terrible wounds.

It was a long, long night, that first of the El Alamein attack. It ran into daylight and then again into darkness, and Thursday scarcely knew when one began and the other ended, nor where the hours went. She worked without stopping, removing bloodstained bandages to reveal deep and jagged wounds – some already showing signs of infection or the dreaded gangrene – or easing a splinted limb with pillows. She washed faces and bodies that were encrusted with desert sand and gunpowder, mixed to a glutinous paste with congealed blood. She smoothed back matted hair from brows that were creased with pain, and smiled into eyes that begged her to put an end to the misery. 'You'll be all right,' she said over and over again, knowing that for many it was not true. 'You're safe now. You'll be all right . . .'

'Stay by this boy, Tilford,' Sister Carrington said, straightening up by one of the new arrivals. She lowered her voice. 'He doesn't have long, I'm afraid. We can't let him go without a friendly face by his side.'

There was a chair nearby and Thursday pulled it close to the bed. She looked down at the young face, ashen beneath the desert tan, and her heart sank. Sister was right, he was barely more than a boy – no more than nineteen, surely – and it was obvious that he was sinking fast. But his eyelids were fluttering and she thought he knew she was there. She took his thin hand in hers – the bones no thicker than a sparrow's leg, she thought and smiled although she knew her lips were trembling and the tears were hot in her eyes.

'It's all right,' she whispered. 'You're safe here in Alexandria. You don't have to fight any more. You're going to be all right.'

The boy's head, covered with a thatch of thick fair hair, turned restlessly from side to side. 'Mairi . . . where's Mairi? I want Mairi.'

Pity swelled up in Thursday's heart. She stroked the hand that trembled in hers and whispered again, 'It's all right. You're going to be all right.'

'Mairi! Where's Mairi? Mairi . . .'

'She'll come soon,' Thursday said desperately. She was giving him no comfort, she knew it. It wasn't her he wanted, it was Mairi – his girlfriend probably – and no one else would do. She stared down at him helplessly, taking in the body that was so thin that she could see his ribs, see the fluttering of his heartbeat just beneath the stretched, sunburned skin. 'Mairi will be here in a minute. Someone's gone to find her.' He wouldn't live long enough to know that she was lying. If it could give him just one small crumb of comfort . . . But he was twisting on the bed, each movement clearly an agony, yet his mental agony all the greater. 'Mairi! Mairi!'

I can't do a thing, Thursday thought. I can't help him at all, and he needs it so much. Oh God, please let me help this poor, poor boy. Please give me strength to help him, please let me say the right words, do the right thing . . . But all she could do was hold his hand, whisper in his ear and watch the twisting restlessness and the rapidly weakening flutter of his heart. 'It's all right. Mairi's coming.' And then, with a final desperate attempt at relieving his anguish, 'She's here now. Look – she's coming through the door. Mairi! Mairi! Over here . . .' And what am I going to do now, she wondered, appalled by her recklessness. I've just made it all worse. And she looked down again, tormented by guilt, knowing that she must tell him the truth and that the truth was the last thing he wanted to hear.

The dark-blue eyes looked up into hers. There was a moment of perfect clarity, of joy. He believed her lie, she thought, dazed, and opened her mouth to confess the truth. And then their expression altered; the pupils widened and the fluttering eyelids faltered. And Thursday looked away and at the fragile chest, just in time to see the final throb of his heart as it stopped for ever.

She sat very still, holding the limp, bony hand. As Sister had said, he had had very little time, and Thursday was not the person he wanted by him in those last few moments. But perhaps she had, after all, given him comfort at the last. Perhaps he had believed that his Mairi was with him. Perhaps, in some strange way, he had actually seen her.

She got up a little stiffly. She had been sitting there longer than she should, as the boy was dead and there was nothing more she could do. Her task now was with the living.

It was on the second, or perhaps the third day, when she was almost dropping with exhaustion, that a new group of casualties arrived. During all that time, Thursday and the other VADs had worked almost ceaselessly, eating when food was thrust in front of them, returning to their quarters only when ordered to go, falling on to their beds for a few hours' sleep then getting up to stumble back into the wards. There they spent hours in the sluice, washing bloodstained bandages, for there would be no more sent out from England while the present emergency continued. They took them into the gardens and festooned them over shrubs and bushes for the sun to bleach them white, and when they went back in there was a new supply waiting to be washed. They began to feel as if their hands would be bloodstained for ever.

'They're giving us some Italian POWs to help out,' Louisa said as they worked. Louisa was always first to get news. The others looked at her in some dismay. 'They're all right really, you know.' She hesitated. 'I went to Italy a couple of times before the war. I knew quite a lot of Italians. They're not like the Germans. They never really wanted to be in the war anyway. And they'll be guarded all the time.'

'I dunno,' Elsie said dubiously. 'Eyeties . . .' But when they came, dark-eyed and black-haired, almost pathetically anxious to help, her heart melted; and like pet dogs they adored the yellow-haired girl and followed her about, vying to carry out her wishes so that the other girls teased her unmercifully about her male harem.

Thursday found herself sitting beside several other men who were obviously not going to survive. With each one she felt more miserably helpless, tortured by the knowledge that it was someone else they cried out for – their wife, their girlfriend, their mother – and more than once she made up her mind to ask Sister not to give her this particular task again. But she could never bring herself to do so. If it isn't me, it'll have to be someone else, she thought, stroking the rough, hairy hand of a man who was surely too old to be a soldier, or the smooth skin of a lad even younger than Mairi's lover. And none of us is going to be the one they want.

'You should go and get some rest, Tilford,' Sister said when Thursday went to report that the latest one had slipped away. 'Go now.'

'But we've got a new batch just arriving – I can do a few more hours,' Thursday said, though in truth she felt dizzy with fatigue. 'I'll stay as long as you want me.'

'An hour, then,' Sister said firmly. 'No more. You're on your honour to leave the ward when the time's up, do you understand? And you mustn't do any more than just sit by their beds.' Her face softened a little. 'It's what you are best at, you know. I don't quite understand why, but they seem to draw a kind of calmness from you – a touch of peace. It's a wonderful gift.'

Thursday stared at her, then stumbled to the nearest bed. A wonderful gift? A calmness – a touch of peace? She shook her head, dismissing the words, and then looked down, expecting to see what she had now so often seen; the blurred grey shadow of death flung like a cobweb across the body that lay there.

Instead, she saw a thin, narrow face with deep brown eyes and a wide mouth, tightened just now with pain. Straight dark hair, dusted with sand, swept across a high forehead. Blood was clotting over the slashed wounds that had laid his cheeks open. A rough splint had been bound on each arm and stained bandages were wrapped around his body.

How badly injured he was, she couldn't at that moment tell. But he was not dying. This man, Thursday knew, was still full of life and energy and determination. It was, perhaps, a good thing that she didn't know then just how determined he could be when he saw a thing he wanted. Nor that in that first brief glance, in pain though he was, he had decided that he wanted her.

Chapter Twelve

Mark Sangster was an Army doctor. He was young for the rank of Lieutenant Colonel, and as his injuries – mostly superficial – healed, he became the star of the ward, his dark eyes gleaming and impertinent as he teased the nurses. He led the rest of the patients in counting loudly whenever a VAD was trying to take a pulse, he deliberately dropped his book or writing-pad on the floor by his bed so that a passing nurse would have to bend over to pick it up, to the accompaniment of cheers and wolf whistles, he distracted Thursday by pointing out of the window and then dipping his thermometer into a cup of hot tea, and he pestered them all for a good night kiss. 'Come on, I know you've got the best kisses in Alex. It'll help me get better. You are *supposed* to help me get better, aren't you?'

Despite his teasing, or maybe because of it, he was a popular patient with the nurses and not least because of his dark good looks and easy manner. It wasn't surprising that they all fell in love with him.

'I'll have to be very careful about Lieutenant Colonel Sangster,' Louisa remarked one day as they washed bandages in the sluice. 'He's the sort that could turn a good girl into a very bad one.'

'Go on, you'll never be a bad girl,' Elsie told her. 'Now me, I could be *very bad indeed*, specially when he gives me one of those looks of his. He's got eyes like a filmstar!'

Thursday said nothing. She was aware of a powerful electric current running through her whenever she caught one of Dr Sangster's dark glances, and it wasn't a joking matter. He looked at her as if they already shared a secret, she thought, and a guilty one at that. It wasn't a feeling she liked. As Louisa had said, he was a man to be wary of, and Thursday made up her mind not to have any more to do with him than she had to.

Lieutenant Colonel Sangster, however, had other ideas.

'So what made you volunteer as a VAD?' he enquired one night, lounging against the end of his bed as Thursday set her hurricane lamp and primus stove on a rickety table and spread a white sheet over her chair to keep off the lurking bed-bugs. 'You're bright enough to have taken State Registration, or gone into the QARMNS.'

Thursday gave him a look. 'It's not a matter of intelligence,' she said crisply. 'I wanted to do something to help.'

'But couldn't you help more if you were properly trained? I mean, you're not much more than a dogsbody here. I wonder you can stand it.'

Thursday faced him. 'I can stand it because someone's got to do these jobs, and I'm not too proud to be the one to do them. I also happen to think that keeping people as comfortable as they can be in hospital is important – whether it means operating on them, giving them medicine or bringing them a bedpan. In fact,' she added with a challenging glance, 'on the whole, they're probably more grateful for the bedpan than for anything else!'

Mark Sangster laughed. 'You're probably right! But don't you ever wish you could do some of the more interesting work? Not have to spend *all* your time emptying bedpans and washing used bandages?'

Thursday stopped to think. In fairness, she had to admit that she had considered training as a Registered Nurse once the war was over. But the war had gone on for so long that, like many other people, she'd almost given up planning for life in peacetime. You couldn't look ahead when you didn't know when peace was going to come, or even if it was going to come. For thousands, perhaps millions, of people, it never had and never would. How could you know that you wouldn't be one of those thousands, those millions? How could you know that you would still be alive this time next week?

'I'll think about that when there's more time,' she said finally. 'Just for the moment I'm quite happy to be doing what I am doing. I know I'm being useful, and that's all that matters. Now, perhaps you'd be kind enough to go to bed. We're keeping the other patients awake, and if Sister comes in she'll be furious to find you still up.'

He made a comical face. 'Oh dear! Mustn't risk Sister's fury, must we?' He winked and lowered his voice. 'I'll tell you what, I'd rather go back to Alamein and face the German guns than face Sister Carrington in one of her furies.' With a smile that turned Thursday's heart over, he climbed into the bed that was uncomfortably close to her chair. 'Come and hold my hand for a while.'

'Certainly not,' she said indignantly, and he put his head on one side.

'Oh, why not? Don't tell me you've already got a sweetheart.' He groaned comically. 'Though it's obvious a pretty girl like you would already be spoken for. Are you engaged?'

'Not exactly,' she admitted. 'Not that it's any of your business – *sir*.' She bit her lip. It wasn't always easy to remember rank with men who were in their pyjamas.

Dr Sangster gave her a bright-eyed look. 'What do you mean, not exactly?'

'Connor's in the Navy,' she said, exasperated. 'Somewhere in the Far East. He gave me a brooch and said he wished it was a ring. But he didn't want to tie me down—' She stopped, wondering why she was telling him this. It was between herself and Connor. 'Look, I think you ought to be asleep. And anyway, I'm not supposed to sit here talking all night.' She sat down and picked up a book.

'You won't mind if I just lie here and look at you, will you? Just to help me fall asleep and give me sweet dreams?'

'So long as you realise that's all they can ever be – dreams,' she answered crisply. As it happened, she minded very much. She was acutely conscious of his gaze, of his nearness. I'm sure he's moved that bed, she thought. I'm sure it wasn't that close last night. She turned away, determined not to let him disturb her, although the way that her heart was thumping told her he'd disturbed her already. Tomorrow, she thought, I'll ask if I can be moved to a different ward.

Next day, however, Mark Sangster was ill, more ill than he'd been even when he had arrived. One of his wounds had been infected by the bite of a sandfly and his temperature shot up. The wound itself turned into a desert sore, a suppurating ulcer that refused to heal, and on top of that he developed jaundice and the dysentery that the sandflies were believed to carry as well as diphtheria. Thursday was told to special him, and spent much of her time by his bed, dressing the sore, keeping his other wounds clear of flies, stamping a damp cake of soap over his sheets to catch bedbugs, monitoring his pulse and temperature and supplying him with a seemingly endless succession of bedpans. Once, through his haze of delirium, he grinned weakly and muttered, 'You were right about the bedpans, Tilford. Just keep 'em coming, won't you!' And Thursday felt the tears come to her eyes.

Allied servicemen weren't the only ones to be brought to Alexandria. There were Germans and Italians too, nursed separately from the others in huts guarded by Indian sentries in turbans. Elsie found herself sent to work there and reported that the Germans were a grim, unyielding lot, angry about their defeat and bitter about their capture. 'Not like that young Heinz Schmidt we had at Haslar that time after Dunkirk,' she said. 'You rather fell for him, didn't you, Thurs?'

'I did not!' Thursday felt a flush of anger and embarrassment, and Elsie looked taken aback. 'I felt sorry for him, that's all. He was just an ordinary boy – too young to be in a war.'

'Sorry, Thurs. I didn't mean anything by it. But these are young too – just kids. Not much over fifteen or sixteen, some of 'em, but they still won't give in. Anyone would think we were going to eat 'em alive.'

'Perhaps that's what they do think,' Louisa said. 'Remember how the ones at Haslar screamed because they thought we were going to operate without anaesthetic? They'd been told all kinds of horror stories, just to make them hate us.'

'Like we were told the Germans ate babies,' Thursday said thoughtfully. 'I'm sure that wasn't true – just people starting rumours.'

The Italians, who had been British allies in the First World War, were allowed to help in the wards. They lived in tents in the grounds and planted flowers in between them, so that their camp looked more like a garden than a POW camp. At night they sang together, often arias that were familiar to those like Louisa who knew about opera, and to girls like Thursday, whose father was fond of classical music and had collected quite a lot of records which he played in the evenings on the gramophone he'd built himself. The sound of the liquid voices floating across the hospital grounds in the darkness brought memories to many of them, and even those who had never heard an operatic aria paused to listen.

'Them Tonis can certainly sing,' Elsie commented. 'I was never much of a one for posh music before, but I reckon I'll go along to the King's Theatre when I get back to Pompey – they have whole weeks of opera there. That's if the King's is still there then,' she added wryly.

Thursday, who hadn't after all asked to be moved, found herself shifted anyway to do night duties on a different ward. She left Mark's bedside with an odd mixture of relief and reluctance and handed him over to Priscilla, who was to special him next, with a list of instructions.

'He likes his lime juice really sharp – hardly any sugar. When you wash him, look out for his right arm – it wasn't broken but it was badly bruised and it's still tender. His temperature tends to go up at—'

'Yes, *all* right,' Priscilla interrupted. 'I have specialled patients before, you know.' She gave Thursday a quizzical look. 'You seem very concerned about Lieutenant Colonel Sangster.'

'No more than I am about any of our patients,' Thursday answered stiffly. She handed over the sheet of paper on which Mark's temperature was recorded. 'There you are, then. I'm not going to be away for long anyway – I'm just relieving for a couple of weeks while Nurse Dawson's getting over that bug she caught. I expect I'll take over again when I come back.'

'Oh, I doubt that,' Priscilla said sweetly. 'He'll be used to me by then – he won't want to change back again.'

Thursday made a face at her. I hope he is, she thought. Anyway, with any luck he won't need a special by then. He'll probably be moved somewhere else. I'll be thankful if he is.

'You shouldn't take any notice of him,' Louisa advised when Thursday told her this. She stretched a pair of rubber gloves over her hands and examined them for holes. 'He's just a natural flirt – can't help it.' She took off the gloves and fished about in a tin box until she found the right-sized patches to stick over the holes. 'Mind you, he does seem to watch you quite a bit more than the others. These gloves are in a terrible state, you know. Good thing I got lots of practice at home, mending my brother's bike punctures!'

Night duties were a strange, lonely time. With no Colonel's rounds to prepare for and only a few medicines to be given out, there was little to do and until the men fell asleep they would talk amongst themselves. A lot of their talk was about their war experiences, and Thursday listened sadly to the stories they told – stories that seemed to grow more horrific as the war progressed. Tanks bombed or mined and set on fire, their crews trapped inside, burning with them. 'You can smell it, nurse, just like roasting meat of a Sunday dinnertime, it is.' Men mown down by enemy tanks, the wide, implacable tracks crushing them into the sand so that there was almost nothing to be salvaged. Men who were still just alive, their bodies booby-trapped by the enemy so that when the stretcher crews ran to pick them up they were all blown to oblivion together. Men in aircraft, shot down and found days or weeks later, still strapped into their seats, having either bled, fried or starved to death. 'You never seen nothing like it. You don't want to, neither.'

'We didn't oughter tell you these things, I know,' a Sergeant said to Thursday one night as she sat by his bed listening to his outpourings. 'But we gotta tell someone, see. It's like it's all festering inside and if we don't talk about it we'll go clean round the bend.' He chuckled. 'You heard what they call blokes what do that, doncher? Harpic – clean round the bend, see?'

Thursday smiled but her heart felt close to breaking. And as she sat through the night in her white-sheeted chair, in sole charge of the ward, she felt the desolation of the desert creep eerily close. All around her were men in varying stages of suffering, some of whom would not survive, all of whom were desperately missing their homes and families. 'It ain't so bad when yer doin' the actual *fightin'*,' one of them explained as she paused by his bed to soothe him with cool water on his parched lips. 'You can't think about nothin' else then, see. But layin' here of a night, with nuffin' to think about but blasted bed-bugs – well, you can't help yer mind wanderin', can yer? An' then when you hears about all them Yanks over in Blighty, you gets to worryin', see. What's the old woman doin' with herself? I mean, I bin away nigh on three years now. She must wonder if she'll ever see me again. And if some bloody Yank swaggers by with a pocket full o' dollars, lookin' for company, well . . .'

'I'm sure you've nothing to worry about,' Thursday tried to

reassure him. 'With a fine man like you for a husband she won't look twice at an American.'

'I ain't so sure,' he said restlessly. 'I ain't so flamin' fine these days, I can tell yer. There's this bloody great scar right across me chops for a start – what's she goin' ter say when she sees that, eh? She was always one for a good-lookin' bloke, was my Edie. What am I goin' ter do if she won't even kiss me, eh? Tell me that.'

'Of course she'll kiss you. I would, if you were my husband. In fact, I'll kiss you now, just to prove it!' And with a swift glance around the ward to make sure that Sister hadn't crept in unnoticed, Thursday bent and laid her lips on the sweating face. She rested her cheek against his for a moment, feeling the puckering of the scar, and just for that instant, poured into him all the love she wanted so desperately to give – to her cousins Mike and Leslie, to poor dead Tony West, to Patsy's Roy, to all the men who lay in hospitals. And, most of all, to Connor.

After that, good night kisses became a part of her duties – albeit unofficially, and always discreetly. Nothing was ever said, and it never became a habit, but always there were one or two men who seemed especially in need for some reason – a worsening in their condition, bad news from home, or sheer aching loneliness. A kiss was the least she could give them – a kiss, a touch on the cheek, a whispered word or two. It was all the comfort there could be.

And then Thursday, having finished her rounds and made sure they were all at least resting, if not asleep, would sit in her chair in the middle of them all, sharply aware of the loneliness all around her and piercingly aware of her own.

Gradually, Mark Sangster's dysentery began to improve and when Nurse Dawson returned to duty Thursday came back to the ward to find him sitting up again, the yellowness fading from his skin and eyes. His thin face lit up when he saw her.

'I thought you'd abandoned me. Was it something I said?'

'It was everything you said,' Thursday replied crisply, dismayed to feel the tingle that went through her as she rested her hand on his shoulder to help him lean forward. 'Just let me shake out your pillow . . . There, is that better?'

'Just seeing you makes me feel better,' he said. He lowered his voice, beckoning, so that she had to move closer. 'You are going to special me, aren't you? You're not going to let Nurse Lacock loose on me again?'

'It doesn't look to me as if you need specialling any more. Anyway, what was wrong with Nurse Lacock? Didn't you get along with her?'

'Get along with her?' He rolled his eyes. 'It was *her* getting along with *me* that was the problem! Honestly, if I'd been able to walk she'd have had me out of here and walking up the aisle in the local church! A man's not safe with her around.'

Thursday laughed. 'Don't be silly! As if she'd look at you, with all these other men in the ward to choose from. Anyway, she's already engaged.'

'Well, she doesn't act like it,' he said, and then added with huge dignity, 'I'll have you know that I've been voted The Man Most Likely To by all the nurses in the ward, so put that in your pipe and smoke it!'

'Most likely to what?' Thursday asked unkindly, and he gave her a haughty look.

'You'll have to ask them that. And much as I like having you stand there with your hand on my shoulder, I think perhaps you ought to remove it, because I've just seen Sister go past the window and she'll be in at any minute.'

Thursday leaped away, her face burning. Hastily, keeping her face turned aside, she began to tidy his locker. Mark chuckled. 'You needn't look so guilty. There's nothing to be ashamed of in giving a man a cuddle.'

'I was not cuddling you!' Her voice came out as a squeak and she lowered it to repeat forcefully, 'I was *not* cuddling you. I just forgot what I was doing for a minute.'

'How unflattering,' he murmured. 'I didn't forget it, not for a second. Most enjoyable. Do it again, sometime.'

Thursday shot him a murderous glance and moved away. Sister had come in by now and was clapping her hands for attention. The nurses stopped what they were doing to listen.

'Colonel's rounds will be early today,' she announced, sending a wave of panic through the ward. 'I want this ward spick and span in ten minutes. All up-patients in bed, please, and no newspapers or magazines or other clutter on show.' She looked around with disfavour. 'The whole place is in the most disgusting mess. Ten minutes, mind!'

Ten minutes! The nurses erupted. Panic-stricken, they scurried around, gathering up overflowing ashtrays, used mugs and plates, orange peel and bags of dates. The patients opened their lockers and thrust in books and half-written letters, and stubbed out their cigarettes. 'Put it in there, nurse. That's right, just give the door a good kick, it'll close. Mind you don't take Major Rodway's teeth, now, he'll need them later for cracking nuts. Don't you go losing that photograph of my best girlfriend, will you.'

'We'll never get rid of it all in time,' Louisa panted, passing Thursday with an armful of assorted bits and pieces. 'I don't know where it's all come from.'

'Shove it under Captain Barry's cradle,' Mark suggested, indicating the man in the next bed, who had a large wooden frame over his leg to keep the bedclothes from touching it. 'He won't mind.'

Louisa hesitated. Thursday whipped up the sheets, revealing the space beneath, and Louisa shoved her load under, taking care not to touch the bandaged leg. Thursday dropped the counterpane back into place and smoothed it down rapidly, and the girls snapped to attention as the Sister came briskly back into the ward, the Colonel beside her.

Two pairs of piercing eyes swept about the room. Thursday, glancing covertly from under her lashes, wondered how they had ever managed to achieve so much in so short a time. Every bed was immaculate, the openings of the pillowslips all turned away from the door, the patients sitting up straight with pyjama jackets neatly buttoned and the sheets folded over to the same depth. The tops of the lockers each had a jug of water and glass placed precisely in the middle and the chairs were exactly at right-angles to the beds. The floors had been swept clean and there was not a bedpan or a urine bottle to be seen anywhere.

Does the Colonel really suppose the ward looks like this all the time, she wondered. Doesn't he realise that there are books and papers strewn around, half-eaten bars of chocolate, mugs of tea? Does he really think the patients just sit to attention all day long, doing absolutely nothing?

The Colonel advanced into the ward. He paused by each bed, shooting gimlet glances but treating each man with the respect to which, as an officer, he was entitled. He asked a few questions, which Sister answered promptly in a deferential voice, and he glanced at the charts. Once or twice, he stopped for several minutes, talking to the patient, until with a nod of satisfaction he proceeded on his way.

He came to Mark's bed. Thursday and Louisa, standing stiffly at the foot, moved aside to allow him to see the chart hung on the end. He glanced at it and pursed his lips.

'You've had a bad dose of dysentery and jaundice, I see. Getting over it now?'

'Yes, sir. Thanks to the good offices of these nurses.'

The Colonel gave Thursday a sharp glance. 'Been your special, has he?'

'He was at the beginning, sir, but I was moved over to C Ward for a fortnight. Lacock's been looking after him since then.'

'But it was Tilford who set me on the road to recovery,' Mark added helpfully, ignoring Thursday's imploring expression. 'I keep telling her, she ought to join the QARMNS.'

The Colonel looked at her from under his brows. 'Well, why didn't you do that? Prefer the Navy, do you?'

'I just wanted to help,' Thursday began helplessly, but he was already moving on. He stopped beside Captain Barry's bed and looked at the hump made by the cradle.

'Burns and a break, hm? Let's have a look.'

Thursday caught her breath and cast Louisa an agonised glance. Louisa was biting her lips and looking as if she was ready either to laugh or to burst into tears. The Sister, standing nearby, gave them both a suspicious stare. Thursday, meeting her eye, saw light dawn and drew in another breath as she stepped forward.

'Sir, you do have a number of patients to see. I don't think there's any need—' But it was too late. The Colonel had motioned to Louisa to draw back the covers, and Louisa had no choice but to obey. Slowly, her face crimson, she pulled down the sheets and revealed the treasure house within.

There was a long silence. Thursday stared at the floor, willing it to open up beneath her feet. She knew that every eye in the ward was riveted upon them. She could imagine exactly the livid fury on Sister's face, the half amused, half appalled guilt on Captain Barry's, the suppressed chuckle on Mark's. I'll kill you for this, she promised him silently. I'll smother you with your pillow. I'll make you eat boiled rice for every meal. I'll load your lime juice with sugar. I'll confiscate your bedpan—

The sound of laughter broke into her murderous thoughts and she lifted her eyes, astonished, to see the Colonel throw back his head and roar with mirth. He flung back the cover, grinning broadly, and turned to Sister.

'That's what happens when you take people by surprise,' he said. 'You force them to use their initiative.' He gave Louisa a nod. 'Well done, girl. But perhaps you'd better clear out some of the rubbish now, hm? And I think we'll call rounds over for this morning, shall we, Sister? As you say, I do have other patients to see, and this lot look disgustingly healthy. Taking up beds!'

He strode out of the ward, followed by the Sister, and the men erupted into laughter. Louisa, her face still scarlet, hastily removed all the offending articles from Barry's bed, aided by suggestions from Mark. Thursday, almost as embarrassed, turned on him. 'That was all your fault! You could have got us into real trouble.'

'I didn't know he was going to want to examine old Barry's bad leg,' Mark protested. 'It's not something I'd want to examine myself, and I'm a doctor! Now if it was yours . . .'

'Oh, for goodness sake! You're impossible!' She turned on her heel. The men were already getting out their papers and books, strewing them about the ward so that it looked just as untidy as it had before. She paused and shook her head. 'What's the use? What *is* the use?'

'None at all,' Mark said cheerfully from behind her. 'It's just so that we don't forget our discipline, that's all. And to stop us degenerating into total chaos. But you must admit, it does look more homely like this, now doesn't it?'

Thursday ignored him. She knew that Sister would be back, and would have some sharp words to say about the clutter hidden under Captain Barry's cradle. In any case, it was time to take the bedpans round again, and after that would come the daily bathing routine. And when that was done, there would be no shortage of bandages to wash, roll and sterilise – and by then they'd be calling out for bottles and bedpans again, and then it would be lunch . . .

Thank heaven Mark Sangster's getting better now, she thought, going to the sluice to collect an armful of pans. At least I don't have to special him any more. With any luck, I can stay at the other end of the ward and keep right out of his way.

Chapter Thirteen

It seemed very strange, with the sound of gunfire in the distance and the knowledge that wounded men were arriving daily at the hospital, to realise that outside the gates quite a different life was being lived.

'You wouldn't think there was a war on at all, to see the way they carry on round here,' Elsie observed as the girls snatched a few hours' relaxation in the town. 'Look at that lot getting out of that Rolls Royce, all dressed up to the nines as if they were going to dinner with the King hisself. I suppose they're going to that posh hotel. And look – there's some Yanks. I didn't know they were here.'

'They look as if they've only just arrived,' Thursday said, gazing at the group of American Army officers, relaxed and fresh-faced in their clean uniforms. 'There's not a speck of sand on them! And don't they look keen and eager.'

'Think they've come to win the war for us,' Elsie said a trifle sourly. 'Pity they didn't join in a bit earlier, it could've been over by now.'

Louisa shook her head. 'You have to be fair. Why should they get involved, when nobody'd actually threatened them?'

'Well, *we* did, didn't we? Come in just to protect Poland and all those little countries. Stand up for our friends, we do, but the Yanks wait till someone knocks them on the head before they'll lift a finger, and then come breezing in like Sir Galahad on a white charger and expect us all to fall about with gratitude.' Elsie threw a disparaging glance in the direction of the Americans, who were lounging on the verandah of one of the restaurants, sipping beer. 'And they all seem to think they're flipping film stars, too! Look as if they're posing for their blooming pictures all the time.'

Thursday laughed. 'You do seem to have it in for them. But you ought to remember they did do all that Lease-Lend, and send us food parcels and things. And you've got to admit we are glad of them now.'

'I bet you won't say no if one of them asks you out for a drink or dinner, either,' Louisa said slyly. 'They *are* rather good-looking, after all – and they have plenty of money. And some of them might even *be* film stars! I've heard people like James Stewart and Clark Gable are joining up.'

'I don't know what you're suggesting,' Elsie said with dignity. 'As if money and good looks would mean anything to me! And I don't know what you think is so funny about that, Thursday Tilford. If you laugh much more, your face'll get stuck.'

'Well, what shall we do anyway?' Thursday asked, trying to control her giggles. 'I don't feel like just sitting in a bar. Let's get a gharry and have a drive out.'

'Or we could have a camel ride,' Elsie suggested. 'We haven't done that yet. The camel park's over there, look. Come on, it'll be fun.'

If fun was to be had, it didn't seem to be shared by the camels. Groaning and complaining, their rubbery lips curled with disdain, they squatted in the sand so that the girls could clamber aboard and then rose grudgingly to their feet and lurched off into the desert. All along the road they were passed by gharries and taxis, each one ringing a little bell or hooting so that the camels snorted with bad temper and hunched their shoulders as if to toss their passengers on to the rough, gritty sand of the track. Thursday, clinging to the hump for dear life, wondered why in the world anyone had ever come to think about riding camels in the first place, and how they'd managed to catch and tame the first ones. Even now, it didn't seem to be a matter of co-operation or mutual enjoyment, like it did with horses. For two pins, she thought, if you let go of these beasts for more than a second they'd be off into the desert and never come back.

'Ships of the desert,' Louisa said. 'That's what they're called, because they can travel miles on the sand. Did you know they can go for days and days without drinking? They store water in their humps, or so I've heard.'

'So do the humps sort of shrink as they get thirstier? And what about those camels without humps?' Elsie asked, but Louisa didn't know. She'd never heard of a camel with no hump.

'It wouldn't really be a camel at all then, would it,' she said thoughtfully. 'Perhaps they don't store the water there after all.'

The desert was a strange place. At first glance, it seemed quite empty, nothing but dunes stretching away endlessly beneath the harsh blue sky, but when you looked more closely you could see that the dunes were rippled by the wind, and that they were continually changing. It really was a bit like the sea in slow motion, Thursday thought, a huge rolling swell of sand, with waves creasing its surface. And in a storm the motion would quicken, the sand swirling up into the air and sweeping into a different shape altogether, so that when it was over the landscape would have completely changed. No wonder people got lost out here in this vast emptiness, far away from habitation with no trees or buildings or landmarks of any kind to guide them.

'Let's go back,' she said suddenly, a strange sense of oppression sweeping over her. 'All this space – it's making me feel queer. I don't like it much.'

Back amongst the buildings, she slid down from the camel's back and grinned a little shamefacedly. 'Sorry, I just felt a bit peculiar out there, I don't know why. I've never been anywhere as *empty* as that before. I felt a bit sick and dizzy – stupid, I know.'

'It's not,' Louisa said. 'I've heard other people say the same thing. It's like the opposite of the claustrophobia Priscilla has. It's all so different from what we're used to – it's bound to affect us a bit.'

Thursday sighed. 'I know, but what about the poor men who feel the same way and have to go anyway, and fight? Oh, Lou, it just makes it all seem so much worse. We don't think about these things when we're at home. We send our boys off to war and we never really know what they're going to have to face. All those terrible stories they tell us in the wards – men being killed so horribly, lying there wounded for hours without help, perhaps dying out there all alone with nobody to look after them. And having to go to sea when they never wanted to, or out into the desert or the jungle. And what for? What's it all *for*?' She shook her head. 'Why did it all start, Lou? Did anyone have any idea it was going to spread like this? Didn't anyone ever *realise*?'

'I don't think they could have done,' Louisa said soberly. 'No one could ever have imagined all this. It's like a machine you don't know how to stop. You press a button, and it starts going and doing all sorts of things you didn't want it to and sucking other things in, and you can't find the button to press to stop it. That's what this war seems to be now. A machine that can't be stopped.'

Mark Sangster was an up-patient now and, since he was a doctor, able to be more helpful than most about the ward. He seemed to be always at Thursday's elbow, ready to hand her whatever instrument she needed, or leaning against the door of the sluice as she embarked yet again on a 'dhobey' of soiled bandages. Disturbed by his presence at first, and annoyed with herself – and therefore him – by her discomfort, she gradually became accustomed to it, but never felt as easy as she did with some of the other patients, nor the servicemen who invited her and the other girls out for a drink or a meal. She knew that this reluctance was unreasonable, but she couldn't explain it to herself, let alone to the other girls.

'I don't know what you've got against him, I really don't,' Elsie told her. 'I mean, he's the best-looking bloke on the ward, he's a good laugh and a perfect gent – and *those* two don't always go together, mark my words! What's more, he obviously fancies you. Why don't you kick over the traces and have a bit of fun?'

'You know why.' Thursday waved the pad of paper on which she was writing her daily epistle to Connor.

'Huh!' Elsie said scornfully. 'Didn't stop you having a bit of a kiss and cuddle with that NCO at the pictures the other night. *I* saw you. And what about all those good night kisses you handed out when you were on nights? I heard about them too. Gave the rest of us a bit to live up to, I can tell you.'

Thursday blushed. 'They don't mean anything, you know they don't. Well . . .' she hesitated and Elsie raised her eyebrows, 'they do at the time because I feel so sorry for the poor chaps. But they don't mean I'm in *love* with them.'

'So what about the NCO? Are you in love with him?'

'No!' Thursday looked down at the writing-pad again. 'Well, I don't know. When I'm with him – with any of them – I feel as if I might be. It's a nice feeling. I *want* to feel in love with someone, I want to kiss and cuddle and all that, but I don't think it's any special man, and I don't think it's serious. It's just – well, fun. You know.'

'Yeah, I know,' Elsie said quietly. 'We all want a bit of loving, the whole lot of us. And whether we've got someone waiting for us at home, or thousands of miles away like your Connor, we still want it. We want it *now* – not in God knows how many years' time, or perhaps never.'

Thursday sighed. 'Oh, Elsie, I don't know what I feel, half the time. I really do love Connor, I'm sure I do, but he's so far away, and we don't know how we'll really feel when we meet again. If we ever do meet again,' she added soberly. 'And meanwhile, here we are, and here are all those men, all of them going back to the fighting after their hospitalisation or their leave, and we'll probably never see them again. By this time next week, they could be dead. It doesn't seem wrong to love them just for a little while – when they're here and alive. It doesn't seem wrong to have fun and enjoy ourselves, just for a little while.'

'It's not wrong,' Elsie said robustly. 'It's natural. And I don't see as it does any harm. In fact, I reckon it does us all good.' She glanced at Thursday. 'So why don't you have some fun with Dr Sangster? Because I'm darned sure you like him, Thurs. I've seen you looking at him.' She waited a moment, watching her friend, and then said quietly, 'I'm right, aren't I? You do like him.'

Thursday looked up and met her eyes. Her face flooded with scarlet. She took in a breath, opened her mouth to speak – and then, quite unexpectedly, flung down the writing-pad and jumped to her feet.

'For heaven's sake, Elsie, leave me alone!' she cried, and stalked towards the door. 'Just don't keep *on* at me, all right?'

Several other girls, also engaged in writing letters or mending stockings or lying on their beds reading, glanced up in surprise. Elsie rolled her eyes at them, then inclined her head towards the wire screen door that Thursday had let swing violently behind her.

'Seems to me someone's getting a bit touchy,' she remarked. 'I wonder why.' She bent and retrieved the pad, placing it face down on the bed. 'Never mind, Connor,' she murmured. 'It won't be long now before she gives way and gets it out of her system. She'll be back then – don't you worry.'

Thursday walked out into the grounds, breathing quickly. Her heart was thumping uncomfortably and she could feel the ache of tears in her throat and the sting of them in her eyes. In all the time they'd known each other, she had never quarrelled with Elsie before. I don't know what's got into me lately, she thought miserably. I snap people's heads off for no reason at all, I feel like crying over the slightest thing and now I've rowed with Elsie. Over nothing.

No. Not over nothing. Over Mark Sangster.

But why should she quarrel with Elsie over him, of all people? Why was he so different from all the others – Johnny on board ship, Geoff the NCO who'd taken her to the pictures, Bob the Sergeant who'd taken her dancing, James the young Lieutenant who'd taken her to dinner in Cairo? She'd enjoyed herself with them, flirting and fluttering her eyelashes, she'd kissed them and let them hold her in their arms, knowing all the time that it would go no further than that, that this delicious feeling of being just slightly in love was doing no one any harm. Knowing too that the tiny undercurrent of danger – that they might really fall in love – added spice to the affair, yet could be kept under control. So why couldn't she let herself fall just slightly, deliciously, in love with Mark Sangster? Why couldn't she enjoy a similar, quite innocent, romance with him?

Because you might not be able to keep it under control, she thought suddenly, and her heart sank as she realised the truth. The attraction was too strong. The danger was more than a tiny undercurrent – it was a tide that could sweep her away. And he knew it too.

She leaned against the wall and stared up at the night sky. Here, close to the desert, the stars were clustered so thickly that you could scarcely have put a pin between them. The tall, fronded palm trees were silhouetted against their brilliance, swaying gently with the soft breeze, whispering a shush-shush; shush-shush. From somewhere beyond the hospital walls she could hear the sound of horses' hooves and the rattle of a gharry's wheels, or the softer plod of a camel. Now and then an Arab would call or the wail of Egyptian music drift across. From the Italian sector came the sweet, liquid sound of singing. A ripple of laughter sounded through the open, wire-screened windows of the building behind her, and she felt suddenly very lonely.

Elsie's right, she thought. We just want to be loved. And, perhaps even more, to *love*. It all seems to be passing us by. Here I am, almost twenty-four and I don't even know what it's like to love a man properly. And Connor might not even *want* me by the time we meet again.

A soft movement nearby made her turn. A tall, dark figure was standing close to the wall and she started in sudden panic. The man moved again and spoke in a quiet voice.

'You're looking very sad, Nurse Tilford. Care to tell me about it?'

'Dr Sangster!' she gasped. 'What – what are you doing out here?'

'The same as you, I imagine. Came out for a breath of air and a look at the stars.' He came to stand close beside her and stared up at the sky. 'Beautiful, aren't they? Millions of them. So magnificent. And so hard to believe there's a war going on down here. It makes me wonder why we do it – all this pitiful struggling and killing – when the universe is so vast and we're so very, very small.'

Thursday said nothing. She could feel the warmth of his arm, almost touching her through the thin cotton of her sleeve. Her heart was thudding and she felt almost sick. She moved away abruptly and said, 'I must go in. And so should you. You – you ought to be in bed.'

He turned his head and looked down at her, and for a moment she was afraid he was going to make one of his wicked remarks, designed to bring a blush to her face. Instead, he reached one hand up and touched her cheek with his fingertip. He let it trail gently down the line of her jaw until it rested beneath her chin, and then he tilted her downcast face up towards him.

'They say your name is Thursday,' he said. 'Is that true?'

'Yes. I was named for Armistice Day – it was the day I was born.'

He nodded. 'You must have interesting parents.'

Nobody had ever said that before. Thursday considered. 'They seem quite ordinary to me.'

'Well, so they would – you're an interesting person too. But it takes quite a lot of imagination and courage to give a baby an unusual name like Thursday.'

'My father was in the First War,' Thursday said. 'He saw a lot of things he never talks about. I think it meant a lot to him that I was born just then.'

'And do you mind if I call you Thursday?'

She felt herself blush. 'We're not supposed to—'

'Fraternise. I know. But I'm a doctor, so perhaps it makes a difference.' It didn't, so far as Thursday could see, but she knew Dr Sangster well enough by now to know that he liked to get his own way. That was one of the things that alarmed her about him.

'And you can call me Mark,' he said.

'Oh no, I—'

'Not on the ward, I know. But when we're off it. When we're together, on our own.'

Thursday stared at him. 'When are we ever going to be off the ward together, on our own?'

'Whenever I can manage it,' he said, and lowered his head to hers and kissed her lips.

Thursday stood very still. She felt his good arm around her shoulders. The damaged one was almost better, the plaster due to come off in a day or so, and then . . . She shivered suddenly and he drew back a little and looked at her. She could see the shine of the starlight in his eyes.

'Cold?'

'No,' she whispered, and laid her head against his chest.

'Thursday,' he murmured against her hair. 'Thursday, Thursday, Thursday . . . It's a beautiful name. A beautiful name for a beautiful girl.'

'No. You mustn't say that.' She lifted her head and stepped away, staring at him with fear in her eyes. 'You mustn't do this. Please.'

'Mustn't?'

'No. Please. I – I ought to go in now. You'd better go back to the ward, they'll be missing you.'

'Just a moment or two longer,' he said quietly, and drew her against his side again. 'Just let's stand here together for a minute or two and look at the stars.'

Thursday stood close, her head lifted. He felt warm and firm against her side, his breathing steady. The kicking of her heart slowed to a more peaceful rhythm and she sighed.

'Better now?' he murmured. 'I don't want to frighten you, Thursday.'

She nodded without speaking, knowing he could feel the movement against his shoulder. After a moment, still gazing at the stars, she said, 'They look so close, don't they? As if you could reach up and touch them.'

Mark released his hold on her shoulders and reached up, his hand open and fingers outstretched as if he were grasping for the brilliant pinpricks of light. Then he closed his fist and lowered it, opening it into Thursday's palm as if depositing something of immense value.

'There,' he said. 'A handful of stardust for you to keep, to remind you of the night of a million stars. Better than diamonds.'

'Yes,' Thursday said, staring down at her palm and imagining the glitter now cradled there. 'Better than diamonds . . .'

Chapter Fourteen

'There were two more poliomyelitis patients today,' Elsie said, sitting down to supper with the others. Having already had experience of infectious diseases in Haslar's Zymotics wards, she had been quickly moved to the same work in the 64th, but she was encountering diseases here that they'd barely heard of at home and sometimes found herself unable to mix with the other girls because of some infectious or contagious illness she was in contact with. She'd already nursed several men through diphtheria, which was a constant scourge, and she'd seen others die from it. Smallpox occurred from time to time, and those patients were removed immediately to isolation – a small hut or tent situated as far away as possible from the main hospital. Elsie had been told the story of one case, kept a mile away, which still managed to spread the infection back to the main buildings.

'Nobody knew how it was getting there. They knew it was coming from this poor bloke, because the new cases were all happening in the nearest ward – even though it was all that distance away. They thought of birds and rats, and set traps and everything, but it still kept coming out – and then the CO went over one day and noticed a trail of ants marching away from the tent. They were carrying bits of scab and stuff off the bloke's skin, and they were taking it all the way back to their nest, right under the hospital walls! Would you believe it? A *mile*. They had to move the isolation tent five miles away to get out of the pesky things' range!'

'Poliomyelitis? Isn't that what they call infantile paralysis?' Thursday asked. 'I thought only children got that.'

'No, older people can get it too. It can leave them paralysed and if it gets into their chest they just can't breathe.' Elsie helped herself to some rice and lowered her voice. 'And listen – don't spread it around – but someone told me today there's a case that might be *plague*.'

'*Plague*? You mean like in London?' Thursday asked, horrified. 'We did it at school. It's terrible—'

'I thought it didn't happen any more,' Priscilla said. 'Wasn't it rats that carried it?' She remembered the rats the QARMN had told them about and gasped, her hand to her mouth. 'But what will they do if it's true? We might all get it!'

'They've put him in isolation,' Elsie said. 'They're giving him M&B. He'll be nursed by volunteers – there's a vaccination, so they should be all right.'

A few days later there were more cases, when some Basutos arrived at the hospital in various stages of the disease. Some of the Zymotics nurses disappeared into isolation with them and Elsie said, 'I reckon they're going to be asking for more volunteers. If they do, I'll go.'

'Elsie! Won't you be scared?'

'Listen, I could get dip, or typhus, or smallpox – anything. Half the time they're in the ward for days before we even know what they've got. And I've had the vaccination.' She rolled up her sleeve to show them. 'Someone's got to go and help the poor blighters.'

Elsie's offer was refused, the Sister saying she was too valuable with the polio patients, but word of the epidemic was spreading around the rest of the hospital. Thursday, going on duty, found the men beginning to panic. Everyone had heard of the Great Plague of London and their injuries seemed like nothing beside this new threat. A young boy, no more than nineteen, reached out to Thursday as she passed and implored her to tell him it wasn't true. 'I learned about it at school. You come up in huge black lumps everywhere and just rot away inside. I'd rather go back to the front lines than that, I'd rather *anything*—'

'It's all right. You won't get it in here.' Thursday smiled at him, praying that it was true. She'd seen a rat outside only the night before. 'They're all in isolation. It's safe here.'

The men weren't convinced. The ward buzzed all morning with increasingly anxious voices, and in the end the Wardmaster himself came in and shouted for quiet. They fell silent at once, eyes fixed on him, but one man whispered to his mate that this was it, they were going to be told it was all over the hospital, it was curtains for the lot of them . . .

'I said, *quiet*!' The Wardmaster's brows came down in a heavy scowl. 'Next man to utter a sound gets put on a charge! Now listen, all of you. This panic about the plague has got to stop. You're acting like a pack of bloody babes in arms. Soldiers? I wouldn't give tuppence for any one of you. Strikes me you've been laying about in bed too long, getting soft. I've a good mind to tell the doctor to discharge the lot of you and send you back, bandages and all.' He paused and glowered at each man in turn. 'I've never seen such a disgraceful shower. And there's young girls like these VADs and QARMNs, not too scared to volunteer to go into the plague wards and nurse the poor blighters who've got it. Put you all to shame, they do.'

The men hung their heads. Thursday, glancing at their downcast faces, felt sorry for them. They'd been through a lot already, fighting in the desert with all its discomforts and then being wounded and brought back to a hospital which was scarcely luxurious. Some of them had lost families at home in the bombing too, or were afraid that their wives and sweethearts would grow tired of waiting for them. The threat of something as terrifying as bubonic plague had been just too much. It was almost too much for her too – like all the nurses, she was just as afraid but knew she mustn't show it.

'It's all right,' she murmured as she went round with lime juice after the wardmaster had gone to harangue another roomful of frightened men. 'They'll get it under control. You won't catch it here.'

That evening they heard that two of the Basutos had died and one of the nurses had caught the disease. They stared at each other in dismay.

'But wasn't she vaccinated?'

'It doesn't always work,' Louisa said grimly. 'Does anyone know who it is?'

'It's one of the QARMNs,' Priscilla said. She hesitated, glanced at Elsie, then added, 'I've volunteered as well. I went to Sister and asked for the vaccination this afternoon.'

'*You*, Priss? But you've always said you hated infectious diseases.'

'Well, so do we all.' She shrugged. 'I just feel I ought to do something – something more. I've been so lucky all my life.' She glanced down at the ring she always wore off duty. 'Quentin's out there risking his life, and I feel I ought to be doing the same. Not to be a heroine, or anything,' she added hastily, 'but to be – well, more worthy of him, if you know what I mean.'

'You're worthy of him already,' Thursday said at last. 'You don't have to put yourself at risk.'

'No, but it's what Elsie said the other day – someone's got to nurse the poor blighters. Anyway, there it is. I've volunteered – can't take it back now.' She gave them all a somewhat tremulous smile and brushed back her pale, spun-gold hair. 'So I shan't be here for breakfast tomorrow, I'm afraid. You can have my sausages between you.'

Thursday looked at her. She hadn't known Priscilla long, and would never have expected to be friendly with a girl from her background. But these days, she thought, you got to know people so quickly and class didn't seem to make any difference any more. Priscilla, Elsie and Louisa were almost like sisters – closer, in some ways, than real sisters. She bit her lip.

'You just be careful,' she said gruffly. 'Don't go taking any daft risks, and come back here the minute you can, see? We can't manage without you, Priss.'

'I'll be all right,' Priscilla said, giving a little nod. 'You don't have to worry about me, Thursday.'

'Worry?' Elsie said in her normal robust tones. 'Who said anything about worrying? I'm just looking forward to all those sausages!'

Once back on the wards, there was no time for worrying about anyone other than the patients.

'Captain Roberts has collapsed – dehydration. Ice!'

The order caught Thursday on her way to the sluice. Immediately, she wheeled round and set off at a fast walk for the other door. Dehydration was always a risk in the heat of the desert: no matter how hard you tried to keep the men's fluid levels up, every now and then someone would succumb to heat stroke and, if not dealt with at once, it could kill.

By the time she ran back, lugging buckets filled with ice and followed by an Indian orderly carrying more, the patient was stretched out on a bed, naked apart from a cotton sheet, with a fan whirring overhead. Sister snatched one of the buckets and tipped it out on to the bed. Thursday did the same with the other and, working swiftly, they began to pack the ice around his body, into his armpits and groin, and along his backbone. Another VAD arrived with the jugs and tubes necessary for a cold enema, and Sister began to set up saline and glucose drips.

'Keep dousing him with cold water,' she instructed Thursday, 'and don't move from his side. His temperature was up to a hundred and ten, so keep taking it. He'll have to be monitored until it comes right down, and then very gradually and gently rewarmed. It's a critical task.' She looked down at the shuddering body. 'I'll be back in ten minutes but if there are any symptoms, anything at all, call me at once, and *don't take your eyes off him for a second*, understand?'

Thursday nodded. She pulled up a chair and sat beside the patient, watching him closely. She knew that he could go into convulsions or even into a coma, and if that happened he would almost certainly die. A young Private had died of heat stroke only a fortnight earlier – he'd been brought in already in a state of collapse, and treatment had simply come too late. The whole ward had been upset by this needless death, not even caused by wounds, and the Wardmaster had decreed that there must be no more such deaths on his ward. Thursday, sitting beside the Captain, replenishing the rapidly melting ice and cooling his overheated body with more cold water, hoped desperately that this would not be the next.

Captain Roberts was beginning to show signs of recovery. His temperature was down a degree or two and Thursday signalled her relief to the Sister the next time she approached. 'That's excellent, Nurse. Now, he'll need very careful monitoring to get him back to normal. We're not out of the wood yet – but at least we can see the edge of the trees.' She felt the patient's pulse and nodded. 'You're doing very well, Tilford. You're an excellent worker.'

She departed again, promising once more to return within ten minutes, and Thursday continued to sponge her patient with cool water. He moved and moaned a little and she bent hastily, laying her palm on his forehead and praying that he wasn't going into a convulsion. With her free hand, she gestured for more cold water and the orderly poured it over the naked skin. Captain Roberts opened his eyes.

'What the hell?' His voice was no more than a mutter.

'You've got heat stroke,' Thursday told him, relief washing over her. 'You'll be all right but I'm going to stay here with you for a while. I'll get them to bring more ice.'

'Ice? If I'd known gin was part of the treatment . . .' His voice faded and Thursday smiled.

'It's not. And you'll be off alcohol for a while anyway. Just lie quietly and go to sleep.' She touched his forehead again and was relieved to find it less burningly hot.

The next time Sister came back, she decreed that he was out of the wood and Thursday was sent off for a brief tea break. She took her cup outside and sat in the shade, half her mind with Priscilla in the plague ward, and half wondering where Mark Sangster was now.

She had not seen him since the evening he had plucked the stardust from the sky. Overcome by a welter of emotion, so tangled that she barely knew what she felt, she had turned and scurried back into the building then and hidden in the washrooms. When she finally crept into the dormitory Elsie was in bed, and Thursday had slipped into her own bunk without disturbing her. The next morning they had been slightly awkward with each other, until Elsie suddenly threw her arms about Thursday and said, 'This is daft! We're not going to let a little thing like a man come between us, are we? I'm sorry I upset you, Thurs.'

'I'm sorry too,' Thursday said, wiping her eyes and grinning shakily. 'I was stupid, going off at half-cock like that.'

She didn't tell Elsie what had happened outside, however, and when she went on duty it was to find his bed already occupied by another patient. She looked at him in some surprise and Sister said, 'Oh, that's Major Lewis. He's a trauma – broken ribs, collar-bone, several shell splinters. He was admitted during the night.'

'What happened to Lieutenant Colonel Sangster?'

'He's gone. Doctor saw him this morning and decided he was fit to leave. He'll be back in, of course, to have his plaster removed and his final check-up, but there was really no need for him to be taking up a bed. I believe he's found a room at one of the local hotels.'

Thursday had gone back to her duties, feeling oddly perturbed. She had lain awake most of the night, her senses awakened by the encounter, reliving his touch and his kiss, hearing his words in her mind again and again. She'd thought of Connor, and her longing for him, for his warm presence, for the love that had grown between them and never been fulfilled, had brought an ache to her heart. I want so much to be loved, she thought, I want so much to love. But it's Connor I want. It is. It *is*.

It's a good thing Dr Sangster's gone, she thought now, as she leaned against the hospital wall and gazed out over the gardens. It's for the best. I shan't have to worry any more, I shan't have to feel guilty because I think about him. If he's not here, I'll be able to forget . . .

But she was wrong. She hadn't been able to forget.

The Battle of El Alamein had lasted for eleven days – eleven days in which the distant roar of gunfire could be heard, eleven days of horror in the desert, eleven days of the steady stream of wounded men being brought back to the hospitals. It had ended on 7 November with Rommel on the run and Lieutenant-General Montgomery – 'Monty' – victorious. His face and name were on the front pages of all the English newspapers and he was the hero of the hour. On 10 November, the day before Thursday's twenty-fourth birthday, he was both knighted and promoted, becoming officially General Sir Bernard Montgomery – but nobody took any notice of that. He was Monty to everyone now, and Monty he would remain.

'It just shows how important it is out here,' Thursday said. 'And Monty – he looks a funny little man when you see him, yet they obviously think he's the bee's knees at home. Fancy making him a knight, just like that. It's really romantic.'

'And we're a part of it,' Louisa agreed. 'It's something we'll always remember – being here during the Battle of El Alamein.'

'Let's celebrate,' Elsie suggested. 'It's your birthday tomorrow, Thurs – let's go out somewhere, somewhere posh. I've saved up a bit of money, we'll treat you. What d'you say, Louie?'

'Good idea. We'll go to the Cecil. Best bibs and tuckers. OK?'

They laughed, knowing they had only their white uniform dresses to wear. However, Louisa had found a local dressmaker not far from the hospital and got a new frock made, still white as per regulation but in sharkskin instead of cotton, and much more smartly cut. Sister had given it a look when Louisa had first worn it on the ward, but said nothing, and now all the girls had been there, marvelling at the cheapness and delighting in their new elegance.

Thursday never counted herself as being a year older until eleven in the morning, knowing that this was the precise minute at which she had been born on 11 November 1918. From early childhood, she had been taught to stay still and quiet during the two minutes' silence of remembrance, and only then allowed to celebrate. On this day, the ward fell silent, each man sombre as he thought of his fallen comrades, and then, as the hands of the ward clock passed the hour, she was startled by an enormous cheer.

'What on earth?'

'Happy Birthday!' shouted the Lance-Corporal in the nearest bed. 'Happy birthday to you!' And with both his arms, one still in plaster, he began to conduct the song, all the others joining in. 'Happy Birthday, dear Tilford, happy birthday to you!'

Thursday stood in the middle, her hands to her face, feeling the blush run up her neck and over her cheeks. 'Who told you?' she demanded, and then caught sight of Louisa grinning in the doorway. 'Oh, you wretch! It was supposed to be a secret.'

'Don't be daft,' the Lance-Corporal said. 'Birthdays shouldn't be secret. Not when it's a pretty young nurse like you, anyway. And not when it's on a day like today. That makes you special.' He foraged with his good arm under his pillow and brought out a box, wrapped in white paper and tied with ribbon. 'Here. This is from all of us.'

Thursday stared at him, then slowly took it. She looked doubtfully at the box and then around the ward.

'From all of you?'

'Thass right. Open it!'

She gave them a suspicious look and they laughed. 'It's all right, nursey! It ain't full of bed-bugs or nothing. You can open it up.'

Thursday untied the knot carefully. The ribbon was blue, and would do to tie in her hair later. She took off the sheet of white paper and smoothed it out. It was good enough to use again, for another present. The box inside was of chocolates – the best sort you could buy in town, and needing to be eaten quickly before the heat melted them. Thursday, beaming from ear to ear although there were also tears in her eyes, went round the entire ward offering the box to the patients.

'Here, no, love, we got them for you. You 'ave 'em tonight when yer off duty. Share 'em with yer pals.'

'I *am* sharing them with my pals,' Thursday said, offering the box again. 'This is my party, see, and you're all invited.'

'Well, all right, then,' said a Sergeant, taking one. 'I was always brought up that it was rude to say no. Thanks, nursey, and a happy birthday to you.' He leaned closer and whispered loudly, 'And we won't split on how old you are. We won't tell a soul you're fifty-two!'

The ward erupted into laughter and Sister appeared in the doorway, her face stern. 'Now what's all this noise? I could hear you all the way from B Ground. Tilford, shouldn't you be blanket-bathing now?'

'Yes, Sister. I'll start right away.' Her cheeks burning, Thursday hurriedly pushed the empty box under the nearest pillow. 'Now see what you've done!' she hissed at the occupant, but the soldier just grinned.

''S all right, love. She knows what was goin' on – I spotted her outside, hanging about waiting for us to give it yer.' He winked. 'Thanks for the party, ducks. Now let's get on with winning the war, eh?'

The newspaper stands in town were blazing their headlines in half a dozen languages. The girls, on their way for their evening out, stopped and grabbed all the English ones they could find, reading them eagerly.

'Look at this!' Louisa waved a copy of the *Egyptian Mail*. ' "ALLIES CAPTURE ORAN NAVAL BASE. *Us Tanks Close on Casablanca. Calm in Algiers after Surrender*." ' Her face was alight. 'They've invaded Algeria! Listen – it says that American troops have been landed all along the North African coast. They've lost a lot of men and some ships – British ones as well – and the French are putting up a terrific resistance, but they're winning and—'

'The *French*?' Elsie broke in. 'But they're supposed to be on our side!'

'Well, this is Algeria. I suppose it's different – they don't want to be invaded. And it's like Vichy France, isn't it? They've gone over to the Germans. I don't really understand it either, Elsie, but that's what it says here. And listen to what Mr Churchill has said about Alamein.' She cleared her throat and read aloud, her voice dropping almost involuntarily into the grave, sonorous tones of the Prime Minister:

' "This is not the end. It is not even the beginning of the end. But it is, perhaps, the end of the beginning." '

'I love the way he talks,' Elsie said after a moment. 'It's so clever – almost like poetry.'

'Anyway, the Allies are winning, that's the main thing.' Louisa folded the paper and grinned triumphantly. 'I'm going to send these papers home to my father. He'll be tickled pink.'

'He'll have heard all about it long before they get there.'

'Doesn't matter. He won't have seen *these* papers.' Louisa gave a little squirm of delight. 'Well, what a celebration for your birthday, Thursday! I think we'll have a bottle of wine, don't you? And something really, really scrumptious to eat.'

'It's a shame Priscilla can't be here,' Thursday said, looking up at the hotel façade. 'She'd have loved this.'

The Cecil Hotel was, as always, crowded with military, RAF and Naval officers, with plenty of their American counterparts. Tonight, the talk was all of the Algerian invasion and excitement was running high. The girls found a table and sat down, fending off a few attempts to occupy the fourth chair. 'Later on, maybe,' Louisa said with a smile at an undeniably good-looking American Lieutenant. 'This is a private celebration.'

'Say, ain't we all got sumpin to celebrate tonight?' he drawled, but he drifted away and the girls were left in peace to order their meal and their bottle of wine.

'It still seems strange to be able to eat like this, while the people at home are on rations for everything,' Thursday said, eyeing the mountain of couscous that had been placed before her. 'I'd never even heard of this before we came to Egypt. I suppose rice is the nearest to it, but we only ever had that as a pudding!'

'I reckon we'll all have some new ideas when we go home,' Elsie said, tucking in. 'And I bet we'll never use any of them. Too glad to get back to good old steak and kidney pie and roast beef! That's if you can still get 'em by then.'

'No, it'll be Spam and corned beef, and sardines on toast. So make the most of it,' Louisa said, giving Thursday a severe look. 'And no feeling guilty – this is your birthday party, remember!'

They were just finishing their ice cream – another thing the family back home wouldn't have seen for years, Thursday thought – and had ordered coffee when a shadow fell across the table. They looked up, expecting to see the American Lieutenant, and Thursday drew in a sharp breath.

'Mark – Dr Sangster!'

'Mark will do,' he said, smiling. 'May I join you?' He glanced at the vacant chair and laid his hand on the back.

'We're just going—' Thursday began, but Louisa smiled and nodded, and Elsie put her own hand on the chair to draw it out, her voice drowning Thursday's confused protests. 'Course you can, sir. We've got hours yet. Have some coffee.'

'I will, and perhaps you'll join me in a brandy to go with it.' He flicked his fingers at a hurrying waiter, then leaned his elbows on the table and smiled round at them. 'And how are you all getting along? What d'you think of the news about Torch?'

'Torch?'

'The invasion of Algeria – Operation Torch.' He grinned. 'I'd love to know how they choose the names for all these different operations – just open a dictionary at random and stick in a pin, I should think.' He glanced at Thursday. 'What do you think, Thursday?'

'Yes, I expect so,' she stammered. 'I don't know . . .' She glanced imploringly at Elsie, who leaped obligingly to the rescue.

'It's Thursday's birthday today, did you know? She was twenty-four at exactly eleven o'clock this morning – the eleventh hour of the eleventh day of the eleventh month. Here, I bet they pushed the boat out on your *eleventh* birthday, didn't they, Thurs? And you should've seen the blokes in the ward this morning, sir. Singing and dancing they were, practically – gave her a big box of chocolates and all. I wasn't there myself, of course, because I'm over in Infectious Diseases, but Louie here'll tell you, won't you, Lou?'

Louisa nodded, smiling. Thursday, looking from one to the other, caught a small conspiratorial grin pass between them, but before she could speak Mark was pulling something out of his pocket. He laid it on the table and she saw that it was a small box, wrapped in delicate silver gauze and tied with the thinnest of silver ribbons.

'I did know it was your birthday, Thursday,' he said quietly. 'You told me, remember? And I wanted to give you a little present.' He lifted her hand from the table and turned it over, placing the box in her cupped palm. 'Happy Birthday.'

Thursday stared at it. She looked up and met his eyes, then looked accusingly at the other two. 'You told him we'd be here! You laid a trap!'

They were both laughing. She felt her cheeks grow hot and bit her lip, not knowing whether to laugh with them or to cry. In her heart was a mixture of anger and a strange, burgeoning delight. In her hand, the little box felt both light and heavy.

'I—'

'Open it,' he said softly, and the other two joined in. 'Go on, Thursday, open it!'

Still scarlet, Thursday fumbled with the wrappings, trying not to tear the fragile gauze. It fell away and she opened the box, her fingers trembling.

'Oh,' she said, and then again, '*Oh . . .*'

'What is it? Let's see.' Elsie was craning over the table. Louisa, next to Thursday, leaned over for a better view. 'Oh, how lovely!'

'It's a star,' Thursday said shakily. 'A little silver star. Oh, *Mark*.'

'I wanted something for you to remember me by,' he said quietly. 'I'll be going back in a day or two. I wanted you to remember the night of the million stars.'

There was a moment of silence. The other two girls had drawn away, and it was as if Mark and Thursday were the only two people in the restaurant. She stared into his eyes, and felt the full force of the attraction he had for her, the passion that could so easily flare between them. Desperately, she tried to think of Connor, but he seemed very small and very far away. Mark was here – and he loved her. She could see it in the darkness of his eyes. And she – did she love him?

'May I take you back tonight, Thursday?' he asked. 'Elsie and Louisa can take a gharry. I want to ride with you under the desert stars and the rising moon, just this once. So that I too have something to remember.'

She was helpless, caught in a spell. She nodded, and the other two girls got up.

'We're going now, Thursday,' Louisa said gently. 'We'll see you back at the hospital.' She glanced at Mark Sangster. 'Look after her, Doctor. She means quite a lot to us, too.'

Then they were gone, their white dresses gleaming in the darkness outside the window. Mark and Thursday looked at each other. She felt a sudden flurry of panic and half rose to her feet. 'I ought to go too.'

'No,' he said, his hand burning on her arm, 'no, don't. Just give me this one evening, Thursday – this one last evening to be with you. It's all I'm asking.'

Thursday sank back into her chair. It was all he was asking. Yet, if he could only see into her heart, he would know that she was ready to give him the world.

'There are terrible things happening out there,' Mark said as the gharry clopped along the desert road. They had left Alexandria behind and, apart from their Arab driver, were alone under the million stars. Thursday was wearing her new brooch, pinned to the right shoulder of her white dress. On the left, she wore the marcasite Naval crown brooch that Connor had given her before he too had gone away to war.

'I know,' she said. 'This war goes on and on, and more and more people are being killed all the time.' She looked up at the velvet sky with its studding of diamonds. 'There must have been almost as many killed as there are stars.'

'I hope not,' he said. 'I hope there'll never be that many.' They were silent for a few moments, then he said, 'It's not just the soldiers, though, and the sailors and airmen – the fighters. It's all the civilians. And worse still, the people who were being ground under Hitler's heel when it all started and still are.'

'The Czechoslovakians, you mean, and the Polish?'

'And the Jews,' he said, 'forced to live in ghettoes, walled away from the rest of the cities, made to wear yellow stars so that they could be recognised in the streets and beaten and kicked. And the little villages where people have dared to resist. An American I met was telling me about a poster that's been going up, showing some poor fellow with a sack over his head, waiting to be shot. It's about a village called Lidice, where all the men were shot, and the women sent to concentration camps and the children to what they called "appropriate centres". And there've been places in France too where old men and women have been shot down in their own homes just because they were working in their gardens when the Germans passed by and didn't stand to attention. That's not war, Thursday, not honest fighting between trained men. It's hideous brutality.'

Thursday tried to find words, but there were none that were adequate. She sat close to him, seeking reassurance in the warmth of his body, and after a moment he slipped his arm around her and held her tightly.

'I'm sorry, sweetheart. I shouldn't be talking like this, not on your birthday and when I've got you to myself for the first time. But it's just because of that – because it's the first time, and it may be the last – that I have to tell you what I feel about it all.' His voice was more serious than she had ever known it. 'I expect you think I'm just a fool, clowning about in the ward, making ridiculous jokes – but there's more to me than that, Thursday. I care very much about what happens in this war. I care about what happens to the people – and I've never forgotten the people we started out fighting for. The ordinary people of those little countries that Hitler overran, the ones who didn't want any part of his regime but had no choice.' He paused, and she sensed that he was fighting down the passion in his heart. 'I just wanted you to hear that, Thursday, so that you know what makes me tick.'

'I think I do know,' she said softly. 'It's the reason I'm here too – why I became a VAD. I wanted to help. We all want to help.'

'And with all of us fighting on the same side,' he said, 'we're bound to win. We're *bound* to.' He turned his face towards her and she lifted hers. The kiss was as natural as breathing, and as soft as a sigh. Yet in the tension of his lips she could feel the desire that simmered in his heart, the longing of his body for hers.

'Oh, Mark,' she said, feeling a rush of all the yearning she had felt in the past months, the yearning that had touched her whenever a man took her in his arms for a dance, and most of all when she had thought of Connor, yet was now, here in Mark's arms with the warmth and hardness of his body against hers, more powerful than she had ever known it. 'Mark, I want you to love me properly. And I want to love *you*.'

He held her very close, his lips moving in her hair, drifting down her cheek and neck and into the softness of the cleft between her breasts. Her blood surged at his touch and a weakness invaded her body, so that her arms loosened about him and she lay back against the leather seat. Her fingers found his hair and she played with it, feeling its softness like tendrils catching at her heart.

He raised his head and kissed her again, then drew back a little. 'This is all there is,' he said quietly. 'I'm not going to ask you to go any further than this, Thursday. Believe me, it wouldn't be fair. But at least I have this to remember – we both have this to remember.'

'You'll come back,' she whispered. 'I know you'll come back.'

'I hope so.' He touched the silver star. 'And until I do, wear this for me. But,' his fingers strayed across her breasts and she shivered, 'you're wearing another man's brooch as well. I don't doubt your feelings for him, and I don't hold it against you. But one day you may have to decide which you'll wear for good, Thursday. One day – if we both come back.'

She stared at him, then hid her face against his shoulder. 'What sort of a girl am I? Connor—'

'He didn't want you to promise. He knew the future was uncertain. And I'm the same, Thursday. I know I may never come back. I just want to stake a claim, so that if I do, you'll give me a chance. Same as him. And if we both come back . . .'

'I don't know what I'll do.'

'You'll know,' he said, smiling down at her, and she could see the stars reflected in his eyes. 'You'll know.'

The gharry turned and made its way back to Alexandria. The two passengers sat very close, their arms wrapped tightly about each other. Thursday, her head resting against Mark's shoulder, felt a strange, poignant sense of loss, mingled with the headiness of passionate love. Of all the men she had known, kissed, flirted with and loved, only these two had really caught her heart. I love them both, she thought with dizzy bewilderment, and then, as if an icy finger had touched, her: *and I may lose them both.*

The gharry stopped at the hospital gates. In sudden anguish, she turned and lifted her face again, and Mark caught her lips with his. In the midst of their passion, she dimly heard the sound of the gate opening and closing, and then to her astonishment, Elsie's voice from close by.

'Thursday! *Thursday*! Come in, quick – we've had some patients brought in, bad burn cases off a ship that's been hit. One of them's asking for you, he wants you. Sister said to come out and find you – please, come quick!'

Thursday lifted her face away from Mark's. Elsie was standing beside the gharry, her eyes wide with anxiety. She held up her hands, begging Thursday to come.

'Someone who knows me? Off a ship? Oh, my God, Elsie – it's not –?'

'Just *come*!' Elsie urged. 'I can tell you as we go, but for God's sake, come quick. He – he –' she gasped and swallowed. 'Sister says he may not last the night.'

Chapter Fifteen

Mark refused to leave her. 'I'm a doctor,' he said. 'And still almost a patient – I don't get full clearance till tomorrow. Of course I'm coming.'

Thursday cast him an agonised glance. He understood immediately. 'It's all right, I'll stay outside. I want to make things easier for you, not more difficult.'

They can't be more difficult, Thursday thought as she raced through the corridors. If it's Connor – and who else could it be? – *nothing* could make things more difficult. Nor any easier. But she was thankful, all the same, for Mark's hand firm around hers.

Elsie paused at the door of the ward. 'He's here. Right by the office.' It was the bed where they put the most gravely ill patients, the ones who needed to be under Sister's eye, with special nursing; the ones who weren't expected to live past the next few hours. Thursday brushed the tears from her eyes, giving Elsie a brief, twisted smile of thanks, took a deep breath and went in.

Sister was by the bed. She rose as Thursday hurried in. 'He came in an hour ago. His ship was set on fire and sunk by an air attack. We've had a number of casualties, mostly burns. They're very extensive, I'm afraid, but he knew you were here and he's been asking for you. He's a member of your family, I believe.'

'My *family*?' Thursday began, and moved towards the bed, her eyes on the swathed figure lying there so still beneath the mosquito net. She stared for a moment, bewildered, then her hand flew to her mouth and she gave a gasp that was almost a tiny scream. 'Oh! Oh!' And then she fell silent, the tears falling thick and fast down her ashen cheeks as she dropped to her knees beside the iron bed.

Elsie's head came round the ward door. 'Thursday? You all

right?' She too looked at the injured man. 'Who is it? Can you recognise him?'

Thursday nodded, her hands covering her face, the tears seeping between her fingers. 'Yes, I can.'

Elsie tiptoed in. She cast another brief glance at the still figure and slid her arms around Thursday's shoulders. 'Who it is? It's not Dr Kirkpatrick, is it?'

'No,' Thursday said, taking her hands away from her face. She felt for a handkerchief and held it against her streaming eyes. 'No, it's not Connor.' She felt a huge wave of relief, followed almost at once by a surge of guilt. She looked up into Elsie's face. 'It's my young cousin's husband, Vic. I didn't even know he was in the Med. I don't suppose Dizzy did either. Oh, Elsie, it's *Vic* . . .'

She stayed by his bed all that night. Mark sat with her, his hand in hers as they watched over the young man who lay there, covered in dressings, a saline drip in his arm to replace the vital fluids he had lost. Thursday gazed at him, her heart filled with pity. Even if he lived, she thought, he would be badly scarred. And she thought of her young cousin, Denise, only just turned eighteen years old, who had defied her parents to marry him two short years ago. Eighteen years old, with a baby of eighteen months, and perhaps before the dawning of her second wedding anniversary, in only a few days' time, she would be a widow.

'It isn't fair,' she said, breaking into tears again. 'It isn't *fair*.'

The figure on the bed stirred, turning its head with difficulty. The burned lips parted and a cracked, almost unintelligible voice whispered her name. 'Thursday? Thursday, is that you?'

She leaned closer, controlling her tears. 'Yes, it's me, Vic. Thursday. Can you hear me?'

'Thursday,' he breathed again. 'Thursday . . .'

She glanced at Mark. 'I don't know if he can hear me.'

'Thursday,' the whisper came again, more insistently. 'I – can hear – Thursday.'

'Oh, Vic. Vic.' She touched his hand, the only unblistered part of him that she could find. 'Vic, you're going to be all right. You are. You're safe now, in hospital, and we'll look after you. *I'll* look after you. We'll patch you up and send you back to Denise as soon as we can. You're going to be all right, I promise, and you're going home to Denise.'

'Dizzy,' he whispered. 'Home to Dizzy.' There was a pause. 'And Leslie. Our Leslie. God, Thursday, don't let me die. Promise you won't let me die.'

'I won't,' she said, and felt the strength of her determination, willing it to flow through her fingers to his. 'I *won't* let you die.'

On that same day, Thursday's twenty-fourth birthday, the Germans marched into Vichy France 'to protect it from Allied invasion' and in the space of twenty-four hours had taken control of almost the entire territory. In Russia, they launched another offensive against the bombed and ruined city of Stalingrad. But in Libya, the Eighth Army, which had sent Rommel on the run, took Bardia without firing a single shot; in the Indian Ocean two Japanese ships were sunk by an Indian minesweeper, and in Papua, New Guinea, the Australian forces killed six hundred Japanese and took the town of Oivi.

The war surged back and forth, sometimes one side winning, sometimes the other. As Mr Churchill had said, it was not the end, nor anywhere close to it.

Sister came in just before the morning duty was due to come on. She laid her hand on Thursday's shoulder. 'You'd better go and get some sleep now, Tilford. You've done wonders to get him through the night. I never thought he'd make it.'

Thursday turned her head stiffly and looked up at her. 'I can't leave him.'

'You must. You've got to rest. I'll stay with him now, until the day staff come on. I'll make sure he has a good special.'

'Louisa,' Thursday said, turning back to Vic. 'Can he have Louisa? Wetherby,' she added in case Sister didn't know Louisa's Christian name.

'Yes, that'll be all right.' Sister looked at Mark. 'And you ought to be going too, Dr Sangster. You're looking as white as a sheet.'

'I know.' He hesitated, glancing at Thursday, who was whispering to Vic that her friend would be here shortly to take care of him, that she'd be back as soon as she could, that he was to stay alive until she did so. 'Thursday, I have to go now. I'm on duty at noon.'

'Yes.' Together, reluctantly, they left the ward. Outside, Mark paused and laid his hands on her shoulders. 'You know what this means?'

'You're going away.'

He nodded. 'This is the last time I'll see you, Thursday. Unless . . .'

She nodded. Neither of them wanted to finish his sentence. It was like asking for bad luck, tempting Fate. She felt her tired eyes fill with tears. 'Oh, Mark.'

'I'm not asking for any promises, Thursday,' he whispered against her hair. 'You've already made one, I know. And last night, when Elsie told you there was someone asking for you, I knew what you thought. It's him you love. Really love. I know that now.' He paused again, 'but keep the little star for me, won't you, and remember me, just once in a while. And if we're meant to be together, we will be.' He kissed her. 'Goodbye, Thursday, my love. Goodbye.'

'Goodbye, Mark,' she whispered and, dazed with tears and tiredness, returned his kiss and then pushed him gently away. Through a blur of tears, she watched him walk along the corridor, and then he turned a corner and was gone.

As she walked back to the dormitory she felt light-headed with fatigue, yet tingling with a strange, febrile energy that she was sure wouldn't let her sleep. I ought to have stayed with him, she thought. I ought to have stayed beside him, holding his hand, willing him to live. Oh, Vic. Poor Vic. And Denise, and little Leslie, who wouldn't even remember his father. I can't let him die.

The other girls were hurrying to get ready for duty. They stopped as she came in, and Elsie and Louisa ran across to her, searching her face. 'How is he?'

'He's still alive. Just.' She sank on to Elsie's bed and looked at Louisa. 'You're to special him. You will keep him going, won't you? He's in a dreadful state, but Sister says that now he's got through the night there's a chance. A – a very small chance.' She buried her face in her hands and her two friends sat down one on each side of her, their arms about her shoulders. 'Oh, Louie, Elsie, it's so awful when it's someone you know. Someone in your own family . . .'

'Ssh, ssh,' they murmured, rocking her gently.

'He looks so pitiful, all wrapped up in dressings. There's hardly a bit of him that hasn't been burned. It must have been so awful on that ship. I know we've seen men just as bad before, but somehow, seeing someone you know, it all comes home to you.' She was crying now, great harsh sobs forcing their way up from deep inside. 'I mean, I *know* him. I've sat and had Christmas dinner with him, my cousin's his wife, they've got a baby . . . I can't let him die, I can't. I'd never be able to face them again.'

'Thursday, Thursday,' Louisa said, holding her close. 'You mustn't upset yourself like this. It won't be your fault. How could it be? All you can do is be with him, like you've been with all those others you sat with. And if he does die—'

'He mustn't! He can't! I can't let him!'

'He won't, of course he won't,' Louisa said soothingly. 'But if he did, at least you'd know you'd given him comfort at the last. And you could tell your cousin that.'

'I can't let him die,' Thursday moaned, shaking her head. 'I *can't* let him die.'

Elsie took charge. 'Now listen to me, Thurs. You're getting yourself all worked up, and that ain't going to help no one, least of all young Vic. Me and Louie have got to go on duty now and what *you've* got to do is get some rest. You won't be no good to man nor beast else. Lou's going to look after him, and when you wake up and go back he'll be on the mend, you see if he's not. Now let's get you into bed.' She forced Thursday gently back against the pillows and began to unbutton her dress. 'Blimey, you've been in this frock all night. And look at this pretty brooch what Dr Sangster give you. I'll put it over here, see, with the other one. No, don't worry about getting up on your own bunk, you can doss down in mine. Why, you're worn out, and no wonder. Look, Lou, she's practically asleep already. Help me get her into bed, there's a pal.'

Thursday lay back, suddenly overwhelmed with fatigue, and felt thankfulness wash over her as the two girls slipped off her petticoat and stockings and spread the cool sheet over her. She felt Elsie sponge her face with water – just as if I were a patient myself, she thought dizzily – and heard a whispered goodbye. The other girls had already left the dormitory, and when the door closed there was silence.

Eyes shut, she lay waiting for sleep, drifting in and out of a tumble of fleeting dreams and memories. Denise as a toddler who won everyone's hearts, Denise growing up, a pretty but wilful schoolgirl, Denise out at work, painting her nails with red varnish, buying lipstick, making herself look older. Denise, meeting Vic Pearce from the Post Office in secret, telling him she was eighteen, letting him make love to her. Denise, pregnant, confessing to her parents, facing her father's wrath, insisting she wanted to get married . . .

Poor Uncle Percy, Thursday thought, half conscious, half dreaming. He hadn't liked it, but that was what had happened, and they'd got married in November – 15 November, the great raid on Coventry overshadowing what muted celebrations there had been. Two years ago next Sunday, Thursday thought, jerking awake. Their second anniversary. He *mustn't* die.

She slept at last, worn out by anxiety and a day that seemed to have gone on for ever. And when she finally woke, it was to find Elsie and Louisa beside her bed, gazing down at her.

Thursday blinked at them. For a moment or two, she couldn't understand what they were doing there, nor why she was in Elsie's bunk instead of her own. Then memory flooded back and she started up.

'What is it? Why are you here? How's Vic? He's not dead?' She stared accusingly at Louisa. 'You haven't let him die – and me not there!'

'Ssh. It's all right.' Louisa reached out to touch her shoulder. 'He's not dead, Thursday. He's very, very ill, and Sister still doesn't know if he'll make it, but he's still alive and he's asking for you. We're here because we're off duty now – you've slept all day – and as soon as you're ready, you can go back on the ward. But,' the pressure of her hand increased, 'Sister says you must have something to eat first. We aren't to let you even think about going back without a good meal inside you.'

Thursday stared at her. Then she nodded and swung her legs out of the bed.

'I will. I'll have a shower, and then I'll get a meal. Then I'll go back.' She stood up and gave them both a hug. 'Thanks, Louie. Thanks, Else. You've been marvellous.'

She hurried off to the washrooms, feeling suddenly hungry and ready for something to eat. It seemed a long time since supper last night. Since the meal at the Cecil.

The Cecil! She stood beneath the cool spray, shocked by the realisation. Was it only yesterday that it had been her birthday, only last night that they had gone out together, the three of them, to celebrate? Only last night that Mark had found them there – by arrangement, she strongly suspected – and given her the star brooch? Only last night that they had driven out to the desert together and kissed under the million stars?

It seems a lifetime away, she thought, reaching for the sponge and squeezing it over her shoulders. And now he's gone. He was leaving at noon. And I may never see him again.

She closed her eyes and felt a tear trickle slowly out between her lids and down her cheek, mingling with the soapy water. At least he didn't ask me for another promise, she thought. And I didn't break the one I had already made.

Not quite.

Thursday stayed beside Vic for seven nights without taking a break, until the Army doctor was as sure as he could be that the young man would survive. 'There can never be absolute certainty,' he told Thursday just outside the ward. 'There could still be complications – heart, kidneys, further shock – but I'd say he's out of the worst of the wood. There are just a few bushes to squeeze through now.' He smiled at her. 'He's a relative of yours, I understand.'

'Yes, sir. My cousin's husband.'

'Well, he and your cousin have a great deal to thank you for, er . . .'

'Tilford, sir.'

'Tilford. Yes. Sister's told me you've nursed him devotedly. She says he would certainly not have come this far without your dedication. We didn't expect him to come through the first night, you know.'

'No, sir, I know.'

'It makes a lot of difference,' he said, 'if a patient has someone beside him, someone who cares. Even if the patient dies, the death itself seems to be easier in some way. I suppose that's why a priest can be so helpful, even if the man isn't religious. But to have someone like you – someone who seems able to give strength as well as comfort,' he patted her shoulder, 'well, it's a great gift, Tilford. A very valuable gift.'

Thursday bit her lip and looked down. She felt suddenly close to tears, and desperately tired. For a week she had spent every spare off-duty moment, as well as all her duty hours, beside Vic's bed, holding his hand, talking to him, telling him everything she could think of about Denise – how she'd been like a fairy child, so small and delicate, how she'd enchanted everyone she met, how she'd grown up able to twist the whole family round her finger – even her father. Until . . . but Thursday had veered away hastily from what had happened after she met Vic. Instead, she'd begun to tell him about her own family, about Steve and Jenny, about her own days as a tailor's apprentice, about her little dog Patch and Auntie Maudie's Jack Russell, Nipper, and Snowy the stately white Persian cat.

On and on she talked, her voice no more than a soft murmur, repeating the same stories over and over again as the nights wore on. She believed and hoped that they kept Vic's brain alive, that as long as she could hold his attention he wouldn't die. He wouldn't want to die. And the longer she kept him alive, the better chance his body had of healing itself, of mending the ravaged flesh.

Sometimes he slept, and she sat quietly, still holding his hand, watching his face for any sign of a change. Gradually, his sleep became more peaceful, more healing, and she knew that her strategy was working. He was staying alive. He was getting better.

On the first morning, she had asked Elsie to go into town to send a telegram to Denise to tell her that Vic was here. After that, she wrote letters every day, telling her cousin of his progress, constantly assuring her of her determination that he would get better, that he would come home again. She didn't tell her how badly burned he was, nor that if he did recover his face and body would be badly scarred. That could come later. For now, it would be enough for Denise to know that he was here and being cared for.

The plague epidemic was almost over. Two Basutos had died and one nurse, but everyone else seemed to be recovering. And then another patient went down with the disease, and the VADs were shocked to learn that it was Priscilla.

'*Prissy!*' Elsie said, running into the mess one suppertime to tell the others. 'We heard this morning. It's awful. I mean, she was vaccinated and everything. I can't believe it.' Tears ran down her cheeks and she sat suddenly on the nearest chair. 'Poor, *poor* Prissy.'

'She'll get better,' Thursday said, wishing she felt sure of it. She'd been eating her supper as quickly as possible so as to go on duty with Vic. 'The others have, haven't they?'

'Not all of them. There was that QARMN, she died.' Elsie stared up at them, her mouth working. 'I can't bear to think about it. Our Prissy, all covered in black lumps. They bleed and ooze pus and—'

'Don't!' Thursday cried, covering her ears. 'It's horrible, *horrible*. She's so pretty. Elsie, she's got to get better, she's got to.'

'Of course she'll get better,' Louisa said. 'Of course she will.'

They stared at each other. Bubonic plague. It was one of the most frightening diseases they had ever heard of. It could kill within days, and not everyone did get better, even if they'd been vaccinated.

'She's engaged too,' Elsie said miserably. 'Quentin.' For once, she spoke the name without trying to sound funny. 'Shouldn't we inform him? I don't even know what ship he's on.'

'I expect Sister knows,' Louisa said. 'They took all our family details when we arrived, didn't they? I told her about Andrew, so she'll know about Quentin.'

Thursday stood up. 'I've got to go on duty. Vic'll be waiting for me. Elsie, you'll let me know if anything happens, won't you?'

'Course I will,' Elsie said. 'She'll be OK in a day or two, Thurs, don't you fret.' But her normally cheerful voice was subdued and she brushed her hand across her eyes again.

Thursday hurried back to the ward, praying that she was right. The thought of that pretty face with its cloud of spun-gold hair, blackened by the plague, the image of those slender arms and legs swollen by buboes, were too horrible to contemplate, yet she couldn't dismiss them from her mind. I've got to though, she thought. I've got to stop thinking about Priscilla and concentrate on Vic. Like the doctor said, he's not completely out of the wood yet. And it's up to me to get him better, for Denise and Leslie.

Vic was sitting up in bed when she came through the door, his dark curls falling over his eyes. His blisters were healing and new skin beginning to form; it seemed that the burns hadn't been so deep as was first thought, although he would certainly be scarred and would not be sent back to the fighting. Instead, once recovered, he would be given support work behind the lines.

As soon as she came in, he began to make his presence felt.

'Time you washed out some of these bandages, Thursday. I've

had this one on since yesterday. Where's that other nice girl, the one who looked after me during the day? Louie, that's the one I mean. She didn't bully me like you do. Always making me wash when I don't want to and sleep when I'm wide awake, and waking me up to give me that horrible medicine. I don't know why I had to fetch up in a ward with my cousin-in-law, I really don't.'

'It's a judgement on you,' Thursday told him briskly, sweeping under his bed. They had developed an easy, bantering relationship, far removed from the deep, anxious bond that had been formed during the early days and which was still there, hidden beneath their teasing. 'And if you don't behave yourself I'll write and tell Denise. She'll have something to say, I can tell you!'

'Go on, she worships the ground I walk on,' he said lightly, and Thursday stopped what she was doing and looked at him.

'Yes,' she said slowly, 'I believe she does.'

There was a moment's silence. Then Vic said quietly, 'And I think the same of her too, you know. I wasn't sure to begin with – I mean, I knew I fancied her a lot, I didn't want any other girl while we were going out together – but when she told me about the baby I was proper shaken. I didn't know what to do. I'd never thought of getting married, not then. And later, when I found out how old she was and thought I might get the police after me, might even get sent to prison – well, I was in a muck sweat. I nearly cut and run, only there was nowhere to run to. And there didn't seem to be anything else to do but get married. It was a proper mess, I don't mind telling you.'

'Yes,' Thursday said, 'it was.'

'And then, when we did get married, living with her mum and dad – it wasn't easy. Not until the day we heard Leslie had been killed.' He paused. 'I was the first one home that day – found her mum in a proper state. After that, it seems awful to say it, but things were a bit better. And then when little Les was born and Dizzy's dad come round to him – well, it all seemed different. And I never thought no more about being trapped or anything like that. Dizzy was my wife and we had a kid, and everything seemed all right after all.' He paused. 'And then I got me papers and got put in the Army, and that was it. Basic training, and then off. I haven't seen her or the kiddy since.' He bit his lips, healed now but pulled a little to one side by the puckering scar that crinkled the whole of one cheek. 'It's all I want,' he said in a low voice, 'just to get home to my wife and kiddy and be a proper family. Get our own place – couple of rooms somewhere, maybe a little house later on – and be a family. Because that's what it's all about, isn't it?' He waved a hand. 'All this fighting and suchlike – it's all about people living ordinary lives, with their families. Isn't it?'

'Yes,' Thursday said, staring at him. 'Yes, that's what it's all about.'

She went on with her sweeping. Families. That was what it was all about – freeing the world so that ordinary people could live peaceful lives with their families.

A simple enough wish. Or so you might think.

Priscilla died the next day. The disease had rampaged through her body, and she had had no chance. The girls clung to each other, weeping, and the entire unit was stunned with grief.

'It's so unfair,' Thursday said. 'She was young and pretty – she had everything to live for. I just don't see why it had to happen.'

'Life isn't fair,' Elsie said bitterly. 'Didn't no one ever tell you that?'

'But Priscilla . . .'

'Listen, we all think that, don't we? What about your Mike? And your Cousin Leslie, shot down in the Battle of Britain? And our Dave?' she added in a lower tone. 'They had everything to live for too, and they were young even if they weren't pretty.'

'I know,' Thursday said, 'but they all died because of the war. That could happen to any of us. But Prissy – getting that horrible disease. Well, it seems different, somehow.'

They were silent. Then Louisa said, 'What about the funeral, Elsie?'

'It's tomorrow. We can't even go – it's got to be in a special place, out in the desert.' Elsie shook her head. 'But there's going to be a service for her next week, in the English church. We can all go, and Sister says we can choose one of the hymns.' Her voice trembled. 'I thought – I thought perhaps "All Things Bright And Beautiful".'

'Bright and beautiful,' Thursday said quietly. 'That's exactly what she was. Yes, Elsie. Let's have that at her service.'

Priscilla was the last person to catch the plague and the service in her memory was the last to be held for its victims. Every nurse, VAD and doctor who could be spared attended, and when they sang the hymn that the girls had chosen, every eye brimmed with tears. Afterwards, the wards were subdued for a day or two and then gradually returned to normal. As the priest who had officiated quoted, 'In the midst of life, we are in death' – but life must, nevertheless, go on.

'Poor Prissy,' Elsie said as they walked in the hospital grounds. 'We didn't know her long, and we laughed at her a bit but she was a smashing girl. It's awful that she should die like that.'

Louisa nodded. 'I'm writing to her people. And Quentin. I'll go and see them when we go home, too. Tell them about some of the times we had together.' She sighed. 'Well, at least it's over for her. She doesn't have to suffer any more.'

It was a poor comfort, Thursday thought, but all they had. And it had been quick, too. But she could not forget the cruelty of it – the cruelty of such a death, come needlessly, a death that Priscilla herself could have avoided by simply not volunteering. 'She was a heroine,' she said quietly. 'Just as much as if she'd been fighting. She deserves a medal.'

Vic's improvement continued. Sooner than Thursday had dared to hope, he was being discharged and returning to his regiment. His left arm was damaged and nothing could be done about his scars, but he was in better shape than many who left the hospital and when he said goodbye to Thursday he held her tightly.

'We never knew each other all that well back home,' he muttered. 'Never had much time, did we? But I reckon we know each other pretty well now. Know things none of the rest of the family do, eh?' He tried to grin, but his mouth twisted and Thursday felt tears sting her eyes. 'I reckon you've been more than an in-law to me, Thurs. More than a cousin, too. More like a sister – a real, good sister.'

'I'm just glad I was here, Vic,' she said, hugging him in return. 'I'm glad I was able to be with you, especially in that first week or two.'

'I tell you what, if you hadn't been I don't reckon I'd be here now. It was you kept me going, Thursday. All that talking you did, about Dizzy and the family and all that – I couldn't slip away, even if I'd wanted to.' He thought for a moment. 'I did want to, you know, when they first brought me in. I didn't think I could take it, you see.

And then I found out where I was, and somehow or other I remembered you were here in the 64th, and I asked if you were around. I wanted to give you a message for Dizzy, tell her I loved her, and then I was going to just hand in my dinner-pail, as they say. Close my eyes and say bye-bye. But you wouldn't let me. Kept on and on at me – "you're not going to die, you're going to be all right, I won't let you die" – and making me want to stay alive so I could go home again, and be with Diz and the kiddy.' He looked into Thursday's wet eyes. 'That's all I want now – to be back home with my family – and it's all because of you, Thursday. You're a heroine, that's what you are.'

'For God's sake, stop blathering and go!' Elsie's voice broke in from behind them. 'You're making her even more big-headed than she is already! We've got to live with her, remember.' She gave Vic an affectionate wallop on his backside. 'Go on, get out of here before we find something else wrong with you.'

Thursday laughed, and Vic grinned and gave Elsie a smacking kiss. 'If I wasn't already spoken for, I might have tried my luck with you,' he told her. 'I always did like the brassy blonde ones.' He shouldered his kitbag and gave them both a salute. 'And remember me to Louie too. I said goodbye to her last night, but she said she might nip out for a minute if she could. I expect she's busy.'

'Yes,' Thursday said. 'I expect she is.' She stood with Elsie and watched him march off down the drive, between its avenue of date palms, and sighed. 'Well, there he goes. At least he won't be fighting any more, but – well, I wonder if he will survive to go back home, Elsie. Nobody knows for certain, do they? Even we don't know what's around the corner for us.'

'And that's probably just as well,' Elsie said bracingly. 'Come on, Thurs – back to work. I'm only over here because I managed to wangle a message to the labs. If I'm not back in two ticks, I'll be jankered!'

Thursday smiled at her. 'And so will I. But the first thing I'm going to do when I come off duty is write to Denise and tell her that Vic's been discharged. You know, I don't think she's ever realised how near to dying he was.' She paused, then added quietly, 'I don't think she ever will.'

Chapter Sixteen

W*hen it's the right one*. The words had come back into Thursday's mind over and over again as she settled back into Haslar during the tumultuous summer of 1944. Connor was the right one, she was certain of it, she *knew* it – and yet . . . And yet there was that other face in her mind, that dark, thin face with the teasing eyes that seemed to see and to know so much. No, she thought, no. I've put Mark Sangster out of my mind. We've said goodbye. He's not coming back for me, and I'll never see him again.

And now, almost two years after they had said goodbye, here he was at Haslar, where she had never dreamed he might come, lying on a trolley and waiting to go into the operating theatre – a casualty of Market Garden, looking to her for comfort.

And still able, with one glance from those dark eyes, to turn her heart over in her breast.

Mark's wounds had looked worse than they were. The gash on his cheek would leave a scar for life – not the ugly puckering that Vic and so many others had been left with, but a thin white line that would probably even enhance his looks. The kind of romantic scar that a Regency buck might have received in a duel, Thursday thought, gazing at him as Surgeon Commander Sharp sewed up the final stitches and straightened himself. There were other cuts and some deep grazes, and he'd broken his arm again – the same one as before – and a couple of ribs, but in a few weeks he would be healed and ready to go back into action. Like a cat, he seemed to have nine lives.

'I can't believe he's here,' Elsie said when she told them. 'I'd have thought he'd be in Italy. What on earth was he doing in France?'

'Wasn't he in the Parachute Regiment?' Louisa asked. 'Perhaps he went over to help bring people back from Arnhem.'

'I suppose he must have done.' Thursday thought of the stories she had heard, of paratroopers shot down as they descended, hanging in trees, impaled on wire fences. She put her hands over her face, fighting the sudden sickness. 'Oh, *Mark* . . .'

The others glanced at each other. Louisa reached out and laid her hand on Thursday's arm and Elsie put her arm around her. Their concern brought tears flooding from her eyes and dripping between her fingers. She drew in a long, shuddering sob. 'Sorry.'

'It's reaction,' Elsie said. 'Reaction' was what they always said when someone broke down unexpectedly. It didn't have to be a reaction to something that had only just happened – everyone knew that it could be delayed, especially if there were a lot of other things going on. But when it was all over and there was time to breathe again, people often did break down. 'We've all been working flat out ever since we got back. And it must've been a shock, seeing him like that with no warning.'

'It was just *thinking* of him, parachuting down and being shot or caught on barbed wire,' Thursday said shakily. 'We've heard such awful things – I just couldn't bear it.'

Elsie and Louisa glanced at each other again. 'He's here now,' Louisa said gently. 'You don't have to worry, Thursday. He's safe.'

'I know. I know. And he isn't even very badly injured.' She took her hands away from her face and gazed at them through still streaming eyes. 'I don't know why I'm behaving like this. I haven't heard from him for nearly two years. I haven't even *thought* of him. Well,' she added honestly, 'I've tried not to. And I never expected to see him again. So why am I crying because he's here? When he's not even badly wounded? Why?'

Elsie looked as if she could have answered that but chose not to. She bit her lip and glanced at Louisa again. Louisa shook her head very slightly. 'It's just because it was so unexpected, Thursday. And you were fond of him, you know. There's nothing wrong in that.'

'Isn't there?' Thursday asked. 'Even when it makes me cry like this – when I can't bear to think of him out there, hanging on some barbed-wire fence, being machine-gunned by German soldiers, bleeding to death and *me not there*?' She stared at them, white-faced. 'I haven't seen him for two years – we said goodbye – I never expected to see him again, and yet when I do, I break down like a lovesick schoolgirl! Because that's what I am – *lovesick*. And I shouldn't be. I've got Connor. Why should I be crying like this over someone else? I've no right to!'

'We can't help who we cry for,' Louisa began, but Thursday shook her head violently.

'We can! We *can*! I wouldn't be like this over Mark if I really loved Connor, I couldn't be.' She waved her hands in despair, then ran them through her brown hair. 'But I do love him, I *do*! I don't understand it!'

Louisa touched her arm again. 'Don't try, Thursday. You've had a shock and it's brought it all back to you. And you've been working hard all day, for weeks now. Elsie's right – we all need a break. You'll feel better when you've had a bit of time off; it'll help you get things back into perspective.'

Thursday stared at her. Then she wiped her eyes with the back of her hand and shook her head again, more slowly. 'I don't think it's going to make any difference. I'm in a muddle now and I'm going to stay in a muddle.' She heaved a sigh and rubbed her hand over her forehead. 'Oh, I'm such a selfish person! Thinking about myself and my own feelings, when all the time Mark – when *all* these poor men— Oh, Elsie!' She broke off and covered her face again, her shoulders shaking. 'Oh, Lou!'

The two friends sat close to her, their arms about her. Over her head, they exchanged silent messages. It was natural, Elsie's eyes said. Thursday was worn out and seeing Dr Sangster had been just the last straw. It didn't really mean anything. She needed a rest, a bit of time at home with her family. Once she'd had that, she'd be herself again, loyal and strong, keeping her promise to Connor Kirkpatrick and looking forward only to his return.

Louisa read the message and sighed. She'd seen the look on Thursday's face after she'd said goodbye to Mark in the desert; she'd seen the longing there and the shadows in her eyes over the past two years, and she'd known that they weren't always for Connor.

It would have been better, she reflected, if Mark Sangster had never come to Haslar.

Thursday dithered for almost a whole day before going to see Mark in his ward. He'd been weaker than expected from his injuries and took some time to recover from the anaesthetic. Ellen Bridges, who was specialling him, told Thursday that he was thought to have been out in the open for some time before being found.

'Has he asked about me at all?' Thursday enquired, trying to appear casual. 'Only he was conscious when he came into theatre and I think he recognised me. I just wondered if he remembered it.'

'Oh, is that what he's been on about?' Ellen said with a grin. 'We thought he'd got a date next Thursday! Keeps on and on, he does. You'd better go and see him, he's driving us all mad.'

Thursday gave her a suspicious look, not sure whether the other girls had told Ellen about her relationship with Mark, but Ellen met her eyes with total guilelessness. The trouble with Ellen was, you never knew when that straight face was real and when it wasn't. But she didn't think Elsie or Louisa would have gossiped.

'He seems a real nice bloke,' Ellen said innocently. 'Ever so good-looking, too. If it was me he was asking for I'd be there like a shot.'

'Well, I'm afraid he'll have to wait,' Thursday said aloofly. 'I can't visit him yet, I've promised to go with Elsie this afternoon to see her mum. I might pop in tonight before I go on duty.'

Ellen sighed. 'I'll tell him. Maybe he'll give me a chance instead.' She rolled her eyes. 'He was saying something about dinner at the Savoy. Not over in Southsea – there's one in London, he says, proper posh.'

Thursday gave her a look of exasperation. 'You're having me on, I know you are! He hasn't said any such thing, and if he does you might as well accept the invitation, because I'm not going to!'

Ellen laughed, and Thursday gave her another look and marched away. Ellen Bridges knew a good deal more than she was letting on, she thought, and if Elsie and Louisa hadn't told her, there was only one other person who could have done. She wondered just what he'd been saying, either when he was still under the anaesthetic and rambling a bit, or when he'd come round.

Elsie's mother was staying with her own mother in Gosport. The old lady lived close to the railway line in a maze of tiny streets. Thursday had often gone to visit the family when they lived in Portsmouth, before the house was bombed and Elsie's brother Dave killed, and had been to her grandmother's house for Christmas dinner soon after, but she'd only managed one visit since returning from Egypt. She cycled beside Elsie along the Avenue and then past the cemetery, turning off just before the slope of the railway arch.

'The only hill in Gosport, that is,' Elsie remarked. 'Dunno why it's called Ann's Hill, or who Ann was. Not much of a hill anyway, but then what d'you expect of Turktown?'

Thursday grinned. As a 'Pompey' girl, Elsie never missed an opportunity to disparage Gosport. Portsmouth people, she'd found, had no time for the smaller town on the other side of the harbour and knew very little about it. Most of them had been across on the ferry at some time and walked up the High Street and, finding no bigger shops than a rather small Woolworths and Littlewoods, had turned and walked back, wondering why they'd wasted their time. Few had ventured as far as Stokes Bay or even Lee-on-the-Solent – why should they, when they had Southsea on their doorstep? – and parts like Rowner, Brockhurst and even Alverstoke might as well have been in a foreign land.

'Doesn't bother us,' Gosport people said, shrugging. 'We can go over to Pompey any time.' And they did, to work, shop, go to the cinema – even though Gosport had three of its own – or to dance. Gosport, with all its fortifications and moats, was left mostly to the Army, the Navy and the Marines – a garrison town.

Thursday rather liked it. When she had first come here she'd been fascinated by the redbrick forts and moats that surrounded the town and enraptured by the sea which turned up in unexpected places, reaching creeks like long fingers right into what looked like ordinary little backstreets far from the shore. You could walk past a row of plain little workman's houses and find yourself suddenly faced with the bobbing masts of a cluster of sailing boats and dinghies. The harbour too was always bustling with ships, with a spectacular view of Portsmouth from the ferry approach: the masts and black rigging of HMS *Victory*, Nelson's flagship, just visible in its dry dock in Portsmouth dockyard, and the square tower of the cathedral tucked behind the rounded bastion of the sallyport, to remind everyone of a glorious past.

'How's Eddy?' she asked as they turned the corner into the little cul de sac where Elsie's grandmother lived. 'Are your mum and dad going to let him come home soon?'

Elsie made a face. 'Not just yet. You can't blame them – not after losing Dave the way they did. He's safer out in the country, Mum says, and I reckon she's right. It might look as if we're winning, but I reckon Hitler's still got a trick or two up his sleeve.'

They propped their bikes against the garden wall and went into the cottage. It was tiny inside, with two small rooms downstairs, two bedrooms above and a scullery tacked on to the back. The lavatory was outside, beyond the scullery, but at least it was a flushing one – at the bottom of the garden was a small wooden hut that had once housed a bucket under a plank of wood with a hole cut in it. Thursday shuddered at the thought of creeping down there at night with a candle. No wonder they'd all kept chamber pots under their beds.

Old Mrs Jenkins was in a chair beside the fireplace, and Mrs Jackson was out in the scullery mixing up a cake. She popped out as soon as she heard the door, her face lighting up. She looked thinner than Thursday remembered her, her cheeks drawn and her eyes shadowed. She still hadn't got over losing her elder son Dave, who had been killed in an air raid as he went up to the house to make cocoa for the family in the Anderson shelter at the bottom of the garden. And she'd been separated from her younger son since then too, sent out to safety in the country. No wonder she looked so unhappy.

However, she was obviously delighted to see her daughter, and pleased to see Thursday as well. She hugged her and then held her away, examining her face. 'You're looking well, Thursday, but you've got thin. Are they feeding you right?'

Thursday laughed. 'I eat like a horse! We all do. It's the hard work that keeps us slim.'

'Well, it don't seem to have done much for our Elsie,' Mrs Jackson said, looking at her daughter's ample figure. 'Perhaps she doesn't work like you do.'

'I flipping well do!' Elsie exclaimed, dipping her finger in the bowl of cake mixture. 'It's just the way I am and always will be. Pleasantly plump.'

'Yes, and you'll be a lot plumper if you eat all that cake mixture before it's even baked,' her mother said, snatching the bowl away. 'There's half our egg ration in that bowl, I'll have you know. Sit down and talk to your gran while I make a cup of tea and I *might* find a couple of broken biscuits in the tin.'

Elsie grinned and plonked herself down in a kitchen chair beside her grandmother, while Thursday lifted the old tabby cat out of the second armchair on the other side of the small fireplace and sat down with him on her lap. Elsie took the shrunken old hand in hers and stroked it gently. 'How are you, Gran? Is our Mum looking after you properly?'

The faded eyes, once cornflower blue like Elsie's, were weak and rheumy and had lost most of their sight, and the old lady's face was a mass of deep wrinkles but her smile lit her whole face. 'Is that our Else? Marge told me you were coming. Brought that nice friend of yours with you, have you? Monday, or whatever her name is?'

'Thursday,' Elsie said with a grin. 'Yes, she's here, sitting right opposite you with old Tibby on her knee. We came over on our bikes.'

'On your bikes? I'd have liked a bike when I was a girl, but all you could get then was either penny-farthings or side-saddle, like horses, and my dad said they were too dangerous for ladies. Your ma had a bike though, went all over the place on it, she did. Dad said they were an abomination. He didn't reckon it was right, young girls being able to go out like that and their parents never knowing where they was.'

'And where d'you reckon she did go, then?' Elsie asked, winking at Thursday. 'Off after the boys, was she?'

'Elsie Jackson! What a thing to say about your own mother.' The cracked old voice tightened with glee. 'Mind you, she was one for the lads, I can't say she wasn't. Gave your grandad and me a few worries, I don't mind telling you.'

'I hope you're not telling those girls any of your daft stories,' Mrs Jackson called from the scullery. 'Don't you believe a word she says, you two. She's wandering.'

'Not as much as you used to, by all accounts,' Elsie retorted. 'I've heard all about it – off on your bike down by St. George's, sparking with soldiers.'

'*Elsie*! How dare you talk like that! I don't know what's got into you since you joined the VADs, you've lost all respect.' Thursday heard the oven door open and close. 'There, that's the sponge in the oven, and now we'll have a cup of tea and I'll see if I can get some better sense out of Thursday here. Honestly, Thursday, I thought when our Elsie brought you home that you might be able to have a bit of influence on her, but it don't seem as if you have. I only hope she's not leading you into her bad ways.' She came through the door, wiping floury hands on her apron. 'Get the biscuit tin out, Else, will you.'

'Thursday doesn't need leading into bad ways,' Elsie said, getting up to open the door of the cupboard by the fireplace. 'She's got enough of her own. One of her old flames turned up at Haslar a day or two ago.'

'Elsie!' Thursday protested, blushing.

'Well, it's true. You had quite a thing going with Dr Sangster out in Egypt. Remember your birthday? You never did tell me and Lou just what went on after we made ourselves scarce.'

'No, and I'm not going to either,' Thursday retorted. 'Not till you spill the beans about that sailor you were dancing with at the Pier the other week. *I've* seen the letters arriving.'

'I can't help it if he writes to me,' Elsie said with some dignity, her blush almost as deep as Thursday's.

'You can help writing back though!' Thursday turned to Mrs Jackson who was setting teacups out on the little table. 'How's Eddy? He must be getting on for twelve now, isn't he?'

'Twelve in November, and shooting up. I'm hoping he'll be home for Christmas, though it'll be a bit of a squeeze. Not that I'll mind that – I miss him something chronic, I don't mind telling you. Elsie's told you we're living over here permanent now, hasn't she? That place they gave us in Pompey after we were bombed wasn't up to much and what with Mum being on her own here and not getting any younger it seemed the sensible thing to do.' She glanced around the tiny room and made a rueful face. 'Never thought I'd end up back here, not after what we had in Copnor. Here's your tea, Thursday.'

'Thanks. Is this where you lived when you were a child, then? I never realised.'

'Oh yes, Gosport girl born and bred, went to Brockhurst School as a kiddy. I worked down Lipton's in the High Street when I left school, and then I met my Bert at a dance and when we got engaged we started looking for a place in Pompey. Couple of rooms in Fratton, that's where we started, till we decided to go in for a house of our own.' She shook her head. 'Not many people bought their own place in those days. Millstone round your neck, that's what

Bert's mates told him, but he wouldn't take any notice, and I was so proud when we moved in, even though money was tight. And now it's gone, smashed to bits, not a thing left. It makes you wonder if it was all worth it.'

'But you'll get some sort of compensation, won't you?' Thursday asked, taking a broken biscuit from the tin Elsie was holding out. 'Insurance or something?'

'Oh yes, but is it going to buy us another place once the war's over? Nobody can tell us that. There's been so many places lost, see, and thousands needing new homes. I don't know how they're going to get them all built in time.' She shook her head again. 'No, I reckon we'll be here for a few years yet. Now look, Mum, I'm putting your tea here on the shelf beside you. Don't try to drink it yet, it's hot.'

'Any apples on the tree?' Elsie asked, her mouth full of biscuit. She turned to Thursday, grinning. 'I brought one of my friends over here for tea with Gran once when I was about nine. Grandad said we could pick up the windfalls to take home, and there were so many we didn't know how to carry them. We wanted to take as many as we could, but we didn't want Grandad telling us off for being greedy, so guess what we did.'

'What?' Thursday asked obediently.

'Stuffed 'em into our knickers! It's surprising how many pounds of apples you could get into those navy-blue bloomers – so long as the elastic holds! We got so many in we could hardly walk, and when we went indoors with half a dozen each in our hands Grandad could hardly keep a straight face. He knew very well what we'd done – not that we realised that, of course. We really thought we'd got away with it as we waddled off up the road. I reckon he and Gran must've split their sides laughing as soon as we got outside the door.'

'I remember that,' old Mrs Jenkins piped up. 'I never saw my Alf laugh so much in all my life. I thought he'd choke himself, I really did.'

Mrs Jackson stared at them. 'You mean you came all the way back on the ferry and the bus like that?'

'No, we fetched 'em out when we got round the corner and carried them in our pinnies. And we ate some on the way, of course.'

'And then you brought them home and put them in the bowl? Without even washing them? And we ate them – after they'd been in your *knickers*?' Mrs Jackson looked so appalled that Thursday burst out laughing, and Elsie grinned.

'It doesn't seem to have done you any harm,' she pointed out. 'Anyway, I promise not to do it again, if you let me and Thursday take some back with us.'

'Well, I should hope not indeed! And of course you can take some with you. I'm sure Thursday knows better than to stuff them into her knickers.' She turned to Thursday. 'And when are you going to be able to go home again? I suppose you haven't had any leave since you got back from Egypt.'

'Well, only the first few days. What with D-Day and then Market Garden the hospital's been at full stretch. But I'm hoping to have some time off in a week or two.'

'You could take Mark with you,' Elsie suggested slyly. 'Introduce him to the folks.'

Thursday turned on her. 'Don't be ridiculous! You know perfectly well I won't do any such thing. All that's over – he doesn't mean a thing to me any more. He never did, not really. We were just friends, you *know* we were. And I haven't even seen him, not since he came into the theatre . . .' She floundered to a stop, her face pink, and Mrs Jackson glanced at her shrewdly and picked up the teapot.

'I'll just freshen this up a bit. You'd like another cup, wouldn't you, love? And another biscuit, if our Elsie hasn't wolfed them all.'

Thursday took a breath and subsided. She gave Elsie an apologetic grin.

'Sorry, Else. I didn't mean to blow up like that.'

'That's all right,' Elsie said. 'It was a daft thing to say.' But the look in her eyes said something different, and Thursday saw it and knew.

She'd flared up like that before when Mark's name was mentioned. His return had brought it all back to her – the nights in the ward, the gharry ride through the darkness of the desert night. And the burning in her heart as his lips touched hers.

Chapter Seventeen

It was late in the evening and the ward was quiet. Thursday trod softly so as not to disturb the patients, some of whom were already asleep; all were recovering from operations. She passed three beds and then stopped.

'Mark?'

The figure in the bed stirred and half sat up, then lay back with a grunt. Thursday was at his side at once, pressing him gently back against his pillows. 'Don't try to sit up – you're not ready for it. Oh, Mark . . .'

He lay gazing up at her. Involuntarily, she reached out one hand and touched his cheek with her forefinger. 'I couldn't believe it when I saw you on the trolley. Do you remember seeing me?'

'Remember?' he whispered huskily. 'It got me through the op. And when I came round, all I wanted was to see you.' To her horror, a tear crept from the corner of his eye and spread into a small, damp patch on the pillow. 'Oh God, this infernal weakness!'

'It's the shock,' Thursday said quietly. 'It doesn't mean anything.'

'My God, d'you think I don't know about shock? I'm a doctor, remember! And it does mean something. It means I was damned glad to see you and damned disappointed not to find you beside me when I surfaced again. Thursday, where the hell have you been?'

Thursday gazed at him. There were tears in her own eyes and she knew that when she spoke her voice would shake. 'I – I've been on duty. And then I went to see Elsie's mum.'

'You went to see Elsie's mum? When I was lying here needing you?' His voice was hoarse and she couldn't tell if he were joking or not. It was the sort of joke he would have made, back in Egypt. She realised that her hand was still on his cheek and removed it hastily, but he reached out with his good hand and snatched it back. 'Don't stop, Thursday. Please don't stop touching me. If you knew how I've longed . . .' He turned his head aside and she saw the tears again, flowing down his cheeks. 'God, it's been so long, so bloody long.'

Thursday sat very still. Her heart was jumping and her skin was hot. She gazed down at his face, noting the small changes – the crow's feet splaying out from the corners of his eyes, where he had been so long in the hot African sun, the few strands of white in his black hair. He was thinner too, his cheeks drawn into deep hollows, one sliced across by the thin, silvery scar he had acquired at El Alamein. His recent injuries had left him with his arm in plaster, just as when she'd first known him, his ribs strapped up and one ear bandaged. There were other wounds too, less serious but probably painful and uncomfortable. She stroked his cheek, her fingers tracing the scar, then slipped her hand over his, and he turned his head back and looked up at her.

'I thought I'd never see you again,' he whispered. 'That night, when your brother-in-law came in . . .'

'Cousin. My cousin's husband.'

'Right, well, when he came in and you thought it was Connor Kirkpatrick, I could see then which way you'd go when he came home.' He paused. 'Is – is he still alive?'

Thursday nodded. 'He hasn't been home yet though. I don't think he will, until the war ends.'

'Well, that may not be so long now. We're on our way, Thursday.' He paused again and Thursday glanced around, fearful that Sister might come in and tell her she must go. She'd been given permission to visit Mark, but he was tiring and she knew that she could easily be forbidden a second visit. She opened her mouth to quieten him, but he was already going on. 'That night, I told you that if we were meant to be together, we would be. And so we are. So we are.'

'Mark—'

'Don't say any more now,' he whispered, and she saw that he was drifting into sleep. 'Don't talk. Just – just stay with me and hold me. Just be here . . .'

His voice faded and she saw that his eyes were closed and he was asleep. Her tears falling fast, she lifted his hand to her mouth and laid her lips on the dry skin.

'Mark,' she whispered in the silence of the ward. 'Oh, Mark.'

As September entered its third week most of the paratroopers who had been trapped in Arnhem managed to escape across the Rhine. Over a thousand had been killed, and nearly six and a half thousand taken prisoner. After the triumph of D-Day it was a dreadful blow, yet in other parts of Europe the Allies were still pushing ahead. In Italy, the Eighth Army, whose fortunes the girls had followed at El Alamein, was thrusting its way north, liberating towns and villages as it went. In Greece, authority had been ceded to the British, and the Germans were being forced out. And on the last day of the month, the news came that the Canadians had taken Calais.

Calais! It was a sign of hope, a cause for celebration. Calais had been the closest the Germans had ever come to invading England; a mere twenty miles or so from Dover, it had been the site for the most massive mortars which had fired their shells across the narrow neck of sea. The girls hugged each other and jumped for joy, and when Thursday went to see Mark she found him sitting up, bright-eyed, waiting for her.

'You've heard the news? Calais! We're on the home straight now, my sweet.'

'Don't call me that!' she whispered, casting an anxious glance around the ward. 'You'll get me into trouble.'

He winked. 'Don't tempt me – we might frighten Sister. All right, all right,' he held up his hand, 'sorry I said that. Put it down to excitement. There are only two things I want now, and d'you know what they are?'

'No,' Thursday said cautiously.

'One,' he held up a finger, 'to get out of here and give you a thorough kissing. And two,' another finger, 'to get back over there for a final crack at those bastards. Sorry about the language, Thursday, but I'm too fired up to watch my words. My God, if I could only get out of this straitjacket,' he indicated the plaster on his arm and the strapping around his chest, 'I'd show 'em what for, I would!'

Thursday gazed at him. 'Haven't you been through enough? I'd have thought you'd be glad of a rest, somewhere safe.'

'Rest? *Safe*? Thursday, I'm a soldier! I didn't join the Army to rest and be safe. For heaven's sake, girl!'

She looked down at her lap, feeling abashed. 'Well, I know that, but surely you must wish sometimes that it was all over. The war, I mean. Don't you want peace, Mark? Do you actually *like* war?'

There was a short silence. She looked up, meeting his eyes, and after a moment he said, 'Of course I want peace. That's what we're fighting for, isn't it?'

'Is it?' she asked quietly.

Mark shifted irritably in his bed. 'Well, of course it is! For God's sake, Thursday, what do you think I am? I don't kill people – I'm a doctor, I go to save their lives. But I'm a soldier too. I can handle a gun, I can kill if I have to, and if I'm in a situation where it's me or an enemy, I kill him, because that's what I'm trained to do. But I don't go looking for people to kill. I don't *enjoy* it.'

'Not the killing, no. But you enjoy being in the thick of it all, don't you? You enjoy the excitement of it.' She frowned. 'I can see it must be exciting, in a way. I remember the air raids – they were terrifying but I felt sort of lifted up, if you know what I mean. As if I'd suddenly got more energy from somewhere, as if I could do anything.'

'That's right,' Mark said, looking at her intently. 'That's exactly what I feel. As if I could do anything.' He paused. 'And then you see what's happening all around you. The poor blighters shot down, trampled by their mates, the paratroopers machine-gunned out of the sky, the kids barely out of nappies killed before they've had time to fire a single shot. And *that's* why I want to get back, Thursday,' he said with sudden force. 'To help bring an end to it all. Yes, it's exciting, yes, more people are going to be killed – but we've got to end it, and this is the only way. What's more, we're doing it. We're *winning*. We've had some setbacks but we're overcoming them. We're ploughing up through Italy and France, we've got them on the run, we're going to win this bloody war, and the sooner the better.' He lay back against his pillows, his breathing ragged. 'And once we've done that,' he said more quietly, 'we can get back to our normal lives and I can ask you to marry me.'

Thursday stared at him. The shock seemed to hit her full in the breast. She put a shaking hand to her cheek. 'What – what did you say?' she whispered.

He met her eyes. His were very dark, the pupils wide. 'I think you heard me, Thursday.'

'No,' she gasped. 'No, you can't say that. You mustn't.' She began to rise to her feet. 'I've got to go.'

His hand shot out and gripped her wrist. 'No, you haven't. You've only been here a few minutes.' He waited while she hesitated, then slowly sat down again. 'I'm sorry, Thursday, I didn't mean to blurt it out like that. Put it down to the excitement of today's news, together with the sheer damned frustration of being trapped in this bed. And we seemed to be getting into quite a deep conversation anyway. But – well, you must have known the way I was thinking.'

She shook her head. 'No. No, I never dreamed . . . Mark, you know I can't even think of it. You know I've already promised . . . We're just friends, no more than that. You mustn't say such things to me.'

'Mustn't I? Why not?' His mouth tightened, like that of a child being denied a new toy. 'Don't I have the right to fall in love, Thursday? Don't I have the right to ask a girl to be my wife? *I* haven't made any promises.' He glinted a look at her. 'Nor, as I understand it, have you.'

Thursday gazed at him, wishing she'd never told him how Connor had said he didn't want to tie her down. 'I did,' she said. 'I made a promise to myself, and I want to keep it. You know that, Mark.'

'It's one of the things I love about you,' he said quietly, and she sighed and covered her face with both hands.

'Mark, please. I can't talk like this. I can't let Connor down. He's thousands of miles away. I can't tell him I don't love him any more, that I'm not going to wait for him. I can't.'

'Plenty of girls do.'

'Yes – they send a *Dear John* and break a poor man's heart when he's miles from home and can't even talk to her about it. I won't do that, Mark, I just won't.'

'But if it were true?' he asked. 'If you'd realised you didn't love him after all – if you realised you loved another man – wouldn't you *have* to do it? How could you go on writing to him, telling him lies? What does a girl like you do in that sort of situation, Thursday?'

'I don't know,' she wailed, her voice muffled.

'Perhaps,' he said, 'it's time for you to start thinking about it.'

There was a small silence. Then she lifted her hands away from her face and looked at him. 'No. No, it's not. Because I *do* love him. I love him very much, and I mean to wait for him.' She stood up, and this time he did not try to detain her. 'I don't think I'd better come to see you again, Mark. I'm sorry.' And she turned and walked away, out of the ward.

Outside, in the unexpected warmth of some mild November sunshine, she felt sick and shaky. She pressed her hand against the red bricks and felt the heat radiate into her cold palm. She leaned her head against the back of her hand, and let the tears run from her eyes and down her bare arm. Deliberately, she tried to conjure up Connor's face, his smiling blue eyes, but to her horror she couldn't put the picture together. It was as if he were swimming away from her.

'What's happening to me?' she whispered to herself. 'What's happening to our love?'

Keeping away from Mark's ward was the hardest thing Thursday had ever done. She longed to be able to go to him, but dreaded what he might say to her. He seemed so certain that they'd been meant to meet again, that they were meant to be together. Suppose he's right, she thought. Suppose there is something – someone – driving us together. But each time she found her thoughts veering in this direction, she remembered Connor and the promise she had made. I meant that promise, she thought, and I'll keep it.

She lay awake at night, trying to stop the thoughts going round and round in her head. They were there all the time, as she ate, as she washed, as she walked or talked with her friends. It was only while she was working, totally absorbed in the operations the surgeon was performing, totally concerned with the patient before her, that she was able to push them aside. Once she came off duty, they all rushed back.

'You're not eating, Thursday,' Louisa said. 'And you're looking as white as a sheet. You're not sickening for something, are you?'

Thursday shook her head. 'There's nothing the matter. I'm all right.'

Elsie and Louisa glanced at each other. 'You're letting it get you down,' Elsie said. 'Go and see him again, Thurs.'

But Thursday shook her head.

Thankful for her work in the underground theatre, she tried not to go near the block where he was, afraid that her steps would take her along that corridor and into the long room with its rows of beds. Instead, she would come up the stairs into the arched stone arcade and walk down the smooth marbled way with its iron tracks, taking the long way round to the dormitories and mess in D Block. Once, she strolled down to the jetty and stood there, gazing across the neck of the harbour towards Portsmouth Cathedral and the sallyport. There was a pinnace there, waiting to ferry people across, and the sailor standing by the wheel looked up and caught her eye.

'Waiting to go ashore, love?'

Thursday shook her head. 'Just going off duty.' It was on a pinnace from Portsmouth that she had first spoken to Connor. 'I wanted a breath of fresh air – I've been down below all night. It's a lovely morning, isn't it?'

He nodded. 'Better make the most of it, the winter'll be setting in any day. Another Christmas with Hitler breathing down our necks. Blimey, you wonder how long it can go on, don't you.'

Thursday shrugged. 'I've almost given up thinking about it. What's the point? We won't know what to do with peace when we do get it. Five years of war. Nobody ever thought it would go on this long, did they?'

He took a packet of Player's Weights from his pocket, offering it to Thursday. She shook her head. 'You seem a bit down, love,' he said kindly. 'Had a row with the boyfriend?'

Thursday gave him a wry look. 'I wish it was that easy. No, I'm all right. Just a bit chokker.'

'We all get like that now and then,' he nodded, striking a match. 'Dare say you're tired. You'll be OK after a bit of grub and a kip.'

'Yes.' She looked again at the skyline of Portsmouth. From here, you couldn't see any of the bomb damage that she knew had laid the centre of the city to waste. The ships moored in the harbour or against the jetty were quiet. Even the sky was empty of aircraft. This is what peace will be like, she thought. Quiet. And with no dread always in your mind about what's going to happen next. We'll be able to go to dances at Southsea without wondering if there'll be a raid before we get home. We'll be able to be as sure as you ever can be that our families are safe and will be there when we go on leave.

Hang on, we won't be going on leave! We'll be home with them, if we want to be, living our own lives. Going where we please, living where we please, loving whomever we like . . .

She was swept by a sudden wave of loneliness. I've had enough of all this, she thought. I've had *enough.*

The matelot was watching her. He took the cigarette from his mouth and tapped the ash into the water.

'You know what you need, love?' he said. 'You need a spot of leave.'

'Yes,' Thursday said, and she nodded. 'You're right. That's exactly what I need.'

Madam had agreed. 'You should have had some before, but when Market Garden happened all that was put aside. However, I think we can spare you now.' Her brown eyes smiled kindly. 'Go home and have a few days' rest, Tilford. You deserve it. You've worked hard. And you're looking pale and tired. Get some good country air.'

Thursday packed her bag and caught the train from Portsmouth to Waterloo. Crossing London was another reminder of how badly the war had struck; despite the efforts of the authorities, there was still bomb damage to be seen everywhere, and now there was the threat of the V2 rockets. They'd been coming for several weeks, apparently, and the resulting explosions were blamed on the gas mains, but now the Government had admitted that they were really another form of air raid, even worse than the doodlebugs. You never knew where or when they would come.

She was thankful to be on the Worcester train at last, heading west through the Cotswolds. The signboards hadn't been replaced yet but as the train rumbled closer to Worcester she began to recognise many of the stations – Oxford, Evesham, where Patsy had come from, then Pershore – and the dull misery she had been feeling during the past week began slowly to dissipate.

Her sister Jenny was waiting on the platform. She jumped with excitement and hugged Thursday as she hauled her suitcase out of the carriage. 'Gosh, it's good to see you. How are you? You should see the dinner Mum's getting ready – I don't know where she's got half the food from. And we've got a surprise for you.'

'A surprise? What's that?'

'Well, it won't be a surprise if I tell you, will it? But you'll never guess, not in a million years.'

Thursday grinned and rose to the challenge. 'You've got engaged.'

'Oh.' Jenny looked disappointed. 'Well – yes, I have, as a matter of fact. I was going to tell you that next. But that isn't *the* surprise.'

'You mean there's something more?'

'Something *else*,' Jenny amended. 'I wouldn't say it was more, exactly.' Her grin broke out again, almost splitting her face, and she bit her lips in an attempt to control it. 'Well – yes, I suppose it is, really. I mean, it's something . . .' She closed her mouth again firmly and her eyes glinted with secrets. 'I'm not saying another word. I mustn't give it away.'

Thursday gave her an exasperated look. 'All right then, tell me about this engagement. Who is he? I didn't even know you were going steady with anyone. Have you got a ring?'

'Of course I have!' Jenny waved her left hand and they both stopped just before the barrier for Thursday to examine it. A woman behind them clicked her tongue and they moved hastily out of the way. 'Solitaire diamond, see.'

Thursday gazed at it enviously. Connor had given her the little silver crown brooch when he'd gone away, saying he wished it could have been a ring. At that moment, Thursday wished it too, with all her heart. If I had a ring on my finger, she thought, Mark would have respected it and we'd never have got into this situation. But Connor didn't want to tie me down . . .

'It's lovely,' she said wistfully as they walked out of the station. 'And what about the lucky man, then? Who is he?'

Jenny gave a little wriggle of joy. 'Well, you know him actually, quite well, in fact. You used to—'

Thursday stared at her. 'You're not going to tell me you're engaged to *Sidney*?' Not Sidney, the rather dull young man Thursday had gone around with before she'd joined the VAD. 'Jenny, you *couldn't*!'

'No, of course it's not Sidney. What on earth d'you take me for? Honestly, Thurs.'

'Well, who is it, then?' They came to the bus stop and Thursday put down her suitcase. 'Come on, Jen, don't keep me in suspense.'

'It's Charlie Harris, next door.' She looked self-conscious. 'I know it sounds daft, marrying the boy next door, but—'

'*Charlie*? But you always hated each other!'

'Well, we don't now. That was when we were kids, anyway.' Charlie had been the sort of boy who ran after girls, pulling their pigtails, and Jenny's had been particularly long and tempting. 'He's different now, honestly, Thurs.'

'So how long's this been going on? You never said a word when I came home in May.' The bus came along and they climbed aboard, squeezing Thursday's case into the little cubby-hole under the stairs and climbing up to the top deck. Jenny lit a cigarette.

'Well, we'd only just started going out then. He's in the RAF, came home on leave at Easter and asked me to go to the pictures with him, for company. We hit it off and went to a dance, and that was when it all started. Then he was in the D-Day landings – giving air cover, you know – and I was so scared he'd get killed that when it was all over and he wangled a forty-eight hour pass I told him we'd got to get married. So he bought me a ring and—'

'You mean you proposed to him?' Thursday stared at her sister, then looked up as the conductor came to collect their fares. She scrabbled in her purse for the money and waited impatiently while he punched out their tickets, then turned back to Jenny and hissed again, 'You *asked* him to marry you?'

'Well, actually I *told* him.' Jenny grinned. 'I said I wanted to know just where I stood. I wanted a ring on my finger, and I wanted to be Mrs Charles Harris. Well, we couldn't get married straight away, obviously, so we went out and got an engagement ring and we're getting married as soon as he can get leave.'

'What do Mum and Dad say about all this? And Mr and Mrs Harris?'

Jenny tossed her head. 'Doesn't matter what they say. I'll be twenty-one in December so there's not much point Dad putting his foot down now. Anyway, they're all pleased so that's OK.' She grinned. 'Mum was scared I'd meet a GI at some dance and go off to America! Lots of girls are doing that, you know.'

Thursday looked at her. Jenny had always been one to go her own way, and she'd always been able to twist her father round her little finger, too. As the eldest child, Thursday had felt that she had responsibilities – it had always been her job to look after her brother and sister. 'Take the baby with you,' her mother would say when Thursday was going out to play with her friends in the street. And Jenny or Steve would toddle out, clinging to her skirts, and be either a nuisance or an asset depending on what games the crowd wanted to play. It was always Thursday's fault if they came back dirty or with their clothes torn, as they invariably did. So Thursday had grown up burdened with a sense of responsibility which Jenny, dancing through life, didn't seem to feel.

'And if you had met a GI, I suppose that's what you'd have done,' she said. 'Swanned off to America without a backward glance. No wonder Mum's pleased you've chosen the boy next door.'

Jenny made a face at her. 'That's not a very nice thing to say, Thursday. Anyone would think I didn't care about my family.'

'Well, of course you do – I didn't mean that. But you would have, wouldn't you? You wouldn't have let anything or anyone stop you, if that's what you wanted to do.'

Jenny took a draw at her cigarette. 'No, of course not. We've got to live our own lives, Thurs, not let other people live them for us. Mum and Dad have had their lives and now we've got ours. Anyway, who's to say me and Charlie are going to stay in Worcester? We might do anything, once the war's over. Go and live in Canada or Australia – anything.'

Thursday looked out of the window. The bus was just crossing the bridge over the River Severn and she could see the great tower of the cathedral on her left. Its reflection shimmered in the smooth water and she thought of the cities that had lost similar beautiful buildings in the so-called 'Baedeker' raids in 1942, when the Germans had deliberately attacked towns that had no military significance, but were famous for their history. She thought of Coventry, not so far away from Worcester, almost razed to the ground in one night, its own cathedral no more than a shell, and thinking of Coventry reminded her of her cousin Denise, who had been married the day after that raid.

'How's Dizzy? And my godson?' she asked.

Jenny's face twitched, almost as though she were trying to suppress a sudden storm of giggles. 'Oh, they're all right. They'll be home when we get there. Everyone's coming to see you, Thursday.'

Thursday stared at her. '*Are* they? Why? I was going to go round to Auntie Flo's tomorrow – I wouldn't have thought they'd all want to trail down specially tonight.' She gave her sister another suspicious look. 'Something's going on, isn't it? This surprise you were on about – it's to do with them. It's not Vic, is it? Is he home? Surely he's in Italy with the Eighth?'

Jenny shook her head. She closed her lips firmly, but her eyes were sparkling and Thursday was sure she was right. 'I promised I wouldn't tell. You'll have to wait. Oh, *Thurs*.' She wrapped her arms around her body, hugging herself tightly. 'I can't wait to see your face!'

They were almost there. The bus trundled to a stop and the girls ran down the stairs. The conductor dragged out Thursday's suitcase and handed it down to her, and they set off for the last few hundred yards to Waterloo Street. They turned the corner and Thursday stared.

'What are all those flags doing, draped over the front of the house? They're not for me, surely! Jenny, what's going on? *Tell* me.' But once again Jenny shook her head, and Thursday quickened her steps. It must be Vic, she thought, but why was he home now, and why had Mum and Dad put all these flags up? Denise and Vic didn't live here.

'Have you got a key yet?' she asked Jenny. Thursday had had to wait for her twenty-first birthday for hers, but she couldn't believe that Jenny would have been satisfied with that, especially as her work at the Royal Infirmary would have meant coming home at all sorts of odd hours. But Jenny shook her head and she saw that the front door was standing ajar, as it always used to and, feeling her heart suddenly kick with excitement, she pushed it open and went inside.

'Here she is!' A great shout went up, and she found herself in a sea of faces and then enveloped by hugs as her family rushed forward to greet her. Laughing, kissing whoever happened to be nearest, she hugged them back and then, with her mother's arms still around her, found herself staring into a face she had thought never to see again.

It was her cousin Mike. Mike, missing believed killed at Dunkirk.

Chapter Eighteen

'Mike!' she whispered, and put both hands to her face. He looked very different from the way he'd been when she last saw him, four long years ago. He was thinner, older, and he'd grown a beard. But she still knew him. His eyes were the same, and when they looked into hers she found disbelief washed away by a sudden rush of incredulous joy.

'*Mike!* But you're dead!' She stared wildly round at the rest of the family. They were all watching her, both tears and smiles twisting the faces of her mother and aunt, and even her father's and uncle's eyes moist. 'Is – is it really Mike? I'm not dreaming?'

'It's me all right,' he said, giving her a hug. 'Hullo, Thursday. Good to see you again.'

'But – but they *said* you were dead!' she stammered again. 'We had a telegram. I don't understand.'

'It's a long story,' he said. 'But I'm alive and I'm here in Worcester, as you can see. And not half glad to be home, I can tell you! Anyway, haven't you got a kiss for your long-lost cousin?'

Thursday, her face streaming with tears, laid her cheek against his, feeling the roughness of his beard, the warmth of his skin. Mike, home again. It seemed impossible. She looked around at the rest of them again. They were all beaming at her, although there were still tears on her mother's face and her Aunt Flo was sobbing. Denise, with little Leslie in her arms, was wiping her eyes on the back of one hand. Jenny, who had managed to keep the secret all the way from the station, was half crying, half giggling.

'Mike,' she said wonderingly. 'It's like a miracle. But – how long – when did you come back? Why didn't anyone let me know?'

'We didn't know ourselves till yesterday,' her mother said. 'It all happened so quick, we've hardly had a chance to get used to it ourselves. Anyway, Thursday love, you sit down and I'll fetch you a cup of tea. You must be tired out after that journey.'

'Me, tired out!' she exclaimed, allowing herself to be pushed into a chair. 'What about the journey Mike's had? Where have you been?' she asked him. 'How did you manage to get home?' She put her hand to her forehead. 'I just can't seem to take it in.'

He grinned. 'I told you, it's a long story. I was left just outside Dunkirk – never even got back to the beach. Got caught in the blast from a bomb, you see, and it blew all my clothes away. Mother-naked, I was, when they picked me up. Most embarrassing moment of my life.' He grinned cheerfully and drank half his own cup of tea with one swallow.

'That's four years ago – where've you been all this time? Were you caught by the Germans? Did you escape?'

'I told you – it's a long story. I was found by a French farmer, lying in one of his fields. God knows how I got there. I was knocked about the head and dazed by the blast. Didn't even know who I was for a few days. He took me home and they put me up in the attic and looked after me until I was fit to move on. By then, they had some idea what had happened.'

'But they must have known about Dunkirk and the Germans occupying France.'

'You'd be surprised how little they did know,' he said. The family had gathered round to listen and Mary handed Thursday a cup of tea. 'Don't forget, they weren't allowed to use their wirelesses, and when the newspapers did start coming out again they were only allowed to publish what the Germans wanted them to publish. And when they realised the British had gone, they felt as if they'd been abandoned.'

'But we had no choice!' Thursday exclaimed, sitting up straight. 'What were we supposed to do, leave our boys there to be slaughtered?'

'They didn't know that,' he pointed out. 'All they knew was that the British had gone, leaving them to the Germans. A lot of French people were really upset about that.'

'I'm surprised they didn't hand you over,' Jenny said. She was sitting in her favourite spot, on the hearthrug, her legs folded under her. 'They were taking quite a risk, looking after you, weren't they?'

He nodded. 'They were risking their lives. And they weren't the only ones. But as some of them began to use their wirelesses again, secretly, and heard the BBC news, they started to see what had happened – and by then they'd come to realise what life was like under the Germans too, and – well, they began to be more keen to help us. And there were British agents getting in as well – men who were there to help us.'

'Us?' Walter asked. 'There were more of you?'

'Yes, quite a lot. Blokes who hadn't been able to get on the boats or were left in the countryside, injured or just lost. We were milling about all over the place.' He grinned. 'It was worse for those who still had their uniforms – they stood out like sore thumbs! At least my family had to give me a few bits and bobs, for decency's sake!'

'And you really were suffering from amnesia?' Jenny asked professionally. 'I mean, you didn't know who you were?'

'Not at first. Combination of shock from the blast and the bang on the head, I suppose. What I did know was that I was English – well, it was the only language I could speak, for a start! – and must be a Tommy. It didn't last long, and they didn't really want to know too much. Anyway, it was more important to get me somewhere safe and back to England.'

'But you were near the coast. Couldn't you just get a boat?' Denise frowned. 'There must have been fishing boats or things that would have brought you over.'

Mike shook his head. 'Look, the beaches were being watched day and night. Don't forget, the French had surrendered by then. They had to co-operate with the Germans. They weren't allowed to use their boats, and if they'd tried they'd have been shot. The Germans weren't going to take any chances of people coming in or out. We just might have invaded again, you know. And the Vichy Government was going along with them. It wasn't safe for the French families.' He shook his head. 'We had to go south, away from occupied France. It was our only chance of getting back home.'

'But that's an enormously long way!' Thursday exclaimed.

He nodded. 'I know. And we had to take it slowly. Me and three other blokes, we made our own way, getting lifts where we could and hiding up during the day. We used to make for the local *abbé* – the priest – when we came to a village. They were usually sympathetic and a lot of them were in touch with the local

Resistance. They could contact people who would help. We worked on farms to get food or money. I got ill the first winter – flu to start with, then pneumonia.'

'Pneumonia!' Flo exclaimed, horrified. 'I always knew you'd have chest trouble!'

'Oh, I was all right. The family I was with then kept me for three months, looking after me. I'd learned a bit of French by then, but by the time I left I could speak it like a native – local accent and all. So then I was useful, see, because I could help other blokes who were trying to get away as well. There were a lot of us left over from Dunkirk, but as time went on there were others too – airmen, shot down, who'd got away, and secret agents who were brought in to find out what was going on and help organise the Resistance movement. I stayed quite a while, working with them.'

The family was silent, listening in fascination. Thursday noticed that her Aunt Flo, sitting close beside her son, was crying quietly. What a shock this must have been for her, having her son come back from the dead. And yet, joyful though it must be, there must be pain as well in knowing that her other son, Leslie, shot down in his Spitfire, couldn't possibly come back as well.

'So what happened then, after you got better?'

Mike looked at her. 'I just kept on going south. We were making for Marseilles. There were safe houses there, and an escape line that would take us over the Pyrenees and into Spain. From there, we'd be able to get a ship to England, or maybe America. So that's what we did, in the end. It just took a hell of a long time.'

And a lot of dangerous adventures along the way, Thursday thought, gazing at him. She tried to imagine the life Mike had been leading during the past few years. Trudging through the endless, unfamiliar countryside, never really sure it was safe to accept lifts; sleeping under hedges or in barns, sometimes in the home of some brave family who were prepared to take a risk. Making cautious contact with those who worked in the Resistance, staying for months, even a year or so, to help other escaping servicemen, when all he really wanted to do was get home himself.

'Couldn't they have let us know?' Flo asked suddenly. 'I mean, just let us know you were alive? It's cruel, letting us go on thinking you were dead.'

Mike looked uncomfortable. 'I know. It upset me a lot, that did.

But they couldn't afford to let anything leak out about the safe houses, see. The people there – they were risking their lives, helping chaps like me escape. They kept them in their own homes, secretly, and if they were found out they'd be arrested. Some of them were,' he added soberly. 'They ended up in places like Buchenwald – concentration camps. They still don't know what goes on in those places, but not many people come out, I can tell you that. There was one man I knew – he and his wife sheltered hundreds of blokes before someone gave him away. He died . . . ' He bit his lip. 'Just one word in the wrong place and hundreds of others could have gone the same way, and I'd have been one of them. It had to be kept secret.'

'I don't see what difference it would have made us knowing, all the same,' Flo said resentfully. 'I've been through years of misery—'

Mike put his arm round her. 'I know, Mum. It's cruel. But war *is* cruel, see, and you know what they say – walls have ears. If someone *had* found out . . . It wasn't just soldiers – I told you, it was airmen as well, chaps who'd been shot down. They had to be got back to England; they were too valuable to lose. What we were doing – what the people who let their houses be used were doing – was really important. We just couldn't risk it being found out. And I *am* alive, and I'm back now, that's the main thing.'

Flo blew her nose and wiped her eyes. 'I suppose so. Well, of course it is.' She gave him a tremulous smile.

Mike kept his arm around her. 'And I was pretty useful by then too, because I could pass for a Frenchman with my country accent. The *abbé* got me some papers and I had a job, working as a handyman, so I could go round meeting people and taking messages between the houses, and I could keep my eyes and ears open for any problems too. There was one bloke they suspected of being a traitor. An Englishman, he was,' he added, looking angry, 'and they reckoned it was him got the poor old codger arrested. I'd like a few minutes on my own with him, I can tell you! I'd show him a thing or two.'

'These safe houses,' Walter said. 'What were they, exactly?'

'I told you – just people's homes. They'd keep blokes in a back room or an attic, somewhere that the neighbours wouldn't notice. They had to be dead quiet and never go near the window or do anything that might make people wonder. You never knew who might give you away, see. And there were all sorts of things you'd never think of that might make someone suspicious – getting enough rations was one, and getting rid of rubbish. Even flushing the lavatories too much. It was even worse once the Germans took over the south as well – the Gestapo were everywhere. They were watching all the time – they knew it was going on, see.'

'Is all this secret?' Thursday asked suddenly. 'Are you allowed to talk about it?'

Mike looked rueful. 'I've probably said more than I should. But I'm not going back – I've had trouble with my chest ever since the pneumonia.' He gave his mother a reassuring grin. 'It's not serious, Mum, you don't have to worry. But I've been a bit off-colour lately so they decided I'd better make tracks. It was tough enough coming across into Spain as it was. I had to report back to barracks of course,' he added. 'I'm still a soldier! I've got to go back to hospital next week to see what they can make of it. But they gave me a couple of days' leave first.'

Thursday turned on her sister. 'How on earth did you manage to keep all this quiet? She never breathed a word, Mum.'

'Well, we only let her go to meet you on condition she promised not to let on. We didn't want to spoil the surprise. You didn't guess, did you?'

'How could I?' Thursday glanced at her cousin. 'I thought it must be Vic, to tell you the truth. Though I couldn't see how he could be home either.'

'Wish he was,' Denise said wistfully. 'Here's our little Les nearly four years old and never seen his daddy, not to know him. And Vic hasn't seen him since he was a tiny baby. He'll be at school before Vic comes home.'

'Oh no,' Thursday said. 'The war's going to be over soon, I'm sure it is. Look at the way we're going through France. *And* Italy. The Germans must give in soon.'

'Don't forget these V2s they're sending over, though,' her father warned. 'That Hitler's still got a few surprises for us, mark my words. And then there's the Japs, too. We've still got them to deal with.'

'I know.' Thursday fell silent, thinking as she always did of Jeanie Brown, possibly in Japanese hands. She felt a light touch on her own knee and turned to see her four-year-old godson looking up at her.

With an exclamation, she scooped him up in her arms and cuddled him against her. 'Leslie! I haven't even said hello to you yet. I was so surprised to see your Uncle Mike, I forgot all about you.' She nuzzled her face against him. 'Give your Auntie Thursday a big kiss now, and tell me what you've been doing.'

'Getting ready for my daddy to come home,' Leslie said importantly. 'He's coming home soon, Mummy says.'

'Is he? Well, won't that be lovely. And have you got a nice photo of your daddy, so that you'll know what he looks like?' Thursday asked, knowing that beside Denise's bed at her parents' house stood a framed photograph of Vic in his Private's uniform. Leslie nodded.

'My daddy's a soldier. Like Uncle Mike,' he added, glancing shyly at the newcomer.

'He thought Mike was Vic when he first saw him,' Denise said in a low voice to Thursday. 'It's the uniform, see. He thinks any soldier in uniform must be his daddy, poor little mite.'

Thursday smiled. '*I've* seen your daddy,' she told Leslie. 'I saw him when I was in Egypt. D'you know where Egypt is?'

'Grandpa showed me on the map. It's over the sea.'

'Yes, a long way over the sea. There's lots and lots of sand there, and your daddy had been out in the middle of all the sand—'

'Was he building sandcastles? I saw a picture of a boy building sandcastles.'

'No, he wasn't building sandcastles. He was – he was doing some work. Soldier work.'

'Killing Germans,' he said, nodding matter-of-factly, and Thursday felt a small shock at hearing a four-year-old boy speaking so casually. He raised his arms, miming the action of holding a rifle to his shoulder. 'Bang-bang, you're dead. My daddy's killed lots of Germans.'

Thursday looked over his head at Denise. Her cousin shrugged. 'It's true, isn't it? He hears about it all the time, on the wireless and people talking. And he's got ears like a hare, he hears everything. You can't help him knowing.'

'That's right,' Mike said unexpectedly. 'Kids like him, they've got to know, Thursday. They've got to know what the world's like. It's no good keeping it from them, like it was kept from us. Pretending it didn't happen. I tell you, if it hadn't been for Dad taking me down the pub one night and giving it to me straight what happened the first time, same as Uncle Walter did with Steve, I'd have gone off without any idea of what war was like. And I'd have felt proper let down. Betrayed. Because someone ought to have told us, someone ought to have said what it was like in the First War, and if we'd all known what it was like maybe there wouldn't have been a second one. Maybe we wouldn't have had to fight and kill, and see our mates ripped to bits by bullets and us not able to do a thing to help them, maybe our Les would still be alive and all the other poor bastards who—' His voice had been rising almost to a shout and he stopped abruptly, his thin cheeks reddening. He glanced around at the ring of startled faces and mumbled, 'Sorry. Didn't mean to go off at half-cock like that. Sorry, Mum. Sorry, Auntie Mary.'

Flo, her hand at her throat, sat down on the only vacant chair. She was breathing quickly, her face pale, and Thursday began to lift Leslie from her lap to go to her. But Denise was already there, holding a cup of tea under her mother's nose.

'Have a sip of this, Mum. You'll be all right in a minute. Mike didn't mean to upset you.'

Percy cleared his throat and glared at his son. 'Now look what you done. I told you, I didn't want her upset. It's always upset her, all that sort of talk.'

'Yes, but Mike's right, you know,' Denise said, still helping her mother to sip the tea. 'People ought to know. *We* ought to have known. And youngsters like Leslie, they ought to know too, so that when all this is over there are no more wars at all, ever. How can we expect them to stop when nobody ever says what it's like?'

'Now look—'

'All right,' Flo said, lifting her face, 'that's enough. I'm all right, Perce. It was just a bit of a shock, that's all, hearing Mike raise his voice like that. But he's right. They all are. I know I got upset whenever you talked about the First War, but for goodness sake, haven't we been through enough in this one for me to be able to take a bit of truth? All the bombing and killing, and all those boys lost, God rest their souls, and us thinking Mike was dead same as Leslie, and not knowing if we'd ever see Steve again. And I've come to think that maybe I *should* have been upset. Why should I be saved from hearing about it when other people have had to go through it and suffer? And Mike's right about children. They've got to know. They've got to be told.'

'But not at four years old,' Mary said, her voice trembling. 'He's too little, too innocent. He doesn't have to know these things just yet.'

'I don't think he understands yet anyway,' Denise said. 'But he will, when he's old enough. And like I said, he hears everything. There's nothing we can do about that.'

Flo got up again. Her colour had returned and she looked around at the family gathering.

'Don't let's argue about it,' she said. 'Don't let's argue about anything. Not now, when our Mike's come back to us and Thursday's here too. Let's just have a lovely time together, like we used to before the war.'

There was a brief silence. Thursday bit her lip and glanced under her lashes at her aunt and uncle. But we're not all together, she thought. Steve and Leslie aren't here, even though Mike is, and Les never will be again. And Denise is missing Vic too, and she doesn't really know if her Leslie will ever see his daddy.

Percy cleared his throat. He laid his hand on his wife's shoulder and spoke a little loudly.

'That's right, Flo, love. It's not often we get together like this and we ought to make the most of it. Let's have a slap-up tea – or as slap-up as tea can ever be, these days – and then a game of cards or something. Something to make us laugh.' He was silent for a moment, and then said more quietly. 'Nobody can change what's already happened, and nobody can bring back those that have gone. But the news is pretty good, for all that, and we've got something to celebrate, so let's make a proper job of it – all right?'

The family, relieved to have the tension of the past few minutes dissipated, broke into a spontaneous cheer. And Thursday, her face once again wet with tears, turned to her cousin and laid her face against his sleeve.

'Oh, Mike,' she said. 'It's *so* good to have you back home.'

Mary had, as promised, put on a good spread for tea and the game of cards had them all laughing, forgetting the war for an hour or two. Thursday had learned a few new games, and they played these, together with the old favourites like Chase the Ace and Where's the Lady? Leslie sat on his grandfather's knee and caused more hilarity with his attempts to help, and it really began to seem like old times.

They finished up with a cup of cocoa all round, and then Flo and Percy said they must go, it was past that young man's bedtime, and they wrapped themselves up in their old winter coats and departed.

'Mind you come round and see us before you go back, Thursday,' her aunt said, kissing her cheek as they stood by the front door. It was dark by now and although the blackout had now become a 'dim-out' you still had to be careful about showing lights. 'And you come too, Mary, before our Mike gets taken off to that Army hospital.'

Thursday gave him an anxious glance. Mike hadn't said much yet about the reason why he had to go to hospital but she didn't like the sound of it. She didn't like the look of him either. He was too thin, too bright-eyed and there were spots of bright red on his gaunt cheeks.

'What's the matter with him?' she asked Jenny when they were in their own room. 'He ought to have got over that pneumonia by now. Has it left him with a weakness?'

'Something more than weakness, I'm afraid.' Jenny was smoothing Ponds cold cream into her face to take off her make-up. 'It looks to me a bit like TB.'

'TB? Oh no!' Thursday was already undressed and in bed, sitting up against her pillows. 'You don't really think so, do you? Does Auntie Flo have any idea?'

'No, and I'm not going to mention it until we know for certain. I could be wrong. Anyway, he's home now and he'll be looked after properly. It could just be because he's had such a hard life these past few years. They'll probably use penicillin – I can't imagine how we got on without that now, can you? It's made such a difference.' Jenny removed the cream with a scrap of cotton wool. She took off her engagement ring and laid it tenderly on the dressing-table. 'What about you, Thursday? There's been so much excitement here I don't think anyone's even asked you about Connor. Have you heard from him lately?'

'Yes, of course. I get letters all the time.' Her defensive tone brought a lift to Jenny's eyebrows. 'He won't be coming home though, not till it's all over.'

'And then you'll get married.' Jenny, peeling off her stockings and examining them for holes or ladders, spoke as though it was taken for granted. Thursday said nothing and after a moment she turned her head. 'Won't you?'

'I don't know. We'll have to wait and see, won't we.'

Jenny laid the stockings on her bed and stared at her. 'What d'you mean? I thought it was all decided.'

'No, it wasn't. It never has been. We're not engaged – I know Connor gave me my brooch and said he wished it was a ring, but it isn't one, is it? And he said he didn't want to tie me down. He *said* that.' Her voice rose a little and she stopped and bit her lip, aware of her sister's curious glance. 'I'm only saying we'll need to see how we feel when we meet each other again. Things might be different. *We* might be different.'

There was a long silence. Jenny put her stockings aside to be washed in the morning and took off her dressing-gown. She climbed into bed beside Thursday and then said quietly, 'Is there someone else, Thurs?'

'No! Of course there's not. Why should you think that?'

'Well, you've never said anything like this before. You've always been so sure . . . Look, I wouldn't blame you. You must be meeting men all the time. It'd be a funny thing if you didn't fancy any of them.'

Thursday said nothing. She slid down in the bed and lay there, her arms behind her head, staring at the ceiling. Jenny sat quietly beside her, filing her nails. At last she said, 'There is someone. An Army doctor. I met him in Alex two years ago and he's just come to Haslar.'

'An *Army* doctor? But what's he doing in Haslar? I thought it was all Navy.'

'He's a patient. Haslar's a clearing hospital – they bring them there first and we do emergency operations and then, when they're fit to be moved, they go on. Mark came in a week or so ago—'

'Mark?'

'Mark Sangster.' Thursday drew in a deep, troubled sigh. 'Oh, Jenny, I don't know what to do! When we were in Alex – well, it was so different there, everything was different, we were so far from home and I hardly knew where Connor was – I almost fell in love with him then. We used to do it all the time – almost fall in love, I mean – with lots of men. You know, go out dancing or driving in a gharry. It was so romantic and we needed it after being in the wards, and they needed it too. It never meant anything. It was just flirting, and it never went any further than that. Except . . .'

'Except with Mark,' Jenny finished for her.

'We never did anything we shouldn't,' Thursday said quickly. 'Not a thing. I didn't want to – well, I *did*, but I never forgot Connor, I couldn't let him down. And Mark understood that. When he went back to the desert, we said goodbye. We didn't think we'd ever see each other again. And I tried to forget him. I *did* forget him – almost. And then he turned up in Haslar and it all came back.'

'And what does he feel about it?'

'He thinks it was meant,' Thursday said miserably. 'He thinks we're meant to be together, and he says he wants to marry me.'

'Oh, lor,' Jenny said after another brief silence. She looked down at Thursday's face. 'You've got yourself into a bit of a muddle, haven't you?'

'I never meant to,' Thursday protested. 'It all just happened. I've always wanted to be true to Connor. I still want to.'

'So why are you bothered about this Mark? Why don't you just tell him to take a running jump?'

'Because I can't,' Thursday said. 'He doesn't deserve it. He's nice, Jenny, really nice. We get along together. And he says he loves me. How can I be nasty to him?'

'You could if you didn't like him so much,' Jenny observed, still filing her nails. She spread her fingers out in front of her, nodded with satisfaction, then put the nail file on the small bedside table. 'You could if you were absolutely sure about Connor.'

'I *am* sure!' Thursday rolled over and punched her pillow. 'Look, I've done all I can. I've told Mark I won't see him any more. I haven't been back to his ward for days. What else can I do?'

'It's not what you do that's important,' Jenny said shrewdly. 'It's what you think. And what you feel.' She waited a moment, then pointed out, 'You don't actually have to marry either of them, you know.'

'Oh, don't make it all more complicated than it is already,' Thursday groaned. 'Honestly, I do want to marry Connor – I've always wanted to. I just think – well, it's been a long time and things have changed so much, and we might be different. We shouldn't rush into anything. And then – I don't know *what* I feel about Mark. I can't seem to sort it out.'

'Don't do anything, then,' Jenny advised. 'Let things sort themselves out. Wait till Connor comes home, and when you see him again you'll know. And tell Mark if he won't wait till then it's just too bad.' She looked down again. 'The other thing to do is what a lot of people are doing – go where the wind blows you. Take what happiness you can get while it's on offer. You might not get the chance again.'

She put out the light and a few minutes later Thursday heard her steady breathing. She lay still, staring at the pale square of the window, her thoughts reeling with the events of the day and the problem that was ever present in her mind.

Keep the promise that Connor hadn't asked her to make – or let her relationship with Mark go ahead, and go where the wind blew?

Chapter Nineteen

Her brief leave over, Thursday returned to Haslar. She spent the train journey deep in thought. The shock of Mike's return still hadn't quite sunk in. All that first evening, she'd kept looking at him, wanting to touch him to make sure he was real. But one look at the faces of her aunt and uncle told her that it was true. They looked dazed with happiness and relief, and Auntie Flo didn't seem able to bear him out of her sight. She sat beside him all the time, and tears trickled out of her eyes every time she turned her head and looked at him.

'It gives us all a bit of hope,' Mary had said as she kissed Thursday goodbye that morning. 'If Mike can come home from the dead like that, anyone can. Well, maybe not *anyone*,' she added, her face shadowing as they both remembered Leslie. 'But it makes you realise good things *can* happen. It helps you to look forward.' She held Thursday close for a moment. 'It'll be Steve next, and Vic, and your chap too. They'll all be coming home.'

Yes, Thursday thought, watching the countryside flash past. They'd all be coming home. Steve, from prison camp. Vic, from Italy. And Connor . . .

She and Jenny hadn't talked any more about Thursday's dilemma. Jenny had gone back to the Royal Infirmary early next morning. She had only one more year to go before finishing her training and would then be a Registered Nurse. 'You could have done this too, you know,' she told Thursday, pinning up her curly hair. 'Didn't you think about it?'

'Not at the time. I've thought about it since, but – I don't know, Jen. I've enjoyed being a VAD but I don't know if I want to go on being a nurse. I don't know *what* I want to do, to tell you the truth.'

Jenny paused and looked at her, sitting up in the bed. Then she laid a hand on Thursday's leg. 'It'll all come out right, Thursday. You'll see. Just stop worrying so much, and enjoy life. That's what I do, and look where it's got me!'

She danced out of the room and down the stairs and a few moments later Thursday heard her calling a cheerful goodbye to Mary. She smiled to herself and snuggled down under the quilt. Jenny was right. She should enjoy life, and she'd start now by having a long, lazy lie-in.

The rest of the time had been taken up with visiting. She went to see all her old friends who were still around, and spent a good deal of time with her Aunt Flo and cousin Mike. Denise was at work at the glove factory, so she played with Leslie and one afternoon took him on the train across the Malvern Hills to Ledbury to visit her Aunt Maudie. Maudie was still nursing at the cottage hospital but hurried home across the road and welcomed them both with tea and fresh scones, while the white Persian cat, Snowy, looked more majestic than ever on the rag rug by the fire.

'You heard Nipper died, I suppose,' Maudie said. 'He was a good age – nearly sixteen. I miss him a lot, but I don't suppose I'll have another, not at my age.'

'Go on, Auntie,' Thursday said, her mouth full of scone, 'you're not old.'

'No, but I would be by the time a new puppy got to the age Nipper was. Anyway, there'll never be another dog like him. Have you still got that little watch I gave you?'

Thursday nodded. She wore the little silver fob watch whenever she was on duty and it had become a talisman, bringing her safely through the war. She would give it back to her aunt when the war was over. Thursday knew that Maudie treasured it.

When the war was over . . . Talk was of peace now, all the time. The Germans had been driven back even further through France and were now defending their positions from the Moselle to the Low Countries. They had been chased out of Finland by the Finns and Soviets, and were retreating across their own borders. At the same time, the war in the Pacific and Far East was being fought ever more vigorously, with the Japanese army on the defensive all over Burma. The Red Army had launched a massive assault on the Baltic coast, prior to their attack on East Prussia. On all fronts, the enemy were caught in pincer movements and fighting, as Jenny remarked with satisfaction, like rats in a corner.

It wasn't all good news, though. On the day before Thursday left to go back to Haslar they heard that a V2 rocket had struck a Woolworth's store in London, killing a hundred and sixty people and injuring at least two hundred more. Poor souls, Mary said, her eyes filling with tears. Just gone out for an afternoon's shopping, the kiddies with them as likely as not, and smashed to rubble without any warning. Not even time to get to a shelter. It wasn't *fair*.

'It's awful,' Mary had said, reading the newspaper out loud. 'There's a young girl here saying what it was like. Things falling out of the sky, she says, bits of things and bits of people. She saw a horse's head lying in the gutter – just its *head*. And a pram all smashed and twisted and a little baby's hand, still in its sleeve.' She laid the paper in her lap, her face twisted with horror. 'Poor little soul. And there was a bus with people still sitting in it in rows, all of them stone dead. And nothing left of Woolworth's at all – just a huge pile of rubble, and people screaming underneath.'

The image had haunted Thursday all night and still overshadowed her mind as she sat in the train. Suppose a V2 hit the train now . . . Well, there was nothing you could do to guard against it, so it was no use worrying. Determinedly, she turned her thoughts back to her own life.

I'm not going to make up my mind about anything at the moment, she thought. I can't, and nobody can force me to. I'll go and see Mark again, but I won't agree to marry him, I won't even think about it until the war's over. But I won't think about marrying Connor either – not until I've seen him, and until we've had time to get to know each other again.

At the back of her mind was the thought planted there by Jenny. She didn't have to marry either of them. She didn't *have* to marry anyone at all.

By the time she crossed the harbour, night had fallen and the wind was whipping the tops off the choppy waves. In spite of the 'dim-out' both towns were in darkness, with barely a glow from the few street-lights that were now permitted. Thursday sat in the pinnace, watching the shadowy bulk of the hospital block out the occasional glitter of stars behind the flying tatters of cloud. How many more times am I going to do this, she wondered.

The other girls had already gone to the mess for supper when she arrived. Tired and suddenly despondent, she dropped her case on the floor beside the bunks, went to the washroom to sluice water over her face and hands, and then walked along to join them. Haslar shepherd's pie was rather a comedown after her mother's cooking, but she'd got to eat. She found the others in their usual places and slipped into her seat.

'Hello, Thursday,' Elsie said, her mouth full of mince and potato. 'You're back, then.'

'I think so,' Thursday said, picking up her knife and fork. 'I think it's me, anyway. What does everyone else think?'

'All right, ask a silly question! Did you have a good time? How're the family?'

Thursday looked around the table. They all appeared much as usual, cheerfully eating their shepherd's pie and sipping their water. There was, after all, no reason why they should look any different. She'd only been away for five days. Yet she felt as if she'd been away for months. As if far more had happened than could possibly have been packed into only five days.

'My cousin's home,' she said baldly. 'Mike. The one we thought was killed at Dunkirk.'

They stopped eating to stare at her. 'The one you thought was killed at Dunkirk? He's *home*? But—'

'You mean you haven't heard from him in all that time? And he's just come home? Out of the blue? But how?'

'You're joking. You're having us on. He *can't* have just turned up, just like that.'

'I don't *understand*.'

'Here, have a bite to eat, Thurs,' Elsie said, watching her. 'You're looking all in. Get some grub inside you and then tell us all about it. I reckon she's had a real shock,' she said to the others, 'and it's only just begun to hit her. Leave her be for a bit while she gets herself together.'

Thursday nodded. She felt suddenly close to tears. It's daft, she thought, trying to hold them back, it's daft to feel like this. It's good news – wonderful news – and I was so pleased, so excited about it. I still am. So why should I break down now, the minute I get back to

Haslar? And I feel so *tired* . . . She leaned her head on one hand and used the other to fork up the meat and potato. Its warmth and solidity gradually penetrated the numb coldness of her body and she began to feel better. After a few more mouthfuls she looked up and grinned shakily.

'All right. I'm OK now. Just felt a bit woozy, that's all.'

'I'm not surprised, after that journey,' Patsy said. 'I remember the first time we came, in all that snow – I thought it was going to take for ever. Now, tell us about your cousin. Has he really come home?'

Thursday nodded and recounted as much of the story as she thought she ought to. 'He's been in France all that time, just dodging the Germans, but he managed to get to Spain and find a ship. He's been ill, too. Jenny, my sister, thinks it may be TB. He's going to the nearest Army hospital.'

'They'll soon sort him out, then,' Elsie said bracingly. 'My goodness, what a story! Imagine being on the run all that time in France! I bet your auntie's over the moon.'

'She is. She thought she'd lost both her boys. She knows Leslie won't come back, of course, but it does give you hope, doesn't it?' She glanced around and caught Patsy's eye and a wave of sorrow struck her. 'Oh, Pats, if only it could happen to Roy.'

'I know it won't, though,' Patsy said sadly. 'They found his body. It was buried somewhere over in Normandy – they say there's huge graveyards stretching for miles with little wooden crosses by each grave. My Roy's in one of them and one day I'll go and see him.' She gave Thursday a wobbly smile. 'But I'm glad about your cousin. Really glad.'

'So am I,' said Elsie, and then Louisa, and then each girl at the table. 'So am I. So am I. So am I.' Even Vera Hapgood, who rarely joined in any congratulations, smiled and nodded, and Thursday felt a warm, all encompassing glow as she looked at them. My friends, she thought, all these girls are my friends.

As she rose from the table, however, she knew that there was another friend to whom she had not yet told the news. Not Connor – she'd written to him twice during her leave, telling him about Mike and all the rest of the family news. No, this friend was here in Haslar, but in order to tell him she would have to walk across to the wards and ask Sister to let her in to see him.

Mark, she thought. I want to tell Mark.

It was too late to go that evening, and she was exhausted anyway. The emotion of the past few days had suddenly caught up with her and she felt almost sick with fatigue. She went back to the dormitory and sat round the big iron stove with the others, sipping cocoa and listening to their chatter. As usual, it was mostly about the hospital and the social life they managed to squeeze into their off-duty hours, and Elsie was coming in for a good deal of attention. Thursday looked at her curiously.

'This sailor – is it serious, then?'

Elsie blushed and nodded her fair head. 'I think it might be, Thurs. Well, you know we've been out a few times since that dance at South Parade Pier. We get on really well. He's a local boy too, comes from Fareham, so he's not going to go disappearing up north or anything like that.'

'And you can check he hasn't already got a wife,' Patsy said wickedly. 'Not round here, anyway.'

Elsie gave her a withering look. 'He hasn't got a wife *anywhere*. Anyway,' her fair skin was suddenly tinged with pink, 'we're thinking of getting engaged at Christmas. Might be going over to Pompey to look at a few rings on Saturday.'

'A *few* rings?' Patsy echoed. 'Crikey, how many d'you want, Elsie? One for every finger? Most people are satisfied with just the one.'

'Oh, shut up, you fool.' Elsie gave her friend a push and Patsy almost spilled her cocoa. She turned to Thursday. 'Honestly, Thurs, I'm glad you're back, at least there's a chance of a bit of sensible conversation.' Ignoring the derisive howl from Patsy, she went on, 'I can't make up me mind between three diamonds or a solitaire, what d'you think?'

'Not a solitaire,' Patsy said, suddenly sober. 'It's unlucky. Everyone I know who had a solitaire got left on her own. Have three diamonds.'

There was a short silence. Nobody could help glancing towards Patsy's hand, where her own tiny solitaire engagement ring winked in the harsh light from the overhead lamp. In a sense it wasn't really an engagement ring, since Roy had bought it for her on their honeymoon – their wedding had been arranged so quickly there hadn't been time for an engagement – but that was what it was meant to be.

'Well, maybe that's what I'll do then,' Elsie said after a moment.

'I think I like them better anyway. Not but what yours isn't really pretty, Pats,' she added hastily, 'but my hands are bigger than yours and one stone will just look lost.'

'I can't believe it,' Thursday said. 'I've only been away a few days. You weren't talking about getting engaged when I went.'

'Not to you lot, no. But we've been thinking about it. I wasn't going to say anything tonight either – it just slipped out. So keep it under your hats.'

'Fat chance of that,' Ellen Bridges said. 'Now we all know it'll be all round the hospital, even if none of us says a word. You know what it's like here – talk about walls having ears! I bet the whole of the ward will hear of it by tomorrow.'

'Well, if they do I'll know who to blame,' Elsie said, fixing Ellen with a stern look.

'So when's the wedding going to be?' Thursday asked quickly. 'I mean, won't Pete be going away soon?'

'No, he's got a desk job in Cambridge Barracks,' Elsie said. 'He copped some shrapnel in his shoulder when his ship was sunk in the spring and he was in the water for seven hours so it did it a bit of no good. They don't reckon it'll ever be properly right again. He'll be there for a while, anyway, so we can take our time. We thought we might make it February the fourteenth.'

'St Valentine's Day!' Joy said. 'Oh, that's so romantic. Are we all invited? I'll need to save up my coupons for a new frock.'

'For cripes' sake!' Elsie exclaimed in exasperation. 'We haven't even got engaged yet! I'm not supposed to have told you any of this. Look, it's almost ten o'clock, I'm going to bed, and Thursday here's almost dropping. Whose turn is it to wash up?'

'Yours!' said several voices, and she groaned and collected up the mugs. Thursday followed her out to the washroom and began to clean her teeth while Elsie swished the mugs under the tap.

'I'm really pleased, Else. I liked Pete the first time I met him. I think you'll be very happy together.'

Elsie rested her hands in the water and looked at her. Her face was unusually serious. 'I hope so, Thurs. I really hope so. You know, there've been a lot of blokes I've fancied before I met Pete, and I've had a bit of a fling with a few of them – well, you know that – but I've never felt the way I do now. I know it's awful to say it when so many other chaps are out there in danger, but I'm just so thankful he's got that bad shoulder and they've put him in the barracks. I don't think I could stand it if he went away and I lost him. I couldn't be as brave as Patsy. I know I couldn't.'

Thursday heard the wobble of tears in her voice. She dried her hands and put her arm around Elsie's shoulders. 'Yes, you could. But you're not going to have to. This is one story that's going to end happily ever after – I know it is.' She laid her cheek against her friend's for a moment. 'Congratulations, Elsie. And mind you do invite us all to the wedding, see? Or you'll have me to reckon with!'

Climbing into her bunk, she thought how good it was to be back amongst her friends, and a wave of sadness washed over her as she realised that in some ways she felt more at home here than she did back in Worcester. It had been lovely to be with her family again – especially with the added joy of Mike's miraculous return – but it hadn't always been easy. There was so much about her life that her family, especially her parents, didn't understand. So much of what in Haslar would have been casual comment or banter, immediately understood by the others, seemed to need explanation that she had begun to find herself weighing her words before uttering them. Even Jenny seemed to have grown away from her. Her training as a Registered Nurse had taken her beyond Thursday's medical knowledge, yet still remained far short of her experience. Jenny had attended numerous lectures, studied piles of books and passed detailed examinations in a number of areas of which Thursday knew very little, but she had never encountered a flood of wounded soldiers, encrusted in blood and sand, nor sat beside a dying sailor as he moaned and wept for his sweetheart. She hadn't helped unload a man with a torn and mutilated face from a small ferry boat after Dunkirk and realised it was her own sweetheart. It was as if they inhabited different worlds. And the rest of the family seemed even further apart, concerned with the difficulties of civilian life and the Home Front.

I've been away too long, Thursday thought. It's nearly five years now since I left home, and two of those years I spent in Egypt. I've changed, and I don't think I'll ever be able to change back. I'm a different person.

She felt the tears seep from her eyes and spread into a damp patch on her pillow. I don't *want* to be different, she mourned. I don't *want* to be the kind of person who can only feel comfortable in a crowd, in a dormitory, in a hospital or some other sort of institution. I want to be ordinary again, to be able to go back to ordinary life after the war and be a wife and mother, just as Mum always meant me to be.

Ordinary life. She didn't even know what that was, any more. And as for being a wife – another whole world of confusion must be settled before that could come about.

She went to see Mark the next morning, before going on duty. Her heart beating fast, she crossed the quad and entered the door of the medical block. Almost running, she joined the throng of nurses going up the stairs and paused at the door of the ward. The QARNN Sister came out and looked at her.

'I'd like to see Lieutenant Colonel Sangster,' Thursday said. 'I've been on leave for a few days. I won't stay long but I'd just like to see him before I go on duty. Just to – to say hello.'

The QARNN looked at her curiously. 'Lieutenant Colonel Sangster? He's not here any more. He's gone.'

Thursday stared at her. Her heart, which had been beating so fast, seemed to give an extra kick and then drop right through her body. 'Gone? But – but where? When? He—' Fear gripped her. 'He's not worse, is he? He was doing so well.'

'No, of course he's not worse. He was fit enough to be moved, that's all. He's gone to the Army hospital.' The Sister paused for a moment. 'I'm surprised he didn't let you know. Since you're such good friends.'

Thursday felt the colour burn her cheeks. 'I've been away, otherwise . . .' She looked at the Sister. 'Do you have an address for him?'

'Sorry,' the QARNN said. 'All I know is that he's gone to the Army hospital, but I'm sure he'll be in touch, if he wants you to know it. Now if you'll excuse me— She was already turning away, anxious to get on with the business of the ward.

'Yes,' Thursday said dully, not missing the sardonic note in the senior nurse's voice. She moved away along the corridor, feeling suddenly bereft. 'Yes, I'm sure he will.'

Chapter Twenty

'Gone?' Elsie echoed. 'You mean he's just buggered off without even telling you?'

'*Elsie!*' Thursday was used to hearing people swear now, but she still didn't like hearing it from her friend. 'Well, yes, I suppose that's about it.' She twisted her mouth wryly. 'I shouldn't be surprised, I suppose. I made it pretty clear I wasn't going to see him again. But I didn't really expect him to *believe* it!' she ended on a wail.

Elsie couldn't help grinning. 'You shouldn't say such things if you don't mean them.'

'I thought I did at the time,' Thursday said despondently. 'Oh, Elsie, I'm in such a muddle! Why couldn't I fall in love with a nice uncomplicated sailor like Pete? Why does it all have to be so *difficult*?'

Elsie watched her. 'Is it? Isn't it just that you've realised there can be more than one Mr Right in the world, and you happen to have come across two of them? Strikes me it doesn't really matter which one you choose, Thurs, you'll have a pretty good life with either.'

Thursday stared at her. 'That's an awful thing to say.'

'I don't see why. I bet it's true. Look, if there's only one man for any of us, out of all the millions of men there are in the world, it's a pretty big coincidence that so many of us happen to meet him, isn't it? Stands to reason there's got to be lots. And what about all the widows who get married again? *They've* met more than one, haven't they? So—'

'Stop it, Elsie, you're making my head ache.' Thursday put the heel of her hand to her forehead. 'Look, I can't think about millions. I can only think about two. And I *don't* know which one's Mr Right, as you call him – or even if *either* of them is. I just don't know what to do, that's all. And I wish Mark hadn't gone off like that without even leaving me his address.'

'Maybe you've convinced him you do know, and thinking he's out of the picture, he's done the decent thing.' Elsie paused. 'Anyway, it wouldn't be that difficult to find him. You know he's gone to an Army hospital. You could easily find out which one.'

Thursday looked at her. 'You think I ought to try to contact him again? Go and see him – wherever he is?'

'Good Lord, *I'm* not saying what you ought to do!' Elsie exclaimed, flapping her hands. 'I'm just saying what you could do. You've got to make up your own mind over this, Thursday.'

Thursday sighed and the two girls parted, Elsie to go to Zymotics and Thursday to the operating theatre. They were still using the underground theatres even though the risk of raids had diminished – apart from the threat of V2 rockets – and she ran down the wide stairs, conscious that she was only just in time. The theatre sister gave her a severe look as she pushed open the big double doors.

'You're almost adrift, Tilford.'

'I know, I'm sorry. I – I wanted to see someone in the wards first and I cut it rather fine.'

'Well, keep your visiting time for off-duty hours. We've got a lot of ops this morning and the boss wants to get started as soon as possible.' The QARNN detailed the morning's work briskly, allocating jobs to the nurses and VADs. Thursday accepted her tasks meekly and set to work, determined to thrust her own problems out of her mind for the next few hours. Wherever Mark was, and wherever Connor was, they would have to stay there without her thoughts. For the time being, while she was on duty, the only men who mattered to her were the patients lying on the table, their lives and their recovery held in the hands of every person in the theatre.

It was almost Christmas. People were beginning to discuss what they were going to do and whether they'd be able to go home. A few people who were due for leave managed to organise it for the two or three days of the holiday, but Thursday, who had already taken her leave, was to stay at Haslar. Since they would both be on duty on Christmas Day itself, Elsie invited her to go to her grandmother's for Boxing Day to help celebrate her engagement to Pete.

'I don't mind being here for Christmas anyway,' she declared as they sat darning their stockings. 'We've had some good times in hospital at Christmas, haven't we? Remember those we had out in Egypt?'

'Do I! It was almost like pre-war with all those coloured paper chains and funny hats. And the *food*! I've never seen such a spread.'

'Mm. It was good, though it seemed funny not to be having turkey or chicken. And sweet potatoes, too – not like our spuds, are they! Still, it was a smashing spread. And couldn't the men just put it away! Got through a few gallons of beer too, if I remember right.'

'I'm surprised you can remember at all,' Thursday said with a grin. 'I know by the time we'd gone carol singing round all the wards we weren't singing the usual words to half of them! But I couldn't help a little weep now and then when I looked at them all. Poor souls, all so far away from home with nobody of their own to come and hold their hands. I'll tell you now, I went back to bed and cried myself to sleep that night.'

'You weren't the only one,' Elsie said quietly. 'And here we are, back where we started, getting ready for yet another Christmas. D'you reckon this really will be the last one, Thurs – the last one of the war, I mean?'

'I hope so,' Thursday said. She rolled her stockings into a ball. 'I've had enough of wartime Christmases. I want to be able to have the whole three days doing just what I like, with a huge spread of turkey and Christmas pudding, and cakes and trifles, and lots of sweets and chocolates, and oranges and bananas, and figs and dates and—'

'Blimey O'Riley,' Elsie said, 'I thought it was me that was the greedy one! You'll burst.'

'I don't care,' Thursday said. 'I want to burst!'

Elsie laughed. 'You're in a good mood today. Had a letter from Connor?'

'No.' Thursday gave her a sideways glance. 'Actually, I've decided to go out somewhere on my next day off. I'm going to Rochester.'

'*Rochester*? But why on earth . . . ?'

Then light dawned in Elsie's eyes. 'Ohhh. There wouldn't be an Army hospital there, by any chance?'

'As a matter of fact,' Thursday said, 'there would.'

'Mark?'

'Yes. I've decided to go and see him. I've got to, Elsie,' she added rather defensively. 'I can't just leave things as they were. I've got to give him his chance. I'm not going to *agree* to anything, mind. I shan't get engaged, or anything like that – I still want to wait till I see Connor again before I make up my mind. But I can't simply walk away from Mark.' She glanced down at the rolled stockings in her lap. 'I just can't.'

'No, you can't,' Elsie said after a moment. 'But – be careful, won't you Thurs? He's got a dangerous look about him, Mark Sangster has. Just watch yourself, all right?'

'Yes,' Thursday said. 'I will.'

She didn't ask Elsie what she meant by the word *dangerous*. She knew only too well. She'd seen it herself in the glint of Mark's dark brown eyes, in the narrow lines of his face; she'd heard it in his voice. He *was* dangerous – dangerous to her heart.

On the day Thursday went to Rochester, news began to come through of the 'Battle of the Bulge'. The US Army, now in the Ardennes, had been attacked by a massive German force and left in disarray. It looked like another step backwards.

On the same day she read in her newspaper of the disappearance of the bandleader Glenn Miller somewhere over the Channel. He'd been flying to Paris to perform for General Eisenhower and somewhere over the freezing sea his plane had vanished. His band had gone in a different plane and were all safe – but what would they do without him, Thursday wondered. With his famous tunes 'String of Pearls', 'Moonlight Serenade', 'American Patrol', and 'In the Mood' he had come to represent the very sound of America at war.

The crowded train rumbled through the countryside. Thursday had never been to Kent before but the scenes outside did little to hold her attention. She tried to read the paper again but the words danced before her eyes and she laid it back in her lap. I wish I knew if I were doing the right thing, she thought restlessly. I wish I knew if Mark really wanted to see me again . . .

Elsie had advised her to let him know she was coming, but Thursday had shaken her head. 'I just want to surprise him – to see what he does. I'll know then if he really loves me.'

'And will you know if *you* love *him*?' Elsie had asked shrewdly, and Thursday had sighed and shaken her head.

'I don't know when I'm going to know that.'

She reached into her bag and reached for an envelope. It was yellow and crumpled with much folding and unfolding. She drew out the sheet of paper inside and stared at it.

My Darling Thursday,

I seem to feel you with me with every step I take. I miss you every moment, more than I can say, more than I can ever show you – but oh, how I long to show you and to love you, and when all this is over I swear we'll never be parted again, never. I love you, my darling.

Her eyes blurred and she bit her lips hard and stared out of the window, determined not to let the tears fall. I wasn't the only one to make a promise, she thought. Connor did too, in this letter. We promised each other.

What was she doing here, with Connor's letter in her bag, going to see another man?

Perhaps Elsie was right. Perhaps there were many men in the world that she could love. It was just bad luck that she'd happened to meet two of them.

The soldier sitting opposite her gave her a sympathetic look. 'Letter from your sweetheart, love?'

'Yes.' She wondered what he would say if he knew the truth. She'd known so many men in Egypt, worrying themselves sick about what their wives and sweethearts might be doing back at home, and she felt a lurch of shame. 'It's an old one, though.'

'Been away a long time?' He nodded. 'Feels like it'll never come to an end, don't it. But don't fret, ducks, it'll all be over soon.' He glanced out of the window. 'One or two more big pushes, that's all it'll take, and we'll smash old Hitler into the dust. They say he's dying on his feet anyway.'

'Do they?'

'Yeah, mate of mine says he's heard he's in a bad way. Get rid of him and the others'll fall to bits. Good riddance to bad rubbish, that'll be. You wouldn't credit one man could make such a mess of the world, would you? Pity old Chamberlain never saw what he was up to – him and his "piece of paper"!' The man snorted with derision. 'Blooming politicians. There's only one thing a devil like that understands, and it ain't appeasement!'

'But so many people have been killed,' Thursday said, and he shrugged.

'That's war, innit. That's what it's all about. Mind you, it's all right for me to talk like that – I'm a Regular, went into it in thirty-six with me eyes open, got proper training. I can see it's rough on the poor sods that got called up straight out of school and didn't even know one end of a gun from the other. Cannon-fodder, that's what they were right enough. But you gotta have it, ain't you? You got to waste the Jerry's ammo on something.' He glanced out of the window and started to get to his feet. 'We're just coming into the station now. Be seeing you, love.' He winked. 'Hope the boyfriend gets back soon.'

'Yes,' Thursday said faintly. 'Yes, so do I.'

She folded Connor's letter – the first real love letter he had written to her, just before Patsy's wedding – and put it carefully away in her bag. For a moment or two she sat staring out of the window, thinking over what the soldier had said.

Cannon-fodder. The lives of young boys, barely trained, used to 'waste' the Germans' ammunition. Was that really how the Army saw war? Was it how the politicians who ran the war – Mr Churchill, Mr Atlee and the others – saw it? Was that all her brother Steve and her Cousin Mike and all those others who had never wanted to be soldiers, meant to those in power?

I hate it, she thought with sudden force. War, and all it means – I *hate* it.

The hospital reminded her of the 64th in Alexandria, with the influence of the Army apparent from the entrance, guarded by Privates instead of matelots, to the ward where eventually Thursday managed to find her way. Almost exhausted by her efforts to persuade the guards and nursing staff that she was a friend of one of the patients – what do they think I am, she wondered crossly, a spy? – she approached the QARMN sister and made her request yet again.

'Lieutenant Colonel Sangster?' The military nurse frowned. 'Yes, he's here. Who are you?'

'I'm a VAD at Haslar Naval Hospital, near Portsmouth. I was

nursing him there, and we knew each other in Egypt too. I'd like to see him.'

The Sister gave her a sharp glance and to Thursday's horror her eyes moved down to inspect her waist. 'It's not that!' she exclaimed in dismay. 'We've never – I've never – I just want to *see* him, that's all. I've come a long way.'

'Did he know you were coming?'

'No – I wanted it to be a surprise. Please,' she begged, 'please let me see him, just for a minute or two. There's something important I have to tell him.'

Suspicion returned to the Sister's eyes. 'I think I ought to ask him if he wants to see you, first. In any case, he already has a visitor.'

'I'll wait,' Thursday said. 'I don't mind waiting. If you could just let him know . . .'

'I'll see. You'd better wait out here. I don't want my patients upset.' She rustled away, leaving Thursday standing in the corridor, at a loss.

There were no chairs to sit on. She stood with her back against the wall, trying to look as if she belonged there. Nurses, doctors, patients and visitors brushed past her, some giving her curious looks, some not even appearing to notice her. I wish I hadn't come, she thought miserably. Elsie was right. I ought to have let him know. It was a crazy thing to do.

The door swung open. She looked up eagerly and saw a woman emerge. She was tall, with a pale, oval face and huge violet eyes. Her hair was set in immaculate Marcel waves and she was swathed in a lush, deep brown fur coat. Her shoes had the highest heels Thursday had ever seen.

She took no notice of Thursday. Instead, her attention was on the man behind her, the man holding the door open for her to pass through. She turned as she came out and lifted her hand to his cheek, and her voice carried clearly to Thursday, standing only a yard or two away.

'Goodbye for now, darling, and take care of yourself. I'll be here to fetch you first thing in the morning, and we'll have our own special Christmas together. Till then . . .' She reached up and kissed the man on the cheek, and then turned and tapped away along the corridor, leaving him looking after her.

Then he turned. His dark brown eyes met Thursday's and she

saw them widen with surprise. For a moment they stared at each other, then he said uncertainly, as if not quite believing what he saw, *'Thursday?'*

Thursday felt as if she had been nailed to the brown linoleum floor. She stared at him, unable to speak, unable to move. Then she pressed the back of her hand to her mouth and shook her head. She turned and began to run along the corridor. Behind her, she heard his voice. 'Thursday, wait! *Thursday!'*

But Thursday couldn't wait. Her whole body burning with shame and humiliation, deeply aware of her old coat and scuffed flat-heeled shoes, her brown hair with only natural waves and the Pond's lipstick that was all she could afford, she wanted nothing but to get away. Away from the hospital, away from Mark and, most of all, away from the rich, beautiful woman with whom he was going to spend Christmas.

You're a fool, Thursday Tilford, she told herself angrily as she made her way back to the station and climbed on board the next train returning to Portsmouth. A stupid, gullible fool. And it serves you right. It serves you *bloody* well right.

Chapter Twenty-One

'She looked like a film star,' she told Elsie when at last she was back at Haslar, shivering by the stove with her hands wrapped round a mug of cocoa. 'All expensive make-up and furs. Honestly, I felt such a fool. Such an *idiot*. Standing there in that old overcoat, looking like a *ragbag*!'

'You don't look like a ragbag. It's a very nice coat.'

'I did, beside her. Honestly, Else. I mean, I'd been travelling all day, I was all covered in smuts from the train, my hair was a mess – I could see what that snooty QARMN Sister thought. This little naval VAD chasing after him all the way from Portsmouth, not even letting him know I was coming. It was as plain as the nose on your face, she thought we'd had a fling and I was after him to marry me. She thought I was expecting a *baby*!' Her voice broke and she leaned her head on her hands and sobbed. 'I have never felt so humiliated in my life, never. It was *awful*.'

Elsie stroked her back sympathetically. 'It must have been. You poor thing. But didn't Mark say anything when he saw you?'

'I didn't give him a chance. I just got out as fast as I could.' Thursday raised a woebegone, tear-streaked face. 'Anyway, what could he have said, Elsie? It was obvious what was going on. They were going to spend *Christmas* together. She called him *darling*. She's his girlfriend, probably his fiancée. Maybe even his *wife*, for all I know. He was just stringing me along, that's what, having a bit of fun, and I was stupid enough to fall for it. Oh, *Elsie*!'

Elsie didn't know what to say. Thursday was probably right, yet she would never have thought Mark was the sort to string a girl along like that. 'He always struck me as a really nice bloke,' she said.

'When we were in Egypt he seemed as straight as a die. I'd have put money on him being really sweet on you.'

'Well, maybe he was,' Thursday agreed. 'And maybe he wasn't.' She remembered the starry nights in the desert, the ride in the gharry, the handful of stardust, and began to cry again. 'Oh, Elsie, I've been such a fool. And I've let Connor down too. I'll have to write and tell him—'

'No!' Elsie was alarmed. 'Don't do that, Thursday! What's the point of upsetting him now? It's all over anyway, he needn't ever know a thing about it. And you haven't done anything wrong. You and Mark – it never went further than a kiss or two. Did it?' she added, a little doubtfully.

'Of course it didn't! But I've let him down all the same. I *wanted* it to,' she confessed miserably. 'And there were times when I – I would have. I don't deserve a decent man like Connor, Elsie. I'll have to tell him.'

'Well, wait till he comes home then. Don't send him a *Dear John* and break his heart while he's thousands of miles away and can't do a thing about it. And if you'll take my advice you won't tell him at all.' Elsie took the mug gently from her hands. 'Look, this has gone cold. I'll make you some more.'

'That's wasteful. I'll drink it.'

'No, you won't. You need something hot inside you. Thursday, promise me you won't write to Connor about this. I bet we've all done some daft things in the past few years. Blimey, look at all the dances we've been to, all the blokes we've met. Look at all those little romances we had on the way out to Egypt. That chap you used to go out and spoon with – what was his name? – Eddy. And the others – you're not going to tell Connor about them, are you?'

'That's different.'

'It seems different now,' Elsie said, mixing cocoa with sugar and a spoonful of milk, 'but it might not in a few months' time. I'm only saying you shouldn't do anything in a rush, not while you're all upset. Once you've got over this, you'll see that it isn't so important after all. I mean, what you have to think about is what you're upset *about*. Is it because you know now you don't have a chance with Mark, or is it because you just feel you've made a fool of yourself?' She took the kettle from the top of the stove and poured it into the mug, stirring briskly.

Thursday took the mug and held it in her hands. She still felt cold, chilled right through to the bone. The journey back had seemed endless, with the train stopping at every tiny station plus a few times, without explanation, in the middle of the countryside with not a light showing anywhere. It had been cold and draughty, and the compartment had been filled with smoke. She'd been unable to stop the tears trickling down her cheeks and a sergeant sitting next to her had tried to offer comfort, but she'd brushed him away.

'I don't know, Elsie,' she said at last. 'I'm in such a muddle. And it was awful – I feel hot and cold every time I think about it. That Sister's face, and that woman, calling him *darling* and kissing him. And me in my old coat. But I wouldn't have gone if I hadn't wanted to see him again, would I? I mean, I wouldn't have gone all that way to see Eddy or the others.' She shook her head. 'I can't sort it out now. I'm just too tired, and I feel all muzzy.'

Elsie gave her a concerned look. 'You'd better get yourself into bed. Look, go and have a quick bath, that'll warm you up a bit, and I'll put a hot water bottle in your bed. I wouldn't be surprised if you hadn't caught a chill. And don't lay there going over it again all night. It's sleep you need. Things'll look better in the morning – they always do.'

Not always, Thursday thought as she rose obediently. Not when your life has been ruined, and you did it yourself.

Thursday had caught more than a chill – she developed a nasty dose of 'flu which kept her in bed for a week. She was moved into the Wrens' ward and became a patient for a while, nursed by – of all people – Vera Hapgood. If that wasn't an incentive to get better fast, she said to Elsie who popped in to see her, bringing a copy of *Woman's Own* and a small bar of chocolate, she didn't know what was.

'Actually, she's not a bad nurse,' she admitted, wiping streaming eyes. 'Not exactly the motherly type, but she does all the right things. Though she did keep me hanging on a long time for my tea this morning.'

'Probably goes against the grain, bringing one of us tea in bed!' Elsie grinned. 'Can't say I'd be in a hurry to do for her, to be honest. Anyway, the main thing is, will you be out in time for Christmas?'

'Oh yes, just about, though Sister says I'll need a few days to get my strength back. 'Flu knocks you right back. She says I might be a bit low for a while too.'

'Well, just remember that and don't start worrying about Connor again. Oh, that reminds me – a letter came for you.' Elsie fished in her pocket and brought out an envelope. 'Dunno who it's from.'

'You mean you haven't read it?' Thursday asked sarcastically, and caught her breath in a coughing fit which lasted a good three minutes. Vera Hapgood came bustling over and bossily dragged her into an upright position, pushing her pillows behind her. She took the letter away from Elsie and put it on Thursday's locker under the magazine.

'You'd better go now. She isn't really fit for visitors.'

'Yes, nurse. No, nurse. Three bags full, nurse,' Elsie said mockingly, but she got up and gave Thursday a grin. 'Got to be moving anyway, me and Pete are going to the pictures. We're going to see *The Way Ahead*. It's got David Niven in it – Pete says he's smarmy but *I* think he's gorgeous.'

Thursday leaned back against her pillows and gave her a faint smile. 'Thanks for coming, Else.'

'That's OK. Had to make sure you weren't being murdered.' Elsie gave a dark glance in the direction of Vera Hapgood, now attending to another patient. 'Anyway, you get better soon, we're missing you. And Gran says you've got to be sure and be better for Boxing Day, or she'll come in herself and drag you out.'

Thursday chuckled a little painfully. 'She would, too. Even Vera Hapgood wouldn't scare your gran when she'd made up her mind.'

Elsie departed and Thursday slid down in the bed and closed her eyes. Sitting up had eased the cough but made her feel faint, and she wanted nothing more than to sleep. She dozed off into an uneasy world of dreams, where she was on an endless train journey trying to reach a destination that grew further and further away and, as she dreamed, tears of weakness trickled from her eyes and soaked into her pillow.

The letter lay beneath the magazine, and when the ward orderly came to tidy up it slipped into her waste bucket and was thrown away.

The fighting continued. For some days there had been a news blackout on the Battle of the Bulge but there was plenty to be heard about the other areas of the war. All over Christmas and into the New Year, the battles in Italy, the Pacific and the South China Sea continued remorselessly, and thousands more people died. Thousands of families torn apart, Thursday thought, thousands of fathers, husbands, brothers killed, thousands of wives made widows and children left fatherless. It was cruel.

On Christmas Day she went round the wards with the others, singing carols in a rather cracked, husky voice, and being kissed under the mistletoe that one of the doctors had brought in from his garden at Hillhead. She had received a telegram from Connor, assuring her yet again of his love, and she carried it in her breast pocket, close to her heart, feeling a mixture of love and guilt. Since being ill, she had managed only to scribble a few short notes, but she was uneasily aware that she'd used her illness as an excuse. I don't know what to say to him any more, she thought. I feel as if everything I say could be a lie.

Boxing Day was a relief. She cycled with Elsie past Alverstoke church, where Patsy and Roy had got married, and down the Avenue to the War Memorial Hospital. The sight of the verandahs where the TB patients sat to get fresh air reminded her of her cousin Mike who had, as Jenny had predicted, been diagnosed with the disease and was in a sanatorium near Worcester. Luckily, the illness wasn't far progressed and he was expected to recover but his war was over, and Auntie Flo had said it was a blessing. At least she knew where he was and could visit him and see that he was being properly looked after.

Thursday was looking forward to seeing him again. She would have her own Christmas leave soon, and would be going home to see the family. Mary had dropped a hint or two in her letters about Jenny and Charlie planning a wedding, and she wanted to see Leslie again – he seemed to change every time she saw him, and Denise had written to say he was talking nineteen to the dozen and kept asking for his Auntie Thirsty.

Thinking of weddings reminded her of Elsie's plans. 'So is it the big day today, then? Is Pete giving you a ring?' Ever since she had told them the news in the dormitory, Elsie had refused to say any more about her engagement. 'Come on, Else, you've been just teasing us all this time. You've got to come clean now.'

'No, I haven't. You just wait and see.' Elsie turned her head to grin at her. Her face was alive with excitement, and Thursday laughed.

'I can see it in your face! Honestly, Elsie, you're like an open book.'

'Well, you just read quietly then. Me and Pete want to announce it properly, all right?' They crossed the road for the final lap along Ann's Hill Road, and she gave Thursday a concerned look. 'You OK?'

Thursday nodded. 'My legs are a bit shaky but I'll make it. I'll be glad to get in by the fire, though.'

Within another ten minutes they were being welcomed into the cottage. Mrs Jackson fussed around them, taking Thursday's coat and exclaiming over her thin, pale face. Mr Jackson pushed her into the second best chair by the fire, opposite old Mrs Jenkins, and she found a cup of tea thrust into her hand and a plate of biscuits – whole ones, not broken – set on the little table beside her. Elsie, who was still in the passage renewing acquaintance with Pete, whom she had not seen for almost forty-eight hours, came in after a few minutes, flushed and smiling, her hair somewhat tousled. Pete followed, his brown hair flopping over his beaming round face.

'Happy Christmas, Mum and Dad. Happy Christmas, Gran. Did you have a nice day yesterday?'

'Well, it wasn't like before the war,' began old Mrs Jenkins, rehearsing a well-worn theme, and then, catching her daughter's eye, 'but it wasn't so bad. Your mum cooked a nice dinner. I done the sprouts – straight out of the garden they were – and the pudding was all right, though she only let me have a bit, said it was bad for me.' The old lady snorted. 'Bad for me, I ask you! Christmas pudding! It's not even as if it was *rich*, not like before—'

'Before the war!' Elsie joined in. 'Never mind, Gran, we've got a nice box of chocolates for you, all soft centres, and you're to have them all to yourself. Here's a box for you too, Mum – Black Magic, your favourite. And some baccy for Dad, that Pete got with his issue. So no more complaints about the war, all right? It's Christmas and we're going to forget all that.'

'Oh, Elsie, you shouldn't have. These must have taken up all your ration for the past two months.'

Elsie patted her tummy. 'Do me good to go without. I need to lose a bit of fat for me wedding.'

There was a tiny silence. Marge and Alf Jackson stared at their daughter and then at Pete, standing self-consciously beside her, while old Mrs Jenkins gave a cackle of laughter and exclaimed that she knew it all along, she'd seen it coming, blest if she hadn't.

'Wedding!' Marge threw her arms round her daughter. 'Oh, Elsie, you naughty girl, you never gave us a clue! And you Pete, you're just as bad, coming in here and not saying a word. It's a good job we've got some sherry and port in for Christmas or we wouldn't even be able to drink your health.'

'And I dunno what happened to asking the father's permission,' Alf added, gripping the young sailor's hand and shaking it hard. 'But we'll say no more about that. Too glad to have someone take her off our hands.'

'Dad! What a thing to say!' But Elsie was laughing, and Thursday caught the sparkle in her eyes. She came forward and gave Elsie a kiss.

'Hey, shouldn't we be congratulating you? Where's the ring?'

Elsie held out her left hand. 'I thought you'd never ask. Well? What d'you think?'

Thursday gazed at it. Three small diamonds, just as Elsie had said she would have, glittered on her third finger. They were no more than tiny specks, but they were real enough and she felt a sudden lump in her throat. 'It's lovely, Elsie.'

Mrs Jackson took Elsie's fingers in hers and inspected the ring. 'It is. I'm really pleased. Congratulations, Pete.'

'Though I'm not sure you know what you're letting yourself in for,' her husband added, giving Elsie a smacking kiss. 'Better not be in too much of a hurry to tie the knot. You know what they say.'

'No, we don't, Dad,' Elsie said cheekily, bending to show her grandmother the ring. 'What do they say?'

'Marry in haste, repent at leisure,' piped up old Mrs Jenkins. 'That's what he means, ain't it? Not that he practised what he preaches, mind. He and our Marge were only engaged six months before they had—'

'Yes, and that's not all they say,' Mrs Jackson interrupted, her cheeks suddenly pink. 'Change your name and not the letter, marry for worse and not for better! Jenkins to Jackson, that's what I did, and look at me now.'

'Go on, love, you haven't done so bad,' her husband said, putting his arm round her plump waist. 'We haven't had a bad life, have we, all things considered.'

Marge Jackson gave him a glance that mixed fondness with mild exasperation. 'No, we haven't, as a matter of fact. If these two youngsters do half as well, they'll be all right.'

'That's true,' Mrs Jenkins agreed, 'but I hope they won't take too long getting round to the wedding. I want to see me granddaughter wed before I die.'

'Don't talk daft, Gran, you're going to live for years yet. But we're not going to hang about, are we, Pete? We've set the date already – St Valentine's Day, ain't that right?'

'Blimey, that don't give us long,' her father said. 'Still, I can see your point, Else, grab him while he's keen. And now what about something to celebrate? Didn't I see you put a bottle of sherry in the cupboard the other day, Marge? I'll get it out now, if young Thursday'll excuse me.' He leaned past her to open the door of the alcove cupboard and brought out the bottle. He poured a measure into each of the glasses that his wife brought in on a little tray, and lifted one into the air. 'Congratulations to the happy couple, and may all your troubles be little ones.'

'Alf! Honestly,' Marge said to Thursday, 'I don't know what to do with him sometimes. I'm already dreading his wedding speech.'

Alf Jackson grinned and then lifted his glass again. This time, his grin faded and his voice was solemn as he said, 'And here's a toast to absent friends.'

'Absent friends,' they echoed, and Thursday saw the moisture in their eyes and felt the tears pricking at her own.

Absent from the family today were Elsie's brothers Dave and Eddy. Dave, who hadn't been able to go into the Forces because of his leg which had never grown properly since he had infantile paralysis, had been killed by the bomb that had flattened their home in Portsmouth during the Blitz. Eddy, who was nearly twelve now, had been sent to the countryside soon after that and stayed there. Thursday knew that his mother had begged for him to come home for Christmas, but Alf had shaken his head. 'Not as things are now, love. Next year – it'll all be over by then. He'll be back for good. It won't be long now.'

Was he right, she wondered, lifting her glass in a private toast to her own 'absent friends' – her family in Worcester, her Cousin Mike in the sanatorium, her brother Steve in a German prisoner-of-war camp and her other cousin, Leslie, lost in his Spitfire. And Connor, somewhere off the coast of Africa.

And there was another absent friend too. Mark, who was no doubt enjoying Christmas with his rich, beautiful lady friend. His fiancée, perhaps. Possibly even, by now, his wife.

The sherry burned her throat and she blinked away the tears.

'That was a smashing day,' Elsie said dreamily as they cycled back through the darkened streets, their lights showing only the faintest glow to reveal the way. 'I think I'll get engaged more often.'

Thursday laughed. 'You're a dope. You just be satisfied with the one you've got. He's a nice chap.'

'Course he is. I only meant I'd get engaged to *him* more often. Anyway, we've got the wedding to think about now, I reckon that'll keep me busy. It's only two months, you know.'

'As you've pointed out at least a dozen times already.' Thursday was beginning to feel tired. It had been a good day but underneath all the celebrations she'd been conscious of a sense of loneliness. I'm missing Connor, she thought. I ought to be used to it by now but it seems to get worse as time goes on. It's been so long.

And she knew too that it wasn't just Connor she was missing. Try as she might, she couldn't push Mark's image out of her mind. His dark, narrow face and deep brown eyes wouldn't be pushed away. It was as if he were trying to force himself into her thoughts, refusing to be forgotten, refusing to be put into the past. It's because we never said a proper goodbye, she thought. And whose fault was that?

'What did that letter say?' Elsie asked suddenly, and Thursday turned her head to stare at her in the darkness.

'What letter?'

'You know – the one I brought you when you had 'flu. Postmarked Rochester. Don't tell me it wasn't from him. I've been waiting all this time for you to tell me,' Elsie added a little reproachfully.

'I don't know what you're talking about. I didn't have a letter.'

'Yes, you did. I brought it to you. I brought you a *Woman's Own* and a Mars bar. Cost me sixpence ha'penny, that lot did, and you say you never had them?'

'No, I'm not. I had them all right, but I never had a letter. Honestly, Elsie.'

'So what happened to it?' Elsie asked after a minute. They passed under the wall of St Mary's Church and cycled past Anglesey creek. 'What on earth happened to it?'

'I don't know. I must have gone to sleep or something. The *Woman's Own* and the Mars were inside my locker when I found them next day. But there wasn't any letter. Why – do you think it came from Mark?'

'Certain it did. Told you, the postmark was Rochester.' Elsie came to a halt and put one foot on the ground. 'Oh, *Thurs*. And I've been waiting all this time, wondering what it said.'

Thursday stopped too and put her head down on her handlebars. She felt a great flood of loneliness and misery engulf her. A letter from Mark. A letter, unread and unanswered. And now she would never know what he had said.

'I don't suppose it would have helped anyway,' she said, as much to herself as to Elsie. 'I expect it was just to tell me he was getting engaged. Or married. I expect it was to say goodbye.'

Chapter Twenty-Two

The battle for the Ardennes continued. In the Pacific, the Japanese began to launch kamikaze raids on American ships, their pilots screaming abuse as they plunged their aircraft into the helpless vessels below. In Italy, the Allies were slowed down by bad weather. In Burma, the British made a continual and steady advance. Back in Europe, Hungary declared war on Germany.

'Blimey,' Elsie said, 'talk about better late than never. Haven't they noticed the war's been going on over five years?'

'They couldn't do it before,' Louisa explained. 'They've only just—' But Elsie flapped her hands at her.

'It's all right, Lou, don't bother. I've given up trying to understand what's going on. All I know is they say we're winning, yet there's all these things happening all over the world and we're still getting the poor blokes here day after day. It don't make any sense to me.'

The Germans were still making raids over Britain. The V2s were inflicting terrible damage wherever they fell and V1s were still coming over too, fired now by Heinkel He-111 aircraft. At the same time, the authorities were, as Elsie said, behaving as though the end of the war must be in sight. The Home Guard had been disbanded before Christmas and paraded in Guildhall Square for their stand-down ceremony, and Portsmouth City Council was already planning the rebuilding of the city. There was talk of people being allowed to sail and boat off the local beaches by spring.

Thursday went home to see in the New Year with the family. As usual, everyone crowded into her parents' front room and Walter handed round glasses of sherry. He and Percy had dropped in at the pub earlier in the evening, but were home by ten, ready for the sandwiches and leftover Christmas cake that Mary and Flo had laid out on the table in the back room.

'Well, here's to another year,' he said, lifting his glass. 'Maybe this is the one that'll see the end of the war at last.'

'Oh, please God, I hope so,' Mary said feelingly. 'We've all had enough of it. Too much. Whoever would have thought, when we had our Thursday's twenty-first birthday party, that it'd still be going on over five years later?'

'It's probably just as well we didn't know,' Flo said. 'If I'd known then all the things that were going to happen – well, I don't know as I could've stood it.' She turned to Denise. 'Mind you, it's not been all bad. At least we've got our little Leslie to bring a bit of sunshine into our lives.'

'And we've done a lot of things we might not have done,' Thursday added. 'I have, anyway. If it hadn't been for the war I'd still be stuck in the tailor's workroom, setting sleeves! Being a VAD's been more interesting than that, specially going to Egypt.'

They sat quietly for a while. Thursday glanced around at the familiar faces, imagining the thoughts that were going on in each head. Her mother would be thinking of Steve, still in the POW camp, robbed of years of his youth but still alive. Auntie Flo would be grieving for Leslie but thankful that Mike had so miraculously returned to them. Denise would be missing Vic while Jenny, curled up on the settee with Charlie's arm around her, was looking forward to her own wedding, set for June.

The clock on the mantelpiece gave the whirring sound that meant it was about to strike. They all turned to look at it and saw the minute hand almost on the figure twelve. Midnight. The threshold of a new year.

'I'd like to propose a toast,' Walter said, clearing his throat. 'To all of us here. To absent friends. And to the end of the war.'

'The end of the war,' they echoed, and raised their glasses to their lips.

The room was quiet. And then Thursday lifted her head and took a little breath. 'Listen! Listen, everybody. They're ringing the bells!'

Denise, who was nearest the front door, scrambled to open it and they rushed outside, closing the door from the habit of five long years so that no light should escape. All along the street, other doors were opening and people coming out, calling greetings to each other and then falling silent to gaze at the stars and listen to the sound that had once been so familiar and was now so rare.

The bells of St John's Church, just around the corner, were ringing out into the frosty air. And over the river, in the city itself, they could hear the deeper tones of the cathedral bells, pealing with joy and hope and promise. Thursday felt the tears spring to her eyes and spill over her cheeks, while a hand groped for hers and gripped it hard.

'Is it really going to finish this year?' Denise whispered in her ear. 'Will Vic and Steve and all the others really be home this time next year, and everything be like it was again?'

'I hope so.' But Thursday didn't really believe that anything could be just as it had been before – not after all that had happened. They were going to have to start from scratch, building a new and different world. There was going to be so much to do . . .

But we'll be part of it, she thought with a sudden thrill of excitement. We're the ones that are going to do it. And as the bells sounded their message of hope, she thought of Connor and sent him a little prayer of love. *Perhaps we'll be part of it, together.*

Would 1945 really be the last year of the war?

It was bitterly cold all through January, and halfway through the month there was a tremendous thunderstorm accompanied by a powerful gale. Thursday and Louisa, deep in the underground theatre, knew little of it until the electricity failed and the hospital's own generators came into hasty operation, but Elsie reported later that it had been the best firework show she'd seen since before the war. 'You'd have thought it was another Blitz, except there were no bombs. There must have been some places struck, though. Honestly, the lightning was all over the sky, great jagged forks just like huge rips in a blackout curtain.'

A week later they woke to find the ground blanketed in snow. It was ankle-deep and all the matelots available were marshalled to clear the footpaths and roads through the hospital grounds. Some of the younger VADs built a snowman on the Quarter Deck and garnished it with a Petty Officer's cap. Thursday stared at it.

'Gosh, remember how we got hauled over the coals just for cycling along there? Do they realise they're dicing with death?'

'I think it's a case of catch 'em first,' Louisa said, looking amused.

'Doesn't it make you feel old, though. Once upon a time it would have been us getting up to tricks like that.'

'Yes, Thurs and me and Patsy, and the SBAs,' Elsie agreed. 'It all seems like a lifetime ago.'

'It was, for the boys.' Of the three of them – Tony West, Doug Brighton and Roy Greenaway – only Doug was still alive. He'd sent Elsie a Christmas card from somewhere in the Far East and asked her to remember him to the others. *Especially Thursday*, he'd scribbled. '*Tell her she's got to wait for me – like she promised!*

'I never did anything of the sort,' Thursday had protested when Elsie showed it to her. 'He's just taking the mickey – he knows we never got on.'

'Maybe he fancied you after all,' Elsie said wickedly. 'Maybe when the war's over he'll come marching back expecting you to fall into his arms and marry him. Then what will you do?'

'Well, that's one thing I *won't* have to worry about!' she retorted. 'I'll tell him to take a running jump, that's what. Anyway, he never will, and you know it. It's you he'll be coming back for, and what are *you* going to do when he asks you why you're a married woman?'

'A married woman,' Elsie sighed. 'Sounds lovely, doesn't it? Oh, I wish we'd decided to do it sooner – February seems ages away.'

But January, with is storms and blizzards, gave them too much to think about to bewail the slowness of time passing. All too soon, the month had drawn to a close and Elsie was beginning to panic.

'I'll never be ready in time! Mum's gone down with 'flu, and she's only got my frock half-made. She'll never get it finished now, and I'm useless with a needle.'

'Well, I'm not,' Thursday said. 'I was apprenticed for five years to a tailor, remember? I'll finish it.'

'Oh, Thurs, would you? Would you really?'

'Course I will. I'll go round every time I'm off duty. It'll be lovely to sew.' Thursday had seen the material for Elsie's wedding dress. It was actually a pair of cream satin curtains donated by a friend of Miss Makepeace, with some net for a veil. It had to be given back afterwards, but not many young women were able to have such a sumptuous wedding dress these days and Elsie knew how lucky she was. She had almost fallen to her knees in gratitude when Madam had given it to her, and had to have the swathe of silky fabric snatched away before her tears fell on it and stained it.

'Don't be silly, Jackson,' Madam had said sharply. 'Get up at once. My friend just happened to have this in a cupboard – no use during the blackout, of course – and she says once the war's over she'll refurbish right through. Naturally, I thought of you.'

'I don't know why, Madam,' Elsie said through her tears. 'I never thought you had that much time for me.'

Madam gazed at her for a moment, her bright brown eyes warm. 'Of course I have a great deal of time for you, Jackson,' she said. 'You're one of my best girls. You deserve something special for your wedding.'

'You can borrow it if you want to, for your wedding,' Elsie said to Thursday as they inspected the half-made dress at her grandmother's cottage. 'Madam says she's going to lend it out to anyone that wants one. She reckons there'll be a lot of Haslar weddings once the war's over.'

'I don't even know if I'm going to have a wedding,' Thursday said. 'I'm not making any decisions. I'm just going to wait and see.'

She had heard no more from Mark. Whatever the missing letter had said, he made no other effort to contact her, and she knew that it must have been goodbye. Even if it hadn't, she thought, he would have taken her silence for one. And she couldn't bring herself to write and tell him that she had never received his letter. The humiliation of another rejection would be too much to bear.

St Valentine's Day was on a Wednesday. Funny day to get married, Elsie said, but never mind. If people couldn't come to the wedding itself at St Mary's Church, they could pop round to the village hall in the evening where everyone was invited. Now that Thursday had taken over the frock, her mum would be able to do a bit of baking, helped by various neighbours and relatives in both Gosport and Portsmouth. Marge still wasn't a hundred per cent, she said, but she could manage a few cakes and sausage rolls, and she'd saved the Christmas cake for the wedding cake. No icing, of course, but icing hadn't been seen for years now and they'd almost forgotten what it looked like. Instead, she covered it in white paper and stood a figure of a sailor and his bride on top. She had shown Thursday the two lead soldiers, rescued from Eddy's old toybox, and while Alf found some dark blue paint to turn one into a matelot Thursday sewed a tiny satin frock on the other and covered its head with a scrap of net.

'It's not the sort of send-off we'd have given her before the war,' old Mrs Jenkins said in her reedy voice, 'but there you are, it's the best we can do, and I do want to see her settled before I die. At least she's getting married in white. And entitled to be, too, I hope,' she added, fixing her daughter with a stern look. 'Not like some I could mention.'

'Isn't it time for your medicine, Mum?' Marge interrupted. 'You know the doctor said every four hours prompt. She wanders a bit,' she added to Thursday in a low voice. 'And she's not been herself at all since Christmas. Keeps going off in a sort of dream, as if she's not quite with us, you know what I mean? I asked our Elsie to have a look at her when she was over yesterday and she said we ought to get the doctor in. But Mum's getting on, when all's said and done – eighty in March. It's a good age.'

Thursday glanced at the old woman. She lay back in her armchair, her eyes closed, and Thursday was alarmed to see how papery and yellow her skin had become, and how it seemed to have shrunk against the bones of her face. Her eyes too had a yellow tinge when she opened them for a moment, and her breathing seemed shallow and difficult.

'Has she had 'flu as well? Elsie didn't say.'

'No, not 'flu. Just going downhill, you know.' Mrs Jackson mouthed the words so that the old woman wouldn't hear them. 'It's old age. The doctor can't do anything.'

'I think you ought to call him, all the same. I mean, I don't know anything about old people but she really doesn't look well. It would be a shame if anything happened before the wedding.'

Marge looked alarmed. 'You think it could be that bad?'

'I don't know. I don't know anything about it. But . . .' Thursday left her sentence unfinished, afraid that the old woman's hearing might be sharper than they supposed. She might not be asleep at all, but listening to every word. Marge frowned anxiously.

'I suppose you and Else see more than we do, not being here all the time. You know, we get used to how she is, we don't see the changes. Oh dear, I don't know what to do for the best.'

'Get the doctor,' Thursday advised. 'I know it costs money, but Elsie would rather have her granny at the wedding than another dozen sausage rolls.' She snapped off her thread of Sylko and began to put away her sewing things. 'I'll have to be going now, Mrs

Jackson. With all this snow and ice still about, I couldn't ride my bike and you can't be sure when the buses will run. I want to get back while it's still light – I don't like walking down Clayhall Road by myself in the dark. It feels haunted.'

'I expect it is,' Mrs Jackson said. 'All those poor sailors who've been along there and through those gates. And ending up in the cemetery,' she added ghoulishly. 'And then never knowing if one of those awful rockets will come down on top of you.'

'Yes, well, I'll be going, then,' Thursday said hastily. Elsie's mother was remarkably like her daughter at times. She bent over the recumbent figure of old Mrs Jenkins and laid her hand on the thin, bony wrist. The pulse felt light and jumpy. 'And you will get the doctor, won't you?'

'Yes, if you think I should.' Marge Jackson stared at her mother, her mouth working a little. 'I can see what you mean. I've been able to see it for days really, only I felt so poorly meself. And I didn't want to think about it, somehow. I mean, she's me mum. She's always been there. I know she's old but – well, you never want to lose your mum, do you?'

'No,' Thursday said, thinking of how terrible it would be to lose her own mother. 'No, you don't.'

She went out of the house and began the walk back to Haslar. It was hardly even worth waiting for a bus, and she would have had to walk the last half mile anyway. The worst half mile, she thought, between those high, haunted walls.

I wish I'd never said that to Mrs Jackson, she thought ruefully. It was bad enough before, just being in the dark and wondering if a rocket was on its way, but now I've got all those dead sailors to think about as well. And those poor young Wrens who were killed in that big raid and buried in the cemetery here. Plus all the others who have died at Haslar over the last two hundred years and whose ghosts may be out on a night like this . . .

It was stupid to think like that, letting her imagination run away with her. But death seemed very much in the air, somehow, and as she half-ran that last half mile she shivered with sudden premonition. Something was going to happen. She was sure of it.

Daylight next morning dispelled Thursday's fears and she scolded herself for being silly. After five years of war, she ought to be used to fear and death – it had become so much a part of daily living that you just pushed it out of your mind – but there had been something particularly eerie about the idea of the dead sailors. Thousands of people were buried at Haslar – it was one of the first things Madam told new arrivals during her welcoming lecture, when she related a little of its history. Even before the hospital had been built, it was a common burial ground, and then most of the sailors who arrived were already dying. In one year alone, nearly two thousand men had died there, and then there were thousands more who came back from Corunna already too far gone with typhus to be saved, and nearly four thousand others in the paddock – and then the Turkish colony which had settled in Gosport . . . No wonder I got the shivers, Thursday thought. You could drive yourself right round the bend, thinking about them all!

Firmly, she thrust her fears away, yet a few shreds still remained, hanging like cobwebs at the edge of her mind, and she couldn't quite rid herself of the sense of dread that had attacked her as she scurried between those high, redbrick walls.

As February came, the fighting continued as bitterly as the winds that scoured the frozen rutted slush still lining the roads. Yet it did seem that the tide was turning the Allies' way. The Red Army had crossed into Germany and were less than a hundred miles from Berlin. The United States, led by General MacArthur, were advancing through the Philippines to Manila, preparing to attack Japan, and the British had raided Japanese-controlled oil refineries in Sumatra. And there were *still* countries joining in – in South America, Ecuador declared war on Germany and Japan, Venezuela was reported to be considering the same action, and it seemed likely that Chile would follow suit before long. As Elsie said, it was better late than never, and if they all joined this new United Nations that was being talked about it would be all to the good.

Not that Elsie had much time to bother about the news these days. When she wasn't in the ward she was entirely wrapped up in wedding preparations. You wouldn't think there'd be so much to do, Thursday thought, when there was so little in the shops and the happy couple weren't even going to set up a proper home together. But they both seemed to have endless numbers of relatives in Portsmouth, Gosport and Fareham, and all would expect to be invited, even if they had to bring their own sandwiches. 'And that wouldn't be a bad idea,' Elsie observed. 'Be easier all round. But you can't ask people to do that, can you, even in wartime. And I don't want to look back in fifty years' time and just remember spam sandwiches!'

In the event, a number of relatives got together and organised a wedding feast, collecting contributions from the rest and spending the final week in a frenzy of baking. They descended on the Memorial Hall the night before the wedding and set up trestle tables, covering them with sheets and an assortment of crockery, and refused to let Elsie in when she and the other girls arrived begging to see how they were getting on. 'Go away,' said a middle-aged lady who seemed to be one of the aunts, although Thursday never made out whether she was Elsie's or Pete's and wasn't convinced that they knew, either. 'Go away. You can't come in. It's to be a surprise.'

'Blimey, what the flipping heck are they up to in there?' Elsie muttered as the two girls turned away. 'All they're supposed to be doing is a few sausage rolls.'

Thursday giggled. 'Maybe the sausages are trying to escape. Come on, let's go to the village inn and have a drink to celebrate your last night of freedom. I don't see why it should be just the man who gets a stag night.'

'And Pete had better not enjoy *his* last night of freedom too much,' Elsie said darkly. 'I've told him, if he turns up with a thick head it's all off.'

They strolled on to the village inn, passing the church where Elsie would be married next day. Thursday felt Patsy close beside her, and squeezed her arm, knowing she must be thinking of her own wedding day. Elsie had been afraid that Patsy wouldn't want to come but Patsy had told her not to be so silly. 'Of course I'm coming to your wedding. I can't moon around here while all the rest of you are having fun. And I don't expect people to stop living just because – because –' It was obviously not going to be easy for her, but Patsy had surprised them all with her courage and Thursday knew that nobody seeing her next day would guess that she nursed a broken heart.

'Looking forward to being a bridesmaid, Thursday?' Louisa enquired as Elsie went to the bar for their drinks. 'It's your second time, isn't it?'

'Yes.' Thursday had been Patsy's bridesmaid too. 'Once more, and that's my chances of ever getting married gone right out of the window. You know what they say – three times a bridesmaid, never a bride!'

'That's a pity,' Louisa said. 'I was going to ask you to be mine too.'

They stared at her. 'When are you getting married? Is Andrew coming back?'

Louisa laughed. 'Not as far as I know. I'm just thinking ahead to the end of the war. There'll be hundreds of weddings then, and I want to be ready for mine – I don't want to wait. How about you, Thursday?'

Thursday flushed. 'I don't know. We've got to see if we still feel the same. And there's his family too – they're so different from mine.'

'What does that matter? They're not marrying each other.'

'No, but it means *we're* different. He's more like you, Lou – in ordinary life, you could have met and gone out together and nobody would have batted an eyelid. But me and Connor, we'd never have come across each other. My family are just working class, and his father's a doctor like him.'

'I don't think that sort of thing'll matter after the war,' Louisa said. 'Class, and all that – it doesn't mean a thing these days. Look at you three, you're as good VADs as the rest of us who come from privileged backgrounds. Better than some. And look at all the working-class girls and men who've gone on to get commissions in the Services. And done good things in civvy life, too. We'll never be able to go back to a class system, with people firmly put back in their boxes.'

Thursday shook her head. 'I don't know. There'll still be a huge amount of working-class people who'll stay there. People in factories and things. How can they ever get out, once things go back to the way they were?'

'But they won't, that's the point. The Government's talking about making education better for everyone, so that you can go to a grammar school just through passing a scholarship exam, and not have to pay. Anyone bright enough will be able to go. *You* three could have gone.'

'Gone where?' Elsie asked, bringing the drinks over.

'To grammar school,' Thursday said. 'Lou says we'll all be posh when the war's over.'

Elsie gave a hoot of laughter. 'That'll be the day! Common as muck I am, always have been and always will be. What are we going to do, take elocution lessons? "How now, brown cow" and all that?'

'No, but your children might,' Louisa said. 'Honestly, this war is going to make a difference. Look at the last one – women did so much then, they just *had* to give them the vote. Well, this time they'll see that it's intelligence and hard work that matter more than inheriting a lot of money.'

'And that's just as well,' Elsie said cheerfully, 'because I'm never likely to inherit money, and neither are my kids. Now look, you've all got a drink in front of you – isn't anyone going to drink my health? It's my wedding day tomorrow, just in case you've forgotten!'

They laughed and raised their glasses. 'To Elsie,' Thursday declared. 'Elsie and Pete. A long life and a happy one.'

Patsy and Louisa echoed her words. They drank, and then set down their glasses. But as the other three began to laugh and chatter, Thursday felt once again that tiny chill of premonition, as if something were about to happen.

Don't be daft, she scolded herself. Of course something's going to happen. Elsie's getting married. That's all. And everything's going to be all right.

Chapter Twenty-Three

Elsie's wedding day dawned bright and sunny, one of those February days when spring seems suddenly to have woken up and rushed to action stations. Thursday, waking early, stretched in her bunk and rolled over to peer down at Elsie on the lower bed. 'Come on, slug-abed. You're getting married, remember?'

Elsie yawned and pulled the blanket over her head. 'I'm getting my sleep in. Don't expect I'll get much tonight.'

'Oh, *Elsie*.' Thursday grinned and slid down to the floor. She took hold of the corner of Elsie's blankets and tugged, leaving her curled up in her pyjamas. 'Hope you've got something a bit daintier than those to wear. Talk about passion-killers!'

'As a matter of fact,' Elsie said, sitting up reluctantly and trying to drag the blankets out of Thursday's grasp, 'I've got a smashing new nightie. Gran gave it to me yesterday. She said she didn't need the coupons so she'd saved them up and they had it in that shop in Stoke Road, kept since before the war. Only found it a few days before, apparently. I meant to show it you.' She gave up trying to get the blankets back and reached under her bunk for her suitcase. 'Look.'

'It's lovely.' Thursday gazed at the shimmering white fabric. 'It's Swiss cotton, isn't it? You mean to say they'd got this hidden away all these years?'

'Yes, you can tell because there are still yellow marks where it's been folded so long, see? Mum gave it a good wash but she couldn't get them all out.' Elsie held the nightgown against herself and swayed dreamily. 'I never thought I'd have anything like this for my wedding night.'

'You'll knock him out,' Thursday declared. 'Show it to the others and then put it away again. There's a lot to do and *you* might be on leave as of now, but me and the others have still got duties to go to. Now look, me and Patsy'll be off at twelve and we'll have our baths then and come straight over to your gran's, all right? Right – you can have your blankets back,' she added, piling them on Elsie's bunk, 'and have your lie-in.'

'Go on, I'll never get back to sleep now. I'll come over to breakfast with you. Got to keep up my strength.' She glanced out of the window. 'It's going to be a nice day! Maybe I'll have a walk along the sea wall first to pass the time. Just you make sure you and Patsy are there by one o'clock. Mum wants us all to have dinner together before we start to get ready.'

Thursday ran down the steps to the operating theatre with a lighter heart. It was just the bad weather that had made her feel a bit down lately, she thought, that and the 'flu she'd had before Christmas. Today, the sun was out and everything seemed brighter. Elsie was getting married, and even though there was still a long way to go, the war really did seem to be coming to an end. Mike was doing well in the sanatorium, Steve was OK in prison camp, Connor was now on his way to Australia as part of the South Pacific Fleet, and Vic was in Italy. She turned her mind away from the things that might yet go wrong. Today wasn't a day for being miserable.

By lunchtime, all those going to Elsie's wedding were in a frenzy. Everyone who could get the afternoon off duty was going, even Vera Hapgood who had apologised (rather ungraciously, but then as Elsie remarked she probably didn't know any other way) for her remarks about Elsie when they'd first returned from Egypt. 'She's not really so bad,' Thursday had said, urging Elsie to include her in the guest list. 'I feel rather sorry for her. She just finds it difficult to make friends, that's all.'

'She could try being nice to people for a start,' Elsie said, but she wrote her name on the list and Vera had responded by giving her a toasting fork as a wedding present and got out her best civvy clothes for the occasion. Being Vera, however, even that hadn't gone right.

'Oh *no*, there's a moth-hole in my green jumper! Look, right in the front.' She held up the garment and they crowded round to look.

'It's not very big,' Ellen said uncertainly, and Vera snorted.

'It'll show, just the same. I'll have to darn it – anyone got any wool that might match?'

Nobody had, and Vera had to darn it with a scrap of navy-blue wool which was all that they could find. 'It'll show even more now,' she moaned. 'I'll have to wear my waistcoat to hide it, and Elsie wore that herself, when Patsy got married!'

Thursday bit her lip and glanced swiftly at Patsy. It was inevitable that there would be reminders of that other wedding day four years ago, but Patsy gave no sign. It was as if she had determined that Elsie's day was to be a happy one, with no sad memories.

'You'll look OK,' Thursday told Vera. 'I think a waistcoat looks smart anyway, and it just picks up the colour of your jumper. Nobody'll notice that darn if you keep it buttoned up.'

She and Patsy, as bridesmaids, were going to the cottage near Ann's Hill, to help Elsie get ready and dress in their own finery. Carried away by her success in finishing Elsie's wedding dress, Thursday had altered two old dance dresses, sent for by Louisa from her own pre-war wardrobe, and when the three girls were all arrayed in the tiny bedroom they looked at each other in amazement.

'Blimey,' Elsie said in an awed tone, 'is this really us? We look proper glamorous.'

'It's this gorgeous material,' Patsy said, touching the satin of Elsie's dress with her fingertips. 'It's like something in a film. And these lovely frocks of Louie's. That colour looks really smashing on you, Thursday.'

'Well, I've always liked green but I was afraid Elsie might not like it for her wedding,' Thursday admitted. 'I mean, you might have thought it was unlucky.'

'Not that colour – it's more of a turquoise, isn't it? Sea-green, anyway. And that rose pink's lovely on you, Pats, with your dark hair.' Elsie turned slowly, trying to glimpse more of her own dress in the dressing-table mirror. 'Mum thought it was a bit funny not having matching bridesmaids but I reckon it's going to look smashing. A rainbow wedding.'

'Yes,' Thursday said slowly. 'A rainbow wedding. Bringing hope – that's what rainbows are supposed to do, aren't they? Hope for the world.'

'Coo, we are getting deep!' Elsie giggled. 'Come on, Thurs, stop going all poetic and come downstairs. You're supposed to be going on ahead with Mum, remember, and then Dad and me in the second taxi, and I don't want to be late, even if it is the bride's privilege. Pete might decide to call it all off while he's still got the chance!'

They went downstairs carefully, trying not to catch their dresses against the walls of the narrow staircase. The Jacksons were waiting in the front room, all arrayed in their Sunday best and with Eddy, home for the occasion, in a jacket handed down from one of his cousins. It was the first time Thursday had seen Eddy since she'd returned from Egypt and she could scarcely believe that this tall, lanky youth was the same noisy little boy she'd first met over in Copnor. He grinned at her self-consciously but there was no time to talk, for the rest of the family were exclaiming over the girls' appearance.

'Oh Elsie, you look beautiful,' Marge Jackson said, her eyes filling with tears. 'Doesn't she, Alf?'

'Looks a proper picture,' he agreed a bit huskily. 'So do you other two, for that matter. If I was young Pete, I'd be hard put to it to know which one to marry, and that's the truth! Now look, the taxi's at the door and you'd all better get in, though it's going to be a bit of a squash with five of you.'

'Let Gran come with us,' Elsie said. 'It's daft having that lot in one car and only you and me in the other one. You can sit in the front, Gran, with the driver.'

'I don't know as I want to come after all,' the old lady said, and Thursday noticed with alarm that her colour seemed bad again, despite the new medicine that the doctor had prescribed. Following her advice, Marge had called the doctor but he'd shaken his head and said there wasn't much he could do, it was old age and nature must take its course. All he could do was prescribe something to help her but all it seemed to do, Marge said, was make her sleep more. Though maybe that wasn't a bad thing; sleep was always good for you.

One of these days, Thursday thought, she's going to go to sleep and not wake up again, and the doctor knows that.

'Not come?' Elsie echoed in dismay. 'Gran, you've got to come. You know you've been wanting to see me married. And you've got all dressed up, too.'

'Perhaps it was too much for her,' Marge said in a low voice. 'All the fuss and bother – she's had enough.'

Elsie went down on her knees beside the old lady. 'Please come, Gran. It won't be the same without you.' She laid her plump hand over the skinny claw and looked into the rheumy, yellowing eyes. 'Please.'

There was a little silence, then the old lady sighed. 'Oh, all right then, seeing as it's you. Get me into the car. But I'm not doing any dancing, mind. Nor any washing up or any of that.'

Elsie laughed. 'You won't have to! Just see me get married and enjoy yourself, that's all I ask. And you won't have to stay late, we'll get a taxi specially to bring you home, whenever you want it.'

Marge looked at the clock on the mantelpiece. 'Come on, you girls, it's time we went!' She kissed her daughter. 'Have a happy life, Elsie,' she said softly. 'If you do half as well as your dad and me you'll be all right. Now, I'll see you in church, and mind out for that dress in the car door!'

The wedding went smoothly from start to finish, not counting the small cousin who cried through the entire service, the row over a piece of wedding cake between two of Elsie's aunts who hadn't spoken for years and ought (Alf Jackson said caustically) to have stayed that way, and the local stray dog which somehow got in and made off with a whole plate of sausage rolls. But everyone agreed that the bride looked lovely, the groom not too hung over and quite overwhelmed when he saw her walk up the aisle, the bridesmaids were pretty and the reception every bit as good as a really posh do. (Better, said Louisa, who'd been to more posh do's than most of them.) And there was plenty to eat and drink, thanks to all the contributions that had been made, and all that was left at the end of the meal were six Spam sandwiches.

'I knew someone'd bring some,' Elsie remarked, helping to clear up for the dancing. 'Even the flaming dog turned its nose up at them.'

'Go away,' Thursday said, giving her a push. 'You're not supposed to be doing this. You're the bride.'

'Once a skivvy, always a skivvy,' Elsie said cheerfully, but went off to find her new husband. 'Come on, Pete, let's get the gramophone going and have a dance.'

'You're not supposed to be doing it either, Thursday,' one of

Elsie's cousins said. 'You're a bridesmaid. Go and find a partner and enjoy yourself. There are plenty of us here to do this.'

Thursday hesitated, then went to join Patsy beside the dance floor. One of Pete's mates was looking after the gramophone and plenty of people had brought records. There seemed to be a bit of everything, from Victor Silvester to Ambrose, and just at the moment he was playing Glenn Miller's 'Little Brown Jug', with everyone singing the words.

'They never found him, did they?' Thursday said sadly. 'He must have been shot down, I suppose.'

'Like that film star Leslie Howard a couple of years ago,' Patsy agreed. 'I liked him, didn't you? He was lovely in *Gone with the Wind*. And *Pimpernel Smith*, and *The First of the Few*. It seems an awful shame when people like that get killed, when all they're trying to do is entertain people.'

They watched the dancers for a few minutes. The record changed to an old Tommy Dorsey, with Frank Sinatra singing. Else and Pete were jitterbugging, to applause from their friends and the amazement of their families. Alf Jackson, his mouth open, blinked as Pete swung his bride over his shoulder, and called out, 'Is that what you get up to at those dance halls? I'd have put my foot down if I'd known!'

'And a fat lot of good it would have done you,' Elsie shouted back. 'Come on, Dad. Have a go!' She dragged him out on to the floor and nodded at Pete's sailor friend to play the record again.

Thursday giggled. She turned to Patsy to say something and then, over Patsy's shoulder, her eye caught the movement of the door opening and she felt her voice die in her throat.

A man had come quietly in. He was tall, with broad shoulders and a dark, narrow face. His glance moved intently around the room, noting first the dancers and then the people who stood or sat around the fringe. As Thursday watched, frozen, he saw her and for a moment of icy, unreal silence, she felt as if the world had stopped.

'Patsy,' she whispered, 'tell me I'm dreaming. Please, for God's sake, tell me I'm dreaming.'

'How did you know where to find me?' she asked as they moved around the dance floor in a slow foxtrot.

Mark smiled down at her. 'I went to Miss Makepeace. She told me you were all here at Elsie's wedding reception.'

'Oh yes, she was at the service, but she went back after that. But – I still don't know why . . .'

'Why I'm here? I came to find you, of course, Thursday.'

She was silent. It was obvious that was what he had come for, but *why* was another question. And it was just one of the tumult of questions flooding her brain, now that the first shock of seeing him was over. The girl at Rochester. The unread letter. Why – why – *why*?

'Why now, after all this time?' she asked, half to herself. 'Why today?'

'Surely you know what day it is,' he said, whirling her round the corner.

'It's Elsie's wedding day. But you didn't know that, did you? And I still don't see—'

'Thursday,' he said gently, 'it's St Valentine's Day. The day for sweethearts to find each other. What better day could there be for me to come and find you?'

St Valentine's Day! She stared at him, shocked. 'It's my godson's birthday,' she said stupidly, her mind veering away from his words. 'Leslie, my cousin Denise's little boy. He's four.'

'It's the day for sweethearts,' he insisted, swirling her around again. 'Thursday, for God's sake let's get out of here. I can't hear myself think with all this racket going on, and I want you to myself, somewhere quiet.'

'But I'm a bridesmaid!'

'The wedding's over. Look, Elsie and her man are getting ready to leave. The party'll be breaking up soon anyway. Come *on*.'

'I've got to be in by ten-thirty.'

'You haven't,' he said. 'I squared it with Miss Makepeace. She says you can have till midnight. Come on, Thursday, we've got things to talk about.'

She stopped in the middle of the floor and stared at him. 'You squared it with Madam? You asked her if I could stop out late, without even knowing if I'd want to? Just who do you think you are, Mark Sangster? Who do you think *I* am?' Only vaguely aware of the other dancers trying to pass them, of people stopping to look, she went on, her voice rising, '*I* decide when I want a late pass, right? *I* decide when I'll stay out late, and who with! And why on earth do you think I should want to stay out late with you anyway? What's all this about? Your glamorous fiancée left you, has she, so you thought you'd slip back to Haslar and see if that little VAD was still in love with you? Well, take it from me she's not! I don't know why you came here, and I don't know why you've gatecrashed Elsie's wedding, and I *don't care*! I never want to see you again – *never*!'

There was a moment of complete silence. Thursday stood glaring at him, panting slightly, her eyes snapping with fury. Mark stared back at her, his lazy eyes open wide. And then the little ring of onlookers who had formed about them broke into spontaneous applause.

'That's it, Thurs! You tell him!' 'Tell him where he gets off!' 'Crikey – don't she look a smasher when she's in a bate!' 'Tell you what, *I* wouldn't like to cross her, matey, straight I wouldn't.' 'Bet she's a right tartar on the wards.'

Thursday glanced around and flushed scarlet. With a little sob, she put both hands up to her burning face and ran towards the door. It opened as if by magic and she ran straight through and out into moonlight. The night air struck like ice against her bare arms and she hesitated, then turned left for the hospital. I don't care if I do catch cold, she thought, I'm not going back in there again. *Nothing* would make me go back in there again.

'Thursday! *Thursday!* Wait a minute!'

The voice only made her run faster. Go away, she thought frantically, stumbling along the slippery pavement, go away. Leave me alone. But as she heard the footsteps behind her draw nearer, she knew it was useless and she stopped and leaned against the cemetery wall, panting and half sobbing. In another moment Mark was beside her, wrapping her coat – the same old blue overcoat that she'd worn to visit him in Rochester – around her shoulders. Gently, he took her in his arms and with one hand pressed her head to his chest, and she gave in and rested there while the sobs turned into real weeping and she trembled against his body.

'There,' he said softly. 'There. It's all right. My sweet, sweet Thursday, everything's all right.'

'It's not all right,' she wept. 'It's not all right at all. I was getting over you. I was *sure* I was getting over you. And now you've come back and – and I don't – I don't know – oh, Mark, what am I to do? What *am* I to do?'

He said nothing for a while. He continued to hold her, his hand stroking her hair. At last her sobs began to diminish and she lifted her tear-streaked face to look at him. He cupped her chin in his hand and bent to kiss her lips.

'I don't know what's going to happen, or what you're going to do,' he said. 'All I know is, I couldn't go away again without seeing you just once more. Without trying to find out,' he paused, 'without trying to find out once and for all just what we mean to each other – even if we mean anything at all. At least,' he laughed a little shakily, 'I know what you mean to me, Thursday. What I don't know, is what I mean to you.'

She stared at him. 'But you do. Why else would I have come all the way to Rochester to see you?'

'So why,' he asked, looking at her very seriously, 'didn't you answer my letter?'

The letter! Thursday had almost forgotten it. With the excitement of Mike's return, followed by the anxiety over his illness, and then Christmas and the hustle of preparing for Elsie's wedding, together with the worry over old Mrs Jenkins's health, she had completely forgotten the letter. In any case, she had made up her mind that it was no more than a formal goodbye, written perhaps from a guilty conscience. It had never occurred to her that Mark might be waiting for an answer.

'I never got your letter,' she said. 'At least, I did – Elsie says I did – but I was ill with 'flu and never saw it. It got lost. I only knew about it when Elsie asked me about it after I came out of the ward.'

'You were ill?' he broke in. 'Badly enough to be in hospital?'

'It was only 'flu,' she said, brushing it aside. 'I'm all right now. But I never saw your letter, Mark. I don't know what it said. And after I saw you with your – your fiancée that day – well, I knew it was all over anyway.' She looked up at him. 'Is that what you've come to tell me? That you're getting married?'

'Getting *married*?' He stared at her, then broke into laughter. 'Thursday, you've got it all wrong. That wasn't my fiancée. That was my . . .' He laughed again. 'This is beginning to sound like an old music-hall joke! Thursday, that wasn't my fiancée, that was my—'

His voice was drowned by a sudden clamour from the direction of the Memorial Hall. They both turned, startled, and saw in the silvery light a little crowd of people spill out on to the pavement, and then heard another voice – Elsie's voice. 'There they are!'

'They're coming after us,' she said, bewildered.

'Thursday!' Elsie's voice sounded again, and she recognised the note of panic in it. 'Thursday – is Mark there with you?'

'Yes,' she called. 'Why? What's happened?'

'We need him! We need a doctor.' Elsie was running towards them, a pale, shimmering ghost in her satin wedding dress. 'It's Gran, she's been took poorly. Louie and Patsy are with her now, but I'm scared. Oh, Thursday, I'm scared she's—'

Thursday gave him a push, but he was already running. The crowd seemed to gather him up, Elsie clinging to his arm as they raced towards the hall, and Thursday followed as quickly as she could, her overcoat still clutched around her shoulders. By the time she reached the door there was a crowd around it, everyone trying to scramble in at once. She thrust her way through, and they recognised her and let her pass. But when she stood at last looking down at the crumpled little figure on the floor, covered now by the coats that had been draped over her to try to keep her warm, she knew the truth. Old Mrs Jenkins had seen her granddaughter married, and then died.

Chapter Twenty-Four

'So why *did* you come?' Thursday asked. She was sitting opposite Mark in the British Restaurant that had been opened in the grammar school premises in Walpole Road. He'd wanted to take her somewhere smarter but, exhausted by the events of the day before and upset by Mrs Jenkins's death, she'd begged to go somewhere simple, close by. And British Restaurant food wasn't bad, after all. Meat and two veg and a pudding to follow, for just one and sixpence.

'I meant to spend more than one and sixpence on taking you out,' Mark said, looking ruefully at the menu. 'Woolton Pie and apple and custard. It's not much of a celebration.'

'I don't know what we're supposed to be celebrating,' Thursday said. She propped one elbow on the table and leaned her aching head on her hand. 'I wouldn't feel like it even if I did know.'

'Oh, come on, Thursday. The old lady was a good age and she had a nice easy death. Think of all the people you've seen die in pain and agony. The young men you've sat beside in hospitals. Look, if anyone asked me how I'd like to die, that's just the way I'd choose – at a party with all my family and friends around me, having just been to the wedding of my favourite grandchild! What more could anyone ask?'

'You've got some then, have you? Grandchildren?' Thursday said with a weak attempt at a joke. 'Oh, I suppose you're right, but well, for the past fortnight I've had this feeling something sad was going to happen, and I've been worried about Mrs Jenkins too. I knew she was poorly. It seems such a shame that it should happen on Elsie's wedding night.'

'Well, that's the way things go,' Mark said. 'It could have been a lot worse. I knew a fellow whose wedding reception was ruined by a bomb falling on it.'

'Oh, no!' Thursday stared at him, horrified. 'Was anyone killed?'

'Most of them. Thursday, you know we can't keep mourning, and Mrs Jenkins had had her life. It's not as if it was a baby or a young person dying.'

'No, you're right.' She took her elbow off the table and leaned back in her chair. 'So why *did* you come, Mark? And what about the letter you sent me? And the person you say isn't your fiancée?'

'Well, she isn't.' He looked at her and shook his head slowly. 'Oh Thursday, Thursday. If only you hadn't rushed off like that it could have been all cleared up there and then. Saved us both a lot of heartache.'

'Who says my heart's been aching?' she demanded at once, sitting up straight, then drooped again as he smiled at her.

'There must have been *some* reason why you came all that way, and it wasn't to bring me a Christmas card! Thursday, let's stop playing games with each other. One of the things I've always liked about you is that you're so straight, so direct. Anyway, I don't mind admitting *my* heart's been aching. Especially when you never replied to my letter.'

'I really didn't get it, Mark. I don't know what happened to it. Elsie said she put it on the locker, and I can only think it got tidied away and lost. Are you going to tell me what it said?'

'Yes,' he said, and reached across the table for her hand. 'But let's start at the beginning, shall we? First of all, let me tell you about Phoebe.'

'Phoebe? Is that the girl I saw you with?'

'Yes. Phoebe, my sister.' He looked at her and Thursday felt a blush run up her neck to cover her cheeks.

'Your *sister*?'

'Yes.'

Thursday bit her lips hard. She looked down at the table with its covering of slippery American cloth and its gravy stains and saw the pattern swim before her eyes. 'Oh, *Mark*.'

'She'd come to take me home,' he said, 'to our parents'. To have our own special Christmas as a family. The first we'd had together since the war began.'

'I've been such a fool,' Thursday said after a moment.

'It was understandable. She's certainly very glamorous – she's married to someone with a country estate – and I can see that it would never occur to you that an ugly devil like me might have a sister like that.'

Thursday's head snapped up. 'You're laughing at me!'

'Well, it *is* quite funny really, isn't it? Now that we're getting things sorted out, anyway – I must admit I hadn't seen the funny side before.' He smiled at her. 'Look, it doesn't matter now – we're together again. Let's enjoy ourselves.'

Thursday shook her head. 'But I feel such an idiot. The way I ran off and wouldn't even listen to you, and then didn't answer your letter. I can't see why you bothered with me after all that. I can't see why you came all this way.'

'I came to say goodbye,' he said quietly.

'*Goodbye*?'

The waitress arrived with their pie and vegetables. She was about fifty, a plain woman with a long, sour face, flat brown eyes and grey hair. She dumped the plates in front of them and went away again.

Mark looked after her ruefully. 'They're not like those girls in the Lyons Corner Houses, are they, these British Restaurant waitresses! Nothing Nippy about them.'

'They're doing their best. All the young women have been called up now. Mark, tell me what you mean. Why have you come just to say goodbye? If you thought I didn't want to hear from you again . . .'

'Not that sort of goodbye,' he said seriously. 'This is the sort of goodbye people say at railway stations. I'm going back on service, Thursday.' He glanced around him and picked up his knife and fork. 'Look, we can't discuss it here. Let's eat and then get out – go for a walk somewhere.'

Thursday ate in silence, her thoughts whirling. Mark had come to see her, still believing she wanted nothing more to do with him. He had written to explain, presumably, and she hadn't replied, yet he'd still come to say goodbye before he went away. He wouldn't have done that if it hadn't meant a lot to him. She looked up at last and found him watching her gravely.

'Tell me about the letter.'

He shrugged. 'It just said what I feel. That I love you and want you for my wife. And hell's teeth, I never meant to say that *here*! He glanced around him again at the bustling, noisy restaurant with its smell of boiled cabbage and custard. 'Honestly, couldn't we have found somewhere a bit more romantic for me to propose to you? Last time I did it, I was in bed and now here we are in the middle of a lot of saucepans!' He sighed with exasperation and Thursday giggled, feeling suddenly light-hearted. This was more like the old Mark, the one who made a joke of everything. He looked back at her and smiled. 'That's better. That's my girl.'

Thursday looked at him helplessly. 'But I'm not your girl, Mark. I never was. And it was because of – of what you said that I stopped coming to visit you. I *can't* promise to marry you.'

'I understand that. You've got this other fellow. But that won't stop me asking you, Thursday. I've got the right to do that. And that was what I said in my letter.' He put down his knife and fork and leaned forward. 'Look, if you're not making any decision about him until after the war, I've got a chance, haven't I? I can at least stand in the queue. And *you've* got the right to think about it,' he added. 'It's your life, Thursday. You've got to be sure you're sharing it with the right person. You need to know who's applying for the position.'

She stared at him, then laughed. 'I'm not offering you a job, Mark!'

'It was a figure of speech,' he said impatiently. 'You know that.'

'Yes.' She looked down again. The Woolton pie, basically just a mixture of oatmeal and vegetables – you never knew quite which ones would be used – was stodgy and unappetising. She sighed and laid down her own knife and fork. 'I'm sorry, I can't eat any more.'

'I'm not surprised,' he said grimly. 'It's bloody awful! Sorry, Thursday, but it is. Look, let's go. I'll get the bill.'

The waitress came over and looked at their plates. 'Didn't you like it?'

'Not much,' Mark said. 'Does anyone? Oh, it's all right, I know you're doing your best, and it filled a hole. But we'd like to pay now, please.'

'Pay? But you 'aven't 'ad your apple and custard.'

'We don't want them, thanks. We're in rather a hurry.'

'But it's all in. You got to 'ave them.'

'No, we haven't. Look, I'm quite happy to pay for them but we're not going to eat them, so . . .' Mark stopped as the waitress turned on her heel and marched away. He looked at Thursday and raised his eyebrows comically. 'And you say they're only calling up the younger ones? She's wasted in Civvy Street – she'd make a first-class Sergeant Major. Oh lor', she's bringing the flipping apple and custard anyway.' He looked up as the woman held the plates out to them, a challenging look in her flat eyes. 'I told you, we don't want them. They'll just be wasted.'

'I got to serve you with them. The dinner's all in – Woolton pie, and apple an' custard to follow, one and six the lot. I can't take the pudding off that.'

'I'm not asking you to. I just don't want to eat the ruddy stuff!' Mark dragged a few coins out of his pocket and slapped them down on the table. 'Look, that's enough to cover the bill *and* give you a tip you don't deserve! Short of strapping us to our chairs and force-feeding us, that's as far as you can go. Give the apple and custard to someone else with my compliments – say it's seconds.' He rose to his feet and pulled Thursday up beside him.

'But we don't *do* seconds!' The waitress's cry of outrage brought looks from everyone around them. Thursday bit her lip hard to repress her laughter and began to sidle towards the door, half expecting to be hauled back to finish her dinner. She glanced around and saw the grins on the faces of other diners.

Mark drew in a deep sigh of exasperation, picked up the bowls and slammed them down in front of a couple at the next table, who were just finishing their own pudding.

'You do now,' he said loudly and, catching Thursday's wrist, marched her towards the door.

Outside, they leaned against the wall, giggling helplessly. 'The look on her face! I thought she was going to explode!' Mark chuckled.

'I'll never be able to go in there again, never!' Thursday said.

'Would you want to?' he asked, pulling himself upright at last. 'I mean to say, Thursday – that pie! It was terrible.'

'It wasn't very good,' she acknowledged. 'But it's all right usually. They just have to use what they can get, and at least it's cheap.'

'Yes, and there's good reason for that!' He tucked her hand into his arm. 'Come on, let's go for a walk. I've got to go back this evening. We've only got a few hours together – don't let's waste them.'

They crossed the street and walked into Walpole Park. The little boating pool still had a few dinghies on it, that you could hire for sixpence an hour, and they walked past these and headed across the grass towards the creek. A thin, chilly wind scoured across the water but Thursday's hand, pressed between Mark's arm and his side, felt warm and secure. Her doubts had vanished, for the moment at least, and she felt a deep contentment wash over her. She leaned her head against his shoulder, and he stopped under a tall tree and took her in his arms.

'Mark, not here!'

'Sorry, I can't wait any longer.' He gathered her against him and pressed his lips against hers. For a moment, she felt a resistance; no man had kissed her like this since Connor had left. And then the firmness of his body against hers, the tenderness of his lips, spread their warmth through her and she felt a flare of desire and let herself soften against him.

'*Thursday . . .*'

'Mark.' She was shivering. Shakily, she tried to pull away. 'Mark, no. Not here.' She glanced around. There were a few people wandering across the grass and a couple of men fishing off the low wall. 'Please, Mark.'

He stared at her. His eyes were almost black, with only the narrowest of brown rims. He was breathing a little quickly and there was a flush on his cheeks. 'Thursday, I love you.'

Thursday bent her head. 'Please don't say that. Please.'

'But why not?' His voice was urgent. 'Look, I have the right to say it. It's what I feel. You can't stop me saying what I feel.' He waited a moment and then said, 'You feel it too. I know you do.'

She faced him, then put one hand to her forehead. 'Look, I can't make up my mind just like that. I can't. Please don't try to force me.'

'I'm not forcing you to do anything,' he said after a moment.

'You are. It feels as though you are.' She sighed and pulled herself from his arms. 'Please, let's just walk. Let's just be together. Tell me about your draft.'

'We don't call it a draft in the Army,' he said a little stiffly, walking beside her.

'Posting, then, or whatever it is. Where are you going?'

'You know I can't tell you that. Europe, somewhere, that's all.' He closed his mouth.

Thursday sighed. She stopped and faced him again. 'Don't let's quarrel. I'm sorry I can't say what you want me to say, but I have to have time to think about it. I have to think about Connor too.' She looked up at him pleadingly. 'Imagine if you were the one who'd gone away years ago, wouldn't you expect me to at least *try*?'

He looked away, his lips still closed, then took a breath and shrugged. 'I suppose so. Well, all right then, I would. In fact, if I were Connor and came home and found you'd gone off with another bloke, I'd probably want to kill him.' He glowered at her.

'Well, then,' Thursday said gently, 'you must see that that's what I've got to do. I am not going to let him come home and find I've gone off with someone else.'

'But I love you, Thursday!'

'Yes,' she said, 'and so does he. At least, I think he does.'

He pounced. 'You only *think* so? You don't know for sure?'

Thursday lost patience. 'How can I know for sure? He's been away for four years! I can't know anything for sure – all I can do is *remember*. I don't know if we'll be the same people when he comes back. I know I've changed – I'm older, I've been abroad, I've seen and done things I'd never dreamed about when we were here together, but I don't really know *how* I've changed, and I don't know how *he's* changed. I don't know if we'll have changed towards each other. And I can't know that until he comes home. I've got to wait!'

'So what you're saying,' Mark said after a long pause, 'is that you loved him then more than you love me now, and you want to see if you still do. And meanwhile, what am I to do? Hang around in the hope that you'll take me as second best?'

Thursday looked at him sadly. 'I didn't say that, Mark.'

'You didn't have to.' He stared moodily across the creek. The big blue gasometer rose on their right, the high slope of Pneumonia Bridge to their left. Across the strip of water lay the clutter of houses, the cemetery and the pig farm of Clayhall, and the high walls of Haslar Hospital and the prison. A few shabby boats bobbed on the chilly water.

He turned suddenly and gripped her arms. 'Thursday, I didn't want to leave without saying goodbye, without making things right between us. When you walked out of the ward that day, after I'd asked you to marry me, I felt as if my world had come to an end. You didn't come back, and when I asked that other nurse where you were, she told me you'd gone on leave. I was transferred to Rochester the next day and I never had a chance even to write you a note. I asked her to give you a message – didn't she tell you?'

Thursday stared at him. 'No, she didn't.'

'Well, maybe she forgot. Anyway, when I didn't hear, I thought you really meant what you said, that you didn't want to see me again. I tried to forget you, but I couldn't,' he said, his eyes burning. 'I couldn't forget. And then, when I came out of the ward that day with Phoebe and saw you standing there, it was like a dream. I couldn't believe it was you. By the time I realised it, you were gone, running as if the hounds of hell were after you. Why did you come, Thursday? Why, if you didn't love me?'

She looked down. 'I don't know. I just felt I had to. I couldn't leave it like that either.' She lifted her eyes to look at him. 'It all seems such a *muddle*.'

'I thought about it so much,' he said in a low voice. 'In the end I decided I had to write to you. I had to try just once more. But you never got my letter.' He met her eyes. 'I poured out my heart to you in that letter, Thursday. I told you all I felt about you, all you meant to me. I asked you again to marry me, or at least to give me a chance. And when you never answered, I thought it was hopeless. I tried to make myself forget you.'

Tears slipped from Thursday's eyes and trickled down her cheeks. She looked down at her hands. Would it have made any difference now if she had been wearing Connor's ring? Would it ever have got beyond an innocent flirtation, out there under the desert stars?

'I couldn't do it,' Mark went on. 'I couldn't forget you, Thursday. And then, when I got my posting, I knew I had to make one more attempt. I had to see you again, if only to say goodbye.'

'Oh, Mark,' she whispered.

He shrugged. 'Well, I know now, don't I? I know where your heart really is. You've made it very clear.'

Thursday shook her head and the tears flew in the wind. 'I haven't. I don't *know* any more. Mark, I was feeling so happy just now – just being with you. Surely that must mean something too. But I don't know what I'm going to feel when – when . . .'

'When Connor comes home,' he said. 'But the very fact that you're saying that tells me the truth, Thursday, can't you see that? If you really loved me, you wouldn't have these doubts. You'd know.'

Thursday was silent for a moment. Then she lifted her head again.

'I'm not going to be rushed into this, Mark,' she said quietly. 'It isn't just a matter of what I feel or who I feel it for. I made a promise. It might have been only to myself, but it's still important to me. I want to wait until Connor comes home. I'm going to see how I feel then. When I see him again, I think I'll know.'

'And suppose *I* don't wait? Suppose when you finally realise it was me, I've gone for good?'

'Then that'll be just my bad luck, won't it,' Thursday said. She looked him in the eye. 'Things are going to be different after the war, Mark. Women have learned what they can do. We've had freedom and independence and we know we can do a lot of different things. We aren't going to be dependent on men, not in the same way as before. We're not going to just accept that we've got to get married and have a man to look after us. We've learned that we can look after ourselves.'

He stared at her. Then he moved his head slightly in acknowledgement. 'Well, we'll see. Maybe you're right, or maybe you'll find that once the men come home things will go back to the way they were, quicker than you expect. But since you're so keen to keep your promises, Thursday, will you make one to me as well?'

'What is it?' she asked doubtfully, and he gave her a crooked smile.

'It's all right, I'm not going to propose to you again! Three times is quite enough, I think. But promise me that you'll see me just once more when all this is over, will you? Promise me you'll give me an equal chance with Connor.'

She thought for a moment, then nodded. 'Yes, Mark. I'll do that. I promise.'

He looked down at her, his expression a mixture of regret and resignation. 'Well, if that's the best I can have, I'll take it. And one more kiss? Just to seal a bargain?'

She smiled and lifted her face. Once again, Mark gathered her close and bent his head so that his lips met hers. Once again, they clung closely together and swung giddily into their own reeling, leaping world, oblivious of the gulls that wheeled about their heads and the wind that cut through their bodies. Thursday, her eyes closed, felt his hands move on her shoulders, and cup the back of her head; she dug her fingers into the thick fabric of his jacket and leaned her body into his, sinking herself into the experience of the moment, trying to store it in her memory to be cherished and treasured in the lonely months to come.

The kiss ended. Mark lifted his head and looked down into her eyes. They gazed at each other and then he broke away.

'I'm going to say goodbye now,' he murmured. 'If I don't, I'll never be able to go. Oh, *Thursday*!'

'Mark!' She clung to him in sudden desperation. Shakily, he reached up his hands and unhooked hers from his shoulders. He bent his head and gave her one last, firm kiss, and then stepped back.

'Just keep that promise, Thursday,' he said huskily. 'That's all I ask. See me one last time before you make up your mind.' And then he turned and began to walk away towards the town.

Thursday watched him. She wanted to run after him, to call him back, to hold him once more and tell him that she'd promise anything, anything he wanted, if he would only stay with her. But once again Connor's face rose in her mind and his voice sounded in her ears. *I love you, Thursday . . . I wish it could have been a ring . . .*

He knew this might happen, she thought, her throat aching with tears. He knew I'd meet other people, he knew I might fall in love. That's why he wouldn't tie me down. But I wanted to be tied down. I tied *myself* down.

And now she had another promise to keep.

Chapter Twenty-Five

By the end of February 1945 almost every country in the world was at war. The plan to form a 'United Nations' amongst all those countries which had declared war by 1 March had resulted in a rush to sign up, from South America to the Middle East. In the last week of the month, Egypt, Uruguay, Syria, Lebanon and Saudi Arabia all declared war on Germany, and some on Japan as well. It was clear that the world wanted peace, and saw that only a concerted and co-operative effort would achieve and maintain such an ideal.

Elsie and Pete enjoyed a brief honeymoon of just two nights out in the country, with Eddy's foster-parents. They came back with their happiness muted by Mrs Jenkins's funeral, and Elsie told Thursday that she'd be back in Haslar by the end of the week. 'Not to sleep, mind,' she said with a wink. 'I'll be going back to Pete's place every night – his mum and dad have given us the front room. Of course, I'll have to move back into the dormitory if there's another emergency, but I'm afraid you won't be seeing so much of me now I'm a married woman.'

'Whereas Pete will see a lot more,' Ellen Bridges said with a grin, and Elsie blushed.

'You've got a dirty mind, Ellen Bridges. Mind you, it's true!' And she laughed her old, raucous laugh.

The news these days was full of the Allied bombings over Germany. On the day of Elsie's wedding, Dresden had been almost destroyed by such heavy bombing that a firestorm had been created, the flames causing their own wind that tore through the streets and fanned them into even greater heat. Over fifty thousand people died in one night, many more times those who had been killed in even the worst of the Blitz on London; even more died in the follow-up raids of the next two days. Berlin was raided over and over again, with the city set ablaze at the end of February by firebombs dropped by over a thousand aircraft.

In Japan, Tokyo too was bombed by American B-29 Superfortresses, with over eighty thousand killed in one attack; fifteen thousand more were killed when the city of Kobe was set alight, and in yet another attack Osaka was completely wiped out. It was almost impossible to count the number of people dead.

'It's getting worse and worse,' Thursday said in dismay, but the others shook their heads.

'We're winning. It's *good* news, Thursday.' But she could only think of those who had died. The old people like Mrs Jenkins, who had no part in the war, the women and children who had no voice. Too many people were being killed. Too many.

Mark had written to her three times since he'd been away. He had rejoined his unit somewhere in Europe. He wasn't required to parachute any more, but to work somewhere behind the lines, setting up hospitals and looking after the wounded. He had only enough time to scribble a few lines, but he always ended with love and a kiss. She read his letters again and again, and put them in her drawer beside Connor's. Then she took them out and put them into another drawer. It didn't seem right to have them there together.

The fighting in Europe was bitter, with the Allies flooding across the borders into Austria and Germany. Russia's Red Army was marching on Berlin, and Montgomery's forces had crossed the Rhine only a day behind those of the American General Patton's. The three major powers were now massing, ready for their final assault. It really did seem as if the Germans were about to lose.

'They won't go down easily, all the same,' Louisa said, studying the newspaper at lunch one day. 'They're still sending those doodlebugs and V2s over.' One had destroyed an entire block of flats in London, and another was shot down over Suffolk. 'Of course, these might be the last ones they send, but we won't know that till it's all over, will we?'

By the beginning of April, it was beginning to look as if the war might be almost over. Five million leaflets had been dropped over the Ruhr, telling the German forces there of the advances being made into the country, and over three hundred thousand were expected to join the mass surrender. Vienna itself was liberated, leaving Berlin as the next and greatest target. In Italy, the Allies had pushed the front line as far as Ravenna, and in Japan too the bombing had intensified. It was said that over a ten-mile square area of Tokyo, not a building had been left standing.

'Guess what!' Elsie came running into the mess waving a newspaper, and the others looked up with a mixture of excitement and anxiety. 'Mr Roosevelt's died!'

'The American President?' Patsy exclaimed, and Elsie threw her a withering look.

'How many Mr Roosevelts d'you know, goof? It says here he just collapsed while he was having his portrait painted. You wouldn't think he'd have time to worry about things like that, would you? Why not just take a photo?' She rushed on without waiting for Thursday's comment that it seemed he hadn't had time after all. 'Mr Truman's been sworn in as the new President and the Germans are jumping for joy. Why d'you suppose they're doing that? It isn't going to make any difference, is it?'

'They probably think the Americans and Russians will start squabbling,' Louisa remarked, stirring a saccharin into her tea. 'They won't, though – not while we've still got Hitler to deal with. Anyway, it's General Eisenhower who's really in charge now. We're still going to win.'

A few days later Thursday heard that the great German prisoner-of-war camp, Colditz, had been liberated by the Americans.

'Colditz!' She raced into the dining mess, shouting and waving the newspaper just as Elsie had done a few days earlier. 'They've opened Colditz! Our Steve'll be home. Louie – Patsy – Joy – Steve's coming home!'

The others leaped up from the table and rushed to hug her. All over the big hall, people were looking up and staring and then, as word went round, calling out and laughing with excitement. Some of them also had relatives in the same camp; they came running to see the newspaper for themselves, and the hall erupted into tumult. It was another real indication that the war was almost over.

'How soon d'you think he'll be home?' Thursday asked, spreading the paper out on the table. 'And look, the Russians are almost in Berlin. They're bombarding it every day, people are having to hide in cellars and creep out at night to get food and water – oh, that sounds terrible – and look at *this*! Hitler's hiding in his bunker and won't come out. He must be just about to give up, he *must*!'

More disturbing reports were coming through too. Colditz was not the only camp to have been opened. The troops had opened the gates of other wired-off settlements and found horrors there that they had never dreamed of. Buchenwald. Belsen. Auschwitz. The names were burned into the minds of all those who read or heard them. The girls looked at the newspapers in appalled silence and Elsie, who had been to the pictures with Pete one night, came in next morning looking pale and sick.

'We saw this newsreel. Honestly, you wouldn't believe it. People as thin as skeletons, you could see their bones sticking through their skin. Laying there in piles, some of them still just alive, just chucked there with the corpses. And the guards, they'd been burying them like it, throwing them into great big pits, and you could tell that some of them weren't properly dead. I've never seen anything so horrible in my life.'

'It's got to be over soon,' Louisa said, shaken. 'They can't let Hitler get away with it any more.'

The last nine days of April saw the greatest battle of all – the battle for Berlin that would finally end the war. Day by day, the Allies advanced, shelling, bombing, sending in tanks and troops to fight their way, street by street, to the very heart of the city. On the last day of all, the Russians took the Reichstag itself, fighting through the rooms and corridors until they possessed every inch. And to signal their victory to all who still stood in the ruined streets, to the country of Germany itself, and to the entire war-torn world, two Red Army Sergeants climbed to a pinnacle of the shattered roof and waved the Red Flag high in bitter triumph.

'It's over,' Thursday said in awe, as they listened to the news on the wireless. 'It really is over.'

'Not quite,' Louisa corrected her. 'There's still Japan.'

But they knew that the victory over Japan must be no more now than a matter of time. The greater part of this long conflict, which had taken up so much of their lives – which had brought them grief and pain, joy and laughter, new experiences, new friends and bitter losses that could never be regained – was over. The Second World War was drawing to an end.

*

The news was coming so fast now, and so mingled with rumour that it was almost impossible to keep track of it all or to sort out fact from fiction. Some of it was so sickening that Thursday felt she would rather not know – yet she was drawn by a horrible fascination to the newspapers and the wireless. She shuddered at the fate of Mussolini, the Italian leader, and his mistress, both shot and mutilated, dangling upside down over a garage forecourt and spat upon or riddled by more bullets from those who had come to jeer. It was such a squalid end. But even she could not feel pity for the suicide of Hitler himself, nor for those who died with him in his bunker. Too many millions had died because of his madness and greed. Too many lives had been wasted.

'It's going to be tomorrow.' The buzz ran round the hospital like wildfire. Mr Churchill was going to broadcast at three in the afternoon, and everyone knew what he was going to say. It seemed impossible to believe. They'd been waiting for this very day for five and a half years yet it seemed, in a way, to have come upon them almost without warning. The past few months had seen such bitter fighting – fighting that was still going on in the Far East – that it was difficult to comprehend a world without it, a world in which people would once more be able to travel safely, to go to bed at night in the knowledge that they would not be woken by air-raid sirens or killed by a rocket. The fear they had learned to live with had been taken away, yet it left a strange vacuum and they didn't know quite what to put in its place.

'No more blackout,' Elsie said gleefully as they walked along the sea wall after their duty. 'Not even a dimout. We'll be able to have lights on without drawing the curtains. Put proper lights on our bikes again. Use torches. Have parties and late dances. They'll be able to ring the church bells whenever they like – remember that time the ones at Alverstoke got rung years ago, because someone thought we were being invaded? Everything's going to be just like it used to be.'

'Andrew will come home,' Louisa said. 'I've started thinking about the wedding already, and you're all invited. How about you, Thursday? When d'you think Connor will be back?'

'I don't know. It'll be quite a while yet. Not till after the Japanese war's over, I suppose.' Now that the time was drawing near Thursday was beginning to experience something very like panic.

'To be honest, I'm not sure I want him to just yet – I don't feel ready. I don't feel ready for anyone.'

Louisa gave her a sympathetic look. 'You're not really over Mark, are you? Still not made up your mind?'

'I'm not even trying to. I decided to stop thinking about it and just wait till I see them both again.' Thursday turned away and stared out over the Solent. As usual, it was full of ships, and she could see men moving about the decks. 'What d'you think they're doing?'

Elsie craned her neck. 'They're putting up flags! Dressing overall. Oh, how gorgeous – d'you think all the ships are doing it?'

'Bound to.' Louisa stood still and lifted both arms above her head, her face glowing with excitement. 'You know what, tomorrow's going to be one huge party! I bet there's people everywhere putting up flags and getting ready for parties. What are we going to do? We can't just go tamely to bed!'

'We could go over to Pompey,' Elsie suggested. 'There's bound to be plenty going on over there. We'll walk up Queen Street and go to the Guildhall Square, that's where all the people will go.'

'I've heard there are going to be street-parties,' Thursday put in, beginning to feel excited herself. 'Will there be one where your mum and dad are, Elsie?'

'Might be. We could go round there first, then get the bus back down to the ferry and go over then. They might want to come with us anyway – we're Pompey folk really, after all.' Elsie gave a little skip and gripped her friends' arms. 'You know, I reckon this is going to be the biggest party any of us has ever seen!'

The other two nodded, and then Thursday said more soberly, 'What about Patsy?'

'Oh.' Elsie stopped jogging up and down. 'Oh, poor Pats. She's bound to feel a bit low, isn't she. What d'you think? We can't leave her moping all by herself, but if she comes, she's going to be thinking about Roy all the time. It'll be miserable for her either way.'

'Well, I think we should make her come,' Louisa decided. 'It's history, isn't it. We're never going to see a day like this again. Nobody ought to stop at home and pretend it's not happening – whatever the circumstances.'

The entire hospital was waiting next day for the moment at 3 p.m.

when Mr Churchill was going to broadcast and make the news official. There were wireless sets in most of the wards and as the hour drew near they were all tuned in and patients and nurses alike gathered round them. Down in the basement, there were no operations and the theatre staff came up and crowded into the rooms just off the arcade to listen. Thursday and Louisa stood together, just behind Surgeon Commander Sharp, holding each other's hands tightly.

It seems only five minutes since we were waiting for Mr Chamberlain to announce that the war was starting, Thursday thought, looking back down the years. And yet at the same time, it seems an eternity. So much has happened since. So many people have been killed, or had their lives changed for ever.

The hour struck. The familiar, sombre voice of the announcer John Snagge said, 'This is London.' And then they heard that other voice which had become so familiar over the years, which had become the voice of wartime Britain itself.

'The German war is over,' Winston Churchill proclaimed, his rolling tones booming over the entire country, and Thursday felt Louisa's fingers tighten. And then, lifting his voice in exhortation: 'Advance Britannia! Long live the cause of freedom! *God Save the King!*'

Immediately, the National Anthem itself was broadcast and everyone stood to attention and saluted. As the last strains died away, all those crowded into the room broke into cheers. Thursday and Louisa hugged each other and then found themselves in the arms of Surgeon Commander Sharp himself. He planted smacking kisses on their cheeks, then let them go and went round the whole room, hugging every person in it, and they all began to do the same. I just want to hug everyone in the whole world, Thursday thought, tears streaming down her face. Well, everyone on our side, of course! 'Oh, Louie! Patsy! Joy! It's over – it's really over!'

'I can't believe it,' Patsy declared, her face alight, and Thursday felt a swift delight that her friend was able to share in the excitement without having it marred by her own sorrow. 'It's finished at last – and we've won! We've *won the war!* Oh, *Thursday*!'

Thursday held her tightly. Patsy had been her first friend at Haslar and even though they had been separated when Thursday was sent to Egypt, there had always been a special bond between them. What would Patsy do now, she wondered. As a widow, she could hardly go back to her parents and live with them as a young daughter. I won't even be able to do that myself, she thought suddenly. I want to make my own life now – but how? Which direction should I go in? Marry, like Louisa, or stay single and enjoy my freedom?

Marriage seemed suddenly to be no more than exchanging one form of service for another. Wives were expected to stay at home, look after their husbands, have children. But for single women, the world was opening up. There would be opportunities – of what kind, she didn't know, but that there would be opportunities she was certain. I don't want to let them pass me by, she thought. Whatever they are, I want to be able to take them.

'Wake up, Thursday!' Louisa was shaking her arm. 'We're going to go round the wards, just like at Christmas. And then we're leaving with Elsie, remember? There'll be parties everywhere and we don't want to miss a minute!'

The party had started in Portsmouth that morning. There'd been a service in the Guildhall Square, led by the Bishop of Portsmouth, with parades of all the Services and, someone told them on seeing their VAD uniforms, a row of nurses along the front of the steps, their red capes, blue dresses and white aprons looking like a bit of the Union Jack itself. Some sailors had climbed up on top of the tower of the Guildhall, burned to a shell in the Blitz of 1941, and hoisted up the White Ensign, which had been flown from the same place on Armistice Day in 1918. The day I was born, Thursday thought. At the very minute I was born, they were flying that flag. She looked up at it and felt a lump in her throat.

The girls had gone over on the ferry. The afternoon had been an endless cacophony of ships' sirens and hooters, church bells and brass bands, and as they went through the streets after their tour of the hospital, they saw that bunting and flags were festooned across almost every house. The ferry boats were dressed overall, just as were the bigger ships, and the harbour was so alive with dancing colour that the steady drizzle didn't matter at all. What was a bit of damp, when you had the end of the war to celebrate!

In the Guildhall Square, the solemnity of the morning's service had abated and there was, as Elsie had predicted, a huge party in full swing. The square was thronged with sailors, marines, soldiers and airmen who were all cheered incessantly, while impromptu bands had been started up and vied with wind-up gramophones to play dance music. Long lines of conga dancers threaded their way through the crowds, breaking and joining up again, and there was a constant hubbub of song, laughter and calls from one to the other. Portsmouth had, it seemed, gone wild with joy.

The girls stayed until long after dark. Finally, with the party still going on behind them, they turned and made their way back down Queen Street to the harbour. The last ferry boat was waiting on one side of the pontoon, and on the other bobbed a pinnace with a lone sailor at the wheel. He grinned at them as they climbed wearily aboard.

'Had a good time, ducks? What a night, eh? All over bar the shouting, as they say. Now all we got to do is clear up the mess, eh!'

Thursday sank down on a thwart between Patsy and Elsie. She looked up at the sky, still lit with spears of light from the searchlights which had been so familiar a sight during the air raids.

She felt suddenly flat. After the joy of the past few hours, there seemed to be nothing ahead but drudgery and toil. The years of emotions, ranging from fear to excitement, had come suddenly to an end and, as the sailor had said, there was nothing left to do but clear up the mess. And what a mess it was.

I've had enough, she thought. I just want it to be properly over, so that I can get on with my own life.

Chapter Twenty-Six

The war might have ended in Europe, but there was still bitter fighting in the Far East, and still patients to be looked after at Haslar. Now that the flow of emergencies had eased, the operating theatres were taking on more commonplace work such as tonsillectomies or hernias, to ease the burden on the little War Memorial hospital in Gosport. After the terrible injuries that had been arriving almost daily for so long, it was both a relief and a comedown to find these filling the lists, and along with many of the VADs Thursday was feeling more and more restless. The urgency that had driven her to volunteer five years ago and kept her ready and willing to work all the hours she was needed, had now faded, and three haemorrhoid cases in a row seemed an anti-climax.

On top of this was the terrible news now coming from the concentration camps in Germany. The girls were appalled by the reports of thousands of prisoners starved down to skin and bone, their limbs like sticks and their bodies hollowed out as if they were already dead. As Elsie had told them after seeing that newsreel, guards had been seen callously tossing live people into deep pits, while those who were still able to walk were forced to crawl to the few standpipes or wells to collect water for themselves and their friends.

'This must be the worst war there's ever been,' Thursday said to her parents when she went home for a few days' leave. 'Even worse than the one you were in, Dad.'

Walter shook his head. 'I don't know that you can say any war's worse than another – there's always cruelty and death involved. We just keep thinking of new ways of killing each other – and more all the time. You know, they said the last one had got to be the war to end all wars, but it wasn't, was it? Now they're saying the same about this one, but they'll forget it soon enough. Seems to me they always do.'

'Well, I'm just thankful it's over,' Mary said. 'Our Steve'll be home any day, and so will Vic. Mike seems to be getting along all right too; they say he'll have to stay in the sanatorium for a few months yet, but he's going to get better. I know it'll take a lot of work to get things back to normal, but at least we can start to do it in peace. Then kiddies like little Leslie will have a better world to look forward to.'

'What are your plans, Thursday?' her father asked. 'I dare say you'll be getting demobbed soon. You'll be coming home, I suppose, until that man of yours comes back?'

Thursday glanced uncomfortably at her mother. 'I'm not exactly sure what I'm going to be doing, Dad. We're not all being demobbed straight away. The married women, and those who're getting married, are going first. And then some girls have decided to stay on and take training to be State Registered Nurses, like our Jenny.'

'You won't be doing that, though,' Mary observed. 'Not much point, is there, if you're getting married.'

'I don't know that I am getting married,' Thursday began, and they both stared at her.

'Not getting married!' Mary exclaimed. 'Don't tell me you've quarrelled! Or have you thrown him over? I must say—'

'No, it's nothing like that. I just don't want to rush into anything.' She looked at them appealingly. 'We haven't seen each other for more than four years. It's a long time . . .'

Her mother gave her a shrewd glance. 'You haven't found someone else, have you? Is that it?'

'No. I don't know.' Thursday got up restlessly and looked out of the window. 'I've just got to take time, that's all. Look, I think I'll walk round and see Denise and Leslie. And Auntie Flo and Uncle Percy,' she added, pulling open the door.

Mary and Walter watched her go and then glanced at each other.

'She's changed,' Mary said sadly. 'She's not the same girl as she was, Walter.'

'None of us is the same as we were. She's right, Mary, four years *is* a long time. It's not as if they knew each other very long before he went away. And there's the different backgrounds to take into consideration as well.'

'It's more than that,' Mary said. 'She couldn't look me in the eye when I asked her if there was someone else. She had that guilty look on her face, the one she used to have when she was a kiddy, remember?' She got up and went out to the kitchen. 'I just hope she's not gone through all those years just to make a fool of herself at the end of it.'

Thursday took her time walking round to her aunt's house. She walked down to the bridge and leaned on the parapet, staring across the shimmering water at the tower of the cathedral. From here, you'd never know there'd been a war at all, she thought. Not like in Portsmouth, where the heart of the city had been blasted away, nor in Plymouth which had been almost flattened, nor in Coventry or all those other places that had been pounded into the ground. Almost no city had escaped damage; almost no part of the country been left untouched in some way. And now it all had to be put right, repaired, rebuilt. After all they'd been through, people still couldn't say it was finished. They had to pick themselves up, weary and bruised, and start all over again.

She strolled slowly through the streets to her aunt's house. Denise was home from her job at the glove factory and welcomed her in, with Leslie jumping up and down behind her. Flo was out visiting her friend in the next street, she explained, leading the way through to the back room.

'I'll make a cup of tea. How are you, Thursday? Glad it's all over?'

'Well, of course.' Thursday followed her cousin out to the kitchen. 'It seems queer, though. I feel sort of flat.'

'I know.' Denise filled the kettle and lit the gas. 'I do, too. And a bit scared. I mean, I'm looking forward to Vic coming home, of course I am, but I feel nervous too. Suppose he doesn't fancy me any more? Suppose he's sorry he's got to come back to me? I mean, it was all such a rush – and I know I was daft, doing what I did. Not that I'm sorry we had Les, never for a minute,' she added quickly, 'but I just worry about how we're all going to settle down together. I mean, Leslie's never even seen him, not to remember.'

The kettle boiled and she swished a drop of hot water in the teapot and tipped it into the sink before spooning in the tea.

Thursday took the cups down from their hooks and went outside to the meatsafe to fetch the milk. She looked at her cousin. 'How d'you feel yourself, Diz? I mean, you're not sorry you got married, are you?'

'No, of course not.' She wrinkled her mouth. 'I think as much of Vic as I ever did – but it's as if everything's been frozen for the past four years, isn't it? We've been through so much – and Vic's had such a different life. He's been wounded and in hospital, he's done all sorts of things, he must be different from what he was. I hope he'll be the same Vic underneath it all, but I can't know that till I see him, can I? I *want* to feel the same,' she continued, pouring the tea, 'but how can I be sure I will? How can I be sure *he* will? And whatever are we going to do if we don't?'

'I think you've got to give yourselves time.' Thursday carried the cups into the back room and sat down in her uncle's chair while Denise took the one on the other side of the fireplace. 'It's bound to seem strange at first. And he's been away for so long, he'll need time to get used to being at home again and in civvies. Will he go back into the Post Office?'

'I don't know. I suppose so – civil servants will get their jobs back, won't they? But that's going to be queer, isn't it, stamping out parcels when he's been fighting in Italy.' Denise shook her head. 'It's going to be queer for everyone. You know, I don't think it will be any easier being at peace than it was being at war! At least there was some excitement then – it just all seems so flat now. And so much hard work to put it all to rights.'

Thursday looked at her thoughtfully. Denise had changed, she thought. A few years ago, when she'd had nothing more in her mind than the latest shade of nail varnish or which boy was going to take her to the pictures, her nickname Dizzy had suited her perfectly. Now, the mother of a small boy, she looked older and more serious. I hope she hasn't lost all her sense of fun though, Thursday thought. That was one of the things Vic loved about her.

'I don't think you need worry that he won't want you any more,' she said. 'I told you before, you were all he thought about when I nursed him in Egypt. He told me that all he wanted was to get home to you and Leslie and find a little home of your own and be together. And I expect he'll be feeling nervous too.'

'*Him* nervous?' Denise repeated, as if it was a new idea. 'But he's got nothing to be nervous about!'

'Well, he thinks he has.' Thursday hesitated. 'Don't forget, he's been burned. He's worried you won't fancy him—'

'Oh, I know all that,' Denise broke in. 'I wrote and told him after you first came home, it doesn't matter *what* he looks like, I'll love him just the same. More, because every time I look at him I'll see what he's been through. But it's the time I'm worried about. The time we've been apart. We're going to be different, Thursday – everyone is. We're *all* going to find it strange, settling down to Civvy Street again.'

'I know,' Thursday said. 'I've been thinking exactly the same myself. It's going to be really strange, and it's going to be hardest of all for the youngest ones, the ones who never really had much ordinary life before it all started. People like you and me, who'd hardly begun our lives – we've got to find out how to live without a war. I don't think it's going to be easy, Diz – I don't think it's going to be easy at all.'

The few days passed quickly, with visits to relatives and old friends. Slowly, Thursday began to feel that it might be possible to settle into civilian life again. But many of her friends seemed to feel the same way as she did: there was a restlessness, combined with a feeling of depression. And there was the knowledge that despite all the celebrating, the war wasn't totally over. There was still Japan.

'They won't give in, you know,' Walter said, spreading the *Daily Express* out on the table after tea. 'It's not in their nature. They think if you give in you might as well be dead. We're going to have to go on and on, hammering at them until there's hardly any left. There's no other way.'

'If we do that, there'll be hardly any of us left either,' Thursday objected. 'There's been thousands and thousands of Allied men killed out there, not to mention the ones in prison camps. They've got to give in.' But her father shook his head. There was no 'got to' about it where the Japs were concerned.

After tea, Mary and Walter liked to settle down to listen to the wireless or have a game of cards. For the first two evenings Thursday and Jenny settled down with them; but on the third, Thursday glanced at her sister. 'Fancy a walk? It's a lovely evening.'

Mary looked up, disappointed. 'I thought we might play crib.'

'Maybe later on, Mum. I just can't settle indoors when it's as nice as this outside.' Thursday gave her mother an apologetic smile. 'I've spent so much time underground since I came back from Egypt, I'm just starving for some sunshine! We won't be late.'

The two girls strolled out and walked down to the river. They crossed the bridge and wandered through the park, looking across at the racecourse. 'I suppose it'll all start again this summer,' Jenny observed. 'All the racing and the pleasure boats and everything. People just want to get back to normal now, don't they?'

'I suppose so.'

Thursday's tone was despondent and Jenny gave her a sharp glance. 'What's up?'

'Oh, I don't know – everything and nothing. I'm being daft, I know I am, but I can't seem to get used to it, somehow – not being at war any more, I mean. Except that we still are at war, aren't we, and there are still men being killed, but nobody's taking much notice. Because it's so far away and we're not in any danger ourselves, it's all been shoved under the carpet. People don't seem to *care* – unless they've got a man out there, and then of course they don't think the war's over at all.'

Jenny gave her a shrewd glance. 'You're worrying about Connor.'

'Well, yes, of course I am – but it's not just that. It's all of it. All the men coming home, expecting to find things the same as when they went away – and they can't be. I mean, some of them haven't even got a home any more, or a wife or family or *anything*. They've been through all that, and they've got to come home to nothing. How are they going to feel? They'll wonder what it was all about. And then there's the ones who come home and find they can't get along with their wives any more. Or their children don't want them. And even if they do, it's all so hard to get going again.' Thursday glanced around at the peaceful scene. 'You don't see much of it here, Jen, but back in Pompey you can see just what the war's done. All those buildings, smashed. All those houses and shops, gone. Everything needing to be put back together again. It's going to take years.'

Jenny looked at her again. 'You're sounding really miserable, Thursday. What's happened?'

The other girl shook her head. 'Nothing, not really. I just feel so flat, and I can't seem to pull myself out of it. I don't know what to *do* with my life, Jenny, not any more. When it all started, we were all so keen to get involved, to do something to help. There were so many opportunities. You could join the women's Services or the VAD or go and work on the land – all sorts of things. Now, suddenly, it's all gone. We're being demobbed and we don't know what else to do.' She stopped and faced her sister. 'Jen, I don't want to just get married and be a housewife like Mum for the rest of my life. I want to *do* something. But I don't know what!'

'You don't want to go on with nursing?'

'It won't be the same. Anyway, I think I've had enough. I want a change.'

They walked slowly on. After a few minutes, Jenny asked tentatively, 'But what about Connor, Thurs? Won't he want to get married? What will he say about all this?'

'It's not really up to him, is it!' Thursday stopped and bit her lip. 'Oh, there I go, flying off the handle when the poor man hasn't even said anything. I don't know what he'll want, Jen. I don't know what *I'll* want, until I see him again. And then there's . . .'

'Someone else,' Jenny said. 'You might as well tell me, Thurs.'

Thursday heaved a sigh. 'All right, then. Yes, there is someone else – an Army doctor. I do seem to go for the medical blokes, don't I! Or they go for me . . . Anyway, his name's Mark and I met him in Egypt. I didn't want it to lead to anything so we broke it off and I didn't see him again till a few months ago when he turned up at Haslar. He'd been at Arnhem. I tried not to let anything happen, but he said it must have been meant and he wouldn't take no for an answer.' She stared at Jenny, her eyes suddenly filled with tears. 'He's gone away again, back to Germany, but he keeps writing to me. He made me promise to give him a chance. Oh, Jenny, I don't know what to do. I think such a lot of them both, and yet sometimes I wish I'd never met either of them!'

They stood quite still staring at one another. Tears had begun to trickle down Thursday's cheeks. Jenny opened her mouth to speak, but before she could say a word a voice hailed them and they both turned in amazement.

'Hello, Thursday. Hello – Jenny, is it? Gosh, you've grown up!' The tall young soldier stood, legs straddled, beaming at them. 'Well, haven't you got anything to say? Haven't you got a kiss for your old sweetheart, Thursday?'

'*Sidney!*' Thursday gasped. 'Sidney – but what are you doing here?'

'I live here, remember? Not all that far from you.' He gave her a cocky look and winked. 'Don't tell me you've forgotten all those nights I walked you home from the pictures.'

Thursday flushed. 'No, I haven't,' she said a little sharply. 'And as far as I remember, nothing ever happened. Anyway, how are you, Sidney? You're looking well.'

'Fit as a flea.' He flexed one arm. 'Shame you can't see the muscles. Being in the Army suits me.'

'I can see that. So where have you been?'

He grinned. 'That'd take a bit of telling. Seen a good bit of action, been around a bit, made some good mates.' He winked again. 'Never thought it was going to last that long, did we? How about you, had a good war? Went for a nurse, didn't you?'

'That's right,' Thursday said shortly, wondering how he could have forgotten. It was the reason they'd split up, when she'd told him she was volunteering as a VAD. 'I've been at Haslar Hospital, near Portsmouth, but I was in Egypt for two years—'

'Egypt! I was out there for a bit, and in Algiers. Talk about sand! And flies, and God knows what else. Then we went on to Italy. The girls are better-looking there!' He winked for a third time.

Thursday looked at him. He had filled out and was no longer the rather weedy Sidney she remembered, and it certainly suited him. I suppose a lot of girls would think he was really good-looking now, she thought, but there was something she didn't like about him. He was too cocky.

'Suppose you've had a few boyfriends since those days, Thurs?' he went on. 'Not the little innocent you were, eh? Didn't know what it was all about, did we! Learned a few tricks since then, I can tell you – bet you have too, eh?'

'Sorry, Sidney,' Thursday said abruptly. 'It's been nice seeing you, but we've got to go now. Mum's waiting for us to go home and play cards.'

He stared at her and gave a short laugh. 'Well, you'd better go then! Mustn't keep Mummy waiting, must you. Shame, I was going to ask you to come round to the Swan With Two Nicks for a drink –

or maybe you're not allowed into pubs yet, eh?' He gave her a rather nasty smile.

'Goodbye, Sidney,' Thursday said and took Jenny's arm. They walked away quickly, and when Thursday turned her head at the corner of the road Sidney had gone.

'Whew!' Jenny said. 'He's even worse than I remember him. What on earth did you ever see in him, Thursday?'

'I don't know. I never did like him all that much anyway – we just got into the habit of going to the pictures together.' Thursday giggled. 'I remember the night we broke up – he took umbrage because I'd volunteered for the VADs without asking him first! I told him he didn't own me and he said he'd just been going to ask me to get engaged. We'd never even kissed properly!'

'I remember Mum being upset that you weren't going to marry him. She liked Sidney.'

'She didn't really know him. She just wanted me to settle down and have a husband.' Thursday looked seriously at her sister. 'I tell you what, Jen – girls aren't going to need to get married any more, not like they used to. We've found out we can do all sorts of different things – we don't need men to look after us any more.'

'I don't know,' Jenny said. 'I don't think it's going to be that easy. We don't get paid as much, do we? How can a girl afford to live on the sort of pay we get? That's why men get so much more – because they'll have a wife and family to keep. Women aren't supposed to need so much.'

'Well, that'll change, surely.'

'I don't know,' Jenny said again. 'Once they're all back, they'll want to take over again. You saw what Sidney was like. Thinks he's God's gift to women. I don't suppose they'll all be like that – my Charlie isn't, for a start – but they're going to want their jobs back, aren't they?' A bus went past and she waved a hand towards the woman driving it. 'I bet *she* won't be driving a bus in six months' time. She'll be back in the kitchen, washing clothes. And so will a lot of other women.'

'It's like I was saying just now,' Thursday said. 'It's not going to be easy, sorting it all out, is it? Nearly six years of war, and not over yet – it leaves a lot of mess behind.'

They walked back slowly. There were other people out walking too, couples strolling arm in arm along the riverbank, children running in front of them. It was a peaceful scene, a scene of contentment, yet all those couples and all those families would be facing their own problems. Peace didn't come easily.

'Do you really not know what you're going to do?' Jenny asked, breaking the silence.

'I've almost given up trying to make up my mind,' Thursday said. 'I think the best thing I can do is just wait and see. Maybe neither of them will want me. Maybe I won't get married at all – ever.'

'Don't be daft!' Jenny said robustly. 'You're just feeling a bit low, that's all. It's what Mum calls "reaction" – you've been working with wounded men for years and you've been in Blitzes and you've been abroad, and now it's all suddenly stopped and you don't know what's going to happen next. And you're worn out. That's all it is.' She squeezed Thursday's arm. 'You'll feel better in a little while. Honestly.'

Thursday gave her a smile. 'I hope so,' she said. 'I really hope so.'

They turned the corner of their own street. The front door stood open and there was a little knot of people gathered round, chattering excitedly. The two girls looked at each other and began to walk faster and as they came to the edge of the crowd a man came to the door and looked out.

'Thursday! Jen!'

Thursday stopped dead. Her heart rose within her breast and she caught her hand to her throat, staring in disbelief. He looked taller than she remembered – but perhaps that was because he was thinner. And he had a beard. He'd always wanted to grow a beard, she thought in bewilderment, and then her brain and her emotions caught up with each other and a huge surge of joy swelled to her lips.

'*Steve!* It's our *Steve!*' She gripped Jenny's arm and they pushed through the little crowd and flung themselves into their brother's arms. 'Oh, Steve, you're back, you're back at last!'

Behind him, her mother was crying with relief and joy, and her father was beaming, his mouth a little twisted with his own emotion and his eyes moist. The neighbours were laughing and chattering, and as Thursday felt his body, so much thinner than she remembered, but whole and alive as they had once thought he would never be again, she felt her depression slip away and a new optimism warm her heart.

Peace wasn't going to be easy. But it was *peace*, and if there was work to be done it could be done with a high heart. The world *could* be rebuilt, and people could learn to live their lives again in safety.

Chapter Twenty-Seven

The results of the General Election, which were announced the day after Steve's return and three weeks after election day itself, surprised everyone and shocked many. Mr Churchill, voted out and forced to resign after all he had done! Labour in power with an overall majority of a hundred and forty-six! Clement Attlee the new Prime Minister, and 'The Red Flag' sung in Parliament at the election of the new Speaker! It was as if the country had been turned upside down.

'I can't make it out,' Walter Tilford said, shaking his head. 'Mr Churchill was good enough in wartime, he ought to be good enough in peacetime. It's an insult to the man.'

'I think people want something different now though,' Thursday said. 'They want things to be better than they were before the war. We had a Depression then, remember. A lot of people were having a really bad time – no jobs, no money, couldn't afford the doctor, couldn't get a proper education. Labour want to change all that. They want children to be able to go to grammar schools if they're bright enough, without their parents having to pay, and they want you to be able to go to the doctor when you're ill and not have to be put on the panel before you get free treatment. They don't think the Conservatives will do that.'

Her father stared at her. 'Don't say you're going over to Labour! We've always been Conservative in this family, always. Never had any truck with trade unions – oh, they were needed in their day, I'll admit that, but once they'd done their job they ought to have closed down, not gone on asking for more and more. I tell you what, now that Labour's in again we'll have nothing but strikes. And where's the money going to come from for all this free education and doctor's visits? From the workers, that's where. It's all very fine to talk big, but who's going to have to put their hands in their pockets, eh? Tell me that.'

Thursday opened her mouth to reply, but caught her mother's eye and closed it again. There was no point in arguing with her father, who was a dyed in the wool Conservative and wouldn't ever change his opinions. Most working-class people favoured Labour, but when you found one who was a Conservative he was usually fixed that way for good.

'Well, let's forget it for now,' she said instead. 'It's my last night and Steve's home again and we just want to enjoy it. Mum and I've been busy all day getting a party ready for tonight, and the others are coming round so let's forget politics. There's nothing we can do about it now, anyway.'

That last evening had been almost like before the war, she thought next day as she boarded the train to return to Haslar. All the family together, except for Mike who was still in hospital, and Leslie who would never be with them again. But little Leslie had been there to win everyone's hearts with his beaming smile and comical remarks, and soon his father would be home again. They'd eaten the tea that Thursday and her mother had prepared, and played games and finished up with a sing-song. Leslie had been almost asleep before the others left, cradled in his grandfather's arms, and Mary had smiled as she closed the door and came back inside.

'What a little love he is. And Percy thinks the world of him, too. Funny, when you think how upset he was when Denise had to get married but like I said, they bring their love with them.' She glanced at her son and daughters. 'I'm looking forward to some grandchildren of my own now.'

'Crikey,' Steve said, 'give us a chance, Mum. I've only just got back from Colditz. I haven't seen a girl in five years, I can hardly remember what it's all about.'

Thursday and Jenny glanced at each other and grinned, but Thursday had felt a pang in her heart as she watched her cousin tending the little boy. I would like children of my own, she thought, I can't deny it. But I'm not getting married just for a family. It's got to be someone I truly love – and he's got to understand that I want my own life as well. I don't want to be just a wife and mother.

Mary and Steve had come to the station to see her off, and she waved until she could no longer see the platform. Then she sat back in her seat and watched the countryside flash by. I wonder if this will be the last time I go back to Haslar, she thought. I wonder if the next time I come home it will be for good. Or if I'll ever come home to live again.

July ran into August and still the war was continuing in Japan. It didn't seem to matter how much the Allies bombed them, the Japanese wouldn't give in. A bit like the British, Thursday thought but didn't say so. Nobody would have liked to be compared with the Japanese.

'How's it ever going to end?' Elsie asked. She was the first of the girls to be demobbed and they watched enviously as she packed her suitcase for the last time. Pete had found a couple of rooms in Gosport and would go to Portsmouth on the ferry every day, and was looking forward to being demobbed himself soon. Then he'd go back to work in the garage where he'd been a mechanic before the war and the pair would settle down in domestic bliss for the rest of their lives. 'Apart from the odd tiff, I dare say,' Elsie grinned, 'but we've found a good way to make up!'

Thursday grinned back, but she felt that little pang of loneliness which had struck her so often just lately as more and more girls announced their engagements and began to prepare for weddings. I'm not surprised people are rushing into marriage, she thought. If it hadn't been for the war, a lot of us would have been married and have children by now. We're fed up with waiting. *I'm* fed up with waiting. I want someone to love and someone to love me, but I'm still not sure about marriage. I'm still not sure about giving up my freedom.

She went with the others to wave goodbye to Elsie and then turned to go for a walk along the sea wall. Haslar would be a different place without Elsie's cheery presence and raucous laugh. I want it to be my turn, she thought. I want to move on: I'm ready to go.

Patsy fell into step beside her. 'It's going to seem queer without Elsie, isn't it?'

'It seems queer anyway. I feel as if we're all in limbo, waiting for something to happen.' They came to the edge of the sea wall and stared out over the Solent towards the Spithead Forts. 'What will you do when you leave here, Patsy?' she asked. 'Will you go back to Evesham?'

'I suppose so. I don't really know what else to do. I'll have to get a job, of course – maybe in a shop or something. I'll just have to see what there is.'

Thursday glanced at her. 'Wouldn't you rather do something else? Something more interesting?'

'Like what?' Patsy asked. 'All the interesting jobs are going to be taken back by the men, aren't they? It stands to reason. And women aren't going to want them anyway. They'll be wanting to start their families.' She sighed and gazed out across the silvery-blue water.

Thursday bit her lip and berated herself once again for her tactlessness and selfishness. There must be thousands of young women like Patsy, widowed before they'd had a chance really to begin their marriages and have a family. Thousands who would like nothing more than to do just what Elsie was doing – set up home in a couple of rooms with a few utility cups and saucers and a toasting fork, knowing that their lives could now take the course they'd dreamed of. Marriage, a modest home and children. Why can't I feel the same, she wondered. Why doesn't it seem to be enough for me?

They turned and walked slowly back to the hospital. The Quarter Deck, that long avenue leading to the little church, was peaceful, its cherry trees in full leaf. They had grown there ever since before the war started, coming into a foam of blossom every spring and turning a burnished bronze each autumn, quite unaffected by the war. Thursday thought of all the times she had gazed at them, drinking in the beauty of the froth of flowers or the coppery leaves against a clear blue sky, and felt a peace enter her soul. Whoever built this hospital, she thought, whoever decided there ought to be trees here and gardens and big open spaces, knew what would heal people as well as medicine. Whoever it was, knew about healing minds and hearts and souls, as well as bodies.

'I hope this place lasts for ever,' she said. 'I'm ready to go now, Pats, but I'm glad we came here. It's a lovely hospital. I'll never forget it.'

They stood for a moment, gazing along the avenue and remembering the time they'd been told off by an officer for running along it, the time they'd been upbraided by Madam for daring to ride their bikes. And then they heard a shout, and turned to see Ellen Bridges and Joy running towards them.

'What? What's the matter?' Thursday and Patsy began to run as well. It was obviously something momentous. Fear clutched at Thursday's heart and she tried angrily to push it away. We've done with that, she thought. We've done with feeling frightened. 'What's happened?'

'They've dropped a huge bomb on Japan.' Ellen stopped and put her hand over her heart, panting out the words. 'It's an atom bomb. It's the biggest bomb there's ever been. They're saying it's destroyed a whole city, and there are thousands of people killed. *Thousands.* They're saying it's going to end the war.'

The first atom bomb, dropped on Hiroshima, didn't end the war, but the second one dropped on Nagasaki three days later did. By then, there was some idea as to the damage done by the first – an entire city obliterated, miles of streets and buildings flattened, the inhabitants killed even more dreadfully than those who had died in Hitler's Blitzes. People whose clothes had been blasted from their bodies, their skin peeled away like an onion's, their brains bursting through their shattered skulls, people simply incinerated where they stood. There had been no chance for them to escape the inferno; even underground shelters offered no protection and of those who had survived, many, many more would die of their terrible injuries.

The girls were shaken by the news. Accustomed as they were to the wounds inflicted by war, these seemed worse than anything they had ever encountered. Thursday, reading an account in the newspaper, felt sickened. If this was the way war was going, what hope could there be for the world? In six years, it had gone from being able to destroy a few houses or a street, to a way of destroying civilisation itself. And now Russia, which had helped to conquer Germany, had joined in to declare war on Japan along with the other Allies. How many more cities would be flattened, how many more innocent civilians burned to death?

But it seemed that two bombs were enough. At midnight on 14 August, the Prime Minister announced that Japan had surrendered. For the first time ever, Emperor Hirohito spoke to his people and explained that they were laying down their arms. '*Should we continue to fight, it would not only result in the ultimate collapse and obliteration of the Japanese nation, but also it would lead to the total extinction of human civilisation.*' He asked his people to '*respond loyally*' to his command to surrender.

The Second World War was finally at an end.

To Thursday, the celebrations had a bittersweet quality. Just as had happened on VE Day, the whole Allied world seemed to go mad with joy. People flooded into the streets, lighting bonfires, setting up parties, bringing out their gramophones and singing and dancing late into the night. In the harbour, every ship sounded its siren madly for an entire hour. Rockets and fireworks soared into the sky, church bells rang, and as people answered their call and thronged to offer prayers of thanksgiving, impromptu church services were held. The little bell of Haslar's own church of St Luke was ringing, a small, pure sound against the cacophony of the sirens and hooters, and Thursday and the others found themselves joining a vast crowd of staff and up-patients in making their way along the footpaths and Quarter Deck towards its glowing windows.

Inside, the church was almost bursting at the seams. The chaplain stood before them and offered prayers of thanks, and the organist played the most rousing hymns, ending with 'O God, Our Help in Ages Past, Our Hope for Years to Come' and then the National Anthem. The tears burned hot in Thursday's eyes and then brimmed over, but she made no attempt to wipe them away, and as the sailors and the officers stood to attention she saw that every other face in the church was wet with similar tears, and nobody felt any shame.

Making their way out, Thursday became separated from the other girls and, thankful for the moment of solitude, lingered until everyone had gone. Then she walked alone down the length of the Quarter Deck and let the memories crowd about her.

Tony West, who had kissed her and then returned from Dunkirk too mutilated ever to kiss again. Doug Brighton, who had never failed to put her back up, and Roy Greenaway who had married Patsy and then left her a widow. Stoker Davis and his enema. The young German, Heinz Schmidt, who had listened to her chatter without revealing until the last day that he understood every word. The men who had flooded back from Dunkirk, wounded and burned and half-drowned. The young Wrens who had been killed in the air raid and buried in the little cemetery.

So many of them, she thought, looking up at the sky, its darkness brightened still by flashes of light and the glow of bonfires. Not so long ago, that glow would have been from burning buildings and there would have been searchlights looking for enemy aircraft. She remembered the night of the Blitz, when she had been up on Portsdown Hill with Connor in a borrowed car, and they'd rushed back and found themselves caught up in the devastation. She remembered Susie, the little girl whose leg Connor had amputated, and wondered where she was now.

And there were all the others as well. The constant flow of wounded sailors who had come through Haslar's gates or been brought to the jetty. And those who had never even made it that far; the Canadians killed at Dieppe, the soldiers who had died at El Alamein and in all the other desert battles. Those in Italy, in France, in Sicily, in Russia, in the Far East . . . The list was too long, and the countries too many.

Thank God it's all over, she thought. And that's all I want to do tonight – thank God. The others can dance in the streets and light fires and sound sirens and hooters, but all I want to do is feel thankful that it's over and do the job I came here to do, until I'm not needed any more.

She came to the main hospital block and turned to go down the basement steps to the operating theatre. There was work to be done still, and Thursday was glad of it.

Chapter Twenty-Eight

'What are you going to do when you get out?'

As summer wore into autumn and then into early winter, the question was being asked every day. Most of the VADs, like so many conscripted servicemen and women, were looking forward eagerly to demobilisation. Some would be returning to their pre-war occupation, others were starting a new life. Some were more reluctant to leave, recognising that the past six years had brought them experiences they didn't want to leave behind. Many, having joined up almost straight from school, had known nothing other than war during their entire working lives and felt strangely nervous about the free-for-all of Civvy Street.

'Let's face it,' Ellen Bridges said as they sat round the iron stove in the mess, 'we've been pretty well looked after all this time. We haven't been paid much but we've had everything found for us – food, clothes, a bed for the night. And plenty of company too. You've got to admit, we've had a pretty good time, by and large.'

'It's been rather like being back at boarding school,' Louisa remarked, glancing up from her writing-pad. 'Plenty of rules, but as long as you either obey them or don't get caught, you can have a lot of fun. More, actually,' she added with a wicked grin. 'There were plenty of boys' schools in Malvern as well as the girls' but we weren't allowed to have anything to do with them!'

'What are you writing?' Thursday asked curiously, and Louisa showed her. 'It's an advertisement for a job, see? *Ex-VAD seeks position requiring initiative. Driving licence, nursing and travel experience*. I thought I might do something while I'm waiting for Andrew to come back.'

'I didn't know you had a driving licence.'

'Well, I haven't yet, but I will have by the time I need it. That nice young Lieutenant's teaching me. It's all right,' she added defensively when they raised their eyebrows, 'that's all he's doing. Anyway, our mothers knew each other at school.'

The others hooted with laughter. 'And that makes him all right?' Patsy chortled. 'I don't think it'd be much recommendation to my mum. You ought to hear her on the subject of some of the girls *she* went to school with!'

'Well, she didn't go to a posh school like Louisa's mum,' Thursday told her. 'I think I might put an advert like that in one of the papers. What d'you think I should say? *Initiative and drive? Camel-riding a speciality? Sandcastles built to order*?'

'If you're thinking of advertising in the *Egyptian Mail*, yes,' Ellen scoffed. 'But seriously, Lou, what sort of job d'you think you'll get from an advert like that? Being a nanny, or something.'

'I don't know. I thought more of a personal secretary. Lots of people have them.' The other girls' blank looks told her that this was a new idea to them. In places like Worcester and Evesham, nobody had personal secretaries and, if they had, wouldn't have known what to do with them. She shrugged. 'Well, some people do, anyway. It's worth a try.'

'I think some of these training schemes sound interesting.' Patsy fished in her bag and pulled out a handful of leaflets. 'Look, I got these from the mess. The Government's fixing up all these classes for training people to do all sorts of things. You can learn shorthand and typing, or cookery, or teaching . . .'

'Teaching?' Thursday said. 'But don't you have to go to college to be a teacher?'

Patsy shook her head. 'Not for infants. Or for the older children at primary schools. It says here there'll be lots of teachers needed because so many of the men were called up and – and won't come back.' Her voice trembled a little but she went on determinedly. 'There are other things too. You can be a District Nurse. Or work in one of the homes and clinics they're setting up for servicemen who've been badly wounded and won't ever get properly better. There's a leaflet here about them – there's one near Portsmouth, and another one in Bristol, and they're looking for girls with experience. Or you can be a midwife – there are going to be a lot of babies born when the men come home!' She looked at the leaflet again, more thoughtfully. 'Actually, that might be a nice thing to do, bringing new babies into the world. Not exactly a nurse, but doing something like it – something *happier*.'

The door opened and Joy came in. She spotted Thursday and called across to her. 'Phone call for you, Thursday. Madam asked me to let you know.'

'Phone? Who is it?' But Joy shook her head and Thursday got up and hurried out. It was probably her mother, with some piece of family news – Vic come home, perhaps. She hoped it wasn't bad news about Mike. She ran up the stairs to Miss Makepeace's office and knocked breathlessly on the door.

'Oh, there you are, Tilford.' The Commandant indicated the receiver lying on her desk. 'You'd better hurry, the gentleman sounds a little impatient. I think he's just about to run out of money.' She smiled and got up to go out of the office. 'I'll leave you to it for a moment.'

The gentleman? Her heart suddenly quickening, Thursday picked up the instrument and put it to her lips. 'Hello?' she said uncertainly. 'Thursday Tilford here.'

There was brief pause, as though the person at the other end was unable to speak at once. Then a deep voice said, 'Thursday? Is that really you?' And then, when she too was unable to answer: 'Don't tell me you don't recognise my voice. It's Connor . . .'

She met him the next evening on Portsmouth Harbour railway station. She stood at the barrier waiting for the train to arrive, trembling with nerves, a chilly wind from the sea whipping her hair around her face. Four years had passed since she saw him last. What would he be like? What would he think of her? Suppose they didn't even like each other any more . . .

It was nonsense, she knew. In many ways, they had grown closer through their letters. You could spend hours with a person and still know nothing about them if you didn't talk to each other, but you couldn't be silent in a letter. You couldn't send sheets of blank paper.

But knowing and liking weren't necessarily the same as loving. And then there had been Mark . . .

The train was arriving now. Her knees weak, Thursday rested her hand on the barrier and stretched her neck to try to catch a glimpse of him in the crowd of people who were now jumping down from the carriages. He would be in uniform, she knew, one Naval officer amongst many. She might not even recognise him. She stared, trying to pick out his familiar face, the face that had smiled at her every day from the photograph beside her bed. She couldn't see him. He wasn't there. The crowd had thinned out, almost passed her by, and he hadn't come. She turned away, her disappointment almost too great to bear.

'*Thursday . . .*'

Unbelievingly, she turned again. And there he was. Tall, his face deeply tanned, a little thinner and more lined than she remembered, but his eyes still the same warm hazel. And as she gazed into them she had the most extraordinary feeling that four years were rolling away from her, like a burden she had been carrying on her back, and that nothing had changed. Nothing.

'Oh, *Connor*,' she said, and put both hands to her cheeks. It was as if she had, at last, truly come home.

There was so much to talk about, so much to tell and so much to hear. Yet on that first evening, they agreed that it could wait. Tonight they would just be together, revelling in the delight of being able to reach out and touch each other, in the sense that this must be just another of the vivid dreams they had each dreamed over the past four years and the swift, joyful realisation that this time it was real, that the waiting was over.

'You haven't changed at all,' he said as they sat on a bench on Southsea sea front, gazing out towards the twinkling lights of Ryde. He turned towards her, tracing the lines of her face with one finger. 'You're exactly the same as you were when I went away.'

'I'm not really. Four years is a long time, Connor. A lot's happened since then.'

'I know. But it hasn't changed us, has it? Not really. It hasn't changed the way things are between us.'

Thursday hesitated. She felt that she should tell him about Mark, that he deserved the truth – but how could she spoil this moment, this precious first evening, by raising doubts? Yet even as the thought slid through her mind, she knew that she had hesitated too long, and saw his brows come together in a frown.

'It *hasn't* changed us, has it? Things are the same?'

'Oh, Connor,' she said, 'I don't think anything's changed at all. Not while I'm here with you. But I've got to get used to it all again – to the war being over and getting demobbed soon, and you being back, and – and everything. I don't want to do anything too quickly. I've got to have time.'

There was a short silence. Then he nodded. 'I can understand that. And don't look so sad, my darling. So long as you give *me* time too – time to be with you, time to tell you I love you. Because that's what kept me going all these years – knowing that you were here. I know I said I didn't want to tie you down, but when you said you'd wait for me it meant the whole world. To know that, meant everything to me, through all the dark nights and the battles and the horror of it all. And look,' he felt in his breast pocket and brought out something small and flat, 'I kept this by my heart every minute of those four years, as a reminder.'

Thursday looked down and saw, held in his palm, her old fabric VAD badge, the one she had taken from her sleeve and given to him in exchange for the little silver crown brooch. It looked worn and rubbed, as if it had had much handling during that time, and she felt her throat ache and the tears come hot to her eyes.

'Oh, Connor,' she said softly.

He kissed her and she clung to him, letting her tears run down her cheeks. 'I'll make your uniform wet,' she said with a tiny laugh, and felt him smile.

'It doesn't matter. A sailor's uniform is used to salt water. Cry all you want to, Thursday, I don't mind. So long as I can hold you against me and comfort you and kiss you, you can cry all you want to. God knows we've both got a lot of crying to make up for – but we've got laughter too, and smiles, and loving. And when the crying's finished, that's what we'll share. Our loving, and our lives.'

Our loving and our lives.

For the next few weeks, Thursday held those words close to her heart. She was sure now that Connor would never willingly leave her life, yet she was still held back from her own final commitment. Whether it was the result of four years' separation, the restlessness that she'd been feeling for some months now or the feeling that she still had one more promise to keep – the one she had made to Mark – she didn't know; but although she felt herself to be as deeply in love as ever with Connor, although she had felt from that first moment of meeting again that they belonged together, she still could not bring herself to take that final step.

Connor was away again, spending his disembarkation leave with his family, and as she continued with her duties at Haslar Thursday felt the restlessness invade her even more strongly. The other girls were beginning to make decisions about their lives, yet she still seemed to be drifting in a strange limbo. It was as if she found herself tangled in invisible cobwebs, unable to free herself.

Patsy had made up her mind to train as a midwife. If she couldn't have babies of her own, she said, she wanted to help other women have theirs. The other girls were sure that Patsy would marry again, but knew that it would take her some time yet to get over Roy's death, and so they encouraged her decision. Louisa had got a job as a secretary to a doctor who was setting up a practice in London, and Ellen Bridges was going back to her old job as a hairdresser. Joy surprised them all by getting engaged to one of the sailors on the gate, and Elsie came in one day and told them she was expecting a baby.

The best news of all came when Miss Makepeace entered the mess one day while they were all off duty and, with her thin face wreathed in smiles and her bright brown eyes alight, announced that Jeanie Brown was coming back from the Japanese prison camp where she had been ever since the fall of Singapore.

'Jeanie!' The girls leaped from their chairs and hugged each other. 'Jeanie's alive! Oh, what wonderful news, what wonderful, wonderful news!'

'She's had a very bad time, poor girl,' Madam said, looking more serious. 'She's in hospital now, being brought back to health, and they say she'll make a complete recovery. They were treated terribly . . . But I understand that she did wonderful work in the camp, helping to nurse the others. I'm very proud of her.' She looked around and her eyes were brighter than ever. 'I'm proud of you all. *All* my girls.'

The news about Jeanie lifted Thursday's spirits, but she still felt as if she were strangely adrift. When Christmas came, with its round of parties and dances, she felt even more lost. She had a few days' leave before the festival itself to spend at home, and then returned to the hospital to join in the usual tour of the wards, with the officers, doctors and surgeons wearing paper hats and singing carols; however, the jollity seemed forced, at least on her part. I've had enough, she thought. The war emergency was over now and although she could still immerse herself in her work in the theatre or nursing the patients, she wanted to get on with her own life.

If only she knew what it was!

New Year's Eve came, with yet another party to go to. Thursday sat on her bed in the cabin she'd been recently allocated – the first time in her life she had ever had a bedroom to herself! – and gazed at Connor's photograph, wishing he could be here to celebrate with her. I don't want to go on my own, she thought. I want you here with me. But Connor was still with his family after his own demobilisation, and although she knew he was planning to come to Haslar the following weekend, it seemed an age away. It's now I want you, she thought, touching the little crown brooch she wore pinned to her dress. *Now.*

Patsy poked her head round the door. 'Come on, Thursday, aren't you ready? We're all going over together.' She looked better than she had for a long time, Thursday thought. A career lay ahead of her and although she was still grieving for Roy she was also looking ahead. Thursday felt ashamed of her own indecision.

As on so many previous occasions, they were going to Kimball's in Southsea. There was a particularly good band performing and the celebrations of the first New Year after the war promised to be hectic. They had decided to splash out and get a taxi from the harbour. 'Can't ride our bikes in our posh frocks,' Patsy said with a grin. 'Don't want them getting caught up in the chains.'

'It seems funny going out in civvies at last.' Thursday said. She had altered one of Louisa's old dresses from a bundle that the other girl had sent for from home and distributed around the mess. 'I feel quite odd – as if no one'll know who I am without my uniform!' She stood up and twirled round so that the skirt, a shimmering gold shot with olive green, flared out in a bronze cloud. 'Lou's a brick, letting us have all these things. I suppose she'll be getting a whole new wardrobe for her trousseau, though I don't know where she's going to get all the coupons from.'

'She's got a cousin in America who's sending her some material.'

Patsy twisted round to view her own dress in Thursday's small mirror. 'Does this look all right at the back?'

'It looks lovely. You'll be the belle of the ball.' Thursday hooked her arm through Patsy's and switched off the light as they went out together. 'D'you realise, this will be the last Christmas and New Year we'll spend here? By this time next year we'll all be living quite different lives. I wonder where we'll be.'

'Wherever it is,' Patsy said, 'we'll always keep in touch. We've made some good friends, haven't we, Thursday? We mustn't forget.'

'We won't,' Thursday said as they went down the stairs and out into the cold night air. 'We'll never forget.'

The dance was almost over. They'd waltzed, tangoed, foxtrotted and jitterbugged. Although many people had gone with partners, there were still plenty of young men anxious to dance with the girls and when they'd all linked hands and sung 'Old Lang Syne' Thursday was glad to slip outside for a few moments of fresh air. She wandered across the road to look at the sea, then caught her breath as someone spoke her name.

'Thursday.'

She turned slowly. The voice was instantly recognisable. Her heart seemed to stop and her blood turn to water. She stared into the darkness and saw him move into the light that spilled from the windows all along the front. When she tried to speak, her voice caught in her throat.

'Mark . . .'

He came closer. 'I've been looking for you everywhere. That Commandant of yours who never seems to sleep told me you'd come out with the other girls, but she didn't know which dance you were coming to. I think I've been to every one in Portsmouth!' He looked down into her face and put his hands on her shoulders. 'You're here with the other girls. Does that mean what I think it means?'

She stared up at him. 'I don't know. I don't know what you think.'

He shook her gently. 'Thursday, you're here on your own. With no partner. What does that mean? Tell me.'

'It doesn't mean anything,' she said, regaining her control. 'If you're asking about Connor, he's in Plymouth. He came home a few weeks ago and he'll be coming to see me again soon. He's expecting to be demobbed soon and go into general practice with his father.' She met his eyes.

'And?' he said quietly.

'And nothing. I kept my promise to him, and I'm keeping the one I made to you too. I haven't decided anything.'

'So I still have a chance!'

'Mark.' She put her hand to her forehead and tried to turn away, but he held her facing him. 'Mark, I don't *know*. I have to have time. Connor understands that.'

'Does he? Well, I don't.' His tone was suddenly harsh. 'Thursday, I don't *have* time! I'm only back for a few days and I've got a lot to do. I have to know soon.'

'Know what? Don't shout at me, Mark.'

'I'm sorry,' he said more quietly, 'I didn't mean to shout. But I have to know whether you'll go back with me. Not at once, I'm not asking that, but—'

'Go back with you?' she broke in. 'Mark, what are you talking about? Go back where?'

'To Germany, of course.' He took a breath, then said, 'Thursday, there's work to do there. I went into the concentration camps when they were first opened. You have no idea what it was like. People like skeletons, barely able to crawl, left to starve. People with terrible diseases coming from malnutrition, ill-treatment and total lack of hygiene. People who will never properly recover but need care and help. We can give it to them. We *have* to give it to them!' He was speaking rapidly, his voice passionate. 'The Army's going to be in Germany for a long time, helping to protect the people there who had no part in the atrocities that went on, the people who suffered so much. I want to be part of that, Thursday, and I want my wife to be part of it with me. I want *you*.'

She stared at him. 'You want me to go to Germany with you? To live? To work as a – a nurse?'

'Yes! Yes, that's what I want. You must come, Thursday. You can't say no. You can't stay here and waste your life as a country GP's wife.'

'Would it be such a waste? They're all human beings.'

'But they can manage, Thursday! They can manage without you. I can't. I want you as my wife, you've known that for years, and I'm not prepared to wait any longer.' He stared at her and she felt a sudden spasm of dismay at the look in his eyes. It was the look of a passionate man, a man whose passion could turn to fanaticism. She thought of Connor and his more restrained understanding. 'If that won't convince you,' he was saying in a low, intense tone, 'let me try this.'

He caught her against him, his arms hard around her body in the thin dress. His lips touched and then crushed hers in a kiss of searing frenzy. Thursday struggled against him, pushing at his chest with both hands.

'Mark! Please! How dare you do that? How dare you!'

'Thursday, I love you!'

'No,' she said, and she was trembling all over with anger. 'You *don't* love me, not as I want to be loved. You just *want* me, that's all. You want a wife who'll want what *you* want, and *do* what you want. Look, what you're going to do sounds wonderful and good and worthwhile, and maybe it's the kind of thing I've been looking for – but there are other good things to do too. I can't make a decision like this all in a moment. I've got to have time to think. And pushing yourself on me like that won't help.'

'Time to *think*?' he broke in. 'For God's sake, haven't you had months – *years* – to think? It's what you always say, Thursday, whenever you're asked to give a definite answer. I'll tell you what *I* think, shall I?' He stepped back a little and glowered into her eyes. 'I think you've already made up your mind, and you just can't face up to telling me. It's *him*, isn't it? You've seen him again, and he's won.'

'There was never any competition,' she said. 'And I *do* need time to think. I'm *entitled* to it! Look, you've been to Germany, you've seen these things with your own eyes – you've had time to think about them. I haven't. I had no idea you were planning to do this.' She lifted her chin and met his angry stare. 'I'm not your possession, to be told what to do and where to go,' she said quietly. 'I'm my own person. *I* decide how much time I need to think about this, and if you can't accept that you'd better take no for my answer.'

She saw his eyes flicker and for a moment she thought that he was about to turn on his heel and walk away. Then his mouth moved a little and she saw his shoulders lift.

'All right. You assert your independence, if you must. Take your time to think, Thursday, but bear in mind that it isn't just me who's setting deadlines. I'm a soldier – not a free person as you're so proud of being. I have to go where I'm sent, and when I'm sent there. I've got ten more days, and I need to have your answer within two. There'll be a lot to arrange.'

'Two *days*?'

'I'm not asking you to pack your bags and come with me,' he said impatiently. 'Wives won't be allowed out there yet. But if you're going to be my wife, Thursday, I want us safely married before I go. There'll be just time. I don't want any more of this dithering!' He stopped and looked at her again. 'Two days.'

'Mark—'

'I'll ring you at Haslar,' he told her and then, as the doors of the dance hall opened and people began to spill out on to the pavement, he turned away. 'I'll leave you to go back with your friends. Happy New Year, Thursday. And if you choose *not* to spend it with me, have a happy life as well.'

'You too,' she whispered, and watched as he marched away into the darkness. 'You too, Mark.'

Connor was demobbed a month later. He had found a position as surgeon in a hospital in Bristol, and was due to start work only a day or two after Thursday's own release from the Voluntary Aid Detachment. It was the middle of February 1946, already a year since Elsie's wedding. The war had been over for six months.

She had refused to be forced into a decision. Mark had telephoned as promised, and she'd told him that he must go to Germany without her. It hurt her to hear his voice, knowing that it was for the last time, but she'd swallowed her sorrow. 'I do love you, Mark,' she'd said, 'in a way. But it's not the way I need. It wouldn't be right for either of us.' And when he'd begun to argue, she'd said a quiet goodbye and then put down the phone. She'd stood very still for a few minutes, taking deep breaths to control herself, and then walked out of Madam's office and down the stairs, knowing that this time it really was over and that the pain was going to be sharper than she had imagined.

I'd have liked to go to Germany, she thought regretfully. I'd have liked to work with those people, knowing I was doing something really worthwhile. But I couldn't marry Mark just for that. It had to be because I loved *him* – not just the life he was offering me. And I don't think I did, not really. He excited me, he made my head swim and my knees go weak, but I don't believe we belonged together. I don't believe it would have lasted us all our lives.

And Connor? She shook her head, unable to think of him just yet. The feeling of belonging she had experienced when they had first met again still warmed her heart – but she had to get over Mark before she could go to him. She had to be able to offer him a whole and honest heart and, as she suffered the pain of having sent Mark away, she began to wonder if she would ever be able to do it.

As the day of their demobilisation drew nearer the girls still remaining at Haslar threw themselves into a frenzy of packing and goodbyes. There were so many 'last times' – the last time cycling over Pneumonia Bridge, the last time at the Swiss Café or the Dive, the last time on the ferry, the last time walking along Stokes Bay. Thursday and Patsy went to see Elsie, now in the throes of early pregnancy and bemoaning her state – 'sick all morning and starving the rest of the day!' – but obviously thrilled about the coming baby. They clung together, eyes swimming with tears, promising to keep in touch. Louisa, who had already left to prepare for her own wedding, sent them a telegram to wish them good luck, and even Vera Hapgood asked for their home addresses, to send Christmas cards.

'I know we've never liked her all that much,' Thursday said, 'but she's not bad really. Just got a funny manner, that's all.'

The dormitory was cluttered with possessions and suitcases. Madam marched up and down the corridor, ready to give a hand where needed and told them over and over again that they must keep in touch. 'I shall want to know what all of you do. I want to be able to go on feeling just as proud of you all.'

'She's going to miss Haslar even more than we are,' Patsy whispered to Thursday. 'I wonder what she'll do in Civvy Street.'

'Stay in the Red Cross, I suppose. There's still plenty of work to do.' Thursday was beginning to feel excited. A letter had come for her that morning that she hadn't yet told anyone about, and she could feel it in her pocket. She went to stand at the window, gazing out over the hospital grounds and past the sea wall to the green bulk of the Isle of Wight across the Solent. This is the last time I'll stand here, she thought. The very last time . . .

Patsy came quietly to stand behind her.

'Well, Thursday, this is it. It's funny – in one way, it seems so long since we first came here, and in another it seems like yesterday. Remember, Thurs? The snow and the ice, and the matelot telling us about port and starboard. We didn't know a thing, did we! We've learned a lot since then. Lived through a lot, too.' Her face was sober.

'Yes.' Thursday slipped her arm round Patsy's shoulders. 'Some of it good, some not so good. But I'm glad we came, aren't you, Patsy?'

Patsy nodded, and then turned her head as someone shouted from the corridor. 'Come on, Thursday. It's time to go.'

They walked down the stairs with their worn brown linoleum and brass strips. At the door to the block, Madam was surrounded by a crowd of girls, some in tears, all vying to shake her hand. She pressed her lips together and gave them all a sharp nod, then said in a voice only slightly less firm than usual, 'Well, off you go then. The pinnace is waiting. Remember, Naval time –'

'Is five minutes early,' they chorused, remembering one of the first lessons they had learned here, and then the crowd broke up and they turned to hurry through the arcade and down the smoothly paved tramway to the quay where the pinnaces were waiting to take them on their last trip across the harbour, to the railway station where they would begin their journey into civilian life.

Their luggage was piled on the quayside. Thursday looked for hers and then, to her surprise, found that it had been detached from the others and set at a little distance. She looked at it uncertainly and then a voice behind her spoke her name.

'Thursday.'

She spun round, staring in disbelief. The voices of the other girls faded from her ears. The quay, the pinnace, the harbour with all its ships, seemed to rock and swing around her and the sky itself tipped on edge. She put both hands to her face and felt the tears spring to her eyes, even as the relief of familiarity and belonging flooded her body and filled her heart with warmth.

In that brief moment, all her doubts, all her indecision, swooped away like a receding tide, and she knew exactly how she wanted to spend the rest of her life, and with whom she wanted to spend it.

'*Connor*,' she breathed, and stepped into his arms.

'And you really will marry me?' he asked for the twentieth time as they sat in a restaurant that evening. He had already arranged rooms for them in one of Portsmouth's hotels, in the hope that she would stay, and Thursday had telegraphed her mother to say she wouldn't be coming home until tomorrow. 'You'll come to Bristol and be my wife? You've made up your mind?'

Thursday smiled and nodded. 'I'm sorry I kept you waiting so long. I had to be sure.'

'I know. I had to be sure too – it just didn't take me so long. I knew the first moment I saw you.' He took her hand. 'I hoped you'd know too, but I've had to be very patient!'

'I did know,' she said. 'It felt so right, being with you again. But I'd promised Mark he should have his chance and I had to keep to it.'

Connor nodded. Thursday had told him about Mark. There could be no secrets between them, she'd said, not if they were to make their lives together. Secrets cast shadows, and they couldn't start a new life with shadows overhanging them.

'And you needed to find something to do for yourself too,' he said. 'You're not the sort of person to sit at home and wait for babies to come along. Are you quite sure that what you've found is right for you?'

Thursday nodded. She took the letter out of her pocket and smoothed it out on the table. It was from the matron of the home for wounded servicemen in Bristol, and it offered her a position working with those who were being rehabilitated. Men who were paralysed or had lost limbs, who needed to be taught to live again. The kind of work Thursday knew, from her experiences at both Haslar and in Egypt, that she would be able to do well.

It's not so very different from the work I might have done in Germany, she thought. But I'll be with Connor – and that makes all the difference in the world.

She looked up and met his eyes. 'We're going to make a good life together,' she said. 'We've waited a long time, but we can start now.' She tightened her fingers around his. 'I love you, Connor. I always will. That's a promise.'

Another promise, she thought, and one made willingly and happily, with a whole and loving heart.

A promise to keep.

Praise for *The Lo*

'Moving and compelling . . . Sebold's vision of death and the afterlife is shiveringly exact . . . *The Lovely Bones* is a bold, fresh, clear-eyed take on the meta-life of death. It will put an imperceptible but steathily insistent hold on you. I sat down in the morning to read the first couple of pages; five hours later, I was still there, book in hand, transfixed'
Sunday Telegraph

'Spare, beautiful and brutal prose . . . *The Lovely Bones* is compulsive enough to read in a single sitting, brilliantly intelligent, elegantly constructed and ultimately intriguing'
The Times

'This book should be bleak, a chunk of ugliness and grief as chilling as the Arctic, but it's just luminous . . . Alice Sebold's words will stay with you long after you finish the last page'
Daily Mail

'Simple and beautiful'
List

'It's a work of extraordinary structural originality, finding a fresh way to combine great tenderness of feeling with the most brutal events. You can sense its poise from the very first sentences'
Evening Standard

'In *The Lovely Bones*, [Alice Sebold] deals with almost unthinkable subjects with humour and intelligence and a kind of mysterious grace'
New York Times Book Review

'[Sebold] has created a novel that is painfully fine and accomplished, one which readers will have their own difficulties relinquishing, long after the last page is turned'
Los Angeles Times

'A keenly observed portrait of familial love and how it endures and changes over time. The novel is an elegy about a vanished place and time and the loss of childhood innocence'
New York Times

'Sebold has worked wonders. Part of the book's appeal is its marvellous pacing; it can be gulped down, devoured in one long evening. Part of it is the dreamy safety-net of Sebold's words... And part of it is that she knows of what she writes'
Entertainment Weekly

[Sebold] manages to evoke awe, terror, sadness, laughter, yearning, wistfulness and ecstasy – sometimes in the space of a single paragraph'
Time Out, New York

'A small but far from minor miracle . . . Sebold's most dazzling stroke, among many bold ones, is to narrate the story from Susie's heaven . . . It might be this that gives Sebold's novel its special flavor, for in Susie's every observation and memory—of the smell of skunk or the touch of spider webs—is the reminder that life is sweet and funny and surprising and almost as irresistible as this book'
Publishers Weekly (starred review)

'Sebold's beautiful novel shows how a tragedy can tear a family apart and bring them back together again. She challenges us to reimagine happy endings, as she brings the novel to a conclusion that is unfalteringly magnificent. And she paints, with an artist's precision, a portrait of a world where the terrible and the miraculous can and do coexist'
Booklist (starred review)

'With an impressive 925,000 copies in print after 11 printings, Alice Sebold's *The Lovely Bones* has outpaced the sales of any other first novel in memory'
Publishers Weekly

THE LOVELY BONES

Alice Sebold is the author of the memoir *Lucky*. She lives in California with her husband, Glen David Gold.

ALSO BY ALICE SEBOLD

Lucky

THE

LOVELY

BONES

a novel

Alice Sebold

PICADOR

Always, Glen

First published 2002 by Little, Brown and Company, USA

First published in Great Britain 2002 by Picador

This paperback edition published 2003 by Picador
an imprint of Pan Macmillan Ltd
Pan Macmillan, 20 New Wharf Road, London N1 9RR
Basingstoke and Oxford
Associated companies throughout the world
www.panmacmillan.com

ISBN 978-0-330-51192-6

1

A CIP catalogue record for this book is available from
the British Library.

Printed and bound in the UK by
CPI Mackays, Chatham ME5 8TD

THE LOVELY BONES

Inside the snow globe on my father's desk, there was a penguin wearing a red-and-white-striped scarf. When I was little my father would pull me into his lap and reach for the snow globe. He would turn it over, letting all the snow collect on the top, then quickly invert it. The two of us watched the snow fall gently around the penguin. The penguin was alone in there, I thought, and I worried for him. When I told my father this, he said, "Don't worry, Susie; he has a nice life. He's trapped in a perfect world."

ONE

My name was Salmon, like the fish; first name, Susie. I was fourteen when I was murdered on December 6, 1973. In newspaper photos of missing girls from the seventies, most looked like me: white girls with mousy brown hair. This was before kids of all races and genders started appearing on milk cartons or in the daily mail. It was still back when people believed things like that didn't happen.

In my junior high yearbook I had a quote from a Spanish poet my sister had turned me on to, Juan Ramón Jiménez. It went like this: "If they give you ruled paper, write the other way." I chose it both because it expressed my contempt for my structured surroundings à la the classroom and because, not being some dopey quote from a rock group, I thought it marked me as literary. I was a member of the Chess Club and Chem Club and burned everything I tried to make in Mrs. Delminico's home ec class. My favorite teacher was Mr. Botte, who taught biology and liked to animate the frogs and crawfish we had to dissect by making them dance in their waxed pans.

I wasn't killed by Mr. Botte, by the way. Don't think every person you're going to meet in here is suspect. That's the problem. You never know. Mr. Botte came to my memorial (as, may I add, did almost the entire junior high school—I was never so popular) and cried quite a bit. He had a sick kid. We all knew this, so when he laughed at his own jokes, which were rusty way before I had him, we laughed too, forcing it sometimes just to make him happy. His daughter died a year and a half after I did. She had leukemia, but I never saw her in my heaven.

My murderer was a man from our neighborhood. My mother liked his border flowers, and my father talked to him once about fertilizer. My murderer believed in old-fashioned things like eggshells and coffee grounds, which he said his own mother had used. My father came home smiling, making jokes about how the man's garden might be beautiful but it would stink to high heaven once a heat wave hit.

But on December 6, 1973, it was snowing, and I took a shortcut through the cornfield back from the junior high. It was dark out because the days were shorter in winter, and I remember how the broken cornstalks made my walk more difficult. The snow was falling lightly, like a flurry of small hands, and I was breathing through my nose until it was running so much that I had to open my mouth. Six feet from where Mr. Harvey stood, I stuck my tongue out to taste a snowflake.

"Don't let me startle you," Mr. Harvey said.

Of course, in a cornfield, in the dark, I was startled. After I was dead I thought about how there had been the light scent of cologne in the air but that I had not been paying attention, or thought it was coming from one of the houses up ahead.

"Mr. Harvey," I said.

"You're the older Salmon girl, right?"

"Yes."

"How are your folks?"

Although the eldest in my family and good at acing a science quiz, I had never felt comfortable with adults.

"Fine," I said. I was cold, but the natural authority of his age, and the added fact that he was a neighbor and had talked to my father about fertilizer, rooted me to the spot.

"I've built something back here," he said. "Would you like to see?"

"I'm sort of cold, Mr. Harvey," I said, "and my mom likes me home before dark."

"It's after dark, Susie," he said.

I wish now that I had known this was weird. I had never told him my name. I guess I thought my father had told him one of the embarrassing anecdotes he saw merely as loving testaments to his children. My father was the kind of dad who kept a nude photo of you when you were three in the downstairs bathroom, the one that guests would use. He did this to my little sister, Lindsey, thank God. At least I was spared that indignity. But he liked to tell a story about how, once Lindsey was born, I was so jealous that one day while he was on the phone in the other room, I moved down the couch—he could see me from where he stood—and tried to pee on top of Lindsey in her carrier. This story humiliated me every time he told it, to the pastor of our church, to our neighbor Mrs. Stead, who was a therapist and whose take on it he wanted to hear, and to everyone who ever said "Susie has a lot of spunk!"

"Spunk!" my father would say. "Let me tell you about spunk," and he would launch immediately into his Susie-peed-on-Lindsey story.

But as it turned out, my father had not mentioned us to Mr. Harvey or told him the Susie-peed-on-Lindsey story.

Mr. Harvey would later say these words to my mother when he

ran into her on the street: "I heard about the horrible, horrible tragedy. What was your daughter's name, again?"

"Susie," my mother said, bracing up under the weight of it, a weight that she naively hoped might lighten someday, not knowing that it would only go on to hurt in new and varied ways for the rest of her life.

Mr. Harvey told her the usual: "I hope they get the bastard. I'm sorry for your loss."

I was in my heaven by that time, fitting my limbs together, and couldn't believe his audacity. "The man has no shame," I said to Franny, my intake counselor. "Exactly," she said, and made her point as simply as that. There wasn't a lot of bullshit in my heaven.

Mr. Harvey said it would only take a minute, so I followed him a little farther into the cornfield, where fewer stalks were broken off because no one used it as a shortcut to the junior high. My mom had told my baby brother, Buckley, that the corn in the field was inedible when he asked why no one from the neighborhood ate it. "The corn is for horses, not humans," she said. "Not dogs?" Buckley asked. "No," my mother answered. "Not dinosaurs?" Buckley asked. And it went like that.

"I've made a little hiding place," said Mr. Harvey.

He stopped and turned to me.

"I don't see anything," I said. I was aware that Mr. Harvey was looking at me strangely. I'd had older men look at me that way since I'd lost my baby fat, but they usually didn't lose their marbles over me when I was wearing my royal blue parka and yellow elephant bell-bottoms. His glasses were small and round with gold frames, and his eyes looked out over them and at me.

"You should be more observant, Susie," he said.

I felt like observing my way out of there, but I didn't. Why didn't I? Franny said these questions were fruitless: "You didn't and that's that. Don't mull it over. It does no good. You're dead and you have to accept it."

"Try again," Mr. Harvey said, and he squatted down and knocked against the ground.

"What's that?" I asked.

My ears were freezing. I wouldn't wear the multicolored cap with the pompom and jingle bells that my mother had made me one Christmas. I had shoved it in the pocket of my parka instead.

I remember that I went over and stomped on the ground near him. It felt harder even than frozen earth, which was pretty hard.

"It's wood," Mr. Harvey said. "It keeps the entrance from collapsing. Other than that it's all made out of earth."

"What is it?" I asked. I was no longer cold or weirded out by the look he had given me. I was like I was in science class: I was curious.

"Come and see."

It was awkward to get into, that much he admitted once we were both inside the hole. But I was so amazed by how he had made a chimney that would draw smoke out if he ever chose to build a fire that the awkwardness of getting in and out of the hole wasn't even on my mind. You could add to that that escape wasn't a concept I had any real experience with. The worst I'd had to escape was Artie, a strange-looking kid at school whose father was a mortician. He liked to pretend he was carrying a needle full of embalming fluid around with him. On his notebooks he would draw needles spilling dark drips.

"This is neato!" I said to Mr. Harvey. He could have been the hunchback of Notre Dame, whom we had read about in French class. I didn't care. I completely reverted. I was my brother Buckley on our day-trip to the Museum of Natural History in New York, where he'd fallen in love with the huge skeletons on display. I hadn't used the word *neato* in public since elementary school.

"Like taking candy from a baby," Franny said.

* * *

I can still see the hole like it was yesterday, and it was. Life is a perpetual yesterday for us. It was the size of a small room, the mud room in our house, say, where we kept our boots and slickers and where Mom had managed to fit a washer and dryer, one on top of the other. I could almost stand up in it, but Mr. Harvey had to stoop. He'd created a bench along the sides of it by the way he'd dug it out. He immediately sat down.

"Look around," he said.

I stared at it in amazement, the dug-out shelf above him where he had placed matches, a row of batteries, and a battery-powered fluorescent lamp that cast the only light in the room—an eerie light that would make his features hard to see when he was on top of me.

There was a mirror on the shelf, and a razor and shaving cream. I thought that was odd. Wouldn't he do that at home? But I guess I figured that a man who had a perfectly good split-level and then built an underground room only half a mile away had to be kind of loo-loo. My father had a nice way of describing people like him: "The man's a character, that's all."

So I guess I was thinking that Mr. Harvey was a character, and I liked the room, and it was warm, and I wanted to know how he had built it, what the mechanics of the thing were and where he'd learned to do something like that.

But by the time the Gilberts' dog found my elbow three days later and brought it home with a telling corn husk attached to it, Mr. Harvey had closed it up. I was in transit during this. I didn't get to see him sweat it out, remove the wood reinforcement, bag any evidence along with my body parts, except that elbow. By the time I popped up with enough wherewithal to look down at the goings-on on Earth, I was more concerned with my family than anything else.

My mother sat on a hard chair by the front door with her mouth open. Her pale face paler than I had ever seen it. Her blue eyes staring. My father was driven into motion. He wanted to know details and to comb the cornfield along with the cops. I still thank God for a small detective named Len Fenerman. He assigned two uniforms to take my dad into town and have him point out all the places I'd hung out with my friends. The uniforms kept my dad busy in one mall for the whole first day. No one had told Lindsey, who was thirteen and would have been old enough, or Buckley, who was four and would, to be honest, never fully understand.

Mr. Harvey asked me if I would like a refreshment. That was how he put it. I said I had to go home.

"Be polite and have a Coke," he said. "I'm sure the other kids would."

"What other kids?"

"I built this for the kids in the neighborhood. I thought it could be some sort of clubhouse."

I don't think I believed this even then. I thought he was lying, but I thought it was a pitiful lie. I imagined he was lonely. We had read about men like him in health class. Men who never married and ate frozen meals every night and were so afraid of rejection that they didn't even own pets. I felt sorry for him.

"Okay," I said, "I'll have a Coke."

In a little while he said, "Aren't you warm, Susie? Why don't you take off your parka."

I did.

After this he said, "You're very pretty, Susie."

"Thanks," I said, even though he gave me what my friend Clarissa and I had dubbed the skeevies.

"Do you have a boyfriend?"

"No, Mr. Harvey," I said. I swallowed the rest of my Coke, which was a lot, and said, "I got to go, Mr. Harvey. This is a cool place, but I have to go."

He stood up and did his hunchback number by the six dug-in

steps that led to the world. "I don't know why you think you're leaving."

I talked so that I would not have to take in this knowledge: Mr. Harvey was no character. He made me feel skeevy and icky now that he was blocking the door.

"Mr. Harvey, I really have to get home."

"Take off your clothes."

"What?"

"Take your clothes off," Mr. Harvey said. "I want to check that you're still a virgin."

"I am, Mr. Harvey," I said.

"I want to make sure. Your parents will thank me."

"My parents?"

"They only want good girls," he said.

"Mr. Harvey," I said, "please let me leave."

"You aren't leaving, Susie. You're mine now."

Fitness was not a big thing back then; *aerobics* was barely a word. Girls were supposed to be soft, and only the girls we suspected were butch could climb the ropes at school.

I fought hard. I fought as hard as I could not to let Mr. Harvey hurt me, but my hard-as-I-could was not hard enough, not even close, and I was soon lying down on the ground, in the ground, with him on top of me panting and sweating, having lost his glasses in the struggle.

I was so alive then. I thought it was *the worst thing in the world* to be lying flat on my back with a sweating man on top of me. To be trapped inside the earth and have no one know where I was.

I thought of my mother.

My mother would be checking the dial of the clock on her oven. It was a new oven and she loved that it had a clock on it. "I can time things to the minute," she told her own mother, a mother who couldn't care less about ovens.

She would be worried, but more angry than worried, at my

lateness. As my father pulled into the garage, she would rush about, fixing him a cocktail, a dry sherry, and put on an exasperated face: "You know junior high," she would say. "Maybe it's Spring Fling." "Abigail," my father would say, "how can it be Spring Fling when it's snowing?" Having failed with this, my mother might rush Buckley into the room and say, "Play with your father," while she ducked into the kitchen and took a nip of sherry for herself.

Mr. Harvey started to press his lips against mine. They were blubbery and wet and I wanted to scream but I was too afraid and too exhausted from the fight. I had been kissed once by someone I liked. His name was Ray and he was Indian. He had an accent and was dark. I wasn't supposed to like him. Clarissa called his large eyes, with their half-closed lids, "freak-a-delic," but he was nice and smart and helped me cheat on my algebra exam while pretending he hadn't. He kissed me by my locker the day before we turned in our photos for the yearbook. When the yearbook came out at the end of the summer, I saw that under his picture he had answered the standard "My heart belongs to" with "Susie Salmon." I guess he had had plans. I remember that his lips were chapped.

"Don't, Mr. Harvey," I managed, and I kept saying that one word a lot. *Don't.* And I said *please* a lot too. Franny told me that almost everyone begged "please" before dying.

"I want you, Susie," he said.

"Please," I said. "Don't," I said. Sometimes I combined them. "Please don't" or "Don't please." It was like insisting that a key works when it doesn't or yelling "I've got it, I've got it, I've got it" as a softball goes sailing over you into the stands.

"Please don't."

But he grew tired of hearing me plead. He reached into the pocket of my parka and balled up the hat my mother had made me, smashing it into my mouth. The only sound I made after that was the weak tinkling of bells.

As he kissed his wet lips down my face and neck and then began to shove his hands up under my shirt, I wept. I began to leave my body; I began to inhabit the air and the silence. I wept and struggled so I would not feel. He ripped open my pants, not having found the invisible zipper my mother had artfully sewn into their side.

"Big white panties," he said.

I felt huge and bloated. I felt like a sea in which he stood and pissed and shat. I felt the corners of my body were turning in on themselves and out, like in cat's cradle, which I played with Lindsey just to make her happy. He started working himself over me.

"Susie! Susie!" I heard my mother calling. "Dinner is ready."

He was inside me. He was grunting.

"We're having string beans and lamb."

I was the mortar, he was the pestle.

"Your brother has a new finger painting, and I made apple crumb cake."

Mr. Harvey made me lie still underneath him and listen to the beating of his heart and the beating of mine. How mine skipped like a rabbit, and how his thudded, a hammer against cloth. We lay there with our bodies touching, and, as I shook, a powerful knowledge took hold. He had done this thing to me and I had lived. That was all. I was still breathing. I heard his heart. I smelled his breath. The dark earth surrounding us smelled like what it was, moist dirt where worms and animals lived their daily lives. I could have yelled for hours.

I knew he was going to kill me. I did not realize then that I was an animal already dying.

"Why don't you get up?" Mr. Harvey said as he rolled to the side and then crouched over me.

His voice was gentle, encouraging, a lover's voice on a late morning. A suggestion, not a command.

I could not move. I could not get up.

When I would not—was it only that, only that I would not follow his suggestion?—he leaned to the side and felt, over his head, across the ledge where his razor and shaving cream sat. He brought back a knife. Unsheathed, it smiled at me, curving up in a grin.

He took the hat from my mouth.

"Tell me you love me," he said.

Gently, I did.

The end came anyway.

TWO

When I first entered heaven I thought everyone saw what I saw. That in everyone's heaven there were soccer goalposts in the distance and lumbering women throwing shot put and javelin. That all the buildings were like suburban northeast high schools built in the 1960s. Large, squat buildings spread out on dismally landscaped sandy lots, with overhangs and open spaces to make them feel modern. My favorite part was how the colored blocks were turquoise and orange, just like the blocks in Fairfax High. Sometimes, on Earth, I had made my father drive me by Fairfax High so I could imagine myself there.

Following the seventh, eighth, and ninth grades of middle school, high school would have been a fresh start. When I got to Fairfax High I would insist on being called Suzanne. I would wear my hair feathered or up in a bun. I would have a body that the boys wanted and the girls envied, but I'd be so nice on top of it all that they would feel too guilty to do anything but worship me. I liked to think of myself—having reached a sort of queenly status—as protecting misfit kids in the cafeteria. When someone taunted Clive Saunders for walking like a girl, I would deliver swift vengeance with my foot to the taunter's less-protected parts. When the boys teased Phoebe Hart for her sizable breasts, I would give a speech on why boob jokes weren't funny. I had to forget that I too had made lists in the margins of my notebook when Phoebe walked by: Winnebagos, Hoo-has, Johnny Yellows. At the end of my reveries, I sat in the back of the car as my father drove. I was beyond reproach. I would overtake high school in a matter of days, not years, or, inexplicably, earn an Oscar for Best Actress during my junior year.

These were my dreams on Earth.

After a few days in heaven, I realized that the javelin-throwers and the shot-putters and the boys who played basketball on the cracked blacktop were all in their own version of heaven. Theirs just fit with mine—didn't duplicate it precisely, but had a lot of the same things going on inside.

I met Holly, who became my roommate, on the third day. She was sitting on the swing set. (I didn't question that a high school had swing sets: that's what made it heaven. And no flat-benched swings—only bucket seats made out of hard black rubber that cradled you and that you could bounce in a bit before swinging.) Holly sat reading a book in a weird alphabet that I associated with the pork-fried rice my father brought home from Hop Fat Kitchen, a place Buckley loved the name of, loved so much he yelled "Hop Fat!" at the top of his lungs. Now I know Vietnamese, and I know that Vietnamese is not what Herman Jade, who owned Hop Fat, was, and that Herman Jade was not Herman Jade's real name but one he adopted when he came to the U.S. from China. Holly taught me all this.

"Hi," I said. "My name is Susie."

Later she would tell me she picked her name from a movie, *Breakfast at Tiffany's.* But that day it rolled right off her tongue.

"I'm Holly," she said. Because she wanted no trace of an accent in her heaven, she had none.

I stared at her black hair. It was shiny like the promises in magazines. "How long have you been here?" I asked.

"Three days."

"Me too."

I sat down on the swing next to her and twisted my body around and around to tie up the chains. Then I let go and spun until I stopped.

"Do you like it here?" she asked.

"No."

"Me either."

So it began.

We had been given, in our heavens, our simplest dreams. There were no teachers in the school. We never had to go inside except for art class for me and jazz band for Holly. The boys did not pinch our backsides or tell us we smelled; our textbooks were *Seventeen* and *Glamour* and *Vogue.*

And our heavens expanded as our relationship grew. We wanted many of the same things.

Franny, my intake counselor, became our guide. Franny was old enough to be our mother—mid-forties—and it took Holly and me a while to figure out that this had been something we wanted: our mothers.

In Franny's heaven, she served and was rewarded by results and gratitude. On Earth she had been a social worker for the homeless and destitute. She worked out of a church named Saint Mary's that served meals to women and children only, and she did everything there from manning the phones to swatting the roaches—karate-chop style. She was shot in the face by a man looking for his wife.

Franny walked over to Holly and me on the fifth day. She

handed us two Dixie Cups of lime Kool-Aid and we drank. "I'm here to help," she said.

I looked into her small blue eyes surrounded by laugh lines and told her the truth. "We're bored."

Holly was busy trying to reach her tongue out far enough to see if it had turned green.

"What do you want?" Franny asked.

"I don't know," I said.

"All you have to do is desire it, and if you desire it enough and understand why — really know — it will come."

It seemed so simple and it was. That's how Holly and I got our duplex.

I hated our split-level on Earth. I hated my parents' furniture, and how our house looked out onto another house and another house and another — an echo of sameness riding up over the hill. Our duplex looked out onto a park, and in the distance, just close enough to know we weren't alone, but not too close, we could see the lights of other houses.

Eventually I began to desire more. What I found strange was how much I desired to know what I had not known on Earth. I wanted to be allowed to grow up.

"People grow up by living," I said to Franny. "I want to live."

"That's out," she said.

"Can we at least watch the living?" asked Holly.

"You already do," she said.

"I think she means whole lives," I said, "from beginning to end, to see how they did it. To know the secrets. Then we can pretend better."

"You won't experience it," Franny clarified.

"Thank you, Brain Central," I said, but our heavens began to grow.

There was the high school still, all the Fairfax architecture, but now there were roads leading out.

"Walk the paths," Franny said, "and you'll find what you need."

So that's when Holly and I set out. Our heaven had an ice cream shop where, when you asked for peppermint stick ice cream, no one ever said, "It's seasonal"; it had a newspaper where our pictures appeared a lot and made us look important; it had real men in it and beautiful women too, because Holly and I were devoted to fashion magazines. Sometimes Holly seemed like she wasn't paying attention, and other times she was gone when I went looking for her. That was when she went to a part of heaven we didn't share. I missed her then, but it was an odd sort of missing because by then I knew the meaning of forever.

I could not have what I wanted most: Mr. Harvey dead and me living. Heaven wasn't perfect. But I came to believe that if I watched closely, and desired, I might change the lives of those I loved on Earth.

My father was the one who took the phone call on December ninth. It was the beginning of the end. He gave the police my blood type, had to describe the lightness of my skin. They asked him if I had any identifying features. He began to describe my face in detail, getting lost in it. Detective Fenerman let him go on, the next news too horrible to interrupt with. But then he said it: "Mr. Salmon, we have found only a body part."

My father stood in the kitchen and a sickening shiver overtook him. How could he tell that to Abigail?

"So you can't be certain that she's dead?" he asked.

"Nothing is ever certain," Len Fenerman said.

That was the line my father said to my mother: "Nothing is ever certain."

For three nights he hadn't known how to touch my mother or what to say. Before, they had never found themselves broken together. Usually, it was one needing the other but not both needing each other, and so there had been a way, by touching, to borrow from the stronger one's strength. And they had never understood, as they did now, what the word *horror* meant.

"Nothing is ever certain," my mother said, clinging to it as he had hoped she might.

My mother had been the one who knew the meaning of each charm on my bracelet—where we had gotten it and why I liked it. She made a meticulous list of what I'd carried and worn. If found miles away and in isolation along a road, these clues might lead a policeman there to link it to my death.

In my mind I had wavered between the bittersweet joy of seeing my mother name all the things I carried and loved and her futile hope that these things mattered. That a stranger who found a cartoon character eraser or a rock star button would report it to the police.

After Len's phone call, my father reached out his hand and the two of them sat in the bed together, staring straight in front of them. My mother numbly clinging to this list of things, my father feeling as if he were entering a dark tunnel. At some point, it began to rain. I could feel them both thinking the same thing then, but neither of them said it. That I was out there somewhere, in the rain. That they hoped I was safe. That I was dry somewhere, and warm.

Neither of them knew who fell asleep first; their bones aching with exhaustion, they drifted off and woke guiltily at the same time. The rain, which had changed several times as the temperature dropped, was now hail, and the sound of it, of small stones of ice hitting the roof above them, woke them together.

They did not speak. They looked at each other in the small light cast from the lamp left on across the room. My mother began to cry, and my father held her, wiped her tears with the pad of his thumbs as they crested her cheekbones, and kissed her very gently on the eyes.

I looked away from them then, as they touched. I moved my

eyes into the cornfield, seeing if there was anything that in the morning the police might find. The hail bent the stalks and drove all the animals into their holes. Not so deep beneath the earth were the warrens of the wild rabbits I loved, the bunnies that ate the vegetables and flowers in the neighborhood nearby and that sometimes, unwittingly, brought poison home to their dens. Then, inside the earth and so far away from the man or woman who had laced a garden with toxic bait, an entire family of rabbits would curl into themselves and die.

On the morning of the tenth, my father poured the Scotch down the kitchen sink. Lindsey asked him why.

"I'm afraid I might drink it," he said.

"What was the phone call?" my sister asked.

"What phone call?"

"I heard you say that thing you always say about Susie's smile. About stars exploding."

"Did I say that?"

"You got kind of goofy. It was a cop, wasn't it?"

"No lies?"

"No lies," Lindsey agreed.

"They found a body part. It might be Susie's."

It was a hard sock in the stomach. "What?"

"Nothing is ever certain," my father tried.

Lindsey sat down at the kitchen table. "I'm going to be sick," she said.

"Honey?"

"Dad, I want you to tell me what it was. Which body part, and then I'm going to need to throw up."

My father got down a large metal mixing bowl. He brought it to the table and placed it near Lindsey before sitting down.

"Okay," she said. "Tell me."

"It was an elbow. The Gilberts' dog found it."

He held her hand and then she threw up, as she had promised, into the shiny silver bowl.

Later that morning the weather cleared, and not too far from my house the police roped off the cornfield and began their search. The rain, sleet, snow, and hail melting and mixing had left the ground sodden; still, there was an obvious area where the earth had been freshly manipulated. They began there and dug.

In places, the lab later found, there was a dense concentration of my blood mixed with the dirt, but at the time, the police grew more and more frustrated, plying the cold wet ground and looking for girl.

Along the border of the soccer field, a few of my neighbors kept a respectful distance from the police tape, wondering at the men dressed in heavy blue parkas wielding shovels and rakes like medical tools.

My father and mother remained at home. Lindsey stayed in her room. Buckley was nearby at his friend Nate's house, where he spent a lot of time these days. They had told him I was on an extended sleepover at Clarissa's.

I knew where my body was but I could not tell them. I watched and waited to see what they would see. And then, like a thunderbolt, late in the afternoon, a policeman held up his earth-caked fist and shouted.

"Over here!" he said, and the other officers ran to surround him.

The neighbors had gone home except for Mrs. Stead. After conferring around the discovering policeman, Detective Fenerman broke their dark huddle and approached her.

"Mrs. Stead?" he said over the tape that separated them.

"Yes."

"You have a child in the school?"

"Yes."

"Could you come with me, please?"

A young officer led Mrs. Stead under the police tape and over the bumpy, churned-up cornfield to where the rest of the men stood.

"Mrs. Stead," Len Fenerman said, "does this look familiar?" He held up a paperback copy of *To Kill a Mockingbird.* "Do they read this at the school?"

"Yes," she said, her face draining of color as she said the small word.

"Do you mind if I ask you . . ." he began.

"Ninth grade," she said, looking into Len Fenerman's slate blue eyes. "Susie's grade." She was a therapist and relied on her ability to hear bad news and discuss rationally the difficult details of her patients' lives, but she found herself leaning into the young policeman who had led her over. I could feel her wishing that she had gone home when the other neighbors had left, wishing that she was in the living room with her husband, or out in the backyard with her son.

"Who teaches the class?"

"Mrs. Dewitt," Mrs. Stead said. "The kids find it a real relief after *Othello.*"

"*Othello?*"

"Yes," she said, her knowledge of the school suddenly very important right now—all the policemen listening. "Mrs. Dewitt likes to modulate her reading list, and she does a big push right before Christmas with Shakespeare. Then she passes out Harper Lee as a reward. If Susie was carrying around *To Kill a Mockingbird* it means she must have turned in her paper on *Othello* already."

All of this checked out.

The police made calls. I watched the circle widen. Mrs. Dewitt had my paper. Eventually, she sent it back to my parents, unmarked, through the mail. "Thought you would want to have this," Mrs.

Dewitt had written on a note attached to it. "I'm so very very sorry." Lindsey inherited the paper because it was too painful for my mother to read. "The Ostracized: One Man Alone," I had called it. Lindsey had suggested "The Ostracized," and I made up the other half. My sister punched three holes down the side of it and fastened each carefully handwritten page into an empty notebook. She put it in her closet under her Barbie case and the box that held her perfect-condition Raggedy Ann and Andy that I'd envied.

Detective Fenerman called my parents. They had found a schoolbook, they believed, that might have been given to me that last day.

"But it could be anyone's," my father said to my mother as they began another restless vigil. "Or she could have dropped it along the way."

Evidence was mounting, but they refused to believe.

Two days later, on December twelfth, the police found my notes from Mr. Botte's class. Animals had carried off the notebook from its original burial site—the dirt did not match the surrounding samples, but the graph paper, with its scribbled theories that I could never understand but still dutifully recorded, had been found when a cat knocked down a crow's nest. Shreds of the paper were laced among the leaves and twigs. The police unbraided the graph paper, along with strips of another kind of paper, thinner and brittle, that had no lines.

The girl who lived in the house where the tree stood recognized some of the handwriting. It was not my writing, but the writing of the boy who had a crush on me: Ray Singh. On his mother's special rice paper Ray had written me a love note, which I never read. He had tucked it into my notebook during our Wednesday lab. His hand was distinct. When the officers came they had to piece together the scraps of my biology notebook and of Ray Singh's love note.

"Ray is not feeling well," his mother said when a detective called his house and asked to speak to him. But they found out what they needed from her. Ray nodded to her as she repeated the policeman's questions to her son. Yes, he had written Susie Salmon a love note. Yes, he had put it in her notebook after Mr. Botte had asked her to collect the pop quiz. Yes, he had called himself the Moor.

Ray Singh became the first suspect.

"That sweet boy?" my mother said to my father.

"Ray Singh is nice," my sister said in a monotone at dinner that night.

I watched my family and knew they knew. It was not Ray Singh.

The police descended on his house, leaning heavily on him, insinuating things. They were fueled by the guilt they read into Ray's dark skin, by the rage they felt at his manner, and by his beautiful yet too exotic and unavailable mother. But Ray had an alibi. A whole host of nations could be called to testify on his behalf. His father, who taught postcolonial history at Penn, had urged his son to represent the teenage experience at a lecture he gave at the International House on the day I died.

At first Ray's absence from school had been seen as evidence of his guilt, but once the police were presented with a list of forty-five attendees who had seen Ray speak at "Suburbia: The American Experience," they had to concede his innocence. The police stood outside the Singh house and snapped small twigs from the hedges. It would have been so easy, so magical, their answer literally falling out of the sky from a tree. But rumors spread and, in school, what little headway Ray had made socially was reversed. He began to go home immediately after school.

All this made me crazy. Watching but not being able to steer the police toward the green house so close to my parents, where Mr. Harvey sat carving finials for a gothic dollhouse he was building. He watched the news and scanned the papers, but he wore his own innocence like a comfortable old coat. There had been a riot inside him and now there was calm.

I tried to take solace in Holiday, our dog. I missed him in a way

I hadn't yet let myself miss my mother and father, my sister and brother. That way of missing would mean that I had accepted that I would never be with them again; it might sound silly but I didn't believe it, would not believe it. Holiday stayed with Lindsey at night, stood by my father each time he answered the door to a new unknown. Gladly partook of any clandestine eating on the part of my mother. Let Buckley pull his tail and ears inside the house of locked doors.

There was too much blood in the earth.

On December fifteenth, among the knocks on the door that signaled to my family that they must numb themselves further before opening their house to strangers—the kind but awkward neighbors, the bumbling but cruel reporters—came the one that made my father finally believe.

It was Len Fenerman, who had been so kind to him, and a uniform.

They came inside, by now familiar enough with the house to know that my mother preferred them to come in and say what they had to say in the living room so that my sister and brother would not overhear.

"We've found a personal item that we believe to be Susie's," Len said. Len was careful. I could see him calculating his words. He made sure to specify so that my parents would be relieved of their first thought—that the police had found my body, that I was, for certain, dead.

"What?" my mother said impatiently. She crossed her arms and braced for another inconsequential detail in which others invested meaning. She was a wall. Notebooks and novels were nothing to her. Her daughter might survive without an arm. A lot of blood was a lot of blood. It was not a body. Jack had said it and she believed: Nothing is ever certain.

But when they held up the evidence bag with my hat inside, something broke in her. The fine wall of leaden crystal that had protected her heart—somehow numbed her into disbelief—shattered.

"The pompom," Lindsey said. She had crept into the living room from the kitchen. No one had seen her come in but me.

My mother made a sound and reached out her hand. The sound was a metallic squeak, a human-as-machine breaking down, uttering last sounds before the whole engine locks.

"We've tested the fibers," Len said. "It appears whoever accosted Susie used this during the crime."

"What?" my father asked. He was powerless. He was being told something he could not comprehend.

"As a way to keep her quiet."

"What?"

"It is covered with her saliva," the uniformed officer, who had been silent until now, volunteered. "He gagged her with it."

My mother grabbed it out of Len Fenerman's hands, and the bells she had sewn into the pompom sounded as she landed on her knees. She bent over the hat she had made me.

I saw Lindsey stiffen at the door. Our parents were unrecognizable to her; everything was unrecognizable.

My father led the well-meaning Len Fenerman and the uniformed officer to the front door.

"Mr. Salmon," Len Fenerman said, "with the amount of blood we've found, and the violence I'm afraid it implies, as well as other material evidence we've discussed, we must work with the assumption that your daughter has been killed."

Lindsey overheard what she already knew, had known since five days before, when my father told her about my elbow. My mother began to wail.

"We'll be working with this as a murder investigation from this point out," Fenerman said.

"But there is no body," my father tried.

"All evidence points to your daughter's death. I'm very sorry."

The uniformed officer had been staring to the right of my father's pleading eyes. I wondered if that was something they'd taught him in school. But Len Fenerman met my father's gaze. "I'll call to check in on you later today," he said.

By the time my father turned back to the living room, he was too devastated to reach out to my mother sitting on the carpet or my sister's hardened form nearby. He could not let them see him. He mounted the stairs, thinking of Holiday on the rug in the study. He had last seen him there. Into the deep ruff of fur surrounding the dog's neck, my father would let himself cry.

That afternoon the three of them crept forward in silence, as if the sound of footsteps might confirm the news. Nate's mother knocked on the door to return Buckley. No one answered. She stepped away, knowing something had changed inside the house, which looked exactly like the ones on either side of it. She made herself my brother's co-conspirator, telling him they would go out for ice cream and ruin his appetite.

At four, my mother and father ended up standing in the same room downstairs. They had come in from opposite doorways.

My mother looked at my father: "Mother," she said, and he nodded his head. He made the phone call to my only living grandparent, my mother's mother, Grandma Lynn.

I worried that my sister, left alone, would do something rash. She sat in her room on the old couch my parents had given up on and worked on hardening herself. *Take deep breaths and hold them. Try to stay still for longer and longer periods of time. Make yourself small and like a stone. Curl the edges of yourself up and fold them under where no one can see.*

My mother told her it was her choice whether she wanted to return to school before Christmas—there was only one week left—but Lindsey chose to go.

On Monday, in homeroom, everyone stared at her as she approached the front of the classroom.

"The principal would like to see you, dear," Mrs. Dewitt confided in a hush.

My sister did not look at Mrs. Dewitt when she was speaking. She was perfecting the art of talking to someone while looking through them. That was my first clue that something would have to give. Mrs. Dewitt was also the English teacher, but more importantly she was married to Mr. Dewitt, who coached boys' soccer and had encouraged Lindsey to try out for his team. My sister liked the Dewitts, but that morning she began looking into the eyes of only those people she could fight against.

As she gathered her things, she heard whispers everywhere. She was certain that right before she left the room Danny Clarke had whispered something to Sylvia Henley. Someone had dropped something near the back of the classroom. They did this, she believed, so that on their way to pick it up and back again, they could say a word or two to their neighbor about the dead girl's sister.

Lindsey walked through the hallways and in and out of the rows of lockers—dodging anyone who might be near. I wished I could walk with her, mimic the principal and the way he always started out a meeting in the auditorium: "Your principal is your pal with principles!" I would whine in her ear, cracking her up.

But while she was blessed with empty halls, when she reached the main office she was cursed with the drippy looks of consoling secretaries. No matter. She had prepared herself at home in her bedroom. She was armed to the teeth for any onslaught of sympathy.

"Lindsey," Principal Caden said, "I received a call from the police this morning. I'm sorry to hear of your loss."

She looked right at him. It was not so much a look as a laser. "What exactly is my loss?"

Mr. Caden felt he needed to address issues of children's crises directly. He walked out from behind his desk and ushered Lindsey onto what was commonly referred to by the students as The Sofa. Eventually he would replace The Sofa with two chairs, when politics swept through the school district and told him, *"It is not good to have a sofa here—chairs are better. Sofas send the wrong message."*

Mr. Caden sat on The Sofa and so did my sister. I like to think she was a little thrilled, in that moment, no matter how upset, to be on The Sofa itself. I like to think I hadn't robbed her of everything.

"We're here to help in any way we can," Mr. Caden said. He was doing his best.

"I'm fine," she said.

"Would you like to talk about it?"

"What?" Lindsey asked. She was being what my father called "petulant," as in, "Susie, don't speak to me in that petulant tone."

"Your loss," he said. He reached out to touch my sister's knee. His hand was like a brand burning into her.

"I wasn't aware I had lost anything," she said, and in a Herculean effort she made the motions of patting her shirt and checking her pockets.

Mr. Caden didn't know what to say. He had had Vicki Kurtz fall apart in his arms the year before. It had been difficult, yes, but now, in hindsight, Vicki Kurtz and her dead mother seemed an artfully handled crisis. He had led Vicki Kurtz to the couch—no, no, Vicki had just gone right over and sat down on it—he had said, "I'm sorry for your loss," and Vicki Kurtz had burst like an overinflated balloon. He held her in his arms as she sobbed, and sobbed, and that night he brought his suit to the dry cleaner's.

But Lindsey Salmon was another thing altogether. She was

gifted, one of the twenty students from his school who had been selected for the statewide Gifted Symposium. The only trouble in her file was a slight altercation early in the year when a teacher reprimanded her for bringing obscene literature—*Fear of Flying*—into the classroom.

"Make her laugh," I wanted to say to him. "Bring her to a Marx Brothers movie, sit on a fart cushion, show her the boxers you have on with the little devils eating hot dogs on them!" All I could do was talk, but no one on Earth could hear me.

The school district made everyone take tests and then decided who was gifted and who was not. I liked to suggest to Lindsey that I was much more pissed off by her hair than by my dumbo status. We had both been born with masses of blond hair, but mine quickly fell out and was replaced with a grudging growth of mousy brown. Lindsey's stayed and acquired a sort of mythical place. She was the only true blonde in our family.

But once called gifted, it had spurred her on to live up to the name. She locked herself in her bedroom and read big books. When I read *Are You There God? It's Me, Margaret,* she read Camus's *Resistance, Rebellion, and Death.* She might not have gotten most of it, but she carried it around, and that made people—including teachers—begin to leave her alone.

"What I'm saying, Lindsey, is that we all miss Susie," Mr. Caden said.

She did not respond.

"She was very bright," he tried.

She stared blankly back at him.

"It's on your shoulders now." He had no idea what he was saying, but he thought the silence might mean he was getting somewhere. "You're the only Salmon girl now."

Nothing.

"You know who came in to see me this morning?" Mr. Caden had held back his big finish, the one he was sure would work. "Mr. Dewitt. He's considering coaching a girls' team," Mr. Caden said. "The idea is all centered around you. He's watched how good you are, as competitive as his boys, and he thinks other girls would come out if you led the charge. What do you say?"

Inside, my sister's heart closed like a fist. "I'd say it would be pretty hard to play soccer on the soccer field when it's approximately twenty feet from where my sister was supposedly murdered."

Score!

Mr. Caden's mouth opened and he stared at her.

"Anything else?" Lindsey asked.

"No, I . . ." Mr. Caden reached out his hand again. There was a thread still—a desire to understand. "I want you to know how sorry we are," he said.

"I'm late for first period," she said.

In that moment she reminded me of a character in the Westerns my father loved, the ones we watched together on late-night TV. There was always a man who, after he shot his gun, raised the pistol to his lips and blew air across the opening.

Lindsey got up and took the walk out of Principal Caden's office slow. The walks away were her only rest time. Secretaries were on the other side of the door, teachers were at the front of the class, students in every desk, our parents at home, police coming by. She would not break. I watched her, felt the lines she repeated over and over again in her head. *Fine. All of it is fine.* I was dead, but that was something that happened all the time—people died. As she left the outer office that day, she appeared to be looking into the eyes of the secretaries, but she was focusing on their misapplied lipstick or two-piece paisley crepe de chine instead.

At home that night she lay on the floor of her room and braced her feet under her bureau. She did ten sets of sit-ups. Then she got into push-up position. Not the girl's kind. Mr. Dewitt had told her about the kind he had done in the Marines, head-up, or one-handed, clapping between. After she did ten push-ups, she went to her shelf and chose the two heaviest books—her dictionary and a world almanac. She did bicep curls until her arms ached. She focused only on her breathing. The in. The out.

I sat in the gazebo in the main square of my heaven (our neighbors, the O'Dwyers, had had a gazebo; I had grown up jealous for one), and watched my sister rage.

Hours before I died, my mother hung on the refrigerator a picture that Buckley had drawn. In the drawing a thick blue line separated the air and ground. In the days that followed I watched my family walk back and forth past that drawing and I became convinced that that thick blue line was a real place—an Inbetween, where heaven's horizon met Earth's. I wanted to go there into the cornflower blue of Crayola, the royal, the turquoise, the sky.

Often I found myself desiring simple things and I would get them. Riches in furry packages. Dogs.

Every day in my heaven tiny dogs and big dogs, dogs of every kind, ran through the park outside my room. When I opened the door I saw them fat and happy, skinny and hairy, lean and hairless even. Pitbulls rolled on their backs, the nipples of the females distended and dark, begging for their pups to come and suckle them, happy in the sun. Bassets tripped over their ears, ambling forward, nudging the rumps of dachshunds, the ankles of greyhounds, and the heads of the Pekingese. And when Holly took her tenor sax, set herself up outside the door that looked onto the park, and played the blues, the hounds all ran to form her chorus.

On their haunches they sat wailing. Other doors opened then, and women stepped out from where they lived alone or with roommates. I would step outside, Holly would go into an endless encore, the sun going down, and we would dance with the dogs—all of us together. We chased them, they chased us. We circled tail to tail. We wore spotted gowns, flowered gowns, striped gowns, plain. When the moon was high the music would stop. The dancing stopped. We froze.

Mrs. Bethel Utemeyer, the oldest resident of my heaven, would bring out her violin. Holly tread lightly on her horn. They would do a duet. One woman old and silent, one woman not past girl yet. Back and forth, a crazy schizoid solace they'd create.

All the dancers would slowly go inside. The song reverberated until Holly, for a final time, passed the tune over, and Mrs. Utemeyer, quiet, upright, historical, finished with a jig.

The house asleep by then; this was my Evensong.

THREE

The odd thing about Earth was what we saw when we looked down. Besides the initial view that you might suspect, the old ants-from-the-skyscraper phenomenon, there were souls leaving bodies all over the world.

Holly and I could be scanning Earth, alighting on one scene or another for a second or two, looking for the unexpected in the most mundane moment. And a soul would run by a living being, touch them softly on the shoulder or cheek, and continue on its way to heaven. The dead are never exactly seen by the living, but many people seem acutely aware of something changed around them. They speak of a chill in the air. The mates of the deceased wake from dreams and see a figure standing at the end of their bed, or in a doorway, or boarding, phantomlike, a city bus.

On my way out of Earth, I touched a girl named Ruth. She went to my school but we'd never been close. She was standing in my path that night when my soul shrieked out of Earth. I could not help but graze her. Once released from life, having lost it in such violence, I couldn't calculate my steps. I didn't have time for contemplation. In violence, it is the getting away that you concentrate on. When you begin to go over the edge, life receding from you as a boat recedes inevitably from shore, you hold on to death tightly, like a rope that will transport you, and you swing out on it, hoping only to land away from where you are.

Like a phone call from the jail cell, I brushed by Ruth Connors—wrong number, accidental call. I saw her standing there near Mr. Botte's red and rusted Fiat. When I streaked by her, my hand leapt out to touch her, touch the last face, feel the last connection to Earth in this not-so-standard-issue teenage girl.

On the morning of December seventh, Ruth complained to her mother about having had a dream that seemed too real to be a dream. When her mother asked her what she meant, Ruth said, "I was crossing through the faculty parking lot, and suddenly, down out of the soccer field, I saw a pale running ghost coming toward me."

Mrs. Connors stirred the hardening oatmeal in its pot. She watched her daughter gesticulating with the long thin fingers of her hands—hands she had inherited from her father.

"It was female, I could sense that," Ruth said. "It flew up out of the field. Its eyes were hollow. It had a thin white veil over its body, as light as cheesecloth. I could see its face through it, the features coming up through it, the nose, the eyes, the face, the hair."

Her mother took the oatmeal off the stove and lowered the flame. "Ruth," she said, "you're letting your imagination get the best of you."

Ruth took the cue to shut up. She did not mention the dream that was not a dream again, even ten days later, when the story of my death began to travel through the halls of the school, receiving add-on nuances as all good horror stories do. They were hard-pressed, my peers, to make the horror any more horrible than it was. But the details were still missing—the what and when and who became hollow bowls to fill with their conjectures. Devil Worship. Midnight. Ray Singh.

Try as I might, I could not point Ruth strongly enough to what no one had found: my silver charm bracelet. I thought it might help her. It lay exposed, waiting for a hand to reach out, a hand that would recognize it and think, *Clue*. But it was no longer in the cornfield.

Ruth began writing poetry. If her mother or her more approachable teachers did not want to hear the darker reality she had experienced, she would cloak this reality in poetry.

How I wished Ruth could have gone to my family and talked to them. In all likelihood, no one but my sister would have even known her name. Ruth was the girl who got chosen next to last in gym. She was the girl who, when a volleyball sailed in her direction, cowered where she stood while the ball hit the gymnasium floor beside her, and her teammates and the gym teacher tried hard not to groan.

As my mother sat in the straight-backed chair in our hallway, watching my father run in and out on his various errands of responsibility—he would now be hyperaware of the movements and the whereabouts of his young son, of his wife, and of his remaining daughter—Ruth took our accidental meeting in the school parking lot and went underground.

She went through old yearbooks and found my class photos, as well as any activities photos like Chem Club, and cut them out with her mother's swan-shaped embroidery scissors. Even as her obsession grew I remained wary of her, until that last week before Christmas when she saw something in the hallway of our school.

It was my friend Clarissa and Brian Nelson. I'd dubbed Brian "the scarecrow" because even though he had incredible shoulders that all the girls mooned over, his face reminded me of a burlap sack stuffed with straw. He wore a floppy leather hippie hat and smoked hand-rolled cigarettes in the student smoking lounge. According to my mother, Clarissa's penchant for baby blue eye shadow was an early warning sign, but I'd always liked her for just this reason. She did things I wasn't allowed to do: she lightened her long hair, she wore platform shoes, she smoked cigarettes after school.

Ruth came upon the two of them, but they didn't see her. She had a pile of huge books she had borrowed from Mrs. Kaplan, the social science teacher. They were all early feminist texts, and she held them with their spines resting against her stomach so that no one could see what they were. Her father, a building contractor, had made her a gift of two super-strong elastic book bands. Ruth had placed two of them around the volumes she planned to read over vacation.

Clarissa and Brian were giggling. His hand was inside her shirt. As he inched it up, her giggling increased, but she thwarted his advances each time by twisting or moving an inch or two away. Ruth stood apart from this, as she did most things. She would have passed it in her usual manner, head down/eyes averted, but everyone knew Clarissa had been my friend. So she watched.

"Come on, honey," Brian said, "just a little mound of love. Just one."

I noticed Ruth's lip curl in disgust. Mine was curling up in heaven.

"Brian, I can't. Not here."

"How 'bout out in the cornfield?" he whispered.

Clarissa giggled nervously but nuzzled the space between his neck and shoulder. For now, she would deny him.

After that, Clarissa's locker was burgled.

Gone were her scrapbook, random photos stuck to the inside of her locker, and Brian's stash of marijuana, which he had hidden there without Clarissa's knowledge.

Ruth, who had never been high, spent that night emptying out the tobacco from her mother's long brown More 100s and stuffing them with pot. She sat in the toolshed with a flashlight, looking at photos of me and smoking more grass than even the potheads at school could suck down.

Mrs. Connors, standing at the kitchen window doing dishes, caught a whiff of the scent coming from the toolshed.

"I think Ruth is making friends at school," she said to her husband, who sat over his copy of the *Evening Bulletin* with a cup of coffee. At the end of his workday he was too tired even to speculate.

"Good," he said.

"Maybe there's hope for her yet."

"Always," he said.

When Ruth tottered in later that night, her eyes bleary from using the flashlight and from the eight More cigarettes she'd smoked, her mother greeted her with a smile and told her there was blueberry pie in the kitchen. It took a few days and some non-Susie-Salmon-focused research, but Ruth discovered why she had eaten the entire pie in one sitting.

The air in my heaven often smelled like skunk—just a hint of it. It was a smell that I had always loved on Earth. When I breathed it in, I could feel the scent as well as smell it. It was the animal's fear and power mixed together to form a pungent, lingering musk. In Franny's heaven it smelled like pure, grade-A tobacco. In Holly's it smelled like kumquats.

I would sit whole days and nights in the gazebo and watch. See Clarissa spin away from me, toward the comfort of Brian. See Ruth staring at her from behind a corner near the home ec room or outside the cafeteria near the nurse's station. At the start, the freedom I had to see the whole school was intoxicating. I would watch the assistant football coach leave anonymous chocolates for the married science teacher, or the head of the cheerleading squad trying to capture the attention of the kid who had been expelled so many times, from so many schools, even he had lost count. I watched the art teacher make love to his girlfriend in the kiln room and the principal moon over the assistant football coach. I concluded that this assistant football coach was a stud in the world of Kennet Junior High, even if his square jaw left me cold.

On the way back to the duplex each night I would pass under old-time street lamps that I had seen once in a play of *Our Town.* The globes of light hung down in an arc from an iron post. I had remembered them because when I saw the play with my family, I thought of them as giant, heavy berries full of light. I made a game in heaven of positioning myself so that my shadow plucked the berries as I made my way home.

After watching Ruth one night I met Franny in the midst of this. The square was deserted, and leaves began to swirl around in an eddy up ahead. I stood and looked at her—at the laugh lines that were clustered near her eyes and mouth.

"Why are you shivering?" Franny asked.

And though the air was damp and chilly I could not say that that was why.

"I can't help thinking of my mother," I said.

Franny took my left hand in both of hers and smiled.

I wanted to kiss her lightly on the cheek or have her hold me, but instead I watched her walk off in front of me, saw her blue dress trail away. I knew that she was not my mother; I could not play pretend.

I turned around and went back to the gazebo. I felt the moist air lace its way up along my legs and arms, lifting, ever so slightly, the ends of my hair. I thought of spider webs in the morning, how they held small jewels of dew, how, with a light movement of the wrist, I used to destroy them without thinking.

On the morning of my eleventh birthday I had woken up very early. No one else was up, or so I thought. I crept downstairs and looked into the dining room, where I assumed my presents would be. But there was nothing there. Same table as yesterday. But as I turned around I saw it lying on my mother's desk in the living room. The fancy desk with an always-clean surface. "The bill-paying desk" was what they called it. Swaddled in tissue paper but not yet wrapped was a camera—what I had asked for with a tinge of whining in my voice, so sure they would not get it for me. I went over to it and stared down. It was an Instamatic, and lying beside it were three cartridges of film and a box of four square flashbulbs. It was my first machine, my starter kit to becoming what I wanted to be. A wildlife photographer.

I looked around. No one. I saw through the front blinds, which my mother always kept at a half-slant—"inviting but discreet"—that Grace Tarking, who lived down the street and went to a private school, was walking with ankle weights strapped to her feet. Hurriedly I loaded the camera and I began to stalk Grace Tarking as I would, I imagined, when I grew older, stalk wild elephants and rhinos. Here I hid behind blinds and windows, there it would be high reeds. I was quiet, what I thought of as stealthy, gathering the long hem of my flannel nightgown up in my free hand. I traced her movements past our living room, front hall, into the den on the other side. As I watched her receding form I had a brainstorm—I would run into the backyard, where I could see her with no barriers.

So I ran on tiptoe into the back of the house, only to find the door to the porch wide open.

When I saw my mother, I forgot all about Grace Tarking. I wish I could explain it better than this, but I had never seen her sitting so still, so *not there* somehow. Outside the screened-in porch she was sitting on an aluminum fold-out chair that was facing the backyard. In her hand she held a saucer and in the saucer was her customary cup of coffee. That morning there were no lipstick marks because there was no lipstick until she put it on for . . . who? I had never thought to ask the question. My father? Us?

Holiday was sitting near the birdbath, panting happily, but he did not notice me. He was watching my mother. She had a stare that stretched to infinity. She was, in that moment, not my mother but something separate from me. I looked at what I had never seen as anything but Mom and saw the soft powdery skin of her face—powdery without makeup—soft without help. Her eyebrows and eyes were a set-piece together. "Ocean Eyes," my father called her when he wanted one of her chocolate-covered cherries, which she kept hidden in the liquor cabinet as her private treat. And now I understood the name. I had thought it was because they were blue, but now I saw it was because they were bottomless in a way that I found frightening. I had an instinct then, not a developed thought, and it was that, before Holiday saw and smelled me, before the dewy mist hovering over the grass evaporated and the mother inside her woke as it did every morning, I should take a photograph with my new camera.

When the roll came back from the Kodak plant in a special heavy envelope, I could see the difference immediately. There was only one picture in which my mother was Abigail. It was that first one, the one taken of her unawares, the one captured before the click startled her into the mother of the birthday girl, owner of the happy dog, wife to the loving man, and mother again to another girl and a cherished boy. Homemaker. Gardener. Sunny neighbor. My mother's eyes were oceans, and inside them there was loss. I thought I had my whole life to understand them, but that was the only day I had. Once upon Earth I saw her as Abigail, and then I let it slip effortlessly back—my fascination held in check by wanting her to be that mother and envelop me as that mother.

I was in the gazebo thinking of the photo, thinking of my mother, when Lindsey got up in the middle of the night and crept across the hall. I watched her as I would a burglar circling a house in a movie. I knew when she turned the knob to my room it would give. I knew she would get in, but what would she do in there? Already my private territory had become a no man's land in the middle of our house. My mother had not touched it. My bed was still unmade from the hurried morning of my death. My flowered hippo lay among the sheets and pillows, and so did an outfit I'd discarded before I chose the yellow bell-bottoms.

Lindsey walked across the soft rug and touched the navy skirt and red and blue crocheted vest that were two separate, heatedly despised balls. She had an orange and green vest made from the same pattern. She took the vest and spread it out flat on the bed, smoothing it. It was ugly and precious all at once. I could see that. She petted it.

Lindsey traced the outline of the gold tray I kept on my dresser, filled with pins from elections and school. My favorite was a pink pin that said "Hippy-Dippy Says Love," which I'd found in the school parking lot but had had to promise my mother I wouldn't wear. I kept a lot of pins on that tray and pinned to a giant felt banner from Indiana University, where my father had gone to school. I thought she would steal them—take one or two to wear—but she didn't. She didn't even pick them up. She just swept her fingertips over everything on the tray. Then she saw it, a tiny white corner sticking out from underneath. She pulled.

It was the picture.

A deep breath rushed out of her, and she sat down on the floor, her mouth still open and her hand still holding the picture. The tethers were rushing and whipping around her, like a canvas tent come loose from its stakes. She too, like me until the morning of that photograph, had never seen the mother-stranger. She had seen the photos right after. My mother looking tired but smiling. My mother and Holiday standing in front of the dogwood tree as the sun shot through her robe and gown. But I had wanted to be the only one in the house that knew my mother was also someone else—someone mysterious and unknown to us.

The first time I broke through, it was an accident. It was December 23, 1973.

Buckley was sleeping. My mother had taken Lindsey to the dentist. That week they had agreed that each day, as a family, they would spend time trying to move forward. My father had assigned himself the task of cleaning the upstairs guest room, which long ago had become his den.

His own father had taught him how to build ships in bottles. They were something my mother, sister, and brother couldn't care less about. It was something I adored. The den was full of them.

All day at work he counted numbers—due diligence for a Chadds Ford insurance firm—and at night he built the ships or read Civil War books to unwind. He would call me in whenever he was ready to raise the sail. By then the ship would have been glued fast to the bottom of the bottle. I would come in and my father would ask me to shut the door. Often, it seemed, the dinner bell rang immediately, as if my mother had a sixth sense for things that didn't include her. But when this sense failed her, my job was to hold the bottle for him.

"Stay steady," he'd say. "You're my first mate."

Gently he would draw the one string that still reached out of the bottle's neck, and, voilà, the sails all rose, from simple mast to clipper ship. We had our boat. I couldn't clap because I held the bottle, but I always wanted to. My father worked quickly then, burning the end of the string off inside the bottle with a coat hanger he'd heated over a candle. If he did it improperly, the ship would be ruined, or, worse still, the tiny paper sails would catch on fire and suddenly, in a giant whoosh, I would be holding a bottle of flames in my hands.

Eventually my father built a balsa wood stand to replace me. Lindsey and Buckley didn't share my fascination. After trying to create enough enthusiasm for all three of them, he gave up and retreated to his den. One ship in a bottle was equal to any other as far as the rest of my family was concerned.

But as he cleaned that day he talked to me.

"Susie, my baby, my little sailor girl," he said, "you always liked these smaller ones."

I watched him as he lined up the ships in bottles on his desk, bringing them over from the shelves where they usually sat. He used an old shirt of my mother's that had been ripped into rags and began dusting the shelves. Under his desk there were empty bottles—rows and rows of them we had collected for our future shipbuilding. In the closet were more ships—the ships he had built with his own father, ships he had built alone, and then those we had made together. Some were perfect, but their sails browned; some had sagged or toppled over after years. Then there was the one that had burst into flames in the week before my death.

He smashed that one first.

My heart seized up. He turned and saw all the others, all the years they marked and the hands that had held them. His dead father's, his dead child's. I watched him as he smashed the rest. He christened the walls and wooden chair with the news of my death, and afterward he stood in the guest room/den surrounded by green glass. The bottles, all of them, lay broken on the floor, the sails and boat bodies strewn among them. He stood in the wreckage. It was then that, without knowing how, I revealed myself. In every piece of glass, in every shard and sliver, I cast my face. My father glanced down and around him, his eyes roving across the room. Wild. It was just for a second, and then I was gone. He was quiet for a moment, and then he laughed—a howl coming up from the bottom of his stomach. He laughed so loud and deep, I shook with it in my heaven.

He left the room and went down the two doors to my bedroom. The hallway was tiny, my door like all the others, hollow enough to easily punch a fist through. He was about to smash the mirror over my dresser, rip the wallpaper down with his nails, but instead he fell against my bed, sobbing, and balled the lavender sheets up in his hands.

"Daddy?" Buckley said. My brother held the doorknob with his hand.

My father turned but was unable to stop his tears. He slid to the floor with the sheets still in his fists, and then he opened up his arms. He had to ask my brother twice, which he had never had to do before, but Buckley came to him.

My father wrapped my brother inside the sheets that smelled of me. He remembered the day I'd begged him to paint and paper my room purple. Remembered moving in the old *National Geographics* to the bottom shelves of my bookcases. (I had wanted to steep myself in wildlife photography.) Remembered when there was just one child in the house for the briefest of time until Lindsey arrived.

"You are so special to me, little man," my father said, clinging to him.

Buckley drew back and stared at my father's creased face, the fine bright spots of tears at the corners of his eyes. He nodded seriously and kissed my father's cheek. Something so divine that no one up in heaven could have made it up; the care a child took with an adult.

My father draped the sheets around Buckley's shoulders and remembered how I would fall out of the tall four-poster bed and onto the rug, never waking up. Sitting in his study in his green chair and reading a book, he would be startled by the sound of my body landing. He would get up and walk the short distance to my bedroom. He liked to watch me sleeping soundly, unchecked by nightmare or even hardwood floor. He swore in those moments that his children would be kings or rulers or artists or doctors or wildlife photographers. Anything they dreamed they could be.

A few months before I died, he had found me like this, but tucked inside my sheets with me was Buckley, in his pajamas, with his bear, curled up against my back, sucking sleepily on his thumb. My father had felt in that moment the first flicker of the strange sad mortality of being a father. His life had given birth to three children, so the number calmed him. No matter what happened to Abigail or to him, the three would have one another. In that way the line he had begun seemed immortal to him, like a strong steel filament threading into the future, continuing past him no matter where he might fall off. Even in deep snowy old age.

He would find his Susie now inside his young son. Give that love to the living. He told himself this—spoke it aloud inside his brain—but my presence was like a tug on him, it dragged him back back back. He stared at the small boy he held in his arms. *"Who are you?"* he found himself asking. *"Where did you come from?"*

I watched my brother and my father. The truth was very different from what we learned in school. The truth was that the line between the living and the dead could be, it seemed, murky and blurred.

FOUR

In the hours after I was murdered, as my mother made phone calls and my father began going door to door in the neighborhood looking for me, Mr. Harvey had collapsed the hole in the cornfield and carried away a sack filled with my body parts. He passed within two houses of where my father stood talking to Mr. and Mrs. Tarking. He kept to the property line in between two rows of warring hedge—the O'Dwyers' boxwood and the Steads' goldenrod. His body brushed past the sturdy green leaves, leaving traces of me behind him, smells the Gilberts' dog would pick up and follow to find my elbow, smells the sleet and rain of the next three days would wash away before police dogs could even be thought of. He carried me back to his house, where, while he went inside to wash up, I waited for him.

After the house changed hands, the new owners tsk-tsked at the dark spot on the floor of their garage. As she brought prospective buyers through, the realtor said it was an oil stain, but it was me, seeping out of the bag Mr. Harvey carried and spilling onto the concrete. The beginning of my secret signals to the world.

It would be some time before I realized what you've undoubtedly already assumed, that I wasn't the first girl he'd killed. He knew to remove my body from the field. He knew to watch the weather and to kill during an arc of light-to-heavy precipitation because that would rob the police of evidence. But he was not as fastidious as the police liked to think. He forgot my elbow, he used a cloth sack for a bloody body, and if someone, anyone, had been watching, maybe they would have thought it strange to see their neighbor walk a property line that was a tight fit, even for children who liked to pretend the warring hedges were a hideout.

As he scoured his body in the hot water of his suburban bathroom—one with the identical layout to the one Lindsey, Buckley, and I shared—his movements were slow, not anxious. He felt a calm flood him. He kept the lights out in the bathroom and felt the warm water wash me away and he felt thoughts of me then. My muffled scream in his ear. My delicious death moan. The glorious white flesh that had never seen the sun, like an infant's, and then split, so perfectly, with the blade of his knife. He shivered under the heat, a prickling pleasure creating goose bumps up and down his arms and legs. He had put me in the waxy cloth sack and thrown in the shaving cream and razor from the mud ledge, his book of sonnets, and finally the bloody knife. They were tumbled together with my knees, fingers, and toes, but he made a note to extract them before my blood grew too sticky later that night. The sonnets and the knife, at least, he saved.

At Evensong, there were all sorts of dogs. And some of them, the ones I liked best, would lift their heads when they smelled an interesting scent in the air. If it was vivid enough, if they couldn't identify it immediately, or if, as the case may be, they knew exactly what it was—their brains going, "Um steak tartare"—they'd track it until they came to the object itself. In the face of the real article, the true story, they decided then what to do. That's how they operated. They didn't shut down their desire to know just because the smell was bad or the object was dangerous. They hunted. So did I.

Mr. Harvey took the waxy orange sack of my remains to a sinkhole eight miles from our neighborhood, an area that until recently had been desolate save for the railroad tracks and a nearby motorcycle repair shop. In his car he played a radio station that looped Christmas carols during the month of December. He whistled inside his huge station wagon and congratulated himself, felt full-up. Apple pie, cheeseburger, ice cream, coffee. Full. Better and better he was getting now, never using an old pattern that would bore him but making each kill a surprise to himself, a gift to himself.

The air inside the station wagon was cold and fragile. I could see the moist air when he exhaled, and this made me want to palpate my own stony lungs.

He drove the reed-thin road that cut between two new industrial lots. The wagon fishtailed coming up out of a particularly deep pothole, and the safe that held the sack that held my body smashed against the inside hub of the wagon's back wheel, cracking the plastic. "Damn," Mr. Harvey said. But he picked up his whistling again without pause.

I had a memory of going down this road with my father at the wheel and Buckley sitting nestled against me—one seat belt serving the two of us—in an illegal joyride away from the house.

My father had asked if any of us kids wanted to watch a refrigerator disappear.

"The earth will swallow it!" he said. He put on his hat and the dark cordovan gloves I coveted. I knew gloves meant you were an adult and mittens meant you weren't. (For Christmas 1973, my mother had bought me a pair of gloves. Lindsey ended up with them, but she knew they were mine. She left them at the edge of the cornfield one day on her way home from school. She was always doing that—bringing me things.)

"The earth has a mouth?" Buckley asked.

"A big round mouth but with no lips," my father said.

"Jack," my mother said, laughing, "stop it. Do you know I caught him outside growling at the snapdragons?"

"I'll go," I said. My father had told me that there was an abandoned underground mine and it had collapsed to create a sinkhole. I didn't care; I liked to see the earth swallow something as much as the next kid.

So when I watched Mr. Harvey take me out to the sinkhole, I couldn't help but think how smart he was. How he put the bag in a metal safe, placing me in the middle of all that weight.

It was late when he got there, and he left the safe in his Wagoneer while he approached the house of the Flanagans, who lived on the property where the sinkhole was. The Flanagans made their living by charging people to dump their appliances.

Mr. Harvey knocked on the door of the small white house and a woman came to answer it. The scent of rosemary and lamb filled my heaven and hit Mr. Harvey's nose as it trailed out from the back of the house. He could see a man in the kitchen.

"Good evening, sir," Mrs. Flanagan said. "Got an item?"

"Back of my wagon," Mr. Harvey said. He was ready with a twenty-dollar bill.

"What you got in there, a dead body?" she joked.

It was the last thing on her mind. She lived in a warm if small house. She had a husband who was always home to fix things and to be sweet on her because he never had to work, and she had a son who was still young enough to think his mother was the only thing in the world.

Mr. Harvey smiled, and, as I watched his smile break across his face, I would not look away.

"Old safe of my father's, finally got it out here," he said. "Been meaning to do it for years. No one remembers the combination."

"Anything in it?" she asked.

"Stale air."

"Back her up then. You need any help?"

"That would be lovely," he said.

The Flanagans never suspected for a moment that the girl they read about in the papers over the next few years—MISSING, FOUL PLAY SUSPECTED; ELBOW FOUND BY NEIGHBORING DOG; GIRL, 14, BELIEVED KILLED IN STOLFUZ CORNFIELD; WARNINGS TO OTHER YOUNG WOMEN; TOWNSHIP TO REZONE ADJOINING LOTS TO HIGH SCHOOL; LINDSEY SALMON, SISTER OF DEAD GIRL, GIVES VALEDICTORIAN SPEECH—could have been in the gray metal safe that a lonely man brought over one night and paid them twenty dollars to sink.

On the way back to the wagon Mr. Harvey put his hands in his pockets. There was my silver charm bracelet. He couldn't remember taking it off my wrist. Had no memory of thrusting it into the pocket of his clean pants. He fingered it, the fleshy pad of his index finger finding the smooth gold metal of the Pennsylvania keystone, the back of the ballet slipper, the tiny hole of the minuscule thimble, and the spokes of the bicycle with wheels that worked. Down Route 202, he pulled over on the shoulder, ate a liverwurst sandwich he'd prepared earlier that day, then drove to an industrial park they were building south of Downingtown. No one was on the construction lot. In those days there was no security in the suburbs. He parked his car near a Port-o-John. His excuse was prepared in the unlikely event that he needed one.

It was this part of the aftermath that I thought of when I thought of Mr. Harvey—how he wandered the muddy excavations and got lost among the dormant bulldozers, their monstrous bulk frightening in the dark. The sky of the earth was dark blue on the night following my death, and out in this open area Mr. Harvey could see for miles. I chose to stand with him, to see those miles ahead as he saw them. I wanted to go where he would go. The snow had stopped. There was wind. He walked into what his builder's instincts told him would soon be a false pond, and he stood there and fingered the charms one last time. He liked the Pennsylvania keystone, which my father had had engraved with my initials—my favorite was the tiny bike—and he pulled it off and placed it in his pocket. He threw the bracelet, with its remaining charms, into the soon-to-be man-made lake.

Two days before Christmas, I watched Mr. Harvey read a book on the Dogon and Bambara of Mali. I saw the bright spark of an idea when he was reading of the cloth and ropes they used to build shelters. He decided he wanted to build again, to experiment as he had with the hole, and he settled on a ceremonial tent like the ones described in his reading. He would gather the simple materials and raise it in a few hours in his backyard.

After smashing all the ships in bottles, my father found him there.

It was cold out, but Mr. Harvey wore only a thin cotton shirt. He had turned thirty-six that year and was experimenting with hard contacts. They made his eyes perpetually bloodshot, and many people, my father among them, believed he had taken to drink.

"What's this?" my father asked.

Despite the Salmon men's heart disease, my father was hardy. He was a bigger man than Mr. Harvey, so when he walked around the front of the green shingled house and into the backyard, where he saw Harvey erecting things that looked like goalposts, he seemed bluff and able. He was buzzing from having seen me in the shattered glass. I watched him cut through the lawn, ambling as school kids did on their way toward the high school. He stopped just short of brushing Mr. Harvey's elderberry hedge with his palm.

"What's this?" he asked again.

Mr. Harvey stopped long enough to look at him and then turned back to his work.

"A mat tent."

"What's that?"

"Mr. Salmon," he said, "I'm sorry for your loss."

Drawing himself up, my father gave back what the ritual demanded.

"Thank you." It was like a rock perched in his throat.

There was a moment of quiet, and then Mr. Harvey, sensing my father had no intention of leaving, asked him if he wanted to help.

So it was that, from heaven, I watched my father build a tent with the man who'd killed me.

My father did not learn much. He learned how to lash arch pieces onto pronged posts and to weave more slender rods through these pieces to form semiarches in the other direction. He learned to gather the ends of these rods and lash them to the crossbars. He learned he was doing this because Mr. Harvey had been reading about the Imezzureg tribe and had wanted to replicate their tents. He stood, confirmed in the neighborhood opinion that the man was odd. So far, that was all.

But when the basic structure was done—a one-hour job—Mr. Harvey went toward the house without giving a reason. My father assumed it was breaktime. That Mr. Harvey had gone in to get coffee or brew a pot of tea.

He was wrong. Mr. Harvey went into the house and up the stairs to check on the carving knife that he had put in his bedroom. It was still in the nightstand, on top of which he kept his sketch pad where, often, in the middle of the night, he drew the designs in his dreams. He looked inside a crumpled paper grocery sack. My blood on the blade had turned black. Remembering it, remembering his act in the hole, made him remember what he had read about a particular tribe in southern Ayr. How, when a tent was made for a newly married couple, the women of the tribe made the sheet that would cover it as beautiful as they could.

It had begun to snow outside. It was the first snow since my death, and this was not lost on my father.

"I can hear you, honey," he said to me, even though I wasn't talking. "What is it?"

I focused very hard on the dead geranium in his line of vision. I thought if I could make it bloom he would have his answer. In my heaven it bloomed. In my heaven geranium petals swirled in eddies up to my waist. On Earth nothing happened.

But through the snow I noticed this: my father was looking toward the green house in a new way. He had begun to wonder.

Inside, Mr. Harvey had donned a heavy flannel shirt, but what my father noticed first was what he carried in his arms: a stack of white cotton sheets.

"What are those for?" my father asked. Suddenly he could not stop seeing my face.

"Tarps," said Mr. Harvey. When he handed a stack to my father, the back of his hand touched my father's fingers. It was like an electric shock.

"You know something," my father said.

He met my father's eyes, held them, but did not speak.

They worked together, the snow falling, almost wafting, down. And as my father moved, his adrenaline raced. He checked what he knew. Had anyone asked this man where he was the day I disappeared? Had anyone seen this man in the cornfield? He knew his neighbors had been questioned. Methodically, the police had gone from door to door.

My father and Mr. Harvey spread the sheets over the domed arch, anchoring them along the square formed by the crossbars that linked the forked posts. Then they hung the remaining sheets straight down from these crossbars so that the bottoms of the sheets brushed the ground.

By the time they had finished, the snow sat gingerly on the covered arches. It filled in the hollows of my father's shirt and lay in a line across the top of his belt. I ached. I realized I would never rush out into the snow with Holiday again, would never push Lindsey on a sled, would never teach, against my better judgment, my little brother how to compact snow by shaping it against the base of his palm. I stood alone in a sea of bright petals. On Earth the snowflakes fell soft and blameless, a curtain descending.

Standing inside the tent, Mr. Harvey thought of how the virgin bride would be brought to a member of the Imezzureg on a camel. When my father made a move toward him, Mr. Harvey put his palm up.

"That's enough now," he said. "Why don't you go on home?"

The time had come for my father to think of something to say. But all he could think of was this: "Susie," he whispered, the second syllable whipped like a snake.

"We've just built a tent," Mr. Harvey said. "The neighbors saw us. We're friends now."

"You know something," my father said.

"Go home. I can't help you."

Mr. Harvey did not smile or step forward. He retreated into the bridal tent and let the final monogrammed white cotton sheet fall down.

FIVE

Part of me wished swift vengeance, wanted my father to turn into the man he could never have been—a man violent in rage. That's what you see in movies, that's what happens in the books people read. An everyman takes a gun or a knife and stalks the murderer of his family; he does a Bronson on them and everyone cheers.

What it *was* like:

Every day he got up. Before sleep wore off, he was who he used to be. Then, as his consciousness woke, it was as if poison seeped in. At first he couldn't even get up. He lay there under a heavy weight. But then only movement could save him, and he moved and he moved and he moved, no movement being enough to make up for it. The guilt on him, the hand of God pressing down on him, saying, *You were not there when your daughter needed you.*

Before my father left for Mr. Harvey's, my mother had been sitting in the front hall next to the statue they'd bought of St.

Francis. She was gone when he came back. He'd called for her, said her name three times, said it like a wish that she would not appear, and then he ascended the steps to his den to jot things down in a small spiral notebook: "A drinker? Get him drunk. Maybe he's a talker." He wrote this next: "I think Susie watches me." I was ecstatic in heaven. I hugged Holly, I hugged Franny. My father knew, I thought.

Then Lindsey slammed the front door more loudly than usual, and my father was glad for the noise. He was afraid of going further in his notes, of writing the words down. The slamming door echoed down the strange afternoon he'd spent and brought him into the present, into activity, where he needed to be so he would not drown. I understood this—I'm not saying I didn't resent it, that it didn't remind me of sitting at the dinner table and having to listen to Lindsey tell my parents about the test she'd done so well on, or about how the history teacher was going to recommend her for the district honors council, but Lindsey was living, and the living deserved attention too.

She stomped up the stairs. Her clogs slammed against the pine boards of the staircase and shook the house.

I may have begrudged her my father's attention, but I respected her way of handling things. Of everyone in the family, it was Lindsey who had to deal with what Holly called the Walking Dead Syndrome—when other people see the dead person and don't see you.

When people looked at Lindsey, even my father and mother, they saw me. Even Lindsey was not immune. She avoided mirrors. She now took her showers in the dark.

She would leave the dark shower and feel her way over to the towel rack. She would be safe in the dark—the moist steam from the shower still rising off the tiles encased her. If the house was quiet or if she heard murmurs below her, she knew she would be undisturbed. This was when she could think of me and she did so in two ways: she either thought *Susie,* just that one word, and cried there, letting her tears roll down her already damp cheeks, knowing no one would see her, no one would quantify this dangerous substance as grief, or she would imagine me running, imagine me getting away, imagine herself being taken instead, fighting until she was free. She fought back the constant question, *Where is Susie now?*

My father listened to Lindsey in her room. Bang, the door was slammed shut. Thump, her books were thrown down. Squeak, she fell onto her bed. Her clogs, boom, boom, were kicked off onto the floor. A few minutes later he stood outside her door.

"Lindsey," he said upon knocking.

There was no answer.

"Lindsey, can I come in?"

"Go away," came her resolute answer.

"Come on now, honey," he pleaded.

"Go away!"

"Lindsey," my father said, sucking in his breath, "why can't you let me in?" He placed his forehead gently against the bedroom door. The wood felt cool and, for a second, he forgot the pounding of his temples, the suspicion he now held that kept repeating itself. *Harvey, Harvey, Harvey.*

In sock feet, Lindsey came silently to the door. She unlocked it as my father drew back and prepared a face that he hoped said "Don't run."

"What?" she said. Her face was rigid, an affront. "What is it?"

"I want to know how you are," he said. He thought of the curtain falling between him and Mr. Harvey, how a certain capture, a lovely blame, was lost to him. He had his family walking through the streets, going to school, passing, on their way, Mr. Harvey's green-shingled house. To get the blood back in his heart he needed his child.

"I want to be alone," Lindsey said. "Isn't that obvious?"

"I'm here if you need me," he said.

"Look, Dad," my sister said, making her one concession for him, "I'm handling this alone."

What could he do with that? He could have broken the code and said, "I'm not, I can't, don't make me," but he stood there for a second and then retreated. "I understand," he said first, although he didn't.

I wanted to lift him up, like statues I'd seen in art history books. A woman lifting up a man. The rescue in reverse. Daughter to father saying, "It's okay. You're okay. Now I won't let anything hurt."

Instead, I watched him as he went to place a call to Len Fenerman.

The police in those first weeks were almost reverent. Missing dead girls were not a common occurrence in the suburbs. But with no leads coming in on where my body was or who had killed me, the police were getting nervous. There was a window of time during which physical evidence was usually found; that window grew smaller every day.

"I don't want to sound irrational, Detective Fenerman," my father said.

"Len, please." Tucked in the corner of his desk blotter was the school picture Len Fenerman had taken from my mother. He had known, before anyone said the words, that I was already dead.

"I'm certain there's a man in the neighborhood who knows something," my father said. He was staring out the window of his upstairs den, toward the cornfield. The man who owned it had told the press he was going to let it sit fallow for now.

"Who is it, and what led you to believe this?" Len Fenerman asked. He chose a stubby, chewed pencil from the front metal lip of his desk drawer.

My father told him about the tent, about how Mr. Harvey had told him to go home, about saying my name, about how weird the neighborhood thought Mr. Harvey was with no regular job and no kids.

"I'll check it out," Len Fenerman said, because he had to. That was the role he played in the dance. But what my father had given him offered him little or nothing to work with. "Don't talk to anyone and don't approach him again," Len warned.

When my father hung up the phone he felt strangely empty. Drained, he opened the door to his den and closed it quietly behind him. In the hallway, for the second time, he called my mother's name: "Abigail."

She was in the downstairs bathroom, sneaking bites from the macaroons my father's firm always sent us for Christmas. She ate them greedily; they were like suns bursting open in her mouth. The summer she was pregnant with me, she wore one gingham maternity dress over and over, refusing to spend money on another, and ate all she wanted, rubbing her belly and saying, "Thank you, baby," as she dribbled chocolate on her breasts.

There was a knock down low on the door.

"Momma?" She stuffed the macaroons back in the medicine cabinet, swallowing what was already in her mouth.

"Momma?" Buckley repeated. His voice was sleepy.

"Mommmmm-maaa!"

She despised the word.

When my mother opened the door, my little brother held on to her knees. Buckley pressed his face into the flesh above them.

Hearing movement, my father went to meet my mother in the kitchen. Together they took solace in attending to Buckley.

"Where's Susie?" Buckley asked as my father spread Fluffernutter on wheat bread. He made three. One for himself, one for my mother, and one for his four-year-old son.

"Did you put away your game?" my father asked Buckley,

wondering why he persisted in avoiding the topic with the one person who approached it head-on.

"What's wrong with Mommy?" Buckley asked. Together they watched my mother, who was staring into the dry basin of the sink.

"How would you like to go to the zoo this week?" my father asked. He hated himself for it. Hated the bribe and the tease—the deceit. But how could he tell his son that, somewhere, his big sister might lie in pieces?

But Buckley heard the word *zoo* and all that it meant—which to him was largely *Monkeys!*—and he began on the rippling path to forgetting for one more day. The shadow of years was not as big on his small body. He knew I was away, but when people left they always came back.

When Len Fenerman had gone door to door in the neighborhood he had found nothing remarkable at George Harvey's. Mr. Harvey was a single man who, it was said, had meant to move in with his wife. She had died sometime before this. He built dollhouses for specialty stores and kept to himself. That was all anyone knew. Though friendships had not exactly blossomed around him, the sympathy of the neighborhood had always been with him. Each split-level contained a narrative. To Len Fenerman especially, George Harvey's seemed a compelling one.

No, Harvey said, he didn't know the Salmons well. Had seen the children. Everyone knew who had children and who didn't, he noted, his head hanging down and to the left a bit. "You can see the toys in the yard. The houses are always more lively," he noted, his voice halting.

"I understand you had a conversation with Mr. Salmon recently," Len said on his second trip to the dark green house.

"Yes, is there something wrong?" Mr. Harvey asked. He

squinted at Len but then had to pause. "Let me get my glasses," he said. "I was doing some close work on a Second Empire."

"Second Empire?" Len asked.

"Now that my Christmas orders are done, I can experiment," Mr. Harvey said. Len followed him into the back, where a dining table was pushed against a wall. Dozens of small lengths of what looked like miniature wainscoting were lined up on top of it.

A little strange, Fenerman thought, *but it doesn't make the man a murderer.*

Mr. Harvey got his glasses and immediately opened up. "Yes, Mr. Salmon was on one of his walks and he helped me build the bridal tent."

"The bridal tent?"

"Each year it's something I do for Leah," he said. "My wife. I'm a widower."

Len felt he was intruding on this man's private rituals. "So I understand," he said.

"I feel terrible about what happened to that girl," Mr. Harvey said. "I tried to express that to Mr. Salmon. But I know from experience that nothing makes sense at a time like this."

"So you erect this tent every year?" Len Fenerman asked. This was something he could get confirmation on from neighbors.

"In the past, I've done it inside, but I tried to do it outside this year. We were married in the winter. Until the snow picked up, I thought it would work."

"Where inside?"

"The basement. I can show you if you want. I have all of Leah's things down there still."

But Len did not go further.

"I've intruded enough," he said. "I just wanted to sweep the neighborhood a second time."

"How's your investigation coming?" Mr. Harvey asked. "Are you finding anything?"

Len never liked questions like this, though he supposed they were the right of the people whose lives he was invading.

"Sometimes I think clues find their way in good time," he said. "If they want to be found, that is." It was cryptic, sort of a Confucius-says answer, but it worked on almost every civilian.

"Have you talked to the Ellis boy?" Mr. Harvey asked.

"We talked to the family."

"He's hurt some animals in the neighborhood, I hear."

"He sounds like a bad kid, I grant you," said Len, "but he was working in the mall at the time."

"Witnesses?"

"Yes."

"That's my only idea," Mr. Harvey said. "I wish I could do more."

Len felt him to be sincere.

"He's certainly a bit tweaked at an angle," Len said when he called my father, "but I have nothing on him."

"What did he say about the tent?"

"That he built it for Leah, his wife."

"I remember Mrs. Stead told Abigail his wife's name was Sophie," my father said.

Len checked his notes. "No, Leah. I wrote it down."

My father doubted himself. Where had he gotten the name Sophie? He was sure he had heard it too, but that was years ago, at a block party, where the names of children and wives flew about like confetti between the stories people told to be neighborly and the introductions to infants and strangers too vague to remember the following day.

He did remember that Mr. Harvey had not come to the block party. He had never come to any of them. This went to his strangeness by the standards of many in the neighborhood but not by my father's own standards. He had never felt completely comfortable at these forced efforts of conviviality himself.

My father wrote "Leah?" in his book. Then he wrote, "Sophie?" Though unaware of it, he had begun a list of the dead.

On Christmas Day, my family would have been more comfortable in heaven. Christmas was largely ignored in my heaven. Some people dressed all in white and pretended they were snowflakes, but other than that, nothing.

That Christmas, Samuel Heckler came to our house on an unexpected visit. He was not dressed like a snowflake. He wore his older brother's leather jacket and a pair of ill-fitting army fatigues.

My brother was in the front room with his toys. My mother blessed the fact that she had gone early to buy his gifts. Lindsey got gloves and cherry-flavored lip gloss. My father got five white handkerchiefs that she'd ordered months ago in the mail. Save Buckley, no one wanted anything anyway. In the days before Christmas the lights on the tree were not plugged in. Only the candle that my father kept in the window of his den burned. He lit it after dark, but my mother, sister, and brother had stopped leaving the house after four o'clock. Only I saw it.

"There's a man outside!" my brother shouted. He'd been playing Skyscraper and it had yet to collapse. "He's got a suitcase."

My mother left her eggnog in the kitchen and came to the front of the house. Lindsey was suffering the mandatory presence in the family room that all holidays required. She and my father played Monopoly, ignoring the more brutal squares for each other's sake. There was no Luxury Tax, and a bad Chance wasn't recognized.

In the front hall my mother pressed her hands down along her skirt. She placed Buckley in front of her and put her arms on his shoulders.

"Wait for the man to knock," she said.

"Maybe it's Reverend Strick," my father said to Lindsey,

collecting his fifteen dollars for winning second prize in a beauty contest.

"For Susie's sake, I hope not," Lindsey ventured.

My father held on to it, on to my sister saying my name. She rolled doubles and moved to Marvin Gardens.

"That's twenty-four dollars," my father said, "but I'll take ten."

"Lindsey," my mother called. "It's a visitor for you."

My father watched my sister get up and leave the room. We both did. I sat with my father then. I was the ghost on the board. He stared at the old shoe lying on its side in the box. If only I could have lifted it up, made it hop from Boardwalk to Baltic, where I always claimed the better people lived. "That's because you're a purple freak," Lindsey would say. My father would say, "I'm proud I didn't raise a snob."

"Railroads, Susie," he said. "You always liked owning those railroads."

To accentuate his widow's peak and tame his cowlick, Samuel Heckler insisted on combing his hair straight back. This made him look, at thirteen and dressed in black leather, like an adolescent vampire.

"Merry Christmas, Lindsey," he said to my sister, and held out a small box wrapped in blue paper.

I could see it happen: Lindsey's body began to knot. She was working hard keeping everyone out, everyone, but she found Samuel Heckler cute. Her heart, like an ingredient in a recipe, was reduced, and regardless of my death she was thirteen, he was cute, and he had visited her on Christmas Day.

"I heard you made gifted," he said to her, because no one was talking. "Me too."

My mother remembered then, and she switched on her autopilot hostess. "Would you like to come sit?" she managed. "I have some eggnog in the kitchen."

"That would be wonderful," Samuel Heckler said and, to Lindsey's amazement and mine, offered my sister his arm.

"What's that?" asked Buckley, trailing behind and pointing to what he thought was a suitcase.

"An alto," Samuel Heckler said.

"What?" asked Buckley.

Lindsey spoke then. "Samuel plays the alto saxophone."

"Barely," Samuel said.

My brother did not ask what a saxophone was. He knew what Lindsey was being. She was being what I called snooty-wooty, as in "Buckley, don't worry, Lindsey's being snooty-wooty." Usually I'd tickle him as I said the word, sometimes burrowing into his stomach with my head, butting him and saying "snooty-wooty" over and over until his trills of laughter flowed down over me.

Buckley followed the three of them into the kitchen and asked, as he had at least once a day, "Where's Susie?"

They were silent. Samuel looked at Lindsey.

"Buckley," my father called from the adjoining room, "come play Monopoly with me."

My brother had never been invited to play Monopoly. Everyone said he was too young, but this was the magic of Christmas. He rushed into the family room, and my father picked him up and sat him on his lap.

"See this shoe?" my father said.

Buckley nodded his head.

"I want you to listen to everything I say about it, okay?"

"Susie?" my brother asked, somehow connecting the two.

"Yes, I'm going to tell you where Susie is."

I began to cry up in heaven. What else was there for me to do?

"This shoe was the piece Susie played Monopoly with," he said. "I play with the car or sometimes the wheelbarrow. Lindsey plays with the iron, and when your mother plays, she likes the cannon."

"Is that a dog?"

"Yes, that's a Scottie."

"Mine!"

"Okay," my father said. He was patient. He had found a way to explain it. He held his son in his lap, and as he spoke, he felt Buckley's small body on his knee—the very human, very warm, very alive weight of it. It comforted him. "The Scottie will be your piece from now on. Which piece is Susie's again?"

"The shoe," Buckley said.

"Right, and I'm the car, your sister's the iron, and your mother is the cannon."

My brother concentrated very hard.

"Now let's put all the pieces on the board, okay? You go ahead and do it for me."

Buckley grabbed a fist of pieces and then another, until all the pieces lay between the Chance and Community Chest cards.

"Let's say the other pieces are our friends."

"Like Nate?"

"Right, we'll make your friend Nate the hat. And the board is the world. Now if I were to tell you that when I rolled the dice, one of the pieces would be taken away, what would that mean?"

"They can't play anymore?"

"Right."

"Why?" Buckley asked.

He looked up at my father; my father flinched.

"Why?" my brother asked again.

My father did not want to say "because life is unfair" or "because that's how it is." He wanted something neat, something that could explain death to a four-year-old. He placed his hand on the small of Buckley's back.

"Susie is dead," he said now, unable to make it fit in the rules of any game. "Do you know what that means?"

Buckley reached over with his hand and covered the shoe. He looked up to see if his answer was right.

My father nodded. "You won't see Susie anymore, honey. None of us will." My father cried. Buckley looked up into the eyes of our father and did not fully understand.

Buckley kept the shoe on his dresser, until one day it wasn't there anymore and no amount of looking for it could turn it up.

In the kitchen my mother finished her eggnog and excused herself. She went into the dining room and counted silverware, methodically laying out the three kinds of forks, the knives, and the spoons, making them "climb the stairs" as she'd been taught when she worked in Wanamaker's bridal shop before I was born. She wanted a cigarette and for her children who were living to disappear for a little while.

"Are you going to open your gift?" Samuel Heckler asked my sister.

They stood at the counter, leaning against the dishwasher and the drawers that held napkins and towels. In the room to their right sat my father and brother; on the other side of the kitchen, my mother was thinking Wedgwood Florentine, Cobalt Blue; Royal Worcester, Mountbatten; Lenox, Eternal.

Lindsey smiled and pulled at the white ribbon on top of the box.

"My mom did the ribbon for me," Samuel Heckler said.

She tore the blue paper away from the black velvet box. Carefully she held it in her palm once the paper was off. In heaven I was excited. When Lindsey and I played Barbies, Barbie and Ken got married at sixteen. To us there was only one true love in everyone's life; we had no concept of compromise, or retrys.

"Open it," Samuel Heckler said.

"I'm scared."

"Don't be."

He put his hand on her forearm and—Wow!—what I felt

when he did that. Lindsey had a cute boy in the kitchen, vampire or no! This was news, this was a bulletin—I was suddenly privy to everything. She never would have told me any of this stuff.

What the box held was typical or disappointing or miraculous depending on the eye. It was typical because he was a thirteen-year-old boy, or it was disappointing because it was not a wedding ring, or it was miraculous. He'd given her a half a heart. It was gold and from inside his Hukapoo shirt, he pulled out the other side. It hung around his neck on a rawhide cord.

Lindsey's face flushed; mine flushed up in heaven.

I forgot my father in the family room and my mother counting silver. I saw Lindsey move toward Samuel Heckler. She kissed him; it was glorious. I was almost alive again.

SIX

Two weeks before my death, I left the house later than usual, and by the time I reached the school, the blacktop circle where the school buses usually hovered was empty.

A hall monitor from the discipline office would write down your name if you tried to get in the front doors after the first bell rang, and I didn't want to be paged during class to come and sit on the hard bench outside Mr. Peterford's room, where, it was widely known, he would bend you over and paddle your behind with a board. He'd asked the shop teacher to drill holes into it for less wind resistance on the downstroke and more pain when it landed against your jeans.

I had never been late enough or done anything bad enough to meet the board, but in my mind as in every other kid's I could visualize it so well my butt would sting. Clarissa had told me that the baby stoners, as they were called in junior high, used the back door to the stage, which was always left open by Cleo, the janitor, who had dropped out of high school as a full-blown stoner.

So that day I crept into the backstage area, watching my step, careful not to trip over the various cords and wires. I paused near some scaffolding and put down my book bag to brush my hair. I'd taken to leaving the house in the jingle-bell cap and then switching, as soon as I gained cover behind the O'Dwyers' house, to an old black watch cap of my father's. All this left my hair full of static electricity, and my first stop was usually the girls' room, where I would brush it flat.

"You are beautiful, Susie Salmon."

I heard the voice but could not place it immediately. I looked around me.

"Here," the voice said.

I looked up and saw the head and torso of Ray Singh leaning out over the top of the scaffold above me.

"Hello," he said.

I knew Ray Singh had a crush on me. He had moved from England the year before but Clarissa said he was born in India. That someone could have the face of one country and the voice of another and then move to a third was too incredible for me to fathom. It made him immediately cool. Plus, he seemed eight hundred times smarter than the rest of us, and he had a crush on me. What I finally realized were affectations—the smoking jacket that he sometimes wore to school and his foreign cigarettes, which were actually his mother's—I thought were evidence of his higher breeding. He knew and saw things that the rest of us didn't see. That morning when he spoke to me from above, my heart plunged to the floor.

"Hasn't the first bell rung?" I asked.

"I have Mr. Morton for homeroom," he said. This explained everything. Mr. Morton had a perpetual hangover, which was at its peak during homeroom. He never called roll.

"What are you doing up there?"

"Climb up and see," he said, removing his head and shoulders from my view.

I hesitated.

"Come on, Susie."

It was my one day in life of being a bad kid—of at least feigning the moves. I placed my foot on the bottom rung of the scaffold and reached my arms up to the first crossbar.

"Bring your stuff," Ray advised.

I went back for my book bag and then climbed unsteadily up.

"Let me help you," he said and put his hands under my armpits, which, even though covered by my winter parka, I was self-conscious about. I sat for a moment with my feet dangling over the side.

"Tuck them in," he said. "That way no one will see us."

I did what he told me, and then I stared at him for a moment. I felt suddenly stupid—unsure of why I was there.

"Will you stay up here all day?" I asked.

"Just until English class is over."

"You're cutting English!" It was as if he said he'd robbed a bank.

"I've seen every Shakespeare play put on by the Royal Shakespeare Company," Ray said. "That bitch has nothing to teach me."

I felt sorry for Mrs. Dewitt then. If part of being bad was calling Mrs. Dewitt a bitch, I wasn't into it.

"I like *Othello,*" I ventured.

"It's condescending twaddle the way she teaches it. A sort of *Black Like Me* version of the Moor."

Ray was smart. This combined with being an Indian from England had made him a Martian in Norristown.

"That guy in the movie looked pretty stupid with black makeup on," I said.

"You mean Sir Laurence Olivier."

Ray and I were quiet. Quiet enough to hear the bell for the end of homeroom ring and then, five minutes later, the bell that meant we should be on the first floor in Mrs. Dewitt's class. As each second passed after that bell, I could feel my skin heat up and Ray's look lengthen out over my body, taking in my royal blue parka and my kelly green miniskirt with my matching Danskin tights. My real shoes sat beside me inside my bag. On my feet I had a pair of fake sheepskin boots with dirty synthetic shearing spilling out like animal innards around the tops and seams. If I had known this was to be the sex scene of my life, I might have prepared a bit, reapplied my Strawberry-Banana Kissing Potion as I came in the door.

I could feel Ray's body leaning toward me, the scaffolding underneath us squeaking from his movement. *He is from England,* I was thinking. His lips moved closer, the scaffold listed. I was dizzy—about to go under the wave of my first kiss, when we both heard something. We froze.

Ray and I lay down side by side and stared at the lights and wires overhead. A moment later, the stage door opened and in walked Mr. Peterford and the art teacher, Miss Ryan, who we recognized by their voices. There was a third person with them.

"We are not taking disciplinary action at this time, but we will if you persist," Mr. Peterford was saying. "Miss Ryan, did you bring the materials?"

"Yes." Miss Ryan had come to Kennet from a Catholic school and taken over the art department from two ex-hippies who had been fired when the kiln exploded. Our art classes had gone from wild experiments with molten metals and throwing clay to day after day of drawing profiles of wooden figures she placed in stiff positions at the beginning of each class.

"I'm only doing the assignments." It was Ruth Connors. I recognized the voice and so did Ray. We all had Mrs. Dewitt's English class first period.

"This," Mr. Peterford said, "was not the assignment."

Ray reached for my hand and squeezed. We knew what they

were talking about. A xeroxed copy of one of Ruth's drawings had been passed around in the library until it had reached a boy at the card catalog who was overtaken by the librarian.

"If I'm not mistaken," said Miss Ryan, "there are no breasts on our anatomy model."

The drawing had been of a woman reclining with her legs crossed. And it was no wooden figure with eyehooks connecting the limbs. It was a real woman, and the charcoal smudges of her eyes—whether by accident or intent—had given her a leering look that made every kid who saw it either highly uncomfortable or quite happy, thank you.

"There isn't a nose or mouth on that wooden model either," Ruth said, "but you encouraged us to draw in faces."

Again Ray squeezed my hand.

"That's enough, young lady," Mr. Peterford said. "It is the attitude of repose in this particular drawing that clearly made it something the Nelson boy would xerox."

"Is that my fault?"

"Without the drawing there would be no problem."

"So it's my fault?"

"I invite you to realize the position this puts the school in and to assist us by drawing what Miss Ryan instructs the class to draw without making unnecessary additions."

"Leonardo da Vinci drew cadavers," Ruth said softly.

"Understood?"

"Yes," said Ruth.

The stage doors opened and shut, and a moment later Ray and I could hear Ruth Connors crying. Ray mouthed the word *go,* and I moved to the end of the scaffold, dangling my foot over the side to find a hold.

That week Ray would kiss me by my locker. It didn't happen up on the scaffold when he'd wanted it to. Our only kiss was like an accident—a beautiful gasoline rainbow.

I climbed down off the scaffold with my back to her. She didn't move or hide, just looked at me when I turned around. She was sitting on a wooden crate near the back of the stage. A pair of old curtains hung to her left. She watched me walk toward her but didn't wipe her eyes.

"Susie Salmon," she said, just to confirm it. The possibility of my cutting first period and hiding backstage in the auditorium was, until that day, as remote as the smartest girl in our class being bawled out by the discipline officer.

I stood in front of her, hat in hand.

"That's a stupid hat," she said.

I lifted the jingle-bell cap and looked at it. "I know. My mom made it."

"So you heard?"

"Can I see?"

Ruth unfolded the much-handled xerox and I stared.

Using a blue ballpoint pen, Brian Nelson had made an obscene hole where her legs were crossed. I recoiled and she watched me. I could see something flicker in her eyes, a private wondering, and then she leaned over and brought out a black leather sketchbook from her knapsack.

Inside, it was beautiful. Drawings of women mostly, but of animals and men too. I'd never seen anything like it before. Each page was covered in her drawings. I realized how subversive Ruth was then, not because she drew pictures of nude women that got misused by her peers, but because she was more talented than her teachers. She was the quietest kind of rebel. Helpless, really.

"You're really good, Ruth," I said.

"Thank you," she said, and I kept looking through the pages of her book and drinking it in. I was both frightened and excited by what existed underneath the black line of the navel in those drawings—what my mother called the "baby-making machinery."

I told Lindsey I'd never have one, and when I was ten I'd spent the better part of six months telling any adult who would listen that I intended on getting my tubes tied. I didn't know what this meant, exactly, but I knew it was drastic, required surgery, and it made my father laugh out loud.

Ruth went from weird to special for me then. The drawings were so good that in that moment I forgot the rules of school, all the bells and whistles, which as kids we were supposed to respond to.

After the cornfield was roped off, searched, then abandoned, Ruth went walking there. She would wrap a large wool shawl of her grandmother's around her under the ratty old peacoat of her father's. Soon she noted that teachers in subjects besides gym didn't report her if she cut. They were happy not to have her there: her intelligence made her a problem. It demanded attention and rushed their lesson plans forward.

And she began to take rides from her father in the mornings to avoid the bus. He left very early and brought his red metal, sloped-top lunchbox, which he had allowed her to pretend was a barn for her Barbies when she was little, and in which he now tucked bourbon. Before he let her out in the empty parking lot, he would stop his truck but keep the heater running.

"Going to be okay today?" he always asked.

Ruth nodded.

"One for the road?"

And without nodding this time she handed him the lunchbox. He opened it, unscrewed the bourbon, took a deep swallow, and then passed it to her. She threw her head back dramatically and either placed her tongue against the glass so very little would make it to her mouth, or took a small, wincing gulp if he was watching her.

She slid out of the high cab. It was cold, bitterly cold, before the sun rose. Then she remembered a fact from one of our classes:

people moving are warmer than people at rest. So she began to walk directly to the cornfield, keeping a good pace. She talked to herself, and sometimes she thought about me. Often she would rest a moment against the chain-link fence that separated the soccer field from the track, while she watched the world come alive around her.

So we met each morning in those first few months. The sun would come up over the cornfield and Holiday, let loose by my father, would come to chase rabbits in and out of the tall dry stalks of dead corn. The rabbits loved the trimmed lawns of the athletic fields, and as Ruth approached she'd see their dark forms line up along the white chalk of the farthest boundaries like some sort of tiny sports team. She liked the idea of this and I did too. She believed stuffed animals moved at night when humans went to sleep. She still thought in her father's lunchbox there might be minute cows and sheep that found time to graze on the bourbon and baloney.

When Lindsey left the gloves from Christmas for me, in between the farthest boundary of the soccer field and the cornfield, I looked down one morning to see the rabbits investigate: sniff at the corners of the gloves lined with their own kin. Then I saw Ruth pick them up before Holiday grabbed them. She turned the bottom of one glove so the fur faced out and held it up to her cheek. She looked up to the sky and said, "Thank you." I liked to think she was talking to me.

I grew to love Ruth on those mornings, feeling that in some way we could never explain on our opposite sides of the Inbetween, we were born to keep each other company. Odd girls who had found each other in the strangest way—in the shiver she had felt when I passed.

Ray was a walker, like me, living at the far end of our development, which surrounded the school. He had seen Ruth Connors walking alone out on the soccer fields. Since Christmas he had come and gone to school as quickly as he could, never lingering. He wanted my killer to be caught almost as much as my parents did. Until he was, Ray could not wipe the traces of suspicion off himself, despite his alibi.

He chose a morning when his father was not going to work at the university and filled his father's thermos with his mother's sweet tea. He left early to wait for Ruth and made a little camp of the cement shot-put circle, sitting on the metal curve against which the shot-putters braced their feet.

When he saw her walking on the other side of the chain-link fence that separated the school from the soccer field and inside which was the most revered of the sports fields—the football one—he rubbed his hands together and prepared what he wanted to say. His bravery this time came not from having kissed me—a goal he'd set himself a full year before its completion—but from being, at fourteen, intensely lonely.

I watched Ruth approach the soccer field, thinking she was alone. In an old home her father had gone to scavenge, he had found her a treat to go along with her new hobby—an anthology of poems. She held them close.

She saw Ray stand up when she was still some distance away.

"Hello, Ruth Connors!" he called and waved his arms.

Ruth looked over, and his name came into her head: Ray Singh. But she didn't know much more than that. She had heard the rumors about the police being over at his house, but she believed what her father had said—"No kid did that"—and so she walked over to him.

"I prepared tea and have it in my thermos here," Ray said. I blushed for him up in heaven. He was smart when it came to *Othello,* but now he was acting like a geek.

"No thank you," Ruth said. She stood near him but with a definite few feet more than usual still in between. Her fingernails were pressed into the worn cover of the poetry anthology.

"I was there that day, when you and Susie talked backstage," Ray said. He held the thermos out to her. She made no move closer and didn't respond.

"Susie Salmon," he clarified.

"I know who you mean," she said.

"Are you going to the memorial service?"

"I didn't know there was one," she said.

"I don't think I'm going."

I was staring hard at his lips. They were redder than usual from the cold. Ruth took a step forward.

"Do you want some lip balm?" Ruth asked.

Ray lifted his wool gloves up to his lips, where they snagged briefly on the chapped surface that I had kissed. Ruth dug her hands in the peacoat pocket and pulled out her Chap Stick. "Here," she said, "I have tons of them. You can keep it."

"That's so nice," he said. "Will you at least sit with me until the buses come?"

They sat together on the shot-putters' cement platform. Again I was seeing something I never would have seen: the two of them together. It made Ray more attractive to me than he had ever been. His eyes were the darkest gray. When I watched him from heaven I did not hesitate to fall inside of them.

It became a ritual for the two of them. On the days that his father taught, Ruth brought him a little bourbon in her father's flask; otherwise they had sweet tea. They were cold as hell, but that didn't seem to matter to them.

They talked about what it was like to be a foreigner in Norristown. They read poems aloud from Ruth's anthology. They talked about how to become what they wanted to be. A doctor for Ray. A painter/poet for Ruth. They made a secret club of the other oddballs they could point out in our class. There were the obvious ones like Mike Bayles, who had taken so much acid no one understood how he was still in school, or Jeremiah, who was from Louisiana and so just as much a foreigner as Ray. Then there were the quiet ones. Artie, who talked excitedly to anyone about the effects of formaldehyde. Harry Orland, who was so painfully shy he wore his gym shorts over his jeans. And Vicki Kurtz, who everyone thought was okay after the death of her mother, but whom Ruth had seen sleeping in a bed of pine needles behind the junior high's regulating plant. And, sometimes, they would talk about me.

"It's so strange," Ruth said. "I mean, it's like we were in the same class since kindergarten but that day backstage in the auditorium was the first time we ever looked at each other."

"She was great," Ray said. He thought of our lips brushing past one another as we stood alone in a column of lockers. How I had smiled with my eyes closed and then almost run away. "Do you think they'll find him?"

"I guess so. You know, we're only like one hundred yards away from where it happened."

"I know," he said.

They both sat on the thin metal rim of the shot-putters' brace, holding tea in their gloved hands. The cornfield had become a place no one went. When a ball strayed from the soccer field, a boy took a dare to go in and get it. That morning the sun was slicing right through the dead stalks as it rose, but there was no heat from it.

"I found these here," she said, indicating the leather gloves.

"Do you ever think about her?" he asked.

They were quiet again.

"All the time," Ruth said. A chill ran down my spine. "Sometimes I think she's lucky, you know. I hate this place."

"Me too," Ray said. "But I've lived other places. This is just a temporary hell, not a permanent one."

"You're not implying . . ."

"She's in heaven, if you believe in that stuff."

"You don't?"

"I don't think so, no."

"I do," Ruth said. "I don't mean la-la angel-wing crap, but I do think there's a heaven."

"Is she happy?"

"It *is* heaven, right?"

"But what does that mean?"

The tea was stone-cold and the first bell had already rung. Ruth smiled into her cup. "Well, as my dad would say, it means she's out of this shithole."

When my father knocked on the door of Ray Singh's house, he was struck dumb by Ray's mother, Ruana. It was not that she was immediately welcoming, and she was far from sunny, but something about her dark hair, and her gray eyes, and even the strange way she seemed to step back from the door once she opened it, all of these things overwhelmed him.

He had heard the offhand comments the police made about her. To their mind she was cold and snobbish, condescending, odd. And so that was what he imagined he would find.

"Come in and sit," she'd said to him when he pronounced his name. Her eyes, on the word *Salmon,* had gone from closed to open doorways—dark rooms where he wanted to travel firsthand.

He almost lost his balance as she led him into the small cramped front room of their house. There were books on the floor with their spines facing up. They came out three rows deep from the wall. She was wearing a yellow sari and what looked like gold lamé capri pants underneath. Her feet were bare. She padded across the wall-to-wall and stopped at the couch. "Something to drink?" she asked, and he nodded his head.

"Hot or cold?"

"Hot."

As she turned the corner into a room he couldn't see, he sat down on the brown plaid couch. The windows across from him under which the books were lined were draped with long muslin curtains, which the harsh daylight outside had to fight to filter through. He felt suddenly very warm, almost close to forgetting why that morning he had double-checked the Singhs' address.

A little while later, as my father was thinking of how tired he was and how he had promised my mother to pick up some long-held dry cleaning, Mrs. Singh returned with tea on a tray and put it down on the carpet in front of him.

"We don't have much furniture, I'm afraid. Dr. Singh is still looking for tenure."

She went into an adjoining room and brought back a purple floor pillow for herself, which she placed on the floor to face him.

"Dr. Singh is a professor?" my father asked, though he knew this already, knew more than he was comfortable with about this beautiful woman and her sparsely furnished home.

"Yes," she said, and poured the tea. It was quiet. She held out a cup to him, and as he took it she said, "Ray was with him the day your daughter was killed."

He wanted to fall over into her.

"That must be why you've come," she continued.

"Yes," he said, "I want to talk to him."

"He's at school right now," she said. "You know that." Her legs in the gold pants were tucked to her side. The nails on her toes were long and unpolished, their surface gnarled from years of dancing.

"I wanted to come by and assure you I mean him no harm," my father said. I watched him. I had never seen him like this before. The words fell out of him like burdens he was delivering, back-logged verbs and nouns, but he was watching her feet curl against the dun-colored rug and the way the small pool of numbed light from the curtains touched her right cheek.

"He did nothing wrong and loved your little girl. A schoolboy crush, but still."

Schoolboy crushes happened all the time to Ray's mother. The teenager who delivered the paper would pause on his bike, hoping that she would be near the door when she heard the thump of the *Philadelphia Inquirer* hit the porch. That she would come out and, if she did, that she would wave. She didn't even have to smile, and she rarely did outside her house—it was the eyes, her dancer's carriage, the way she seemed to deliberate over the smallest movement of her body.

When the police had come they had stumbled into the dark front hall in search of a killer, but before Ray even reached the top of the stairs, Ruana had so confused them that they were agreeing to tea and sitting on silk pillows. They had expected her to fall into the grooves of the patter they relied on with all attractive women, but she only grew more erect in posture as they tried harder and harder to ingratiate themselves, and she stood upright by the windows while they questioned her son.

"I'm glad Susie had a nice boy like her," my father said. "I'll thank your son for that."

She smiled, not showing teeth.

"He wrote her a love note," he said.

"Yes."

"I wish I had known enough to do the same," he said. "Tell her I loved her on that last day."

"Yes."

"But your son did."

"Yes."

They stared at each other for a moment.

"You must have driven the policemen nuts," he said and smiled more to himself than to her.

"They came to accuse Ray," she said. "I wasn't concerned with how they felt about me."

"I imagine it's been hard for him," my father said.

"No, I won't allow that," she said sternly and placed her cup back on the tray. "You cannot have sympathy for Ray or for us."

My father tried to stutter out a protest.

She placed her hand in the air. "You have lost a daughter and come here for some purpose. I will allow you that and that only, but trying to understand our lives, no."

"I didn't mean to offend," he said. "I only . . ."

Again, the hand up.

"Ray will be home in twenty minutes. I will talk to him first and prepare him, then you may talk to my son about your daughter."

"What did I say?"

"I like that we don't have much furniture. It allows me to think that someday we might pack up and leave."

"I hope you'll stay," my father said. He said it because he had been trained to be polite from an early age, a training he passed on to me, but he also said it because part of him wanted more of her, this cold woman who was not exactly cold, this rock who was not stone.

"With all gentleness," she said, "you don't even know me. We'll wait together for Ray."

My father had left our house in the midst of a fight between Lindsey and my mother. My mother was trying to get Lindsey to go with her to the Y to swim. Without thinking, Lindsey had blared, "I'd rather die!" at the top of her lungs. My father watched as my mother froze, then burst, fleeing to their bedroom to wail behind the door. He quietly tucked his notebook in his jacket pocket, took the car keys off the hook by the back door, and snuck out.

In those first two months my mother and father moved in opposite directions from each other. One stayed in, the other went out. My father fell asleep in his den in the green chair, and when he woke he crept carefully into the bedroom and slid into bed. If my mother had most of the sheets he would lie without them, his body curled up tight, ready to spring at a moment's notice, ready for anything.

"I know who killed her," he heard himself say to Ruana Singh.

"Have you told the police?"

"Yes."

"What do they say?"

"They say that for now there is nothing but my suspicion to link him to the crime."

"A father's suspicion . . ." she began.

"Is as powerful as a mother's intuition."

This time there were teeth in her smile.

"He lives in the neighborhood."

"What are you doing?"

"I'm investigating all leads," my father said, knowing how it sounded as he said it.

"And my son . . ."

"Is a lead."

"Perhaps the other man frightens you too much."

"But I have to do something," he protested.

"Here we are again, Mr. Salmon," she said. "You misinterpret me. I am not saying you are doing the wrong thing by coming here. It is the right thing in its way. You want to find something soft, something warm in all this. Your searching led you here. That's a good thing. I am only concerned that it be good, too, for my son."

"I mean no harm."

"What is the man's name?"

"George Harvey." It was the first time he'd said it aloud to anyone but Len Fenerman.

She paused and stood. Turning her back to him, she walked over to first one window and then the other and drew the curtains back. It was the after-school light that she loved. She watched for Ray as he walked up the road.

"Ray will come now. I will go to meet him. If you'll excuse me I need to put on my coat and boots." She paused. "Mr. Salmon," she said, "I would do exactly what you are doing: I would talk to everyone I needed to, I would not tell too many people his name. When I was sure," she said, "I would find a quiet way, and I would kill him."

He could hear her in the hallway, the metal clank of hangers as she got her coat. A few minutes later the door was opened and closed. A cold breeze came in from the outside and then out on the road he could see a mother greet her son. Neither of them smiled. Their heads bent low. Their mouths moved. Ray took in the fact that my father was waiting for him inside his home.

At first my mother and I thought it was just the obvious that marked Len Fenerman as different from the rest of the force. He was smaller than the hulking uniforms who frequently accompanied him. Then there were the less obvious traits too—the way he often seemed to be thinking to himself, how he wasn't much for joking or trying to be anything but serious when he talked about me and the circumstances of the case. But, talking with my mother, Len Fenerman had shown himself for what he was: an optimist. He believed my killer would be caught.

"Maybe not today or tomorrow," he said to my mother, "but someday he'll do something uncontrollable. They are too uncontrolled in their habits not to."

My mother was left to entertain Len Fenerman until my father arrived home from the Singhs'. On the table in the family room Buckley's crayons were scattered across the butcher paper my mother had laid down. Buckley and Nate had drawn until their heads began to nod like heavy flowers, and my mother had plucked them up in her arms, first one and then the other, and brought them over to the couch. They slept there end to end with their feet almost touching in the center.

Len Fenerman knew enough to talk in hushed whispers, but he wasn't, my mother noted, a worshiper of children. He watched her carry the two boys but did not stand to help or comment on them the way the other policemen always did, defining her by her children, both living and dead.

"Jack wants to talk to you," my mother said. "But I'm sure you're too busy to wait."

"Not too busy."

I saw a black strand of her hair fall from where she had tucked it behind her ear. It softened her face. I saw Len see it too.

"He went over to that poor Ray Singh's house," she said and tucked the fallen hair back in its proper place.

"I'm sorry we had to question him," Len said.

"Yes," she said. "No young boy is capable of . . ." She couldn't say it, and he didn't make her.

"His alibi was airtight."

My mother took up a crayon from the butcher paper.

Len Fenerman watched my mother draw stick figures and stick dogs. Buckley and Nate made quiet sounds of sleep on the couch. My brother curled up into a fetal position and a moment later placed his thumb in his mouth to suck. It was a habit my mother had told us all we must help him break. Now she envied such easy peace.

"You remind me of my wife," Len said after a long silence, during which my mother had drawn an orange poodle and what looked like a blue horse undergoing electroshock treatment.

"She can't draw either?"

"She wasn't much of a talker when there was nothing to say."

A few more minutes passed. A yellow ball of sun. A brown house with flowers outside the door—pink, blue, purple.

"You used the past tense."

They both heard the garage door. "She died soon after we were married," he said.

"Daddy!" Buckley yelled, and leapt up, forgetting Nate and everyone else.

"I'm sorry," she said to Len.

"I am too," he said, "about Susie. Really."

In the back hall my father greeted Buckley and Nate with high cheers and calls for "Oxygen!" as he always did when we besieged him after a long day. Even if it felt false, elevating his mood for my brother was often the favorite part of his day.

My mother stared at Len Fenerman while my father walked toward the family room from the back. *Rush to the sink,* I felt like saying to her, stare down the hole and look into the earth. I'm down there waiting; I'm up here watching.

Len Fenerman had been the one that first asked my mother for my school picture when the police thought I might be found alive. In his wallet, my photo sat in a stack. Among these dead children and strangers was a picture of his wife. If a case had been solved he had written the date of its resolution on the back of the photo. If the case was still open—in his mind if not in the official files of the police—it was blank. There was nothing on the back of mine. There was nothing on his wife's.

"Len, how are you?" my father asked. Holiday up and wiggling back and forth for my father to pet him.

"I hear you went to see Ray Singh," Len said.

"Boys, why don't you go play up in Buckley's room?" my mother suggested. "Detective Fenerman and Daddy need to talk."

SEVEN

"Do you see her?" Buckley asked Nate as they climbed the stairs, Holiday in tow. "That's my sister."

"No," Nate said.

"She was gone for a while, but now she's back. Race!"

And the three of them—two boys and a dog—raced the rest of the way up the long curve of the staircase.

I had never even let myself yearn for Buckley, afraid he might see my image in a mirror or a bottle cap. Like everyone else I was trying to protect him. "Too young," I said to Franny. "Where do you think imaginary friends come from?" she said.

For a few minutes the two boys sat under the framed grave rubbing outside my parents' room. It was from a tomb in a London graveyard. My mother had told Lindsey and me the story of how my father and she had wanted things to hang on their walls and an old woman they met on their honeymoon had taught them how to do grave rubbings. By the time I was in double digits most of the grave rubbings had been put down in the basement for storage, the spots on our suburban walls replaced with bright graphic prints meant to stimulate children. But Lindsey and I loved the grave rubbings, particularly the one under which Nate and Buckley sat that afternoon.

Lindsey and I would lie down on the floor underneath it. I would pretend to be the knight that was pictured, and Holiday was the faithful dog curled up at his feet. Lindsey would be the wife he'd left behind. It always dissolved into giggles no matter how solemn the start. Lindsey would tell the dead knight that a wife had to move on, that she couldn't be trapped for the rest of her life by a man who was frozen in time. I would act stormy and mad, but it never lasted. Eventually she would describe her new lover: the fat butcher who gave her prime cuts of meat, the agile blacksmith who made her hooks. "You are dead, knight," she would say. "Time to move on."

"Last night she came in and kissed me on the cheek," Buckley said.

"Did not."

"Did too."

"Really?"

"Yeah."

"Have you told your mom?"

"It's a secret," Buckley said. "Susie told me she isn't ready to talk to them yet. Do you want to see something else?"

"Sure," said Nate.

The two of them stood up to go to the children's side of the house, leaving Holiday asleep under the grave rubbing.

"Come look," Buckley said.

They were in my room. The picture of my mother had been taken by Lindsey. After reconsideration, she had come back for the "Hippy-Dippy Says Love" button too.

"Susie's room," Nate said.

Buckley put his fingers to his lips. He'd seen my mother do this when she wanted us to be quiet, and now he wanted that from Nate. He got down on his belly and gestured for Nate to follow, and they wriggled like Holiday as they made their way beneath the dust ruffle of my bed into my secret storage space.

In the material that was stretched on the underside of the box spring, there was a hole, and stuffed up inside were things I didn't want anyone else to see. I had to guard it from Holiday or he would scratch at it to try and pry the objects loose. This had been exactly what happened twenty-four hours after I went missing. My parents had searched my room hoping to find a note of explanation and then left the door open. Holiday had carried off the licorice I kept there. Strewn beneath my bed were the objects I'd kept hidden, and one of them only Buckley and Nate would recognize. Buckley unwrapped an old handkerchief of my father's and there it was, the stained and bloody twig.

The year before, a three-year-old Buckley had swallowed it. Nate and he had been shoving rocks up their noses in our backyard, and Buckley had found a small twig under the oak tree where my mother strung one end of the clothesline. He put the stick in his mouth like a cigarette. I watched him from the roof outside my bedroom window, where I was sitting painting my toenails with Clarissa's Magenta Glitter and reading *Seventeen*.

I was perpetually assigned the job of watching out for little brother. Lindsey was not thought to be old enough. Besides, she was a burgeoning brain, which meant she got to be free to do things like spend that summer afternoon drawing detailed pictures of a fly's eye on graph paper with her 130-pack of Prisma Colors.

It was not too hot out and it was summer, and I was going to spend my internment at home beautifying. I had begun the morning by showering, shampooing, and steaming myself. On the roof I air-dried and applied lacquer.

I had on two coats of Magenta Glitter when a fly landed on the bottle's applicator. I heard Nate making dare and threat sounds, and I squinted at the fly to try to make out all the quadrants of his eyes that Lindsey was coloring inside the house. A breeze came up, blowing the fringe on my cutoffs against my thighs.

"Susie, Susie!" Nate was yelling.

I looked down to see Buckley on the ground.

It was this day that I always told Holly about when we talked about rescue. I believed it was possible; she did not.

I swung my legs around and scrambled through my open window, one foot landing on the sewing stool and the other immediately in front of that one and on the braided rug and then down on my knees and out of the blocks like an athlete. I ran down the hall and slid down the banister as we'd been forbidden to do. I called Lindsey's name and then forgot her, ran out to the backyard through the screened-in porch, and jumped over the dog fence to the oak tree.

Buckley was choking, his body bucking, and I carried him with Nate trailing into the garage, where my father's precious Mustang sat. I had watched my parents drive, and my mother had shown me how a car went from park to reverse. I put Buckley in the back and grabbed the keys from the unused terra-cotta pots where my father hid them. I sped all the way to the hospital. I burned out the emergency brake, but no one seemed to care.

"If she hadn't been there," the doctor later told my mother, "you would have lost your little boy."

Grandma Lynn predicted I'd have a long life because I had saved my brother's. As usual, Grandma Lynn was wrong.

"Wow," Nate said, holding the twig and marveling at how over time red blood turned black.

"Yeah," said Buckley. His stomach felt queasy with the memory of it. How much pain he had been in, how the faces of the adults changed as they surrounded him in the huge hospital bed. He had seen them that serious only one other time. But whereas in the hospital, their eyes had been worried and then later not, shot through with so much light and relief that they'd enveloped him, now our parents' eyes had gone flat and not returned.

I felt faint in heaven that day. I reeled back in the gazebo, and my eyes snapped open. It was dark, and across from me stood a large building that I had never been in.

I had read *James and the Giant Peach* when I was little. The building looked like the house of his aunts. Huge and dark and Victorian. It had a widow's walk. For a moment, as I readjusted to the darkness, I thought I saw a long row of women standing on the widow's walk and pointing my way. But a moment later, I saw differently. Crows were lined up, their beaks holding crooked twigs. As I stood to go back to the duplex, they took wing and followed me. Had my brother really seen me somehow, or was he merely a little boy telling beautiful lies?

EIGHT

For three months Mr. Harvey dreamed of buildings. He saw a slice of Yugoslavia where thatched-roofed dwellings on stilts gave way to rushing torrents of water from below. There were blue skies overhead. Along the fjords and in the hidden valley of Norway, he saw wooden stave churches, the timbers of which had been carved by Viking boat-builders. Dragons and local heroes made from wood. But there was one building, from the Vologda, that he dreamed about most: the Church of the Transfiguration. And it was this dream—his favorite—that he had on the night of my murder and on the nights following until the others came back. The *not still* dreams—the ones of women and children.

I could see all the way back to Mr. Harvey in his mother's arms, staring out over a table covered with pieces of colored glass. His father sorted them into piles by shape and size, depth and weight. His father's jeweler's eyes looked deeply into each specimen for cracks and flaws. And George Harvey would turn his attention to the single jewel that hung from his mother's neck, a large oval-shaped piece of amber framed by silver, inside of which sat a whole and perfect fly.

"A builder" was all Mr. Harvey said when he was young. Then he stopped answering the question of what his father did. How could he say he worked in the desert, and that he built shacks of broken glass and old wood? He lectured George Harvey on what made a good building, on how to make sure you were constructing things to last.

So it was his father's old sketchbooks that Mr. Harvey looked at when the not still dreams came back. He would steep himself in the images of other places and other worlds, trying to love what he did not. And then he would begin to dream dreams of his mother the last time he had seen her, running through a field on the side of the road. She had been dressed in white. White capri pants and a tight white boat-neck shirt, and his father and she had fought for the last time in the hot car outside of Truth or Consequences, New Mexico. He had forced her out of the car. George Harvey sat still as stone in the back seat—eyes wide, no more afraid than a stone, watching it all as he did everything by then—in slow-mo. She had run without stopping, her white body thin and fragile and disappearing, while her son clung on to the amber necklace she had torn from her neck to hand him. His father had watched the road. "She's gone now, son," he said. "She won't be coming back."

NINE

My grandmother arrived on the evening before my memorial in her usual style. She liked to hire limousines and drive in from the airport sipping champagne while wearing what she called her "thick and fabulous animal"—a mink she had gotten secondhand at the church bazaar. My parents had not so much invited her as included her if she wanted to be there. In late January, Principal Caden had initiated the idea. "It will be good for your children and all the students at school," he had said. He took it upon himself to organize the event at our church. My parents were like sleepwalkers saying yes to his questions, nodding their heads to flowers or speakers. When my mother mentioned it on the phone to her mother, she was surprised to hear the words "I'm coming."

"But you don't have to, Mother."

There was a silence on my grandmother's end. "Abigail," she said, "this is Susan's funeral."

* * *

Grandma Lynn embarrassed my mother by insisting on wearing her used furs on walks around the block and by once attending a block party in high makeup. She would ask my mother questions until she knew who everyone was, whether or not my mother had seen the inside of their house, what the husband did for a living, what cars they drove. She made a solid catalog of the neighbors. It was a way, I now realized, to try to understand her daughter better. A miscalculated circling, a sad, partnerless dance.

"Jack-y," my grandmother said as she approached my parents on the front porch, "we need some stiff drinks!" She saw Lindsey then, trying to sneak up the stairs and gain a few more minutes before the required visitation. "Kid hates me," Grandma Lynn said. Her smile was frozen, her teeth perfect and white.

"Mother," my mother said. And I wanted to rush into those ocean eyes of loss. "I'm sure Lindsey is just going to make herself presentable."

"An impossibility in this house!" said my grandmother.

"Lynn," said my father, "this is a different house than last time you were here. I'll get you a drink, but I ask you to respect that."

"Still handsome as hell, Jack," my grandmother said.

My mother took my grandmother's coat. Holiday had been closed up in my father's den as soon as Buckley had yelled from his post at the upstairs window—"It's Grandma!" My brother bragged to Nate or anyone who would listen that his grandmother had the biggest cars in the whole wide world.

"You look lovely, Mother," my mother said.

"Hmmmm." While my father was out of earshot, my grandmother said, "How is he?"

"We're all coping, but it's hard."

"Is he still muttering about that man having done it?"

"He still thinks so, yes."

"You'll be sued, you know," she said.

"He hasn't told anyone but the police."

What they couldn't see was that my sister was sitting above them on the top step.

"And he shouldn't. I realize he has to blame someone, but . . ."

"Lynn, seven and seven or a martini?" my father said, coming back out into the hallway.

"What are you having?"

"I'm not drinking these days, actually," my father said.

"Now there's your problem. I'll lead the way. No one has to tell me where the liquor is!"

Without her thick and fabulous animal, my grandmother was rail thin. "Starved down" was how she put it when she'd counseled me at age eleven. "You need to get yourself starved down, honey, before you keep fat on for too long. Baby fat is just another way to say ugly." She and my mother had fought about whether I was old enough for benzedrine—her own personal savior, she called it, as in, "I am offering your daughter my own personal savior and you deny her?"

When I was alive, everything my grandmother did was bad. But an odd thing happened when she arrived in her rented limo that day, opened up our house, and barged in. She was, in all her obnoxious finery, dragging the light back in.

"You need help, Abigail," my grandmother said after having eaten the first real meal my mother had cooked since my disappearance. My mother was stunned. She had donned her blue dishwashing gloves, filled the sink with sudsy water, and was preparing to do every dish. Lindsey would dry. Her mother, she assumed, would call upon Jack to pour her an after-dinner drink.

"Mother, that is so nice of you."

"Don't mention it," she said. "I'll just run out to the front hall and get my bag o' magic."

"Oh no," I heard my mother say under her breath.

"Ah, yes, the bag o' magic," said Lindsey, who had not spoken the whole meal.

"Please, Mother!" my mother protested when Grandma Lynn came back.

"Okay, kids, clear off the table and get your mother over here. I'm doing a makeover."

"Mother, that's crazy. I have all these dishes to do."

"Abigail," my father said.

"Oh no. She may get you to drink, but she's not getting those instruments of torture near me."

"I'm not drunk," he said.

"You're smiling," my mother said.

"So sue him," Grandma Lynn said. "Buckley, grab your mother's hand and drag her over here." My brother obliged. It was fun to see his mother be bossed and prodded.

"Grandma Lynn?" Lindsey asked shyly.

My mother was being led by Buckley to a kitchen chair my grandmother had turned to face her.

"What?"

"Could you teach me about makeup?"

"My God in heaven, praise the Lord, yes!"

My mother sat down and Buckley climbed up into her lap. "What's wrong, Mommy?"

"Are you laughing, Abbie?" My father smiled.

And she was. She was laughing and she was crying too.

"Susie was a good girl, honey," Grandma Lynn said. "Just like you." There was no pause. "Now lift up your chin and let me have a look at those bags under your eyes."

Buckley got down and moved onto a chair. "This is an eyelash curler, Lindsey," my grandmother instructed. "I taught your mother all of these things."

"Clarissa uses those," Lindsey said.

My grandmother set the rubber curler pads on either side of my mother's eyelashes, and my mother, knowing the ropes, looked upward.

"Have you talked to Clarissa?" my father asked.

"Not really," said Lindsey. "She's hanging out a lot with Brian Nelson. They cut class enough times to get a three-day suspension."

"I don't expect that of Clarissa," my father said. "She may not have been the brightest apple in the bunch, but she was never a troublemaker."

"When I ran into her she reeked of pot."

"I hope you're not getting into that," Grandma Lynn said. She finished the last of her seven and seven and slammed the highball glass down on the table. "Now, see this, Lindsey, see how when the lashes are curled it opens up your mother's eyes?"

Lindsey tried to imagine her own eyelashes, but instead saw the star-clumped lashes of Samuel Heckler as his face neared hers for a kiss. Her pupils dilated, pulsing in and out like small, ferocious olives.

"I stand amazed," Grandma Lynn said, and put her hands, one still twisted into the awkward handles of the eyelash curler, on her hips.

"What?"

"Lindsey Salmon, you have a boyfriend," my grandmother announced to the room.

My father smiled. He was liking Grandma Lynn suddenly. I was too.

"Do not," Lindsey said.

My grandmother was about to speak when my mother whispered, "Do too."

"Bless you, honey," my grandmother said, "you should have a boyfriend. As soon as I'm done with your mother, I'm giving you the grand Grandma Lynn treatment. Jack, make me an apéritif."

"An apéritif is something you . . ." my mother began.

"Don't correct me, Abigail."

My grandmother got sloshed. She made Lindsey look like a

clown or, as Grandma Lynn said herself, "a grade-A 'tute." My father got what she called "finely drunkened." The most amazing thing was that my mother went to bed and left the dirty dishes in the sink.

While everyone else slept, Lindsey stood at the mirror in the bathroom, looking at herself. She wiped off some of the blush, blotted her lips, and ran her fingers over the swollen, freshly plucked parts of her formerly bushy eyebrows. In the mirror she saw something different and so did I: an adult who could take care of herself. Under the makeup was the face she'd always known as her own, until very recently, when it had become the face that reminded people of me. With lip pencil and eyeliner, she now saw, the edges of her features were delineated, and they sat on her face like gems imported from some far-off place where the colors were richer than the colors in our house had ever been. It was true what our grandmother said—the makeup brought out the blue of her eyes. The plucking of the eyebrows changed the shape of her face. The blush highlighted the hollows beneath her cheekbones ("The hollows that could stand some more hollowing," our grandmother pointed out). And her lips—she practiced her facial expressions. She pouted, she kissed, she smiled wide as if she too had had a cocktail, she looked down and pretended to pray like a good girl but cocked one eye up to see how she looked being good. She went to bed and slept on her back so as not to mess up her new face.

Mrs. Bethel Utemeyer was the only dead person my sister and I ever saw. She moved in with her son to our development when I was six and Lindsey five.

My mother said that she had lost part of her brain and that

sometimes she left her son's house and didn't know where she was. She would often end up in our front yard, standing under the dogwood tree and looking out at the street as if waiting for a bus. My mother would sit her down in the kitchen and make tea for the two of them, and after she calmed her she would call her son's house to tell them where she was. Sometimes no one was home and Mrs. Utemeyer would sit at our kitchen table and stare into the centerpiece for hours. She would be there when we came home from school. Sitting. She smiled at us. Often she called Lindsey "Natalie" and reached out to touch her hair.

When she died, her son encouraged my mother to bring Lindsey and me to the funeral. "My mother seemed to have a special fondness for your children," he wrote.

"She didn't even know my name, Mom," Lindsey whined, as our mother buttoned up the infinite number of round buttons on Lindsey's dress coat. *Another impractical gift from Grandma Lynn,* my mother thought.

"At least she *called* you a name," I said.

It was after Easter, and a spring heat wave had set in that week. All but the most stubborn of that winter's snow had seeped into the earth, and in the graveyard of the Utemeyers' church snow clung to the base of the headstones, while, nearby, buttercup shoots were making their way up.

The Utemeyers' church was fancy. "High Catholic," my father had said in the car. Lindsey and I thought this was very funny. My father hadn't wanted to come but my mother was so pregnant that she couldn't drive. For the last few months of her pregnancy with Buckley she was unable to fit behind the wheel. She was so uncomfortable most of the time that we avoided being near her for fear we'd be thrown into servitude.

But her pregnancy allowed her to get out of what Lindsey and I couldn't stop talking about for weeks and what I kept dreaming about for long after that: viewing the body. I could tell my father and mother didn't want this to happen, but Mr. Utemeyer made a beeline for the two of us when it was time to file past the casket. "Which one of you is the one she called Natalie?" he asked. We stared at him. I pointed to Lindsey.

"I'd like you to come say goodbye," he said. He smelled of a perfume sweeter than what my mother sometimes wore, and the sting of it in my nose, and my sense of exclusion, made me want to cry. "You can come too," he said to me, extending his hands so we would flank him in the aisle.

It wasn't Mrs. Utemeyer. It was something else. But it *was* Mrs. Utemeyer too. I tried to keep my eyes focused on the gleaming gold rings on her fingers.

"Mother," Mr. Utemeyer said, "I brought the little girl you called Natalie."

Lindsey and I both admitted later that we expected Mrs. Utemeyer to speak and that we had decided, individually, that if she did we were going to grab the other one and run like hell.

An excruciating second or two and it was over and we were released back to our mother and father.

I wasn't very surprised when I first saw Mrs. Bethel Utemeyer in my heaven, nor was I shocked when Holly and I found her walking hand in hand with a small blond girl she introduced as her daughter, Natalie.

The morning of my memorial Lindsey stayed in her room for as long as she could. She didn't want my mother to see the still-applied makeup until it would be too late to make her wash it off. She had also told herself it would be okay to take a dress from my closet. That I wouldn't mind.

But it was weird to watch.

She opened the door to my room, a vault that by February was being disturbed more and more, though no one, not my mother or father, nor Buckley or Lindsey, confessed to entering, nor to taking things that they didn't plan on returning. They were blind to the clues that each of them came and visited me there. Any disturbance, even if it could not possibly be blamed on Holiday, was blamed on him.

Lindsey wanted to look nice for Samuel. She opened the double doors to my closet and reviewed the mess. I hadn't been exactly orderly, so every time my mother told us to clean up, I'd shoved whatever was on the floor or bed into my closet.

Lindsey had always wanted the clothes I owned first-run but had gotten them all as hand-me-downs.

"Gosh," she said, whispering into the darkness of my closet. She realized with guilt and glee that everything she saw before her was hers now.

"Hello? Knock-knock," said Grandma Lynn.

Lindsey jumped.

"Sorry to disturb you, hon," she said. "I thought I heard you in here."

My grandmother stood in what my mother called one of her Jackie Kennedy dresses. She had never understood why unlike the rest of us her mother had no hips—she could slide into a straight-cut dress and fill it out just enough, even at sixty-two, to look perfect in it.

"What are you doing in here?" Lindsey asked.

"I need help with this zipper." Grandma Lynn turned, and Lindsey could see what she had never seen on our own mother. The back of Grandma Lynn's black bra, the top of her half-slip. She walked the step or two over to our grandmother and, trying not to touch anything but the zipper tab, zipped her up.

"How about that hook and eye up there," said Grandma Lynn. "Can you get that?"

There were powdery smells and Chanel No. 5 sprinkled all around our grandmother's neck.

"It's one of the reasons for a man—you can't do this stuff yourself."

Lindsey was as tall as our grandmother and still growing. As she took the hook and eye in either hand, she saw the fine wisps of dyed blond hair at the base of my grandmother's skull. She saw the downy gray hair trailing along her back and neck. She hooked the dress and then stood there.

"I've forgotten what she looked like," Lindsey said.

"What?" Grandma Lynn turned.

"I can't remember," Lindsey said. "I mean her neck, you know, did I ever look at it?"

"Oh honey," Grandma Lynn said, "come here." She opened up her arms, but Lindsey turned into the closet.

"I need to look pretty," she said.

"You are pretty," Grandma Lynn said.

Lindsey couldn't get her breath. One thing Grandma Lynn never did was dole out compliments. When they came, they were unexpected gold.

"We'll find you a nice outfit in here," Grandma Lynn said and strode toward my clothes. No one could shop a rack like Grandma Lynn. On the rare occasions that she visited near the start of the school year she would take the two of us out. We marveled at her as we watched her nimble fingers play the hangers like so many keys. Suddenly, hesitating only for a moment, she would pull out a dress or shirt and hold it up to us. "What do you think?" she'd ask. It was always perfect.

As she considered my separates, plucked and posed them against my sister's torso, she talked:

"Your mother's a wreck, Lindsey. I've never seen her like this before."

"Grandma."

"Hush, I'm thinking." She held up my favorite church dress. It was blackwatch wool with a Peter Pan collar. I liked it mostly because the skirt was so big I could sit in the pew cross-legged and flounce the hem down to the ground. "Where did she get *this* sack?" my grandmother asked. "Your dad, he's a mess too, but he's mad about it."

"Who was that man you asked Mom about?"

She stiffened on the question. "What man?"

"You asked Mom if Dad still was saying that *that* man did it. What man?"

"Voilà!" Grandma Lynn held up a dark blue minidress that my sister had never seen. It was Clarissa's.

"It's so short," Lindsey said.

"I'm shocked at your mother," Grandma Lynn said. "She let the kid get something stylish!"

My father called up from the hallway that he expected everyone downstairs in ten minutes.

Grandma Lynn went into preparation overdrive. She helped Lindsey get the dark blue dress over her head, and then they ran back to Lindsey's room for shoes, and then, finally, in the hallway, under the overhead light, she fixed the smudged eyeliner and mascara on my sister's face. She finished her off with firmly pressed powder, whisking the cotton pad lightly in an upward direction along either side of Lindsey's face. It wasn't until my grandmother came downstairs and my mother commented on the shortness of Lindsey's dress while looking suspiciously at Grandma Lynn that my sister and I realized Grandma Lynn didn't have a spot of makeup on her own face. Buckley rode between them in the back seat, and as they neared the church he looked at Grandma Lynn and asked what she was doing.

"When you don't have time for rouge, this puts a little life into them," she said, and so Buckley copied her and pinched his cheeks.

* * *

Samuel Heckler was standing by the stone posts that marked the path to the church door. He was dressed all in black, and beside him his older brother, Hal, stood wearing the beat-up leather jacket Samuel had worn on Christmas Day.

His brother was like a darker print of Samuel. He was tanned, and his face was weathered from riding his motorcycle full-tilt down country roads. As my family approached, Hal turned quickly and walked away.

"This must be Samuel," my grandmother said. "I'm the evil grandma."

"Shall we go in?" my father said. "It's nice to see you, Samuel."

Lindsey and Samuel led the way, while my grandmother dropped back and walked on the other side of my mother. A united front.

Detective Fenerman was standing by the doorway in an itchy-looking suit. He nodded at my parents and seemed to linger on my mother. "Will you join us?" my father asked.

"Thank you," he said, "but I just want to be in the vicinity."

"We appreciate that."

They walked into the cramped vestibule of our church. I wanted to snake up my father's back, circle his neck, whisper in his ear. But I was already there in his every pore and crevice.

He had woken up with a hangover and turned over on his side to watch my mother's shallow breathing against the pillow. His lovely wife, his lovely girl. He wanted to place his hand on her cheek, smooth her hair back from her face, kiss her—but sleeping, she was at peace. He hadn't woken a day since my death when the day wasn't something to get through. But the truth was, the memorial service day was not the worst kind. At least it was honest. At least it was a day shaped around what they were so preoccupied by: my absence. Today he would not have to pretend he was getting back to normal—whatever normal was. Today he could walk tall with grief and so could Abigail. But he knew that as soon as she woke up he would not really look at her for the rest of the day, not really look into her and see the woman he had known her to be before the day they had taken in the news of my death. At nearly two months, the idea of it as news was fading away in the hearts of all but my family—and Ruth.

She came with her father. They were standing in the corner near the glass case that held a chalice used during the Revolutionary War, when the church had been a hospital. Mr. and Mrs. Dewitt were making small talk with them. At home on her desk, Mrs. Dewitt had a poem of Ruth's. On Monday she was going to the guidance counselor with it. It was a poem about me.

"My wife seems to agree with Principal Caden," Ruth's father was saying, "that the memorial will help allow the kids to accept it."

"What do you think?" Mr. Dewitt asked.

"I think let bygones be bygones and leave the family to their own. But Ruthie wanted to come."

Ruth watched my family greet people and noted in horror my sister's new look. Ruth did not believe in makeup. She thought it demeaned women. Samuel Heckler was holding Lindsey's hand. A word from her readings popped into her head: *subjugation.* But then I saw her notice Hal Heckler through the window. He was standing out by the oldest graves in the front and pulling on a cigarette butt.

"Ruthie," her father asked, "what is it?"

She focused again and looked at him. "What's what?"

"You were staring off into space just now," he said.

"I like the way the graveyard looks."

"Ah kid, you're my angel," he said. "Let's grab a seat before the good ones get taken."

Clarissa was there, with a sheepish-looking Brian Nelson, who was wearing a suit of his father's. She made her way up to my family, and when Principal Caden and Mr. Botte saw her they fell away and let her approach.

She shook hands with my father first.

"Hello, Clarissa," he said. "How are you?"

"Okay," she said. "How are you and Mrs. Salmon?"

"We're fine, Clarissa," he said. *What an odd lie,* I thought. "Would you like to join us in the family pew?"

"Um"—she looked down at her hands—"I'm with my boyfriend."

My mother had entered some trancelike state and was staring hard at Clarissa's face. Clarissa was alive and I was dead. Clarissa began to feel it, the eyes boring into her, and she wanted to get away. Then Clarissa saw the dress.

"Hey," she said, reaching out toward my sister.

"What is it, Clarissa?" my mother snapped.

"Um, nothing," she said. She looked at the dress again, knew she could never ask for it back now.

"Abigail?" my father said. He was attuned to her voice, her anger. Something was off.

Grandma Lynn, who stood just a bit behind my mother, winked at Clarissa.

"I was just noticing how good Lindsey looked," Clarissa said.

My sister blushed.

The people in the vestibule began to stir and part. It was the Reverend Strick, walking in his vestments toward my parents.

Clarissa faded back to look for Brian Nelson. When she found him, she joined him out among the graves.

Ray Singh stayed away. He said goodbye to me in his own way: by looking at a picture—my studio portrait—that I had given him that fall.

He looked into the eyes of that photograph and saw right through them to the backdrop of marbleized suede every kid had to sit in front of under a hot light. What did dead mean, Ray wondered. It meant lost, it meant frozen, it meant gone. He knew that no one ever really looked the way they did in photos. He knew he didn't look as wild or as frightened as he did in his own. He came to realize something as he stared at my photo—that it was not me. I was in the air around him, I was in the cold mornings he had now with Ruth, I was in the quiet time he spent alone between studying. I was the girl he had chosen to kiss. He wanted, somehow, to set me free. He didn't want to burn my photo or toss it away, but he didn't want to look at me anymore, either. I watched him as he placed the photograph in one of the giant volumes of Indian poetry in which he and his mother had pressed dozens of fragile flowers that were slowly turning to dust.

At the service they said nice things about me. Reverend Strick. Principal Caden. Mrs. Dewitt. But my father and mother sat through it numbed. Samuel kept squeezing Lindsey's hand, but she didn't seem to notice him. She barely blinked. Buckley sat in a small suit borrowed for the occasion from Nate, who had attended a wedding that year. He fidgeted and watched my father. It was Grandma Lynn who did the most important thing that day.

During the final hymn, as my family stood, she leaned over to Lindsey and whispered, "By the door, that's him."

Lindsey looked over.

Standing just behind Len Fenerman, who was now inside the doorway and singing along, stood a man from the neighborhood. He was dressed more casually than anyone else, wearing flannel-lined khaki trousers and a heavy flannel shirt. For a moment Lindsey thought she recognized him. Their eyes locked. Then she passed out.

In all the commotion of attending to her, George Harvey slipped between the Revolutionary War gravestones behind the church and walked away without being noticed.

TEN

At the statewide Gifted Symposium each summer, the gifted kids from seventh to ninth grade would get together for a four-week retreat to, as I always thought of it, hang out in the trees and pick one another's brains. Around the campfire they sang oratorios instead of folk songs. In the girls' showers they would swoon over the physique of Jacques d'Amboise or the frontal lobe of John Kenneth Galbraith.

But even the gifted had their cliques. There were the Science Nerds and the Math Brains. They formed the superior, if somewhat socially crippled, highest rung of the gifted ladder. Then came the History Heads, who knew the birth and death dates of every historical figure anyone had ever heard of. They would pass by the other campers voicing cryptic, seemingly meaningless life spans: "1769 to 1821," "1770 to 1831." When Lindsey passed the History Heads she would think the answers to herself. "Napoleon." "Hegel."

There were also the Masters of Arcane Knowledge. Everyone begrudged their presence among the gifteds. These were the kids that could break down an engine and build it back again—no diagrams or instructions needed. They understood things in a real, not theoretical, way. They seemed not to care about their grades.

Samuel was a Master. His heroes were Richard Feynman and his brother, Hal. Hal had dropped out of high school and now ran the bike shop near the sinkhole, where he serviced everyone from Hell's Angels to the elderly who rode motorized scooters around the parking lots of their retirement homes. Hal smoked, lived at home over the Hecklers' garage, and conducted a variety of romances in the back of his shop.

When people asked Hal when he was going to grow up, he said, "Never." Inspired by this, when the teachers asked Samuel what he wanted to be, he would say: "I don't know. I just turned fourteen."

Almost fifteen now, Ruth Connors knew. Out in the aluminum toolshed behind her house, surrounded by the doorknobs and hardware her father had found in old houses slated for demolition, Ruth sat in the darkness and concentrated until she came away with a headache. She would run into the house, past the living room, where her father sat reading, and up to her room, where in fits and bursts she would write her poetry. "Being Susie," "After Death," "In Pieces," "Beside Her Now," and her favorite—the one she was most proud of and carried with her to the symposium folded and refolded so often that the creases were close to cuts—"The Lip of the Grave."

Ruth had to be driven to the symposium because that morning, when the bus was leaving, she was still at home with an acute attack of gastritis. She was trying weird all-vegetable regimes and the night before had eaten a whole head of cabbage for dinner. Her mother refused to kowtow to the vegetarianism Ruth had taken up after my death.

"This is not Susie, for Chrissakes!" her mother would say, plunking down an inch-thick sirloin in front of her daughter.

Her father drove her first to the hospital at three A.M. and then to the symposium, stopping home on the way to pick up the bag her mother had packed and left at the end of their driveway.

As the car pulled up into the camp, Ruth scanned the crowd of kids lining up for nametags. She spotted my sister among an all-male group of Masters. Lindsey had avoided putting her last name on her nametag, choosing to draw a fish instead. She wasn't exactly lying that way, but she hoped to meet a few kids from the surrounding schools who didn't know the story of my death or at least wouldn't connect her to it.

All spring she'd worn the half-a-heart pendant while Samuel wore the other half. They were shy about their affection for each other. They did not hold hands in the hallways at school, and they did not pass notes. They sat together at lunch; Samuel walked her home. On her fourteenth birthday he brought her a cupcake with a candle in it. Other than that, they melted into the gender-subdivided world of their peers.

The following morning Ruth was up early. Like Lindsey, Ruth was a floater at gifted camp. She didn't belong to any one group. She had gone on a nature walk and collected plants and flowers she needed help naming. When she didn't like the answers one of the Science Nerds provided, she decided to start naming the plants and flowers herself. She drew a picture of the leaf or blossom in her journal, and then what sex she thought it was, and then gave it a name like "Jim" for a simple-leaved plant and "Pasha" for a more downy flower.

By the time Lindsey stumbled in to the dining hall, Ruth was in line for a second helping of eggs and sausage. She had made a big stink about no meat at home and she had to hold to it, but no one at the symposium knew of the oath she'd sworn.

Ruth hadn't talked to my sister since before my death, and then it was only to excuse herself in the hallway at school. But she'd seen Lindsey walking home with Samuel and seen her smile with him. She watched as my sister said yes to pancakes and no to everything else. She had tried to imagine herself being my sister as she had spent time imagining being me.

As Lindsey walked blindly to the next open spot in line, Ruth interceded. "What's the fish for?" Ruth asked, nodding her head toward my sister's nametag. "Are you religious?"

"Notice the direction of the fish," Lindsey said, wishing simultaneously that they had vanilla puddings at breakfast. They would go great with her pancakes.

"Ruth Connors, poet," Ruth said, by way of introduction.

"Lindsey," Lindsey said.

"Salmon, right?"

"Please don't," Lindsey said, and for a second Ruth could feel the feeling a little more vividly—what it was like to claim me. How people looked at Lindsey and imagined a girl covered in blood.

Even among the gifteds, who distinguished themselves by doing things differently, people paired off within the first few days. It was mostly pairs of boys or pairs of girls—few serious relationships had begun by fourteen—but there was one exception that year. Lindsey and Samuel.

"K-I-S-S-I-N-G!" greeted them wherever they went. Unchaperoned, and with the heat of the summer, something grew in them like weeds. It was lust. I'd never felt it so purely or seen it move so hotly into someone I knew. Someone whose gene pool I shared.

They were careful and followed the rules. No counselor could say he had flashed a light under the denser shrubbery by the boys' dorm and found Salmon and Heckler going at it. They set up little meetings outside in back of the cafeteria or by a certain tree that they'd marked up high with their initials. They kissed. They wanted to do more but couldn't. Samuel wanted it to be special. He was aware that it should be perfect. Lindsey just wanted to get it over with. Have it behind her so she could achieve adulthood—transcend the place and the time. She thought of sex as the *Star Trek* transport. You vaporized and found yourself navigating another planet within the second or two it took to realign.

"They're going to do it," Ruth wrote in her journal. I had pinned hopes on Ruth's writing everything down. She told her journal about me passing by her in the parking lot, about how on that night I had touched her—literally, she felt, reached out. What I had looked like then. How she dreamed about me. How she had fashioned the idea that a spirit could be a sort of second skin for someone, a protective layer somehow. How maybe if she was assiduous she could free us both. I would read over her shoulder as she wrote down her thoughts and wonder if anyone might believe her one day.

When she was imagining me, she felt better, less alone, more connected to something out there. To someone out there. She saw the cornfield in her dreams, and a new world opening, a world where maybe she could find a foothold too.

"You're a really good poet, Ruth," she imagined me saying, and her journal would release her into a daydream of being such a good poet that her words had the power to resurrect me.

I could see back to an afternoon when Ruth watched her teenage cousin undress to take a bath while Ruth sat on the bathroom rug, locked in the bathroom so her cousin could babysit her as she'd been told. Ruth had longed to touch her cousin's skin and hair, longed to be held. I wondered if this longing in a three-year-old had sparked what came at eight. That fuzzy feeling of difference, that her crushes on female teachers or her cousin were more real than the other girls' crushes. Hers contained a desire beyond sweetness and attention, it fed a longing, beginning to flower green and yellow into a crocuslike lust, the soft petals opening into her awkward adolescence. It was not so much, she would write in her journal, that she wanted to have sex with women, but that she wanted to disappear inside of them forever. To hide.

The last week of the symposium was always spent developing a final project, which the various schools would present in competition on the night before the parents returned to pick the students up. The competition wasn't announced until the Saturday breakfast of that final week, but the kids had already begun planning for it anyway. It was always a better-mousetrap competition, and so the stakes were raised year after year. No one wanted to repeat a mousetrap that had already been built.

Samuel went in search of the kids with braces. He needed the tiny rubber bands orthodontists doled out. They would work to keep the tension tight on the guiding arm of his mousetrap. Lindsey begged clean tinfoil from the retired army cook. Their trap involved reflecting light in order to confuse the mice.

"What happens if they like the way they look?" Lindsey asked Samuel.

"They can't see that clearly," Samuel said. He was stripping the paper off the wire twists from the camp garbage bag supply. If a kid looked strangely at ordinary objects around the camp, he or she was most likely thinking of how it would serve the ultimate mousetrap.

"They're pretty cute," Lindsey said one afternoon.

Lindsey had spent the better part of the night before gathering field mice with string lures and putting them under the wire mesh of an empty rabbit hutch.

Samuel watched them intently. "I could be a vet, I guess," he said, "but I don't think I'd like cutting them open."

"Do we have to kill them?" Lindsey asked. "It's a better mouse*trap,* not a better mouse death camp."

"Artie's contributing little coffins made out of balsa wood," Samuel said, laughing.

"That's sick."

"That's Artie."

"He supposedly had a crush on Susie," Lindsey said.

"I know."

"Does he talk about her?" Lindsey took a long thin stick and poked it through the mesh.

"He's asked about you, actually," Samuel said.

"What did you tell him?"

"That you're okay, that you'll be okay."

The mice kept running from the stick into the corner, where they crawled on top of one another in a useless effort to flee. "Let's build a mousetrap with a little purple velvet couch in it and we can rig up a latch so that when they sit on the couch, a door drops and little balls of cheese fall down. We can call it Wild Rodent Kingdom."

Samuel didn't press my sister like the adults did. He would talk in detail about mouse couch upholstery instead.

By that summer I had begun to spend less time watching from the gazebo because I could still see Earth as I walked the fields of heaven. The night would come and the javelin-throwers and shot-putters would leave for other heavens. Heavens where a girl like me didn't fit in. Were they horrific, these other heavens? Worse than feeling so solitary among one's living, growing peers? Or were they the stuff I dreamed about? Where you could be caught in a Norman Rockwell world forever. Turkey constantly being brought to a table full of family. A wry and twinkling relative carving up the bird.

If I walked too far and wondered loud enough the fields would change. I could look down and see horse corn and I could hear it then—singing—a kind of low humming and moaning warning me back from the edge. My head would throb and the sky would darken and it would be that night again, that perpetual yesterday lived again. My soul solidifying, growing heavy. I came up to the lip of my grave this way many times but had yet to stare in.

I did begin to wonder what the word *heaven* meant. I thought, if this were heaven, truly heaven, it would be where my grandparents lived. Where my father's father, my favorite of them all, would lift me up and dance with me. I would feel only joy and have no memory, no cornfield and no grave.

"You can have that," Franny said to me. "Plenty of people do."

"How do you make the switch?" I asked.

"It's not as easy as you might think," she said. "You have to stop desiring certain answers."

"I don't get it."

"If you stop asking why you were killed instead of someone else, stop investigating the vacuum left by your loss, stop wondering what everyone left on Earth is feeling," she said, "you can be free. Simply put, you have to give up on Earth."

This seemed impossible to me.

Ruth crept into Lindsey's dorm that night.

"I had a dream about her," she whispered to my sister.

Lindsey blinked sleepily at her. "Susie?" she asked.

"I'm sorry about the incident in the dining hall," Ruth said.

Lindsey was on the bottom of a three-tiered aluminum bunk bed. Her neighbor directly above her stirred.

"Can I get into bed with you?" Ruth asked.

Lindsey nodded.

Ruth crawled in next to Lindsey in the narrow sliver of the bed.

"What happened in your dream?" Lindsey whispered.

Ruth told her, turning her face so that Lindsey's eyes could make out the silhouette of Ruth's nose and lips and forehead. "I was inside the earth," Ruth said, "and Susie walked over me in the cornfield. I could feel her walking over me. I called out to her but my mouth filled with dirt. She couldn't hear me no matter how much I tried to yell. Then I woke up."

"I don't dream about her," Lindsey said. "I have nightmares about rats nibbling at the ends of my hair."

Ruth liked the comfort she felt next to my sister—the heat their bodies created.

"Are you in love with Samuel?"

"Yes."

"Do you miss Susie?"

Because it was dark, because Ruth was facing away from her, because Ruth was almost a stranger, Lindsey said what she felt. "More than anyone will ever know."

The principal of Devon Junior High was called away on a family matter, and it was left up to the newly appointed assistant principal of Chester Springs School to create, overnight, that year's challenge. She wanted to do something different from mousetraps.

CAN YOU GET AWAY WITH CRIME? HOW TO COMMIT THE PERFECT MURDER, announced her hurriedly drawn-up flier.

The kids loved it. The musicians and poets, the History Heads and artists, were teeming and bubbling about how to begin. They shoveled down their bacon and eggs at breakfast and compared the great unsolved murders of the past or thought of ordinary objects that could be used for fatal wounds. They began to think of whom they could plot to kill. It was all in good fun until 7:15, when my sister walked in.

Artie watched her get in line. She was still unaware, just picking up on the excitement in the air—figuring the mousetrap competition had been announced.

He kept his eye on Lindsey and saw the closest flier was posted at the end of the food line over the utensils tray. He was listening to a story about Jack the Ripper that someone at the table was relaying. He stood to return his tray.

When he reached my sister, he cleared his throat. All my hopes were pinned on this wobbly boy. "Catch her," I said. A prayer going down to Earth.

"Lindsey," Artie said.

Lindsey looked at him. "Yes?"

Behind the counter the army cook held out a spoon full of scrambled eggs to plop on her tray.

"I'm Artie, from your sister's grade."

"I don't need any coffins," Lindsey said, moving her tray down the metalwork to where there was orange juice and apple juice in big plastic pitchers.

"What?"

"Samuel told me you were building balsa wood coffins for the mice this year. I don't want any."

"They changed the competition," he said.

That morning Lindsey had decided she would take the bottom off of Clarissa's dress. It would be perfect for the mouse couch.

"To what?"

"Do you want to go outside?" Artie used his body to shadow her and block her passage to the utensils. "Lindsey," he blurted. "The competition is about murder."

She stared at him.

Lindsey held on to her tray. She kept her eyes locked on Artie.

"I wanted to tell you before you read the flier," he said.

Samuel rushed into the tent.

"What's going on?" Lindsey looked helplessly at Samuel.

"This year's competition is how to commit the perfect murder," Samuel said.

Samuel and I saw the tremor. The inside shakeoff of her heart. She was getting so good the cracks and fissures were smaller and smaller. Soon, like a sleight-of-hand trick perfected, no one would see her do it. She could shut out the whole world, including herself.

"I'm fine," she said.

But Samuel knew she wasn't.

He and Artie watched her back as she departed.

"I was trying to warn her," Artie said weakly.

Artie returned to his table. He drew hypodermics, one after another. His pen pressed harder and harder as he colored in the embalming fluid inside, as he perfected the trajectory of the three drops squirting out.

Lonely, I thought, *on Earth as it is in heaven.*

"You kill people by stabbing and cutting and shooting," Ruth said. "It's sick."

"Agreed," Artie said.

Samuel had taken my sister away to talk. Artie had seen Ruth at one of the outside picnic tables with her big blank book.

"But there are good reasons to kill," Ruth said.

"Who do you think did it?" Artie asked. He sat on the bench and braced his feet up under the table on the crossbar.

Ruth sat almost motionless, right leg crossed over left, but her foot jiggled ceaselessly.

"How did you hear?" she asked.

"My father told us," Artie said. "He called my sister and me into the family room and made us sit down."

"Shit, what did he say?"

"First he said that horrible things happened in the world and my sister said, 'Vietnam,' and he was quiet because they always fight about that whenever it comes up. So he said, 'No, honey, horrible things happen close to home, to people we know.' She thought it was one of her friends."

Ruth felt a raindrop.

"Then my dad broke down and said a little girl had been killed. I was the one who asked who. I mean, when he said 'little girl,' I pictured *little,* you know. Not us."

It was a definite drop, and they began to land on the redwood tabletop.

"Do you want to go in?" Artie asked.

"Everyone else will be inside," Ruth said.

"I know."

"Let's get wet."

They sat still for a while and watched the drops fall around them, heard the sound against the leaves of the tree above.

"I knew she was dead. I sensed it," Ruth said, "but then I saw a mention of it in my dad's paper and I was sure. They didn't use her name at first. Just 'Girl, fourteen.' I asked my dad for the page but he wouldn't give it to me. I mean, who else and her sister hadn't been in school all week?"

"I wonder who told Lindsey?" Artie said. The rain picked up. Artie slipped underneath the table. "We're going to get soaked," he yelled up.

And then as quickly as the rain had started, it ceased. Sun came through the branches of the tree above her, and Ruth looked up past them. "I think she listens," she said, too softly to be heard.

It became common knowledge at the symposium who my sister was and how I had died.

"Imagine being stabbed," someone said.

"No thanks."

"I think it's cool."

"Think of it—she's famous."

"Some way to get famous. I'd rather win the Nobel Prize."

"Does anyone know what she wanted to be?"

"I dare you to ask Lindsey."

And they listed the dead they knew.

Grandmother, grandfather, uncle, aunt, some had a parent, rarer was a sister or brother lost young to an illness—a heart irregularity—leukemia—an unpronounceable disease. No one knew anyone who had been murdered. But now they knew me.

Under a rowboat that was too old and worn to float, Lindsey lay down on the earth with Samuel Heckler, and he held her.

"You know I'm okay," she said, her eyes dry. "I think Artie was trying to help me," she offered.

"You can stop now, Lindsey," he said. "We'll just lie here and wait until things quiet down."

Samuel's back was flush against the ground, and he brought my sister close into his body to protect her from the dampness of the quick summer rain. Their breath began to heat the small space beneath the boat, and he could not stop it—his penis stiffened inside his jeans.

Lindsey reached her hand over.

"I'm sorry . . ." he began.

"I'm ready," my sister said.

At fourteen, my sister sailed away from me into a place I'd never been. In the walls of my sex there was horror and blood, in the walls of hers there were windows.

"How to Commit the Perfect Murder" was an old game in heaven. I always chose the icicle: the weapon melts away.

ELEVEN

When my father woke up at four A.M., the house was quiet. My mother lay beside him, lightly snoring. My brother, the only child, what with my sister attending the symposium, was like a rock with a sheet pulled up over him. My father marveled at what a sound sleeper he was — just like me. While I was still alive, Lindsey and I had had fun with that, clapping, dropping books, and even banging pot lids to see if Buckley would wake up.

Before leaving the house, my father checked on Buckley — to make sure, to feel the warm breath against his palm. Then he suited up in his thin-soled sneakers and light jogging outfit. His last task was to put Holiday's collar on.

It was still early enough that he could almost see his breath. He could pretend at that early hour that it was still winter. That the seasons had not advanced.

The morning dog walk gave him an excuse to pass by Mr. Harvey's house. He slowed only slightly — no one would have noticed save me or, if he had been awake, Mr. Harvey. My father was sure that if he just stared hard enough, just looked long enough, he would find the clues he needed in the casements of the windows, in the green paint coating the shingles, or along the driveway, where two large stones sat, painted white.

By late summer 1974, there had been no movement on my case. No body. No killer. Nothing.

My father thought of Ruana Singh: "When I was sure, I would find a quiet way, and I would kill him." He had not told this to Abigail because the advice made a sort of baseline sense that would frighten her into telling someone, and he suspected that someone might be Len.

Ever since the day he'd seen Ruana Singh and then had come home to find Len waiting for him, he'd felt my mother leaning heavily on the police. If my father said something that contradicted the police theories—or, as he saw them, the lack of them—my mother would immediately rush to fill the hole left open by my father's idea. "Len says that doesn't mean anything," or, "I trust the police to find out what happened."

Why, my father wondered, did people trust the police so much? Why not trust instinct? It was Mr. Harvey and he knew it. But what Ruana had said was *when I was sure.* Knowing, the deep-soul knowing that my father had, was not, in the law's more literal mind, incontrovertible proof.

The house that I grew up in was the same house where I was born. Like Mr. Harvey's, it was a box, and because of this I nurtured useless envies whenever I visited other people's homes. I dreamed about bay windows and cupolas, balconies, and slanted attic ceilings in a bedroom. I loved the idea that there could be trees in a yard taller and stronger than people, slanted spaces under stairs, thick hedges grown so large that inside there were hollows of dead branches where you could crawl and sit. In my heaven there were verandas and circular staircases, window ledges with iron rails, and a campanile housing a bell that tolled the hour.

I knew the floor plan of Mr. Harvey's by heart. I had made a warm spot on the floor of the garage until I cooled. He had brought my blood into the house with him on his clothes and skin. I knew the bathroom. Knew how in my house my mother had tried to decorate it to accommodate Buckley's late arrival by stenciling battleships along the top of the pink walls. In Mr. Harvey's house the bathroom and kitchen were spotless. The porcelain was yellow and the tile on the floor was green. He kept it cold. Upstairs, where Buckley, Lindsey, and I had our rooms, he had almost nothing. He had a straight chair where he would go to sit sometimes and stare out the window over at the high school, listen for the sound of band practice wafting over from the field, but mostly he spent his hours in the back on the first floor, in the kitchen building dollhouses, in the living room listening to the radio or, as his lust set in, sketching blueprints for follies like the hole or the tent.

No one had bothered him about me for several months. By that summer he only occasionally saw a squad car slow in front of his house. He was smart enough not to alter his pattern. If he was walking out to the garage or the mailbox, he kept on going.

He set several clocks. One to tell him when to open the blinds, one when to close them. In conjunction with these alarms, he would turn lights on and off throughout the house. When an occasional child happened by to sell chocolate bars for a school competition or inquire if he would like to subscribe to the *Evening Bulletin,* he was friendly but businesslike, unremarkable.

He kept things to count, and this counting reassured him. They were simple things. A wedding ring, a letter sealed in an envelope, the heel of a shoe, a pair of glasses, an eraser in the shape of a cartoon character, a small bottle of perfume, a plastic bracelet, my Pennsylvania keystone charm, his mother's amber pendant. He would take them out at night long after he was certain that no newsboy or neighbor would knock on his door. He would count them like the beads on a rosary. For some he had forgotten the names. I knew the names. The heel of the shoe was from a girl named Claire, from Nutley, New Jersey, whom he had convinced to walk into the back of a van. She was littler than me. (I like to think I wouldn't have gone into a van. Like to think it was my curiosity about how he could make a hole in the earth that wouldn't collapse.) He had ripped the heel off her shoe before he let Claire go. That was all he did. He got her into the van and took her shoes off. She started crying, and the sound drove into him like screws. He pleaded with her to be quiet and just leave. Step magically out of the van barefoot and uncomplaining while he kept her shoes. But she wouldn't. She cried. He started working on one of the heels of the shoes, prying it loose with his penknife, until someone pounded on the back of the van. He heard men's voices and a woman yelling something about calling the police. He opened the door.

"What the hell are you doing to that kid?" one of the men yelled. This man's buddy caught the little girl as she flew, bawling, out of the back.

"I'm trying to repair her shoe."

The little girl was hysterical. Mr. Harvey was all reason and calm. But Claire had seen what I had—his look bearing down—his wanting something unspoken that to give him would equal our oblivion.

Hurriedly, as the men and woman stood confused, unable to see what Claire and I knew, Mr. Harvey handed the shoes to one of the men and said his goodbyes. He kept the heel. He liked to hold the small leather heel and rub it between his thumb and forefinger—a perfect worry stone.

* * *

I knew the darkest place in our house. I had climbed inside of it and stayed there for what I told Clarissa was a whole day but was really about forty-five minutes. It was the crawlspace in the basement. Inside ours there were pipes coming down that I could see with a flashlight and tons and tons of dust. That was it. There were no bugs. My mother, like her own, employed an exterminator for the slightest infestation of ants.

When the alarm had gone off to tell him to shut the blinds and then the next alarm, which told him to shut off most of the lights because the suburbs were asleep after that, Mr. Harvey would go down into the basement, where there were no cracks that light could peek through and people could point to, to say he was strange. By the time he killed me he had tired of visiting the crawlspace, but he still liked to hang out in the basement in an easy chair that faced the dark hole beginning halfway up the wall and reaching to the exposed baseboards of his kitchen floor. He would often drift off to sleep there, and there he was asleep when my father passed the green house at around 4:40 A.M.

Joe Ellis was an ugly little tough. He had pinched Lindsey and me under water in the pool and kept us from going to swim parties because we hated him so much. He had a dog that he dragged around no matter what the dog wanted. It was a small dog and couldn't run very fast, but Ellis didn't care. He would hit it or lift it painfully by the tail. Then one day it was gone, and so was a cat that Ellis had been seen taunting. And then animals from all over the neighborhood began disappearing.

What I discovered, when I followed Mr. Harvey's stare to the crawlspace, were these animals that had gone missing for more than a year. People thought it stopped because the Ellis boy had been sent to military school. When they let their pets loose in the morning, they returned in the evening. This they held as proof. No one could imagine an appetite like the one in the green house. Someone who would spread quicklime on the bodies of cats and dogs, the sooner for him to have nothing left but their bones. By counting the bones and staying away from the sealed letter, the wedding ring, the bottle of perfume, he tried to stay away from what he wanted most—from going upstairs in the dark to sit in the straight chair and look out toward the high school, from imagining the bodies that matched the cheerleaders' voices, which pulsated in waves on fall days during football games, or from watching the buses from the grammar school unload two houses down. Once he had taken a long look at Lindsey, the lone girl on the boys' soccer team out running laps in our neighborhood near dark.

What I think was hardest for me to realize was that he had tried each time to stop himself. He had killed animals, taking lesser lives to keep from killing a child.

By August, Len wanted to establish some boundaries for his sake and for my father's. My father had called the precinct too many times and frustrated the police into irritation, which wouldn't help anyone be found and just might make the whole place turn against him.

The final straw had been a call that came in the first week of July. Jack Salmon had detailed to the operator how, on a morning walk, his dog had stopped in front of Mr. Harvey's house and started howling. No matter what Salmon had done, went the story, the dog wouldn't budge from the spot and wouldn't stop howling. It became a joke at the station: Mr. Fish and his Huckleberry Hound.

Len stood on the stoop of our house to finish his cigarette. It was still early, but the humidity from the day before had intensified. All week rain had been promised, the kind of thunder and lightning rainstorm the area excelled at, but so far the only moisture of which Len was aware was that covering his body in a damp sweat. He had made his last easy visit to my parents' house.

Now he heard humming—a female voice from inside. He stubbed out his cigarette against the cement under the hedge and lifted the heavy brass knocker. The door opened before he let go.

"I smelled your cigarette," Lindsey said.

"Was that you humming?"

"Those things will kill you."

"Is your father home?"

Lindsey stood aside to let him in.

"Dad!" my sister yelled into the house. "It's Len!"

"You were away, weren't you?" Len asked.

"I just got back."

My sister was wearing Samuel's softball shirt and a pair of strange sweatpants. My mother had accused her of returning home without one single item of her own clothing.

"I'm sure your parents missed you."

"Don't bet on it," Lindsey said. "I think they were happy to have me out of their hair."

Len knew she was right. He was certainly sure my mother had seemed less frantic when he had visited the house.

Lindsey said, "Buckley's made you the head of the police squad in the town he built under his bed."

"That's a promotion."

The two of them heard my father's footsteps in the hallway above and then the sounds of Buckley begging. Lindsey could tell that whatever he'd asked for our father had finally granted.

My father and brother descended the stairs, all smiles.

"Len," he said, and he shook Len's hand.

"Good morning, Jack," Len said. "And how are you this morning, Buckley?"

My father took Buckley's hand and stood him in front of Len, who solemnly bent down to my brother.

"I hear you've made me chief of police," Len said.

"Yes sir."

"I don't think I deserve the job."

"You more than anyone," my father said breezily. He loved it when Len Fenerman dropped by. Each time he did, it verified for my father that there was a consensus—a group behind him—that he wasn't alone in all this.

"I need to talk to your father, kids."

Lindsey took Buckley back into the kitchen with the promise of cereal. She herself was thinking of what Samuel had shown her; it was a drink called a jellyfish, which involved a maraschino cherry at the bottom of some sugar and gin. Samuel and Lindsey had sucked the cherries up through the sugar and booze until their heads hurt and their lips were stained red.

"Should I get Abigail? Can I make you some coffee or something?"

"Jack," Len said, "I'm not here with any news—just the opposite. Can we sit?"

I watched my father and Len head into the living room. The living room seemed to be where no living ever actually occurred. Len sat on the edge of a chair and waited for my father to take a seat.

"Listen, Jack," he said. "It's about George Harvey."

My father brightened. "I thought you said you had no news."

"I don't. I have something I need to say on behalf of the station and myself."

"Yes."

"We need you to stop making calls about George Harvey."

"But . . ."

"*I* need you to stop. There is nothing, no matter how much we stretch it, to connect him to Susie's death. Howling dogs and bridal tents are not evidence."

"I know he did it," my father said.

"He's odd, I agree, but as far as we know he isn't a killer."

"How could you possibly know that?"

Len Fenerman talked, but all my father could hear was Ruana Singh saying what she had to him, and of standing outside Mr. Harvey's house and feeling the energy radiating out to him, the coldness at the core of the man. Mr. Harvey was at once unknowable and the only person in the world who could have killed me. As Len denied it, my father grew more certain.

"You are stopping your investigation of him," my father said flatly.

Lindsey was in the doorway, hovering as she'd done on the day Len and the uniformed officer had brought my hat with the jingle bell, the twin of which she owned. That day she had quietly shoved this second hat into a box of old dolls in the back of her closet. She never wanted my mother to hear the sound of those beadlike bells again.

There was our father, the heart we knew held all of us. Held us heavily and desperately, the doors of his heart opening and closing with the rapidity of stops on an instrument, the quiet felt closures, the ghostly fingering, practice and practice and then, incredibly, sound and melody and warmth. Lindsey stepped forward from her place by the door.

"Hello again, Lindsey," Len said.

"Detective Fenerman."

"I was just telling your father . . ."

"That you're giving up."

"If there was any good reason to suspect the man . . ."

"Are you done?" Lindsey asked. She was suddenly the wife to our father, as well as the oldest, most responsible child.

"I just want you all to know that we've investigated every lead."

My father and Lindsey heard her, and I saw her. My mother coming down the stairs. Buckley raced out of the kitchen and charged, propelling his full weight into my father's legs.

"Len," my mother said, pulling her terry-cloth robe tighter when she saw him, "has Jack offered you coffee?"

My father looked at his wife and Len Fenerman.

"The cops are punting," Lindsey said, taking Buckley gently by the shoulders and holding him against her.

"Punting?" Buckley asked. He always rolled a sound around in his mouth like a sourball until he had its taste and feel.

"What?"

"Detective Fenerman is here to tell Dad to stop bugging them."

"Lindsey," Len said, "I wouldn't put it like that."

"Whatever," she said. My sister wanted out, now, into a place where gifted camp continued, where Samuel and she, or even Artie, who at the last minute had won the Perfect Murder competition by entering the icicle-as-murder-weapon idea, ruled her world.

"Come on, Dad," she said. My father was slowly fitting something together. It had nothing to do with George Harvey, nothing to do with me. It was in my mother's eyes.

That night, as he had more and more often, my father stayed up by himself in his study. He could not believe the world falling down around him—how unexpected it all was after the initial blast of my death. "I feel like I'm standing in the wake of a volcano eruption," he wrote in his notebook. "Abigail thinks Len Fenerman is right about Harvey."

As he wrote, the candle in the window kept flickering, and despite his desk lamp the flickering distracted him. He sat back in the old wooden school chair he'd had since college and heard the reassuring squeak of the wood under him. At the firm he was failing to even register what was needed of him. Daily now he faced column after column of meaningless numbers he was supposed to make square with company claims. He was making mistakes with a frequency that was frightening, and he feared, more than he had in the first days following my disappearance, that he would not be able to support his two remaining children.

He stood up and stretched his arms overhead, trying to concentrate on the few exercises that our family doctor had suggested. I watched his body bend in uneasy and surprising ways I had never seen before. He could have been a dancer rather than a businessman. He could have danced on Broadway with Ruana Singh.

He snapped off the desk light, leaving only the candle.

In his low green easy chair he now felt the most comfortable. It was where I often saw him sleep. The room like a vault, the chair like a womb, and me standing guard over him. He stared at the candle in the window and thought about what to do; how he had tried to touch my mother and she had pulled away over to the edge of the bed. But how in the presence of the police she seemed to bloom.

He had grown used to the ghostly light behind the candle's flame, that quivering reflection in the window. He stared at the two of them — real flame and ghost — and began to work toward a doze, dozing in thought and strain and the events of the day.

As he was about to let go for the night, we both saw the same thing: another light. Outside.

It looked like a penlight from that distance. One white beam slowly moving out across the lawns and toward the junior high. My father watched it. It was after midnight now, and the moon was not full enough, as it often was, to see the outlines of the trees and houses. Mr. Stead, who rode his bike late at night with a flashing light on the front powered by his pedals, would never degrade the lawns of his neighbors that way. It was too late for Mr. Stead anyway.

My father leaned forward in the green chair in his study and watched the flashlight move in the direction of the fallow cornfield.

"Bastard," he whispered. "You murderous bastard."

He dressed quickly from the storage closet in his study, putting on a hunting jacket that he hadn't had on since an ill-fated hunting trip ten years earlier. Downstairs he went into the front hall closet and found the baseball bat he'd bought for Lindsey before she favored soccer.

First he shut off the porch light they kept on all night for me and that, even though it had been eight months since the police said I would not be found alive, they could not bring themselves to stop leaving on. With his hand on the doorknob, he took a deep breath.

He turned the knob and found himself out on the dark front porch. Closed the door and found himself standing in his front yard with a baseball bat and these words: *find a quiet way.*

He walked through his front yard and across the street and then into the O'Dwyers' yard, where he had first seen the light. He passed their darkened swimming pool and the rusted-out swing set. His heart was pumping, but he could not feel anything but the knowledge in his brain. George Harvey had killed his last little girl.

He reached the soccer field. To his right, far into the cornfield but not in the vicinity he knew by heart—the area that had been roped off and cleared and combed and bulldozed—he saw the small light. He clenched his fingers tighter around the bat by his side. For just a second he could not believe what he was about to do, but then, with everything in him, he knew.

The wind helped him. It swept along the soccer field alongside the cornfield and whipped his trousers around the front of his legs; it pushed him forward despite himself. Everything fell away. Once he was among the rows of corn, his focus solely on the light, the wind disguised his presence. The sound of his feet crushing the stalks was swept up in the whistle and bustle of the wind against the broken plants.

Things that made no sense flooded his head—the hard rubber sound of children's roller skates on pavement, the smell of his father's pipe tobacco, Abigail's smile when he met her, like light piercing his confused heart—and then the flashlight shut off and everything went equal and dark.

He took a few more steps, then stopped.

"I know you're here," he said.

I flooded the cornfield, I flashed fires through it to light it up, I sent storms of hail and flowers, but none of it worked to warn him. I was relegated to heaven: I watched.

"I'm here for it," my father said, his voice trembling. That heart bursting in and out, blood gorging the rivers of his chest and then cinching up. Breath and fire and lungs seizing, releasing, adrenaline saving what was left. My mother's smile in his mind gone, mine taking its place.

"Nobody's awake," my father said. "I'm here to finish it."

He heard whimpering. I wanted to cast down a spotlight like they did in the school auditorium, awkwardly, the light not always hitting the right place on the stage. There she would be, crouching and whimpering and now, despite her blue eye shadow and Western-style boots from Bakers', wetting her pants. A child.

She didn't recognize my father's voice infused with hate. "Brian?" Clarissa's quavering voice came out. "Brian?" It was hope like a shield.

My father's hand loosened on the bat, letting it fall.

"Hello? Who's there?"

With wind in his ears, Brian Nelson, the beanstalk scarecrow, parked his older brother's Spyder Corvette in the school lot. Late, always late, sleeping in class and at the dinner table but never when a boy had a *Playboy* or a cute girl walked by, never on a night when he had a girl waiting for him out in the cornfield. Still, he took his time. The wind, glorious blanket and cover for what he had planned, whipped past his ears.

Brian moved toward the cornfield with his giant torch light from his mother's under-the-sink disaster kit. Finally he heard what he would later say were Clarissa's cries for help.

My father's heart was like a stone there, heavy, carried inside his chest as he ran and fumbled toward the sound of the girl's whimpering. His mother was knitting him mittens, Susie was asking for gloves, so cold in the cornfield in winter. Clarissa! Susie's silly friend. Makeup, prissy jam sandwiches, and her tropical tan skin.

He ran blind into her and knocked her down in the darkness. Her screaming filled his ear and poured into the empty spaces, ricocheting inside of him. "Susie!" he screamed back.

Brian ran when he heard my name—full-speed-ahead awake. His light hopped over the cornfield, and, for one bright second, there was Mr. Harvey. No one but me saw him. Brian's light hit his back as he crawled into the high stalks and listened, again, for the sound of whimpering.

And then the light hit target and Brian dragged my father up and off Clarissa to hit him. Hit him on the head and back and face with the survival-kit flashlight. My father shouted and yelped and moaned.

And then Brian saw the bat.

I pushed and pushed against the unyielding borders of my heaven. I wanted to reach out and lift my father up, away, to me.

Clarissa ran and Brian swung. My father's eyes caught Brian's but he could barely breathe.

"You fucker!" Brian was black and white with blame.

I heard mumblings in the dirt. I heard my name. I thought I could taste the blood on my father's face, reach out to draw my fingers across his cut lips, lie down with him in my grave.

But I had to turn my back in heaven. I could do nothing—

trapped in my perfect world. The blood I tasted was bitter. Acid. I wanted my father's vigil, his tight love for me. But also I wanted him to go away and leave me be. I was granted one weak grace. Back in the room where the green chair was still warm from his body, I blew that lonely, flickering candle out.

TWELVE

I stood in the room beside him and watched him sleep. During the night the story had come unwound and spun down so that the police understood: Mr. Salmon was crazy with grief and had gone out to the cornfield seeking revenge. It fit what they knew of him, his persistent phone calls, his obsession with the neighbor, and Detective Fenerman having visited that same day to tell my parents that for all intents and purposes my murder investigation had entered a sort of hiatus. No clues were left to pursue. No body had been found.

The surgeon had to operate on his knee to replace the cap with a purselike suture that partially disabled the joint. As I watched the operation I thought of how much like sewing it seemed, and I hoped that my father was in more capable hands than if he had been brought to me. In home ec my hands had been clumsy. Zipper foot or baster, I got them all confused.

But the surgeon had been patient. A nurse had filled him in on the story as he washed and scrubbed his hands. He remembered reading about what had happened to me in the papers. He was my father's age and had children of his own. He shivered as he stretched his gloves out over his hands. How alike he and this man were. How very different.

In the dark hospital room, a fluorescent bar light buzzed just behind my father's bed. As dawn approached it was the only light in the room until my sister walked in.

My mother and sister and brother woke to the sounds of the police sirens and came down into the dark kitchen from their bedrooms.

"Go wake your father," my mother said to Lindsey. "I can't believe he slept through this."

And so my sister had gone up. Everyone now knew where to look for him: in only six months, the green chair had become his true bed.

"Dad's not here!" my sister yelled as soon as she realized. "Dad's gone. Mom! Mom! Dad's gone!" For a rare moment Lindsey was a frightened child.

"Damn!" my mother said.

"Mommy?" Buckley said.

Lindsey rushed into the kitchen. My mother faced the stove. Her back was a riddled mass of nerves as she went about making tea.

"Mom?" Lindsey asked. "We have to do something."

"Don't you see . . . ?" my mother said, stopping for a moment with a box of Earl Grey suspended in the air.

"What?"

She put the tea down, switched on the burner, and turned around. She saw something herself then: Buckley had gone to cling to my sister as he anxiously sucked his thumb.

"He's gone off after that man and gotten himself in trouble."

"We should go out, Mom," Lindsey said. "We should go help him."

"No."

"Mom, we have to help Daddy."

"Buckley, stop milking your thumb!"

My brother burst into hot panicked tears, and my sister reached her arms down to pull him in tighter. She looked at our mother.

"I'm going out to find him," Lindsey said.

"You are doing no such thing," my mother said. "He'll come home in good time. We're staying out of this."

"Mom," Lindsey said, "what if he's hurt?"

Buckley stopped crying long enough to look back and forth from my sister to my mother. He knew what hurt meant and who was missing from the house.

My mother gave Lindsey a meaningful look. "We are not discussing this further. You can go up to your room and wait or wait with me. Your choice."

Lindsey was dumbfounded. She stared at our mother and knew what she wanted most: to flee, to run out into the cornfield where my father was, where I was, where she felt suddenly that the heart of her family had moved. But Buckley stood warm against her.

"Buckley," she said, "let's go back upstairs. You can sleep in my bed."

He was beginning to understand: you were treated special and, later, something horrible would be told to you.

When the call came from the police, my mother went immediately to the front closet. "He's been hit with our own baseball bat!" she said, grabbing her coat and keys and lipstick. My sister felt more alone than she had ever been but also more responsible. Buckley couldn't be left by himself, and Lindsey wasn't even able to drive. Besides, it made the clearest sense in the world. Didn't the wife belong most at the husband's side?

But when my sister was able to get Nate's mother on the line—after all, the commotion in the cornfield had awakened the whole neighborhood—she knew what she would do. She called Samuel next. Within an hour, Nate's mother arrived to take Buckley, and Hal Heckler pulled up to our house on his motorcycle. It should have been exciting—clutching on to Samuel's gorgeous older brother, riding on a motorcycle for the first time—but all she could think of was our father.

My mother was not in his hospital room when Lindsey entered; it was just my father and me. She came up and stood on the other side of his bed and started to cry quietly.

"Daddy?" she said. "Are you okay, Daddy?"

The door opened a crack. It was Hal Heckler, a tall handsome slash of a man.

"Lindsey," he said, "I'll wait for you out in the visitors' area in case you need a ride home."

He saw her tears when she turned around. "Thanks, Hal. If you see my mother . . ."

"I'll tell her you're in here."

Lindsey took my father's hand and watched his face for movement. My sister was growing up before my eyes. I listened as she whispered the words he had sung to the two of us before Buckley was born:

> Stones and bones;
> snow and frost;
> seeds and beans and polliwogs.
> Paths and twigs, assorted kisses,
> We all know who Daddy misses!

His two little frogs of girls, that's who.
They know where they are, do you, do you?

I wish a smile had come curling up onto my father's face, but he was deep under, swimming against drug and nightmare and waking dream. For a time leaden weights had been tied by anesthesia to the four corners of his consciousness. Like a firm waxen cover it had locked him away tight into the hard-blessed hours where there was no dead daughter and no gone knee, and where there was also no sweet daughter whispering rhymes.

"When the dead are done with the living," Franny said to me, "the living can go on to other things."

"What about the dead?" I asked. "Where do we go?"

She wouldn't answer me.

Len Fenerman had rushed to the hospital as soon as they put the call through. Abigail Salmon, the dispatcher said, requesting him.

My father was in surgery, and my mother was pacing back and forth near the nurses' station. She had driven to the hospital in her raincoat with only her thin summer nightgown beneath it. She had her beating-around-the-yard ballet flats on her feet. She hadn't bothered to pull her hair back, and there hadn't been any hair elastics in her pockets or purse. In the dark foggy parking lot of the hospital she had stopped to check her face and applied her stock red lipstick with a practiced hand.

When she saw Len approaching from the end of the long white corridor, she relaxed.

"Abigail," he said when he grew closer.

"Oh, Len," she said. Her face puzzled up on what she could say next. His name had been the sigh she needed. Everything that came next was not words.

The nurses at their station turned their heads away as Len and my mother touched hands. They extended this privacy veil habitually, as a matter of course, but even so they could see this man meant something to this woman.

"Let's talk in the visitors' area," Len said and led my mother down the corridor.

As they walked she told him my father was in surgery. He filled her in on what had happened in the cornfield.

"Apparently he said he thought the girl was George Harvey."

"He thought Clarissa was George Harvey?" My mother stopped, incredulous, just outside the visitors' area.

"It was dark out, Abigail. I think he only saw the girl's flashlight. My visit today couldn't have helped much. He's convinced that Harvey is involved."

"Is Clarissa all right?"

"She was treated for scratches and released. She was hysterical. Crying and screaming. It was a horrible coincidence, her being Susie's friend."

Hal was slumped down in a darkened corner of the visitors' area with his feet propped up on the helmet he'd brought for Lindsey. When he heard the voices approaching he stirred.

It was my mother and a cop. He slumped back down and let his shoulder-length hair obscure his face. He was pretty sure my mother wouldn't remember him.

But she recognized the jacket as Samuel's and for a moment thought, *Samuel's here,* but then thought, *His brother.*

"Let's sit," Len said, indicating the connected modular chairs on the far side of the room.

"I'd rather keep walking," my mother said. "The doctor said it will be an hour at least before they have anything to tell us."

"Where to?"

"Do you have cigarettes?"

"You know I do," Len said, smiling guiltily. He had to seek out her eyes. They weren't focusing on him. They seemed to be preoccupied, and he wished he could reach up and grab them and train them on the here and now. On him.

"Let's find an exit, then."

They found a door to a small concrete balcony near my father's room. It was a service balcony for a heating unit, so even though it was cramped and slightly chilly, the noise and the hot exhaust of the humming hydrant beside them shut them into a capsule that felt far away. They smoked cigarettes and looked at each other as if they had suddenly and without preparation moved on to a new page, where the pressing business had already been highlighted for prompt attention.

"How did your wife die?" my mother asked.

"Suicide."

Her hair was covering most of her face, and watching her I was reminded of Clarissa at her most self-conscious. The way she behaved around boys when we went to the mall. She would giggle too much and flash her eyes over at them to see where they were looking. But I was also struck by my mother's red mouth with the cigarette going up and away from it and smoke trailing out. I had seen this mother only once before—in the photograph. This mother had never had us.

"Why did she kill herself?"

"That's the question that preoccupies me most when I'm not preoccupied by things like your daughter's murder."

A strange smile came across my mother's face.

"Say that again," she said.

"What?" Len looked at her smile, wanted to reach out and trace the corners of it with his fingertips.

"My daughter's murder," my mother said.

"Abigail, are you okay?"

"No one says it. No one in the neighborhood talks about it. People call it the 'horrible tragedy' or some variation on that. I just want it to be spoken out loud by somebody. To have it said aloud. I'm ready—I wasn't ready before."

My mother dropped her cigarette onto the concrete and let it burn. She took Len's face in her hands.

"Say it," she said.

"Your daughter's murder."

"Thank you."

And I watched that flat red mouth move across an invisible line that separated her from the rest of the world. She pulled Len in to her and slowly kissed him on the mouth. He seemed to hesitate at first. His body tensed, telling him NO, but that NO became vague and cloudy, became air sucked into the intake fan of the humming hydrant beside them. She reached up and unbuttoned her raincoat. He placed his hand against the thin gauzy material of her summer gown.

My mother was, in her need, irresistible. As a child I had seen her effect on men. When we were in grocery stores, stockers volunteered to find the items on her list and would help us out to the car. Like Ruana Singh, she was known as one of the pretty mothers in the neighborhood; no man who met her could help but smile. When she asked a question, their beating hearts gave in.

But still, it had only ever been my father who stretched her laughter out into the rooms of the house and made it okay, somehow, for her to let go.

By tacking on extra hours here and there and skipping lunches, my father had managed to come home early from work every Thursday when we were little. But whereas the weekends were family time, they called that day "Mommy and Daddy time." Lindsey and I thought of it as good-girl time. It meant no peeps out of us as we stayed quiet on the other side of the house, while we used my father's then sparsely filled den as our playroom.

My mother would start preparing us around two.

"Bath time," she sang, as if she were saying we could go out to play. And in the beginning that was how it felt. All three of us would rush up to our rooms and put on bathrobes. We would meet in the hallway—three girls—and my mother would take us by the hands and lead us into our pink bathroom.

Back then she talked to us about mythology, which she had studied in school. She liked to tell us stories about Persephone and Zeus. She bought us illustrated books on the Norse gods, which gave us nightmares. She had gotten her master's in English—having fought tooth and nail with Grandma Lynn to go so far in school—and still held on to vague ideas of teaching when the two of us were old enough to be left on our own.

Those bath times blur together, as do all the gods and goddesses, but what I remember most is watching things hit my mother while I looked at her, how the life she had wanted and the loss of it reached her in waves. As her firstborn, I thought it was me who took away all those dreams of what she had wanted to be.

My mother would lift Lindsey out of the tub first, dry her, and listen to her chatter about ducks and cuts. Then she would get me out of the tub and though I tried to be quiet the warm water made my sister and me drunk, and we talked to my mother about everything that mattered to us. Boys that teased us or how another family down the block had a puppy and why couldn't we have one too. She would listen seriously as if she were mentally noting the points of our agenda on a steno pad to which she would later refer.

"Well, first things first," she summed up. "Which means a nice nap for the two of you!"

She and I would tuck Lindsey in together. I stood by the bed as she kissed my sister on her forehead and brushed back her hair from her face. I think competition started there for me. Who got the better kiss, the longer time after the bath with Mom.

Luckily, I always won this. When I look back now I see that my mother had become—and very quickly after they moved into that house—lonely. Because I was the oldest, I became her closest friend.

I was too little to know what she was really saying to me, but I loved to be hushed to sleep by the soft lullaby of her words. One of the blessings of my heaven is that I can go back to these moments, live them again, and be with my mother in a way I never could have been. I reach my hand across the Inbetween and take the hand of that young lonely mother in mine.

What she said to a four-year-old about Helen of Troy: "A feisty woman who screwed things up." About Margaret Sanger: "She was judged by her looks, Susie. Because she looked like a mouse, no one expected her to last." Gloria Steinem: "I feel horrible, but I wish she'd trim those nails." Our neighbors: "An idiot in tight pants; oppressed by that prig of a husband; typically provincial and judgmental of everyone."

"Do you know who Persephone is?" she asked me absently one Thursday. But I didn't answer. By then I'd learned to hush when she brought me into my room. My sister's and my time was in the bathroom as we were being toweled off. Lindsey and I could talk about anything then. In my bedroom it was Mommy's time.

She took the towel and draped it over the spindle knob of my four-poster bed. "Imagine our neighbor Mrs. Tarking as Persephone," she said. She opened the drawer of the dresser and handed me my underpants. She always doled out my clothes piecemeal, not wanting to pressure me. She understood my needs early. If I was aware I would have to tie laces I would not have been able to put my feet into socks.

"She's wearing a long white robe, like a sheet draped over her shoulders, but made out of some nice shiny or light fabric, like silk. And she has sandals made of gold and she's surrounded by torches which are light made out of flames . . ."

She went to the drawer to get my undershirt and absentmindedly put it over my head instead of leaving it to me. Once my mother was launched I could take advantage of it—be the baby again. I never protested and claimed to be grown up or a big girl. Those afternoons were about listening to my mysterious mother.

She pulled back the tough-cord Sears bedspread, and I scooted over to the far side along the wall. She always checked her watch then and afterward she would say, "Just for a little while," and slide off her shoes and slip in between the sheets with me.

For both of us it was about getting lost. She got lost in her story. I got lost in her talk.

She would tell me about Persephone's mother, Demeter, or Cupid and Psyche, and I would listen to her until I fell asleep. Sometimes my parents' laughter in the room beside me or the sounds of their late-afternoon lovemaking would wake me up. I would lie there in half-sleep, listening. I liked to pretend that I was in the warm hold of a ship from one of the stories my father read to us, and that all of us were on the ocean and the waves were rolling gently up against the sides of the ship. The laughter, the small sounds of muffled moaning, would usher me back under into sleep.

But then my mother's escape, her half-measure return to the outside world, had been smashed when I was ten and Lindsey nine. She'd missed her period and had taken the fateful car trip to the doctor. Underneath her smile and exclamations to my sister and me were fissures that led somewhere deep inside her. But because I didn't want to, because I was a child, I chose not to follow them. I grabbed the smile like a prize and entered the land of wonder of whether I would be the sister to a little boy or to a little girl.

If I had paid attention, I would have noticed signs. Now I see the shifting, how the stack of books on my parents' bedside table changed from catalogs for local colleges, encyclopedias of mythology, novels by James, Eliot, and Dickens, to the works of Dr. Spock. Then came gardening books and cookbooks until for her birthday two months before I died, I thought the perfect gift was *Better Homes and Gardens Guide to Entertaining.* When she realized she was pregnant the third time, she sealed the more mysterious mother off. Bottled up for years behind that wall, that needy part of her had grown, not shrunk, and in Len, the greed to get out, to smash, destroy, rescind, overtook her. Her body led, and in its wake would be the pieces left to her.

It was not easy for me to witness, but I did.

Their first embrace was hurried, fumbled, passionate.

"Abigail," Len said, his two hands now on either side of her waist underneath the coat, the gauzy gown barely a veil between them. "Think of what you're doing."

"I'm tired of thinking," she said. Her hair was floating above her head because of the fan beside them—in an aureole. Len blinked as he looked at her. Marvelous, dangerous, wild.

"Your husband," he said.

"Kiss me," she said. "Please."

I was watching a beg for leniency on my mother's part. My mother was moving physically through time to flee from me. I could not hold her back.

Len kissed her forehead hard and closed his eyes. She took his hand and placed it on her breast. She whispered in his ear. I knew what was happening. Her rage, her loss, her despair. The whole life lost tumbling out in an arc on that roof, clogging up her being. She needed Len to drive the dead daughter out.

He pushed her back into the stucco surface of the wall as they kissed, and my mother held on to him as if on the other side of his kiss there could be a new life.

* * *

On my way home from the junior high, I would sometimes stop at the edge of our property and watch my mother ride the ride-on mower, looping in and out among the pine trees, and I could remember then how she used to whistle in the mornings as she made her tea and how my father, rushing home on Thursdays, would bring her marigolds and her face would light up yellowy in delight. They had been deeply, separately, wholly in love—apart from her children my mother could reclaim this love, but with them she began to drift. It was my father who grew toward us as the years went by; it was my mother who grew away.

Beside his hospital bed, Lindsey had fallen asleep while holding our father's hand. My mother, still mussed, passed by Hal Heckler in the visitors' area, and a moment later so did Len. Hal didn't need more than this. He grabbed his helmet and went off down the hall.

After a brief visit to the ladies' room, my mother was heading in the direction of my father's room when Hal stopped her.

"Your daughter's in there," Hal called out. She turned.

"Hal Heckler," he said, "Samuel's brother. I was at the memorial service."

"Oh, yes, I'm sorry. I didn't recognize you."

"Not your job," he said.

There was an awkward pause.

"So, Lindsey called me and I brought her here an hour ago."

"Oh."

"Buckley's with a neighbor," he said.

"Oh." She was staring at him. In her eyes she was climbing back to the surface. She used his face to climb back to.

"Are you okay?"

"I'm a little upset—that's understandable, right?"

"Perfectly," he said, speaking slowly. "I just wanted to let you know that your daughter is in there with your husband. I'll be in the visitors' area if you need me."

"Thank you," she said. She watched him turn away and paused for a moment to listen to the worn heels of his motorcycle boots reverberate down the linoleum hall.

She caught herself then, shook herself back to where she was, never guessing for a second that that had been Hal's purpose in greeting her.

Inside the room it was dark now, the fluorescent light behind my father flickering so slightly it lit only the most obvious masses in the room. My sister was in a chair pulled up alongside the bed, her head resting on the side of it with her hand extended out to touch my father. My father, deep under, was lying on his back. My mother could not know that I was there with them, that here were the four of us so changed now from the days when she tucked Lindsey and me into bed and went to make love to her husband, our father. Now she saw the pieces. She saw that my sister and father, together, had become a piece. She was glad of it.

I had played a hide-and-seek game of love with my mother as I grew up, courting her attention and approval in a way that I had never had to with my father.

I didn't have to play hide-and-seek anymore. As she stood in the darkened room and watched my sister and father, I knew one of the things that heaven meant. I had a choice, and it was not to divide my family in my heart.

Late at night the air above hospitals and senior citizen homes was often thick and fast with souls. Holly and I watched sometimes on the nights when sleep was lost to us. We came to realize how these deaths seemed choreographed from somewhere far away. Not our heaven. And so we began to suspect that there was a place more all-encompassing than where we were.

Franny came to watch with us in the beginning.

"It's one of my secret pleasures," she admitted. "After all these years I still love to watch the souls that float and spin in masses, all of them clamoring at once inside the air."

"I don't see anything," I said that first time.

"Watch closely," she said, "and hush."

But I felt them before I saw them, small warm sparks along my arms. Then there they were, fireflies lighting up and expanding in howls and swirls as they abandoned human flesh.

"Like snowflakes," Franny said, "none of them the same and yet each one, from where we stand, exactly like the one before."

THIRTEEN

When she returned to junior high in the fall of 1974, Lindsey was not only the sister of the murdered girl but the child of a "crackpot," "nutcase," "looney-tunes," and the latter hurt her more because it wasn't true.

The rumors Lindsey and Samuel heard in the first weeks of the school year wove in and out of the rows of student lockers like the most persistent of snakes. Now the swirl had grown to include Brian Nelson and Clarissa who, thankfully, had both entered the high school that year. At Fairfax Brian and Clarissa clung to each other, exploiting what had happened to them, using my father's debasement as a varnish of cool they could coat themselves with by retelling throughout the school what had happened that night in the cornfield.

Ray and Ruth walked by on the inside of the glass wall that looked out on the outdoor lounge. On the false boulders where the supposed bad kids sat, they would see Brian holding court. His walk that year went from anxious scarecrow to masculine strut. Clarissa, giggly with both fear and lust, had unlocked her privates and slept with Brian. However haphazardly, everyone I'd known was growing up.

Buckley entered kindergarten that year and immediately arrived home with a crush on his teacher, Miss Koekle. She held his hand so gently whenever she had to lead him to the bathroom or help explain an assignment that her force was irresistible. In one way he profited—she would often sneak him an extra cookie or a softer sit-upon—but in another he was held aloft and apart from his fellow kindergartners. By my death he was made different among the one group—children—in which he might have been anonymous.

Samuel would walk Lindsey home and then go down the main road and thumb his way to Hal's bike shop. He counted on buddies of his brother's to recognize him, and he reached his destination in various pasted-together bikes and trucks that Hal would fine-tune for the driver when they pulled up.

He did not go inside our house for a while. No one but family did. By October my father was just beginning to get up and around. His doctors had told him that his right leg would always be stiff, but if he stretched and stayed limber it wouldn't present too much of an obstacle. "No running bases, but everything else," the surgeon said the morning after his surgery, when my father woke to find Lindsey beside him and my mother standing by the window staring out at the parking lot.

Buckley went right from basking in the shine of Miss Koekle home to burrow in the empty cave of my father's heart. He asked ceaseless questions about the "fake knee," and my father warmed to him.

"The knee came from outer space," my father would say. "They brought pieces of the moon back and carved them up and now they use them for things like this."

"Wow," Buckley would say, grinning. "When can Nate see?"

"Soon, Buck, soon," my father said. But his smile grew weak.

When Buckley took these conversations and brought them to our mother—"Daddy's knee is made out of moonbone," he would tell her, or "Miss Koekle said my colors were really good"—she would nod her head. She had become aware of what she did. She cut carrots and celery into edible lengths. She washed out thermoses and lunchboxes, and when Lindsey decided she was too old for a lunchbox, my mother caught herself actually happy when she found wax-lined bags that would keep her daughter's lunch from seeping through and staining her clothes. Which she washed. Which she folded. Which she ironed when necessary and which she straightened on hangers. Which she picked up from the floor or retrieved from the car or untangled from the wet towel left on the bed that she made every morning, tucking the corners in, and fluffing the pillows, and propping up stuffed animals, and opening the blinds to let the light in.

In the moments when Buckley sought her out, she often made a barter of it. She would focus on him for a few minutes, and then she would allow herself to drift away from her house and home and think of Len.

By November, my father had mastered what he called an "adroit hobble," and when Buckley egged him on he would do a contorted skip that, as long as it made his son laugh, didn't make him think of how odd and desperate he might look to an outsider or to my mother. Everyone save Buckley knew what was coming: the first anniversary.

Buckley and my father spent the crisp fall afternoons out in the fenced-in yard with Holiday. My father would sit in the old iron lawn chair with his leg stretched out in front of him and propped up slightly on an ostentatious boot scraper that Grandma Lynn had found in a curio shop in Maryland.

Buckley threw the squeaky cow toy while Holiday ran to get it. My father took pleasure in the agile body of his five-year-old son and Buckley's peals of delight when Holiday knocked him over and nudged him with his nose or licked his face with his long pink tongue. But he couldn't rid himself of one thought: this too — this perfect boy — could be taken from him.

It had been a combination of things, his injury not the least among them, that had made him stay inside the house on an extended sick leave from his firm. His boss acted differently around him now, and so did his coworkers. They trod gently outside his office and would stop a few feet from his desk as if, should they be too relaxed in his presence, what had happened to him would happen to them — as if having a dead child were contagious. No one knew how he continued to do what he did, while simultaneously they wanted him to shut all signs of his grief away, place it in a file somewhere and tuck it in a drawer that no one would be asked to open again. He called in regularly, and his boss just as easily agreed that he could take another week, another month if he had to, and he counted this as a blessing of always having been on time or willing to work late. But he stayed away from Mr. Harvey and tried to curb even the thought of him. He would not use his name except in his notebook, which he kept hidden in his study, where it was surprisingly easily agreed with my mother that she would no longer clean. He had apologized to me in his notebook. "I need to rest, honey. I need to understand how to go after this man. I hope you'll understand."

But he had set his return to work for December 2, right after Thanksgiving. He wanted to be back in the office by the anniversary of my disappearance. Functioning and catching up on work—in as public and distracting a place as he could think of. And away from my mother, if he was honest with himself.

How to swim back to her, how to reach her again. She was pulling and pulling away—all her energy was against the house, and all his energy was inside it. He settled on building back his strength and finding a strategy to pursue Mr. Harvey. Placing blame was easier than adding up the mounting figures of what he'd lost.

Grandma Lynn was due for Thanksgiving, and Lindsey had kept to a beautifying regime Grandma had set up for her through letters. She'd felt silly when she first put cucumbers on her eyes (to diminish puffiness), or oatmeal on her face (to cleanse the pores and absorb excess oils), or eggs yolks in her hair (to make it shine). Her use of groceries had even made my mother laugh, then wonder if she too should start to beautify. But that was only for a second, because she was thinking of Len, not because she was in love with him but because being with him was the fastest way she knew to forget.

Two weeks before Grandma Lynn's arrival, Buckley and my father were out in the yard with Holiday. Buckley and Holiday were romping from one large pile of burnished oak leaves to another in an increasingly hyper game of tag. "Watch out, Buck," my father said. "You'll make Holiday nip." And sure enough.

My father said he wanted to try something out.

"We have to see if your old dad can carry you piggyback style again. Soon you'll be too big."

So, awkwardly, in the beautiful isolation of the yard, where if my father fell only a boy and a dog who loved him would see, the two of them worked together to make what they both wanted—this return to father/son normalcy—happen. When Buckley stood on the iron chair—"Now scoot up my back," my father said, stooping forward, "and grab on to my shoulders," not knowing if he'd have the strength to lift him up from there—I crossed my fingers hard in heaven and held my breath. In the cornfield, yes, but, in this moment, repairing the most basic fabric of their previous day-to-day lives, challenging his injury to take a moment like this back, my father became my hero.

"Duck, now duck again," he said as they galumphed through the downstairs doorways and up the stairs, each step a balance my father negotiated, a wincing pain. And with Holiday rushing past them on the stairs, and Buckley joyous on his mount, he knew that in this challenge to his strength he had done the right thing.

When the two of them—with dog—discovered Lindsey in the upstairs bathroom, she whined a loud complaint.

"Daaaaddd!"

My father stood up straight. Buckley reached up and touched the light fixture with his hand.

"What are you doing?" my father said.

"What does it look like I'm doing?"

She sat on the toilet lid wrapped in a large white towel (the towels my mother bleached, the towels my mother hung on the line to dry, the towels she folded, and placed in a basket and brought up to the linen closet . . .). Her left leg was propped up on the edge of the tub, covered with shaving cream. In her hand she held my father's razor.

"Don't be petulant," my father said.

"I'm sorry," my sister said, looking down. "I just want a little privacy is all."

My father lifted Buckley up and over his head. "The counter, the counter, son," he said, and Buckley thrilled at the illegal halfway point of the bathroom counter and how his muddy feet soiled the tile.

"Now hop down." And he did. Holiday tackled him.

"You're too young to shave your legs, sweetie," my father said.

"Grandma Lynn started shaving at eleven."

"Buckley, will you go in your room and take the dog? I'll be in in a while."

"Yes, Daddy."

Buckley was still a little boy who my father could, with patience and a bit of maneuvering, get up on his shoulders so they could be a typical father and son. But he now saw in Lindsey what brought a double pain. I was a little girl in the tub, a toddler being held up to the sink, a girl who had forever stopped just short of sitting as my sister did now.

When Buckley was gone, he turned his attention to my sister. He would care for his two daughters by caring for one: "Are you being careful?" he asked.

"I just started," Lindsey said. "I'd like to be alone, Dad."

"Is that the same blade that was on it when you got it from my shaving kit?"

"Yes."

"Well, my beard stubble dulls the blade. I'll go get you a fresh one."

"Thanks, Dad," my sister said, and again she was his sweet, piggyback-riding Lindsey.

He left the room and went down the hallway to the other side of the house and the master bathroom that he and my mother still shared, though they no longer slept in the same room together. As he reached up into the cabinet for the package of fresh razors, he felt a tear in his chest. He ignored it and focused on the task. There was only a flicker of a thought then: *Abigail should be doing this.*

He brought the razor blades back, showed Lindsey how to change them, and gave her a few pointers on how best to shave. "Watch out for the ankle and the knee," he said. "Your mother always called those the danger spots."

"You can stay if you want," she said, ready now to let him in.

"But I might be a bloody mess." She wanted to hit herself. "Sorry, Dad," she said. "Here, I'll move—you sit."

She got up and went to sit on the edge of the tub. She ran the tap, and my father lowered himself onto the toilet lid.

"It's okay, honey," he said. "We haven't talked about your sister in a while."

"Who needs to?" my sister said. "She's everywhere."

"Your brother seems to be all right."

"He's glued to you."

"Yes," he said, and he realized he liked it, this father-courting his son was doing.

"Ouch," Lindsey said, a fine trickle of blood beginning to spread into the white foam of the shaving cream. "This is a total hassle."

"Press down on the nick with your thumb. It stops the bleeding. You could do just to the top of your knee," he offered. "That's what your mother does unless we're going to the beach."

Lindsey paused. "You guys never go to the beach."

"We used to."

My father had met my mother when they were both working at Wanamaker's during the summer break from college. He had just made a nasty comment about how the employee's lounge reeked of cigarettes when she smiled and brought out her then-habitual pack of Pall Malls. "Touché," he said, and he stayed beside her despite the reeking stink of her cigarettes enveloping him from head to toe.

"I've been trying to decide who I look like," Lindsey said, "Grandma Lynn or Mom."

"I've always thought both you and your sister looked like my mother," he said.

"Dad?"

"Yes."

"Are you still convinced that Mr. Harvey had something to do with it?"

It was like a stick finally sparking against another stick—the friction took.

"There is no doubt in my mind, honey. None."

"Then why doesn't Len arrest him?"

She drew the razor sloppily up and finished her first leg. She hesitated there, waiting.

"I wish it was easy to explain," he said, the words coiling out of him. He had never talked at length about his suspicion to anyone. "When I met him that day, in his backyard, and we built that tent—the one he claimed he built for his wife, whose name I thought was Sophie and Len took down as Leah—there was something about his movements that made me sure."

"Everyone thinks he's kind of weird."

"True, I understand that," he said. "But then everyone hasn't had much to do with him either. They don't know whether his weirdness is benign or not."

"Benign?"

"Harmless."

"Holiday doesn't like him," Lindsey offered.

"Exactly. I've never seen that dog bark so hard. The fur on his back stood straight up that morning."

"But the cops think you're nuts."

" 'No evidence' is all they can say. Without evidence and without—excuse me, honey—a body, they have nothing to move on and no basis for an arrest."

"What would be a basis?"

"I guess something to link him to Susie. If someone had seen him in the cornfield or even lurking around the school. Something like that."

"Or if he had something of hers?" Both my father and Lindsey were heatedly talking, her second leg lathered but left unshaved, because what radiated as the two sticks of their interest sparked flame was that I was in that house somewhere. My body—in the basement, first floor, second floor, attic. To keep from acknowledging that horrible—but oh, if it were true, so blatant so perfect so conclusive as evidence—thought, they remembered what I wore that day, remembered what I carried, the Frito Bandito eraser I prized, the David Cassidy button I'd pinned inside my bag, the David Bowie one I had pinned on the outside. They named all the clutter and accessories that surrounded what would be the best, most hideous evidence anyone could find—my corpse cut up, my blank and rotting eyes.

My eyes: the makeup Grandma Lynn had given her helped but did not solve the problem of how much everyone could see my eyes in Lindsey's. When they presented themselves—a compact flashing past her when in use by a girl at a neighboring desk, or an unexpected reflection in the window of a store—she looked away. It was particularly painful with my father. What she realized as they talked was that as long as they were on this subject—Mr. Harvey, my clothes, my book bag, my body, me—the vigilance to my memory made my father see her as Lindsey and not as a tragic combination of his two daughters.

"So you would want to be able to get in his house?" she said.

They stared at each other, a flicker of recognition of a dangerous idea. In his hesitation, before he finally said that that would be illegal, and no, he hadn't thought of that, she knew he was lying. She also knew he needed someone to do it for him.

"You should finish shaving, honey," he said.

She agreed with him and turned away, knowing what she'd been told.

Grandma Lynn arrived on the Monday before Thanksgiving. With the same laser-beam eyes that immediately sought out any unsightly blemish on my sister, she now saw something beneath the surface of her daughter's smile, in her placated, tranquilized movements and in how her body responded whenever Detective Fenerman or the police work came up.

When my mother refused my father's help in cleaning up after dinner that night, the laser eyes were certain. Adamantly, and to the shock of everyone at the table and the relief of my sister—Grandma Lynn made an announcement.

"Abigail, I am going to help you clean up. It will be a mother/daughter thing."

"What?"

My mother had calculated that she could let Lindsey off easily and early and then she would spend the rest of the night over the sink, washing slowly and staring out the window until the darkness brought her own reflection back to her. The sounds of the TV would fade away and she would be alone again.

"I just did my nails yesterday," Grandma Lynn said after tying on an apron over her camel-colored A-line dress, "so I'll dry."

"Mother, really. This isn't necessary."

"It is necessary, believe me, sweetie," my grandmother said. There was something sober and curt in that *sweetie.*

Buckley led my father by the hand into the adjoining room where the TV sat. They took up their stations and Lindsey, having been given a reprieve, went upstairs to call Samuel.

It was such a strange thing to see. So out of the ordinary. My grandmother in an apron, holding a dish towel up like a matador's red flag in anticipation of the first dish coming her way.

They were quiet as they worked, and the silence—the only sounds being the splash of my mother's hands plunging into the scalding water, the squeak of plates, and the clank of the silver—made a tension fill the room which grew unbearable. The noises of the game from the nearby room were just as odd to me. My father had never watched football; basketball his only sport. Grandma Lynn had never done dishes; frozen meals and takeout menus were her weapons of choice.

"Oh Christ," she finally said. "Take this." She handed the just-washed dish back to my mother. "I want to have a real conversation but I'm afraid I'm going to drop these things. Let's take a walk."

"Mother, I need to . . ."

"You need to take a walk."

"After the dishes."

"Listen," my grandmother said, "I know I'm whatever I am and you're whatever you are, which isn't me, which makes you happy, but I know some things when I see them and I know something is going on that isn't kosher. *Capisce?*"

My mother's face was wavering, soft and malleable—almost as soft and malleable as the image of her that floated on the sullied water in the sink.

"What?"

"I have suspicions and I don't want to talk about them here."

Ten-four, Grandma Lynn, I thought. I'd never seen her nervous before.

It would be easy for the two of them to leave the house alone. My father, with his knee, would never think to join them, and, these days, where my father went or did not go, my brother, Buckley, followed.

My mother was silent. She saw no other option. As an afterthought they removed their aprons in the garage and piled them on the roof of the Mustang. My mother bent down and lifted the garage door.

It was still early enough so the light would hold for the beginning of their walk. "We could take Holiday," my mother tried.

"Just you and your mother," my grandmother said. "The most frightening pairing imaginable."

They had never been close. They both knew it, but it wasn't something they acknowledged very much. They joked around it like two children who didn't particularly like each other but were the only children in a large, barren neighborhood. Now, never having tried to before, having always let her daughter run as fast as she could in whatever direction she wished, my grandmother found that she was suddenly catching up.

They had passed by the O'Dwyers' and were near the Tarkings' before my grandmother said what she had to say.

"My humor buried my acceptance," my grandmother said. "Your father had a long-term affair in New Hampshire. Her first initial was F and I never knew what it stood for. I found a thousand options for it over the years."

"Mother?"

My grandmother kept walking, didn't turn. She found that the crisp fall air helped, filling her lungs until they felt cleaner than they had just minutes before.

"Did you know that?"

"No."

"I guess I never told you," she said. "I didn't think you needed to know. Now you do, don't you think?"

"I'm not sure why you're telling me this."

They had come to the bend in the road that would lead them back around the circle. If they went that way and did not stop, eventually they would find themselves in front of Mr. Harvey's house. My mother froze.

"My poor, poor sweetie," my grandmother said. "Give me your hand."

They were awkward. My mother could count on her fingers how many times her tall father had leaned down and kissed her as a child. The scratchy beard that smelled of a cologne that, after years of searching, she could never identify. My grandmother took her hand and held on as they walked the other way.

They walked into an area of the neighborhood where newer families seemed to be moving in more and more. The anchor houses, I remembered my mother calling them, because they lined the street that led into the whole development—anchored the neighborhood to an original road built before the township was a township. The road that led to Valley Forge, to George Washington and the Revolution.

"Susie's death brought your father's back to me," my grandmother said. "I never let myself mourn him properly."

"I know," my mother said.

"Do you resent me for it?"

My mother paused. "Yes."

My grandmother patted the back of my mother's hand with her free one. "Good, see, that's a nugget."

"A nugget?"

"Something that's coming out of all this. You and me. A nugget of truth between us."

They passed the one-acre lots on which trees had been growing for twenty years. If not exactly towering, they were still twice as tall as the fathers who had first held them and stomped the dirt around them with their weekend work shoes.

"Do you know how alone I've always felt?" my mother asked her mother.

"That's why we're walking, Abigail," Grandma Lynn said.

My mother focused her eyes in front of her but stayed connected to her mother with her hand. She thought of the solitary nature of her childhood. How, when she had watched her two daughters tie string between paper cups and go to separate rooms to whisper secrets to each other, she could not really say she knew how that felt. There had been no one else in the house with her but her mother and father, and then her father had gone.

She stared at the tops of the trees, which, miles from our development, were the tallest things around. They stood on a high hill that had never been cleared for houses and on which a few old farmers still dwelled.

"I can't describe what I'm feeling," she said. "To anyone."

They reached the end of the development just as the sun was going down over the hill in front of them. A moment passed without either of them turning around. My mother watched the last light flicker in a drain-off puddle at the end of the road.

"I don't know what to do," she said. "It's all over now."

My grandmother was not sure what she meant by "it," but she did not press harder.

"Shall we head back?" my grandmother offered.

"How?" my mother said.

"To the house, Abigail. Head back to the house."

They turned and began walking again. The houses one after another, identical in structure. Only what my grandmother thought of as their accessories marked them as different. She had never understood places like this—places where her own child had chosen to live.

"When we get to the turn to the circle," my mother said, "I want to walk past it."

"His house?"

"Yes."

I watched Grandma Lynn turn when my mother turned.

"Would you promise me not to see the man anymore?" my grandmother asked.

"Who?"

"The man you're involved with. That's what I've been talking about."

"I'm not involved with anyone," my mother said. Her mind flew like a bird from one rooftop to the next. "Mother?" she said, and turned.

"Abigail?"

"If I needed to get away for a while, could I use Daddy's cabin?"

"Have you been listening to me?"

They could smell something in the air, and again my mother's anxious, agile mind slipped away. "Someone is smoking," she said.

Grandma Lynn was staring at her child. The pragmatic, prim mistress that my mother had always been was gone. She was flighty and distracted. My grandmother had nothing left to say to her.

"They're foreign cigarettes," my mother said. "Let's go find them!"

And in the fading light my grandmother stared, flabbergasted, as my mother began to follow the scent to its source.

"I'm heading back," my grandmother said.

But my mother kept walking.

She found the source of the smoke soon enough. It was Ruana Singh, standing behind a tall fir tree in her backyard.

"Hello," my mother said.

Ruana did not start as I thought she would. Her calmness had become something practiced. She could make a breath last through the most startling event, whether it was her son being accused of murder by the police or her husband running their dinner party as if it were an academic committee meeting. She had told Ray he could go upstairs, and then she had disappeared out the back door and not been missed.

"Mrs. Salmon," Ruana said, exhaling the heady smell of her cigarettes. In a rush of smoke and warmth my mother met Ruana's extended hand. "I'm so glad to see you."

"Are you having a party?" my mother asked.

"My husband is having a party. I am the hostess."

My mother smiled.

"This is a weird place we both live," Ruana said.

Their eyes met. My mother nodded her head. Back on the road somewhere was her own mother, but for right now she, like Ruana, was on a quiet island off the mainland.

"Do you have another cigarette?"

"Absolutely, Mrs. Salmon, yes." Ruana fished into the pocket of her long black cardigan and held out the pack and her lighter. "Dunhills," she said. "I hope that's all right."

My mother lit her cigarette and handed the blue package with its golden foil back to Ruana. "Abigail," she said as she exhaled. "Please call me Abigail."

Up in his room with his lights off, Ray could smell his mother's cigarettes, which she never accused him of pilfering, just as he never let on that he knew she had them. He heard voices downstairs—the loud sounds of his father and his colleagues speaking six different languages and laughing delightedly over the oh-so-American holiday to come. He did not know that my mother was out on the lawn with his mother or that I was watching him sit in his window and smell their sweet tobacco. Soon he would turn away from the window and switch on the small light by his bed to read. Mrs. McBride had told them to find a sonnet they'd like to write a paper on, but as he read the lines of those available to him in his *Norton Anthology* he kept drifting back to the moment he wished he could take back and do over again. If he had just kissed me on the scaffold, maybe everything would have turned out differently.

Grandma Lynn kept on the course she had set with my mother, and, eventually, there it was—the house they tried to forget while living two houses down. *Jack was right,* my grandmother thought. She could even feel it in the dark. The place radiated something malevolent. She shivered and began to hear the crickets and see the fireflies gathering in a swarm above his front flower beds. She thought suddenly that she would do nothing but sympathize with her daughter. Her child was living inside the middle of a ground zero to which no affair on her own husband's part could offer her insight. She would tell my mother in the morning that the keys to the cabin would always be there for her if she needed them.

That night my mother had what she considered a wonderful

dream. She dreamed of the country of India, where she had never been. There were orange traffic cones and beautiful lapis lazuli insects with mandibles of gold. A young girl was being led through the streets. She was taken to a pyre where she was wound in a sheet and placed up on a platform built from sticks. The bright fire that consumed her brought my mother into that deep, light, dreamlike bliss. The girl was being burned alive, but, first, there had been her body, clean and whole.

FOURTEEN

For a week Lindsey cased my killer's house. She was doing exactly what he did to everyone else.

She had agreed to train with the boys' soccer team all year in preparation for the challenge Mr. Dewitt and Samuel encouraged her to take on: qualifying to play in the all-male high school soccer league. And Samuel, to show his support, trained alongside her with no hope of qualifying for anything, he said, other than "fastest guy in shorts."

He could run, even if kicking and fielding and noticing a ball anywhere within his vicinity were all beyond him. And so, while they did laps around the neighborhood, each time Lindsey shot a look toward Mr. Harvey's house, Samuel was out in front, setting the pace for her — unaware of anything else.

Inside the green house, Mr. Harvey was looking out. He saw her watching and he began to itch. It had been almost a year now, but the Salmons remained bent on crowding him.

It had happened before in other towns and states. The family of a girl suspected him but no one else did. He had perfected his patter to the police, a certain obsequious innocence peppered with wonder about their procedures or useless ideas that he presented as if they might help. Bringing up the Ellis boy with Fenerman had been a good stroke, and the lie that he was a widower always helped. He fashioned a wife out of whichever victim he'd recently been taking pleasure in in his memory, and to flesh her out there was always his mother.

He left the house every day for an hour or two in the afternoon. He would pick up any supplies he needed and then drive out to Valley Forge Park and walk the paved roads and the unpaved trails and find himself suddenly surrounded by school tours at George Washington's log cabin or the Washington Memorial Chapel. This would buoy him up—these moments when the children were eager to see history, as if they might actually find a long silver hair from Washington's wig caught on the rough end of a log post.

Occasionally one of the tour guides or teachers would notice him standing there, unfamiliar even if amiable, and he would be met with a questioning stare. He had a thousand lines to give them: "I used to bring my children here." "This is where I met my wife." He knew to ground whatever he said in connection to some imagined family, and then the women would smile at him. Once an attractive, heavy woman tried to engage him in conversation while the park guide told the children about the winter of 1776 and the Battle of the Clouds.

He had used the story of widowhood and talked about a woman named Sophie Cichetti, making her his now-deceased wife and true love. It had been like luscious food to this woman, and, as he listened to her tell him about her cats and her brother, who had three children, whom she loved, he pictured her sitting on the chair in his basement, dead.

After that, when he met a teacher's questioning glare he would shyly back off and go somewhere else inside the park. He watched mothers with their children still in strollers walk briskly along the exposed paths. He saw teenagers who were cutting school necking in the uncut fields or along the interior trails. And at the highest point of the park was a small wood beside which he sometimes parked. He would sit in his Wagoneer and watch lonely men pull up beside him and get out of their cars. Men in suits on their lunch hour or men in flannel and jeans would walk quickly into that wood. Sometimes they would cast a look back in his direction—an inquiry. If they were close enough, these men could see, through his windshield, what his victims saw—his wild and bottomless lust.

On November 26, 1974, Lindsey saw Mr. Harvey leaving the green house, and she began to hang back from the pack of running boys. Later she could claim she had gotten her period and all of them would hush up, even be satisfied that this was proof that Mr. Dewitt's unpopular plan—a girl at regionals!—would never work out.

I watched my sister and marveled. She was becoming everything all at once. A woman. A spy. A jock. The Ostracized: One Man Alone.

She walked, clutching her side in a false cramp, and waved the boys on when they turned to notice her. She kept walking with her hand on her waist until they turned the corner at the far end of the block. At the edge of Mr. Harvey's property was a row of tall, thick pines that had been left untrimmed for years. She sat down by one of them, still feigning exhaustion in case any neighbor was looking out, and then, when she felt the moment was right, she curled up in a ball and rolled in between two pines. She waited. The boys had one more lap. She watched them pass her and followed them with her eyes as they cut up through the vacant lot and back to the high school. She was alone. She calculated she had forty-five minutes before our father would begin to wonder when she'd be home. The agreement had been that if she trained with the boys' soccer team, Samuel would escort her home and have her back by five o'clock.

The clouds had hung heavy in the sky all day, and the late-fall cold raised goose bumps along her legs and arms. The team runs always warmed her, but when she reached the locker room where she shared the showers with the field hockey team, she would begin to shiver until the hot water hit her body. But on the lawn of the green house, her goose bumps were also from fear.

When the boys cut up the path, she scrambled over to the basement window at the side of Mr. Harvey's house. She had already thought of a story if she was caught. She was chasing a kitten that she'd seen dart in between the pine trees. She would say it was gray, that it was fast, that it had run toward Mr. Harvey's house and she'd followed it without thinking.

She could see inside to the basement, where it was dark. She tried the window, but the latch lock was pushed in. She would have to break the glass. Her mind racing, she worried about the noise, but she was too far along to stop now. She thought of my father at home, ever mindful of the clock near his chair, and took her sweatshirt off and balled it around her feet. Sitting down, she braced her body with her arms and then kicked once, twice, three times with both feet until the window smashed—a muffled cracking.

Carefully, she lowered herself down, searching the wall for a foothold but having to jump the final few feet onto the broken glass and concrete.

The room appeared tidy and swept, different from our own basement, where heaps of holiday-marked boxes—EASTER EGGS AND GREEN GRASS, CHRISTMAS STAR/ORNAMENTS—never made it back on the shelves my father had built.

The cold air from outside came in, and she felt the draft along her neck pushing her out of the shimmering semicircle of shattered glass and into the rest of the room. She saw the easy chair and a little table beside it. She saw the large alarm clock with luminous numbers sitting on the metal shelving. I wanted to guide her eyes to the crawlspace, where she would find the bones of the animals, but I knew, too, that regardless of drawing a fly's eyes on graph paper and excelling that fall in Mr. Botte's biology class, she would imagine the bones were mine. For this, I was glad she went nowhere near them.

Despite my inability to appear or whisper, push or usher, Lindsey, all alone, felt something. Something charged the air in the cold, dank basement and made her cringe. She stood only a few feet from the open window, knowing that she would, no matter what, be walking farther in and that she had to, no matter what, calm and focus herself to look for clues; but right then, for one moment, she thought of Samuel running ahead, having thought he would find her on his last lap, then running back toward the school, thinking he would find her outside, and then assuming, but with the first trace of a doubt, that she was showering, and so he too would be showering now, and then waiting for her before he did anything else. How long would he wait? As her eyes mounted the stairs to the first floor before her feet followed, she wished that Samuel were there to climb down after her and trace her movements, erasing her solitude as he went, fitting into her limbs. But she had not told him on purpose—had told no one. What she was doing was beyond the pale—criminal—and she knew it.

If she thought about it later, she would say that she had needed air and so that was what had gotten her up the stairs. Small flecks of white dust collected at the tips of her shoes as she mounted the stairs, but she didn't notice them.

She twisted the knob of the basement door and reached the

first floor. Only five minutes had passed. She had forty left, or so she thought. There was still a bit of light seeping in through the closed blinds. As she stood, again, hesitating, in this house identical to our own, she heard the thwack of the *Evening Bulletin* hit the stoop and the delivery boy ring the bell on his bike as he passed.

My sister told herself that she was inside a series of rooms and spaces that, gone through methodically, might yield what she needed, provide her the trophy she could take home to our father, earning her freedom from me that way. Competition always, even between the living and the dead. She saw the flagstones in the hall—the same dark green and gray as ours—and imagined crawling after me when she was a baby and I was just learning to walk. Then she saw my toddler body running delightedly away from her and into the next room, and she remembered her own sense of reaching out, of taking her first steps as I teased her from the living room.

But Mr. Harvey's house was much emptier than ours, and there were no rugs to lend warmth to the decor. Lindsey stepped from the flagstones onto the polished pine floors of what in our house was the living room. She made echoes up the open front hall, the sound of every movement reaching back for her.

She couldn't stop the memories slamming into her. Every one had a brutal report. Buckley riding piggyback on my shoulders down the stairs. Our mother steadying me as Lindsey looked on, jealous that I could reach, with the silver star in my hands, the top of the Christmas tree. Me sliding down the banister and asking her to join. Both of us begging the comics off our father after dinner. All of us running after Holiday as he barked and barked. And the countless exhausted smiles awkwardly dressing our faces for photos at birthdays, and holidays, and after school. Two sisters dressed identically in velvet or plaid or Easter yellows. We held baskets of bunnies and eggs we had sunk in dye. Patent leather shoes with straps and hard buckles. Smiling hard as our mother tried to focus her camera. The photos always fuzzy, our eyes bright red spots. None of them, these artifacts left to my sister, would hold for posterity the moments before and the moments after, when we two girls played in the house or fought over toys. When we were sisters.

Then she saw it. My back darting into the next room. Our dining room, the room that held his finished dollhouses. I was a child running just ahead of her.

She hurried after me.

She chased me through the downstairs rooms and though she was training hard for soccer, when she returned to the front hall she was unable to catch her breath. She grew dizzy.

I thought of what my mother had always said about a boy at our bus stop who was twice as old as us but still in the second grade. "He doesn't know his own strength, so you need to be careful around him." He liked to give bear hugs to anyone who was nice to him, and you could see this dopey love drop into his features and ignite his desire to touch. Before he was removed from regular school and sent somewhere else no one talked about, he had picked up a little girl named Daphne and squeezed her so hard that she fell into the road when he let go. I was pushing so hard on the Inbetween to get to Lindsey that I suddenly felt I might hurt her when I meant to help.

My sister sat down on the wide steps at the bottom of the front hall and closed her eyes, focused on regaining her breath, on why she was in Mr. Harvey's house in the first place. She felt encased in something heavy, a fly trapped in a spider's funnel web, the thick silk binding up around her. She knew that our father had walked into the cornfield possessed by something that was creeping into her now. She had wanted to bring back clues he could use as rungs to climb back to her on, to anchor him with facts, to ballast his sentences to Len. Instead she saw herself falling after him into a bottomless pit.

She had twenty minutes.

Inside that house my sister was the only living being, but she was not alone, and I was not her only company. The architecture of my murderer's life, the bodies of the girls he'd left behind, began to reveal itself to me now that my sister was in that house. I stood in heaven. I called their names:

Jackie Meyer. Delaware, 1967. Thirteen.

A chair knocked over, its underside facing the room. Lying curled toward it, she wore a striped T-shirt and nothing else. Near her head, a small pool of blood.

Flora Hernandez. Delaware, 1963. Eight.

He'd only wanted to touch her, but she screamed. A small girl for her age. Her left sock and shoe were found later. The body, unrecovered. The bones lay in the earthen basement of an old apartment house.

Leah Fox. Delaware, 1969. Twelve.

On a slipcovered couch under a highway on-ramp, he killed her, very quietly. He fell asleep on top of her, lulled by the sound of cars rushing above them. Not until ten hours later, when a vagrant knocked on the small shack Mr. Harvey had built out of discarded doors—did he begin to pack himself and Leah Fox's body up.

Sophie Cichetti, Pennsylvania, 1960. Forty-nine.

A landlady, she had divided her upstairs apartment into two by erecting a Sheetrock wall. He liked the half-circle window this created, and the rent was cheap. But she talked too much about her son and insisted on reading him poems from a book of sonnets. He made love to her on her side of the divided room, smashed her skull in when she started to talk, and brought her body to the bank of a creek nearby.

Leidia Johnson. 1960. Six.

Buck's County, Pennsylvania. He dug an arched cave inside a hill near the quarry and waited. She was the youngest one.

Wendy Richter. Connecticut, 1971. Thirteen.

She was waiting for her father outside a bar. He raped her in the bushes and then strangled her. That time, as he grew conscious, coming up out of the stupor that often clung on, he heard noises. He turned the dead girl's face toward his, and as the voices grew closer he bit down on her ear. "Sorry, man," he heard two drunk men say as they walked into the nearby bushes to take a leak.

I saw now that town of floating graves, cold and whipped by winds, where the victims of murder went in the minds of the living. I could see his other victims as they occupied his house—those trace memories left behind before they fled this earth—but I let them go that day and went to my sister.

Lindsey stood up the moment I focused back on her. Together the two of us walked the stairs. She felt like the zombies in the movies Samuel and Hal loved. One foot in front of the other and staring blankly straight ahead. She reached what was my parents' bedroom in our house and found nothing. She circled the hallway upstairs. Nothing. Then she went into what had been my bedroom in our house, and she found my killer's.

It was the least barren room in the house, and she did her best not to displace anything. To move her hand in between the sweaters stacked on the shelf, prepared to find anything in their warm insides—a knife, a gun, a Bic pen chewed on by Holiday. Nothing. But then, as she heard something but could not identify what it was, she turned toward the bed and saw the bedside table and, lying in the circle of light from a reading lamp left on, his sketchbook. She walked toward it and heard another sound, again, not putting the sounds together. Car pulling up. Car braking with a squeak. Car door slamming shut.

She turned the pages of the sketchbook and looked at the inky drawings of crossbeams and braces or turrets and buttresses, and she saw the measurements and notes, none of which meant anything to her. Then, as she flipped a final page, she thought she heard footsteps outside and very close.

As Mr. Harvey turned the key in the lock of his front door, she saw the light pencil sketch on the page in front of her. It was a small drawing of stalks above a sunken hole, a detail off to the side of a shelf and how a chimney could draw out smoke from a fire, and the thing that sunk into her: in a spidery hand he had written "Stolfuz cornfield." If it were not for the articles in the paper after the discovery of my elbow, she would not have known that the cornfield was owned by a man named Stolfuz. Now she saw what I wanted her to know. I had died inside that hole; I had screamed and fought and lost.

She ripped out the page. Mr. Harvey was in the kitchen making something to eat—the liverwurst he favored, a bowl of sweet green grapes. He heard a board creak. He stiffened. He heard another and his back rose and blossomed with sudden understanding.

The grapes dropped on the floor to be crushed by his left foot, while my sister in the room above sprang to the aluminum blinds and unlocked the stubborn window. Mr. Harvey mounted the stairs two at a time, and my sister smashed out the screen, scrambling onto the porch roof and rolling down it as he gained the upstairs hall and came barreling toward her. The gutter broke when her body tipped past it. As he reached his bedroom, she fell into the bushes and brambles and muck.

But she was not hurt. Gloriously not hurt. Gloriously young. She stood up as he reached the window to climb out. But he stopped. He saw her running toward the elderberry. The silk-screened number on her back screamed out at him. 5! 5! 5!

Lindsey Salmon in her soccer shirt.

Samuel was sitting with my parents and Grandma Lynn when Lindsey reached the house.

"Oh my God," my mother said, the first to see her through the small square windows that lined either side of our front door.

And by the time my mother opened it Samuel had rushed to fill the space, and she walked, without looking at my mother or even my father hobbling forward, right into Samuel's arms.

"My God, my God, my God," my mother said as she took in the dirt and the cuts.

My grandmother came to stand beside her.

Samuel put his hand on my sister's head and smoothed her hair back.

"Where have you been?"

But Lindsey turned to our father, lessened so now—smaller, weaker, than this child who raged. How alive she was consumed me whole that day.

"Daddy?"

"Yes, sweetheart."

"I did it. I broke into his house." She was shaking slightly and trying not to cry.

My mother balked: "You what?"

But my sister didn't look at her, not once.

"I brought you this. I think it might be important."

She had kept the drawing in her hand, crumpled tightly into a ball. It had made her landing harder, but she had come away anyway.

A phrase my father had read that day appeared in his mind now. He spoke it aloud as he looked into Lindsey's eyes.

"There is no condition one adjusts to so quickly as a state of war."

Lindsey handed him the drawing.

"I'm going to pick up Buckley," my mother said.

"Don't you even want to look at this, Mom?"

"I don't know what to say. Your grandmother is here. I have shopping to do, a bird to cook. No one seems to realize that we have a family. We have a family, a family and a son, and I'm going."

Grandma Lynn walked my mother to the back door but did not try to stop her.

My mother gone, my sister reached her hand out to Samuel. My father saw what Lindsey did in Mr. Harvey's spidery hand: the possible blueprint of my grave. He looked up.

"Do you believe me now?" he asked Lindsey.

"Yes, Daddy."

My father—so grateful—had a call to make.

"Dad," she said.

"Yes."

"I think he saw me."

I could never have imagined a blessing greater to me than the physical safety of my sister that day. As I walked back from the gazebo I shivered with the fear that had held me, the possibility of her loss on Earth not just to my father, my mother, Buckley, and Samuel, but, selfishly, the loss of her on Earth to me.

Franny walked toward me from the cafeteria. I barely raised my head.

"Susie," she said. "I have something to tell you."

She drew me under one of the old-fashioned lampposts and then out of the light. She handed me a piece of paper folded into four.

"When you feel stronger, look at it and go there."

Two days later, Franny's map led me to a field that I had always walked by but which, though beautiful, I'd left unexplored. The drawing had a dotted line to indicate a path. Searching nervously, I looked for an indentation in the rows and rows of wheat. Just ahead I saw it, and as I began to walk between the rows the paper dissolved in my hand.

I could see an old and beautiful olive tree just up ahead.

The sun was high, and in front of the olive tree was a clearing. I waited only a moment until I saw the wheat on the other side begin to pulse with the arrival of someone who did not crest the stalks.

She was small for her age, as she had been on Earth, and she wore a calico dress that was frayed at the hem and the cuffs.

She paused and we stared at each other.

"I come here almost every day," she said. "I like to listen to the sounds."

All around us, I realized, the wheat was rustling as it moved against itself in the wind.

"Do you know Franny?" I asked.

The little girl nodded solemnly.

"She gave me a map to this place."

"Then you must be ready," she said, but she was in *her* heaven too, and that called for twirling and making her skirt fly out in a circle. I sat on the ground under the tree and watched her.

When she was done she came toward me and breathlessly sat herself down. "I was Flora Hernandez," she said. "What was your name?"

I told her, and then I began to cry with comfort, to know another girl he had killed.

"The others will be here soon," she said.

And as Flora twirled, other girls and women came through the field in all directions. Our heartache poured into one another like water from cup to cup. Each time I told my story, I lost a bit, the smallest drop of pain. It was that day that I knew I wanted to tell the story of my family. Because horror on Earth is real and it is every day. It is like a flower or like the sun; it cannot be contained.

FIFTEEN

At first no one stopped them, and it was something his mother enjoyed so much, the trill of her laughter when they ducked around the corner from whatever store and she uncovered and presented the pilfered item to him, that George Harvey joined in her laughter and, spying an opportunity, would hug her while she was occupied with her newest prize.

It was a relief for both of them, getting away from his father for the afternoon and driving into the nearby town to get food or other supplies. They were scavengers at best and made their money by collecting scrap metal and old bottles and hauling them into town on the back of the elder Harvey's ancient flatbed truck.

When his mother and he were caught for the first time, the two of them were treated graciously by the woman at the cash register. "If you can pay for it, do. If you can't, leave it on the counter as good as new," she said brightly and winked at the eight-year-old George Harvey. His mother took the small glass bottle of aspirin out of her pocket and placed it sheepishly on the counter.

Her face sank. "No better than the child," his father often reprimanded her.

Getting caught became another moment in his life that brought fear—that sick feeling curling into his stomach like eggs being folded into a bowl—and he could tell by the closed faces and hard eyes when the person walking down the aisle toward them was a store employee who had seen a woman stealing.

And she began handing him the stolen items to hide on his body, and he did it because she wanted him to. If they got outside and away in the truck, she would smile and bang the steering wheel with the flat of her hand and call him her little accomplice. The cab would fill with her wild, unpredictable love, and for a little while—until it wore off and they spied something glinting on the side of the road that they would have to investigate for what his mother called its "possibilities"—he did feel free. Free and warm.

He remembered the advice she gave him the first time they drove a stretch of road in Texas and saw a white wooden cross along the road. Around the base of it were clusters of fresh and dead flowers. His scavenger's eye had been drawn immediately by the colors.

"You have to be able to look past the dead," his mother said. "Sometimes there are good trinkets to take away from them."

Even then, he could sense they were doing something wrong. The two of them got out of the truck and went up to the cross, and his mother's eyes changed into the two black points that he was used to seeing when they were searching. She found a charm in the shape of an eye and one in the shape of a heart and held them out for George Harvey to see.

"Don't know what your father would make of them, but we can keep them, just you and me."

She had a secret stash of things that she never showed his father.

"Do you want the eye or the heart?"

"The eye," he said.

"I think these roses are fresh enough to save, nice for the truck."

That night they slept in the truck, unable to make the drive back to where his father was working a temporary job splitting and riving boards by hand.

The two of them slept curled into each other as they did with some frequency, making the inside of the cab an awkward nest. His mother, like a dog worrying a blanket, moved around in her seat and fidgeted. George Harvey had realized after earlier struggles that it was best to go limp and let her move him as she wished. Until his mother was comfortable, no one slept.

In the middle of the night, as he was dreaming about the soft insides of the palaces in picture books he'd seen in public libraries, someone banged on the roof, and George Harvey and his mother sat bolt upright. It was three men, looking through the windows in a way George Harvey recognized. It was the way his own father looked when he was drunk sometimes. It had a double effect: the whole gaze was leveled at his mother and simultaneously absented his son.

He knew not to cry out.

"Stay quiet. They aren't here for you," she whispered to him. He began to shiver underneath the old army blankets that covered them.

One of the three men was standing in front of the truck. The other two were banging on either side of the truck's roof, laughing and lolling their tongues.

His mother shook her head vehemently, but this only enraged them. The man blocking the truck started rocking his hips back and forth against the front end, which caused the other two men to laugh harder.

"I'm going to move slow," his mother whispered, "and pretend I'm getting out of the truck. I want you to reach forward and turn the keys in the ignition when I say so."

He knew he was being told something very important. That she needed him. Despite her practiced calm, he could hear the metal in her voice, the iron breaking up through fear now.

She smiled at the men, and as they sent up whoops and their bodies relaxed, she used her elbow to knock the gear shift into place. "Now," she said in a flat monotone, and George Harvey reached forward and turned the keys. The truck came to life with its rumbling old engine.

The faces of the men changed, fading from an acquisitive joy and then, as she reversed back to a good degree and they stared after her, uncertainty. She switched into drive and screamed, "On the floor!" to her son. He could feel the bump of the man's body hitting the truck only a few feet from where he lay curled up inside. Then the body was pitched up onto the roof. It lay there for a second until his mother reversed again. He had had a moment of clarity about how life should be lived: not as a child or as a woman. They were the two worst things to be.

His heart had beat wildly as he watched Lindsey make for the elderberry hedge, but then immediately he had calmed. It was a skill his mother, not his father, had taught him—to take action only after calculating the worst possible outcome of each choice available. He saw the notebook disturbed and the missing page in his sketchbook. He checked the bag with the knife. He took the knife with him to the basement and dropped it down the square hole that was drilled through the foundation. From the metal shelving, he retrieved the group of charms that he kept from the women. He took the Pennsylvania keystone charm from my bracelet and held it in his hand. Good luck. The others he spread out on his white handkerchief, and then he brought the four ends together to form a small hobo sack. He put his hand inside the hole under the foundation and got down on the floor on his stomach to push his arm in all the way to the shoulder. He groped, feeling with the free fingers of his hand as the other held the hobo sack, until he found a rusty jut of a metal support over which the workmen had poured the cement. He hung his trophy bag there and then withdrew his arm and stood. The book of sonnets he had buried earlier that summer in the woods of Valley Forge Park, shedding evidence slowly as he always did; now, he had to hope, not too slowly.

Five minutes at the most had gone by. That could be accounted for by shock and anger. By checking what everyone else thought to be valuables—his cuff links, his cash, his tools. But he knew no more time than that could be overlooked. He had to call the police.

He worked himself up. He paced briefly, drew his breath in and out rapidly, and when the operator answered he set his voice on edge.

"My home has been broken into. I need the police," he said, scripting the opening of his version of the story as inside he calculated how quickly he could leave and what he would carry with him.

When my father called the station, he requested Len Fenerman. But Fenerman couldn't be located. My father was informed that two uniforms had already been sent out to investigate. What they found when Mr. Harvey answered his door was a man who was tearfully upset and who in every aspect, save a certain repellent quality that the officers attributed to the sight of a man allowing himself to cry, seemed to be responding rationally to the reported events.

Even though the information about the drawing Lindsey had taken had come in over the radio, the officers were more impressed by Mr. Harvey's readily volunteering to have his home searched. He also seemed sincere in his sympathy for the Salmon family.

The officers grew uncomfortable. They searched the house perfunctorily and found nothing except both the evidence of what they took to be extreme loneliness and a room full of beautiful dollhouses on the second floor, where they switched topics and asked him how long he had been building them.

They noticed, they said later, an immediate and friendly change in his demeanor. He went into his bedroom and got the sketchbook, not mentioning any stolen drawing. The police took note of his increasing warmth as he showed them the sketches for the dollhouses. They asked their next question delicately.

"Sir," an officer said, "we can take you down to the station for further questioning, and you do have the right to have a lawyer present but—"

Mr. Harvey interrupted him. "I would be happy to answer anything here. I am the wronged party, though I have no wish to press charges against that poor girl."

"The young woman that broke in," the other officer began, "she did take something. It was a drawing of the cornfield and a sort of structure in it . . ."

The way it hit Harvey, the officers would tell Detective Fenerman, was all at once and very convincing. He had an explanation that fit so perfectly, they did not see him as a flight risk—largely because they did not see him first and foremost as a murderer.

"Oh, the poor girl," he said. He placed his fingers to his pursed lips. He turned to his sketchbook and flipped through it until he came to a drawing that was very much like the one Lindsey had taken.

"There, it was a drawing similar to this one, correct?" The officers—now audience—nodded. "I was trying to figure it out," Mr. Harvey confessed. "I admit the horror of it has obsessed me. I think everyone in the neighborhood has tried to think how they could have prevented it. Why they didn't hear something, see something. I mean, surely the girl screamed.

"Now here," he said to the two men, pointing to his drawing with a pen. "Forgive me, but I think in structures, and after hearing about how much blood there was in the cornfield and the churned-up nature of that area where it was found, I decided that perhaps . . ." He looked at them, checking their eyes. Both officers were following him. They wanted to follow him. They had had no leads, no body, no clues. Perhaps this strange man had a workable theory. "Well, that the person who did it had built something underground, a hole, and then I confess I began to worry at it and detail it the way I do the dollhouses, and I gave it a chimney and a shelf, and, well, that's just my habit." He paused. "I have a lot of time to myself."

"So, did it work out?" one of the two officers asked.

"I always did think I had something there."

"Why didn't you call us?"

"I wasn't bringing back their daughter. When Detective Fenerman interviewed me I mentioned how I suspected the Ellis boy, and I turned out to be dead wrong. I didn't want to meddle with any more of my amateur theories."

The officers apologized for the fact that the following day Detective Fenerman would be calling again, most likely wanting to go over the same material. See the sketchbook, hear Mr. Harvey's assertions about the cornfield. All of this Mr. Harvey took as part of being a dutiful civilian, even if it had been he who was victimized. The officers documented my sister's path of break-in from the basement window and then out through the bedroom window. They discussed the damages, which Mr.

Harvey said he would take care of out-of-pocket, stressing his awareness of the overwhelming grief the Salmon father had displayed several months ago, and how it now seemed to be infecting the poor girl's sister.

I saw the chances of Mr. Harvey's capture diminish as I watched the end of my family as I had known it ignite.

After picking up Buckley from Nate's house, my mother stopped at a payphone outside the 7-Eleven on Route 30. She told Len to meet her at a loud and raucous store in the mall near the grocery store. He left immediately. As he pulled out of his driveway, the phone in his house was ringing but he didn't hear it. He was inside the capsule of his car, thinking of my mother, of how wrong it all was and then of how he could not say no to her for reasons he couldn't hold on to long enough to analyze or disclaim.

My mother drove the short distance from the grocery store to the mall and led Buckley by the hand through the glass doors to a sunken circle where parents could leave their children to play while they shopped.

Buckley was elated. "The circle! Can I?" he said, as he saw his peers jumping off the jungle gym and turning somersaults on the rubber-covered floor.

"Do you really want to, honey?" she asked him.

"Please," he said.

She phrased it as a motherly concession. "All right," she said. And he went off in the direction of a red metal slide. "Be good," she called after him. She had never allowed him to play there without her.

She left his name with the monitor who watched over the play circle and said that she would be shopping on the lower level near Wanamaker's.

While Mr. Harvey was explaining his theory of my murder, my mother felt a hand brush across the back of her shoulders inside a trashy store called Spencer's. She turned with expectant relief, only to see Len Fenerman's back as he made his way out of the store. Passing glow-in-the-dark masks, black plastic eight balls, fuzzy troll keychains, and a large laughing skull, my mother followed after him.

He did not turn around. She kept following him, at first excited and then annoyed. In between footfalls there was enough time to think, and she did not want to think.

Finally, she saw him unlock a white door that was set flush into the wall, which she had never noticed before.

She could tell by the noises up ahead in the dark corridor that Len had brought her into the inner workings of the mall—the air filtration system or the water pumping plant. She didn't care. In the darkness she imagined herself to be within her own heart, and a vision of the enlarged drawing from her doctor's office entered her head and simultaneously she saw my father, in his paper gown and black socks, perched on the edge of the examining table as the doctor had explained to them the dangers of congestive heart failure. Just as she was about to let go into grief, cry out, and stumble and fall into confusion, she came to the end of the corridor. It opened into a huge room three stories high that throbbed and buzzed and throughout which there were tiny lights mounted higgledy-piggledy on metal tanks and drums. She paused and listened for any sound other than the deafening thrumming of air being sucked out of the mall and reconditioned to be pushed back in. Nothing.

I saw Len before she did. Standing alone in the almost-darkness he watched her for a moment, locating the need in her eyes. He was sorry for my father, for my family, but he fell into those eyes. "I could drown in those eyes, Abigail," he wanted to say to her, but he knew that this he would not be allowed.

My mother began to make out more and more shapes within the bright interconnected jumble of metal, and for a moment I could feel the room begin to be enough for her, the foreign territory enough to soothe her. It was the feeling of being unreachable.

If it had not been for Len's hand stretching out and grazing her fingers with the tips of his own, I might have kept her to myself there. The room could have remained simply a brief vacation from her life as Mrs. Salmon.

But he did touch her, and she did turn. Still, she could not really look at him. He accepted this absence on her part.

I swirled as I watched it and held on to the bench in the gazebo, gulping air. She could never know, I thought, that while she was clutching Len's hair and he was reaching his hand around to the small of her back, bringing her in closer, that the man who had murdered me was escorting two officers out his front door.

I felt the kisses as they came down my mother's neck and onto her chest, like the small, light feet of mice, and like the flower petals falling that they were. Ruinous and marvelous all at once. They were whispers calling her away from me and from her family and from her grief. She followed with her body.

While Len took her hand and brought her away from the wall into the tangle of pipes where the noise overhead added its chorus, Mr. Harvey began to pack his belongings; my brother met a small girl playing Hula-Hoop in the circle; my sister and Samuel lay beside each other on her bed, fully dressed and nervous; my grandmother downed three shots in the empty dining room. My father watched the phone.

My mother grabbed at Len's coat and shirt greedily, and he helped her. He watched as she tugged at her own clothes, pulling her sweater over her head, then her mother-jumper, and her turtleneck, until she was left in her underpants and camisole. He stared at her.

Samuel kissed the back of my sister's neck. She smelled of soap and Bactine, and he wanted, even then, never to leave her.

Len was about to say something; I could see my mother notice his lips just as they parted. She shut her eyes and commanded the world to shut up—screaming the words inside her skull. She opened her eyes again and looked at him. He was silent, his mouth set. She took her cotton camisole over the top of her head and stepped out of her underwear. My mother had my body as it would never become. But she had her own moonlit skin, her ocean eyes. She was hollow and lost and abandoned up.

Mr. Harvey left his house for the final time while my mother was granted her most temporal wish. To find a doorway out of her ruined heart, in merciful adultery.

SIXTEEN

A year to the day after my death, Dr. Singh called to say he would not be home for dinner. But Ruana would do her exercises no matter what. If, as she stretched out on the rug in the one warm spot that the house seemed to hold in the winter, she could not help but turn over and over again her husband's absences in her mind, she would let them consume her until her body pled for her to let him go and to focus—as she leaned forward, her arms outstretched toward her toes now—and move, to shut her brain off and forget everything but the slight and pleasant yearning of muscles stretching and her own body bending.

Reaching almost to the floor, the window in the dining room was interrupted only by the metal baseboard for the heat, which Ruana liked to keep turned off because the noises it made disturbed her. Outside, she could see the cherry tree, its leaves and flowers all gone. The empty bird feeder swung slightly on its branch.

She stretched until she was quite warm and she'd forgotten herself, and the home she stood in fell away from her. Her age.

Her son. But still, creeping in on her was the figure of her husband. She had a premonition. She did not believe it was a woman, or even a student who worshiped him, that made him late more and more often. She knew what it was because it was something she too had had and had severed herself from after having been injured long ago. It was ambition.

She heard sounds now. Holiday barking two streets over and the Gilberts' dog answering him and Ray moving around upstairs. Blessedly, in another moment, Jethro Tull erupted again, shutting out all else.

Except for the occasional cigarette, which she smoked as secretly as she could so as not to give Ray license, she had kept herself in good health. Many of the women in the neighborhood commented on how well she kept herself and some had asked her if she would mind showing them how, though she had always taken these entreaties merely as their way of making conversation with their lone foreign-born neighbor. But as she sat in Sukhasana and her breath slowed to a deep rhythm, she could not fully release and let go. The niggling idea of what she would do as Ray grew older and her husband worked increasingly long hours crept up the inside of her foot and along her calf to the back of her knee and began to climb into her lap.

The doorbell rang.

Ruana was happy for the escape, and though she was someone to whom order was also a sort of meditation, she hopped up, wrapped a shawl that was hanging on the back of a chair around her waist, and, with Ray's music barreling down the stairs, walked to the door. She thought only for a moment that it might be a neighbor. A complaining neighbor—the music—and she, dressed in a red leotard and shawl.

Ruth stood on the stoop, holding a grocery sack.

"Hello," Ruana said. "May I help you?"

"I'm here to see Ray."

"Come in."

All of this had to be half-shouted over the noise coming from upstairs. Ruth stepped into the front hall.

"Go on up," Ruana shouted, pointing to the stairs.

I watched Ruana take in Ruth's baggy overalls, her turtleneck, her parka. *I could start with her,* Ruana thought to herself.

Ruth had been standing in the grocery store with her mother when she saw the candles among the paper plates and plastic forks and spoons. At school that day she had been acutely aware of what day it was and even though what she had done so far—lain in bed reading *The Bell Jar,* helped her mother clean out what her father insisted on calling his toolshed and what she thought of as the poetry shed, and tagged along to the grocery store—hadn't consisted of anything that might mark the anniversary of my death, she had been determined to do something.

When she saw the candles she knew immediately that she would find her way over to Ray's house and ask him to come with her. Because of their meetings at the shot-put circle, the kids at school had made them a couple despite all evidence to the contrary. Ruth could draw as many female nudes as she might wish and fashion scarves on her head and write papers on Janis Joplin and loudly protest the oppression of shaving her legs and armpits. In the eyes of her classmates at Fairfax, she remained a weird girl who had been found K-I-S-S-I-N-G a weird boy.

What no one understood—and they could not begin to tell anyone—was that it had been an experiment between them. Ray had kissed only me, and Ruth had never kissed anyone, so, united, they had agreed to kiss each other and see.

"I don't feel anything," Ruth had said afterward, as they lay in the maple leaves under a tree behind the teachers' parking lot.

"I don't either," Ray admitted.

"Did you feel something when you kissed Susie?"

"Yes."

"What?"

"That I wanted more. That night I dreamed of kissing her again and wondered if she was thinking the same thing."

"And sex?"

"I hadn't really gotten that far yet," Ray said. "Now I kiss you and it's not the same."

"We could keep trying," Ruth said. "I'm game if you don't tell anyone."

"I thought you liked girls," Ray said.

"I'll make you a deal," Ruth said. "You can pretend I'm Susie and I will too."

"You are so entirely screwed up," Ray said, smiling.

"Are you saying you don't want to?" Ruth teased.

"Show me your drawings again."

"I may be screwed up," Ruth said, dragging out her sketchbook from her book bag—it was now full of nudes she'd copied out of *Playboy,* scaling various parts up or down and adding hair and wrinkles where they had been airbrushed out—"but at least I'm not a perv for charcoal."

Ray was dancing around his bedroom when Ruth walked in. He wore his glasses, which at school he tried to do without because they were thick and his father had only sprung for the least expensive, hard-to-break frames. He had on a pair of jeans that were baggy and stained and a T-shirt that Ruth imagined, and I knew, had been slept in.

He stopped dancing as soon as he saw her standing at the doorway holding the grocery bag. His hands went up immediately and collected his glasses, and then, not knowing what to do with them, he waved them at her and said, "Hello."

"Can you turn it down?" Ruth screamed.

"Sure!"

When the noise ceased her ears rang for a second, and in that second she saw something flicker across Ray's eyes.

He now stood on the other side of the room, and in between them was his bed, where sheets were rumpled and balled and over which hung a drawing Ruth had done of me from memory.

"You hung it up," Ruth said.

"I think it's really good."

"You and me and nobody else."

"My mom thinks it's good."

"She's intense, Ray," Ruth said, putting down the bag. "No wonder you're so freak-a-delic."

"What's in the bag?"

"Candles," said Ruth. "I got them at the grocery store. It's December sixth."

"I know."

"I thought we might go to the cornfield and light them. Say goodbye."

"How many times can you say it?"

"It was an idea," Ruth said. "I'll go alone."

"No," Ray said. "I'll go."

Ruth sat down in her jacket and overalls and waited for him to change his shirt. She watched him with his back toward her, how thin he was but also how the muscles seemed to pop on his arms the way they were supposed to and the color of his skin, like his mother's, so much more inviting than her own.

"We can kiss for a while if you want."

And he turned, grinning. He had begun to like the experiments. He was not thinking of me anymore—though he couldn't tell that to Ruth.

He liked the way she cursed and hated school. He liked how smart she was and how she tried to pretend that it didn't matter to her that his father was a doctor (even though not a real doctor, as she pointed out) and her father scavenged old houses, or that the Singhs had rows and rows of books in their house while she was starved for them.

He sat down next to her on the bed.

"Do you want to take your parka off?"

She did.

And so on the anniversary of my death, Ray mashed himself against Ruth and the two of them kissed and at some point she looked him in the face. "Shit!" she said. "I think I feel something."

When Ray and Ruth arrived at the cornfield, they were silent and he was holding her hand. She didn't know whether he was holding it because they were observing my death together or because he liked her. Her brain was a storm, her usual insight gone.

Then she saw she had not been the only one to think of me. Hal and Samuel Heckler were standing in the cornfield with their hands jammed in their pockets and their backs turned toward her. Ruth saw yellow daffodils on the ground.

"Did you bring those?" Ruth asked Samuel.

"No," Hal said, answering for his brother. "They were already here when we got here."

Mrs. Stead watched from her son's upstairs bedroom. She decided to throw on her coat and walk out to the field. It was not something she even tried to judge, whether or not she belonged there.

Grace Tarking was walking around the block when she saw Mrs. Stead leaving her house with a poinsettia. They talked briefly in the street. Grace said that she was going to stop at home but she would come and join them.

Grace made two phone calls, one to her boyfriend, who lived a short distance away in a slightly richer area, and one to the

Gilberts. They had not yet recovered from their strange role in the discovery of my death—their faithful lab having found the first evidence. Grace offered to escort them, since they were older and cutting across neighbors' lawns and over the bumpy earth of the cornfield would be a challenge to them, but yes, Mr. Gilbert had said, he wanted to come. They needed this, he told Grace Tarking, his wife particularly—though I could see how crushed he was. He always covered his pain by being attentive to his wife. Though they had thought briefly of giving their dog away, he was too much comfort to both of them.

Mr. Gilbert wondered if Ray, who ran errands for them and was a sweet boy who had been badly judged, knew, and so he called the Singh household. Ruana said she suspected her son must already be there but that she would be along herself.

Lindsey was looking out the window when she saw Grace Tarking with her arm in Mrs. Gilbert's and Grace's boyfriend steadying Mr. Gilbert as the four of them cut across the O'Dwyers' lawn.

"Something's going on in the cornfield, Mom," she said.

My mother was reading Molière, whom she had studied so intensely in college but hadn't looked at since. Beside her were the books that had marked her as an avant-garde undergraduate: Sartre, Colette, Proust, Flaubert. She had pulled them off the shelves in her bedroom and promised herself she would reread them that year.

"I'm not interested," she said to Lindsey, "but I'm sure your father will be when he gets home. Why don't you go up and play with your brother?"

My sister had dutifully hovered for weeks now, paying court to our mother regardless of the signals she gave. There was something on the other side of the icy surface. Lindsey was sure of it. She stayed by my mother, sitting by her chair and watching our neighbors outside the window.

* * *

By the time darkness fell, the candles the latecomers had had the foresight to bring lit the cornfield. It seemed like everyone I'd ever known or sat next to in a classroom from kindergarten to eighth grade was there. Mr. Botte saw that something was happening when he'd come out of the school after preparing his classroom for the next day's annual animal digestion experiment. He'd strolled over, and, when he realized what it was, he let himself back into the school and made some calls. There had been a secretary who had been overcome by my death. She came with her son. There had been some teachers who hadn't come to the official school memorial.

The rumors of Mr. Harvey's suspected guilt had begun to make their way from neighbor to neighbor on Thanksgiving night. By the next afternoon it was the only thing the neighbors could talk about—was it possible? Could that strange man who had lived so quietly among them have killed Susie Salmon? But no one had dared approach my family to find out the details. Cousins of friends or fathers of the boys who cut their lawn were asked if they knew anything. Anyone who might know what the police were doing had been buddied up to in the past week, and so my memorial was both a way to mark my memory and a way for the neighbors to seek comfort from one another. A murderer had lived among them, passed them on the street, bought Girl Scout cookies from their daughters and magazine subscriptions from their sons.

In my heaven I buzzed with heat and energy as more and more people reached the cornfield and lit their candles and began to hum a low, dirgelike song for which Mr. O'Dwyer called back to the distant memory of his Dublin grandfather. My neighbors were awkward at first, but the secretary from the school clung to Mr. O'Dwyer as his voice gave forth, and she added her less melodious one. Ruana Singh stood stiffly in an outer circle away from her son. Dr. Singh had called as she was leaving to say he would be sleeping overnight in his office. But other fathers, coming home from their offices, parked their cars in their driveways only to get out and follow their neighbors. How could they both work to support their families and watch their children to make sure they were safe? As a group they would learn it was impossible, no matter how many rules they laid down. What had happened to me could happen to anyone.

No one had called my house. My family was left undisturbed. The impenetrable barrier that surrounded the shingles, the chimney, the woodpile, the driveway, the fence, was like a layer of clear ice that coated the trees when it rained and then froze. Our house looked the same as every other one on the block, but it was not the same. Murder had a blood red door on the other side of which was everything unimaginable to everyone.

When the sky had turned a dappled rose, Lindsey realized what was happening. My mother never lifted her eyes from her book.

"They're having a ceremony for Susie," Lindsey said. "Listen." She cracked the window open. In rushed the cold December air and the distant sound of singing.

My mother used all her energy. "We've had the memorial," she said. "That's done for me."

"What's done?"

My mother's elbows were on the armrests of the yellow winged-back chair. She leaned slightly forward and her face moved into shadow, making it harder for Lindsey to see the expression on her face. "I don't believe she's waiting for us out there. I don't think lighting candles and doing all that stuff is honoring her memory. There are other ways to honor it."

"Like what?" Lindsey said. She sat cross-legged on the rug in front of my mother, who sat in her chair with her finger marking her place in Molière.

"I want to be more than a mother."

Lindsey thought she could understand this. She wanted to be more than a girl.

My mother put the Molière book on top of the coffee table and scooted forward on the chair until she lowered herself down onto the rug. I was struck by this. My mother did not sit on the floor, she sat at the bill-paying desk or in the wing chairs or sometimes on the end of the couch with Holiday curled up beside her.

She took my sister's hand in hers.

"Are you going to leave us?" Lindsey asked.

My mother wobbled. How could she say what she already knew? Instead, she told a lie. "I promise I won't leave you."

What she wanted most was to be that free girl again, stacking china at Wanamaker's, hiding from her manager the Wedgwood cup with the handle she broke, dreaming of living in Paris like de Beauvoir and Sartre, and going home that day laughing to herself about the nerdy Jack Salmon, who was pretty cute even if he hated smoke. The cafés in Paris were full of cigarettes, she'd told him, and he'd seemed impressed. At the end of that summer when she invited him in and they had, both for the first time, made love, she'd smoked a cigarette, and for the joke he said he'd have one too. When she handed him the damaged blue china to use as an ashtray, she used all her favorite words to embellish the story of breaking and then hiding, inside her coat, the now homely Wedgwood cup.

"Come here, baby," my mother said, and Lindsey did. She leaned her back into my mother's chest, and my mother rocked her awkwardly on the rug. "You are doing so well, Lindsey; you are keeping your father alive." And they heard his car pull into the drive.

Lindsey let herself be held while my mother thought of Ruana Singh out behind her house, smoking. The sweet scent of Dunhills had drifted out onto the road and taken my mother far away. Her last boyfriend before my father had loved Gauloises. He had been a pretentious little thing, she thought, but he had also been oh-so-serious in a way that let her be oh-so-serious as well.

"Do you see the candles, Mom?" Lindsey asked, as she stared out the window.

"Go get your father," my mother said.

My sister met my father in the mud room, hanging up his keys and coat. Yes, they would go, he said. Of course they would go.

"Daddy!" My brother called from the second floor, where my sister and father went to meet him.

"Your call," my father said as Buckley bodychecked him.

"I'm tired of protecting him," Lindsey said. "It doesn't feel real not to include him. Susie's gone. He knows that."

My brother stared up at her.

"There is a party for Susie," Lindsey said. "And me and Daddy are taking you."

"Is Mommy sick?" Buckley asked.

Lindsey didn't want to lie to him, but she also felt it was an accurate description of what she knew.

"Yes."

Lindsey agreed to meet our father downstairs while she brought Buckley into his room to change his clothes.

"I see her, you know," Buckley said, and Lindsey looked at him.

"She comes and talks to me, and spends time with me when you're at soccer."

Lindsey didn't know what to say, but she reached out and grabbed him and squeezed him to her, the way he often squeezed Holiday.

"You are so special," she said to my brother. "I'll always be here, no matter what."

My father made his slow way down the stairs, his left hand tightening on the wooden banister, until he reached the flagstone landing.

His approach was loud. My mother took her Molière book and crept into the dining room, where he wouldn't see her. She read her book, standing in the corner of the dining room and hiding from her family. She waited for the front door to open and close.

My neighbors and teachers, friends and family, circled an arbitrary spot not far from where I'd been killed. My father, sister, and brother heard the singing again once they were outside. Everything in my father leaned and pitched toward the warmth and light. He wanted so badly to have me remembered in the minds and hearts of everyone. I knew something as I watched: almost everyone was saying goodbye to me. I was becoming one of many little-girl-losts. They would go back to their homes and put me to rest, a letter from the past never reopened or reread. And I could say goodbye to them, wish them well, bless them somehow for their good thoughts. A handshake in the street, a dropped item picked up and retrieved and handed back, or a friendly wave from a distant window, a nod, a smile, a moment when the eyes lock over the antics of a child.

Ruth saw my three family members first, and she tugged on Ray's sleeve. "Go help him," she whispered. And Ray, who had met my father on his first day of what would prove a long journey to try to find my killer, moved forward. Samuel came away too. Like youthful pastors, they brought my father and sister and brother into the group, which made a wide berth for them and grew silent.

My father had not been outside the house except to drive back and forth to work or sit out in the backyard, for months, nor had he seen his neighbors. Now he looked at them, from face to face, until he realized I had been loved by people he didn't even recognize. His heart filled up, warm again as it had not been in what seemed so long to him—save small forgotten moments with Buckley, the accidents of love that happened with his son.

He looked at Mr. O'Dwyer. "Stan," he said, "Susie used to stand at the front window during the summer and listen to you singing in your yard. She loved it. Will you sing for us?"

And in the kind of grace that is granted, but rarely, and not when you wish it most—to save a loved one from dying—Mr. O'Dwyer wobbled only a moment on his first note, then sang loud and clear and fine.

Everyone joined in.

I remembered those summer nights my father spoke of. How the darkness would take forever to come and with it I always hoped for it to cool down. Sometimes, standing at the open window in the front hall, I would feel a breeze, and on that breeze was the music coming from the O'Dwyers' house. As I listened to Mr. O'Dwyer run through all the Irish ballads he had ever learned, the breeze would begin to smell of earth and air and a mossy scent that meant only one thing: a thunderstorm.

There was a wonderful temporary hush then, as Lindsey sat in her room on the old couch studying, my father sat in his den reading his books, my mother downstairs doing needlepoint or washing up.

I liked to change into a long cotton nightgown and go out onto the back porch, where, as the rain began falling in heavy drops against the roof, breezes came in the screens from all sides and swept my gown against me. It was warm and wonderful and the lightning would come and, a few moments later, the thunder.

My mother would stand at the open porch door, and, after she said her standard warning, "You're going to catch your death of cold," she grew quiet. We both listened together to the rain pour down and the thunder clap and smelled the earth rising to greet us.

"You look invincible," my mother said one night.

I loved these times, when we seemed to feel the same thing. I turned to her, wrapped in my thin gown, and said:

"I am."

SNAPSHOTS

With the camera my parents gave me, I took dozens of candids of my family. So many that my father forced me to choose which rolls I thought should be developed. As the cost of my obsession mounted, I began keeping two boxes in my closet. "Rolls to be sent out" and "Rolls to hold back." It was, my mother said, the only hint of any organizational skills I possessed.

I loved the way the burned-out flashcubes of the Kodak Instamatic marked a moment that had passed, one that would now be gone forever except for a picture. When they were spent, I took the cubed four-corner flashbulbs and passed them from hand to hand until they cooled. The broken filaments of the flash would turn a molten marble blue or sometimes smoke the thin glass black. I had rescued the moment by using my camera and in that way had found a way to stop time and hold it. No one could take that image away from me because I owned it.

* * *

On a summer evening in 1975, my mother turned to my father and said:

"Have you ever made love in the ocean?"

And he said, "No."

"Neither have I," my mother said. "Let's pretend it is the ocean and that I am going away and we might never see each other again."

The next day she left for her father's cabin in New Hampshire.

That same summer, Lindsey or Buckley or my father would open the front door and find a casserole or a bundt cake on the front stoop. Sometimes an apple pie—my father's favorite. The food was unpredictable. The casseroles Mrs. Stead made were horrible. The bundt cakes Mrs. Gilbert made were overly moist but bearable. The apple pies from Ruana: heaven on Earth.

In his study during the long nights after my mother left, my father would try to lose himself by rereading passages from the Civil War letters of Mary Chestnut to her husband. He tried to let go of any blame, of any hope, but it was impossible. He did manage a small smile once.

"Ruana Singh bakes a mean apple pie," he wrote in his notebook.

In the fall he picked up the phone one afternoon to hear Grandma Lynn.

"Jack," my grandmother announced, "I am thinking of coming to stay."

My father was silent, but the line was riddled with his hesitation.

"I would like to make myself available to you and the children. I've been knocking around in this mausoleum long enough."

"Lynn, we're just beginning to start over again," he stammered. Still, he couldn't depend on Nate's mother to watch Buckley forever. Four months after my mother left, her temporary absence was beginning to take on the feel of permanence.

My grandmother insisted. I watched her resist the remaining slug of vodka in her glass. "I will contain my drinking until"— she thought hard here—"after five o'clock, and," she said, "what the hell, I'll stop altogether if you should find it necessary."

"Do you know what you're saying?"

My grandmother felt a clarity from her phone hand down to her pump-encased feet. "Yes, I do. I think."

It was only after he got off the phone that he let himself wonder, *Where will we PUT her?*

It was obvious to everyone.

By December 1975, a year had passed since Mr. Harvey had packed his bags, but there was still no sign of him. For a while, until the tape dirtied or the paper tore, store owners kept a scratchy sketch of him taped to their windows. Lindsey and Samuel walked in the neighborhood or hung out at Hal's bike shop. She wouldn't go to the diner where the other kids went. The owner of the diner was a law and order man. He had blown up the sketch of George Harvey to twice its size and taped it to the front door. He willingly gave the grisly details to any customer who asked—young girl, cornfield, found only an elbow.

Finally Lindsey asked Hal to give her a ride to the police station. She wanted to know what exactly they were doing.

They bid farewell to Samuel at the bike shop and Hal gave Lindsey a ride through a wet December snow.

From the start, Lindsey's youth and purpose had caught the police off guard. As more and more of them realized who she was, they gave her a wider and wider berth. Here was this girl, focused, mad, fifteen. Her breasts were perfect small cups, her legs gangly but curved, her eyes like flint and flower petals.

While Lindsey and Hal waited outside the captain's office on a wooden bench, she thought she saw something across the room that she recognized. It was on Detective Fenerman's desk and it stood out in the room because of its color. What her mother had always distinguished as Chinese red, a harsher red than rose red, it was the red of classic lipsticks, rarely found in nature. Our mother was proud of her ability to wear Chinese red, noting each time she tied a particular scarf around her neck that it was a color even Grandma Lynn dared not wear.

"Hal," she said, every muscle tense as she stared at the increasingly familiar object on Fenerman's desk.

"Yes."

"Do you see that red cloth?"

"Yes."

"Can you go and get it for me?"

When Hal looked at her, she said: "I think it's my mother's."

As Hal stood to retrieve it, Len entered the squad room from behind where Lindsey sat. He tapped her on the shoulder just as he realized what Hal was doing. Lindsey and Detective Fenerman stared at each other.

"Why do you have my mother's scarf?"

He stumbled. "She might have left it in my car one day."

Lindsey stood and faced him. She was clear-eyed and driving fast toward the worst news yet. "What was she doing in your car?"

"Hello, Hal," Len said.

Hal held the scarf in his hand. Lindsey grabbed it away, her voice growing angry. "Why do you have my mother's scarf?"

And though Len was the detective, Hal saw it first—it arched over her like a rainbow—Prisma Color understanding. The way it happened in algebra class or English when my sister was the first person to figure out the sum of *x* or point out the double entendres to her peers. Hal put his hand on Lindsey's shoulder to guide her. "We should go," he said.

And later she cried out her disbelief to Samuel in the back room of the bike shop.

When my brother turned seven, he built a fort for me. It was something the two of us had said we would always do together and something my father could not bring himself to do. It reminded him too much of building the tent with the disappeared Mr. Harvey.

A family with five little girls had moved into Mr. Harvey's house. Laughter traveled over into my father's study from the built-in pool they had poured the spring after George Harvey ran. The sound of little girls—girls to spare.

The cruelty of it became like glass shattering in my father's ears. In the spring of 1976, with my mother gone, he would shut the window of his den on even the hottest evenings to avoid the sound. He watched his solitary little boy in among the three pussy-willow bushes, talking to himself. Buckley had brought empty terra-cotta pots from the garage. He hauled the boot scraper out from where it lay forgotten at the side of the house. Anything to make walls for the fort. With the help of Samuel and Hal and Lindsey, he edged two huge boulders from the front of the driveway into the backyard. This was such an unexpected windfall that it prompted Samuel to ask, "How are you going to make a roof?"

And Buckley looked at him in wonder as Hal mentally scanned the contents of his bike shop and remembered two scrap sheets of corrugated tin he had leaning up against the back wall.

So one hot night my father looked down and didn't see his son anymore. Buckley was nestled inside his fort. On his hands and knees, he would pull the terra-cotta pots in after him and then prop a board against them that reached almost up to the wavy roof. Just enough light came in to read by. Hal had obliged him and painted in big black spray paint letters KEEP OUT on one side of the plywood door.

Mostly he read the Avengers and the X-Men. He dreamed of being Wolverine, who had a skeleton made of the strongest metal in the universe and who could heal from any wound overnight. At the oddest moments he would think about me, miss my voice, wish I would come out from the house and pound on the roof of his fort and demand to be let in. Sometimes he wished Samuel and Lindsey hung out more or that my father would play with him as he once had. Play without that always-worried look underneath the smile, that desperate worry that surrounded everything now like an invisible force field. But my brother would not let himself miss my mother. He tunneled into stories where weak men changed into strong half-animals or used eye beams or magic hammers to power through steel or climb up the sides of skyscrapers. He was the Hulk when angry and Spidey the rest of the time. When he felt his heart hurt he turned into something stronger than a little boy, and he grew up this way. A heart that flashed from heart to stone, heart to stone. As I watched I thought of what Grandma Lynn liked to say when Lindsey and I rolled our eyes or grimaced behind her back. "Watch out what faces you make. You'll freeze that way."

One day, Buckley came home from the second grade with a story he'd written: "Once upon a time there was a kid named Billy. He liked to explore. He saw a hole and went inside but he never came out. The End."

My father was too distracted to see anything in this. Mimicking my mother, he taped it to the fridge in the same place Buckley's long-forgotten drawing of the Inbetween had been. But my brother knew something was wrong with his story. Knew it by how his teacher had reacted, doing a double take like they did in his comic books. He took the story down and brought it to my old room while Grandma Lynn was downstairs. He folded it into a tiny square and put it inside the now-empty insides of my four-poster bed.

On a hot day in the fall of 1976, Len Fenerman visited the large safety box in the evidence room. The bones of the neighborhood animals he had found in Mr. Harvey's crawlspace were there, along with the lab confirmation of evidence of quicklime. He had supervised the investigation, but no matter how much they dug, or how deep, no other bones or bodies had been found on his property. The blood stain on the floor of his garage was my only calling card. Len had spent weeks, then months, poring over a xerox of the sketch Lindsey had stolen. He had led a team back into the field, and they had dug and then dug again. Finally they found an old Coke bottle at the opposite end of the field. There it was, a solid link: fingerprints matching Mr. Harvey's prints, which were all over his house, and fingerprints matching those on my birth certificate. There was no question in his mind: Jack Salmon had been right from the beginning.

But no matter how hard he looked for the man himself, it was as if George Harvey had evaporated into thin air when he hit the property line. He could find no records with that name attached. Officially, he did not exist.

What he had left behind were his dollhouses. So Len called the man who sold them for him, and who took commissions from select stores, and the wealthy people who ordered replicas of their own homes. Nothing. He had called the makers of the miniature chairs, the tiny doors and windows with beveled glass and brass hardware, and the manufacturer of the cloth shrubs and trees. Nothing.

He sat down among the evidence at a barren communal desk in the basement of the station. He looked through the stack of extra fliers that my father had made up. He had memorized my face, but still he looked at them. He had come to believe that the best hope in my case might be the recent rise in development in the area. With all the land churning and changing, perhaps other clues would be found that would provide the answer he needed.

In the bottom of the box was the bag with my jingle-bell hat. When he'd handed it to my mother, she had collapsed on the rug. He still couldn't pinpoint the moment he'd fallen in love with her. I knew it was the day he'd sat in our family room while my mother drew stick figures on butcher paper and Buckley and Nate slept toe to toe on the couch. I felt sorry for him. He had tried to solve my murder and he had failed. He had tried to love my mother and he had failed.

Len looked at the drawing of the cornfield that Lindsey had stolen and forced himself to acknowledge this: in his cautiousness, he had allowed a murderer to get away. He could not shake his guilt. He knew, if no one else did, that by being with my mother in the mall that day he was the one to blame for George Harvey's freedom.

He took his wallet out of his back pocket and laid down the photos of all the unsolved cases he had ever worked on. Among them was his wife's. He turned them all face-down. "Gone," he wrote on each one of them. He would no longer wait for a date to mark an understanding of who or why or how. He would never understand all the reasons why his wife had killed herself. He would never understand how so many children went missing. He placed these photos in the box with my evidence and turned the lights off in the cold room.

But he did not know this:

In Connecticut on September 10, 1976, a hunter on his way back to his car saw something shiny on the ground. My

Pennsylvania keystone charm. Then he saw that the ground nearby had been partially dug up by a bear. Exposed by the bear were the unmistakable bones of a child's foot.

My mother made it through only one winter in New Hampshire before she got the idea of driving all the way to California. It was something she had always thought she would do but had never done. A man she met in New Hampshire had told her about the work to be had in wineries in the valleys above San Francisco. It was easy to get, it was physical, and it could be, if you wanted it to be, very anonymous. All three sounded good to her.

This man had also wanted to sleep with her, but she said no. By then, she knew this wasn't the road out anymore. From the first night with Len in the innards of the mall she had known the two of them weren't building anything. She could not even really feel him.

She packed her bags for California and sent cards to my brother and sister from every town she stopped in. "Hello, I'm in Dayton. Ohio's state bird is the cardinal." "Reached the Mississippi last night at sunset. It certainly is a big river."

In Arizona, when she was eight states beyond the farthest she had ever been, she paid for her room and brought a bucket of ice with her from the machine outside. The next day she would reach California, and to celebrate she had bought herself a bottle of champagne. She thought of what the man in New Hampshire had said, how he had spent one whole year scraping the mold out of the giant casks that held wine. He had lain flat on his back and had to use a knife to peel back the layers of mold. The mold had the color and consistency of liver, and no matter how hard he bathed he would still attract fruit flies for hours afterward.

She sipped champagne from a plastic cup and looked at herself in the mirror. She forced herself to look.

She remembered sitting in our living room then, with me and my sister, my brother and father, on the first New Year's Eve that all five of us had stayed up. She had shaped the day around making sure Buckley got enough sleep.

When he woke up after dark he was sure that someone better than Santa would come that night. In his mind he held a big bang image of the ultimate holiday, when he would be transported to toyland.

Hours later, as he yawned and leaned into my mother's lap and she finger-combed his hair, my father ducked into the kitchen to make cocoa and my sister and I served German chocolate cake. When the clock struck twelve and there was only distant screaming and a few guns shot into the air in our neighborhood, my brother was unbelieving. Disappointment so swiftly and thoroughly overtook him that my mother was at a loss for what to do. She thought of it as sort of an infant Peggy Lee's "Is that all there is?" and then bawling.

She remembered my father had lifted Buckley up into his arms and started singing. The rest of us joined in. "Let ole acquaintance be forgot and never brought to mind, should ole acquaintance be forgot and days of auld lang syne!"

And Buckley had stared at us. He captured the foreign words like bubbles floating above him in the air. "Lang syne?" he said with a look of wonder.

"What does that mean?" I asked my parents.

"The old days," my father said.

"Days long past," my mother said. But then, suddenly, she had started pinching the crumbs of her cake together on her plate.

"Hey, Ocean Eyes," my father said. "Where'd you go on us?"

And she remembered that she had met his question with a closing off, as though her spirit had a tap—twist to the right and she was up on her feet asking me to help her clean up.

In the fall of 1976, when she reached California, she drove

directly to the beach and stopped her car. She felt like she had driven through nothing but families for four days—squabbling families, bawling families, screaming families, families under the miraculous strain of the day by day—and she was relieved to see the waves from the windshield of her car. She couldn't help thinking of the books she had read in college. *The Awakening.* And what had happened to one writer, Virginia Woolf. It all seemed so wonderful back then—filmy and romantic—stones in the pocket, walk into the waves.

She climbed down the cliffs after tying her sweater loosely around her waist. Down below she could see nothing but jagged rocks and waves. She was careful, but I watched her feet more than the view she saw—I worried about her slipping.

My mother's desire to reach those waves, touch her feet to another ocean on the other side of the country, was all she was thinking of—the pure baptismal goal of it. Whoosh and you can start over again. Or was life more like the horrible game in gym that has you running from one side of an enclosed space to another, picking up and setting down wooden blocks without end? She was thinking *reach the waves, the waves, the waves,* and I was watching her feet navigate the rocks, and when we heard her we did so together—looking up in shock.

It was a baby on the beach.

In among the rocks was a sandy cove, my mother now saw, and crawling across the sand on a blanket was a baby in knitted pink cap and singlet and boots. She was alone on the blanket with a stuffed white toy—my mother thought a lamb.

With their backs to my mother as she descended were a group of adults—very official and frantic-looking—wearing black and navy with cool slants to their hats and boots. Then my wildlife photographer's eye saw the tripods and silver circles rimmed by wire, which, when a young man moved them left or right, bounced light off or on the baby on her blanket.

My mother started laughing, but only one assistant turned to notice her up among the rocks; everyone else was too busy. This was an ad for something, I imagined, but what? New fresh infant girls to replace your own? As my mother laughed and I watched her face light up, I also saw it fall into strange lines.

She saw the waves behind the girl child and how both beautiful and intoxicating they were—they could sweep up so softly and remove this girl from the beach. All the stylish people could chase after her, but she would drown in a moment—no one, not even a mother who had every nerve attuned to anticipate disaster, could have saved her if the waves leapt up, if life went on as usual and freak accidents peppered a calm shore.

That same week she found work at the Krusoe Winery, in a valley above the bay. She wrote my sister and brother postcards filled with the bright fragments of her life, hoping in a postcard's limited space she would sound cheery.

On her days off, she would walk down the streets of Sausalito or Santa Rosa—tiny upscale towns where everyone was a stranger—and, no matter how hard she tried to focus on the hopeful unfamiliar, when she walked inside a gift shop or café the four walls around her would begin to breathe like a lung. She would feel it then, creeping up the side of her calves and into her gut, the onslaught, the grief coming, the tears like a small relentless army approaching the front lines of her eyes, and she would breathe in, taking a large gulp of air to try to stop herself from crying in a public place. She asked for coffee and toast in a restaurant and buttered it with tears. She went into a flower shop and asked for daffodils, and when there were none she felt robbed. It was such a small wish—a bright yellow flower.

The first impromptu memorial in the cornfield opened in my father the need for more. Yearly now, he organized a memorial, to which fewer and fewer neighbors and friends came. There were the regulars, like Ruth, and the Gilberts, but more and more the group was filled out by kids from the high school who, as time went by, knew only my name and even that only as a large dark rumor invoked as a warning to any student that might prove too much a loner. Especially girls.

Each time my name was said by these strangers it felt like a pinprick. It was not the pleasant sensation that it could be when my father said it or when Ruth wrote it in her journal. It was the sensation of being simultaneously resurrected and buried within the same breath. As if in an economics class I had been ushered over into a column of transmutable commodities: the Murdered. A few teachers, like Mr. Botte, remembered me as a real girl. Sometimes on his lunch hour he would go and sit in his red Fiat and think about the daughter he had lost to leukemia. In the distance, out past his window, the cornfield loomed. Often, he would say a prayer for me.

In just a few short years, Ray Singh grew so handsome that a spell radiated from him when he walked into a crowd. His adult face had still not settled on him, but, now that he was seventeen, it was just around the corner. He exuded a dreamy asexuality that made him attractive to both men and women, with his long lashes and hooded eyelids, his thick black hair, and the same delicate features that were still a boy's.

I would watch Ray with a longing different from that which I had for anyone else. A longing to touch and hold him, to understand the very body that he examined with the coldest of eyes. He would sit at his desk and read his favorite book—*Gray's Anatomy*—and depending on what he was reading about he would use his fingers to palpate his carotid artery or his thumb to press down and follow the longest muscle in his body—the sartorius, which ran from the outside of his hip to the inside of his knee. His thinness was a boon to him then, the bones and muscles clearly distinguished beneath the skin.

By the time he packed his bags for Penn, he had committed so many words and their definitions to memory that I grew worried. With all that, how could his mind contain anything else? Ruth's friendship, his mother's love, my memory would be pushed to the back as he made way for the eye's crystalline lens and its capsule, the semicircular canals of the ear, or my favorite, the qualities of the sympathetic nervous system.

I need not have worried. Ruana cast about the house for something, anything, that her son might bring with him that was equal in heft and weight to *Gray's* and that would, she hoped, keep the flower-gathering side of him alive. Without his knowing, she tucked the book of Indian poetry into his luggage. Inside was the long-forgotten photo of me. When he unpacked inside Hill House dormitory, my picture fell on the floor by his bed. Despite how he could dissect it—the vessels of the globe of my eye, the surgical anatomy of my nasal fossae, the light tincture of my epidermis—he could not avoid them, the lips he had once kissed.

In June 1977, on the day of what would have been my graduation, Ruth and Ray were already gone. The day classes ended at Fairfax, Ruth moved to New York City with her mother's old red suitcase full of new black clothes. Having graduated early, Ray was already at the end of his freshman year at Penn.

In our kitchen that same day, Grandma Lynn gave Buckley a book on gardening. She told him about how plants came from seeds. That radishes, which he hated, grew fastest, but that flowers, which he loved, could grow from seeds as well. And she began to teach him the names: zinnias and marigolds, pansies and lilacs, carnations and petunias, and morning glory vines.

* * *

Occasionally my mother called from California. My parents had hurried and difficult conversations. She asked after Buckley and Lindsey and Holiday. She asked how the house was holding up and whether there was anything he needed to tell her.

"We still miss you," he said in December 1977, when the leaves had all fallen and been blown or raked away but even still, with the ground waiting to receive it, there had been no snow.

"I know that," she said.

"What about teaching? I thought that was your plan."

"It was," she conceded. She was on the phone in the office of the winery. Things had slowed up after the lunch crowd, but five limos of old ladies, three sheets to the wind, were soon due in. She was silent and then she said something that no one, least of all my father, could have argued with. "Plans change."

In New York, Ruth was living in an old woman's walk-in closet on the Lower East Side. It was the only thing she could afford, and she had no intention of spending much time there anyway. Daily she rolled her twin-sized futon into the corner so she could have a little floor space in which to dress. She visited the closet only once a day, and she never spent any time there if she could help it. The closet was for sleeping and having an address, a solid if tiny perch in the city.

She worked service bar and walked every inch of Manhattan on her off hours. I watched her pound the cement in her defiant boots, sure that women were being murdered wherever she went. Down in stairwells and up inside beautiful highrises. She would linger at streetlights and scan the facing street. She wrote small prayers in her journal at the cafés and the bars, where she stopped to use the bathroom after ordering the cheapest thing on the menu.

She had become convinced that she had a second sight that no one else had. She didn't know what she would do with it, save taking copious notes for the future, but she had grown unafraid. The world she saw of dead women and children had become as real to her as the world in which she lived.

In the library at Penn, Ray read about the elderly under the boldface heading "The Conditions of Death." It described a study done in nursing homes in which a large percentage of patients reported to the doctors and nurses that they saw someone standing at the end of their bed at night. Often this person tried to talk to them or call their name. Sometimes the patients were in such a high state of agitation during these delusions that they had to be given a sedative or strapped to their beds.

The text went on to explain that these visions were a result of small strokes that often preceded death. "What is commonly thought of by the layman as the Angel of Death, when discussed at all with the patient's family, should be presented to them as a small series of strokes compounding an already precipitous state of decline."

For a moment, with his finger marking the place in the book, Ray imagined what it would be like if, standing over the bed of an elderly patient, remaining as open as he could to possibility, he might feel something brush past him as Ruth had so many years ago in the parking lot.

Mr. Harvey had been living wild within the Northeast Corridor from the outlying areas of Boston down to the northern tips of the southern states, where he would go to find easier work and fewer questions and make an occasional attempt to reform. He had always liked Pennsylvania and had crisscrossed the long state, camping sometimes behind the 7-Eleven just down the local highway from our development, where a ridge of woods survived between the all-night store and the railroad tracks, and where he found more and more tin cans and cigarette butts each time he passed through. He still liked to drive close to the old neighborhood when he could. He took these risks early in the morning or late at night, when the wild pheasants that had once been plentiful still traversed the road and his headlights would catch the hollow glowing of their eye sockets as they skittered from one side of the road to the other. There were no longer teenagers and young children sent to pick blackberries just up to the edge of our development, because the old farm fence that had hung so heavily with them had been torn down to make room for more houses. He had learned to pick wild mushrooms over time and gorged on them sometimes when staying overnight in the overgrown fields of Valley Forge Park. On a night like this I saw him come upon two novice campers who had died after eating the mushrooms' poisonous look-alikes. He tenderly stripped their bodies of any valuables and then moved on.

Hal and Nate and Holiday were the only ones Buckley had ever allowed into his fort. The grass died underneath the boulders and when it rained, the insides of the fort were a fetid puddle, but it stayed there, though Buckley went there less and less, and it was Hal who finally begged him to make improvements.

"We need to waterproof it, Buck," Hal said one day. "You're ten—that's old enough to work a caulking gun."

And Grandma Lynn couldn't help herself, she loved men. She encouraged Buck to do what Hal said, and when she knew Hal would be coming to visit, she dressed up.

"What are you doing?" my father said one Saturday morning, lured out of his den by the sweet smell of lemons and butter and golden batter rising in pans.

"Making muffins," Grandma Lynn said.

My father did a sanity check, staring at her. He was still in his robe and it was almost ninety degrees at ten in the morning, but she had pantyhose and makeup on. Then he noticed Hal in an undershirt out in the yard.

"My God, Lynn," he said. "That boy is young enough . . ."

"But he's de-lec-ta-ble!"

My father shook his head and sat down at the kitchen table. "When will the love muffins be done, Mata Hari?"

In December 1981, Len did not want to get the call he got from Delaware, where a murder in Wilmington had been connected to a girl's body found in 1976 in Connecticut. A detective, working overtime, had painstakingly traced the keystone charm in the Connecticut case back to a list of lost property from my murder.

"It's a dead file," Len told the man on the other end.

"We'd like to see what you have."

"George Harvey," Len said out loud, and the detectives at neighboring desks turned toward him. "The crime was in December 1973. The murder victim was Susie Salmon, fourteen."

"Any body for the Simon girl?"

"Salmon, like the fish. We found an elbow," Len said.

"She have a family?"

"Yes."

"Connecticut has teeth. Do you have her dentals?"

"Yes."

"That may save the family some grief," the man told Len.

Len trekked back to the evidence box he had hoped never to look at again. He would have to make a phone call to my family. But he would wait as long as possible, until he was certain the detective in Delaware had something.

* * *

For almost eight years after Samuel told Hal about the drawing Lindsey had stolen, Hal had quietly worked through his network of biker friends to track George Harvey down. But he, like Len, had vowed not to report anything until he was sure it might be a lead. And he had never been sure. When late one night a Hell's Angel named Ralph Cichetti, who admitted freely he had spent some time in prison, said that he thought his mother had been killed by a man she rented a room to, Hal began asking his usual questions. Questions that held elements of elimination about height and weight and preoccupations. The man hadn't gone by the name George Harvey, though that didn't mean anything. But the murder itself seemed too different. Sophie Cichetti was forty-nine. She was killed in her home with a blunt object and her body had been found intact nearby. Hal had read enough crime books to know that killers had patterns, peculiar and important ways they did things. So as Hal adjusted the timing chain of Cichetti's cranky Harley, they moved on to other topics, then fell silent. It was only when Cichetti mentioned something else that every hair on Hal's neck stood up.

"The guy built dollhouses," Ralph Cichetti said.

Hal placed a call to Len.

Years passed. The trees in our yard grew taller. I watched my family and my friends and neighbors, the teachers whom I'd had or imagined having, the high school I had dreamed about. As I sat in the gazebo I would pretend instead that I was sitting on the topmost branch of the maple under which my brother had swallowed a stick and still played hide-and-seek with Nate, or I would perch on the railing of a stairwell in New York and wait for Ruth to pass near. I would study with Ray. Drive the Pacific Coast Highway on a warm afternoon of salty air with my mother. But I would end each day with my father in his den.

I would lay these photographs down in my mind, those gathered from my constant watching, and I could trace how one thing—my death—connected these images to a single source. No one could have predicted how my loss would change small moments on Earth. But I held on to those moments, hoarded them. None of them were lost as long as I was there watching.

At Evensong one night, while Holly played her sax and Mrs. Bethel Utemeyer joined in, I saw him: Holiday, racing past a fluffy white Samoyed. He had lived to a ripe old age on Earth and slept at my father's feet after my mother left, never wanting to let him out of his sight. He had stood with Buckley while he built his fort and had been the only one permitted on the porch while Lindsey and Samuel kissed. And in the last few years of his life, every Sunday morning, Grandma Lynn had made him a skillet-sized peanut butter pancake, which she would place flat on the floor, never tiring of watching him try to pick it up with his snout.

I waited for him to sniff me out, anxious to know if here, on the other side, I would still be the little girl he had slept beside. I did not have to wait long: he was so happy to see me, he knocked me down.

SEVENTEEN

At twenty-one Lindsey was many things I would never become, but I barely grieved this list anymore. Still, I roved where she roved. I collected my college diploma and rode on the back of Samuel's bike, clinging on to him with my arms wrapped around his waist, pressing into his back for warmth . . .

Okay, it was Lindsey. I realized that. But in watching her I found I could get lost more than with anyone else.

On the night of their graduation from Temple University, she and Samuel rode his bike back to my parents' house, having promised my father and Grandma Lynn repeatedly that they would not touch the champagne tucked inside the bike's pannard until they reached the house. "After all, we're college graduates!" Samuel had said. My father was soft in his trust with Samuel—years had gone by when the boy had done nothing but right by his surviving daughter.

But on the ride back from Philadelphia down Route 30, it began to rain. Lightly at first, small pinpricks flashing into my sister and Samuel at fifty miles per hour. The cool rain hit the hot dry tar of the road and lifted up smells that had been baked in all day under the hot June sun. Lindsey liked to rest her head between Samuel's shoulder blades and take in the scent of the road and the scrappy shrubs and bushes on either side. She had been remembering how the breeze in the hours before the storm had filled all the white gowns of the graduating seniors as they stood outside Macy Hall. Everyone looked poised, for just a moment, to float away.

Finally, eight miles away from the turnoff that led to our house, the rain grew heavy enough to hurt, and Samuel shouted back to Lindsey that he was going to pull off.

They passed into a slightly more overgrown stretch of road, the kind that existed between two commercial areas and that gradually, by accretion, would be eliminated by another strip mall or auto parts store. The bike wobbled but did not fall on the wet gravel of the shoulder. Samuel used his feet to help brake the bike, then waited, as Hal had taught him, for my sister to get off and step a few feet away before he got off himself.

He opened the visor of his helmet to yell to her. "This is no good," he said, "I'm going to roll her under those trees."

Lindsey followed behind him, the sound of rain hushed inside her padded helmet. They picked their way through the gravel and mud, stepping over branches and litter that had gathered at the side of the road. The rain seemed to be getting heavier still, and my sister was glad she had changed out of the dress she'd worn to commencement and into the leather pants and jacket that Hal had insisted on getting her despite her protests that she looked like a pervert.

Samuel wheeled the bike into the stand of oaks close to the road, and Lindsey followed. They had gone the week before to get haircuts at the same barber shop on Market Street, and though Lindsey's hair was lighter and finer than Samuel's, the barber had given them identical short, spiky cuts. Within a moment of removing their helmets their hair caught the large drops that filtered through the trees, and Lindsey's mascara began to bleed. I watched as Samuel used his thumb to wipe the traces from Lindsey's cheek. "Happy graduation," he said in the darkness, and stooped to kiss her.

Since their first kiss in our kitchen two weeks after my death, I had known that he was—as my sister and I had giggled with our Barbies or while watching Bobby Sherman on TV—her one and only. Samuel had pressed himself into her need, and the cement between the two of them had begun to set immediately. They had gone to Temple together, side by side. He had hated it and she had pushed him through. She had loved it and this had allowed him to survive.

"Let's try and find the densest part of this underbrush," he said.

"What about the bike?"

"Hal will probably have to rescue us when the rain stops."

"Shit!" Lindsey said.

Samuel laughed and grabbed her hand to start walking. The moment they did, they heard the first thunderclap and Lindsey jumped. He tightened his hold on her. The lightning was in the distance still, and the thunder would grow louder on its heels. She had never felt about it the way I did. It made her jumpy and nervous. She imagined trees split down the middle and houses on fire and dogs cowering in basements throughout the suburbs.

They walked through the underbrush, which was getting soaked despite the trees. Even though it was the middle of the afternoon, it was dark except for Samuel's safety light. Still they felt the evidence of people. Their boots crunched down on top of tin cans and pushed up against empty bottles. And then, through the thick weeds and darkness both of them saw the broken window panes that ran along the top of an old Victorian house. Samuel shut off the safety light immediately.

"Do you think there's someone inside?" Lindsey asked.

"It's dark."

"It's spooky."

They looked at each other, and my sister said what they both were thinking. "It's dry!"

They held hands in the heavy rain and ran toward the house as fast as they could, trying not to trip or slide in the increasing mud.

As they drew closer, Samuel could make out the steep pitch of the roof and the small wooden cross work that hung down from the gables. Most of the windows on the bottom floor had been covered over with wood, but the front door swung back and forth on its hinges, banging against the plaster wall on the inside. Though part of him wanted to stand outside in the rain and stare up at the eaves and cornices, he rushed into the house with Lindsey. They stood a few feet inside the doorway, shivering and staring out into the presuburban forest that surrounded them. Quickly I scanned the rooms of the old house. They were alone. No scary monsters lurked in corners, no wandering men had taken root.

More and more of these undeveloped patches were disappearing, but they, more than anything, had marked my childhood. We lived in one of the first developments to be built on the converted farmland in the area—a development that became the model and inspiration for what now seemed a limitless number—but my imagination had always rested on the stretch of road that had not been filled in with the bright colors of shingles and drainpipes, paved driveways and super-size mailboxes. So too had Samuel's.

"Wow!" Lindsey said. "How old do you think this is?"

Lindsey's voice echoed off the walls as if they stood alone in a church.

"Let's explore," said Samuel.

The boarded-up windows on the first floor made it hard to see anything, but with the help of Samuel's safety light they could pick out both a fireplace and the chair rail along the walls.

"Look at the floor," Samuel said. He knelt down, taking her with him. "Do you see the tongue and groove work? These people had more money than their neighbors."

Lindsey smiled. Just as Hal cared only for the inner workings of motorcycles, Samuel had become obsessed with carpentry.

He ran his fingers over the floor and had Lindsey do it too. "This is a gorgeous old wreck," he said.

"Victorian?" Lindsey asked, making her best guess.

"It blows my mind to say this," Samuel said, "but I think it's gothic revival. I noticed cross-bracing on the gable trim, so that means it was after 1860."

"Look," said Lindsey.

In the center of the floor someone had once, long ago, set a fire.

"And *that* is a tragedy," Samuel said.

"Why didn't they use the fireplace? There's one in every room."

But Samuel was busy looking up through the hole the fire had burned into the ceiling, trying to make out the patterns of the woodwork along the window frames.

"Let's go upstairs," he said.

"I feel like I'm in a cave," said Lindsey as they climbed the stairs. "It's so quiet in here you can barely hear the rain."

Samuel bounced the soft side of his fist off the plaster as he went. "You could wall someone into this place."

And suddenly it was one of those awkward moments that they had learned to let pass and I lived to anticipate. It begged a central question. Where was I? Would I be mentioned? Brought up and discussed? Usually now the answer was a disappointing no. It was no longer a Susie-fest on Earth.

But something about the house and the night—markers like graduations and birthdays always meant that I was more alive, higher up in the register of thoughts—made Lindsey dwell on me more in that moment than she normally might. Still, she didn't mention it. She remembered the heady feeling she had had in Mr.

Harvey's house and that she had often felt since—that I was with her somehow, in her thoughts and limbs—moving with her like a twin.

At the top of the stairs they found the entrance to the room they had stared up at.

"I want this house," Samuel said.

"What?"

"This house needs me, I can feel it."

"Maybe you should wait until the sun comes out to decide," she said.

"It's the most beautiful thing I've ever seen," he said.

"Samuel Heckler," my sister said, "fixer of broken things."

"One to talk," he said.

They stood for a moment in silence and smelled the damp air coming through the chimney and flooding the room. Even with the sound of rain, Lindsey still felt hidden away, tucked safely in an outside corner of the world with the one person she loved more than anyone else.

She took his hand, and I traveled with them up to the doorway of a small room at the very front. It jutted out over what would be the entrance hall of the floor below and was octagonal in shape.

"Oriels," Samuel said. "The windows"—he turned to Lindsey—"when they're built out like that, like a tiny room, that's called an oriel."

"Do they turn you on?" Lindsey asked, smiling.

I left them in the rain and darkness. I wondered if Lindsey noticed that when she and Samuel began to unzip their leathers the lightning stopped and the rumble in the throat of God—that scary thunder—ceased.

In his den, my father reached out to hold the snow globe in his hand. The cold glass against his fingers comforted him, and he shook it to watch the penguin disappear and then slowly be uncovered by the gently falling snow.

Hal had made it back from the graduation ceremonies on his motorcycle but instead of calming my father—providing some assurance that if one motorcycle could maneuver the storm and deliver its rider safe to his door, another one could too—it seemed to stack the probabilities in the reverse in his mind.

He had taken what could be called a painful delight in Lindsey's graduation ceremony. Buckley had sat beside him, dutifully prompting him when to smile and react. He often *knew* when, but his synapses were never as quick now as normal people's—or at least that was how he explained it to himself. It was like reaction time in the insurance claims he reviewed. There was an average number of seconds for most people between when they saw something coming—another car, a rock rolling down an embankment—and when they reacted. My father's response times were slower than most, as if he moved in a world where a crushing inevitability had robbed him of any hope of accurate perception.

Buckley tapped on the half-open door of my father's den.

"Come in," he said.

"They'll be okay, Dad." At twelve, my brother had become serious and considerate. Even if he didn't pay for the food or cook the meals, he managed the house.

"You looked good in your suit, son," my father said.

"Thanks." This mattered to my brother. He had wanted to make my father proud and had taken time with his appearance, even asking Grandma Lynn that morning to help trim the bangs that fell in his eyes. My brother was in the most awkward stage of adolescence—not boy, not man. Most days he hid his body in big T-shirts and sloppy jeans, but he had liked wearing the suit that day. "Hal and Grandma are waiting for us downstairs," he said.

"I'll be down in a minute."

Buckley closed the door all the way this time, letting the latch snap into place.

That fall my father had developed the last roll of film that I'd kept in my closet in my "rolls to hold back" box, and now, as he often did when he begged just a minute before dinner or saw something on TV or read an article in the paper that made his heart ache, he drew back his desk drawer and gingerly lifted the photos in his hand.

He had lectured me repeatedly that what I called my "artistic shots" were foolhardy, but the best portrait he ever had was one I took of him at an angle so his face filled the three-by-three square when you held it so it was a diamond.

I must have been listening to his hints on camera angles and composition when I took the pictures he held now. He had had no idea what order the rolls were in or what they were of when he had them developed. There were an inordinate number of photos of Holiday, and many a shot of my feet or the grass. Gray balls of blurs in the air which were birds, and a grainy attempt at a sunset over the pussy-willow tree. But at some point I had decided to take portraits of my mother. When he'd picked the roll up at the photo lab my father sat in the car staring at photos of a woman he felt he barely knew anymore.

Since then he had taken these photos out too many times to count, but each time he looked into the face of this woman he had felt something growing inside him. It took him a long time to realize what it was. Only recently had his wounded synapses allowed him to name it. He had been falling in love all over again.

He didn't understand how two people who were married, who saw each other every day, could forget what each other looked like, but if he had had to name what had happened—this was it. And the last two photos in the roll provided the key. He had come home from work—I remember trying to keep my mother's attention as Holiday barked when he heard the car pull into the garage.

"He'll come out," I said. "Stay still." And she did. Part of what I loved about photography was the power it gave me over the people on the other side of the camera, even my own parents.

Out of the corner of my eye I saw my father walk through the side door into the yard. He carried his slim briefcase, which, years before, Lindsey and I had heatedly investigated only to find very little of interest to us. As he set it down I snapped the last solitary photo of my mother. Already her eyes had begun to seem distracted and anxious, diving under and up into a mask somehow. In the next photo, the mask was almost, but not quite, in place and the final photo, where my father was leaning slightly down to give her a kiss on the cheek—there it was.

"Did I do that to you?" he asked her image as he stared at the pictures of my mother, lined up in a row. "How did that happen?"

"The lightning stopped," my sister said. The moisture of the rain on her skin had been replaced by sweat.

"I love you," Samuel said.

"I know."

"No, I mean I love you, and I want to marry you, and I want to live in this house!"

"What?"

"That hideous, hideous college shit is over!" Samuel screamed. The small room absorbed his voice, barely bouncing back an echo from its thick walls.

"Not for me, it isn't," my sister said.

Samuel got up off the floor, where he had been lying beside my sister, and came to his knees in front of her. "Marry me."

"Samuel?"

"I'm tired of doing all the right things. Marry me and I'll make this house gorgeous."

"Who will support us?"

"We will," he said, "somehow."

She sat up and then joined him kneeling. They were both half-dressed and growing colder as their heat began to dissipate.

"Okay."

"Okay?"

"I think I can," my sister said. "I mean, yes!"

Some clichés I understood only when they came into my heaven full speed. I had never seen a chicken with its head cut off. It had never meant much to me except something else that had been treated much the same as me. But that moment I ran around my heaven like . . . a chicken with its head cut off! I was so happy I screamed over and over and over again. My sister! My Samuel! My dream!

She was crying, and he held her in his arms, rocking her against him.

"Are you happy, sweetheart?" he asked.

She nodded against his bare chest. "Yes," she said, then froze. "My dad." She raised her head and looked at Samuel. "I know he's worried."

"Yes," he said, trying to switch gears with her.

"How many miles is it to the house from here?"

"Ten maybe," Samuel said. "Maybe eight."

"We could do that," she said.

"You're nuts."

"We have sneakers in the other pannard."

They could not run in leather, so they wore their underwear and T-shirts, as close to streakers as anyone in my family would ever be. Samuel, as he had for years, set a pace just ahead of my sister to keep her going. There were hardly any cars on the road, but when one passed by a wall of water would come up from the puddles near the side of the road and make the two of them gasp to get air back in their lungs. Both of them had run in rain before but never rain this heavy. They made a game of who could gain the most shelter as they ran the miles, waltzing in and out to gain cover under any overhanging trees, even as the dirt and grime of the road covered their legs. But by mile three they were silent, pushing their feet forward in a natural rhythm they had both known for years, focusing on the sound of their own breath and the sound of their wet shoes hitting the pavement.

At some point as she splashed through a large puddle, no longer trying to avoid them, she thought of the local pool of which we had been members until my death brought the comfortably public existence of my family to a close. It had been somewhere along this road, but she did not lift her head to find the familiar chain-link fence. Instead, she had a memory. She and I were under water in our bathing suits with their small ruffled skirts. Both of our eyes were open under water, a new skill—newer for her—and we were looking at each other, our separate bodies suspended under water. Hair floating, small skirts floating, our cheeks bulging with captured air. Then, together, we would grab on to each other and shoot up out of the water, breaking the surface. We sucked air into our lungs—ears popping—and laughed together.

I watched my beautiful sister running, her lungs and legs pumping, and the skill from the pool still there—fighting to see through the rain, fighting to keep her legs lifting at the pace set by Samuel, and I knew she was not running away from me or toward me. Like someone who has survived a gut-shot, the wound had been closing, closing—braiding into a scar for eight long years.

By the time the two of them were within a mile of my house, the rain had lightened and people were beginning to look out their windows toward the street.

Samuel slowed his pace and she joined him. Their T-shirts were locked onto their bodies like paste.

Lindsey had fought off a cramp in her side, but as the cramp lifted she ran with Samuel full-out. Suddenly she was covered in goose bumps and smiling ear to ear.

"We're getting married!" she said, and he stopped short, grabbed her up in his arms, and they were still kissing when a car passed them on the road, the driver honking his horn.

When the doorbell rang at our house it was four o'clock and Hal was in the kitchen wearing one of my mother's old white chef's aprons and cutting brownies for Grandma Lynn. He liked being put to work, feeling useful, and my grandmother liked to use him. They were a simpatico team. While Buckley, the boy-guard, loved to eat.

"I'll get it," my father said. He had been propping himself up during the rain with highballs, mixed, not measured, by Grandma Lynn.

He was spry now with a thin sort of grace, like a retired ballet dancer who favored one leg over the other after long years of one-footed leaps.

"I was so worried," he said when he opened the door.

Lindsey was holding her arms over her chest, and even my father had to laugh while he looked away and hurriedly got the extra blankets kept in the front closet. Samuel draped one around Lindsey first, as my father covered Samuel's shoulders as best he could and puddles collected on the flagstone floor. Just as Lindsey had covered herself up, Buckley and Hal and Grandma Lynn came forward into the hallway.

"Buckley," Grandma Lynn said, "go get some towels."

"Did you manage the bike in this?" Hal asked, incredulous.

"No, we ran," Samuel said.

"You what?"

"Get into the family room," my father said. "We'll set a fire going."

* * *

While the two of them sat with their backs to the fire, shivering at first and drinking the brandy shots Grandma Lynn had Buckley serve them on a silver tray, everyone heard the story of the bike and the house and the octagonal room with windows that had made Samuel euphoric.

"And the bike's okay?" Hal asked.

"We did the best we could," Samuel said, "but we'll need a tow."

"I'm just happy that the two of you are safe," my father said.

"We ran home for you, Mr. Salmon."

My grandmother and brother had taken seats at the far end of the room, away from the fire.

"We didn't want anyone to worry," Lindsey said.

"Lindsey didn't want you to worry, specifically."

The room was silent for a moment. What Samuel had said was true, of course, but it also pointed too clearly to a certain fact—that Lindsey and Buckley had come to live their lives in direct proportion to what effect it would have on a fragile father.

Grandma Lynn caught my sister's eye and winked. "Hal and Buckley and I made brownies," she said. "And I have some frozen lasagna I can break out if you'd like." She stood and so did my brother—ready to help.

"I'd love some brownies, Lynn," Samuel said.

"Lynn? I like that," she said. "Are you going to start calling Jack 'Jack'?"

"Maybe."

Once Buckley and Grandma Lynn had left the room, Hal felt a new nervousness in the air. "I think I'll pitch in," he said.

Lindsey, Samuel, and my father listened to the busy noises of the kitchen. They could all hear the clock ticking in the corner, the one my mother had called our "rustic colonial clock."

"I know I worry too much," my father said.

"That's not what Samuel meant," Lindsey said.

Samuel was quiet and I was watching him.

"Mr. Salmon," he finally said—he was not quite ready to try "Jack." "I've asked Lindsey to marry me."

Lindsey's heart was in her throat, but she wasn't looking at Samuel. She was looking at my father.

Buckley came in with a plate of brownies, and Hal followed him with champagne glasses hanging from his fingers and a bottle of 1978 Dom Perignon. "From your grandmother, on your graduation day," Hal said.

Grandma Lynn came through next, empty-handed except for her highball. It caught the light and glittered like a jar of icy diamonds.

For Lindsey, it was as if no one but herself and my father were there. "What do you say, Dad?" she asked.

"I'd say," he managed, standing up to shake Samuel's hand, "that I couldn't wish for a better son-in-law."

Grandma Lynn exploded on the final word. "My God, oh, honey! Congratulations!"

Even Buckley let loose, slipping out of the knot that usually held him and into a rare joy. But I saw the fine, wavering line that still tied my sister to my father. The invisible cord that can kill.

The champagne cork popped.

"Like a master!" my grandmother said to Hal, who was pouring.

It was Buckley, as my father and sister joined the group and listened to Grandma Lynn's countless toasts, who saw me. He saw me standing under the rustic colonial clock and stared. He was drinking champagne. There were strings coming out from all around me, reaching out, waving in the air. Someone passed him a brownie. He held it in his hands but did not eat. He saw my shape and face, which had not changed—the hair still parted down the middle, the chest still flat and hips undeveloped—and wanted to call out my name. It was only a moment, and then I was gone.

* * *

Over the years, when I grew tired of watching, I often sat in the back of the trains that went in and out of Suburban Station in Philadelphia. Passengers would get on and off as I listened to their conversations mix with the sounds of the train doors opening and closing, the conductors yelling their stops, and the shuffle and staccato of shoe soles and high heels going from pavement to metal to the soft *thump thump* on the carpeted train aisles. It was what Lindsey, in her workouts, called an active rest; my muscles were still engaged but my focus relaxed. I listened to the sounds and felt the train's movement and sometimes, by doing this, I could hear the voices of those who no longer lived on Earth. Voices of others like me, the watchers.

Almost everyone in heaven has someone on Earth they watch, a loved one, a friend, or even a stranger who was once kind, who offered warm food or a bright smile when one of us had needed it. And when I wasn't watching I could hear the others talking to those they loved on Earth: just as fruitlessly as me, I'm afraid. A one-sided cajoling and coaching of the young, a one-way loving and desiring of their mates, a single-sided card that could never be signed.

The train would be still or stop-starting from 30th Street to near Overbrook, and I could hear them say names and sentences: "Now be careful with that glass." "Mind your father." "Oh, look how big she looks in that dress." "I'm with you, Mother," ". . . Esmeralda, Sally, Lupe, Keesha, Frank . . ." So many names. And then the train would gain speed, and as it did the volume of all these unheard phrases coming from heaven would grow louder and louder; at its height between stations, the noise of our longing became so deafening that I had to open my eyes.

I saw women hanging or collecting wash as I peered from the windows of the suddenly silent trains. They stooped over baskets and then spread white or yellow or pink sheets along the line. I counted men's underwear and boys' underwear and the familiar lollipop cotton of little girls' drawers. And the sound of it that I craved and missed—the sound of life—replaced the endless calling of names.

Wet laundry: the snap, the yank, the wet heaviness of double- and queen-sized sheets. The real sounds bringing back the remembered sounds of the past when I had lain under the dripping clothes to catch water on my tongue or run in between them as if they were traffic cones through which I chased Lindsey or was chased by Lindsey back and forth. And this would be joined by the memory of our mother attempting to lecture us about the peanut butter from our hands getting on the good sheets, or the sticky lemon-candy patches she had found on our father's shirts. In this way the sight and smell of the real, of the imagined, and of the remembered all came together for me.

After I turned away from Earth that day, I rode the trains until I could think of only one thing:

"Hold still," my father would say, while I held the ship in the bottle and he burned away the strings he'd raised the mast with and set the clipper ship free on its blue putty sea. And I would wait for him, recognizing the tension of that moment when the world in the bottle depended, solely, on me.

EIGHTEEN

When her father mentioned the sinkhole on the phone, Ruth was in the walk-in closet that she rented on First Avenue. She twirled the phone's long black cord around her wrist and arm and gave short, clipped answers of acknowledgment. The old woman that rented her the closet liked to listen in, so Ruth tried not to talk much on the phone. Later, from the street, she would call home collect and plan a visit.

She had known she would make a pilgrimage to see it before the developers closed it up. Her fascination with places like the sinkhole was a secret she kept, as was my murder and our meeting in the faculty parking lot. They were all things she would not give away in New York, where she watched others tell their drunken bar stories, prostituting their families and their traumas for popularity and booze. These things, she felt, were not to be passed around like disingenuous party favors. She kept an honor code with her journals and her poems. "Inside, inside," she would whisper quietly to herself when she felt the urge to tell, and she would end up taking long walks through the city, seeing instead the Stolfuz cornfield or an image of her father staring at his pieces of rescued antique molding. New York provided a perfect background for her thoughts. Despite her willed stomping and pitching in its streets and byways, the city itself had very little to do with her interior life.

She no longer looked haunted, as she had in high school, but still, if you looked closely at her eyes you could see the skittery rabbit energy that often made people nervous. She had an expression of someone who was constantly on the lookout for something or someone that hadn't yet arrived. Her whole body seemed to slant forward in inquiry, and though she had been told at the bar where she worked that she had beautiful hair or beautiful hands or, on the rare occasions when any of her patrons saw her come out from behind the bar, beautiful legs, people never said anything about her eyes.

She dressed hurriedly in black tights, a short black skirt, black boots, and a black T-shirt, all of them stained from serving double-duty as work clothes and real clothes. The stains could be seen only in the sunlight, so Ruth was never really aware of them until later, when she would stop at an outdoor café for a cup of coffee and look down at her skirt and see the dark traces of spilled vodka or whiskey. The alcohol had the effect of making the black cloth blacker. This amused her; she had noted in her journal: "booze affects material as it does people."

Once outside the apartment, on her way for a cup of coffee on First Avenue, she made up secret conversations with the bloated lap dogs—Chihuahuas and Pomeranians—that the Ukrainian women held on their laps as they sat on their stoops. Ruth liked the antagonistic little dogs, who barked ardently as she passed.

Then she walked, walked flat out, walked with an ache coming up through the earth and into the heel of her striking foot. No one said hello to her except creeps, and she made a game of how many streets she could navigate without having to stop for traffic. She would not slow down for another person and would vivisect crowds of NYU students or old women with their laundry carts, creating a wind on either side of her. She liked to imagine that when she passed the world looked after her, but she also knew how anonymous she was. Except when she was at work, no one knew where she was at any time of day and no one waited for her. It was an immaculate anonymity.

She would not know that Samuel had proposed to my sister and, unless it trickled down to her through Ray, the sole person she had kept in touch with from school, she would never find out. While still at Fairfax she had heard my mother had left. A fresh ripple of whispers had gone through the high school, and Ruth had watched my sister cope with them as best she could. Occasionally the two of them would meet up in the hallway. Ruth would say a few words of support if she could manage them without doing what she thought of as harming Lindsey by talking to her. Ruth knew her status as a freak at school and knew that their one night at the gifted symposium had been exactly what it felt like—a dream, where elements let loose came together unbidden outside the damning rules of school.

But Ray was different. Their kisses and early pushing and rubbings were objects under glass to her—memories that she kept preserved. She saw him every time she visited her parents and had known immediately that it would be Ray she took when she went back to see the sinkhole. He would be happy for the vacation from his constant studying grind, and, if she was lucky, he would describe, as he often did, a medical procedure that he had observed. Ray's way of describing such things made her feel as if she knew exactly what it felt like—not just what it looked like. He could evoke everything for her, with small verbal pulse points of which he was completely unaware.

Heading north on First, she could tick off all the places she'd formerly stopped and stood, certain that she had found a spot where a woman or girl had been killed. She tried to list them in her journal at the end of each day, but often she was so consumed with what she thought might have happened in this or that dark overhang or tight alleyway that she neglected the simpler, more obvious ones, where she had read about a death in the paper and visited what had been a woman's grave.

She was unaware that she was somewhat of a celebrity up in heaven. I had told people about her, what she did, how she observed moments of silence up and down the city and wrote small individual prayers in her journal, and the story had traveled so quickly that women lined up to know if she had found where they'd been killed. She had fans in heaven, even though she would have been disappointed to know that often these fans, when they gathered, resembled more a bunch of teenagers poring over an issue of *TeenBeat* than Ruth's image of low dirgelike whisperings set to a celestial timpani.

I was the one who got to follow and watch, and, as opposed to the giddy choir, I often found these moments as painful as they were amazing. Ruth would get an image and it would burn into her memory. Sometimes they were only bright flashes—a fall down the stairs, a scream, a shove, the tightening of hands around a neck—and at other times it was as if an entire scenario spun out in her head in just the amount of time that it took the girl or woman to die.

No one on the street thought anything of the downtown girl dressed in black who had paused in the middle of midtown foot traffic. In her art student camouflage she could walk the entire length of Manhattan and, if not blend in, be classified and therefore ignored. Meanwhile, for us, she was doing important work, work that most people on Earth were too frightened even to contemplate.

The day after Lindsey and Samuel's graduation I joined her on her walk. By the time she got up to Central Park it was well past lunchtime, but the park was still busy. Couples sat on the clipped grass of the sheep meadow. Ruth peered at them. Her ardentness was off-putting on a sunny afternoon, and when the open faces of young men caught sight of her they closed down or looked away.

She zigzagged up and across the park. There were obvious places where she could go, like the rambles, to document the history of violence there without even leaving the trees, but she preferred those places people considered safe. The cool shimmering surface of the duck pond tucked into the busy southeast corner of the park, or the placid man-made lake, where old men sailed beautiful hand-carved boats.

She sat on a bench on a path leading to the Central Park Zoo and looked out across the gravel at children with their nannies and lone adults reading books in various patches of shade or sun. She was tired from the walk uptown, but still she took her journal out from her bag. She placed it open on her lap, holding the pen as her thinking prop. It was better to look like you were doing something when you stared into the distance, Ruth had learned. Otherwise it was likely that strange men would come over and try to talk to you. Her journal was her closest and most important relationship. It held everything.

Across from her a little girl had strayed from the blanket where her nanny slept. She was making her way for the bushes that lined a small rise before giving way to a fence separating the park from Fifth Avenue. Just as Ruth was about to enter the world of human beings whose lives impinged on one another by calling out to the nanny, a thin cord, which Ruth had not seen, warned the nanny to wake. She immediately sat bolt upright and barked an order at the little girl to return.

In moments like this she thought of all the little girls who grew into adulthood and old age as a sort of cipher alphabet for all of those who didn't. Their lives would somehow be inextricably attached to all the girls who had been killed. It was then, as the nanny packed up her bag and rolled up the blanket, preparing for whatever came next in their day, that Ruth saw her—a little girl who had strayed for the bushes one day and disappeared.

She could tell by the clothes that it had happened some time ago, but that was all. There was nothing else—no nanny or mother, no idea of night or day, only a little girl gone.

I stayed with Ruth. Her journal open, she wrote it down. "Time? Little girl in C.P. strays toward bushes. White lace collar, fancy." She closed the journal and tucked it into her bag. Close at hand was a place that soothed her. The penguin house at the zoo.

We spent the afternoon together there, Ruth sitting on the carpeted seat that ran the length of the exhibit, her black clothes making only her face and hands visible in the room. The penguins tottered and clucked and dived, slipping off the habitat rocks like amiable hams but living under water like tuxedoed muscles. Children shouted and screamed and pressed their faces against the glass. Ruth counted the living just as much as she counted the dead, and in the close confines of the penguin house the joyous screams of the children echoed off the walls with such vibrancy that, for a little while, she could drown out the other kinds of screams.

That weekend my brother woke early, as he always did. He was in the seventh grade and bought his lunch at school and was on the debate team and, like Ruth had been, was always picked either last or second to last in gym. He had not taken to athletics as Lindsey had. He practiced instead what Grandma Lynn called his "air of dignification." His favorite teacher was not really a teacher at all but the school librarian, a tall, frail woman with wiry hair who drank tea from her thermos and talked about having lived in England when she was young. After this he had affected an

English accent for a few months and shown a heightened interest when my sister watched *Masterpiece Theatre.*

When he had asked my father that year if he could reclaim the garden my mother had once kept, my father had said, "Sure, Buck, go crazy."

And he had. He had gone extraordinarily, insanely crazy, reading old Burpee catalogs at night when he was unable to sleep and scanning the few books on gardening that the school library kept. Where my grandmother had suggested respectful rows of parsley and basil and Hal had suggested "some plants that really matter"—eggplants, cantaloupes, cucumbers, carrots, and beans—my brother had thought they were both right.

He didn't like what he read in books. He saw no reason to keep flowers separated from tomatoes and herbs segregated in a corner. He had slowly planted the whole garden with a spade, daily begging my father to bring him seeds and taking trips to the grocery with Grandma Lynn, where the price of his extreme helpfulness in fetching things would be a quick stop at the greenhouse for a small flowering plant. He was now awaiting his tomatoes, his blue daisies, his petunias, and pansies and salvias of all kinds. He had made his fort a sort of work shed for the garden, where he kept his tools and supplies.

But my grandmother was preparing for the moment when he realized that they couldn't grow all together and that some seeds would not come up at certain times, that the fine downy tendrils of cucumber might be abruptly stopped by the thickening underground bosses of carrot and potato, that the parsley might be camouflaged by the more recalcitrant weeds, and bugs that hopped about could blight the tender flowers. But she was waiting patiently. She no longer believed in talk. It never rescued anything. At seventy she had come to believe in time alone.

Buckley was hauling up a box of clothes from the basement and into the kitchen when my father came down for his coffee.

"What ya got there, Farmer Buck?" my father said. He had always been at his best in the morning.

"I'm making stakes for my tomato plants," my brother said.

"Are they even above ground yet?"

My father stood in the kitchen in his blue terry-cloth robe and bare feet. He poured his coffee from the coffee maker that Grandma Lynn set up each morning, and sipped at it as he looked at his son.

"I just saw them this morning," my brother said, beaming. "They curl up like a hand unfolding."

It wasn't until my father was repeating this description to Grandma Lynn as he stood at the counter that he saw, through the back window, what Buckley had taken from the box. They were my clothes. My clothes, which Lindsey had picked through for anything she might save. My clothes, which my grandmother, when she had moved into my room, had quietly boxed while my father was at work. She had put them down in the basement with a small label that said, simply, SAVE.

My father put down his coffee. He walked out through the screened-in porch and strode forward, calling Buckley's name.

"What is it, Dad?" He was alert to my father's tone.

"Those clothes are Susie's," my father said calmly when he reached him.

Buckley looked down at my blackwatch dress that he held in his hand.

My father stepped closer, took the dress from my brother, and then, without speaking, he gathered the rest of my clothes, which Buckley had piled on the lawn. As he turned in silence toward the house, hardly breathing, clutching my clothes to him, it sparked.

I was the only one to see the colors. Just near Buckley's ears and on the tips of his cheeks and chin he was a little orange somehow, a little red.

"Why can't I use them?" he asked.

It landed in my father's back like a fist.

"Why can't I use those clothes to stake my tomatoes?"

My father turned around. He saw his son standing there, behind him the perfect plot of muddy, churned-up earth spotted with tiny seedlings. "How can you ask me that question?"

"You have to choose. It's not fair," my brother said.

"Buck?" My father held my clothes against his chest.

I watched Buckley flare and light. Behind him was the sun of the goldenrod hedge, twice as tall as it had been at my death.

"I'm tired of it!" Buckley blared. "Keesha's dad died and she's okay!"

"Is Keesha a girl at school?"

"Yes!"

My father was frozen. He could feel the dew that had gathered on his bare ankles and feet, could feel the ground underneath him, cold and moist and stirring with possibility.

"I'm sorry. When did this happen?"

"That's not the point, Dad! You don't get it." Buckley turned around on his heel and started stomping the tender tomato shoots with his foot.

"Buck, stop!" my father cried.

My brother turned.

"You don't get it, Dad," he said.

"I'm sorry," my father said. "These are Susie's clothes and I just . . . It may not make sense, but they're hers—something she wore."

"You took the shoe, didn't you?" my brother said. He had stopped crying now.

"What?"

"You took the shoe. You took it from my room."

"Buckley, I don't know what you're talking about."

"I saved the Monopoly shoe and then it was gone. You took it! You act like she was yours only!"

"Tell me what you want to say. What's this about your friend Keesha's dad?"

"Put the clothes down."

My father laid them gently on the ground.

"It isn't about Keesha's dad."

"Tell me what it is about." My father was now all immediacy. He went back to the place he had been after his knee surgery, coming up out of the druggie sleep of painkillers to see his then-five-year-old son sitting near him, waiting for his eyes to flicker open so he could say, "Peek-a-boo, Daddy."

"She's dead."

It never ceased to hurt. "I know that."

"But you don't act that way. Keesha's dad died when she was six. Keesha said she barely even thinks of him."

"She will," my father said.

"But what about us?"

"Who?"

"Us, Dad. Me and Lindsey. Mom left because she couldn't take it."

"Calm down, Buck," my father said. He was being as generous as he could as the air from his lungs evaporated out into his chest. Then a little voice in him said, *Let go, let go, let go*. "What?" my father said.

"I didn't say anything."

Let go. Let go. Let go.

"I'm sorry," my father said. "I'm not feeling very well." His feet had grown unbelievably cold in the damp grass. His chest felt hollow, bugs flying around an excavated cavity. There was an echo in there, and it drummed up into his ears. *Let go.*

My father dropped down to his knees. His arm began to tingle on and off as if it had fallen asleep. Pins and needles up and down. My brother rushed to him.

"Dad?"

"Son." There was a quaver in his voice and a grasping outward toward my brother.

"I'll get Grandma." And Buckley ran.

My father whispered faintly as he lay on his side with his face twisted in the direction of my old clothes: "You can never choose. I've loved all three of you."

That night my father lay in a hospital bed, attached to monitors that beeped and hummed. Time to circle around my father's feet and along his spine. Time to hush and usher him. But where?

Above his bed the clock ticked off the minutes and I thought of the game Lindsey and I had played in the yard together: "he loves me/he loves me not" picked out on a daisy's petals. I could hear the clock casting my own two greatest wishes back to me in this same rhythm: "Die for me/don't die for me, die for me/don't die for me." I could not help myself, it seemed, as I tore at his weakening heart. If he died, I would have him forever. Was this so wrong to want?

At home, Buckley lay in bed in the dark and pulled the sheet up to his chin. He had not been allowed past the emergency room where Lindsey had driven them, following the shrieking ambulance inside which lay our father. My brother had felt a huge burden of guilt descend in the silences from Lindsey. In her two repeated questions: "What were you talking about? Why was he so upset?"

My little brother's greatest fear was that the one person who meant so much to him would go away. He loved Lindsey and Grandma Lynn and Samuel and Hal, but my father kept him stepping lightly, son gingerly monitoring father every morning and every evening as if, without such vigilance, he would lose him.

We stood—the dead child and the living—on either side of my father, both wanting the same thing. To have him to ourselves forever. To please us both was an impossibility.

My father had only missed nighttimes twice in Buckley's life. Once after he had gone into the cornfield at night looking for Mr. Harvey and now as he lay in the hospital and they monitored him in case of a second heart attack.

Buckley knew he should be too old for it to matter, but I sympathized with him. The good-night kiss was something at which my father excelled. As my father stood at the end of the bed after closing the venetian blinds and running his hands down them to make sure they were all down at the same slant—no rebel venetian stuck to let the sunlight in on his son before he came to wake him—my brother would often get goose bumps on his arms and legs. The anticipation was so sweet.

"Ready, Buck?" my father would say, and sometimes Buckley said "Roger," or sometimes he said "Takeoff," but when he was most frightened and giddy and waiting for peace he just said "Yes!" And my father would take the thin cotton top sheet and bunch it up in his hands while being careful to keep the two corners between his thumb and forefinger. Then he would snap it out so the pale blue (if they were using Buckley's) or lavender (if they were using mine) sheet would spread out like a parachute above him and gently, what felt wonderfully slowly, it would waft down and touch along his exposed skin—his knees, his forearms, his cheeks and chin. Both air and cover somehow there in the same space at the same time—it felt like the ultimate freedom and protection. It was lovely, left him vulnerable and quivering on some edge and all he could hope was that if he begged him, my father would oblige and do it again. Air and cover, air and cover—sustaining the unspoken connection between them: little boy, wounded man.

That night his head lay on the pillow while his body was curled in the fetal position. He had not thought to close the blinds himself, and the lights from the nearby houses spotted the hill. He stared across his room at the louvered doors of his closet, out of which he had once imagined evil witches would escape to join the dragons beneath his bed. He no longer feared these things.

"Please don't let Daddy die, Susie," he whispered. "I need him."

When I left my brother, I walked out past the gazebo and under the lights hanging down like berries, and I saw the brick paths branching out as I advanced.

I walked until the bricks turned to flat stones and then to small, sharp rocks and then to nothing but churned earth for miles and miles around me. I stood there. I had been in heaven long enough to know that something would be revealed. And as the light began to fade and the sky turn a dark, sweet blue as it had on the night of my death, I saw someone walking into view, so far away I could not at first make out if it was man or woman, child or adult. But as moonlight reached this figure I could make out a man and, frightened now, my breathing shallow, I raced just far enough to see. Was it my father? Was it what I had wanted all this time so desperately?

"Susie," the man said as I approached and then stopped a few feet from where he stood. He raised his arms up toward me.

"Remember?" he said.

I found myself small again, age six and in a living room in Illinois. Now, as I had done then, I placed my feet on top of his feet.

"Grandaddy," I said.

And because we were all alone and both in heaven, I was light enough to move as I had moved when I was six and he was fifty-six and my father had taken us to visit. We danced so slowly to a song that on Earth had always made my grandfather cry.

"Do you remember?" he asked.

"Barber!"

"Adagio for Strings," he said.

But as we danced and spun—none of the herky-jerky awkwardness of Earth—what I remembered was how I'd found him crying to this music and asked him why.

"Sometimes you cry, Susie, even when someone you love has been gone a long time." He had held me against him then, just briefly, and then I had run outside to play again with Lindsey in what seemed like my grandfather's huge backyard.

We didn't speak any more that night, but we danced for hours in that timeless blue light. I knew as we danced that something was happening on Earth and in heaven. A shifting. The sort of slow-to-sudden movement that we'd read about in science class one year. Seismic, impossible, a rending and tearing of time and space. I pressed myself into my grandfather's chest and smelled the old-man smell of him, the mothball version of my own father, the blood on Earth, the sky in heaven. The kumquat, skunk, grade-A tobacco.

When the music stopped, it could have been forever since we'd begun. My grandfather took a step back, and the light grew yellow at his back.

"I'm going," he said.

"Where?" I asked.

"Don't worry, sweetheart. You're so close."

He turned and walked away, disappearing rapidly into spots and dust. Infinity.

NINETEEN

When she reached Krusoe Winery that morning, my mother found a message waiting for her, scrawled in the imperfect English of the caretaker. The word *emergency* was clear enough, and my mother bypassed her morning ritual of an early coffee drunk while staring out at the grapevines grafted on row upon row of sturdy white crosses. She opened up the part of the winery reserved for public tastings. Without turning on the overhead, she located the phone behind the wooden bar and dialed the number in Pennsylvania. No answer.

Then she dialed the operator in Pennsylvania and asked for the number of Dr. Akhil Singh.

"Yes," Ruana said, "Ray and I saw an ambulance pull up a few hours ago. I imagine they're all at the hospital."

"Who was it?"

"Your mother, perhaps?"

But she knew from the note that her mother had been the one who *called*. It was one of the children or it was Jack. She thanked

Ruana and hung up. She grabbed the heavy red phone and lifted it up from underneath the bar. A ream of color sheets that they passed out to customers—"Lemon Yellow = Young Chardonnay, Straw-colored = Sauvignon Blanc . . ."—fell down and around her feet from where they had been kept weighted by the phone. She had habitually arrived early ever since taking the job, and now she gave a quick thanks that this was so. After that, all she could think of were the names of the local hospitals, so she called the ones to which she had rushed her young children with unexplained fevers or possible broken bones from falls. At the same hospital where I had once rushed Buckley: "A Jack Salmon was seen in emergency and is still here."

"Can you tell me what happened?"

"What is your relationship to Mr. Salmon?"

She said the words she had not said in years: "I'm his wife."

"He had a heart attack."

She hung up the phone and sat down on the rubber-and-cork mats that covered the floor on the employee side. She sat there until the shift manager arrived and she repeated the strange words: *husband, heart attack.*

When she looked up later she was in the caretaker's truck, and he, this quiet man who barely ever left the premises, was barreling toward San Francisco International Airport.

She paid for her ticket and boarded a flight that would connect to another in Chicago and finally land her in Philadelphia. As the plane gained height and they were buried in the clouds, my mother listened distantly to the signature bells of the plane which told the crew what to do or what to prepare for, and she heard the cocktail cart jiggling past, but instead of her fellow passengers she saw the cool stone archway at the winery, behind which the empty oak barrels were stored, and instead of the men who often sat inside there to get out of the sun she imagined my father sitting there, holding the broken Wedgwood cup out toward her.

By the time she landed in Chicago with a two-hour wait, she had steadied herself enough to buy a toothbrush and a pack of cigarettes and place a call to the hospital, this time asking to speak to Grandma Lynn.

"Mother," my mother said. "I'm in Chicago and on my way."

"Abigail, thank God," my grandmother said. "I called Krusoe again and they said you were headed for the airport."

"How is he?"

"He's asking for you."

"Are the kids there?"

"Yes, and Samuel. I was going to call you today and tell you. Samuel has asked Lindsey to marry him."

"That's wonderful," my mother said.

"Abigail?"

"Yes." She could hear her mother's hesitation, which was always rare.

"Jack's asking for Susie, too."

She lit a cigarette as soon as she walked outside the terminal at O'Hare, a school tour flooding past her with small overnight bags and band instruments, each of which had a bright yellow nametag on the side of the case. HOME OF THE PATRIOTS, they read.

It was muggy and humid in Chicago, and the smoky exhaust of double-parked cars made the heavy air noxious.

She burned through the cigarette in record time and lit another, keeping one arm tucked hard across her chest and the other one extended on each exhale. She was wearing her winery outfit: a pair of faded but clean jeans and a pale orange T-shirt with KRUSOE WINERY embroidered over the pocket. Her skin was darker now, which made her pale blue eyes seem even bluer in contrast, and she had taken to wearing her hair in a loose ponytail at the base of her neck. I could see small wisps of salt and pepper hair near her ears and at her temples.

She held on to two sides of an hourglass and wondered how this could be possible. The time she'd had alone had been gravitationally circumscribed by when her attachments would pull her back. And they had pulled now—double-fisted. A marriage. A heart attack.

Standing outside the terminal, she reached into the back pocket of her jeans, where she kept the man's wallet she had started carrying when she got the job at Krusoe because it was easier not to worry about stowing a purse beneath the bar. She flicked her cigarette into the cab lane and turned to find a seat on the edge of a concrete planter, inside of which grew weeds and one sad sapling choked by fumes.

In her wallet were pictures, pictures she looked at every day. But there was one that she kept turned upside down in a fold of leather meant for a credit card. It was the same one that rested in the evidence box at the police station, the same one Ray had put in his mother's book of Indian poetry. My class photo that had made the papers and been put on police fliers and in mailboxes.

After eight years it was, even for my mother, like the ubiquitous photo of a celebrity. She had encountered it so many times that I had been neatly buried inside of it. My cheeks never redder, my eyes never bluer than they were in the photograph.

She took the photo out and held it face-up and slightly cupped in her hand. She had always missed my teeth—their small rounded serrations had fascinated her as she watched me grow. I had promised my mother a wide-open smile for that year's picture, but I was so self-conscious in front of the photographer that I had barely managed a close-lipped grin.

She heard the announcement for the connecting flight over the outdoor speaker. She stood. Turning around she saw the tiny, struggling tree. She left my class portrait propped up against its trunk and hurried inside the automatic doors.

On the flight to Philadelphia, she sat alone in the middle of a row of three seats. She could not help but think of how, if she were a mother traveling, there would be two seats filled beside her. One for Lindsey. One for Buckley. But though she was, by definition, a mother, she had at some point ceased to be one too. She couldn't claim that right and privilege after missing more than half a decade of their lives. She now knew that being a mother was a calling, something plenty of young girls dreamed of being. But my mother had never had that dream, and she had been punished in the most horrible and unimaginable way for never having wanted me.

I watched her on the plane, and I sent a wish into the clouds for her release. Her body grew heavy with the dread of what would come but in this heaviness was at least relief. The stewardess handed her a small blue pillow and for a little while she fell asleep.

When they reached Philadelphia, the airplane taxied down the runway and she reminded herself both where she was and what year it was. She hurriedly clicked through all the things she might say when she saw her children, her mother, Jack. And then, when they finally shivered to a halt, she gave up and focused only on getting off the plane.

She barely recognized her own child waiting at the end of the long ramp. In the years that had passed, Lindsey had become angular, thin, every trace of body fat gone. And standing beside my sister was what looked like her male twin. A bit taller, a little more meat. Samuel. She was staring so hard at the two of them, and they were staring back, that at first she didn't even see the chubby boy sitting off to the side on the arm of a row of waiting-area seats.

And then, just before she began walking toward them—for they all seemed suspended and immobile for the first few moments, as if they had been trapped in a viscous gelatin from which only her movement might free them—she saw him.

She began walking down the carpeted ramp. She heard announcements being made in the airport and saw passengers, with their more normal greetings, rushing past her. But it was as if she were entering a time warp as she took him in. 1944 at Camp Winnekukka. She was twelve, with chubby cheeks and heavy legs—all the things she'd felt grateful her daughters had escaped had been her son's to endure. So many years she had been away, so much time she could never recover.

If she had counted, as I did, she would have known that in seventy-three steps she had accomplished what she had been too afraid to do for almost seven years.

It was my sister who spoke first:

"Mom," she said.

My mother looked at my sister and flashed forward thirty-eight years from the lonely girl she'd been at Camp Winnekukka.

"Lindsey," my mother said.

Lindsey stared at her. Buckley was standing now, but he looked first down at his shoes and then over his shoulder, out past the window to where the planes were parked, disgorging their passengers into accordioned tubes.

"How is your father?" my mother asked.

My sister had spoken the word *Mom* and then frozen. It tasted soapy and foreign in her mouth.

"He's not in the greatest shape, I'm afraid," Samuel said. It was the longest sentence anyone had said, and my mother found herself disproportionately grateful for it.

"Buckley?" my mother said, preparing no face for him. Being who she was—whoever that was.

He turned his head toward her like a racheted gun. "Buck," he said.

"Buck," she repeated softly and looked down at her hands.

Lindsey wanted to ask, *Where are your rings?*

"Shall we go?" Samuel asked.

The four of them entered the long carpeted tunnel that would bring them from her gate into the main terminal. They were headed toward the cavernous baggage claim when my mother said, "I didn't bring any bags."

They stood in an awkward cluster, Samuel looking for the right signs to redirect them back to the parking garage.

"Mom," my sister tried again.

"I lied to you," my mother said before Lindsey could say anything further. Their eyes met, and in that hot wire that went from one to the other I swore I saw it, like a rat bulging, undigested, inside a snake: the secret of Len.

"We go back up the escalator," Samuel said, "and then we can take the overhead walkway into the parking lot."

Samuel called for Buckley, who had drifted off in the direction of a cadre of airport security officers. Uniforms had never lost the draw they held for him.

They were on the highway when Lindsey spoke next. "They won't let Buckley in to see Dad because of his age."

My mother turned around in her seat. "I'll try and do something about that," she said, looking at Buckley and attempting her first smile.

"Fuck you," my brother whispered without looking up.

My mother froze. The car opened up. Full of hate and tension—a riptide of blood to swim through.

"Buck," she said, remembering the shortened name just in time, "will you look at me?"

He glared over the front seat, boring his fury into her.

Eventually my mother turned back around and Samuel, Lindsey, and my brother could hear the sounds from the passenger seat that she was trying hard not to make. Little peeps and a choked sob. But no amount of tears would sway Buckley. He had been keeping, daily, weekly, yearly, an underground storage room of hate. Deep inside this, the four-year-old sat, his heart flashing. Heart to stone, heart to stone.

"We'll all feel better after seeing Mr. Salmon," Samuel said, and then, because even he could not bear it, he leaned forward toward the dash and turned on the radio.

It was the same hospital that she had come to eight years ago in the middle of the night. A different floor painted a different color, but she could feel it encasing her as she walked down the hall—what she'd done there. The push of Len's body, her back pressed into the sharp stucco wall. Everything in her wanted to run—fly back to California, back to her quiet existence working among strangers. Hiding out in the folds of tree trunks and tropical petals, tucked away safely among so many foreign plants and people.

Her mother's ankles and oxford pumps, which she saw from the hallway, brought her back. One of the many simple things she'd lost by moving so far away, just the commonplace of her mother's feet—their solidity and humor—seventy-year-old feet in ridiculously uncomfortable shoes.

But as she walked forward into the room, everyone else—her son, her daughter, her mother—fell away.

My father's eyes were weak but fluttered open when he heard her enter. He had tubes and wires coming out of his wrist and shoulder. His head seemed so fragile on the small square pillow.

She held his hand and cried silently, letting the tears come freely.

"Hello, Ocean Eyes," he said.

She nodded her head. This broken, beaten man—her husband.

"My girl," he breathed out heavily.

"Jack."

"Look what it took to get you home."

"Was it worth it?" she said, smiling bleakly.

"We'll have to see," he said.

To see them together was like a tenuous belief made real.

My father could see glimmers, like the colored flecks inside my mother's eyes—things to hold on to. These he counted among the broken planks and boards of a long-ago ship that had struck something greater than itself and sunk. There were only remnants and artifacts left to him now. He tried to reach up and touch her cheek, but his arm felt too weak. She moved closer and laid her cheek in his palm.

My grandmother knew how to move silently in heels. She tiptoed out of the room. As she resumed her normal stride and approached the waiting area, she intercepted a nurse with a message for Jack Salmon in Room 582. She had never met the man but knew his name. "Len Fenerman, will visit soon. Wishes you well." She folded the note neatly. Just before she came upon Lindsey and Buckley, who had gone to join Samuel in the waiting room, she popped open the metal lip of her purse and placed it between her powder and comb.

TWENTY

By the time Mr. Harvey reached the tin-roofed shack in Connecticut that night, it promised rain. He had killed a young waitress inside the shack several years before and then bought some new slacks with the tips he'd found in the front pocket of her apron. By now the rot would have been eclipsed, and it was true, as he approached the area, that no rank smell greeted him. But the shack was open and inside he could see the earth had been dug up. He breathed in and approached the shack warily.

He fell asleep beside her empty grave.

At some point, to counter the list of the dead, I had begun keeping my own list of the living. It was something I noticed Len Fenerman did too. When he was off duty he would note the young girls and elderly women and every other female in the rainbow in between and count them among the things that sustained him. That young girl in the mall whose pale legs had grown too long for her now-too-young dress and who had an aching vulnerability that went straight to both Len's and my own heart. Elderly women, wobbling with walkers, who insisted on dyeing their hair unnatural versions of the colors they had in youth. Middle-aged single mothers racing around in grocery stores while their children pulled bags of candy off the shelves. When I saw them, I took count. Living, breathing women. Sometimes I saw the wounded—those who had been beaten by husbands or raped by strangers, children raped by their fathers—and I would wish to intervene somehow.

Len saw these wounded women all the time. They were regulars at the station, but even when he went somewhere outside his jurisdiction he could sense them when they came near. The wife in the bait-'n'-tackle shop had no bruises on her face but cowered like a dog and spoke in apologetic whispers. The girl he saw walk the road each time he went upstate to visit his sisters. As the years passed she'd grown leaner, the fat from her cheeks had drained, and sorrow had loaded her eyes in a way that made them hang heavy and hopeless inside her mallowed skin. When she was not there it worried him. When she was there it both depressed and revived him.

He had not had much to write in my file for a long time, but a few items had joined the log of old evidence in the last few months: the name of another potential victim, Sophie Cichetti, the name of her son, and an alias of George Harvey's. There was also what he held in his hands: my Pennsylvania keystone charm. He moved it around inside the evidence bag, using his fingers, and found, again, my initials. The charm had been checked for any clues it could provide, and, besides its presence at the scene of another girl's murder, it had come up clean under the microscope.

He had wanted to give the charm back to my father from the first moment he was able to confirm it was mine. Doing so was breaking the rules, but he had never had a body for them, just a sodden schoolbook and the pages from my biology book mixed in with a boy's love note. A Coke bottle. My jingle-bell hat. These he had cataloged and kept. But the charm was different, and he meant to give it back.

A nurse he'd dated in the years after my mother left had called him when she noticed the name Jack Salmon on a list of patients admitted. Len had determined that he would visit my father in the hospital and bring my charm along with him. In Len's mind he saw the charm as a talisman that might speed my father's recovery.

I couldn't help but think, as I watched him, of the barrels of toxic fluids that had accrued behind Hal's bike shop where the scrub lining the railroad tracks had offered local companies enough cover to dump a stray container or two. Everything had been sealed up, but things were beginning to leak out. I had come to both pity and respect Len in the years since my mother left. He followed the physical to try to understand things that were impossible to comprehend. In that, I could see, he was like me.

Outside the hospital, a young girl was selling small bouquets of daffodils, their green stems tied with lavender ribbons. I watched as my mother bought out the girl's whole stock.

Nurse Eliot, who remembered my mother from eight years ago, volunteered to help her when she saw her coming down the hall, her arms full of flowers. She rounded up extra water pitchers from a supply closet and together she and my mother filled them with water and placed the flowers around my father's room while he slept. Nurse Eliot thought that if loss could be used as a measure of beauty in a woman, my mother had grown even more beautiful.

Lindsey, Samuel, and Grandma Lynn had taken Buckley home

earlier in the evening. My mother was not ready to see the house yet. She focused solely on my father. Everything else would have to wait, from the house and its silent reproach to her son and daughter. She needed something to eat and time to think. Instead of going to the hospital cafeteria, where the bright lights made her think only of all the futile efforts that hospitals contained to keep people awake for more bad news—the weak coffee, the hard chairs, the elevators that stopped on every floor—she left the building and walked down the sloped sidewalk leading away from the entrance.

It was dark out now, and the parking lot where she had once driven in the middle of the night in her nightgown was spotted with only a few cars. She hugged the cardigan her mother had left behind tightly to her.

She crossed the parking lot, looking into the dark cars for signs of who the people inside the hospital were. There were cassette tapes spread out on the passenger seat of one car, the bulky shape of a baby's carseat in another. It became a game to her then, seeing what she could in each car. A way not to feel so alone and alien, as if she were a child playing a spy game in the house of her parents' friends. Agent Abigail to Mission Control. I see a fuzzy dog toy, I see a soccer ball, I see a woman! There she was, a stranger sitting in the driver's side behind the wheel. The woman did not see my mother looking at her, and as soon as she saw her face my mother turned her attention away, focusing on the bright lights of the old diner she had as her goal. She did not have to look back to know what the woman was doing. She was girding herself up to go inside. She knew the face. It was the face of someone who wanted more than anything to be anywhere but where she was.

She stood on the landscaped strip between the hospital and the emergency room entrance and wished for a cigarette. She had not questioned anything that morning. Jack had had a heart attack;

she would go home. But now here, she didn't know what she was supposed to do anymore. How long would she have to wait, what would have to happen, before she could leave again? Behind her in the parking lot, she heard the sound of a car door opening and closing—the woman going in.

The diner was a blur to her. She sat in a booth alone and ordered the kind of food—chicken-fried steak—that didn't seem to exist in California.

She was thinking about this when a man directly across from her gave her the eye. She registered every detail of his appearance. It was automatic and something she didn't do out west. While living in Pennsylvania after my murder, when she saw a strange man whom she didn't trust, she did an immediate breakdown in her mind. It was quicker—honoring the pragmatics of fear—than pretending she shouldn't think this way. Her dinner arrived, the chicken-fried steak and tea, and she focused on her food, on the gritty breading around the rubbery meat, on the metallic taste of old tea. She did not think she could handle being home more than a few days. Everywhere she looked she saw me, and at the booth across from her she saw the man who could have murdered me.

She finished the food, paid for it, and walked out of the diner without raising her eyes above waist level. A bell mounted on the door jingled above her, and she started, her heart jumping up in her chest.

She made it back across the highway in one piece, but she was breathing shallowly as she passed back across the parking lot. The car of the apprehensive visitor was still there.

In the main lobby, where people rarely sat, she decided to sit down and wait for her breathing to come back again.

She would spend a few hours with him and when he woke, she would say goodbye. As soon as her decision was made, a welcome coolness flew through her. The sudden relief of responsibility. Her ticket to a far-away land.

It was late now, after ten, and she took an empty elevator to the fifth floor, where the hall lights had been dimmed. She passed the nurses' station, behind which two nurses were quietly gossiping. She could hear the lilt and glee of nuanced rumors being exchanged between them, the sound of easy intimacy in the air. Then, just as one nurse was unable to suppress a high-pitched laugh, my mother opened my father's door and let it swing shut again.

Alone.

It was as if there was a vacuum hush when the door closed. I felt I did not belong, that I should go too. But I was glued.

Seeing him sleeping in the dark, with only the low-wattage fluorescent light on at the back of the bed, she remembered standing in this same hospital and taking steps to sever herself from him.

As I saw her take my father's hand, I thought of my sister and me sitting underneath the grave rubbing in the upstairs hallway. I was the dead knight gone to heaven with my faithful dog and she was the live wire of a wife. "How can I be expected to be trapped for the rest of my life by a man frozen in time?" Lindsey's favorite line.

My mother sat with my father's hand in hers for a long while. She thought how wonderful it would be to climb up on the fresh hospital sheets and lie beside him. And how impossible.

She leaned close. Even under the smells of antiseptics and alcohol, she could smell the grassy smell of his skin. When she'd left, she had packed her favorite shirt of my father's and would sometimes wrap it around her just to have something of his on. She never wore it outside, so it kept his scent longer than it might have. She remembered one night, when she missed him most, buttoning it over a pillow and hugging it to her as if she were still a high school girl.

In the distance beyond the closed window she could hear the hum of far-off traffic on the highway, but the hospital was shutting down for the night. Only the rubber soles of the night nurses' shoes made sounds as they passed in the hallway.

Just that winter she had found herself saying to a young woman who worked with her at the tasting bar on Saturdays that between a man and a woman there was always one person who was stronger than the other one. "That doesn't mean the weaker one doesn't love the stronger," she'd pleaded. The girl looked at her blankly. But for my mother what mattered was that as she spoke, she had suddenly identified herself as the weaker one. This revelation sent her reeling. What had she thought all those years but the opposite?

She pulled her chair as close to his head as she could and laid her face on the edge of his pillow to watch him breathing, to see the flutter of his eye beneath his eyelid when he dreamed. How could it be that you could love someone so much and keep it secret from yourself as you woke daily so far from home? She had put billboards and roads in between them, throwing roadblocks behind her and ripping off the rearview mirror, and thought that that would make him disappear? erase their life and children?

It was so simple, as she watched him, as his regular breathing calmed her, that she did not even see it happening at first. She began to think of the rooms in our house and the hours that she had worked so hard to forget spent inside of them. Like fruit put up in jars and forgotten about, the sweetness seemed even more distilled as she returned. There on that shelf were all the dates and silliness of their early love, the braid that began to form of their dreams, the solid root of a burgeoning family. The first solid evidence of it all. Me.

She traced a new line on my father's face. She liked the silvering of his temples.

Shortly after midnight, she fell asleep after trying as hard as she could to keep her eyes open. To hold on to everything all at once while she looked at that face, so that when he woke she could say goodbye.

When her eyes were closed and they both slept silently together, I whispered to them:

> Stones and bones;
> snow and frost;
> seeds and beans and polliwogs.
> Paths and twigs, assorted kisses,
> We all know who Susie misses . . .

Around two A.M. it began to rain, and it rained down on the hospital and on my old home and in my heaven. On the tin-roofed shack where Mr. Harvey slept, it was raining too. As the rain beat its tiny hammers above his head, he dreamed. He did not dream of the girl whose remains had been removed and were now being analyzed but of Lindsey Salmon, of the 5! 5! 5! hitting the border of elderberry. He had this dream whenever he felt threatened. It had been in the flash of her soccer shirt that his life had begun to spin out of control.

It was near four when I saw my father's eyes open and saw him feel the warmth of my mother's breath on his cheek even before he knew she was asleep. We wished together that he could hold her, but he was too weak. There was another way and he took it. He would tell her the things he had felt after my death—the things that came into his mind so frequently but that no one knew but me.

But he did not want to wake her. The hospital was silent except for the sound of rain. Rain was following him, he felt, darkness and damp—he thought of Lindsey and Samuel at the doorway, soaked and smiling, having run all that way to relieve him. He often found himself repeatedly commanding himself back to center. Lindsey. Lindsey. Lindsey. Buckley. Buckley. Buckley.

The way the rain looked outside the windows, lit up in circular patches by the lights in the hospital parking lot, reminded him of the movies he had gone to see as a boy—Hollywood rain. He closed his eyes with the breath of my mother reassuringly exhaling against his cheek and listened to it, the slight patter on the slim metal window sills, and then he heard the sound of birds—small birds chirping, but he could not see them. And the idea of this, that there might be a nest right outside his window where baby birds had woken in the rain and found their mother gone, made him want to rescue them. He felt my mother's limp fingers, which had loosened their hold on his hand in sleep. She was here, and this time, despite all, he was going to let her be who she was.

It was then that I slipped inside the room with my mother and father. I was present somehow, as a person, in a way I had never been. I had always hovered but had never stood beside them.

I made myself small in the darkness, unable to know if I could be seen. I had left him for hours every day for eight and a half years as I had left my mother or Ruth and Ray, my brother and sister, and certainly Mr. Harvey, but he, I now saw, had never left me. His devotion to me had made me know again and again that I had been beloved. In the warm light of my father's love I had remained Susie Salmon—a girl with my whole life in front of me.

"I thought if I was very quiet I would hear you," he whispered. "If I was still enough you might come back."

"Jack?" my mother said, waking. "I must have fallen asleep."

"It's wonderful to have you back," he said.

And my mother looked at him. Everything stripped away. "How do you do it?" she asked.

"There's no choice, Abbie," he said. "What else can I do?"

"Go away, start over again," she said.

"Did it work?"

They were silent. I reached out my hand and faded away.

"Why don't you come lie down up here?" my father said. "We have a little time before the enforcers come on duty and kick you out."

She didn't move.

"They've been nice to me," she said. "Nurse Eliot helped me put all the flowers in water while you slept."

He looked around him and made out their shapes. "Daffodils," he said.

"It's Susie's flower."

My father smiled beautifully. "See," he said, "that's how. You live in the face of it, by giving her a flower."

"That's so sad," my mother said.

"Yes," he said, "it is."

My mother had to balance somewhat precariously on one hip near the edge of his hospital bed, but they managed. They managed to stretch out together beside each other so they could stare into each other's eyes.

"How was it seeing Buckley and Lindsey?"

"Incredibly hard," she said.

They were silent for a moment and he squeezed her hand.

"You look so different," he said.

"You mean older."

I watched him reach up and take a strand of my mother's hair and loop it around her ear. "I fell in love with you again while you were away," he said.

I realized how much I wished I could be where my mother was. His love for my mother wasn't about looking back and loving something that would never change. It was about loving my mother for everything—for her brokenness and her fleeing, for her being there right then in that moment before the sun rose and the hospital staff came in. It was about touching that hair with the side of his fingertip, and knowing yet plumbing fearlessly the depths of her ocean eyes.

My mother could not bring herself to say "I love you."

"Will you stay?" he asked.

"For a while."

This was something.

"Good," he said. "So what did you say when people asked you about family in California?"

"Out loud I said I had two children. Silently I said three. I always felt like apologizing to her for that."

"Did you mention a husband?" he asked.

And she looked at him. "No."

"Man," he said.

"I didn't come back to pretend, Jack," she said.

"Why did you come back?"

"My mother called me. She said it was a heart attack and I thought about your father."

"Because I might die?"

"Yes."

"You were sleeping," he said. "You didn't see her."

"Who?"

"Someone came in the room and then left. I think it was Susie."

"Jack?" my mother asked, but her alarm was only at half-mast.

"Don't tell me you don't see her."

She let go.

"I see her everywhere," she said, breathing out her relief. "Even in California she was everywhere. Boarding buses or on the streets outside schools when I drove by. I'd see her hair but it didn't match the face or I'd see her body or the way she moved. I'd see older sisters and their little brothers, or two girls that looked like sisters and I imagined what Lindsey wouldn't have in her life—the whole relationship gone for her and for Buckley, and then that would just hit me, because I had left too. It would just spin onto you and even to my mother."

"She's been great," he said, "a rock. A spongelike rock, but a rock."

"So I gather."

"So if I tell you that Susie was in the room ten minutes ago, what would you say?"

"I'd say you were insane and you were probably right."

My father reached up and traced the line of my mother's nose and brought his finger over her two lips. As he did, the lips parted ever so slightly.

"You have to lean down," he said, "I'm still a sick man."

And I watched as my parents kissed. They kept their eyes open as they did, and my mother was the one to cry first, the tears dropping down onto my father's cheeks until he wept too.

TWENTY-ONE

After I left my parents in the hospital, I went to watch Ray Singh. We had been fourteen together, he and I. Now I saw his head on his pillow, dark hair on yellow sheets, dark skin on yellow sheets. I had always been in love with him. I counted the lashes of each closed eye. He had been my almost, my might-have-been, and I did not want to leave him any more than I did my family.

On the listing scaffold behind the stage, with Ruth below us, Ray Singh had gotten close enough to me so that his breath was near mine. I could smell the mixture of cloves and cinnamon that I imagined he topped his cereal with each morning, and a dark smell too, the human smell of the body coming at me where deep inside there were organs suspended by a chemistry separate from mine.

From the time I knew it would happen until the time it did, I had made sure not to be alone with Ray Singh inside or outside school. I was afraid of what I wanted most—his kiss. That it would not be good enough to match the stories everyone told or those I read in *Seventeen* and *Glamour* and *Vogue.* I feared that I would not be good enough—that my first kiss would equal rejection, not love. Still, I collected kiss stories.

"Your first kiss is destiny knocking," Grandma Lynn said over the phone one day. I was holding the phone while my father went to get my mother. I heard him in the kitchen say "three sheets to the wind."

"If I had it to do over again I would have worn something stupendous—like Fire and Ice, but Revlon didn't make that lipstick back then. I would have left my mark on the man."

"Mother?" my mother said into the bedroom extension.

"We're talking kiss business, Abigail."

"How much have you had?"

"See, Susie," Grandma Lynn said, "if you kiss like a lemon, you make lemonade."

"What was it like?"

"Ah, the kiss question," my mother said. "I'll leave you to it." I had been making my father and her tell it over and over again to hear their different takes. What I came away with was an image of my parents behind a cloud of cigarette smoke—the lips only vaguely touching inside the cloud.

A moment later Grandma Lynn whispered, "Susie, are you still there?"

"Yes, Grandma."

She was quiet for a while longer. "I was your age, and my first kiss came from a grown man. A father of a friend."

"Grandma!" I said, honestly shocked.

"You're not going to tell on me, are you?"

"No."

"It was wonderful," Grandma Lynn said. "He knew how to kiss. The boys who kissed me I couldn't even tolerate. I'd put my hand flat against their chests and push them away. Mr. McGahern knew how to use his lips."

"So what happened?"

"Bliss," she said. "I knew it wasn't right, but it was wonderful—at least for me. I never asked him how he felt about it, but then I never saw him alone after that."

"But did you want to do it again?"

"Yes, I was always searching for that first kiss."

"How about Grandaddy?"

"Not much of a kisser," she said. I could hear the clink of ice cubes on the other end of the phone. "I've never forgotten Mr. McGahern, even though it was just for a moment. Is there a boy who wants to kiss you?"

Neither of my parents had asked me this. I now know that they knew this already, could tell, smiled at each other when they compared notes.

I swallowed hard on my end. "Yes."

"What's his name?"

"Ray Singh."

"Do you like him?"

"Yes."

"Then what's the holdup?"

"I'm afraid I won't be good at it."

"Susie?"

"Yes?"

"Just have fun, kid."

But when I stood by my locker that afternoon and I heard Ray's voice say my name—this time behind me and not above me—it felt like anything but fun. It didn't feel not fun either. The easy states of black and white that I had known before did not apply.

I felt, if I were to say any word, churned. Not as a verb but as an adjective. Happy + Frightened = Churned.

"Ray," I said, but before the name had left my mouth, he leaned into me and caught my open mouth in his. It was so unexpected, even though I had waited weeks for it, that I wanted more. I wanted so badly to kiss Ray Singh again.

The following morning Mr. Connors cut out an article from the paper and saved it for Ruth. It was a detailed drawing of the Flanagan sinkhole and how it was going to be filled in. While Ruth dressed, he penned a note to her. "This is a crock of shit," it said. "Someday some poor sap's car is going to fall into it all over again."

"Dad says this is the death knell for him," Ruth said to Ray, waving the clipping at him as she got into Ray's ice blue Chevy at the end of her driveway. "Our place is going to be swallowed up in subdivision land. Get this. In this article they have four blocks like the cubes you draw in beginning art class, and it's supposed to show how they're going to patch the sinkhole up."

"Nice to see you too, Ruth," Ray said, reversing out of the driveway while making eyes at Ruth's unbuckled seat belt.

"Sorry," Ruth said. "Hello."

"What does the article say?" Ray asked.

"Nice day today, beautiful weather."

"Okay, okay. Tell me about the article."

Every time he saw Ruth after a few months had passed, he was reminded of her impatience and her curiosity—two traits that had both made and kept them friends.

"The first three are the same drawing only with different arrows pointing to different places and saying 'topsoil,' 'cracked limestone,' and 'dissolving rock.' The last one has a big headline that says, 'Patching it' and underneath it says, 'Concrete fills the throat and grout fills the cracks.' "

"Throat?" Ray said.

"I know," said Ruth. "Then there's this other arrow on the other side as if this was such a huge project that they had to pause a second so readers could understand the concept, and this one says, 'Then the hole is filled with dirt.'"

Ray started laughing.

"Like a medical procedure," Ruth said. "Intricate surgery is needed to patch up the planet."

"I think holes in the earth draw on some pretty primal fears."

"I'll say," Ruth said. "They have throats, for God's sake! Hey, let's check this out."

A mile or so down the road there were signs of new construction. Ray took a left and drove into the circles of freshly paved roads where the trees had been cleared and small red and yellow flags waved at intervals from the tops of waist-high wire markers.

Just as they had lulled themselves into thinking that they were alone, exploring the roads laid out for a territory as yet uninhabited, they saw Joe Ellis walking up ahead.

Ruth didn't wave and neither did Ray, nor did Joe make a move to acknowledge them.

"My mom says he still lives at home and can't get a job."

"What does he do all day?" Ray asked.

"Look creepy, I guess."

"He never got over it," Ray said, and Ruth stared out into the rows and rows of vacant lots until Ray connected with the main road again and they crossed back over the railroad tracks moving toward Route 30, which would take them in the direction of the sinkhole.

Ruth floated her arm out the window to feel the moist air of the morning after rain. Although Ray had been accused of being involved in my disappearance, he had understood why, knew that the police were doing their job. But Joe Ellis had never recovered from being accused of killing the cats and dogs Mr. Harvey had killed. He wandered around, keeping a good distance from his neighbors and wanting so much to take solace in the love of cats and dogs. For me the saddest thing was that these animals smelled the brokenness in him—the human defect—and kept away.

Down Route 30 near Eels Rod Pike, at a spot that Ray and Ruth were about to pass, I saw Len coming out of an apartment over Joe's barbershop. He carried a lightly stuffed student knapsack out to his car. The knapsack had been the gift of the young woman who owned the apartment. She had asked him out for coffee one day after they met down at the station as part of a criminology course at West Chester College. Inside the knapsack he had a combination of things—some of which he would show my father and some that no child's parent needed to see. The latter included the photos of the graves of the recovered bodies—both elbows there in each case.

When he had called the hospital, the nurse had told him Mr. Salmon was with his wife and family. Now his guilt thickened as he pulled his car into the hospital parking lot and sat for a moment with the hot sun coming through the windshield, baking in the heat.

I could see Len working on how to state what he had to say. He could work with only one assumption in his head—after almost seven years of ever more dwindling contact since late 1975, what my parents would hope for most was a body or the news that Mr. Harvey had been found. What he had to give them was a charm.

He grabbed his knapsack and locked up the car, passing by the girl outside with her replenished buckets of daffodils. He knew the number of my father's room, so he did not bother announcing himself to the fifth-floor nurses' station but merely tapped lightly on my father's open door before walking in.

My mother was standing with her back toward him. When she turned, I could see the force of her presence hit him. She was holding my father's hand. I suddenly felt terribly lonely.

My mother wobbled a bit when she met Len's eyes, and then she led with what came easiest.

"Is it *ever* wonderful to see you?" she tried to joke.

"Len," my father managed. "Abbie, will you tilt me up?"

"How are you feeling, Mr. Salmon?" Len asked as my mother pressed the up arrow button on the bed.

"Jack, please," my father insisted.

"Before you get your hopes up," Len said, "we haven't caught him."

My father visibly deflated.

My mother readjusted the foam pillows behind my father's back and neck. "Then why are you here?" she asked.

"We found an item of Susie's," Len said.

He had used almost the same sentence when he'd come to the house with the jingle-bell hat. It was a distant echo in her head.

The night before, as first my mother watched my father sleeping and then my father woke to see her head beside his on his pillow, they had both been staving off the memory of that first night of snow and hail and rain and how they had clung to each other, neither of them voicing aloud their greatest hope. Last night it had been my father who'd finally said it: "She's never coming home." A clear and easy piece of truth that everyone who had ever known me had accepted. But he needed to say it, and she needed to hear him say it.

"It's a charm off her bracelet," Len said. "A Pennsylvania keystone with her initials on it."

"I bought that for her," my father said. "At Thirtieth Street Station when I went into the city one day. They had a booth, and a man wearing safety glasses etched in initials for free. I brought Lindsey one too. Remember, Abigail?"

"I remember," my mother said.

"We found it near a grave in Connecticut."

My parents were suddenly still for a moment—like animals trapped in ice—their eyes frozen open and beseeching whoever walked above them to release them now, please.

"It wasn't Susie," Len said, rushing to fill the space. "What it means is that Harvey has been linked to other murders in Delaware and Connecticut. It was at the grave site outside Hartford where we found Susie's charm."

My father and mother watched as Len fumbled to open the slightly jammed zipper of his knapsack. My mother smoothed my father's hair back and tried to catch his eye. But my father was focused on the prospect Len presented—my murder case reopening. And my mother, just when she was beginning to feel on more solid ground, had to hide the fact that she'd never wanted it to begin again. The name George Harvey silenced her. She had never known what to say about him. For my mother, connecting her life to his capture and punishment spoke more about choosing to live with the enemy than about having to learn to live in the world without me.

Len pulled out a large Ziploc bag. At the bottom corner of the bag my parents could see the glint of gold. Len handed it to my mother, and she held it in front of her, slightly away from her body.

"Don't you need this, Len?" my father asked.

"We did all the tests on it," he said. "We've documented where it was found and taken the required photographs. The time may come when I would have to ask for it back, but until then, it's yours to keep."

"Open it, Abbie," my father said.

I watched my mother hold open the bag and lean over the bed. "It's for you, Jack," she said. "It was a gift from you."

As my father reached in, his hand shook, and it took him a

second to feel the small, sharp edges of the keystone against the flesh of his fingers. The way he drew it out of the bag reminded me of playing the game Operation with Lindsey when we were little. If he touched the sides of the Ziploc bag an alarm would go off and he would have to forfeit.

"How can you be sure he killed these other girls?" my mother asked. She stared at the tiny ember of gold in my father's palm.

"Nothing is ever certain," Len said.

And the echo rang in her ears again. Len had a fixed set of phrases. It was this same phrase that my father had borrowed to soothe his family. It was a cruel phrase that preyed on hope.

"I think I want you to leave now," she said.

"Abigail?" my father queried.

"I can't hear anymore."

"I'm very glad to have the charm, Len," my father said.

Len doffed an imaginary cap to my father before turning to go. He had made a certain kind of love to my mother before she went away. Sex as an act of willful forgetting. It was the kind he made more and more in the rooms above the barbershop.

I headed south toward Ruth and Ray, but I saw Mr. Harvey instead. He was driving an orange patchwork car that had been pieced together from so many different versions of the same make and model that it looked like Frankenstein's monster on wheels. A bungee cord held the front hood, which fluttered up and down as it caught the oncoming air.

The engine had resisted anything but a shimmer above the speed limit no matter how hard he pressed the gas pedal. He had slept next to an empty grave, and while he'd been sleeping he had dreamed of the 5! 5! 5!, waking near dawn to make the drive to Pennsylvania.

The edges of Mr. Harvey seemed oddly blurred. For years he

had kept at bay the memories of the women he killed, but now, one by one, they were coming back.

The first girl he'd hurt was by accident. He got mad and couldn't stop himself, or that was how he began to weave it into sense. She stopped going to the high school that they were both enrolled in, but this didn't seem strange to him. By that time he had moved so many times that he assumed that was what the girl had done. He had regretted it, this quiet, muffled rape of a school friend, but he didn't see it as something that would stay with either one of them. It was as if something outside him had resulted in the collision of their two bodies one afternoon. For a second afterward, she'd stared. It was bottomless. Then she put on her torn underpants, tucking them into her skirt's waistband to keep them in place. They didn't speak, and she left. He cut himself with his penknife along the back of his hand. When his father asked about the blood, there would be a plausible explanation. "See," he could say, and point to the place on his hand. "It was an accident."

But his father didn't ask, and no one came around looking for him. No father or brother or policeman.

Then what I saw was what Mr. Harvey felt beside him. This girl, who had died only a few years later when her brother fell asleep smoking a cigarette. She was sitting in the front seat. I wondered how long it would take before he began to remember me.

The only signs of change since the day Mr. Harvey had delivered me up to the Flanagans' were the orange pylons set around the lot. That and the evidence that the sinkhole had expanded. The house's southeast corner sloped downward, and the front porch was quietly sinking into the earth.

As a precaution, Ray parked on the other side of Flat Road,

under a section of overgrown shrubbery. Even so, the passenger side skimmed the edge of the pavement. "What happened to the Flanagans?" Ray asked as they got out of his car.

"My father said the corporation that bought the property gave them a settlement and they took off."

"It's spooky around here, Ruth," Ray said.

They crossed the empty road. Above them the sky was a light blue, a few smoky clouds dotting the air. From where they stood they could just make out the back of Hal's bike shop on the other side of the railroad tracks.

"I wonder if Hal Heckler still owns that?" Ruth said. "I had a crush on him when we were growing up."

Then she turned toward the lot. They were quiet. Ruth moved in ever-diminishing circles, with the hole and its vague edge as their goal. Ray trailed just behind Ruth as she led the way. If you saw it from a distance, the sinkhole seemed innocuous—like an overgrown mud puddle just starting to dry out. There were spots of grass and weeds surrounding it and then, if you looked close enough, it was as if the earth stopped and a light cocoa-colored flesh began. It was soft and convex, and it drew in items placed on top of it.

"How do you know it won't swallow us?" Ray asked.

"We're not heavy enough," Ruth said.

"Stop if you feel yourself sinking."

Watching them I remembered holding on to Buckley's hand the day we went to bury the refrigerator. While my father was talking to Mr. Flanagan, Buckley and I walked up to the point where the earth sloped down and softened, and I swore I felt it give ever so slightly beneath my feet. It had been the same sensation as walking in the graveyard of our church and suddenly sinking into the hollow tunnels that the moles had dug among the headstones.

Ultimately it was the memory of those very moles—and the

pictures of their blind, nosy, toothsome selves that I sought out in books — that had made me accept more readily being sunk inside the earth in a heavy metal safe. I was mole-proof, anyway.

Ruth tiptoed up to what she took to be the edge, while I thought of the sound of my father's laughter on that long-ago day. I made up a story for my brother on the way home. How underneath the sinkhole there was a whole village inside the earth that no one knew about and the people who lived there greeted these appliances like gifts from an Earthly heaven. "When our refrigerator reaches them," I said, "they will praise us, because they are a race of tiny repairmen who love to put things back together again." My father's laughter filled the car.

"Ruthie," Ray said, "that's close enough."

Ruth's toes were on the soft part, her heels were on the hard, and there was a sense as I watched her that she might point her fingers and raise her arms and dive right in to be beside me. But Ray came up behind her.

"Apparently," he said, "the earth's throat burps."

All three of us watched the corner of something metal as it rose.

"The great Maytag of 'sixty-nine," Ray said.

But it was not a washer or a safe. It was an old red gas stove, moving slow.

"Do you ever think about where Susie Salmon's body ended up?" asked Ruth.

I wanted to walk out from underneath the overgrown shrubs that half-hid their ice blue car and cross the road and walk down into the hole and back up and tap her gently on the shoulder and say, "It's me! You've done it! Bingo! Score!"

"No," Ray said. "I leave that to you."

"Everything is changing here now. Every time I come back something is gone that made it not just every other place in the country," she said.

"Do you want to go inside the house?" Ray asked, but he was thinking of me. How his crush had come when he was thirteen. He had seen me walking home from school ahead of him, and it was a series of simple things: my awkward plaid skirt, my peacoat covered in Holiday's fur, the way what I thought of as my mousy brown hair caught the afternoon sun so that the light moved fluidly from spot to spot as we walked home, one behind the other. And then, a few days later, when he had stood in social science class and accidentally read from his paper on *Jane Eyre* instead of the War of 1812—I had looked at him in a way he thought was nice.

Ray walked toward the house that would soon be demolished, and that had already been stripped of any valuable doorknobs and faucets late one night by Mr. Connors, but Ruth stayed by the sinkhole. Ray was already inside the house when it happened. As clear as day, she saw me standing there beside her, looking at the spot Mr. Harvey had dumped me.

"Susie," Ruth said, feeling my presence even more solidly when she said my name.

But I said nothing.

"I've written poems for you," Ruth said, trying to get me to stay with her. What she had wished for her whole life happening, finally. "Don't you want anything, Susie?" she asked.

Then I vanished.

Ruth stood there reeling, waiting in the gray light of the Pennsylvania sun. And her question rang in my ears: "Don't you want anything?"

On the other side of the railroad tracks, Hal's shop was deserted. He had taken the day off and brought Samuel and Buckley to a bike show in Radnor. I could see Buckley's hands move over the curved front-wheel casing of a red minibike. It would be his birthday soon, and Hal and Samuel watched him. Hal had wanted to give Samuel's old alto sax to my brother, but my Grandma Lynn had intervened. "He needs to bang on things, honey," she said. "Save the subtle stuff." So Hal and Samuel had chipped in together and bought my brother a secondhand set of drums.

Grandma Lynn was at the mall trying to find simple yet elegant clothes that she might convince my mother to wear. With fingers made dexterous from years of practice, she pulled a near-navy dress from a rack of black. I could see the woman near her alight on the dress in greenish envy.

At the hospital, my mother was reading aloud to my father from a day-old *Evening Bulletin,* and he was watching her lips move and not really listening. Wanting to kiss her instead.

And Lindsey.

I could see Mr. Harvey take the turn into my old neighborhood in broad daylight, past caring who spotted him, even depending on his standard invisibility—here, in the neighborhood where so many had said they would never forget him, had always thought of him as strange, had come easily to suspect that the dead wife he spoke of by alternate names had been one of his victims.

Lindsey was at home alone.

Mr. Harvey drove by Nate's house inside the anchor area of the development. Nate's mother was picking the wilted blossoms from her front kidney-shaped flower bed. She looked up when the car passed. She saw the unfamiliar, patched-together car and imagined it was a college friend of one of the older children home for the summer. She had not seen Mr. Harvey in the driver's seat. He turned left onto the lower road, which circled around to his old street. Holiday whined at my feet, the same kind of sick, low moan he would let out when we drove him to the vet.

Ruana Singh had her back to him. I saw her through the dining room window, alphabetizing stacks of new books and placing them in carefully kept bookshelves. There were children out in their yards on swings and pogo sticks and chasing one another with water pistols. A neighborhood full of potential victims.

He rounded the curve at the bottom of our road and passed the small municipal park across from where the Gilberts lived. They were both inside, Mr. Gilbert now infirm. Then he saw his old house, no longer green, though to my family and me it would always be "the green house." The new owners had painted it a lavendery mauve and installed a pool and, just off to the side, near the basement window, a gazebo made out of redwood, which overflowed with hanging ivy and children's toys. The front flower beds had been paved over when they expanded their front walk, and they had screened in the front porch with frost-resistant glass, behind which he saw an office of some sort. He heard the sound of girls laughing out in the backyard, and a woman came out of the front door carrying a pair of pruning shears and wearing a sun hat. She stared at the man sitting in his orange car and felt something kick inside her—the queasy kick of an empty womb. She turned abruptly and went back inside, peering at him from behind her window. Waiting.

He drove down the road a few houses further.

There she was, my precious sister. He could see her in the upstairs window of our house. She had cut all her hair off and grown thinner in the intervening years, but it was her, sitting at the drafting board she used as a desk and reading a psychology book.

It was then that I began to see them coming down the road.

While he scanned the windows of my old house and wondered where the other members of my family were—whether my father's leg still made him hobble—I saw the final vestiges of the animals and the women taking leave of Mr. Harvey's house. They straggled forward together. He watched my sister and thought of the sheets he had draped on the poles of the bridal tent. He had stared right in my father's eyes that day as he said my name. And the dog—the one that barked outside his house—the dog was surely dead by now.

Lindsey moved in the window, and I watched him watching her. She stood up and turned around, going farther into the room to a floor-to-ceiling bookshelf. She reached up and brought another book down. As she came back to the desk and he lingered on her face, his rearview mirror suddenly filled with a black-and-white cruising slowly up the street behind him.

He knew he could not outrace them. He sat in his car and prepared the last vestiges of the face he had been giving authorities for decades—the face of a bland man they might pity or despise but never blame. As the officer pulled alongside him, the women slipped in the windows and the cats curled around his ankles.

"Are you lost?" the young policeman asked when he was flush with the orange car.

"I used to live here," Mr. Harvey said. I shook with it. He had chosen to tell the truth.

"We got a call, suspicious vehicle."

"I see they're building something in the old cornfield," Mr. Harvey said. And I knew that part of me could join the others then, swoop down in pieces, each body part he had claimed raining down inside his car.

"They're expanding the school."

"I thought the neighborhood looked more prosperous," he said wistfully.

"Perhaps you should move along," the officer said. He was embarrassed for Mr. Harvey in his patched-up car, but I saw him jot the license plate down.

"I didn't mean to scare anyone."

Mr. Harvey was a pro, but in that moment I didn't care. With each section of road he covered, I focused on Lindsey inside reading her textbooks, on the facts jumping up from the pages and into her brain, on how smart she was and how whole. At Temple she had decided to be a therapist. And I thought of the mix of air that was our front yard, which was daylight, a queasy mother and a cop—it was a convergence of luck that had kept my sister safe so far. Every day a question mark.

Ruth did not tell Ray what had happened. She promised herself she would write it in her journal first. When they crossed the road back to the car, Ray saw something violet in the scrub halfway up a high dirt berm that had been dumped there by a construction crew.

"That's periwinkle," he said to Ruth. "I'm going to clip some for my mom."

"Cool, take your time," Ruth said.

Ray ducked into the underbrush by the driver's side and climbed up to the periwinkle while Ruth stood by the car. Ray wasn't thinking of me anymore. He was thinking of his mother's smiles. The surest way to get them was to find her wildflowers like this, to bring them home to her and watch her as she pressed them, first opening their petals flat against the black and white of dictionaries or reference books. Ray walked to the top of the berm and disappeared over the side in hopes of finding more.

It was only then that I felt a prickle along my spine, when I saw his body suddenly vanish on the other side. I heard Holiday, his fear lodged low and deep in his throat, and realized it could not have been Lindsey for whom he had whined. Mr. Harvey crested the top of Eels Rod Pike and saw the sinkhole and the orange pylons that matched his car. He had dumped a body there. He remembered his mother's amber pendant, and how when she had handed it to him it was still warm.

Ruth saw the women stuffed in the car in blood-colored gowns. She began walking toward them. On that same road where I had been buried, Mr. Harvey passed by Ruth. All she could see were the women. Then: blackout.

That was the moment I fell to Earth.

TWENTY-TWO

Ruth collapsing into the road. Of this I was aware. Mr. Harvey sailing away unwatched, unloved, unbidden—this I lost.

Helplessly I tipped, my balance gone. I fell through the open doorway of the gazebo, across the lawn and out past the farthest boundary of the heaven I had lived in all these years.

I heard Ray screaming in the air above me, his voice shouting in an arc of sound. "Ruth, are you okay?" And then he reached her and grabbed on.

"Ruth, Ruth," he yelled. "What happened?"

And I was in Ruth's eyes and I was looking up. I could feel the arch of her back against the pavement, and scrapes inside her clothes where flesh had been torn away by the gravel's sharp edges. I felt every sensation—the warmth of the sun, the smell of the asphalt—but I could not see Ruth.

I heard Ruth's lungs bubbling, a giddiness there in her stomach, but air still filling her lungs. Then tension stretching out the body. Her body. Ray above, his eyes—gray, pulsing, looking up and down the road hopelessly for help that was not coming. He had not seen the car but had come through the scrub delighted, carrying a bouquet of wildflowers for his mother, and there was Ruth, lying in the road.

Ruth pushed up against her skin, wanting out. She was fighting to leave and I was inside now, struggling with her. I willed her back, willed that divine impossible, but she wanted out. There was nothing and no one that could keep her down. Flying. I watched as I had so many times from heaven, but this time it was a blur beside me. It was lust and rage yearning upward.

"Ruth," Ray said. "Can you hear me, Ruth?"

Right before she closed her eyes and all the lights went out and the world was frantic, I looked into Ray Singh's gray eyes, at his dark skin, at his lips I had once kissed. Then, like a hand unclasping from a tight lock, Ruth passed by him.

Ray's eyes bid me forward while the watching streamed out of me and gave way to a pitiful desire. To be alive again on this Earth. Not to watch from above but to be—the sweetest thing—beside.

Somewhere in the blue blue Inbetween I had seen her—Ruth streaking by me as I fell to Earth. But she was no shadow of a human form, no ghost. She was a smart girl breaking all the rules.

And I was in her body.

I heard a voice calling me from heaven. It was Franny's. She ran toward the gazebo, calling my name. Holiday was barking so loud that his voice would catch and round in the base of his throat with no break. Then, suddenly, Franny and Holiday were gone and all was silent. I felt something holding me down, and I felt a hand in mine. My ears were like oceans in which what I had known, voices, faces, facts, began to drown. I opened my eyes for the first time since I had died and saw gray eyes looking back at me. I was still as I came to realize that the marvelous weight weighing me down was the weight of the human body.

I tried to speak.

"Don't," Ray said. "What happened?"

I died, I wanted to tell him. How do you say, "I died and now I'm back among the living"?

Ray had kneeled down. Scattered around him and on top of me were the flowers he'd been gathering for Ruana. I could pick out their bright elliptical shapes against Ruth's dark clothes. And then Ray leaned his ear to my chest to listen to me breathing. He placed a finger on the inside of my wrist to check my pulse.

"Did you faint?" he asked when these checked out.

I nodded. I knew I would not be granted this grace on Earth forever, that Ruth's wish was only temporary.

"I think I'm fine," I tried, but my voice was too faint, too far away, and Ray did not hear me. My eyes locked on to his then, opening as wide as I could make them. Something urged me to lift up. I thought I was floating back to heaven, returning, but I was trying to stand up.

"Ruth," Ray said. "Don't move if you feel weak. I can carry you to the car."

I smiled at him, one-thousand-watted. "I'm okay," I said.

Tentatively, watching me carefully, he released my arm but continued to hold on to my other hand. He went with me as I stood, and the wildflowers fell to the pavement. In heaven, women were throwing rose petals as they saw Ruth Connors.

I watched his beautiful face break into a stunned smile. "So you're all right," he said. Cautious, he came close enough to kiss me, but he told me he was checking my pupils to see if they were equal in size.

I was feeling the weight of Ruth's body, both the luscious bounce of breasts and thighs but also an awesome responsibility. I was a soul back on Earth. AWOL a little while from heaven, I had been given a gift. By force of will I stood as straight as I could.

"Ruth?"

I tried to get used to the name. "Yes," I said.

"You've changed," he said. "Something's changed."

We stood near the center of the road, but this was my moment. I wanted so much to tell him, but what could I say then? "I'm Susie, I have only a little time." I was too afraid.

"Kiss me," I said instead.

"What?"

"Don't you want to?" I reached my hands up to his face and felt the light stubble of a beard that had not been there eight years ago.

"What's happened to you?" he said, bewildered.

"Sometimes cats fall ten flights out of the windows of highrises and land on their feet. You only believe it because you've seen it in print."

Ray stared at me, mystified. He leaned his head down and our lips touched, tender. At the roots I felt his cool lips deep down inside me. Another kiss, precious package, stolen gift. His eyes were so close to me I saw the green flecks in the gray.

I took his hand, and we walked back to the car in silence. I was aware that he dragged behind, stretching my arm out behind me as we held hands and scanning Ruth's body to make sure she was walking fine.

He opened the door of the passenger side, and I slid into the seat and placed my feet on the carpeted floor. When he came around to his side and ducked inside he looked hard at me once more.

"What's wrong?" I asked.

He kissed me lightly again, on the lips. What I had wanted for so long. The moment slowed down, and I drank it in. The brush of his lips, the slight stubble of his beard as it grazed me, and the sound of the kiss—the small smack of suction as our lips parted after the pushing together and then the more brutal breaking away. It reverberated, this sound, down the long tunnel of loneliness and making do with watching the touch and caress of others on Earth. I had never been touched like this. I had only been hurt by hands past all tenderness. But spreading out into my heaven after death had been a moonbeam that swirled and blinked on and off—Ray Singh's kiss. Somehow Ruth knew this.

My head throbbed then, with the thought of it, with me hiding inside Ruth in every way but this—that when Ray kissed me or as our hands met it was my desire, not Ruth's, it was *me* pushing out at the edges of her skin. I could see Holly. She was laughing, her head tilted back, and then I heard Holiday howling plaintively, for I was back where we had both once lived.

"Where do you want to go?" Ray asked.

And it was such a wide question, the answer so vast. I knew I did not want to chase after Mr. Harvey. I looked at Ray and knew why I was there. To take back a piece of heaven I had never known.

"Hal Heckler's bike shop," I stated firmly.

"What?"

"You asked," I said.

"Ruth?"

"Yes?"

"Can I kiss you again?"

"Yes," I said, my face flushing.

He leaned over as the engine warmed and our lips met once more and there she was, Ruth, lecturing a group of old men in berets and black turtlenecks while they held glowing lighters in the air and called her name in a rhythmic chant.

Ray sat back and looked at me. "What is it?" he asked.

"When you kiss me I see heaven," I said.

"What does it look like?"

"It's different for everyone."

"I want details," he said, smiling. "Facts."

"Make love to me," I said, "and I'll tell you."

"Who are you?" he asked, but I could tell he didn't know what he was asking yet.

"The car is warmed up," I said.

His hand grabbed the shiny chrome stick on the side of the steering wheel and then we drove—normal as day—a boy and a girl together. The sun caught the broken mica in the old patched pavement as he made the U-turn.

We drove down to the bottom of Flat Road, and I pointed to the dirt path on the other side of Eels Rod Pike, which led up to a place where we could cross the railroad tracks.

"They'll have to change this soon," Ray said as he shot across the gravel and up onto the dirt path. The railroad stretched to Harrisburg in one direction and Philadelphia in the other, and all along it buildings were being razed and old families were moving out and industrial tenants in.

"Will you stay here," I asked, "after you're done with school?"

"No one does," Ray said. "You know that."

I was almost blinded by it, this choice; the idea that if I'd remained on Earth I could have left this place to claim another, that I could go anywhere I wanted to. And I wondered then, was it the same in heaven as on Earth? What I'd been missing was a wanderlust that came from letting go?

We drove onto the slim patch of cleared earth that ran along either side of Hal's bike shop. Ray stopped and braked the car.

"Why here?" Ray asked.

"Remember," I said, "we're exploring."

I led him around to the back of the shop and reached up over the doorjamb until I felt the hidden key.

"How do you know about that?"

"I've watched hundreds of people hide keys," I said. "It doesn't take a genius to guess."

Inside it was as I remembered it, the smell of bike grease heavy in the air.

I said, "I think I need to shower. Why not make yourself at home?"

I walked past the bed and turned on the light switch on the cord—all the tiny white lights above Hal's bed glittered then, the only light save the dusty light coming from the small back window.

"Where are you going?" Ray asked. "How do you know about this place?" His voice had a frantic sound it hadn't just a moment before.

"Give me just a little time, Ray," I said. "Then I'll explain."

I walked into the small bathroom but kept the door slightly ajar. As I took Ruth's clothes off and waited for the hot water to heat up, I hoped that Ruth could see me, could see her body as I saw it, its perfect living beauty.

It was damp and musty in the bathroom, and the tub was stained from years of having anything but water poured down its drain. I stepped up into the old claw-foot tub and stood under the water. Even at the hottest I could make it, I still felt cold. I called Ray's name. I begged him to step inside the room.

"I can see you through the curtain," he said, averting his eyes.

"It's okay," I said. "I like it. Take your clothes off and join me."

"Susie," he said, "you know I'm not like that."

My heart seized up. "What did you say?" I asked. I focused my eyes on his through the white translucent liner Hal kept for a curtain—he was a dark shape with a hundred small pinpoints of light surrounding him.

"I said I'm not that kind."

"You called me Susie."

There was silence, and then a moment later he drew back the curtain, being careful to look only at my face.

"Susie?"

"Join me," I said, my eyes welling up. "Please, join me."

I closed my eyes and waited. I put my head under the water

and felt the heat of it prickling my cheeks and neck, my breasts and stomach and groin. Then I heard him fumbling, heard his belt buckle hit the cold cement floor and his pockets lose their change.

I had the same sense of anticipation then as I sometimes had as a child when I lay down in the back seat and closed my eyes while my parents drove, sure we would be home when the car stopped, that they would lift me up and carry me inside. It was an anticipation born of trust.

Ray drew back the curtain. I turned to face him and opened my eyes. I felt a marvelous draft on the inside of my thighs.

"It's okay," I said.

He stepped slowly into the tub. At first he did not touch me, but then, tentatively, he traced a small scar along my side. We watched together as his finger moved down the ribbony wound.

"Ruth's volleyball incident, nineteen seventy-five," I said. I shivered again.

"You're not Ruth," he said, his face full of wonder.

I took the hand that had reached the end of the cut and placed it under my left breast.

"I've watched you both for years," I said. "I want you to make love to me."

His lips parted to speak, but what was on his lips now was too strange to say out loud. He brushed my nipple with his thumb, and I pulled his head toward me. We kissed. The water came down between our bodies and wet the sparse hair along his chest and stomach. I kissed him because I wanted to see Ruth and I wanted to see Holly and I wanted to know if they could see me. In the shower I could cry and Ray could kiss my tears, never knowing exactly why I shed them.

I touched every part of him and held it in my hands. I cupped his elbow in my palm. I dragged his pubic hair out straight between my fingers. I held that part of him that Mr. Harvey had forced inside me. Inside my head I said the word *gentle,* and then I said the word *man.*

"Ray?"

"I don't know what to call you."

"Susie."

I put my fingers up to his lips to stop his questioning. "Remember the note you wrote me? Remember how you called yourself the Moor?"

For a moment we both stood there, and I watched the water bead along his shoulders, then slip and fall.

Without saying anything further, he lifted me up and I wrapped my legs around him. He turned out of the path of the water to use the edge of the tub for support. When he was inside of me, I grabbed his face in my hands and kissed him as hard as I could.

After a full minute, he pulled away. "Tell me what it looks like."

"Sometimes it looks like the high school did," I said, breathless. "I never got to go there, but in my heaven I can make a bonfire in the classrooms or run up and down the halls yelling as loud as I want. But it doesn't always look like that. It can look like Nova Scotia, or Tangiers, or Tibet. It looks like anything you've ever dreamed."

"Is Ruth there?"

"Ruth is doing spoken word, but she'll come back."

"Can you see yourself there?"

"I'm here right now," I said.

"But you'll be gone soon."

I would not lie. I bowed my head. "I think so, Ray. Yes."

We made love then. We made love in the shower and in the bedroom and under the lights and fake glow-in-the-dark stars. While he rested, I kissed him across the line of his backbone and blessed each knot of muscle, each mole and blemish.

"Don't go," he said, and his eyes, those shining gems, shut and I could feel the shallow breath of sleep from him.

"My name is Susie," I whispered, "last name Salmon, like the fish." I leaned my head down to rest on his chest and sleep beside him.

When I opened my eyes, the window across from us was dark red and I could feel that there was not much time left. Outside, the world I had watched for so long was living and breathing on the same earth I now was. But I knew I would not go out. I had taken this time to fall in love instead—in love with the sort of helplessness I had not felt in death—the helplessness of being alive, the dark bright pity of being human—feeling as you went, groping in corners and opening your arms to light—all of it part of navigating the unknown.

Ruth's body was weakening. I leaned on one arm and watched Ray sleeping. I knew that I was going soon.

When his eyes opened a short while later, I looked at him and traced the edge of his face with my fingers.

"Do you ever think about the dead, Ray?"

He blinked his eyes and looked at me.

"I'm in med school."

"I don't mean cadavers, or diseases, or collapsed organs, I mean what Ruth talks about. I mean us."

"Sometimes I do," he said. "I've always wondered."

"We're here, you know," I said. "All the time. You can talk to us and think about us. It doesn't have to be sad or scary."

"Can I touch you again?" He shook the sheets from his legs to sit up.

It was then that I saw something at the end of Hal's bed. It was cloudy and still. I tried to convince myself that it was an odd trick of light, a mass of dust motes trapped in the setting sun. But when Ray reached out to touch me, I didn't feel anything.

Ray leaned close to me and kissed me lightly on the shoulder. I didn't feel it. I pinched myself under the blanket. Nothing.

The cloudy mass at the end of the bed began to take shape now. As Ray slipped out of the bed and stood, I saw men and women filling the room.

"Ray," I said, just before he reached the bathroom. I wanted to say "I'll miss you," or "don't go," or "thank you."

"Yes."

"You have to read Ruth's journals."

"You couldn't pay me not to," he said.

I looked through the shadowy figures of the spirits forming a mass at the end of the bed and saw him smile at me. Saw his lovely fragile body turn and walk through the doorway. A tenuous and sudden memory.

As the steam began to billow out from the bathroom, I made my way, slowly, to the small child's desk where Hal stacked bills and records. I began to think of Ruth again, how I hadn't seen any of it coming—the marvelous possibility that Ruth had dreamed of since our meeting in the parking lot. Instead, I saw how hope was what I had traded on in heaven and on Earth. Dreams of being a wildlife photographer, dreams of winning an Oscar in junior year, dreams of kissing Ray Singh once more. Look what happens when you dream.

In front of me I saw a phone and picked it up. Without thinking, I punched in the number to my house, like a lock whose combination you know only when you spin the dial in your hand.

On the third ring, someone picked up.

"Hello?"

"Hello, Buckley," I said.

"Who is this?"

"It's me, Susie."

"Who's there?"

"Susie, honey, your big sister."

"I can't hear you," he said.

I stared at the phone for a minute, and then I felt them. The room was full now of these silent spirits. Among them were children as well as adults. "Who are you? Where did you all come from?" I asked, but what had been my voice made no noise in the room. It was then that I noticed it. I was sitting up and watching the others, but Ruth was lying sprawled across the desk.

"Can you throw me a towel?" Ray yelled after shutting off the water. When I did not answer he pulled back the curtain. I heard him get out of the tub and come to the doorway. He saw Ruth and ran toward her. He touched her shoulder and, sleepily, she roused. They looked at each other. She did not have to say anything. He knew that I was gone.

I remembered once, with my parents and Lindsey and Buckley, riding backward on a train into a dark tunnel. That was how it felt to leave Earth the second time. The destination somehow inevitable, the sights seen in passing so many times. But this time I was accompanied, not ripped away, and I knew we were taking a long trip to a place very far away.

Leaving Earth again was easier than coming back had been. I got to see two old friends silently holding each other in the back of Hal's bike shop, neither of them ready to say aloud what had happened to them. Ruth was both more tired and more happy than she had ever been. For Ray, what he had been through and the possibilities this opened up for him were just starting to sink in.

TWENTY-THREE

The next morning the smell of his mother's baking had sneaked up the stairs and into Ray's room where he and Ruth lay together. Overnight, their world had changed. It was that simple.

After leaving Hal's bike shop, being careful to cover any trace that they had ever been there, Ray and Ruth drove in silence back to Ray's house. Later that night, when Ruana found the two of them curled up together asleep and fully clothed, she was glad that Ray had at least this one weird friend.

Around three A.M., Ray had stirred. He sat up and looked at Ruth, at her long gangly limbs, at the beautiful body to which he had made love, and felt a sudden warmth infuse him. He reached out to touch her, and just then a bit of moonlight fell across the floor from the window where I had watched him sit and study for so many years. He followed it. There on the floor was Ruth's bag.

Careful not to wake her, he slid off the bed and walked over to it. Inside was her journal. He lifted it out and began to read:

"At the tips of feathers there is air and at their base: blood. I hold up bones; I wish like broken glass they could court light . . . still I try to place these pieces back together, to set them firm, to make murdered girls live again."

He skipped ahead:

"Penn Station, bathroom stall, struggle which led to the sink. Older woman.

"Domestic. Ave. C. Husband and wife.

"Roof on Mott Street, a teenage girl, gunshot.

"Time? Little girl in C.P. strays toward bushes. White lace collar, fancy."

He grew incredibly cold in the room but kept reading, looking up only when he heard Ruth stir.

"I have so much to tell you," she said.

Nurse Eliot helped my father lower himself into the wheelchair while my mother and sister fussed about the room, collecting the daffodils to take home.

"Nurse Eliot," he said, "I'll remember your kindness but I hope it will be a long time before I see you again."

"I hope so too," she said. She looked at my family gathered in the room, standing awkwardly about. "Buckley, your mother's and sister's hands are full. It's up to you."

"Steer her easy, Buck," my father said.

I watched the four of them begin to trail down the hall to the elevator, Buckley and my father first while Lindsey and my mother followed behind, their arms full of dripping daffodils.

In the elevator going down, Lindsey stared into the throats of the bright yellow flowers. She remembered that Samuel and Hal had found yellow daffodils lying in the cornfield on the afternoon of the first memorial. They had never known who placed them there. My sister looked at the flowers and then my mother. She could feel my brother's body touching hers, and our father, sitting in the shiny hospital chair, looking tired but happy to be going home. When they reached the lobby and the doors opened I knew they were meant to be there, the four of them together, alone.

While Ruana's hands grew wet and swollen paring apple after apple, she began to say the word in her mind, the one she had avoided for years: *divorce*. It had been something about the crumpled, clinging postures of her son and Ruth that finally freed her. She could not remember the last time she had gone to bed at the same time as her husband. He walked in the room like a ghost and like a ghost slipped in between the sheets, barely creasing them. He was not unkind in the ways that the television and newspapers were full of. His cruelty was in his absence. Even when he came and sat at her dinner table and ate her food, he was not there.

She heard the sound of water running in the bathroom above her and waited what she thought was a considerate interval before calling up to them. My mother had called that morning to thank her for having talked to her when she called from California, and Ruana had decided to drop off a pie.

After handing a mug of coffee each to Ruth and Ray, Ruana announced that it was already late and she wanted Ray to accompany her to the Salmons', where she intended to run quietly to the door and place a pie on their doorstep.

"Whoa, pony," Ruth managed.

Ruana stared at her.

"Sorry, Mom," Ray said. "We had a pretty intense day yesterday." But he wondered, might his mother ever believe him?

Ruana turned toward the counter and brought one of two pies she had baked to the table, where the scent of it rose in a steamy mist from the holes cut into the crust. "Breakfast?" she said.

"You're a goddess!" said Ruth.

Ruana smiled.

"Eat your fill and then get dressed and both of you can come with me."

Ruth looked at Ray while she said, "Actually, I have somewhere to go, but I'll drop by later."

Hal brought the drum set over for my brother. Hal and my grandmother had agreed. Though it was still weeks before Buckley turned thirteen, he needed them. Samuel had let Lindsey and Buckley meet my parents at the hospital without him. It would be a double homecoming for them. My mother had stayed with my father for forty-eight hours straight, during which the world had changed for them and for others and would, I saw now, change again and again and again. There was no way to stop it.

"I know we shouldn't start too early," Grandma Lynn said, "but what's your poison, boys?"

"I thought we were set up for champagne," Samuel said.

"We are later," she said. "I'm offering an apéritif."

"I think I'm passing," Samuel said. "I'll have something when Lindsey does."

"Hal?"

"I'm teaching Buck the drums."

Grandma Lynn held her tongue about the questionable sobriety of known jazz greats. "Well, how about three scintillating tumblers of water?"

My grandmother stepped back into the kitchen to get their drinks. I had come to love her more after death than I ever had on Earth. I wish I could say that in that moment in the kitchen she decided to quit drinking, but I now saw that drinking was part of what made her who she was. If the worst of what she left on Earth was a legacy of inebriated support, it was a good legacy in my book.

She brought the ice over to the sink from the freezer and splurged on cubes. Seven in each tall glass. She ran the tap to make the water as cold as it would come. Her Abigail was coming home again. Her strange Abigail, whom she loved.

But when she looked up and through the window, she swore she saw a young girl wearing the clothes of her youth sitting outside Buckley's garden-shed fort and staring back at her. The next moment the girl was gone. She shook it off. The day was busy. She would not tell anyone.

When my father's car pulled into the drive, I was beginning to wonder if this had been what I'd been waiting for, for my family to come home, not to me anymore but to one another with me gone.

In the afternoon light my father looked smaller somehow, thinner, but his eyes looked grateful in a way they had not in years.

My mother, for her part, was thinking moment by moment that she might be able to survive being home again.

All four of them got out at once. Buckley came forward from the rear passenger seat to assist my father perhaps more than he needed assistance, perhaps protecting him from my mother. Lindsey looked over the hood of the car at our brother—her habitual check-in mode still operating. She felt responsible, just as my brother did, just as my father did. And then she turned back and saw my mother looking at her, her face lit by the yellowy light of the daffodils.

"What?"

"You are the spitting image of your father's mother," my mother said.

"Help me with the bags," my sister said.

They walked to the trunk together as Buckley led my father up the front path.

Lindsey stared into the dark space of the trunk. She wanted to know only one thing.

"Are you going to hurt him again?"

"I'm going to do everything I can not to," my mother said, "but no promises this time." She waited until Lindsey glanced up and looked at her, her eyes a challenge now as much as the eyes of a child who had grown up fast, run fast since the day the police had said too much blood in the earth, your daughter/sister/child is dead.

"I know what you did."

"I stand warned."

My sister hefted the bag.

They heard shouting. Buckley ran out onto the front porch. "Lindsey!" he said, forgetting his serious self, his heavy body buoyant. "Come see what Hal got me!"

He banged. And he banged and he banged and he banged. And Hal was the only one still smiling after five minutes of it. Everyone else had glimpsed the future and it was loud.

"I think now would be a good time to introduce him to the brush," Grandma Lynn said. Hal obliged.

My mother had handed the daffodils to Grandma Lynn and gone upstairs almost immediately, using the bathroom as an excuse. Everyone knew where she was going: my old room.

She stood at the edge of it, alone, as if she were standing at the edge of the Pacific. It was still lavender. The furniture, save for a reclining chair of my grandmother's, was unchanged.

"I love you, Susie," she said.

I had heard these words so many times from my father that it shocked me now; I had been waiting, unknowingly, to hear it from my mother. She had needed the time to know that this love would not destroy her, and I had, I now knew, given her that time, could give it, for it was what I had in great supply.

She noticed a photograph on my old dresser, which Grandma Lynn had put in a gold frame. It was the very first photograph I'd ever taken of her—my secret portrait of Abigail before her family woke and she put on her lipstick. Susie Salmon, wildlife photographer, had captured a woman staring out across her misty suburban lawn.

She used the bathroom, running the tap noisily and disturbing the towels. She knew immediately that her mother had bought these towels—cream, a ridiculous color for towels—and monogrammed—also ridiculous, my mother thought. But then, just as quickly, she laughed at herself. She was beginning to wonder how useful her scorched-earth policy had been to her all these years. Her mother was loving if she was drunk, solid if she was vain. When was it all right to let go not only of the dead but of the living—to learn to accept?

I was not in the bathroom, in the tub, or in the spigot; I did not hold court in the mirror above her head or stand in miniature at the tip of every bristle on Lindsey's or Buckley's toothbrush. In some way I could not account for—had they reached a state of bliss? were my parents back together forever? had Buckley begun to tell someone his troubles? would my father's heart truly heal?—I was done yearning for them, needing them to yearn for me. Though I still would. Though they still would. Always.

Downstairs Hal was holding Buckley's wrist as it held the brush stick. "Just pass it over the snare lightly." And Buckley did and looked up at Lindsey sitting across from him on the couch.

"Pretty cool, Buck," my sister said.

"Like a rattlesnake."

Hal liked that. "Exactly," he said, visions of his ultimate jazz combo dancing in his head.

My mother arrived back downstairs. When she entered the room she saw my father first. Silently she tried to let him know she was okay, that she was still breathing the air in, coping with the altitude.

"Okay, everyone!" my grandmother shouted from the kitchen, "Samuel has an announcement to make, so sit down!"

Everyone laughed and before they realigned into their more closed selves—this being together so hard for them even if it was what they all had wanted—Samuel came into the room along with Grandma Lynn. She held a tray of champagne flutes ready to be filled. He glanced at Lindsey briefly.

"Lynn is going to assist me by pouring," he said.

"Something she's quite good at," my mother said.

"Abigail?" Grandma Lynn said.

"Yes?"

"It's nice to see you too."

"Go ahead, Samuel," my father said.

"I wanted to say that I'm happy to be here with you all."

But Hal knew his brother. "You're not done, wordsmith. Buck, give him some brush." This time Hal let Buckley do it without assistance, and my brother backed Samuel up.

"I wanted to say that I'm glad that Mrs. Salmon is home, and that Mr. Salmon is home too, and that I'm honored to be marrying their beautiful daughter."

"Hear! Hear!" my father said.

My mother stood to hold the tray for Grandma Lynn, and together they distributed the glasses across the room.

As I watched my family sip champagne, I thought about how their lives trailed backward and forward from my death and then, I saw, as Samuel took the daring step of kissing Lindsey in a room full of family, became borne aloft away from it.

These were the lovely bones that had grown around my absence: the connections—sometimes tenuous, sometimes made at great cost, but often magnificent—that happened after I was gone. And I began to see things in a way that let me hold the world without me in it. The events that my death wrought were merely the bones of a body that would become whole at some unpredictable time in the future. The price of what I came to see as this miraculous body had been my life.

My father looked at the daughter who was standing there in front of him. The shadow daughter was gone.

With the promise that Hal would teach him to do drum rolls after dinner, Buckley put up his brush and drumsticks, and the seven of them began to trail through the kitchen into the dining room, where Samuel and Grandma Lynn had used the good plates to serve her trademark Stouffer's frozen ziti and Sara Lee frozen cheesecake.

"Someone's outside," Hal said, spotting a man through the window. "It's Ray Singh!"

"Let him in," my mother said.

"He's leaving."

All of them save my father and grandmother, who stayed together in the dining room, began to go after him.

"Hey, Ray!" Hal said, opening the door and nearly stepping directly in the pie. "Wait up!"

Ray turned. His mother was in the car with the engine running.

"We didn't mean to interrupt," Ray said now to Hal. Lindsey and Samuel and Buckley and a woman he recognized as Mrs. Salmon were all crowded together on the porch.

"Is that Ruana?" my mother called. "Please ask her in."

"Really, that's fine," Ray said and made no move to come closer. He wondered, *Is Susie watching this?*

Lindsey and Samuel broke away from the group and came toward him.

By that time my mother had walked down the front path to the driveway and was leaning in the car window talking to Ruana.

Ray glanced at his mother as she opened the car door to go inside the house. "Anything but pie for the two of us," she said to my mother as they walked up the path.

"Is Dr. Singh working?" my mother asked.

"As usual," Ruana said. She watched to see Ray walking, with Lindsey and Samuel, through the door of the house. "Will you come smoke stinky cigarettes with me again?"

"It's a date," my mother said.

"Ray, welcome, sit," my father said when he saw him coming through the living room. He had a special place in his heart for the boy who had loved his daughter, but Buckley swooped into the chair next to my father before anyone else could get to him.

Lindsey and Samuel found two straight chairs from the living room and brought them in to sit by the sideboard. Ruana sat between Grandma Lynn and my mother and Hal sat alone on one end.

I realized then that they would not know when I was gone, just as they could not know sometimes how heavily I had hovered in a particular room. Buckley had talked to me and I had talked back. Even if I hadn't thought I'd been talking to him, I had. I became manifest in whatever way they wanted me to be.

And there she was again, alone and walking out in the cornfield while everyone else I cared for sat together in one room. She would always feel me and think of me. I could see that, but there was no longer anything I could do. Ruth had been a girl haunted and now she would be a woman haunted. First by accident and now by choice. All of it, the story of my life and death, was hers if she chose to tell it, even to one person at a time.

* * *

It was late in Ruana and Ray's visit when Samuel started talking about the gothic revival house that Lindsey and he had found along an overgrown section of Route 30. As he told Abigail about it in detail, describing how he had realized he wanted to propose to Lindsey and live there with her, Ray found himself asking, "Does it have a big hole in the ceiling of the back room and cool windows above the front door?"

"Yes," Samuel said, as my father grew alarmed. "But it can be fixed, Mr. Salmon, I'm sure of it."

"Ruth's dad owns that," Ray said.

Everyone was quiet for a moment and then Ray continued.

"He took out a loan on his business to buy up old places that aren't already slated for destruction. He wants to restore them," Ray said.

"My God," Samuel said.

And I was gone.

BONES

You don't notice the dead leaving when they really choose to leave you. You're not meant to. At most you feel them as a whisper or the wave of a whisper undulating down. I would compare it to a woman in the back of a lecture hall or theater whom no one notices until she slips out. Then only those near the door themselves, like Grandma Lynn, notice; to the rest it is like an unexplained breeze in a closed room.

Grandma Lynn died several years later, but I have yet to see her here. I imagine her tying it on in her heaven, drinking mint juleps with Tennessee Williams and Dean Martin. She'll be here in her own sweet time, I'm sure.

If I'm to be honest with you, I still sneak away to watch my family sometimes. I can't help it, and sometimes they still think of me. They can't help it.

After Lindsey and Samuel got married they sat in the empty house on Route 30 and drank champagne. The branches of the overgrown trees had grown into the upstairs windows, and they huddled beneath them, knowing the branches would have to be cut. Ruth's father had promised he would sell the house to them only if Samuel paid him in labor as his first employee in a restoration business. By the end of that summer, Mr. Connors had cleared the lot with the help of Samuel and Buckley and set up a trailer, which during the day would be his work quarters and at night could be Lindsey's study room.

In the beginning it was uncomfortable, the lack of plumbing and electricity, and having to go home to either one of their parents' houses to take showers, but Lindsey buried herself in school work and Samuel buried himself in tracking down the right era doorknobs and light pulls. It was a surprise to everyone when Lindsey found out she was pregnant.

"I thought you looked fatter," Buck said, smiling.

"You're one to talk," Lindsey said.

My father dreamed that one day he might teach another child to love ships in bottles. He knew there would be both sadness and joy in it; that it would always hold an echo of me.

I would like to tell you that it is beautiful here, that I am, and you will one day be, forever safe. But this heaven is not about safety just as, in its graciousness, it isn't about gritty reality. We have fun.

We do things that leave humans stumped and grateful, like Buckley's garden coming up one year, all of its crazy jumble of plants blooming all at once. I did that for my mother who, having stayed, found herself facing the yard again. Marvel was what she did at all the flowers and herbs and budding weeds. Marveling was what she mostly did after she came back—at the twists life took.

And my parents gave my leftover possessions to the Good Will, along with Grandma Lynn's things.

They kept sharing when they felt me. Being together, thinking and talking about the dead, became a perfectly normal part of their life. And I listened to my brother, Buckley, as he beat the drums.

Ray became Dr. Singh, "the real doctor in the family," as Ruana liked to say. And he had more and more moments that he chose not to disbelieve. Even if surrounding him were the serious surgeons and scientists who ruled over a world of black and white, he maintained this possibility: that the ushering strangers that sometimes appeared to the dying were not the results of strokes, that he had called Ruth by my name, and that he had, indeed, made love to me.

If he ever doubted, he called Ruth. Ruth, who had graduated from a closet to a closet-sized studio on the Lower East Side. Ruth, who was still trying to find a way to write down whom she saw and what she had experienced. Ruth, who wanted everyone to believe what she knew: that the dead truly talk to us, that in the air between the living, spirits bob and weave and laugh with us. They are the oxygen we breathe.

Now I am in the place I call this wide wide Heaven because it includes all my simplest desires but also the most humble and grand. The word my grandfather uses is *comfort.*

So there are cakes and pillows and colors galore, but underneath this more obvious patchwork quilt are places like a quiet room where you can go and hold someone's hand and not have to say anything. Give no story. Make no claim. Where you can live at the edge of your skin for as long as you wish. This wide wide Heaven is about flathead nails and the soft down of new leaves, wild roller coaster rides and escaped marbles that fall then hang then take you somewhere you could never have imagined in your small-heaven dreams.

* * *

One afternoon I was scanning Earth with my grandfather. We were watching birds skip from top to top of the very tallest pines in Maine and feeling the bird's sensations as they landed then took flight then landed again. We ended up in Manchester, visiting a diner my grandfather remembered from his days traveling up and down the East Coast on business. It had gotten seedier in the fifty intervening years and after taking stock we left. But in the instant I turned away, I saw him: Mr. Harvey coming out of the doors of a Greyhound bus.

He went into the diner and ordered a cup of coffee at the counter. To the uninitiated, he still looked every bit as ordinary as he could, except around the eyes, but he no longer wore his contacts and no one took the time to look past his thick lenses anymore.

As an older waitress passed him a Styrofoam cup full of boiling coffee, he heard a bell over the door behind him tinkle and felt a cold blast of air.

It was a teenage girl who had sat a few rows ahead of him for the last few hours, playing her Walkman and humming along with the songs. He sat at the counter until she was done using the bathroom, and then he followed her out.

I watched him trail her in the dirty snow along the side of the diner and out to the back of the bus station, where she would be out of the wind for a smoke. While she stood there, he joined her. She wasn't even startled. He was another boring old man in bad clothes.

He calculated his business in his mind. The snow and cold. The pitched ravine that dropped off immediately in front of them. The blind woods on the other side. And he engaged her in conversation.

"Long ride," he said.

She looked at him at first as if she couldn't believe he was talking to her.

"Um hmmm," she said.

"Are you traveling alone?"

It was then that I noticed them, hanging above their heads in a long and plentiful row. Icicles.

The girl put out her cigarette on the heel of her shoe and turned to go.

"Creep," she said, and walked fast.

A moment later, the icicle fell. The heavy coldness of it threw him off balance just enough for him to stumble and pitch forward. It would be weeks before the snow in the ravine melted enough to uncover him.

But now let me tell you about someone special:

Out in her yard, Lindsey made a garden. I watched her weed the long thick flower bed. Her fingers twisted inside the gloves as she thought about the clients she saw in her practice each day—how to help them make sense of the cards life had dealt them, how to ease their pain. I remembered that the simplest things were the ones that often eluded what I thought of as her big brain. It took her forever to figure out that I always volunteered to clip the grass inside the fence so I could play with Holiday while we did yard work. She remembered Holiday then, and I followed her thoughts. How in a few years it would be time to get her child a dog, once the house was settled and fenced-in. Then she thought about how there were now machines with whipcords that could trim a fence post to post in minutes—what it had taken us hours of grumbling to achieve.

Samuel walked out to Lindsey then, and there she was in his arms, my sweet butterball babe, born ten years after my fourteen years on Earth: Abigail Suzanne. Little Susie to me. Samuel placed Susie on a blanket near the flowers. And my sister, my Lindsey, left me in her memories, where I was meant to be.

* * *

And in a small house five miles away was a man who held my mud-encrusted charm bracelet out to his wife.

"Look what I found at the old industrial park," he said. "A construction guy said they were bulldozing the whole lot. They're afraid of more sinkholes like that one that swallowed the cars."

His wife poured him some water from the sink as he fingered the tiny bike and the ballet shoe, the flower basket and the thimble. He held out the muddy bracelet as she set down his glass.

"This little girl's grown up by now," she said.

Almost.

Not quite.

I wish you all a long and happy life.

ACKNOWLEDGMENTS

I owe a debt to my passionate early readers: Judith Grossman, Wilton Barnhardt, Geoffrey Wolff, Margot Livesey, Phil Hay, and Michelle Latiolais. As well as the workshop at the University of California, Irvine.

To those who joined the party late but brought the most awesome refreshments: Teal Minton, Joy Johannessen, and Karen Joy Fowler.

To the pros: Henry Dunow, Jennifer Carlson, Bill Contardi, Ursula Doyle, Michael Pietsch, Asya Muchnick, Ryan Harbage, Laura Quinn, and Heather Fain.

Abiding thanks to: Sarah Burnes, Sarah Crichton, and the glorious MacDowell Colony.

A smarty-pants badge of honor to my informants: Dee Williams, Orren Perlman, Dr. Carl Brighton, and the essential facts-on-file team of Bud and Jane.

And to my continuing troika, whose sustaining friendship and rigorous reading and rereading are, next to tapioca and coffee, what keep me going on a day-to-day basis: Aimee Bender, Kathryn Chetkovich, Glen David Gold.

And a *woof!* to Lilly.